SUPERHEROES IN DENIM

Published by Clockwork Dragon Books
www.clockworkdragon.net

First printing, June 2016
Second printing, January 2018

Superheroes In Denim, *Maze Beset*, *Dragons In Pieces*, *Interlude at the Farm*, *Dragons In Chains*, and *Dragons In Flight* are a works of fiction. Names, places, and incidents are either products of the author's imagination or used fictitiously. No endorsement of any kind should be inferred by existing locations or organizations used within it.

No dragons, squirrels, goats, superheroes, or government agents were harmed in the writing of this book.

ISBN: 978-1-944334-05-5

SUPERHEROES IN DENIM

LEE FRENCH

Dedication

For all the ordinary people with extraordinary powers locked inside. May you discover them without having to be framed for murder.

Table of Contents

DRAGONS IN PIECES

Chapter 1

Today called for a cold beer. Sadly, Bobby wasn't old enough to have one. That didn't always stop him, but it did at work. Sitting in the passenger seat of the delivery truck, he idly sipped at his water bottle, wishing Verne would get the damned air conditioning fixed already. That would mean taking the truck out of service for a couple of days, though, and that would mean no deliveries for a couple of days, and that would mean all these poor people would have to wait a couple of extra days to get their damned crap.

"What's next?" Jimbo drove—he was older and that made the insurance cheaper. The truck stopped for a light and he peered over as Bobby picked up the clipboard with the list.

Bobby sighed heavily. "Washer and dryer. I'll take stairs in and out."

"No bet," Jimbo groaned, "not today. They definitely got stairs inside and outside. Probably have to go up three flights or something. Man, why they always gotta get this stuff when it's hotter'n Satan's balls or raining all to heck?"

"Momma always says suffering builds character."

"Yeah, well, I got enough character to last me 'til infinity, then."

Bobby snorted with amusement and shook his head. "Probably don't got a/c, neither. Maybe if it's a hot housewife, we can get some lemonade outta her."

Jimbo smirked. "You ain't old enough to be talking about hot housewives."

"And you ain't single enough to. Don't mean we can't." Bobby grinned broadly.

"Oh yeah? What about Mandy?"

The grin died, fast and hard, and fell into a mild scowl. Bobby turned to stare out the side window.

When he didn't answer, Jimbo nudged him with an elbow. "What happened? I thought you were crazy about her."

Bobby shrugged and sighed. "She up and left for New York City, like she been talking about for months."

"Damn. How long ago?"

"A week now. That was last Monday."

"Shoulda said something, Bobby. I'd'a gotten you a beer or something, at least."

Shrugging again, he couldn't come up with a good response to that and kept his mouth shut while watching the city go past the window. It hadn't been the worst thing that ever happened to him. Still, he didn't really care for what she said when she dumped him. A guy had to have aspirations, apparently. Dreams. Hopes for something better. Plans.

If she'd asked him to go with her, he would have. She made it clear his services as a boyfriend were no longer required or wanted. That first few hours, he walked around in a daze. Then he slept on it, then he spent Tuesday making up dozens of different plans to chase after her. Momma set him straight. She'd been there when Mandy dumped him. It still sucked to be told he had no worth.

"I guess this explains why you been a little quiet lately. All a'sudden not getting laid anymore'll do that to a guy."

Yeah, he missed that part. Didn't so much miss having to do the stupid chick crap to get some. He thought they were fine, then she up and says he's a lazy good-for-nothing Momma's boy and she wants to be a star up in lights. He'd only hold her back and slow her down. So long and thanks for the sex.

"Aw, come on, boy. She weren't special, right? Just a good lay. You can get that anywhere."

Bobby grunted. "I just need to burn up a little steam is all."

"That's what I'm saying." Jimbo gave him a manly shove on the arm and nodded his satisfaction. Another few minutes later, they reached a nice house in the nice subdivision. They carried out the old washer and dryer, then brought in and hooked up new ones. It had steps up to the front door, but at least the laundry room had been put on the main floor. For once, the house had air conditioning, and they lingered for a few minutes under the guise of double-checking the connections and tweaking the feet to make them level. If only the Hispanic maid had been young and hot, they would have had a reason to dawdle even more.

Two more deliveries later, they returned the used appliances to the shop. In there, Kenny would either fix them up to sell used, or scavenge parts, sell what they could for scrap, and trash the rest. With that kind of back end money, delivery came for free with everything. Bobby liked the job. He put on muscle, had Jimbo around to talk to, and got a decent paycheck with benefits.

After eight hours of deliveries, rearranging the showroom, and shifting store stock around, he walked home from his bus stop with his hands in the pockets of his loose denim shorts, too worn out from working all day in this heat to pay much attention to anything. When he got home, all he wanted to do was collapse in a chair and stare at nothing.

He gazed longingly at the two wicker chairs on the porch, but went inside anyway. "I'm home, Momma," he called as he stepped out of his shoes just inside the front door. They didn't have air conditioning, but they did have a bunch of fans, and right now, the ceiling fan in the living room could be his best friend.

"Haul your butt into the kitchen and you can have cold lemonade, boy."

Pausing at the couch, just about to flop onto it, he sighed and shuffled to the other room where Momma worked on dinner. He got a glass and the pitcher and poured himself a cup. "What're we having?"

"Sandwiches with a salad and popcorn. That sound alright?" She stood shorter than him by about half a foot, but he wasn't tall, only about five foot ten. She had dirty blonde hair and light green eyes nothing like his own icy blue ones. In her fifties now, she showed some wear even though her job—bookkeeper—wasn't too hard on her. Bobby, on the other hand, had been hard on her. Her husband, too, for being away all the time and getting himself killed almost eight years back. Still, he thought she was pretty: just a little plump without being fat, took care of herself, didn't let life get her down much.

"I s'pose. Ain't really hungry, though."

"Gotta eat anyway, boy." She set two plates and a bowl down on the table and he got salad dressing out while putting the lemonade pitcher away. They both sat down. "Lord, we're grateful for everything we've got and can live without everything we don't."

Bobby bowed his head while Momma said her version of Grace over the meal. "Amen." None of the food was exciting or wonderful, but he appreciated that she made it for him when she didn't have to. "How's things at work?"

"Oh, same old, same old." She shrugged a little. "Mr. Peterson is getting a little pushy again, but it's nothing to worry about."

A grunt of disapproval escaped Bobby. "I oughta beat the crap outta him," he grumbled.

Momma looked at him sternly over her sandwich. "You'll do no such thing. He's just a man, acting like a man. And he's my boss. Won't do us no good for you to lose me my job."

Simmering, he crunched a handful of popcorn. Mr. Peterson had a wife and a family. Not only that, and more importantly, Momma didn't like him that way. "He oughtn't be doing that is all. Ain't right."

She reached over and patted his hand with her own. "You're a good boy, but I can handle myself. You leave him alone. I'm gonna have words with his wife if he doesn't stop soon."

More wordless little grumbles pushed their way out of him, but he stopped talking about it. If she didn't want to get into it, he wouldn't keep needling. Man needed to be dealt with, though. This had been going on for a few months now, so far as he knew, and no one else would stand up for her. Grandpa passed a few years ago, and she had no brothers. Dad's family didn't have much to do with them; Bobby wasn't his son and they never did get along with Momma.

"How was your day?"

The question pulled him out of brooding and he looked up with a shrug. "Hotter'n heck. There's a new dryer in, might be cheap if'n Kenny can fix it up."

She shook her head and waved the suggestion off. "I don't mind using the line. So long as there's enough hours in the day to get done what I need to, I don't want a machine doing it for me."

She'd said this before, so Bobby nodded and picked up a handful of popcorn. "Probably going out with Jimbo sometime soon." The popcorn had no butter and a shake of salt, the way he liked it best.

"You finally tell him about Mandy, then?"

"Yeah, it done came up."

"You tell him I don't want you coming home drunk. You drink that much, you can sleep on his couch or something."

"Yes, ma'am."

Reaching over, she cuffed him upside the head with a smirk. "Don't sass me, boy."

He grinned, like he always did. "Sorry, Momma."

"I just ain't cleaning up after you like that, hear?"

"Yes, Momma." It happened once. He threw up all over the place. Since then, he kept it down to a drink here and there, mostly to help with the heat. That scolding, combined with things he later discovered he'd done while drunk, put the fear of God in him about alcohol.

She nodded her satisfaction and picked up dishes. If he didn't interfere, she'd clean everything up herself. Sometimes he stopped her and sometimes he didn't. It depended on how much of a pain he thought he'd been in her behind that day. Right now, he figured it reached the level of 'enough', so he shooed her off and took care of the dishes himself. After he stacked the last clean dish in the drying rack, he grabbed a beer out of the fridge and walked out to find her sitting on the couch, relaxed and content with the TV on.

Not wanting to disturb her and uninterested in the show, he went to his room and sat down on the bed, popping open the beer and taking a long drink. His head needed to settle before he'd get to sleep tonight, though it didn't matter. Tomorrow was his day off. People didn't need new appliances so much on Tuesdays for some reason he'd never know. Thursdays, too, and he also got that day off.

That Peterson, he needed to stop bugging Momma. It'd be one thing if she liked it, though that'd be wrong to bust up his family. If she liked it, though, he wouldn't care because it wouldn't be any of his business. She didn't. The more he thought about that man, with his foofy hair and fake smile, his smarmy handshake and suits with 'funny' ties, the more he wanted to punch the guy in the face. In fact, he wanted to go do that right this damned minute. Bastard needed to know he did something wrong. Dog craps on the rug, you smack it on the nose.

He looked over at his clock: only 6:30 yet. The fire of determination got him off the bed. Empty beer bottle in hand, he stalked out. "'M going out," he tossed towards the living room. Without waiting for a reply, he headed out the door and walked to the bus stop. Time like this made him wish he had a car or motorcycle, but he didn't, and getting bothered about it wouldn't help anything. It was really Peterson's fault they didn't have one. He could cut Momma a deal on one, so they could have it for emergencies. Not Mr. Peterson. Employees got paid already. So he said.

As he walked the two blocks to the bus stop, he imagined that jerk grabbing Momma. Peterson's face had an oily smirk and Momma shied away. She needed someone to make him stop, because she had too much fear for her job to do it herself. He flung the beer bottle at the sidewalk, the smash of the glass feeding his anger rather than venting it.

The bus came along shortly after he reached the stop, not giving him time to think more before getting on and swiping his pass. Only a few other people rode it, normal for this neighborhood at this time of day. Even though it had plenty of empty seats, he felt too fidgety and cranky to take one. Instead, he grabbed a pole and stood glowering out the window, watching the scenery go by and thinking more about Momma putting up with Peterson's sloppy advances. Bastard.

Not long after it trundled out of his neighborhood, the bus reached the dealership, and he boiled off—a dark cloud looking for someone to storm all over. Peterson could take those hands and shove them where the sun doesn't shine, and that's exactly what he would to help the man do. No, Peterson didn't deserve the word 'man'.

Once he reached the lot, it only took him a minute to find that prick, showing some unsuspecting couple around. His navy suit had him sweating up a storm in this flat heat while he tried to get them to pick the expensive car over that cheaper one they seemed more interested in. That his hand touched the woman's shoulder made Bobby's blood boil.

The husband caught sight of him first. The guy put his hands protectively on his young wife, the woman with the rounded belly. It must have been obvious who Bobby headed for, because the guy pulled his wife a few steps out of the way without doing anything else. That movement alerted Peterson. He looked around, then put up a hand in a placating gesture. Bobby ignored it and clocked him across the jaw.

Back in school, Bobby got into scrapes all the time. Everybody liked to pick on the small kid, even when he bounced up and fought back. He'd thrown plenty of punches in his time, and knew how to do it. Peterson went down. He hit the ground with his ass and stayed there.

"Who the Hell do you think you are," Bobby spat at him. "You touch my Momma again, and I'll come back here and kill you, hear?"

"Hi, Bobby," Peterson said with a grimace. Touching his lip, his hand came away with a smear of blood.

Bobby stood there, ready to kick the prick if he didn't say something more useful. "She ain't interested. And if you fire her, you and me are gonna have more words for that, too."

Peterson nodded and pulled out a handkerchief to press it against his mouth. "I didn't—" He stopped when Bobby's eyes narrowed and his foot twitched. With a gulp, he scrabbled back a few inches. "I hear you. She's off limits, I got it."

It seemed clear he'd say or do anything to not get walloped again. Bobby decided to take the words at face value anyway. "This ain't the kinda thing that expires, neither." Now he'd gotten that punch out of his system, he lost his taste for it. Guy gave his word and acted helpless. He didn't beat guys when they were already down. It reminded him too much of some of his own beatings. He needed another beer.

"Yeah, yeah, I get you." Peterson wobbled to his feet and flashed an apologetic smile at the young couple. "Sorry, folks. Little personal squabble, that's all."

Bobby shut his mouth and glared at Peterson another few seconds, then turned and stalked away. Nowhere would serve him alcohol except home, and he didn't want Momma to see him all frothed up like this. He stuffed his hands in his pockets and let his feet carry him. Peterson got what he deserved, and things would be better for Momma from here. Now what? No idea. If he still had Mandy, he'd go to her place.

But he didn't. Since last Monday night when she dumped him, he'd been ignoring that. She was just gone for a week or two, he told himself, and things would be alright. He didn't have to tell Momma—she overheard them arguing and Mandy told her straight up about it. Momma had been nice to her, that's what she said. She deserved to know the truth, instead of whatever he'd tell her. Because, obviously, he would lie.

Now that Jimbo knew, it hit home and couldn't be ignored anymore. They dated for seven months, and in that time, she never told him he was dumb, no matter what he said. They went to the park sometimes and stared up at the stars and she'd talk his ear off for an hour, her voice a soothing drone that erased whatever worries he fretted over. The sex had been great, too.

She walked up and said something. He remembered it as clearly as yesterday. One warm summer day thirteen months ago, he sat out back at the store on his lunch break. This girl went past with two friends and smiled at him. Sunlight glinted off her long blonde hair. Short shorts showed off bronzed legs with the right amount of meat for his tastes. He smiled back to be polite. They went on their way, then she returned five minutes later by herself. Her red shirt had the top three buttons undone, enough to give him an eyeful.

Before that day, he'd dated four girls. None of those lasted more than three dates. All of them picked him out of pity for the little guy with the bloody nose or black eye. Mandy never saw that. She saw the guy with a regular job, who could pick her up and would sit through dumb romance movies. He did whatever she wanted, believing he could never hope to find another girl half as pretty who'd let him anywhere near her. It helped that she pushed her breasts in his face that day, and gave him her real phone number.

Having walked a fair distance, he climbed up out of his reverie to see where he'd gotten to and didn't recognize the area. He saw a gas station ahead, at least. Inside, he asked the guy working the register where he could find the nearest bus stop and got himself a Coke since he couldn't buy a beer. He waited a good ten minutes for the bus to show up, and went straight to bed when he got home a half hour later.

Chapter 2

Bobby sat on the porch, too hot to care about anything more than how he probably ought to be wearing shorts instead of jeans. His glass of lemonade had only been sitting there with him for maybe ten minutes, but it was already tepid, the ice gone so fast he almost missed it being there by just blinking. What he wouldn't give right now for someone to just walk up and douse him with a supersoaker full of ice. He spent his day off mostly feeling sorry for himself, with a little light housework thrown in. A few things needed fixing, so he fixed them, the best he could do to take his mind off things.

Momma went to work and came back already, and now puttered inside. Peterson must not have mentioned Bobby's visit, because she didn't say anything. Actually, she seemed in a really good mood, so probably she had her needlework keeping her company. Doing it reminded her of Dad some, and best to do that sort of thing when she wouldn't dwell on the bad stuff.

An Atlanta police cruiser pulled up in front of the house and stopped there. Two uniformed officers got out and started up the walk. Bobby couldn't think of anything he'd done recently to warrant that kind of attention, other than maybe decking Peterson, so he frowned at them without getting up. It was too damned hot to run anyway, so if they wanted him in that air conditioned car to take to the air conditioned station, he didn't have a lot of incentive to resist. "Can I help you officers?"

"Robert Mitchell?" The first one had his hand on his weapon, the second one stayed far enough behind him to be in a good position in case Bobby decided to take off.

"Yes, sir." He did have to admire the two cops for being dressed in dark blue uniforms in this heat and not looking like they would rather be back in their cruiser. "What's it to ya?"

"Son, you're under arrest for vandalism at Bailey's Package Store."

Bobby blinked and still didn't get up. "Huh?" In fairness to these fine officers of the law, he had committed a few minor acts of what they might call vandalism over the years, but nothing since he started dating Mandy, and he hadn't felt the urge since she left. The name of the store didn't ring any bells, either. "I got no idea what you're talking about. Why're you picking me up for it? I got no reason to even go to a package store, I'm underage."

"Funny." The first cop took his hand off his gun to grab his handcuffs. "C'mon, son, don't make this hard on us. It's too hot to wrangle or chase you down."

Heaving out a sigh, Bobby lifted his hands for the restraints, acquiescing to being arrested. "My Momma's inside, can we at least tell her before you haul me off for something I didn't do?"

"I'll handle it," the second cop said, and he hustled up the steps and inside. He knocked as he walked in, calling out, "Mrs. Mitchell?".

Bobby cooperated with being stuffed into the back seat of the cop car. His mother came out of the house with the second cop, staying on the porch and watching while he got in the cruiser. Bobby watched her cover her mouth in shock and stand there, stunned. Though he felt confident he'd be home in time for dinner, he watched until he couldn't see her anymore. Something inexplicable about the situation made him unable to tear his eyes from her.

For the rest of the ride, he ignored the two cops and watched the scenery go by. He'd been taken down for questioning before, but never arrested. This time, he had no idea why it went to an arrest from the start. They couldn't possibly have any actual evidence he'd done something. He had no idea where this Bailey's place might even be.

Nothing for it but to wait and see what happened. The cops hauled him through the station with a hand balled up in the back of his shirt, then tossed him into a dingy little closet with a table and two chairs. One kicked the back of his knee while the other shoved him down into a chair. The rough treatment surprised him, since he had no record. Then again, if they mixed him up with one of his 'buddies', it made sense they'd treat him like some kind of hard core asshole. Further reinforcing the mistaken identity theory, they left his handcuffs on.

"I ain't never been to that store that I know of," he told them, now getting truly worried. "I been clean for more'n half a year, on account of a girl."

"Don't care." The two cops left the room and shut the door. About five minutes of solitary silence passed before a plain clothes cop walked in. This surprised him more, since he didn't think they usually did this kind of interrogation for something like vandalism. Then again, all he really knew about that came from watching TV, and that usually involved homicides.

"Robert, I'm Detective Cornell." He laid a file folder on the table, currently shut. At a guess it had ten or fifteen pages inside it.

"Nice to meet you, aside from the how." So far as Bobby could see, there wasn't any harm in being polite. "Everybody calls me 'Bobby.'"

"Bobby, then. Right now, I have a witness statement putting you at the scene of a crime, some vandalism at a liquor store. There's also a spray can with your prints on it, so I can get you for that. Truth of the matter, though, is I don't give a rat's ass about that, it's kiddie stuff. What I do care about is I got two witnesses that saw you have an altercation with one Jerry Peterson."

Bobby sighed heavily. "Come on, really? That sonofabitch pressed charges? He's the one harassing Momma."

"No." Cornell opened his folder, and the top page had a glossy color image of Mr. Peterson, badly beaten and covered in blood. "He's dead. According to two witnesses, you said you would kill him if he didn't back off your mother."

"Whoa." Bobby blanched and gulped. "I didn't mean it like that." He'd never seen a real dead person before, not even in pictures. The sight made him queasy. Worse, they thought he did it.

"They said you were pretty angry."

"Well yeah, heck yeah I was angry. Bastard's been schmoozing on Momma for months! Touching her and saying things and stuff. But I didn't kill him. Jesus, I hit him once, then I left."

"Right. From there you walked to a gas station." Cornell pulled out another picture, this one from a security camera. It showed him walking up to the front door, looking perturbed, and had a time stamp in the corner. "The attendant said you were agitated and unhappy, asked for directions to the nearest bus stop, bought a Coke, and left. Jerry Peterson's body was found behind that gas station, with the garbage, time of death about the time you left." He slapped another picture down, from the same security camera, showing him leaving and heading around back.

"I didn't kill nobody. I just hit him once, I swear, at the

dealership." Panicking, he showed his knuckles with their light bruising. "The bus stop was that way, and I didn't see nothing or nobody back there when I went past."

Cornell snorted at him. "Fine, stick to your story. A jury sees this and they'll lock you up and throw away the key." A knock on the door made him turn. It opened as he stood. The man barging in held a badge in a wallet, but Bobby wasn't looking. He had no idea what to think or do, and his head filled with images of the awful things everyone knows happen in prison.

"FBI Special Agent Steve Privek. I'm taking custody of your prisoner. You don't have a choice. He's on the Terrorist Watch List." The Fed walked right in, grabbed Bobby by the arm and hauled him to his feet.

Cornell took a moment to digest that, then he reached over and grabbed Bobby's other arm. "You can't just take my murder suspect."

"Yes, actually, I can." Privek yanked Bobby forward, smacked Cornell's hand, and produced some papers Bobby didn't get to see. "If we're ever done with him, we'll return him to the state of Georgia."

"Wait, what?" Bewildered even more than before, Bobby stumbled after Privek, still handcuffed. Privek and another guy in the same suit bodily hauled him off, and he realized that as soon as he got into their car, he was basically dead to the world. Terrorist? Heck, they'd throw him in a deep, dark hole and not give a crap about guilty or innocent. He threw himself into suit and lurched to run for it, but they had a good grip. Still, he wouldn't go quietly, not for this.

Privek punched him in the face, hard enough to draw blood. It knocked him for a loop, and his wits didn't regroup until he'd already been stuffed into their black SUV. Somewhere in there, the Feds replaced his handcuffs with zip ties and tossed the cuffs back at the cops.

Reaching up to rub at his face, he discovered a sore spot and some blood on his lip. “You pack a heckuva wallop.”

“You wouldn’t calm down.” Bobby couldn’t really tell one Fed from the other and didn’t bother trying.

“I ain’t no terrorist, and I didn’t kill nobody.”

The Fed looked unamused, unimpressed, and unrepentant. “What did you do to get on the Watch List?”

“You’re asking me?” Bobby snorted. “Heck if I know. Sure didn’t blow anything up, or whatever else qualifies these days. Unless sneaking a beer counts. This has gotta be some kind of crazy misunderstanding.”

“Nobody winds up on that list by accident, kid. Nobody.”

“Always a first time for everything.” Bobby muttered. He glared at the smirk Privek gave him. When the agent said nothing else, Bobby set himself on the task of not freaking out. Someone made a mistake, and they’d realize it before he got waterboarded or whatever other crazy stuff they did to suspected terrorists these days.

They drove through the streets of Atlanta, past places Bobby rarely saw. He lived on the outer edges of the city, and had no reason to go in deeper. They pulled into a parking garage and hustled him into an office building. In the basement, they forced him to strip down and put on an itchy orange jumpsuit and too loose white socks with shoes he didn’t think he’d like to be caught dead in. His new threads kept him company while he waited in a holding cell by himself.

Sitting there, he thought his bizarre journey would continue with more interrogation. Why else would they bring him here, instead of a jail? For an hour he stewed, imagining Momma hearing about this. She’d be horrified at her son. He hoped she’d deny it and protest his innocence. Then again, they might not tell her anything. It could be kept quiet. Her son would never come home, and she’d never know why. He had no idea which would be worse.

When they came back, he cooperated, unable to see an upside to resisting, or a way to get free. They hustled him into a van where he was chained down in the back like a… Rabid dogs got treated better than this, he thought. At least he hadn't been crammed into a cage? The two agents gave him nothing, nor did they stop for anything. They drove for long enough that it got dark out. Bobby, bored out of his mind, fell asleep. A boot to his middle parts woke him up to see harsh lights in a parking garage. They shuffled him through a door that put them in an elevator. Privek removed his handcuffs and tossed him into a new cell.

It had to be the weirdest cell he'd ever seen. It stunk of bleach and other cleaning chemicals, enough that he had to cover his nose to breathe. In the back, it had a blank wall, white painted cinder blocks or something like it. The two side walls were some kind of thick glass or plastic, completely see-through. The front wall was made of shiny silver metal bars. A three foot wide space separated his bars from the bars of another cell. This area had a total of five on each side, so ten cells. Bobby's was the second from one end. In the one closest to the wall on that side, another guy sat on the floor, arms crossed, scowling in his own orange jumpsuit. He had a kind of a Native American look to him, and was in good shape, like he lifted weights all the time. Across from Bobby was a girl, Asian of some sort, and pretty, though the orange didn't do much for her. The cell across from the other guy had another Asian girl.

"Hey, any of you know what's going on?" Bobby moved to the bars and grabbed them with both hands, finding the cold somehow comforting. The were solid and real and so far, the only thing out of all this that made sense and did what he expected.

"No." The guy grunted out the word, sounding tired and cranky. Not that Bobby blamed him for it. "They told me I'm a terrorist," he growled. The queer thing about the guy, though, was his eyes.

Bobby knew he had unusual eyes. They had an almond shape, which he'd seen on other people, but with an extra bit of tilt and uptick at the outer corners. He remembered seeing some posters for some online game or something with elves, and his eyes looked a lot more like theirs than any Arabic or Asian person. So far as he knew, nothing else marked him as strange.

This guy had the same eyes with the same icy blue color. On Bobby, a light brown haired white kid, the blue didn't look off, and most people barely noticed. On this other guy, with his darker skin and hair, they looked downright weird. Now that he took a peek, the two girls had the same funky blue eyes, too. It made them look weird, too.

"Yeah," the closer, slighter one said with a nod. "We all have the same freaky eyes. We noticed that, too." She didn't have an Asian accent, which surprised him. Most of the Asian folks Bobby had heard talk before were on TV and in movies, and they always had an accent. He never met any in his neighborhood, except for the one family that ran the Chinese place. She also didn't have a Southern accent of any kind.

"And they think we're all terrorists? Any of you ever do anything at all like that? I been a little rough around the edges sometimes, but never nothing That came from the shorter, heavier girl. She wasn't chunky, just meaty where the other one was slight and waifish. That one had no Asian or Southern accent, too. "I have better things to do than get into trouble."

"How'd you get arrested, then? I'm Bobby, by the way."

"Alice. My car had a brake light out, and some bored cop pulled me over for it. Asshole. When he came back with my license, he arrested me, said I was wanted on a federal warrant."

"I'm Ai. I was getting on a plane with my parents to go visit relatives in Japan. I got stopped in security and pulled off to the side because I was the on the Watch List."

The guy sat there, nodding. "Name's Jayce. I was getting on a plane, too."

"Huh. So they ain't actively looking for us, just when we showed up in the system someplace where they check stuff like that, they grabbed us up. Weird."

"What's weirder," Alice said dryly, "is that all four of us are wanted for terrorism when we aren't terrorists and have the same eyes."

Ai nodded. "And we all happened to get picked up now. Why didn't I get flagged when I got my passport? I just got it about three months ago."

The door at the other end of the cells banged open, cutting Bobby off from agreeing with them. Three men in Army uniforms walked up the aisle between the cells. Two had rifles in hand, the other had a pack he carried to Bobby's cell. "Stand back," he ordered. His name patch read 'Carver', and he seemed older, with salt and pepper hair. To emphasize his demand, the other two lifted their weapons and pointed them at Bobby.

Suddenly faced with the prospect of being shot, multiple times, Bobby let go of the bars, put his hands up, and stepped back. "What's going on?"

"You're going to do exactly what I tell you to, or they're going to hurt you. We clear? "

Bobby gulped. "Um, yessir."

Voice full of indignant outrage, Alice snarled at them. "You can't just do whatever you want to us, we're American citizens. We have rights."

Instead of responding, Carver snapped a latex glove on and

pulled a needle out of his pack. Bobby backed up until he hit the rear wall, and then flattened himself against it.

"Stand still, Mitchell." He opened the cell door and grabbed Bobby's arm with a steely grip, his two goons right behind him with their weapons pointed.

Bobby gulped. "What're you gonna do?"

Carver pushed Bobby's sleeve aside and stuck the needle into his arm. Blood splashed into the little tube attached to it, which filled him with relief. Taking his blood gave him much less cause to worry than an unknown injection. Confusion followed swiftly on its heels. What did they want his blood for? When the tube filled, he pulled the needle out and stuck a small bandage on the site, then directed Bobby to fold his arm to stop any bleeding. "Do you normally have trouble sleeping?"

"Uh, no?"

"Are you asking me or telling me?" Carver demanded.

"Go to Hell," Alice growled.

Carver let the question go and pulled out a swab. "Open up."

Bobby gulped. They wanted his DNA, too? Couldn't they get that from the blood? "This ain't gonna include a cavity search, is it?"

"Not unless you give me a hard time."

Bobby opened his mouth and let the guy use the swab on his cheek. Carver gave no further orders and left the cell, taking his two goons with him. The door clanged shut and Bobby slid to the floor, wondering what the heck was going on. Stuck ina daze as the three men did exactly the same thing to the other three, he rested his chin on his knees and stared. Ai cooperated, and so did Jayce, but Alice had to be held down and got a smack across the face for her struggles.

Up to the moment he'd been forced to give up bodily fluids, Bobby still held onto a shred of hope that this would turn out to all be some giant misunderstanding. Suddenly, it was very serious and not going to go away. Alice cried softly in a corner. Ai paced. Jayce stood against the wall, flexing his fists. Bobby laid himself down on the blank concrete floor and stared at the ceiling, hoping someone would come along and at least explain something about this nightmare.

Time crawled past, and he had no way to measure it. If they meant to break the four of them with boredom, he thought it might work. Between threads of panic, he had the thought to start conversation with the others a thousand times. His mouth opened, then he closed it again, not knowing what to say. He could talk about himself, or Momma, maybe his job. None of them had any reason to care, and if one of them started to do the same, he'd tune it out, too.

His thoughts went fuzzy after a while. A weird thump from Jayce's cell interrupted it. He spent several seconds blinking, trying to understand through the haze of dozing. Sitting up, he looked over to see the large man had fallen down and lay in a crumpled heap. "Hey, Jayce, you okay?" Fresh panic surged through him and he sprang to his hands and knees. Crawling to the glass, called it out again, louder, but got no response. He pounded on the glass and still got nothing.

"Is he dead?" Ai breathed, the words laced with terror.

"Shoot, I don't know." Bobby shook his head, suddenly dizzy. Maybe Jayce keeled over from the fumes of whatever they sprayed this place down with. Why a beefy guy like that would drop before a scrawny guy like himself or a thin little girl like Ai, he had no idea. "Alice, you okay still?"

"Yeah, but I feel like crap." Her voice cracked, but that might have been from the crying.

"Hey!" Bobby turned and called out, hoping some FBI agent had the crappy job of listening to them. "He needs help! Something's wrong with him!" No one came running. Either they weren't being monitored, or… Bobby shuddered as it occurred to him that maybe this happened on purpose. It looked like his blood had been drawn. What if Carver injected something at the same time? He didn't get his blood drawn very often, and didn't know for sure what the doodlydad was supposed to look like.

"Nobody—" Alice dropped over in the middle of saying something. Bobby saw her eyes roll up and her body go limp. It was the creepiest thing he'd ever witnessed.

"Oh, God. We're all going to die," Ai wailed.

Too panicked in his own right to reassure her, Bobby shut his eyes and curled up in a little ball. Within a minute, Ai went quiet.

Chapter 3

Bobby's skin felt cold and clammy. His heart raced like he'd had the worst nightmare ever, but he had no such memory. Nothing happened between panicking in that cell and waking up now. An annoying beeping noise matched his racing heart beat and slowed as he woke up. He tried to move his hand to rub his eyes, but it wouldn't do what he wanted.

It took trying to sit up and forcing his eyes to flutter open to realize he'd been strapped down. There was a strap across his chest, another one at each wrist, one over his waist, one over his thighs, and two more at his ankles. His right arm had an IV in it, and several wires snaked down into various places on his body. He could see them all by lifting his head because he'd been left naked. They didn't even give him the modesty of a sheet over his privates.

"Hey! What's going on?" Eyes darting around, he saw machines, white curtains, a fluorescent light surrounded by industrial ceiling tiles, and tray table with silver tools on it. He'd been strapped to something hard enough to qualify more for the word 'board' than 'bed'. What kind of hospital did they take him to? One that used dentists instead of doctors?

"Where am I?" Ai's groggy voice came from the left.

"I dunno, I just done woke up."

"Oh God, are you strapped down, too?"

"Yeah." He struggled against the bindings, trying to pull one or the other hand loose. "Good and stuck."

"Calm down, you're quite secure." Bobby didn't recognize this man's voice. A figure stepped through a break in the curtain and scared the heck out of Bobby. Surgical blue covered him from head to toe, with a mask hiding his face, work glasses covering his eyes, a hat, a gown, and gloves. "The more you thrash about, the more chance you have of hurting yourself. Just relax."

"Relax? The heck? You crazy or something? I ain't gonna relax when I'm strapped naked to a bed 'gainst my will!" Panic hitting him full force, Bobby bucked and strained to get free.

The covered man sighed and brandished a needle, then stuck it into the IV draining into Bobby's arm. Within seconds, Bobby felt a soft, fuzzy malaise stealing over him. His eyelids got heavier with each passing moment. "You'll cooperate, Mitchell, one way or another."

The last thing he heard this time was Ai making little mewling noises of panic. He woke briefly with agonizing pain in his left foot and a light shining in his eyes. Another time, he seemed to be floating as if he'd been submerged in water. A third time, he couldn't open his eyes and heard a woman screaming in pain and terror. The fourth time, he felt like he might really be awake; he saw the curtains and machines and ceiling with nothing weird. Without waiting to see what might happen, he launched into full-throttle struggling. If he could just get free before They came back, he'd be able to make a run for it. Or something.

Quite unexpectedly, his body exploded. Sort of. His body separated into hundreds of tiny pieces, and each one was him, while they were also not him. Something else had a kind of control over his individual parts, yet he still could direct each one. All the parts, each the size of a quarter, made a swarming cloud of tiny silver creatures that all were him, yet also not. His mind, the part that he identified as himself, floated in the middle of it all, detached. Trying to explain this to someone else would be a major challenge.

Figuring this out could wait. He was free! The straps and wires and needles couldn't hold him down as a swarm of tiny pieces. The cloud responded to his desires, floating off the bed and flowing under the curtain. He/they found Ai, strapped naked to a board just like he'd been. Needles had been jammed into her in six different places, a tube ran under her nose. Her eyes darted around under her eyelids, making her appear to be dreaming. Could he free her like this, or would he need thumbs? He sure couldn't carry her like this. Instinctively, he knew the little parts couldn't handle any more weight than he could all together, and it would be harder for them to carry something. They weren't good at that. They were good at doing lots of small things at once.

He sent his little parts to work undoing her straps and pulling out needles and wires and things. Quick and clever, they dated about, using tiny front claws to manipulate the objects in small groups. When she didn't wake up right away, he directed the swarm to find and free anyone else who might be here. Leaving Jayce or Alice behind… He had no intention of allowing anyone else to go through any of this if he could prevent or stop it.

As they surged under the next curtain, he noticed the lights had been dimmed. It might be night, with no one around, so there might be a good chance of escaping. He found Jayce next and the swarm freed him, though the little pieces noted his skin had turned a funny color, an odd shade of brown with black streaks.

They found Alice last, and her skin had a weirder color: blue. Not a bright blue, but rather the purplish blue of a dead body. Did they kill her and not get around to disposing of the body yet? No, her bare chest rose and fell with even breaths, and the monitors still showed her heart beating slowly and steadily. He floated the swarm in closer and parts touched down to do their job. The first jumped off the moment it touched, finding her flesh ice cold. Another found the same thing and they all backed away.

This was a job for thumbs, maybe. How did he get back into his body? Could he get back into his body? Maybe he was stuck like this forever. He heard Jayce's groggy voice say, "What now?"

Bobby desperately wanted to answer him. All the tiny mouths opened and made tiny chirps, trills and shrieks. Admittedly, a lot of tiny little mouths made all that noise at once, ensuring he'd been heard. Understood, on the other hand… He needed to be able to talk. Without a body, he couldn't take a deep breath, clench his jaws together, or make fists. Instead, he thought about how doing each of those things felt, wanting to make them all reality and wanting to be Bobby again. The little pieces somehow understood, and he could somehow tell.

It made no sense. At the same time, it made perfect sense. Despite being separate pieces, they all made up Bobby. The swarm flew together and melted into each other, forming his body. As the pieces came together, he lost the feeling of being detached, then he stood as himself again, staring at his hand.

"I got free," he hissed, resolving to wonder about what happened to him later. "Come help me with Alice. Something's funky about her."

"Her? What about me? I'm…I don't know what I am." Jayce stumbled into the curtain and thrashed to get through it. As soon as he did, there stood Jayce, the same brown as the board he'd been strapped to, complete with grain lines on his skin. His hair was the same, his lips, everything—really everything—but his eyes. The eyes stayed that same icy blue. "What did they do to us?"

"I got no clue. Look at Alice, though. And she's freezing." Bobby grasped a frozen needle and tugged. It refused to budge. He let go and rubbed his fingers to warm them. "The heck?"

Jayce unbuckled the straps, finding them cold and stiff. "This is insane."

"Don't I know it." Bobby tried wiggling one needle, then finally yanked as hard as he could. It came away with a jagged chunk of ice attached to it, the crystals appearing to be skin and blood. "Damn. She's made outta ice now?"

Jayce pulled at a wire sensor pad and found it to be stuck, too. "I think it's frozen to her." He patted her face. "Alice, wake up."

"Can I pull the tube off the needle, or will that make stuff worse?"

"I'm a security guard, I've got no idea. Try it and see what happens."

Bobby nodded and pulled out tubes. For good measure, he yanked the power cords of the machines out of the outlets in the floor. "Ai, you awake yet?"

Ai groaned. "Am I dead?"

"Don't think so. If you are, so am I, and this is the weirdest afterlife I could imagine. You're free, see if you can walk and come this way."

"I'm naked."

Jayce rolled his eyes. "That's what she's worried about right now," he muttered. Reaching over, he yanked a curtain down and ripped it apart, then another one. His effort produced four pieces of white cloth suitable for covering themselves up.

Bobby took one to Ai, who blushed when she saw him and wrapped it around herself immediately. She didn't look any different, but her hand shook so fast it blurred as she used it to avert her eyes from his own nakedness. “Sorry,” he mumbled, taking his own section of curtain and wrapping it around his waist like a towel.

Alice sucked in a breath, and Bobby turned to go back to her side. Ai took a step in that direction, then Bobby felt a breeze blow past him. The remaining curtains ruffled in the breeze and Ai disappeared.

“What was that?” Now with his own curtain fastened around his waist, Jayce pushed the still hanging curtain between them aside. “Where’s Ai?”

Another breeze blew past them and Ai reappeared. “Oh my God, oh my God, oh my God, oh my—”

Bobby grabbed her hands and held them firmly. “Calm down. What happened?”

Ai squeezed her eyes shut and shook her head. “I went so fast I couldn’t— It was crazy.”

“This is all crazy,” Bobby pointed out. “Tell me something here that ain’t crazy.”

Alice groaned, getting everyone’s attention. “Who turned the heat up? Hey, we’re free.” She looked down at her hands and her eyes went wide. “I… I’m…”

“Icy,” Bobby supplied helpfully. “Look, this is all freaky, but we gotta get while the getting is good, yeah?”

“Seconded,” Jayce nodded. “Can you pull the needles and things off?”

Alice focused on the simple question and tugged at one. For her, the needle slid right out. “Yeah.” She quickly yanked it all out and off and hopped to her feet. Where they touched the floor, ice formed. She gulped. “My hands are itchy, like…” Putting one out, she grimaced with confused effort and a spray of ice shards shot from them. Her mouth opened and shut wordlessly.

“We’re superheroes,” Ai breathed. “Bobby, what can you do?

How did you get free? ”

“Later.” He waved off the question and started moving. Someone had to. Otherwise, they’d all stand around, freaked out by themselves and each other, until someone came back and drugged them again. “There’s gotta be a door here someplace.”

“Oh! This way.” Leading by pointing, Ai walked with Bobby across a room full of computers and equipment that put him in mind of a modern torture chamber. Vague, dream-like snatches of memory made him think they’d used at least a few of these things on him.

“Where are we?” Alice looked around in horrified wonder. “The island of Dr. Moreau?”

“Don’t know what that means, but we gotta be careful getting out or else they’ll put us all down before we get anyplace.” Bobby went to the door and put his ear against it. He heard nothing. It might have been too thick to hear through. “Anybody got any bright ideas?”

“We don’t know enough about the facility to make a plan.” Jayce reached out and checked the knob. “It’s not locked, we should at least open it and take a look. If anybody sees a weapon, I’ve got experience handling them.”

“I’ve fired a rifle a time or two,” Bobby nodded, “but it’s been a while.”

Alice gulped. “I…guess…I can shoot ice at people.”

“Don’t worry, the goal here is to get out of this place, whatever it is, not to kill nobody or nothing.”

“Anybody.”

“What?” Bobby blinked at Alice, confused.

“Not to kill anybody.” She hugged herself and rocked on her heels, giving the impression she thought most of her sanity had already leaked out and she had to clutch at what remained. “You said ‘nobody.’”

Jayce rolled his eyes. "I'm opening the door." He grabbed the knob again and turned it slowly. The silver color of the knob infected his hand, then sped up his arm. Bobby imagined an invisible man with spray paint cans assaulting him. When it reached his shoulder, it spread across him until his entire body took on that color. He tapped a thumb and forefinger together and it made a metallic tinging sound. "Huh."

Deciding not to get sidetracked by that, Bobby took over and pushed the door open. From there, they crept through a labyrinth of epic proportions, though it had all been laid out in grids, like any other building. Ai sped ahead by accident several times. Alice left icy footprints. Jayce avoided touching things, as the weird change seemed to only happen through his hands. Nothing happened to Bobby. He decided those little parts must have been a fluke, or his imagination.

They trudged up three flights of stairs, checking each floor as they went, before finally finding a dark window. This place reminded Bobby of horror movies in sanitariums. Every door they passed made him wonder if a lunatic with rubber gloves and an axe or a chainsaw would lunge out. As they went, most sections, including the stairwell, had been left in darkness. Those few with lights had little of it, dim bulbs straining against the inky blackness of dank underground passages.

Jayce checked the first window they found for an alarm trigger and found one. "Okay," he whispered. The room they'd slipped into had a narrow path circling around stacked filing cabinets. "We can't go out the window without raising an alarm for whoever is monitoring the place. I could try breaking the glass, but I'm not sure what kind of alarm it is. I can just tell there is one."

Bobby peered out the window into the night, able to make out three cars in the reflected light. "It don't look like there's anything to really stop us once we're out of the building. The parking lot ain't very big, and I don't see no fence."

"I'd rather get out without them noticing, if we can." Jayce also peered out, frowning. "They'll find we're missing soon enough, but not as soon as if we set off the alarm. A few hours' head start could make a very big difference."

While they spoke, Ai poked through filing cabinets. Her newfound speed didn't manifest during this activity, and she picked random folders to open and leaf through. "Hey," she pulled a page out, "this one has my name on it. And here, Robert Mitchell, right? Yours is on here, too."

Footsteps went by the door, the sounds of someone patrolling the hallway outside. They all froze, except Ai, who shoved the one page down the front of her makeshift dress. It must have made enough noise to catch the sentry's attention, because the footsteps stopped, then approached the door. The doorknob turned and the door opened, a flashlight clicked on and shined in. By that time, all four of them had hidden among the cabinets, but the one drawer hung open. "Somebody in here?" The man's voice was deep and, to Bobby, sounded dangerous, though that might have been his imagination.

Despite their silence, the sentry walked in to investigate. So much for getting out without a fuss. Bobby didn't want to hurt the guy, but maybe if he got walloped without realizing what happened, they could still get away more or less clean. The guard paced to the filing cabinet and looked it over, then pushed it shut.

A whoosh of air announced that Ai took her chance and ran out the door. The guard turned to look, shining the light. Jayce and Bobby both surged at the guard, the bigger man reaching him first and shoving him against a file cabinet. He staggered into Bobby, who followed up with a slug to the gut.

This guy had to be in good shape, because he failed to fall to the floor. Instead, he doubled over and waved the flashlight around. "Hey," he shouted, "help!" Jayce socked him in the face, which shut him up and dropped him to the floor. Bobby grabbed what he could from the man's pockets and belt: keys, baton, radio. Alice picked up the flashlight where the guard had dropped it.

"Come on," Jayce hissed. "Let's get out of here." The three of them found themselves face to face with another guard who had his baton out already. Ai was nowhere to be seen.

This new guard stared, blinked, then pointed. "Hey, who are you? What are you doing here?"

"Leaving," Jayce snarled as he charged forward. The guard's eyes popped wide as he took in the sight. The metal man plowed into the poor guy, sending him flying backwards into the wall. He made a dent and fell to the floor in a heap. "Move it," he called back. "There could be more."

They rounded the next corner and found a gate of iron bars between them and the solid white front door. Ai stood at the gate, holding the bars and shaking them so fast she blurred. Bobby ran for the security booth where the second guard must have been and slid into the seat. He checked the camera feeds and looked over the buttons and knobs and things. In a stroke of good luck, everything had a label.

"Should we try to erase camera footage?"

"Is there an obvious way to do that?" Alice followed him in and peered around. Jayce stopped a step behind Ai, trying to calm her down.

"Um…well, it's a computer. You're a college student, right? You got any ideas?"

"Sure, medical students are all about hacking."

"Hey, I barely scraped through high school, like I know what people do in college."

"Argue later," Jayce called in. "Just open the damned door."

Bobby nodded and hit the button for the gate. They'd just have to hope that whatever got caught on tape wasn't especially useful in tracking them down. Jayce held the gate open while they all filed out and through the front door. "Maybe we should steal a car," Ai suggested, pointing at the four vehicles parked near the door. "We have that one guy's keys, right?"

Bobby held the ring of keys up and flipped through them. "These are all just building keys, ain't no car keys here." Since they weren't useful, he tossed them into the landscaping, leaving him with a baton and radio. The radio didn't seem useful, either, but he held onto it. Might be worth something in trade to someone for something. No question the baton could be useful.

The four of them ran for it. Ai either couldn't spark her super speed or managed not to so she could stay with the group. They crossed the parking lot and hustled across some grass with scattered trees that led to a patch of woods, then found a street and crossed it and kept going. Alice couldn't keep up the pace for very long, so they slowed to a walk and looked around as they went.

Perhaps two hours later, when dawn gave the eastern sky a rosy glow, Bobby said, "Where in heckbiscuits are we?"

"'Heckbiscuits'?"

Bobby shrugged and gave Alice a sheepish grin. "It's something my Momma says."

Alice rolled her eyes. "Who knows." They walked down the side of a tree-lined road with no signs so far, other than a white one with nothing but a number. Grasses and shrubs grew all the way to the edge, and the asphalt had cracks with scraggly weeds growing in them.

"We should have gone a different direction," Jayce grumbled.

Ai whined. “My feet hurt.”

Bobby frowned and looked around more. “Anybody see a house or something? Can’t just be nothing. There’s a road. Roads don’t get put where there’s nothing.”

Alice groaned, plodding along in front of him, her head hanging with exhaustion. “What are we going to do? Knock on the door and ask to borrow some sugar?”

“Hey, it’s not like I ever broke outta a secret experimental facility before. How’m I supposed to know what to do?”

“I see a house.” Jayce pointed at a building in the distance, one they wouldn’t have to cross the road to reach. “Alice has a point, though. We should decide what to say.”

Ai pouted. “Maybe just one of us should walk up and ask how far to the next town?”

Alice stopped. “Okay, look, we need to make some decisions. Just going without a plan isn’t going to work.”

Everyone else stopped too, and Bobby sighed. “Fair point.” He looked at his three fellow escapees and took in the sight of them. “Okay, imagine you’re a regular person and somebody walks up to you wearing a ripped down curtain, chewed up and spit out, and says they need directions.” The three of them mirrored his thoughts with their disapproval and disappointment. “Yeah, we need a plan. In the movies, folks always steal clothes and then pretend they’re normal.”

“I don’t want to steal,” Alice declared. “I have a bank account. For that matter, I have a family. We should just find a phone and call home.”

Jayce scratched at his chin, a week’s worth of beard growth making the metal-on-metal sound raspy. “We were picked up by FBI agents. That means this is the government trying to experiment on us. They’ll want us back.”

“We gotta stay off grid,” Bobby nodded. Alice and Ai both

looked unhappy about that, but neither disputed him. "What do we really need?"

Ai pulled the list she grabbed out of her curtain-dress and scanned it. "There's more to it than that. There's a Jayce Westbrook on here, and an Alice Fielding. Is that you two?" Both nodded. "Okay, there are…thirty-five names on this list. What about all the rest? Once they find we're gone, will they just go and try picking up four more? Or eight more? Or all the rest? Shouldn't we do something about that?"

"What all is on that page? Just our names?" Bobby stepped closer to peer over the top.

"This is my Social Security number, and the city I live in, and my birthdate."

"Dang."

Jayce nodded for everyone to follow him a short distance farther, where the wild forest dropped away from the side of the road in favor of grass and a farmer's field. He sat himself down with a clank. "I wouldn't wish what happened to us on anyone. They should at least be warned. We're not really in any position to mount a rescue, though. Come with us, we have nothing and nowhere to go, but we're hiding, too! No, it's a crappy sell. I'd slam the door in my face."

The other three paced over and sat down with Jayce. "We need some clothes," Bobby suggested, "some money, and a place to go. Transportation and phones would be good, too."

"Can't we go talk to the press?" Alice picked at the spot where Bobby ripped out a little piece of her flesh. It had scabbed over when she reverted back from being blue during the walk.

"I don't know I want people knowing about what I can do." Ai shivered. "You've heard of the X-Men, right? Regular people hate them because they have superpowers."

"How do they have a list with all that on it," Bobby mused. "I mean, what're the odds that all four of us, with these eyes, just wind up on the same list with that much information about us? "

"They knew we were different," Alice nodded. "They knew there was a reason to have us on a list."

"We must have something else in common then. I know my daddy wasn't my daddy," Bobby offered. "My Momma met him when I was three."

"My father died when I was young, but I've seen pictures of him, and he didn't have these eyes." Jayce tapped his temple.

Alice sighed lightly. "I was adopted, my parents are white."

They all looked at Ai, and she shrugged. "If my parents aren't my parents, they never told me, but yeah, neither of them has these eyes."

Alice pursed her lips. "I'm only *pre*-med, but I do know the odds of us having the same highly unusual eyes and not being related somehow are pretty small."

"That means the folks on that list are our family. Even if it's the decent thing to do to warn 'em, that makes it the right thing to do, too." Bobby shrugged. "I don't know if we should be public about ourselves or not, but I feel like that's a decision we ought to make as a whole group, not just four of us taking it 'pon ourselves to bat our baby blues at the camera."

"That's a good point," Jayce nodded. "We should be careful not to elect ourselves leaders of the whole group."

Bobby looked to the girls to make sure they didn't disagree, and found them nodding. "M'kay, well, we all got pretty obvious superpowers—"

Alice interrupted by poking him in the arm. "Except you. You said later, it's later."

Bobby pursed his lips, but he nodded. He knew what they could do, it was only fair they know what he could do. Even if he still hoped it hadn't been real. One deep breath followed another, then he came apart. Some of the swarm had to break free of his modesty curtain, but once it did, the little critters romped about in the grass and the air. The other three reacted with sharp intakes of breath. Ai held out her hand, so he directed one to land there, and it walked on her palm.

"They're cute! How cool is it to be made of tiny little silver dragons?" The one on her palm reared up on its hind legs and splayed its wings out.

"You win the prize for weirdest superpower." Alice shrank away, so he directed them to leave her alone.

Jayce held up a finger, and when one landed there, he brought it close to his face. "They look like they're robotic, even. Do they need to eat separate from you? Actually, Bobby, can you talk through them?"

Bobby made the effort to re-form, doing his best to put himself together under the curtain scrap. He adjusted it as soon as his hands were whole. "No, least I can't figure how. They can make a little noise, though. Dunno if they need to eat. Guess I'll find out at some point. I think I might be able to do just part of me at a time, but I'm not sure how to control it like that yet. Probably take practice. Anyway, I was trying to make a point. Which is that if any of the others ain't got their superpower yet, or it takes something they injected into us, we all got visible powers that we can use to show 'em we're not just crazy."

Alice pointed her hand away from the group and made a shower of ice shards skitter across the road. On the heated blacktop, then melted into puddles. "Yeah. Not crazy. We need clothes and money, then. We're back to that problem. If we *have* to steal, can we at least try to keep it to stealing from people who can afford it?"

"Sounds fair."

Chapter 4

They skipped the house and kept going in hopes of something better. Like Alice, the act of walking a long distance eventually let Jayce lose his silver sheen in favor of his normal cinnamon skin. About an hour after dawn, a beat-up old pickup truck drove by. It stopped less than a hundred feet in front of them. When Bobby, who wound up in the lead, saw an older man in jeans and a t-shirt with a concerned look on his face getting out, he perked up. Either they'd have to beat the crap out of him to take his keys, or they could get a ride someplace.

"You kids need some help?" He had a mild Southern accent, which made Bobby guess Virginia, Tennessee, or a nearby state.

Bobby threw down some good old Southern 'aw shucks'. Momma called it him a punk when he did it, then she'd tousle his hair and tell him to go fix something. "We're totally lost, sir, and real embarrassed. Car broke down, so we thought we'd have a little romp in the woods, ya know? Make the best of it while we wait for a tow.

"Bad storm hit while we was, er, *busy*, and all our clothes got blown away. When we got back to where we left the car, it was gone, only we got no clue where to. This is the best we could do to avoid walking around naked." Ai reached him first, so he slid his arm around her waist and she tried not to be surprised by this. Behind him, Jayce stopped with Alice and set his hands on her, suggesting a claim on her.

The older man raised bushy eyebrows, and then cracked a grin and chuckled. "That's a streak of bad luck. Hop in, I'll give you a lift to the next town."

The truck had a bench seat, offering only enough space for three across. Ai perched on Bobby's lap and he placed his hands carefully on her waist. "This is mighty kind of you, sir. Most folks'd just drive on by. What's the next town?"

"Purcellville. Where were you headed to?"

The town name was unfamiliar, giving Bobby nothing to work with. "Oh, we come up from the Atlanta area and we're just kinda taking a road trip to nowhere in particular. I guess we found it, huh?"

While the old man chuckled, Jayce asked, "You from this area?"

"Born and raised, Virginia's in my blood, through and through. You kids come up through Gainesville?"

"No, sir, we've been driving up the country roads, mostly." Northern Virginia, then. Bobby didn't know Virginia too well, but he knew where Gainesville was. "Last big city was Charlottesville. Nice place."

"Sure is." The man filled the truck with chatter for the next half hour, telling them about family he had in Charlottesville. Bobby had no interest in his four granddaughters and two grandsons, all of whom apparently had won awards, science fairs, beauty pageants, or talent contests. Ai had the presence of mind to make appropriate noises, keeping him talking and not asking about them.

Purcellville didn't have much, but it did have a gas station, which was good enough. Jayce politely wished the man well when they climbed out, and he went on his way. The teenager manning the gas station stared at them all, and Jayce went over to talk to the guy while Bobby took the girls around back. He saw a garbage dumpster and decided he might as well take a look. Worn, dirty shoes would be better than barefoot.

He hopped up and climbed inside, finding it to be free of anything terribly disgusting. It looked like most of what got dumped back here was packaging from this and that, and it must have been emptied within the past few days. "There's cardboard in here, we could use that for shelter if we gotta."

"I live in an apartment." Alice whined. "I have money. Not a lot, but enough to afford an apartment. This is not fair."

"You're talking like fair matters," Ai said. "Fair left the building the second we were arrested."

Finding nothing other than cardboard and clear plastic, Bobby levered himself back out again and hopped to the ground. "Sorry, ladies, no designer dresses inside."

Alice glared at him, Ai snorted. Jayce found them, carrying a paper cup. "Best I could do was some clean water to drink." He offered the cup to Ai, who took a few sips before passing it on. "I asked what's in this town. He said there's a diner, a doughnut shop, a bar, and a few small stores. Most people drive someplace else to do their major shopping. There are two churches, so we could maybe try them for a little charity, but the more we ask for, the more risk we run of being remembered or recognized.

"I ain't going to a church with the story I fed that old guy." Bobby smirked and handed the cup to Alice to finish off.

Jayce chuckled. "No, probably not the best choice for that. Any other excuse I can come up with, though, is something we should go to the cops for."

"Even that excuse, we ought to be going to the cops for, to

find the car. Hate to say it, but stealing's probably our only real option. We kinda need a city, I think, but I got the impression we ain't exactly near one."

"No, we're not. There's a map up inside. We're in the north part of the state. Washington, DC is relatively close, but outside walking distance. The border with West Virginia is only a mile or two straight north. We're not quite in the Appalachians here."

"That kinda makes sense, I guess. If'n you were gonna set up a secret government lab for human experimentation, you'd put it in the middle of nowhere, but not far from someplace like DeeCee or a military base or something."

Jayce nodded. "One of the shops might be willing to trade for that radio, but one of us really needs to be wearing clothes."

"This isn't really that bad." Ai futzed with her makeshift dress. "With some kind of cord for my waist, maybe a little effort with folding, it could pass for a dress. I still don't have any shoes, though."

"I know we don't want to take from folks if we can help it, but you can go so fast..." Bobby shrugged uncomfortably. "You could probably swipe something without being seen."

Ai opened her mouth to say something, then shut it.

"These people are probably not in a great situation, economically speaking." Alice tossed the empty cup up into the dumpster behind her. "Small towns is where recessions hit the hardest, usually."

"Yeah, well, we got nothing." Bobby turned to Ai. "Just grab some sandals, maybe a shirt or something. I can go airborne, I guess, and have a look around, maybe even find out how fast I can go like that. If I get the chance, maybe I can grab something, too."

Jayce looked around. "We'll stay back here. It's out of sight."

"Okay." Ai took a deep breath and squinted off into the distance. "Here goes nothing." She shot off faster than the eye could track, leaving a small whoosh of wind in her wake.

"Yeah, me too." Bobby handed over the radio and baton, then exploded out into dragons and went up. Focused like this, and with nothing in the way, they actually moved pretty fast. To avoid being seen, he had the swarm spread out. He got images from all the different eyes, and his mind somehow—he chose not to think about it—put them together without making his head explode. Wherever that might be. As a result, he had a birds' eye view of the town and the sky for miles around.

As an experiment, he picked five dragons and sent them off to investigate specific spots, on a mission to find food. Right now, he'd be willing to grab anything edible. The rest of the swarm kept spreading out until he covered a sizable area. Instead of seeing through all the dragons, he saw through the majority of them in the large swarm. If he was whole and had a skull with a brain inside it, he'd say there were five little tickles in the back of his head to let him know five dragons had gone elsewhere.

By focusing on one in particular, he saw what it saw and heard what it heard. A queer sensation, to be sure, since he got the distinct impression the tiny dragon had something of a mind of its own. Not an advanced intellect, but instincts and a kind of intelligence. It could solve simple puzzles, probably, without his input. He had to wonder at that, but not for long, because this one found a dumpster with food in it. Another of the 'tickles' got excited, so as he started the swarm moving towards the first scout, he focused on the second. It had found a rusty old car with the hood stuck open.

Why, exactly, that would make the dragon excited when he sent it for food, he had no idea. Until it dove in, grabbed a small gear, and devoured it. Oh. The dragons needed to eat, and they ate metal things. Great. If the dragons ate, would that fill him up, too? How about the other way around? Only one way to find out. Since he wasn't sure exactly what the dragons needed, he went for the people food. Re-forming at that dumpster, he found himself naked again, this time in an otherwise empty alley.

This dragon had found stale baked goods, fruit past its prime, and floppy vegetables. Starving, he ate without caring about the mushy, moldy spot on the apple or the bites out of a mushy grilled cheese sandwich. He started with the stuff that looked the least appetizing and went from there. For the moment, he had to know if filling himself up also filled up the dragons, or he'd have another problem. The others could wait.

Once he'd taken the edge of his hunger off, he looked down at himself. He had four other dragons still out there, and that ought to equate to four bits of him missing. With a brief inspection, he discovered each foot had the two smallest toes missing. Apparently, each dragon didn't correspond to a specific part of his body, which struck him as both interesting and disturbing.

He sated his belly enough to trust it would last a few hours, then blew out into dragons again. Except for that one, all of them gurgled with hunger to his mind. Damn. At least it seemed they could go for a while yet. From listening to them, he got a small child vibe, reminding him of the grandkids of some of Momma's friends.

When he touched down and re-formed, Ai had already returned, now in a red shirt and sandals with her curtain serving as a skirt. Alice had a pair of the same sandals on, without the shirt. Jayce handed Bobby his curtain piece without a word.

"Looks like you did alright. The dumpster behind the diner has some food that's decent and free. I went ahead and filled myself up because I got a new issue. Apparently, my dragons need to eat separate from me."

Alice gave him a flat look. "That makes no sense."

"Tell me how you spitting ice from your hands makes sense."

Bobby shrugged, because the amount of logic his life operated on now didn't much matter to him. "Anyway, I'mma go off and see if I can find something for them while you all do what you gotta do." Before any of them could object, he blew out into the swarm again. Somehow, he'd have to figure out a way to bring clothes along with him. It wasn't the best possible way ever to travel if he couldn't manage that, but it did still beat walking around barefoot.

He saw the other three head off in the direction of the diner and trusted they could take care of themselves. With four scouts already out, he sent ten more, looking for whatever they wanted to eat. The one that found its meal rejoined the swarm, carrying another gear it found. It could barely manage the weight and other dragons helped by converging and devouring it. By the time it was truly back with the swarm, he had fifteen happy dragons and no gear. At that rate, these things would be a plague of locusts for metal. He was made up of hundreds of the things, maybe even thousands. Hopefully, they didn't need to eat very often.

Twenty minutes later, he noticed his three fellow escapees leaving the alley behind the diner. Jayce licked his fingers. The girls had no such issues. Few of his scouts had managed to find anything he considered acceptable to take. Functioning machinery needed to be left alone, and people needed to be avoided. Aside from a handful of old cars with a few gears and cogs, they had nothing to eat. Most of the swarm remained cranky, so he dove down to the alley and re-formed there.

"Just get cash if you can, but if you see something that would help us a lot, try to swap for as much as you can." Jayce handed the radio over to Ai. He tossed Bobby's curtain at him without looking.

Ai and Alice both nodded. Ai took a deep breath and grabbed Alice's hand, tugging her across the street and into the general store a few buildings up.

Bobby sighed lightly as he watched them. "I didn't find nothing worth going for."

"At least the girls have shoes now." Jayce leaned his bare back against the wall of the building behind him. "What do you really think about hunting down the people on that list?"

The question made Bobby raise his brow and blink a few times. "I said what I meant. It'd be crappy if anybody else had to go through this. Even worse if they decided their superpowers made 'em above the law in a big way. Imagine if Alice decided she just wanted stuff and took it."

Jayce crossed his arms over his chest, looming over him. "Ai already did that. You encouraged her to, even."

"Just for survival, though." Bobby had been intimidated and beaten up by badder guys than Jayce. He shrugged. "I wouldn't tell her to go get a 'spensive handbag or something if she wanted it. I think we really just need to get clothes, then start finding the others. They won't have the same problems getting their own money as we do. They'll be able to pack a bag, even."

"True. If we did want to wreak some havoc, though, we could do quite a bit."

"Oh, sure. I can see that. Ai could rob a place blind. You can probably kill a person with your fist. Alice, she's pretty deadly, or plenty of chaos. Me, I can be a horde of gremlins and the ultimate big brother, both at once. We're real dangerous, and we need to keep everybody else from realizing that. 'Cause the second they do, we're not walking free anymore, we're either in a cage or hiding."

"I'm glad you see that." Jayce gave him a small smile. "Alice and Ai, I'm not so sure they really do. Alice seems more in denial than anything else. Ai… The small theft she did do seemed like it left her more excited than I feel comfortable with. As far as our continued survival is concerned, anyway. I really don't care if she steals a Gucci handbag, I just care whether her stealing it leads to someone deciding I need to be in a hole in the ground."

The girls backed out of the store with the radio still in hand and hurried to the alley, cutting off Bobby's reponse. He frowned and gestured for Jayce to duck farther into the alley with him. The obvious question was obvious, so he didn't bother voicing it, and neither did the bigger man.

"They had a TV on inside," Ai whispered. "It had a breaking news report. They called us federal fugitives, extremely dangerous. I don't think the guy working there saw us before we backed out."

"They had pictures of us." Alice wrung her hands together. "Why are they saying we're dangerous?"

Bobby looked past them, reflexively wanting to see the TV somehow, and recognized the front end of a cop cruiser. "Come on, we need to move." He noticed Jayce saw it, too, and they both herded the girls away from the mouth of the alley. "I guess it's safe to say they noticed we were missing by now."

Alice snorted. "Ya think?"

"Maybe we should split up." Ai peered out the other end of the alley, checking both ways before waving to indicate the way was clear. "I can get pretty far in a short time."

Jayce shook his head. "I don't think that's a good idea. We'll be better off if we stick together."

"Even if we aren't, at least if one of us gets nabbed, the others'll know. And shoot, facing all this alone is kinda crappy." Bobby checked behind them and saw another cop car driving past the alley. He wasn't sure if the cops inside saw them, but how could they not? Likewise, before they had to cross that last street, the cops —he amended himself to use the word 'deputies', because this car had 'Loudoun County Sheriff' plastered on the side—in that other car had to have seen them, also. "Why ain't they getting out and pointing guns at us?"

"Are you upset about that?"

"No, it just…" Bobby stopped. "Hold up a sec." He could see they considered that a dumb idea, and he held up a hand to ask for a minute's grace. "Just listen for a minute. S'posing the deputies," he pitched a thumb over his shoulder to where the car went past, "are here in this podunkville because that old guy heard about us on the radio and called it in. Now, we walked here from that lab, right? So we ain't real far from it. If I was the bad guys here, I'd have a van or something, full of guys with big guns, just waiting to scream out to wherever we got sighted."

Jayce narrowed his eyes as she stared at the mouth of the alley. "You think they're herding us."

Bobby nodded. "It makes sense, and explains why these deputies ain't all trying to be heroes by taking down the known terrorists."

Ai rubbed her face and mewled. Alice's eyes watered and she hugged herself.

Jayce, on the other hand, kept staring, his eyes gone hard. "If we engage them here, they'll get a good handle on what we can do."

"How can we avoid it?" Ai shook her head. "Scratch that. How can you all avoid it? I can just run right by."

"And I can fly away." Bobby frowned and tried hard to think. "We gotta go backwards, or do something unexpected. Come on." The quartet hurried back the way they'd come for one block. Instead of sticking to the alley, they turned down the next street and ducked into the first open door they came across. It was somebody's house, and a voice came from farther inside almost immediately.

"Rich, is that you," a woman's voice called out. "Did you forget something?" They heard the babbling of a young child, too. While this place might be better for a few minutes than running up the street, it sucked as a hidey-hole. Before any of them did more than make a face to express unhappiness at this turn of events, the owner of the voice turned the corner and stopped, her expression comically surprised. She turned out to be a pretty, petite, and very pregnant brunette.

"Ma'am, we don't mean you no harm at all, and we ain't here to rob you or nothing." Bobby put up his hands in the universal sign of 'I'm harmless'. Thank goodness Jayce hid the baton and radio behind his back. Thinking fast, he searched for words to make this better instead of worse. "We had a bit of trouble, and are really just lost and confused and stuff. I gotta admit, we were hoping to get a drink of clean water and maybe use the phone, and if you weren't here, we mighta took some clothes, but that's all, I swear on my daddy's grave."

The woman stood there, blinking in stupid shock. "We don't have a lot, but, um, if all you want is a drink of water, I…um, suppose that's…not a problem."

He hurried down the hallway to her, mostly to make sure she didn't slip in a phone call to 911, while doing his best to keep looking harmless. "Hi there," he said cheerfully to the little girl in the high chair, her hand stuck in a bowl of dry cereal. He waved to her, she waved back. "She about eighteen months?" Glancing back, he met Ai's eyes and jerked his chin for her to join him. She struck him as the most harmless looking of the group.

"Um, nineteen, yes," the woman said with a nod, her wide eyes darting between them. She edged towards the little girl.

"I swear we will not harm you, or her, or the one yet to come." He gestured to her belly. "We're just really having a rough time right now. It ain't your fault, and we ain't gonna put it on you." He could see Alice and Jayce having a whispered conversation out of the corner of his eye, probably around the topic of what to do now, and ignored it.

Moving slowly and keeping her hands in plain sight, Ai got herself a cup from a cabinet that hung open already and filled it with tap water. She gulped the water down and gave a satisfied sigh as she refilled it. "This is a really nice house. And you have good water. The water at my parents' house is really crappy, we have to use a filter."

"Thanks." The woman put her rather substantial girth between Bobby and the little girl, her hands reaching behind her to grip the tray of the high chair. "What do you want from us?"

"Not much." Bobby looked around the kitchen and imagined Momma in it. She'd be tickled pink to have this much space. When his eyes fell back on her, he realized that made him appear to be casing the place. He threw on his 'aw shucks' smile. "Not calling the cops would be real nice."

"Why are the police after you?"

Bobby felt Ai watching him and thought for a moment how to answer the question. "We ain't rightly sure. It seems like a mistake to all of us, but they sure do seem to want us."

For the first time, the woman's eyes traveled down his body. He hoped that meant he'd managed to get her to relax enough to not scream the second they left. Even better, she appreciated what she saw. His job did, after all, having him doing manual labor five days a week. She tore her eyes away from his bare chest and cleared her throat. "How did you lose your clothes?"

"We all woke up naked in a lab and broke out." In reaction to this, Ai goggled at him. She turned away to avoid letting the woman see it. He scratched at the back of his neck to keep Ai from distracting both of them. As he'd hoped, the woman found his flexing bicep more interesting than Ai's sudden movement. "Don't rightly know what they were doing to us, don't rightly much want to know, we just wanted to be outta there."

"Oh my goodness, that's horrible. Who would do that?" The woman let go of the high chair and held her hands out in a kind of low-key invitation. "Are you hungry? You know, my husband, he's not that much bigger than you. Some of his clothes might fit you reasonably well. Sweatpants, maybe." She pointed and tried to lead them out of the kitchen.

Bobby put up a hand to stop her. "You should stay with your daughter, ma'am. If you don't mind us just taking something to wear, we appreciate that, and we won't take nothing else." Out of the corner of his eye, he saw Jayce head off in the direction he saw some stairs. "I swear I'm being honest."

Ai huffed in exasperation. "Why are you explaining this stuff?"

"I don't know." He sighed and shook his head. "I guess I figured if I told somebody, it would make more sense or something."

"I've never seen an Oriental person with blue eyes before." The woman decided to sit down beside her daughter, her hand on her belly. The little girl ignored everyone in the room and stuffed more cereal in her mouth.

"Japanese." Ai filled the glass back up and handed it to Bobby. "Nobody in my family has blue eyes but me. We don't know how it happened."

"There's…well, you know. A…usual sort of way for— For that to happen." The woman shifted as she spoke, and dropped her eyes to their feet.

Bobby chuckled, hoping to disarm her more. "Yes, ma'am, there sure is. Right now, our eyes seems like the main reason why they want to experiment on us, though."

Brow furrowed, the woman lifted her head again and cocked her head to one side. "Isn't that the kind of thing the Nazis did? Experimenting on people because of their genetics. Twins and all."

"I didn't do all that great in school, but that sounds about like what I heard of 'em."

One corner of Ai's mouth curled into a scowl. "Our government has done plenty of that kind of thing, too."

Bobby heard Jayce making his way back and turned in time to catch the pair of boxer shorts thrown at his face. "We really do appreciate your kindness," Jayce said politely. "We'll get out of your home shortly."

"Yeah. Do you mind if we use your bathroom before we go?"

Chapter 5

It was good to have underwear, Bobby thought as they hurried through backyards to avoid being seen on the streets. He hoped that saint of a woman got the long, happy life she deserved. Maybe someday, he'd come back here and do something nice for her and her family. All because he now had boxers, shorts, and a t- shirt —a significant improvement over the curtain kilt. Without shoes, he still had to watch where he walked, but at least he didn't have to worry about flashing anyone anymore.

Jayce now had flip-flops, putting extra bounce in his step. The sweatpants and plain shirt fit tighter on the bigger guy, making his buff physique somehow more obvious than it had been without. The girls got underwear, too, which made both of them instantly less cranky. For whatever reason. Bobby didn't really understand women that much.

"Do you think she'll call?" Alice took Jayce's help to get over a low fence the rest of them had no trouble hopping.

"'Course she'll call."

She frowned. "Why all the talking, then? We could have just backed out again and tried another house or something."

Bobby opened his mouth to give her the same reason he had

given Ai. Someplace between his brain and his mouth, he realized there had been more to it. “It ain’t never killed no one to be polite. ‘Sides, she’s gonna wait a few minutes, I’d wager.”

Jayce grunted in agreement. “She’ll give us a head start, maybe ten minutes or so.”

“What makes you so sure?” Ai peered around, but they hadn’t yet seen any sort of official vehicles tracking them, or even trolling along looking for them.

“She didn’t feel threatened,” Jayce said.

Bobby grinned and let the unspoken compliment sustain him for a minute or two. They dashed across a street and plunged through more backyards, skirting around a house surrounded by hedges. “I say, next time we see cops, we go towards ‘em.”

Alice panted, having trouble keeping up as they kept moving without a break. “Are you crazy? They have guns.”

“We got superpowers.” He wagged his eyebrows at her, feeling clever. “I been thinking, you know, those lab guys must have some clue what we can do already. They maybe don’t know the limits, but they must know what kinda things we got up our sleeves.”

“If that’s true,” Jayce nodded as he hopped over a kid’s bicycle, “we won’t lose much by using them.”

“‘Specially on regular cops what ain’t going to believe what they saw anyway.” Bobby spent so much time paying attention to everything else, he jogged into a tree. His body exploded into tiny dragons and his clothes fell to the ground.

Jayce stopped and scooped the clothes up. “You need to figure out a way to take these with you, Bobby,” he groused. “Might as well stay that way for now.” His eyes rested on a metal swing set in the backyard they stood in. “Actually, I might as well be something else, too.” He gripped one of the legs, sending white painted aluminum spreading down and across his body.

Ai stopped and leaned against a shed near it, and Alice dropped to the ground to take a break. Apparently, she spent all her time with books and none of it with exercise.

Rising up into the sky, the swarm spread out. Bobby watched Jayce give Alice a hand up, then he flew along with them as they hurried through yards again. He saw the cruiser half a second before everyone else did, and they all followed the plan to converge on it.

Ai disappeared, a handful of leaves blown around by her passage. The cruiser bucked like a bronco and the front dented like a rock fell on it. Bobby's best guess had her jumping on the hood.

The two Sheriff's deputies scrambled out of the car, both reaching for their weapons. Jayce put his head down and charged them, plowing into one and throwing him to the ground. Something smacked into the other deputy, knocking him on his ass and sending his gun spinning away across the asphalt. Alice ran up to the car, screwed her eyes shut and grimaced, then flung ice shards at it, ripping two of the tires apart.

It looked to Bobby like the three of them had the situation under control. He sent the dragons in to swarm the deputies anyway, so Ai could grab the gun if she wanted to. The dragons behaved like a big pile of flies on rotting garbage, provoking a lot of swatting and cringing from one. The other seemed to be down for the count, so he left the poor guy alone.

"Damn," Jayce said as he stooped to check for a pulse, "I hit hard. He's still alive, though." The metal man hurried around to the other side of the car, where Bobby had the other deputy distracted. Bobby pulled the swarm away and Jayce punched him in the jaw. The dragons caught the deputy as he fell, and set his limp body on the ground.

Bobby re-formed and grabbed the boxers from Jayce. "We should see what they got."

Ai picked up the gun, holding it gingerly and away from her body. She cringed and asked, "Do we want this?"

"I'll take it." Jayce traded her the baton for the gun.

"I… I could kill someone," Alice whimpered, staring at her hands.

Bobby climbed into the car and checked for anything useful. Catching sight of the radio, he did as much damage to it as he could. He found some spare clips of ammunition in the glove box, and guessed there might be something worth taking in the trunk. He popped the release and went to take a look. "I think we could all kill people pretty easy if we put our minds to it." Inside the trunk, he found flares, vests, jumper cables, all kinds of things. A red canvas bag caught his eye. "Whatever we want, we got something to carry it in." He grabbed it and tossed it to Alice.

She watched the bag hit her arm and fall to the ground. "This is wrong. Really, really wrong."

Bobby pursed his lips and looked her over. The girl's eyes seemed stuck on the nearest unconscious deputy, wide and horrified. Taking a step closer, he poked her with a finger. "Do I gotta slap ya? "

She gulped and shook her head, then bent and picked up the bag. "No."

"Good. My Momma says only assholes hit girls."

Jayce helped him pull out everything that seemed useful. As the strongest, he'd carry it, so his opinion of the weight mattered the most. "We should check their wallets and take whatever cash they've got."

Ai zipped away while they did all this, checking all the closest streets. She breezed through several times, crossing back and forth.

"We can't do that," Alice whined. "We can't steal from the *police*."

Bobby rolled his eyes and knelt beside one deputy, yanking

his wallet out of his pocket. "This one's got thirty-three bucks." He left the guy with three ones. "I left him with snack money, you happy?"

Alice flared her nostrils and scowled hard enough to be sulking. "No."

"We don't have time for this argument right now," Jayce said.

"Ain't that the truth." Bobby took both the deputy's spare clips for his gun, then moved to the other one. He had another two spare clips, and two twenties in his wallet. In a show for Alice's benefit, he left the five and two ones. "We got fifty bucks now. That ain't much, but it's something." All of it, he handed over to Jayce. "Which way ya think?"

Alice paced back and forth between the cruiser and the sidewalk, wringing her hands and muttering. He thought she said something about medical school. Treating her as a distraction, he gave Jayce his full attention.

"Depends." Jayce hefted the bag over his shoulder and looked around. "We could head for a city, or we could go into the wilderness. So long as we don't go east, we'll hit The Appalachian Trail at some point. We could get lost there for a while and probably survive one way or another. That would mean abandoning the others like us, though."

"I don't see that as an option. City, then. We ain't really that far from DeeCee." Bobby shrugged back into the shorts and shirt as he spoke. "You got the list, or Ai still have it? If there's one in DeeCee, we maybe got a serious destination."

Jayce pulled the crumpled page from his pocket and ran his finger down it. "Jasmine Milani is in Washington."

"Sounds like a plan, then. That's east." Looking up at the sky through the trees, he pointed. "More or less that way." He looked back at the beat up cruiser. "Shame about that."

"Alice is going to have a heart attack, but we should steal a car."

Bobby pursed his lips and checked up and down the street. He saw a beat up old Nova on the street, even pointing in the right direction. Must be fate. "You smash the window, I'll hot wire it."

"You've boosted a car?" Jayce raised his brow and smirked.

"Nah," Bobby shrugged. "Girlfriend broke the key off in her ignition once, couldn't afford to get it fixed."

Chuckling, Jayce led the way. He rammed an elbow through the passenger side window and unlocked it. After tossing the loot into the back seat, he leaned against the car and watched Alice with a sigh.

Bobby slid into the driver's seat and grinned. "Suck it up, I got work to do."

"Yeah, yeah." Jayce patted the car and jogged away.

Five minutes later, Alice sat clenched up in the backseat with Ai hunkered down on the floor beside her. Jayce leaned back in the passenger seat with the brim of a Nationals ball cap they found in the car lowered over his face. No one should look at three kids in a car with the windows down on a warm summer day and think anything of it.

Bobby drove them towards the nation's capital. For the first time since they broke out of that lab, they finally managed to be accomplishing something and getting somewhere. They had a goal and plan, of sorts. He spared a thought to wonder and how many more cops they were going to have to beat up to get it all done. Cities should be relatively safe, he thought. They could blend in around the homeless, and probably find folks willing to trade for what they had now.

Construction on the other side of the highway made him think of roadblocks. He kept the car going near the speed limit, and paid attention to the other cars. After a half hour of this hypervigilance, he decided they hadn't yet realized the car had been stolen. They'd keep the search focused around that town until someone noticed, he guessed.

"I'm thinking we should ditch the car pretty quick. Soon as somebody notices it's missing, they'll have plates to look for."

"Good plan," Jayce nodded.

Alice grunted. "This is all screwed up."

"Ayup." She reminded Bobby of this girl he knew back home: prim and proper, and wouldn't date him to save her life because he occasionally strayed from the straight and narrow. That would ruin her reputation, of course. He glanced in the rearview mirror and saw she stared out the window and had let her arms relax enough to no longer have them crossed over her chest.

"I'm going to Stanford."

"Yeah, you told us that," Ai snapped, "like, fifty times already. I'm sure that makes you five hundred times better than the rest of us."

"I worked my ass off to get into that school!"

"And now you're a superhero who can make ice instead of just being made of it," Ai sneered. "Grow up, seriously. Like this is only happening to you or something. We're all sooooo sorry your carefully planned and manicured life is all messed up. News flash, ours are, too."

Alice scowled and huffed and glared out the window. Bobby and Jayce both chose not to get involved. The exchange and the silence that followed it made the car awkward and uncomfortable, so Bobby switched on the radio to find it tuned to a station with a male announcer talking.

"...considered extremely dangerous. The four fugitives are ages nineteen to twenty-one, two males and two females. The two females are of Asian descent, one male is white with light brown hair, the other is of Native American descent. All four have blue eyes with a shape being described as 'somewhat unusual'. We've got pictures on our website—"

Jayce clicked the radio back off. "We could split up to deal with contacting the rest of the people on the list. We might have enough money to get some cheap pre-paid cellphones to keep in touch with."

"I think we'll need more than we got for that."

"Oh, great," Alice growled, "we can just go steal some more. What a brilliant plan. I guess we've already done grand theft auto, so why not a little more assault and battery?"

"Alice, if'n you wanna get outta the car and let them pick you back up so they can stick you with needles again, that's fine. Just say the word, I can pull over anytime. If'n you got a better idea, we're listening. 'Til then, we're kinda stuck. None of us even has ID, and even if we did, using it would just lead 'em to us."

"Be part of the solution or get out of the way," Ai said.

Alice glared at the window in silence.

Chapter 6

The bridge over the Potomac had a toll. Bobby took an exit in Arlington and found a place to park. They piled out and left it behind, the bag slung over Jayce's shoulder. Walking across the bridge slowed them down, but a toll would take cash they couldn't afford to spend on something avoidable. Time cost nothing.

As Bobby hoped, the area had endless city, and he felt confident a body could get lost and never found here. This helped them and complicated their mission. With only fifty bucks and no phone, computer, or transportation, they had to find one particular person. The best option seemed to be hitting an internet cafe and using the time there to look up addresses for everyone on the list.

Alice took the ball cap from Jayce and went to go pay for internet access by herself, in the hope that one of them alone might not get noticed. Bobby went for a flight, leaving his clothes behind with Jayce, who sat on a park bench, trying to look like he had every reason to be there. It was midday by then, and Ai ran off and swiped them a couple of sandwiches. She got enough from multiple places for all of them to eat when Bobby and Alice returned.

From above, Bobby could feel the dragons getting impatient about eating. The vast horde dwarfed the tiny group of satisfied dragons. He sent scouts again, looking for them to find enough food for the whole swarm. For a while, he drifted around, watching cars and people moving around.

One scout hit the jackpot, finding a junkyard. Eager to reach it, the little things flew at a good clip, faster than they had before. Motivation put a fire under their tails. The swarm slipped into the back of the junkyard and slipped through. Dragons stopped and settled as the mass wormed its way through, delighted at finding pieces to devour.

He noticed they ignored most of the large metal pieces, choosing mainly gears and cogs and other small, shaped parts. It seemed to be certain kinds of metal, and the thickness mattered. They might be less picky in a pinch. This particular junkyard, though, offered more than enough of their preferred 'food'. Each one gorged itself and streaked up when it could eat nothing more. When the last dragon, happy and sated, rejoined the swarm, he directed it back to the park.

"I scored for the dragons," he told the other three when he'd re-formed behind the bench.

Jayce held up his clothes, and he shrugged into them before a cop could notice and get annoying about his nakedness. "There's a sandwich for you, and some carrots and juice."

"I managed to get addresses for all the names, but I have no idea if they're all the right people, or current. In cases where there were multiple choices, I wrote them all down. I also made copies, so we all have one." Alice handed Bobby his copy as he hopped over the bench to claim his lunch and sit down with them.

"Not sure how I'm gonna carry it with me." He stuffed his face with sandwich and his pocket with the paper.

"Just don't lose it." Jayce patted the red bag beside him. "We should go together to try to trade the stuff, I think. Stick to the sketchy parts of the city and we should be okay."

"I think we should split up," Ai said. "I'll go find Jasmine."

"I'll go with you," Bobby told Jayce. He crunched a carrot stick, then looked to Alice. "You should come with us, too. Let Ai go zippity and you get to have a say in what we get for what we got."

Alice pursed her lips and furrowed her brow. "I guess."

Bobby wanted to say something friendly, something that would make her feel more welcome, maybe. He scratched his head and tried to think of what might be taken well right now and came up empty. Chewing his bite of sandwich, he decided to be grateful she'd left some of her attitude behind in the car and leave it at that.

Jayce, who'd been looking at a city map for a while now, suggested a place they could meet back up that he felt confident had to be a lousy part of town. Ai took off before Bobby finished eating, and the trio set off with his hands and mouth full of food and juice. When he finished what he had, he knew he could pack more away without feeling full. The next time they sent Ai to swipe food, he'd ask her to grab extra for him.

An hour later, they still had twenty bucks, and Jayce and Bobby had jeans and t-shirts, combat boots, and trenchcoats with pockets. Alice had pants and a shirt and a sports bra, along with regular, cheap shoes. They got the same for Ai. They also had four super-cheap pre-paid cellphones. The bag had been replaced with a gray backpack, and now held a set of basic tools, the extra clips for the gun Jayce hid in his trenchcoat, the baton, and a battery-free wind-up flashlight.

The meeting place turned out to be a gathering point for homeless people, and Bobby looked around with interest at their tactical approaches to life without stuff. Actually, a lot of them had plenty of stuff, in shopping carts and shabby wheeled packs. With nothing better to do while waiting, he sat down next to a guy in an old Army jacket and asked about the weather. Nearby, Jayce leaned against a streetlight and watched everything happening around him.

Alice hugged herself and took excessive care to not touch anyone or anything. She gave the impression of a fish out of water—one with disdain for its new surroundings. Bobby noticed a woman deliberately bump into Alice, then stop and growl at her, too low to be overheard.

Brushing her arm off, Alice stepped away and shook her head. She used both hands to ward the woman off and kept taking small steps towards Bobby. Jayce's head shimmered to the same mottled gray as the lamppost and he stood away from it.

"You come down here for a school project, Princess?"

"No, wait, I know, court ordered community service!"

"Some new church come to save our souls?"

"Some new church come to save our souls?" Several different people bumped Alice around, all unhappy to see her here.

"Stop touching me!" She covered her head and repeated the plaintive wail over and over.

Jayce pushed one man aside without using his full strength, his low voice murmuring something soothing. His action had no effect, and the group pushed Alice around until she screamed. With the scream, which Bobby recognized from having heard it before in the lab, the air temperature dropped like a rock. Ice shot out of her in jagged shards and covering everything with frost.

The ice smashed into Jayce, his body protecting everyone behind himself. It tore through the four people directly harassing her, ripping them to shreds in seconds. Those farther away suffered less deadly cuts and scrapes, and several slipped and fell.

"Alice," Bobby cried out, far enough away to be safe, "Stop it, you're killing them! " He rushed in to check on the woman nearest to him while Jayce dropped down to check for a pulse on the other one next to him. "You killed them."

Shaking all over, Alice's eyes had gone wide and wild and her flesh had turned deathly blue. Her mouth hung open, panting breaths coming out in frozen puffs of cloudy vapor. She slowly stood from a crouch and turned around on the spot, surveying the disaster. "They wouldn't stop," she whispered. "They wouldn't stop."

Ai showed up out of nowhere and slipped on the frost covering everything. She fell on her ass, letting out a squawk of surprise. A dead body stopped her slide, leaking blood all over the ground. The moment she noticed, she scrabbled away from it, through the pool of blood. Despite her mouth moving, no sound came out.

"Let's go, we gotta go now." Bobby nodded for Jayce to take control of Alice while he hauled Ai to her feet and hustled her away. "Where's Jasmine," he asked as they kept moving. When she didn't answer, he squeezed her arms a little. "Do I gotta slap ya?" It worked before.

Shaking her head, Ai took a deep breath. "She invited us to dinner. When I got there, I was a little confused about what to say, so it kind of came out all wrong. I should have gone over what to say with you first. What happened back there?"

"Alice freaked out and blew up."

"She killed those people."

"Yeah. As if things weren't screwed up enough before. Which way to Jasmine's place?"

Ai pointed and they walked. Jayce herded Alice along in silence. She had nothing to say all the way to Jasmine's apartment complex. It was a big place with lots of shade trees around three tall buildings. Bobby would call the neighborhood nice, though he suspected Alice needed more to be impressed. Rather, she would if she wasn't so busy being numb. Little Miss Follows The Rules had to be exploding inside from what she just did, and when it came out, the mess wouldn't to be pretty.

"Is she nice?"

"She's sweet," Ai nodded, "really nice, yeah."

"Let's go in, then."

Jasmine answered the buzzer with a voice so cheerful it felt weird. She also let Ai in without question. In the middle of a middle floor, the door had a sticker of a squirrel with a word bubble over its head, the word 'hi' printed in large block letters inside.

The woman who answered the door had a squirrel in her hands, and stood aside so the four of them could come in. She smiled and greeted each of them, delighted to see them all for no apparent reason. Jayce steered Alice to the couch and forced her to sit, then sat himself down on the floor, away from her. Jasmine hugged Ai enthusiastically. "I didn't expect you back so soon! Is everything okay?"

Her olive complexion hinted at Mediterranean ancestry, and she had long brown hair in a perky ponytail that hung to halfway down her back with the ends forming loose curls. Bright and pleasant, her open face welcomed them as much as her words did, and Bobby found himself smiling at the pretty lady in the ruffled floral blouse despite what they'd just dealt with.

"This is Jasmine," Ai explained. "Jayce, Bobby, and Alice."

"Hi." Jasmine gave them all a really cheerful wave instead of shaking hands with any of them. "What she said sounds pretty serious." She bobbed her head and seemed disturbed by the idea anything could actually *be* serious.

"Have you had an episode recently where you woke up cold but sweating all over, without remembering having had a nightmare?" Jayce spoke up first, a fact Bobby appreciated. They needed to discuss how to have this conversation.

"Oh!" Jasmine rubbed her cheek on the squirrel still in her hands. It seemed content there, not struggling or squirming. "Yes! About a week ago, I scared Will half to death, he said I passed out and he thought I was dead for a minute."

"Who's Will?"

"My boyfriend. We live together. He's a veterinarian." Jasmine pronounced the last word very carefully, like she'd had to practice saying it a lot, or had to say it that way to get it right.

Bobby scratched his forehead. "That kinda complicates things."

Jayce waved Bobby off. "And has something unusual happened to you since then? Like, I can do this." He touched a finger to a button of his trenchcoat and the pattern flowed up his hand. After a short delay, during which it must have spread to the rest of him, it covered his face. Then it dropped away and he looked normal again.

Jasmine nodded earnestly and set the squirrel on the counter, where it sat gazing up at her. She scrunched her eyes shut and made fists. In the space of about two seconds, her body shrank in on itself until a normal squirrel stood there instead of Jasmine. All four of them blinked down at her, then she sprang back up into herself. "Will says I'm a very healthy squirrel." She leaned in and used a loud whisper to say, "He said I shouldn't tell anyone, but if you all have superpowers, too, it's probably okay."

Bobby recovered first, downright jealous—she got to keep her clothes when she did that. "Dang, that's pretty cool. I don't suppose we could meet Will?"

She picked her squirrel up again and cheerfully rubbed noses with it. "He's at work, but he'll be home for dinner."

Out of thirty-one names, the first one they picked happened to be a really sweet, trusting girl who already knew she was special and could do something so unbelievable and obviously real, she didn't reject any of it. Not to mention the understanding boyfriend in a medical field. Bobby had to stop himself from staring in awe of this happy accident. It took no effort to smile, though. "That sounds great. I'd really like to meet him. Maybe he can have a look at my dragons and help me out."

"I love having guests for dinner!" Jasmine clapped around her squirrel and danced into the postage stamp kitchen. "Will is very smart. If anybody can help with dragons, it's my Will." She gently hugged the squirrel in her hands, then rushed over again to show it to Bobby. "This is Walnut. I rescued him when he was just a baby." Fortunately, she set him on the floor, and he scampered over to a cardboard box full of shredded paper, jumped in, and scratched around. If he'd been expected to touch it or something, Bobby wasn't sure what he would've done. Where he came from, squirrels were for shooting.

"He's cute," Bobby said, trying to be nice. "So, I guess Ai said we're kinda all in danger from the government?"

Jasmine nodded earnestly. "She said the government is going around arresting people for having eyes like us."

Ai ducked her head. "I didn't really know what to say."

"Uh-huh." Bobby smirked. "It seems all of us are on a list." Pulling his copy out of his pocket, he laid it out on the counter for Jasmine to see. "That there's me, that's Alice, Jayce, and Ai."

"Oh, and there's me!"

This news, in Bobby's mind, didn't seem right for excitement. He plodded on, hoping he could make her understand the gravity of the situation. "The government is using laws meant to deal with terrorists to pick us all up offa this list. We four got arrested like that a few days back. They took us to some kind of creepy horror movie lab and stuck us with needles and stuff. It was really bad. We escaped in the middle of the night, found this list on the way out, and figured the best thing to do was see about not letting those guys get their hands on anybody else, especially not anybody as nice are you."

"Oh my gosh, that's terrible." She covered her mouth. "You think they'll want to do that to me?" Bobby wanted to pat her on the head and hug her and tell her everything would turn out alright. Whoever this Will guy was, if he turned out to be a jerk, Bobby would deck him, hard and repeatedly.

"Pretty sure, yeah."

Jasmine sucked in a breath and her eyes popped wide. "What do I do?"

"We aren't rightly sure what you should do, Jasmine. So far, we're kinda on the run. Our faces got put up on the TV. They're out there, looking for us. You, though, we don't know when they'll come for you. We're just sure they're gonna."

Her eyes bounced from one somber face to another, and she gulped. A moment later, she smacked the counter and nodded with firm determination. "Will will know what to do." With that, she turned to the kitchen, the matter apparently settled and out of her mind already. Bobby watched her open the fridge, worries and cares slipping off her shoulders like rain off an umbrella. Inside the fridge, he saw pink and yellow post-it notes on several things, including the door itself. "Do any of you eat tofu, or should I make it just vegetables?"

She moved on to other things, so Bobby got out of her way. "Whatever's fine." He could follow simple directions, and knew nothing else about cooking. Scanning the room, he decided somebody needed to do something about Alice, and since Ai bustled into the kitchen to help Jasmine and Jayce seemed to be meditating or otherwise ignoring the problem, that left him.

He sat down next to Alice and rested his forearms on his

knees. Momma called it his 'thoughtful pose', since he always sank into it when he had to think a lot. "You wanna talk about it? "

Alice shook her head, but otherwise stayed curled up in a little ball.

"It looked kinda intense," he offered. "All of 'em pushing and stuff. Jayce tried to wade in, but they were kinda being difficult about it." He paused and rubbed his chin, the stubble there feeling strange even though he noticed it hours ago. They saw a newspaper, so they knew they'd missed five days. Wrapping his head around that took some effort. "I imagine it's hard to control something like what you got under a circumstance like that."

"Cut it out," Alice snapped. "I said I don't want to talk about it."

For a few seconds, only the sounds of Jasmine and Ai banging around in the kitchen filled the air. Jayce sighed and raked a hand through his dark hair. "They know we're here now, or will shortly. How long before they figure out why?"

"Hopefully, a while. They don't know we got that list. Even if they do, they probably don't expect us to start using it right away. Not while we're still trying to get basic things. 'Sides, that spot is pretty far from here. They'll find the car soon enough and know we're on foot again."

"If they do know we have that list, they might come here to look for us, just on the off chance."

Bobby looked over at Jasmine, happily cutting up some kind of vegetable. "They'll swipe her if they come here."

"We won't let them," Alice growled. Her jaw set with determination and she glowered and the floor.

A beat passed while both men stared at her in surprise. Bobby lifted his hand to reach out and pat her on the shoulder or knee. Before it got there, he thought better of it and settled for thumping his own knee. "No, we sure won't. A fight here would be a bit less than ideal, though."

"They might leave her alone with Will here," Jayce said. "Dealing with him when she clearly hasn't done anything wrong could be more trouble than they want to get into."

"You think we ought to hide if'n they show up."

Jayce nodded. "In such a way that if they decide to grab her, we can resist on her behalf."

"Sounds like a plan. Means we need to decide where to hide out now, instead of later." What they really needed right now, Bobby thought, were scouts. But if he was dragons, he couldn't actually be here or relay a warning. Before, he managed to re-form with four missing. Could he just send a few off without having to blow up into a whole swarm? That would certainly be handy. It would mean that even if he got caught, he could have a dragon on the outside. It would mean he could get into all kinds of things without having to be a swarm.

"Easy enough for you," Jayce snorted. "You just explode into dragons and fly out the window. I can probably do low level camouflage, the kind that wouldn't stand up to close scrutiny, but will do fine with just a glance. Ai can run out when they open the door. That just leaves Alice." Again, the two men looked at her.

"I can hide in the bathroom," she grumped.

Bobby nodded his satisfaction and held up his finger and stared at it. He thought about getting just one dragon to separate. For a good five minutes, he concentrated on the idea of one of them going off on its own. Nothing changed, and he couldn't feel their little minds or bodies at all.

He needed a different approach. If he wanted to use a fork or a pencil, he also needed a different hand. Switching to his left hand, he held up a finger and thought about what would entice him to come out and play. As soon as he considered it that way in his head, he watched in horrified amazement as the tip of his thumb turned into a tiny silver dragon and climbed onto his index finger. Its tiny claws tickled.

"That…it's…I mean—" Alice stared with a grimace, shying away from him.

"Yeah, I know. And it's me doing it."

Jayce blinked once, then shrugged, sighed, and returned to meditation.

"They are cute little guys, thought, ain't they?" It trilled at him, a tiny little noise to say 'hi' to its master.

"You do know that 'ain't' isn't actually a word, right?"

Bobby rolled his eyes and ignored her. He took a deep breath and got four more to separate, each taking its own fingertip with it. "Okay, little guys, I need y'all to watch for cops and stuff. You think you can do that for us? It's really important." With the words, he thought about what he wanted them to be alert for. The tiny dragons all trilled their acceptance of the mission and flew out the open window.

Jayce raised an eyebrow. "You gave them more instructions than just that, right?"

"Ayup." Bobby reached up to tap his forehead. With his finger missing the part past the last knuckle, the gesture felt awkward. "I think at 'em," he added.

"Good to know."

Alice took his hand and examined the smooth nubs on the ends of his fingers. "Where does your brain go?"

"Heck if I know. It's like a hive mind thing going on, but I'm still aware and in control. Mostly. They got little minds of their own."

"I didn't mean to kill those people."

"'Course not."

"They wouldn't leave me alone."

"I saw."

"I was outnumbered."

"Ayup."

Alice went quiet for a beat, then threw his hand back at him and snarled. "Why aren't you outraged?" Her shouting made Ai and Jasmine turned to look. "I just killed four people, and you're acting like it's nothing worse than running a stop sign, for fuck's sake! They're dead because I'm a twink-eyed freak!"

She took a breath to rant more. Bobby started talking in the hopes she'd stop and think instead. "They're dead because they were poking a tiger with a stick and didn't know it. And I don't mind you calling me a 'twink-eyed freak', but you should make sure everybody in the room don't mind before you start tossing that around. Jasmine is a real nice person, and I ain't gonna sit here silent-like while you say something like that about her. Also, I don't think you ought to be cussing like that in her house. My Momma says you don't do that when you're a guest in somebody's house, less you know it's okay already. It's rude."

Alice goggled at him for a second, then she got up and went to use the bathroom. Ai whispered to Jasmine and they turned back to their cooking.

Jayce chuckled. "I don't think she was expecting calm."

Bobby shrugged. "I got a lot to say about Alice, but not much of it is nice, and Momma was pretty clear on that sorta thing, too."

"Mmhmm. My mom said things like that, too, but I didn't always listen."

"I got a selective memory, just like anybody else." Bobby smirked. "We gotta learn to deal with each other, though, 'cause we're stuck together, like it or not. Can't see how letting her get all riled up is helping that. 'Course, it's a thing, killing somebody. I never done it, got no idea what it does to ya. She's gotta figure that out for herself. Preferably without yelling at any of us."

"No argument here." Jayce moved to the couch. "You know, now that we're superheroes, maybe we should have superhero names."

"What, you mean like Batman and Superman?"

Jayce snorted. "Yeah, only original."

"I s'pose." Bobby shrugged. "ZippityGirl, Dragon, MetalMan, and Frosty The Snowgirl. And Squirrel."

Jayce grinned. "Frosty the Snowgirl, I like that one. I'll come up with my own, though, thanks."

"Don't rightly matter much, since they already know who we are."

The front door opened, cutting Jayce off. Bobby recognized the man who walked in from pictures around the apartment. Everything about him, from his short, neat blond hair to his slacks and polo shirt screamed out 'respectable professional'. His hazel eyes caught Ai in the kitchen, then swept into the living room to notice Bobby and Jayce, and Alice as she emerged from the bathroom.

Jasmine squealed with delight and jumped on him. Apparently expecting this, he had an arm out and ready, and he caught and squeezed her close. "Hey sweetheart, are we having guests for dinner tonight?"

"Yes!" She planted a kiss on his lips and introduced everyone. "This is Will," she told the room with a delighted smile while bouncing from foot to foot.

Bobby stood and shook his hand. "I'm sure this is a surprise, and we don't meant to be an inconvenience. We're here, though—"

"Because of the eyes? Are you…?"

"Heh, yeah, we are. Different, but yeah." Bobby held up his hand with the missing fingertips and let another dragon pop out, taking another knuckle with it. "You wanna sit down with us, we can tell you what's going on, as much as we know, while the girls finish up dinner."

Will stared at the dragon, watching it climb on Bobby's hand, then re-form back onto his finger. "Yes, I believe I'd like to hear what you have to say." He sat down with Bobby and Jayce, and he listened carefully while they told him everything that happened since they were arrested, the things they knew and the things they guessed. Bobby showed him the list they had, and Jayce shared their suspicions. When they finished, the girls stood in the kitchen with drinks, chatting while waiting for the food to be done.

Sitting back in the chair, Will frowned. "You're kind of asking me to leave my practice. I understand that's not really what you're saying, but I can't send Jasmine off to who knows where and just go on with my life without her. If I knew it would only be a week or two, then sure, yeah, hide her away and bring her back. But indefinitely, no, I can't do that." Where Jasmine wouldn't see it, he pulled out a little ring box and showed Bobby and Jayce, then tucked it back into his pocket. "I just haven't found the right time yet," he murmured.

Part of our problem," Jayce said, "is that we're not sure what to do with ourselves. Constantly being on the run isn't going to work, but if we stand still, they'll find us, and we aren't completely sure we can avoid capture, or escape again if necessary."

Will nodded. "If you're going to ask people who haven't been through what you have to leave their lives for their own safety, you really need someplace for them to actually go. What about taking over an abandoned property somewhere, until you can figure out how to buy it without revealing yourselves?"

Bobby scratched his cheek and considered the problems that immediately leaped to mind: water, electricity, food, defense. On the other hand, a solid destination would change the ball game. "It's worth giving some thought."

"I agree," Jayce nodded.

"Were you going to ask any of us?" Ai reminded Bobby of Momma right then, when she found out he did something stupid.

"Sure," he said with an easy smile. "You want to think about it, too? Plenty of—" He blinked and had to focus on one of his dragons. What he saw through its eyes made him sit up straight. "They're here, pretty sure. It's two guys in suits and six more in tac gear. So much for hoping they wouldn't bother.

"Will, if they try to grab Jasmine, you gotta trust us to deal with them. We don't want you getting hurt or took yourself." With that, he poofed out into full dragon swarm, leaving his clothes behind. He heard Jayce ask Will to give him a hand collecting those up, then he dove out the window.

From his new vantage point, saw eight men heading for the building and going inside. The two suits went in front. It occurred to him that if he wanted to help rescue Jasmine, he needed to know whether rescue became necessary. He sent one dragon back inside, and had another zoom off to follow the men in. That would give him two different angles to see and hear the episode. For the moment, he focused on the one following the men in. They all trooped into the elevator and one of the suits punched the button for Jasmine's floor.

"This is the signal to storm in," Suit Number One said as he made a hand gesture of two fingers together, pointing forward. Not terribly subtle as signals went, but knowing it would give him an advantage. Somehow. If he could figure out how to use it. "Miss Milani is not a target at this time, so don't treat her like a suspect without a reason to."

"How far back do you want us to stand until there's a signal?" one of the SWAT guys asked.

"Stay out of sight if you can, as close as possible. We're hoping you're not needed at all, but if you are, we want you close. These people are capable of causing serious damage."

"Yes, sir." The SWAT guys looked unconcerned and ready for anything. His dad had been like that: always ready for the unexpected and never showing fear. It had probably been what got Marine Sergeant Edward Mitchell killed in Afhganistan.

The elevator doors opened and the SWAT guys poured out around the two suits, lined up half on each side of the apartment door. When they were ready, they nodded to the suits, and one of them knocked on the door. About two seconds passed before Will answered it.

"Can I help you?" He had a properly confused and suspicious look, Bobby thought. One that said 'who the heck are you and why are you knocking on my door?'

One of the suits said, "We'd like to speak with Miss Jasmine Milani."

"And you are?"

Suit Number One pulled a badge wallet out and held it up. When he tried to whisk it away, Will snatched it out of his hand.

Will's brow furrowed as he examined the badge. "Do you have a warrant?"

"We don't need a warrant to speak with someone."

"You do if you want to come inside to do it," Will told them with a frown. "I know my rights, and hers, too."

Suit Number Two made a face. "Can you ask her to come to the door, then, please? We'd just like a few words."

"What's this about?" Bobby had to admire Will for being obnoxious about all this. He knew they had men with them even though he probably didn't see them. Would he be this paranoid about the whole thing if they hadn't been here to warn him?

"We just want to ask her a few questions. Who are you,

exactly?"

"Her boyfriend." Will handed the badge back. "I'll talk to her. Just a minute." He shut the door and locked it. Bobby heard the deadbolt clack home.

"Are we going in?" a SWAT guy hissed to the suits.

"Not yet."

After several long seconds, Jasmine cracked the door open enough to see out without letting them see in. "What do you want?" she breathed, her voice small and scared. Bobby had a feeling it might not be an act.

"Miss Milani, have you been contacted by any of these people?" Suit Number Two held up a piece of paper Bobby couldn't see. He assumed it had pictures of the four of them.

Taking the paper, Jasmine ran her fingertips over it. "They have eyes like mine."

Both suits blinked at her. "Ah, yes, Miss Milani, we noticed that, too. Have you seen any of them? "

"That would be so neat! I've never met anyone with eyes like mine before. They're like Persians'. Mom has eyes a little like this, but not blue and less," she lifted a hand and made a funny little motion to suggest the unusual tilt her eyes had.

"Miss Milani, can you focus please? This is important." Suit Number Two tapped the paper again. "These people are dangerous, and we want to help you stay safe. Have you seen any of them?"

"What kind of dangerous? Do they have guns or bombs or something?"

"They may have one or more guns, yes. More importantly, they may come here to try to harm you specifically." Suit Number One fished a business card out of his pocket. He paused in the act of handing it to her when someone inside sneezed. It sounded too high pitched to be Will. "You have company, Miss Milani?"

"No, I'm a waitress." Her answer came from so far out of nowhere that Bobby couldn't help but wonder if she was kinda dumb or kinda brilliant. It made no sense in such a remarkable way that he thought a person would have to stand and stare and forget about everything else until they understood.

"What?" Suit Number One, apparently not as entranced or impressed as Bobby, gave the hand signal.

Bobby did what he could: the little dragon in the hall trilled a warning. At that noise, someone yanked Jasmine out of the door and slammed it shut. The deadbolt locked while the SWAT guys moved. Bobby sent the swarm back into the window. If they needed him in there, he'd be in there.

The SWAT guys looked around for the source of the noise. One aimed his weapon at the doorknob and fired three times. Two shoved the door open. Bobby recognized the signs of Ai's passage in the form of men shoved off balance for no apparent reason. The door slammed shut.

As the lead SWAT guy kicked the door in again and pointed his rifle straight at Jayce's chest, Suit Number One staggered back into the shut elevator doors. His phone disappeared from his hand. Suit Number Two dropped to the floor with a grunt of surprise for no apparent reason.

"I wouldn't," Jayce said to the SWAT guy, his flesh silvery. He grabbed the barrel of the gun and squeezed it, crunching the metal with an unpleasant creaking, shrieking noise. The SWAT guy pulled the weapon back and tried to kick Jayce in the privates, but he hit solid metal. Jayce grabbed his foot and shoved him back. "We don't want any Girl Scout cookies, gentlemen," he told the hallway. "No means no."

The swarm flowed around Jayce and into the hallway. It must have looked to the SWAT guys like the tiny dragons came from him, somehow. He split the swarm into two halves and surrounded the Suit Twins, focused on their heads and hands so they couldn't accomplish anything at all. They swiped at the dragons , and it was so ineffectual Bobby wanted to laugh. The dragons made little chirps and trills and growls of amusement in his stead, filling the hallway with a cacophony.

Stepping into the hallway, Jayce paused while a SWAT guy punched him. The guy pulled his hand back with a yelp of pain, while Jayce failed to react. Another fired his weapon. The bullet bounced right off Jayce, though it put a hole in his shirt. With that, the SWAT guys backed away, in both directions.

The one on the floor put up a hand to ward him off and scrabbled backwards. "Stand down," he shouted at the rest, "stand down and back off!"

"Gentlemen." Jayce held his fists ready, yet made no move to charge anyone down and use them. "You're doing the bidding of men who want to perform experiments on us. We have no quarrel with you, or even with them, we just aren't excited to be treated like lab animals. All of us are patriots; we love this country and have no intention of doing anything against it. So long as it decides not to do anything against us."

Figuring the fight had, more or less, ended, Bobby let the two suits go and re-formed there in the hallway. Much to his surprise, he still wore the boxer shorts this time. Maybe he just needed time with clothes he felt comfortable in to have them defy physics with him. The boxers fit well enough and had been with him for several hours now.

Movement to the side made him look to see Suit Number One backing away. Suit Number Two, sitting on the floor next to him, jammed something into his thigh. His fingers worked frantically to push the plunger of a needle down.

Jayce stepped in and shoved the suit away while Bobby stumbled back. His fingers managed to grip the needle and pulled it out, then tripped and fell to the floor. He met Jayce's eyes and they shared a look, a nod, then he blinked a lot. One blink, he heard the sounds of fighting. Two blinks, Jayce growled angrily. Three blinks, he felt a strong breeze. Four blinks, Ai patted his cheek.

"C'mon, Bobby, we have to go. It's a mess and we have to get out of here. Jasmine and Will are packing their stuff up, Jayce and Alice are helping."

"Whu'uppen?" Everything felt heavy, and his mouth refused to do what he wanted.

"One of them stuck you with something. In your leg. It knocked you out, but not completely." She held up the syringe, half-full of clear liquid. "Jayce smashed that guy's head into the wall, the cops tried to take him down, they retreated. I saw them outside, they're hanging around by their van. Will and Jasmine have a car, were going to try to get to it with their stuff. Jayce and I will go out first and clear the way, to keep them from stopping any of us."

"Alice?" Bobby remembered not seeing her in the apartment when stuff started going down. He caught a whiff of an unpleasant, pungent smell, one his brain couldn't put its finger on.

Ai sighed. "She's curled up in a ball in the bathtub. We're kind of ignoring her until we're ready to go."

Bobby put his hands out and tried to lever himself up and get to his feet. "Wha's in tha' thing?" He sounded drunk. He felt drunk, too, the kind that came from five too many beers.

"No idea." Ai shrugged. "I'm an accountant, Jim, not a chemist."

Bobby frowned. "Who's Jim?"

"Forget it. It's a joke. Maybe some water will help." She happened to have a glass and handed it to him.

He chugged down half the glass. His vision continued to clear along with his head. The smell got stronger, too. To the side, he noticed a a small pile and associated spray of vomit next to the body with its skull smashed and brains splattered across the wall and floor. Oh, that must be the smell.

"Who threw up?"

Ai coughed as she draped his arm over her shoulders and helped him stand. Between her and the wall, it worked. "That was me. I saw him do it." She averted her eyes from the whole sight and helped him lurch into the apartment.

"Damn." Just inside the door, he realized he still had two scouts out. He stopped and leaned against the wall, waving Ai off. Each scout had a different view of the parking lot. Picking one, he focused on it. "They're talking to someone on their radios."

Ai nodded. "Jayce thinks if we go charge them now, they'll bring a nuke next time."

"Jayce also thinks we're about ready to go, except for Alice." The man himself stood there with a large bag full of stuff slung over his shoulder. "They're leaving a lot behind. Jasmine will go squirrel in the car to save space, and we're hoping you can handle following along as your swarm. Nice job keeping the boxers, by the way."

"Thanks." Bobby grinned, now tired more than woozy. "I'll see if'n I can talk Alice out. And yeah, I can go as dragons."

"I'm going to try running alongside the car," Ai said.

"Good deal." Bobby lurched toward the bathroom. Ai left him there with an encouraging smile. "Alice," he called in, "we gotta go or they're gonna take us down." When she gave no answer, he opened the door and leaned against the frame. He saw here curled up in the bathtub, as promised. "Whatever they stuck me with, it's a doozy, and they'll be able to stick you with it, too."

"I can't do this," Alice whispered. Her voice cracked in the middle.

"You got two choices, Alice, you know that, you just don't wanna deal with it. Choice one, you let 'em take you. They do whatever they want and you're just a guinea pig. Choice two, you run for it. We're running, you can come with us if you want. At some point, we'll stop running and make a stand and take what rights we're owed, but we gotta find someplace and the rest of our kind, and do it all together.

"One of us on our own is gonna get took. Five of us working together can run. Thirty-five of us, shoot, we can do a lot more'n that. But we gotta get up and get going now if we're gonna have that chance. Your choice." He waited, feeling himself recovering with every second that passed. Thank goodness he didn't get the full dose. "I know you're shook up. I ain't gonna let you curl up and die on account of it. We're in this together, and don't nobody hate you or nothing."

She sniffled while he stood there, waiting. He checked on the two scouts, making sure they had no lingering effects from the drug. It seemed they hadn't been affected at all, which he figured could only be a good thing.

Jayce tapped him on the shoulder and gave him a significant look, then nodded towards the front door. Bobby nodded and held up two fingers. In return, Jayce shook his head and held up one. They needed to get going now, not ten minutes from now. He nodded again.

"Look, Alice, there's guys out there that'll be happy to shoot you. They'll either kill you or knock you down, just 'cause there's so many of 'em. If they just take you down, then you'll wind up hogtied and poked and prodded again. Guaranteed. The rest of us, we're not looking for that. We're gonna go ahead and resist. In order to do that, we gotta leave now, before anyone else comes to back these guys up."

Standing away from the wall, Bobby found he still needed it to brace himself. He took three steps before Alice croaked out, "Wait. I don't want to die."

"Then get your ass up, hon, 'cause we're getting while the getting's not too bad." He put one foot in front of the other, heaving with the effort.

Behind him, she scrabbled out of the tub and hurried to slip under his arm. "Lean on me," she murmured. "I'll get you out."

"Thanks." He considered saying something like 'welcome back'. Walking took too much energy to waste it on something stupid like that, especially when she had to still be raw on the inside. In her position, being the one ripped up about all this, he felt confident it'd piss him off something fierce.

Out in the hallway, they had two full size suitcases and a carry-on stacked up and ready to go, all with wheels. That would make getting them to the car doable, given how that had to happen. "If nobody minds, I'm gonna give my dragons as much time to recover as I can before I make 'em work. I got two outside, watching for us, they seem fine, but I ain't keen on finding out the hard way that dragons on this fly drunk."

Still silver and carrying the one bag again, Jayce nodded. "Works for me. The plan is I go out first and make it clear we're not surrendering. If any fighting needs to happen, Ai will assist. When we're clear enough, everyone else goes for the car, it gets loaded up, then we drive away. Ai and Bobby stay there as deterrents until the car is on the road."

No one stood guard at the elevator on the ground floor, and Jayce left his bag outside the front door. Will picked it up and handed the other suitcase off to Alice, who left Bobby to sit for another minute or two. He took a deep breath. This moment seemed important to him. They'd tangled with cops for the first time, and

Jayce killed someone in a fight. After this, anyone they tangled with would leave the kid gloves at home.

He focused on a scout dragon, watching while Jayce walked up to the group of SWAT guys and smiled at them. “We’re leaving. You can assault the apartment as much as you want, but none of us are staying behind there, so you won’t find much. You can try to stop us, even follow us if you want, but I think you already know we’re not going without a fight, and we will kill to stop you from taking us.”

The lead SWAT guy, the one whose weapon got crunched, nodded. “Message received, loud and clear. Westbrook, right?” At Jayce’s nod, the man continued. “We have orders to bring you and the others in and are authorized to use lethal force if necessary to protect ourselves. Just so you understand the position we’re in.”

“Officer, nothing would make me happier than knowing you get to go home to your family tonight, something none of us will be able to do. With that in mind, I strongly recommend you don’t follow us and suggest to your superiors that we’re not worth the effort. I’m not completely certain what I can withstand or not, but I’m willing to bet you’ll need a nuke to take me down, and even that might not work. The others are going to be pretty hard to take down, too. Something to keep in mind.”

“Sir, I don’t think we have much choice here.”

Jayce nodded. “You should listen to him.”

The leader thought about it for a second or two, then nodded. “We won’t follow you, but I can’t guarantee anything else.”

“Just pass on the warning.” Jayce turned and went for the car.

Bobby huffed in relief. At the questioning looks around him, he said, “They’re backing off, at least for now. Let’s git.”

Chapter 7

For three hours, Bobby followed the car from above. They drove on the main highways to Philadelphia, where they could find the next closest person on the list. The little car pulled into a parking lot for a small apartment complex and he dropped down to re-form. His belly growled so hard it hurt, and Jasmine bounced out of the car to shove a granola bar into his mouth. She did the same when Ai stopped in front of the car and slumped against it.

Everyone else piled out of the car and produced what remained of the food they'd been eating along the way: pita chips with hummus, vegetable curry, bananas, apples, and a salad. The pile seemed impressive, yet it had been picked over already. Bobby let Ai eat her fill, knowing he could eat nearly anything and not grouse about it. What she left barely took the edge off his hunger for now. He'd find more as soon as he knew what kind of plan they'd cooked up.

"It seems to us," Alice said, surprising him by speaking up, "that odds are good they'll ignore us now and go for trying to take the others by surprise."

Nodding, Bobby stepped into his clothes. "We need to find a base location and split up, get to as many of them as possible as fast as possible."

"Yes, exactly," Jayce agreed. "Another of ours lives in that building." The small complex had two floors and a fence around it. "We're hoping that not only do we not have another run-in here, but that we might be able to crash here for the night. If you can keep things in a pocket on you come morning, we can split up more."

"I'm good with that. My guess is I gotta feel like it's mine for it to stay with me, or something like that. Hoping, anyway. Who's gonna do the intro?" They all looked at him. Of course he should do it, since he hadn't been around to veto the idea. He sighed and nodded, too tired to resist. "Yeah, fine, okay. Jasmine, you're harmless looking, you come with me." He scraped himself up off the asphalt and trudged that way.

Jasmine squealed with delight, like she'd been chosen first for dodgeball. The fence had been designed to keep out casual riffraff. Bobby had no trouble with it. He'd hopped fences worse than this when he was fourteen and could handle this one with a hand tied behind his back. Being ready to conk out for the night barely slowed him down.

Taking the easier route, Jasmine went squirrel and walked through the bars. "What do you want me to do?"

He sighed and hoped he be able to keep his clothes while swarming soon. "Stand there being yourself. Say something if it seems right. Turn into a squirrel when I ask you to."

She nodded earnestly and smiled. "I hope she's nice."

"Me too. That'll make this all tons easier." He checked numbers and found the right one on the ground floor. A pretty girl answered the door, showing them polite interest. "Hannah Parson, my name is Bobby, this is Jasmine, we'd like to talk to you for a minute, if you don't mind." Damn if he wasn't getting surrounded by gorgeous women.

Hannah had that girl-next-door kind of look. Her straight, blonde hair had been put up in a casual ponytail and her pink tee and shorts suggested she had no plans to go out tonight. Her eyes, of course, were the same blue as theirs, and she noticed that sameness right away. "Are you selling something?"

"Not in the way I'm pretty sure you mean." Bobby reached up and tapped beside his eye. "The two of us and a few others, we all have the same eyes, just like you." He pulled his now crumpled list from his pocket and offered it to her. "All of us are on this list, and some part of the government is hunting us down because of it. They'll come for you, sooner or later, and we'd like to help you avoid becoming a lab rat for some kind of crazy experimentation."

She smoothed the list out and used her finger to scan it. When she reached her own name, she tapped it. "You're nuts."

"Yes, ma'am," he agreed. "Don't mean I ain't right."

With one eyebrow quirked, she smirked at him.

"Not exactly. Jasmine, this is the time." Since he'd already seen the show, he watched Hannah to see her reaction. Her smirk disappeared and she said something his Momma would smack him for. He picked the squirrel up gently and offered her to Hannah for a closer look. Adding to the experience, he popped a dragon off his thumb and it buzzed around them once, then returned to him. "Can we come in? "

"Whoa. Um, yeah, okay. Sure." Five minutes later, the entire group sat at her table, on her couch, and on her floor. Jasmine chose to remain a squirrel, and attacked a can of mixed nuts Hannah happened to have. Like they'd done for Will, Bobby and Jayce told the story, now with what happened at Jasmine and Will's apartment added on.

She listened without interrupting and showed no signs of denial or rejection. "That waking up thing happened to me yesterday, actually. In the middle of the night. I woke up cold and sweaty, except I was trapped and couldn't move. One panicked freakout later, it stopped and I could move. Now…"

Lifting her hands, she flicked them out, the same way Bobby did to spritz Momma while washing the dishes. A near-transparent blue edged disk about four feet in diameter popped into existence with a brief hum to announce itself. "It's a force field. Blocks everything in both directions. So far, that's all I can do with it, but it's only been a day. I think when I woke up, I was encased in it, so I'm guessing I can shape it if I try hard enough."

"That would make an excellent shield to hide behind if we get shot at again." Jayce reached out and poked it. His finger shimmered blue, then stopped. "Nope, can't take that on. Such a shame."

Hannah shrugged. "I haven't thought much about how to use it yet." She grabbed her laptop from the nearby counter and opened it. "I'll see what I can find for properties we might be able to use."

Bobby raised his eyebrows. "You don't want to think about pulling up your stakes and trucking off with us?"

"After everything you just told me? Are you nuts? I'd have to be six kinds of stupid to stay here and wait for them to come grab me. Even if they didn't want to experiment on me, can you imagine the military getting their hands on us? No, thanks. If I'm going to serve my country, it'll be willingly, and after I figure out how to use this power, not with them constantly pushing me with what they think I might be able to do. The second I realized what I'm capable of last night, I started thinking about running for it, I just didn't have a clue where to go. Now, I have a clue."

"This was easier'n I expected it to be."

Hannah laughed. "Maybe we could make a video and send it to everyone, so they all know they aren't crazy as soon as possible and can make their own way to wherever this base winds up being."

Will said, "That's not a bad idea, actually. Getting it into the right hands and not the wrong ones is the biggest problem."

"Not in the wrong ones is the problem," Jayce agreed. "We could just put it up on the internet and get it to everybody it needs to, but our would-be captors will see it, then."

"I was joking, but if you all want to try to figure something out, I have a laptop." Hannah gestured to the machine in question for emphasis. "First things first, though. You can all crash wherever, but my bed is my bed. It's not really big enough for anyone else, either. Besides that, where do you want to put this base?"

"Someplace in the middle of nowhere," Alice said.

Ai added, "Not too far from a city, though. We'll still need to get supplies and stuff."

"Middle of the country somewhere," Bobby suggested. "It'll need to be big, too. Lotsa space so we got a buffer 'tween us and the neighbors. Ten acres ought to be enough, I expect."

"At least ten acres, within…we'll say 75 miles of a big city, in the middle of the country. Okay, I can work with that."

Bobby shifted so he could see the screen. "What is it you do for a living?"

She smirked. "I'm a secretary for a real estate agency."

Grinning, he huffed a quiet laugh and noticed everyone staking out their spot for sleeping. Will and Jasmine settled together on the couch, Jayce grabbed some floorspace off to the side, Ai commandeered the easy chair, Alice curled up on the other end of the couch. Bobby figured he'd wind up doing what Jayce did, and probably soon.

Hannah paused in her churning through web pages and leaned over. "If you promise not to do anything," she muttered, "you can share the bed with me. One hand starts wandering, though, and I'll shove you on the floor. I would have offered to one of the others, but you seem like the nicest of the lot, aside from Jasmine, and she's doing fine."

"Thanks, that's nice of ya. Don't want to make you uncomfortable, though. I'll just take a pillow."

With a shrug, she returned to flipping through property listings. "It's really okay if you change your mind."

"Good to know." He pointed to the picture of a derelict farmhouse she clicked onto. "What's that one?"

She peered at the screen and scrolled down the page. "Thirty miles from Fort Morgan, Colorado. Fifty acres, they want half a million for it."

"Dollars?" He goggled at the picture.

"Yeah." She chuckled. "That's a lot of land, and it's not so far out of the way as to be the total boonies. Let me see if I can find out who 'they' is."

Bobby kept watching the screen as she clicked and typed and typed and clicked. Within fifteen minutes, his head nodded and eyes drooped enough that he noticed. He saw Jayce lying on the floor probably already asleep. It looked inviting, compared to the chair he sat in. His eyes drifted to Hannah and her offer popped back into his head. Thanks to her generosity, he could sleep on a soft bed tonight. It sounded like heaven after the past week. "I'm gonna take you up on that offer after all," he told Hannah softly.

She nodded and checked the time. "I should get some sleep myself." After shutting her laptop and setting it aside, she led him to her bedroom. Five steps in, she paused and looked him over. Her hands moved toward her hips, then shifted in mid-motion and she crossed her arms.

The last time Bobby felt this awkward in a girl's bedroom, the night had gone less than stellar. She never spoke to him again. He had no intention of doing anything like that here. As much as he found her attractive overall, he needed sleep too much to think about her as anything other than a nice host. To put an end to the uncomfortable moment, he turned his back on her and looked down at himself to decide how much to strip down. The more he kept on overnight, the more likely he thought the dragons would let him keep it.

After half a minute of deliberation, he pulled off the boots and trenchcoat. He could sleep in jeans and a shirt, and this would be the last time she slept in this bed anyway. It occurred to him that he might have a harder time getting is clothes washed if the swarm rejected something afterwards. That problem could wait, though. He sat on the edge of the bed and sighed with pleasure at the softness.

A beautiful woman climbed into the bed next to him, and he had to resist the urge to touch her. It had nothing to do with sex and everything to do with wanting to check this all was real. The creepy doctors could be playing tricks on his brain, or he could have passed out on the side of the road, or something else. How touching her would prove that, he couldn't say, but it made sense in his head. The urge to start a conversation bubbled up next. To kill it, he shut his eyes and thought about dragons. It surprised him when Hannah shook his shoulder a few seconds later.

"Breakfast is ready. I didn't have the heart to wake you sooner. You seemed really peaceful."

Bobby rubbed his face. "I'm thankful for that. I did plenty yesterday, and today promises to be more."

He sat up and took a deep breath of cinnamon and coffee. For that reason alone, today started better than yesterday. His belly growled and his bladder pressed, which helped him to get up and get moving. A few minutes later, he grabbed a bowl of oatmeal and some fruit. The chair he'd used last night remained empty, and he took it.

"So," Hannah said as she turned her screen to show him, "this property is owed by the state of Colorado. I didn't find the whole story, but the main gist is that it was seized by eminent domain for some energy project that failed due to budget cuts. The owners were already reimbursed and moved on, so the state just held onto it in case the project went forward.

"At some point, I expect everyone forgot about it. Now it's just sitting there, growing wild. We'll have to do a lot of work to make it livable, and there won't be any electricity, possibly no running water unless we can figure out how to set ourselves up with that. Odds are really good, though, that by the time anyone notices we're using it, we can defend it from anyone who wants to evict us."

Alice groaned. Ai shrugged. Jasmine bounced in her seat with a delighted smile. Will sighed, nodding his acquiescence. Jayce sighed. "If that's the best we can do, then it's the best we can do."

"We should split up here, I think." Bobby looked around the room. "I can fly on my own, Ai can run. Hannah, you have a vehicle?"

"I have a van, yeah."

"That's two cars. Y'all can split up however you want. Ai and I can go west and see who else we can convince. The rest of you go up and down the coast and stuff, hit as many people as you can as quick as you can. We keep in touch by phone, so everybody knows who's been visited and no one wastes any time.

"Tell folks to get money and as much of their stuff as they can, point out what the conditions'll be like. No sense in springing that on 'em. Maybe we get lucky and someone can do something about power and water. We all got pretty obvious powers, so we can all demonstrate. If'n anybody else is willing to go around and find more of us what's also got an obvious power, get 'em to do it. Otherwise, send 'em there.

No one objected.

"Will you all stay and help me pack my stuff?" Hannah asked the room. "I have a van because I've moved a bunch of times in the past few years, and it's just cheaper this way. I can go from living here to being packed in the van in a day, but it'll go a lot faster with help."

Jayce nodded. "Bobby, you and Ai go ahead. I'll help pack and go with Hannah in the van."

The group spent the next ten minutes discussing how to explain this to others. After that, Bobby, Alice, and Ai sat down and divided the names into four lists based on location while everyone else helped Hannah pack. Bobby would take a southern track to the west coast, starting in Baton Rouge. Ai would take a northern one, starting in Chicago. He'd be the one who got to go out to Honolulu, and she'd go up to Juneau. Jayce and Hannah would go north from here, Will and Jasmine would go south. Alice decided to ride with Will and Jasmine, for safety. And because Jayce failed to fully smother a frown at the idea of her coming with him.

"That's that, then," Bobby said around a mouthful of reheated Chinese takeout. Breakfast had already worn thin, and he took a few minutes to stuff his face with food Hannah would otherwise have to throw out. Dumping the empty box into the garbage, he blew out into dragons to see what stayed and what came along. Much to his surprise, nothing fell under the swarm. He had no idea how it worked and had no intention of questioning it; somehow, all his clothing and everything in his pockets got gobbled up by the dragons. He re-formed with a grin, stuffed more things into his pockets, and saluted the others before going swarm again and setting off.

Bobby knew he had about three thousand miles to cross, plus however much father for Hawaii. He'd have to sleep, and eat, and had no idea how far he could push himself before he'd have to stop or fall on his face. Faces. Wings, maybe? Whatever. Without knowing his speed for sure, he could only guess how long it would take. Besides, he had to go down and around, and stop to talk to the others on top of sleeping and eating. His best guess put him at their new base in two weeks.

He went up. The dragons had no problem with heights, so he kept going until the highway he needed to follow became a tiny ribbon cut across the land. Nothing should see him up here, other than maybe people in an airplane. The hardest part, he figured, would be turning at the right points. Without a map in hand to keep track of his path, he'd need to stop often to check his progress and stay on course. At first, he put the ocean at his back. That approach only worked for a while, then he had to rely on his limited knowledge of the region.

Flying felt different up here. Going at full speed with nothing to stop them, he reveled in the freedom. His dragons flew with their mouths open, letting the air stream out the back somehow, gears on the inside using it to propel them faster. That made no sense to him, considering the fact they ate metal. Where did it go? Resolving not to think about it, he let his mind go blank and enjoyed the simple sensations.

Eventually, he noticed the sun had climbed high enough to guess it must be around noon. He ought to be hungry. Without a belly, maybe he couldn't feel that. Despite being made from his body, the dragons had no connection to it. Suddenly concerned about starving to death by accident, he sent the swarm diving into the nearest city. In a run-down part, he flooded into an alley and re-formed himself. His stomach hurt so much from emptiness, he groaned and had to double over.

One of the things he'd pocketed at Hannah's happened to be an apple, which he grabbed and devoured. He ate everything but the seeds and stem, spitting those out onto the ground. It took the pain away without curbing his hunger, and he went looking for more. He also looked for something to tell him where he was, a map or signs. At the mouth of the alley, he found a newspaper dispenser for the Charlotte Observer next to one for the Charlotte Post.

When he looked at the map on Hannah's laptop, he hadn't noticed his route might take him right over his own house. In a direct-line path, Atlanta sat squarely on the way from here to Baton Rouge. He could stop in, tell Momma everything was okay, grab a few things, and be on his way. Maybe empty his bank account. What would the cops have told her? Would he be better off sneaking in and out and not seeing her? What if she believed this garbage about him being a terrorist?

Questions circled around his mind, refusing to answer themselves and give him peace, so he walked. Normal people passed him on the street, doing normal things with their normal friends and families. He wanted to stop someone and shake them, to tell them what their government had done to him. What would any of them do about it? Nothing. Their lives, as he could plainly see, weren't affected by any of it. If someone else asked him for help with this, he liked to think he'd try, but knew well enough he wouldn't.

He happened across a park with a group offering free meals and joined the line. When he reached the table, he encountered kids his own age spooning up pasta and salad and some kind of casserole. They all had that hippie college look, with hair in dreadlocks and weird piercings all over their faces and bold patches on their clothes. The hand drawn sign proclaimed them to be 'Food Not Bombs' in large blocky letters. A week ago, he knew he would have passed these people by with a sneer. Not because they fed the homeless; because they looked like hippie college students.

"Is that enough?" The girl with the ladle smiled at him.

He glanced back at the line and saw plenty of people still

waiting. "I reckon it'll do, yeah. Thanks." His belly growled loudly enough to be heard a few feet away.

She picked up an extra plate and covered it with food. "Here, let me help you." Carrying the plate, she led him to a nearby bench and sat down beside him, offering the plate. Another person stepped in and took her place.

"This is real kind, but why're you sitting with me?" His stomach refused to be ignored, so he started feeding it.

"Most of these people," she waved at those eating and waiting, "are regulars. We come here every week and see the same faces. I've never seen you before, and you haven't had it rough for very long, I think. At the same time, you look awful, like someone killed your puppy or best friend." She patted his knee, and it managed to not seem condescending. "I thought maybe you might want to talk to someone. You know, instead of finding a bottle or a needle to climb inside of."

He sat and ate, and she sat and waited. When he emptied his plate, she traded with him. "It's kinda complicated."

"Everybody's life is kinda complicated." She shrugged. "It's okay if you don't want to talk to me. But you should really talk to someone. Soon."

"Yeah." He sighed. "I lost everything, I guess, and there was cops involved, and I'm not sure about going home to my Momma. She's gonna be real disappointed."

The girl gave him an encouraging smile. "She's your mom. Just tell her you love her and, if you think you need to, ask her to forgive you."

Bobby took a deep breath and nodded. "Yeah." He took another bite and knew he had to stop home, if only for a few minutes. "Thanks."

"No problem." She took his plates and squeezed his shoulder.

"Good luck."

His belly full, he got up and found an empty spot to flow out into the swarm. After orienting himself, he headed straight for Atlanta, then got his bearings again and made for the 'burbs. The hop took him about an hour and a half, and he landed in his own backyard. The wash hung out on the clothesline, flapping gently in a light breeze. The herb and vegetable garden seemed fine. Her sunflowers would be dropping seeds soon.

Inside, a shadow passed behind the kitchen curtains. Despite the girl's suggestion, he'd been hoping she might not be here. She deserved a full explanation, and he didn't have long enough to give it to her. Hanging his head, he trudged around to the front door. At least he could avoid adding scaring the crap out of her to the list of things he'd done wrong recently. The five seconds it took her to get to the front door stretched out, making them the longest of his life.

"Bobby," Momma breathed. She wrapped her arms around him, hugging him the way she did when he fell off his bike or got beat up. "They said some really terrible things."

His eyes burned as he sagged with relief and squeezed her. "I know, Momma, I'm sorry. I didn't mean to make you worry and stuff."

She let him decide when the embrace ended, then pulled back and put a hand on his cheek. Just a few inches shorter than his own five feet, nine inches, she had to look up, but he'd never felt bigger than the woman that raised him. "There's ghosts in your eyes, boy. Come on in and sit down."

"Yes, Momma." How would he explain any of this? Should he explain any of this? Could he leave it all vague? He sat down on the couch obediently. "Nice the heat broke some," he observed. The day he left had been at least ten degrees hotter, and he could never have worn a trenchcoat in that.

"Don't you try to distract me with things like that." Brenda Mitchell planted her feet on the floor and loomed over him with her arms crossed. "Those policemen said you were hauled off by Feds, that you're a terrorist, that you killed Mr. Peterson."

He winced and hung his head again. "Yes, Momma, I know. I ain't no terrorist, though, and I didn't do nothing more than punch Mr. Peterson once." This reminded him of the time he found the cookie jar broken, knocked off the counter by a gust of wind, and went ahead and ate all the cookies.

"I told you to leave him alone, boy."

Knowing that tone, he hunched down and mumbled, "I know." He scratched the back of his neck and squirmed. "I just—Never mind. I gotta ask you something, Momma." He looked up at her and sighed at how much trouble he'd caused her. It'd only get worse from here, too. "Am I adopted?"

Frowning at him, she asked, "What's that got to do with anything?"

"Something happened out there, Momma, and it's hard to explain. I ain't normal, and I'm trying to figure out why. Did you adopt me?"

She turned away to stare at…maybe another time or place. "No." Taking a deep breath, she sat down beside him and clasped her hands together in her lap. "You were born of my body, but I don't know who your daddy rightly was. To be honest, I'm not a hundred percent sure you and me are actually related by blood."

He shifted into his thinking pose and tried not to get upset. Whenever he looked at a picture of them, he figured he took more after his real father, whoever that might be. Edward came into their lives before his fourth birthday, and he never thought to ask about the mystery man before then. After, she'd always brush off any questions with an admonition to think of Edward as Dad.

One of her hands moved to settle on his. "I was young, and I fell in with a bad crowd. I wound up on the drugs, and on the street, and all that. These nice ladies scooped a bunch of us up and asked us to participate in an experimental program. They said they'd help us clean up, get some job training, give us health insurance for five years, and help us find jobs. All we had to do was be a test subject for six months.

"In the position I was in, I said yes. The experimentation was with in-vitro fertilization. They were making test tube babies, and the process was still new then. We were told the chance of actually conceiving was small, less than one percent. While I was there, I was the only one I ever saw actually get pregnant. They said they'd help me give you up for adoption if I wanted to, but I wanted to keep the baby that grew in my body. I stayed there, with those nice people, until you were six months old, then they helped me get a job and find decent child care for you."

Stunned, Bobby let his jaw hang open and stared at her. "But..." No other words came out of his mouth.

"I got no idea if they used my eggs or not, Bobby, but it don't matter to me. You're my boy. You already knew Eddie wasn't your daddy, but he raised you good anyway, and that's what matters."

Taken on its own, the story was crazy. Compared to the last few days, though, it made sense. Sort of. Why anyone would do this, he had no idea, nor could he imagine how. Sitting there, he made a choice and held up his hand. One dragon popped off the end of his thumb. "Momma, I ain't rightly human, exactly."

Her eyes went wide as she stared at the tiny creature. She crossed herself and leaned back away from him, showing the fear he'd dearly hoped she wouldn't. "They said to watch out for anything unusual, but I thought they meant you might get sick."

Swallowing down the taste of bile from her reaction, he stood with a resigned sigh. "I'm just gonna grab a few things, then I'mma go. They didn't let me out, I escaped." Out of the corner of his eye, he saw her reach for him, but stop before her hand got close enough. He fled for his bedroom, tossing the door shut behind himself, and paced its short length a few times, trying not to let that rejection sting. There wasn't time for this. He needed to be strong and get to Baton Rouge, where he'd pick up another guy, then New Orleans, then Little Rock.

This room belonged to his old life. Souvenir beer and soda bottles wouldn't help him. Neither would his high school yearbooks or pictures from parties at work. Clothes would be helpful, he figured, and he stuffed a few pairs of socks and underwear into his coat pockets. He grabbed a keychain flashlight and all the spare cash he kept in a drawer. Since it fit, he took a spare shirt and a bandanna. The FBI still had his best shoes and jeans, and his wallet. Maybe someday, he'd take them back.

For the rest, he hoped Momma would hold onto it. All this would get sorted, eventually. He had to believe that, just as he had to believe Momma would overcome her reaction. The alternative meant a lifetime on the run, always looking over his shoulder. Shaking his head to banish those thoughts, he tried to think of anything else that might be useful in the house. The doorbell rang, making him think of the small tool set in the garage he'd used to repair it a few weeks ago. One part paranoid and one part curious, he cracked his bedroom door open to hear as Momma opened the door.

He watched Momma draw herself up and point her finger at them. "You got a lot of nerve, staking out my house to watch for my boy coming back."

"Ma'am, it's important. He's wanted for—"

"I don't give a damn what he's wanted for. He's an ungrateful bastard of a boy, and he swiped money from my purse and ran out the back five minutes ago. You want to actually catch him, you best be on your way." She slammed the door in their faces and hurried to his room, holding out money. "Boy, you take this and you get going. They're gonna bust in here, probably, and it'll be best for me if you're gone by then."

Heart full of…something, he couldn't decide what, Bobby hugged his Momma and kissed her cheek. "I love you, Momma. Put my stuff in boxes, yeah? I'll be back sometime for it."

She smiled and ruffled his hair. "Get going, boy. Stay safe."

He hurried to the window and popped the screen out. Without waiting for her to leave, he dissolved into dragons and they spiraled up and out. Seeing her expression of awe, this time with no crossing herself, filled his heart, and he knew it had been the right choice to stop. Nothing like a hug from Momma to make everything seem better.

On top of everything else, she gave him money, and he knew she couldn't afford to do that. The top bill had been a twenty, so he had at least thirty-five dollars now. If he really needed something, he could get it, one way or another. And he could do his laundry. Should he chance the bank? His savings account had almost three thousand dollars he'd been saving up to someday get a car. No, he'd leave that for now. Odds were, he'd get stuck there, and that would only make things worse. 'Escaped terrorist robs bank', the headline would read. Besides, he had no ID to get the money with anyway.

He put Atlanta behind him, hopefully not for the last time, and headed west. Trying to judge how long he could go without eating had him stopping several times along the way. After doing this several times, it seemed to him that he could go two to three hours between meals. Dumpsters near eateries saved him, over and over. So many people tossed so much perfectly edible food, especially bakeries.

By the time he hit Baton Rouge, the sun had disappeared. Time to look up Andrew Roulet and give him the spiel. It took half an hour to find a gas station with a map he could open up and use to find an address. The little old lady behind the register gave him a dirty look for doing it. He ignored her and took care to fold it up properly before putting it back.

Andrew had had the not-nightmare experience, but hadn't noticed any kind of superpower. Bobby's story horrified him. The dragons fascinated him. When he stuck his hand into the cloud made by Bobby's arm, they all snapped back to Bobby, and while he stayed touching that arm, Bobby couldn't make even one dragon pop out. With that, Andrew let him eat and crash on the couch and started packing up to move himself to Colorado. In the morning, Bobby made sure he had the directions right, wished him luck, and took the short hop to New Orleans.

Chapter 8

"'Scuse me, ma'am, I'm looking for Raymond Beller." Bobby stood on the porch of a crappy old house, one that had managed to survive Katrina. From the outside it looked fine, at least. In a relative sort of way, anyhow. This neighborhood had a lot of houses that needed serious repairs, alongside a handful of empty lots with scattered debris. These folks had to be barely scraping along to ignore the damage for so many years.

The young black woman who answered the door when he knocked wore a gray uniform dress, marking her as likely to be a hotel maid. Her belly showed just enough of a bump that he felt confident guessing she might be pregnant. What caught his attention were her bloodshot eyes, and the way her shoulders sagged. "Are you a cop?"

Given his clothes and week's worth of beard, Bobby couldn't imagine why she might think that. Also, given the area, it surprised him she'd ask with hope instead of suspicion. "No, ma'am. I'm just—"

She reached out and touched his arm hesitantly, interrupting him. "Please stop calling me 'ma'am'. It's Belinda."

Bobby nodded, now more confused by her. "Yes, ma'am. Belinda. Maybe you noticed I got the same eyes as him?" When she nodded, he kept going. “That’s why I’m looking for him. I just want to talk to him about that. Is he here, or at work, maybe? If you tell me where he works, I can go find him there instead and stop bugging you.”

“I don’t know where he is.” She crossed her arms and leaned against the door frame. “He never came home from work last night. I called all the hospitals, the morgue, the cops, his work, friends, everywhere, but he’s just gone. Nobody saw anything, nobody knows anything. Gone.” She snapped her fingers. “Just like that. Left work for the day and disappeared. Cops won’t look into it,” she spat, “because there’s no sign of foul play and he hasn’t been missing for twenty-four hours yet.”

Bobby paled. Two days ago, they tried to grab Jasmine and Jayce warned them. Yesterday, someone took Raymond Beller. It couldn’t be a coincidence. Had he warned Andrew in time? He had to get out of here and get to the next name. Now. They started a race to collect people at Jasmine’s apartment without knowing it. “I’m sorry.”

Belinda seemed nice. He didn’t want to know anything else about her. Didn’t want to know about that baby, didn’t want to know if she was his wife or just his girlfriend, or even his sister staying with him. Didn’t want to know how she’d manage to make ends meet without him around. Didn’t want to know. He stumbled a few steps back, watching her frown at him. “I’m sorry,” he said again, not sure what he was sorry for.

He took off running without a backward glance and didn’t stop until he got far enough away to be sure she wouldn’t follow or find him by cruising the neighborhood. He pulled out his phone and called Hannah. She needed to know.

“Hi Bobby,” Hannah said, cheerful and bright. “What’s up?”

“Raymond Beller, in New Orleans? He’s missing.”

"Missing? Missing how?"

"Just gone. Belinda— Um, his girl, she said he just up and vanished like smoke in the wind. Yesterday, after work." He doubled over, panic keeping him from being able to catch his breath.

"Okay, Bobby. Calm down. It's not your fault. Nobody saw anything?"

He shook his head, then remembered she couldn't see that. "No. She called around to everywhere she could think of already. I ain't gonna find nothing by doing it all over again."

"No, you won't. Just get yourself to the next one, Bobby. He's gone. We'll find him, but we need a clue to where he is first."

He glanced around, expecting to see a suit tailing him. Instead, he saw few locals ignoring him. "Okay. Right. Just gotta focus."

"I'm on my way to Colorado right now, okay? Sam and I—she's from New York city—split from Jayce, he's going up to Boston on the train. Have you sent anyone to the base yet?"

"Yeah. One so far. He left from Baton Rouge maybe an hour or two ago." He should have come to New Orleans first. Except Raymond went missing early yesterday, and he couldn't have gotten here that fast, not even by skipping Momma's house. Damn.

"Okay, we'll do our best to make good speed, then. Watch your back, Bobby. If you find someone who can keep up with you, consider teaming up so you're not alone."

"Yeah. That's a good idea. Thanks."

"I'll see you soon, Bobby."

"Yeah." He hung up and dropped the phone back into his pocket. Panic helped nothing. Taking a deep breath, he tried to think about it more. The suits had been able to grab a SWAT team, so they must have plenty of resources. They reached New Orleans faster than he did, so they probably had access to at least one plane. Did the guys running the lab send out hit teams as soon as they noticed the four of them went missing? Man, would he love to get one of them strapped to a board naked. See how they like it.

Shaking off the thoughts that wouldn't lead anywhere good, he took a deep breath and looked around. No one around, not really. He burst into the swarm and headed up. Time to get himself to Little Rock. Two of them lived there, Elizabeth Caulfield and Daniel Jarvis, at the same address. It wasn't a terribly long way, he touched down in Little Rock at lunch time, hungry and on the lookout for a map. Problem number one was solved in the alley behind an Italian restaurant, problem number two at a gas station.

Elizabeth and Daniel's house sat outside the city limits of Little Rock, by itself in a semi-rural area. Tucked in behind a bunch of trees, it reminded him of the kind of place teenagers went to in a horror movie. The walls needed paint, the roof had partially collapsed in one corner, the roof needed shingles here and there, a few shutters hung from just one point instead of two, some windows had been boarded up, and the porch didn't look anything like safe to walk on. A cracked tire hung on a frayed rope from a big oak tree and a rusty old car without tires sat on blocks off to one side. Momma would tsk at the state of the yard especially, with weeds and grass higher than his waist in some places. He'd never seen dandelions that big before.

Bobby landed and re-formed next to the mailbox on the road, stuffing his hands into the pockets of his trenchcoat. Movies, he sternly reminded himself, had nothing to do with real life. People who lived in places like this usually suffered from poverty more than insanity. At least it had no dead rodents hanging from the roof or trees. If he saw something like, he thought he might turn around and walk away. Duty or no, he hadn't igned up to collect crazy people.

Taking a deep breath, one that brought him the scent of dry

earth and old leaves and damp wood, he forced himself to the front door. At the porch, he tested each step before putting his weight on it. It had no button for a bell, so he gulped and knocked. His prayers hadn't been paid much attention recently, but he offered one up to not encounter a serial killer here.

Daniel's appearance reminded Bobby a lot of himself. They had the same hair, eyes, facial structure, coloring, height, and build. Looking at him felt a lot like looking in a mirror, except Daniel seemed to have tiny differences that made him more rough and rugged, in the way he suspected a lot of women preferred. "Who're you?" From his raised brow, Bobby figured Daniel noticed that, too.

"Name's Bobby. You must be Daniel Jarvis. Is Elizabeth Caulfield here, too?"

Daniel's eyes narrowed and his brow furrowed. "Dan. What's it to ya?" His Southern accent even sounded similar to Bobby's.

"Dan, then. I'm here because we all got the same eyes, and stuff's happening on account of that. I'd really rather just tell you both the whole story at once, if that's alright. You're both in danger, though, you ought to know that right off."

"Danger? From who?" Dan peered around at the bushes and trees, maybe thinking he'd spot ninjas lurking there.

Bobby shrugged. "I ain't rightly sure who they are. Can I come in and explain to you and Lizzie? What I do know, I'll tell you everything."

Dan looked Bobby over critically, then he shrugged and stood aside to let him in. "Sure, whatever. Lizzie! C'mere," he hollered into the house.

The girl that stepped into view through a nearby doorway had fat red curls dripping off her head to frame a face with high cheekbones and a delicate, pert nose. Her faded red tank top left her fire engine red bra straps visible, and her tight little denim miniskirt made her legs seem a mile long. "Yeah? Who's this?"

Bobby stared as she draped an arm over Dan's shoulders and rubbed against his side. He'd seen girls like this before. In porn. On her, the exotic eyes enhanced everything and his gaze wound up falling from her full, pouting lips down to her chest. She stood with it thrust out, on display. If he wanted to, he could look right down her shirt.

Dan said something, but he missed it. Lizzie smiled at him, then Dan shoved her away and smacked her on the ass. "Sorry, she's just messing with you."

"What? Oh. Right. Sorry," Bobby coughed and looked down, "I just never seen a girl like that in real life before."

He laughed. "She's a wildfire in the sack, too."

Lizzie slipped around behind Dan and stuck her hands in the front pockets of his jeans. Peeking out over his shoulder, she let her eyes travel down Bobby's body, taking him in the same way he'd done to her. "What did you come to tell us?"

Her gaze unnerved him. Although it seemed like Dan controlled her, he got the feeling she actually ran the show between them. More than that, though, she watched him like a predator: a cat hiding in plain sight to catch a mouse. To heck with that; he wasn't a mouse, he was a swarm of dragons. He straightened and pulled the list out of his pocket.

They listened while he told them the whole story, from getting arrested to finding out Raymond was missing. "So, here's my proof." He let his whole left hand dissolve into dragons that buzzed the room before re-forming into him again.

"Lizzie can start fires with her mind," Dan said with a shrug. He made it sound as noteworthy as a talent for playing the piano. "I can't do anything special yet. Haven't had that waking up sweaty thing yet. Sounds like I will at some point."

She could start fires with her mind. Bobby tried not to think too hard about that. Girl like that could probably already get most anything she wanted by posing and pouting. Now she could blow stuff up, too. "We're all going to this place in Colorado, to meet up and make decisions and defend ourselves together."

"I don't wanna be part of a freak brigade," Lizzie sneered. She slipped her hand out of Dan's pocket and stuck it down the front of his jeans. "Dan, you promised we'd go do something fun soon."

Dan smirked and kept his eyes on Bobby, maybe used to her grabbing him while he tried to do something else. Crazy thing to get used to. "This could be something fun. You like road trips, baby."

Bobby looked away and coughed, hoping to cover how disturbing he found the pair of them. "If'n you stay here, uh, odds are good they'll come for you. Maybe, um, maybe you can defend yourselves and all, but it'd be better for all of us if they don't get a good idea what we all can do for as long as possible." He rubbed his forehead, unable to stop himself from imagining Lizzie doing all sorts of other things, to him and Dan both, and bothered by that. "It's possible we're all half brothers and sisters, so, this is, well, it's about family."

"We can just go see what it's like, baby, and if it sucks, we can leave."

"Is that true?" Lizzie stared at him, her eyes piercing and sharp. "If we don't like it, we can leave?"

Bobby nodded. "Not like we could stop you. We ain't the government or nothing." He pulled out the page with his copy of the directions to the place and offered it to them. "This is where everybody is. You wanna make a copy of that, you can decide for yourselves while I go on to the next person on the list. Don't let nobody know where you're going or lose the directions or nothing."

Dan took the page and read it over. "You got better

handwriting than me, baby, go take care of that."

"Sure." Lizzie snatched the paper with a mild scowl and swished her butt out of the room.

Bobby watched her go, unable to tear his eyes away. When she turned a corner, he scratched the back of his neck and found Dan smirking at him with his arms crossed over his chest. "You think you'll go? "

"Yeah." Dan nodded. "She's just being obnoxious 'cause I told her not to play with you. Once we're on the road, she'll get into it."

Whatever 'play' meant to Lizzie, Bobby thought he ought to be grateful to Dan for putting him off limits for it. "Only name I can really give you for sure is Hannah. She seems to be good at the organization thing, so she's the one that's acting kinda in charge, but she ain't really in charge, so don't give her no crap for that."

"Cool." Dan nodded again and shook hands with Bobby. "Its cool you're out doing this. Coulda just run for the hills yourself and left the rest of us to swing in the wind. Says something about a man when he risks his own butt for total strangers."

"'Specially when it's a nice, tight butt," Lizzie said, returning already. She walked into Bobby's personal space and thumped his paper onto his chest. She got so close he could smell peppermint on her breath. "You look just like Dan, you know." Her tongue flicked out. "I could mistake you for him easy." She squealed and danced away backwards.

Dan's arm pulled her back by the waistband of her skirt until she thumped into his chest. "No, baby, you couldn't." He kissed her neck and wrapped an arm around her waist, holding her close and tight.

"I'll get going, then. See you there, I guess." He backed out, pulling the door shut to the sound of Lizzie moaning. As he hurried to the road, a repressed shiver worked its way across his entire body.

People didn't normally creep him out, but those two did. Jasmine was nice, he reminded himself, and so was Hannah. With thirty-five of them, some being freakish shouldn't come as a big shock.

Feeling dirty, he rubbed his hands on his jeans, then broke apart into the swarm. If he ever wound up in the position where a hot girl sticking her hand down his pants happened so often he ignored it to get other things done, he wanted to be put out of his misery. Dallas, he had to get to Dallas. Pulling out his list, he checked the name: Stephen Cant.

He sent up a prayer for Stephen to be less creepy.

Chapter 9

Three hours later, Bobby walked up to the front door of a grand two story house in a wealthy neighborhood. Stephen's house, like many of the others in this Dallas development, had a wraparound porch and a manicured yard with a patch of green grass. His stomach rumbled, threatening to embarrass him in front of whatever society person happened to answer the door. He judged getting to Stephen as more important than eating. Besides, he might be able to wrangle a meal out of the guy.

An older lady answered the door. Her clothes, a light tan pantsuit with a light blue blouse and pearls, marked her as someone who probably had an important job, like a lawyer or a doctor or an executive. "Can I..." Her light green eyes zeroed in on his own and she sucked in a breath. "Stephen isn't here."

"Okay." Bobby stared at her, blinking.

She put a hand on her pearls and frowned. "Are you his brother?"

He figured that for a weird question to come from the woman he presumed to be Stephen's momma. Stifling a shrug, he ran with it anyway. "Yes, ma'am. Know where I can find him?"

"I'm sorry," she breathed, "so sorry. I didn't know he had one."

Still lost, Bobby raised his brow. "You didn't know he had a place to stay?"

She shook her head sadly. "No, a brother. I would have adopted you both if I'd known."

This conversation suddenly made much more sense. "Oh. It's alright, ma'am. I just really need to find him and I don't know where he's gone. It's kinda urgent-like."

"Of course." She gave him an address. "It's our church, I've been going there for a very long time. He's always felt at home there. Pastor Chris can help you."

"Thank you, ma'am." Bobby turned away, took two steps.

"Are you hungry?"

Her voice made him stop and look back to see a grimace of guilt on her face. She wrung her hands together and seemed to desperate to atone for some sin. Although he really did want something to eat, he figured finding Stephen rated higher than his stomach. "Not really, no, but thanks for the offer. Is there something I can deliver to Stephen for you, though?"

Her lip quivered and her eyes crinkled, giving him the impression she might burst into tears at any moment. She nodded and disappeared, then stepped back into sight with a brown leather purse. He walked back to the door while she rooted through it. The wad of cash she pressed into his hand felt thicker than he'd ever had before. "Take it, use it for both of you."

Only a few days ago he had nothing at all, not even clothes. Looking down at the twenty folded over more bills, he had an urge to give it back. He'd lied to her, at least a tiny bit, and inadvertently given her guilt. This money felt like it came from a dishonest place. When he stole, he preferred to do it because he had no other choice. She owed him nothing, no matter what she thought.

On the other hand, Stephen didn't deserve to be deprived of

money his momma wanted him to have for lack of being here to take it. He tucked it into his pocket. "I swear on my Daddy's grave he'll get this."

She covered her mouth and he noticed her eyes watering. "Tell him I love him, very much, all of us do, and we miss him. We all hope he finds what he's looking for. A phone call every so often to let us know he's okay would be— We'd all really like that."

"Yes, ma'am," he ducked his head. "I'll see about getting him to call. I'm sure he's fine." He really ought to see about calling Momma himself once in a while. It had to be hard on her, not knowing. On the other hand, some form of cops had to be tapping her phone, maybe even those suits.

She nodded and kept watching him with that unhappy, pitying smile. Not wanting to see that anymore, or to take anything else from her, he turned and walked away. From the sidewalk, he tossed a wave over his shoulder, then hurried up the street. Her behavior puzzled him, in part. What happened to Stephen that she adopted him and felt that much guilt for missing his brother?

Around the corner, he ducked behind a tree and broke apart into dragons. He re-formed half an hour later, down the street from the Second Baptist Church of Dallas. The neighborhood contrasted sharply with the one where Stephen's momma lived. It had tiny little houses with tiny little yards, many in need of paint and sweeping and minor repairs. None of them had grass. He wondered how the Cants went from this church to that neighborhood, and why they never switched churches to a closer one.

The church, a plain brick building with no ornate decoration, fit in with its neighbors. The landscaping had weeds and needed mowing, the lone fir tree had dead branches in need of pruning. Black plastic covered one window. Without the sign and a couple of crosses here and there, he might have mistaken it for a struggling business of some kind, or a small, underfunded school.

Finding the front door unlocked, he walked into a single large room with stacks of folded chairs leaning against one wall with a microphone stand, folding tables leaning against the other wall, and an empty, footed bathtub at one end. It had three other doors, two marked as restrooms and the third with a piece of paper taped to it that read 'Kitchen'. At the end opposite the bathtub, an area had been blocked off with half-height bookshelves. He saw small bean bag chairs, battered books, a worn shag throw rug over the industrial pseudo-marble floor, and bins in cubbyholes with toys poking out.

On his hands and knees with yellow rubber gloves, a sponge, a spray bottle, and a roll of paper towels, a man in jeans and a white button-down shirt worked hard to clean something off that piece of carpet. He looked up at the soft chime made by the door opening. Friendly green eyes under shaggy brown hair smiled at Bobby in welcome. Sitting up on his feet and swiping the back of his arm across his forehead, he said, "Hi there, I'm Pastor Chris, can I help you?"

"I surely hope so, Pastor." Bobby stuck his hands in his trenchcoat pockets and echoed the Pastor's smile. "I'm looking for Stephen Cant. His momma said he might be here, or you might know where to find him."

"Ah." His smile faded. "Why are you looking for him?" It was a wary, guarded question, like he half expected Bobby to say it was to kill him or something along those lines.

Bobby shrugged, wondering if that tension in his voice meant the Pastor had him hidden in the basement for some reason. "It's complicated. I gotta talk to him about stuff."

Pastor Chris scanned Bobby from head to toe and nodded. "Life is full of complicated stuff."

"I s'pose that's true."

"If you'd like to talk about it, I can listen."

"Not really." Bobby reached up and scratched his beard. "I dunno. I just—" Unwilling to keep looking at Chris while he tried to ignore the things tumbling around in his head, he swept his eyes around the room, hoping to find a distraction. The makeshift altar grabbed his attention. "How come you don't got no crucifix inside here?"

Pastor Chris smirked. "Because, fool that I am, I spend the church money on other things, like bills and an aide for the day care I run here."

"You don't got no church ladies to run a bake sale for it, huh?"

"I do," Chris chuckled, "but there are always more important things than decorations that need the money. I haven't even been able to replace the window yet." He gestured to the black plastic as he pulled his rubber gloves off and stood up. "If you're willing to finish cleaning this up for me, I'd be happy to share my dinner table with you."

Bobby had no interest in taking anything away from this tiny, cash-strapped church. He could graze elsewhere. "How about if I do that, you tell me where to find Stephen?"

Chris nodded, disappointment showing. "Alright, I'll tell you what I can. Would you like anything at all, though?"

"Nah, save it for yourself. 'Sides, I ain't as raggedy as I look."

"That's comforting." Chris grinned and passed Bobby the rubber gloves. As he did, his eyes flicked to Bobby's. "What's your name?"

"Bobby. I'm Stephen's half-brother." It seemed safest to stick to the same maybe- kinda-lie he told Stephen's momma. He pulled the gloves on and knelt down to see what he'd gotten himself into.

"It's grape juice. I'm mostly worried about ants." Chris stood there and watched Bobby get to work. "I didn't know he had a half-brother."

"Yeah, he don't, neither. I didn't 'til a few days ago."

"So you came to meet him?"

"Yeah, that's part of it."

"Hm." Chris paced away, leaving him to the work. It took no skill, only elbow grease. Several minutes later, he decided he'd done as much as a body could do. Chris came back out of the kitchen with a tray that he set on the floor while pulling out a table and two chairs. "Looks like my timing is good."

"If you get ants, it ain't gonna be because of this." He pulled off the gloves and picked up all the cleaning supplies. Eyeing the second chair and the plate set in front of it, he sighed. "You don't gotta feed me."

"At least have a glass of water. You can take something with you if you want. Set that stuff by the kitchen door and come sit with me. Eating alone gets tiresome after a while."

"This is why you can't afford nothing," Bobby shook his head and gave him half a smirk. He could smell the lasagna and it made his stomach growl. Once that gave him away, he sat down and picked up a fork. Along with a large slab of lasagna, he'd been given a biscuit and a small salad with two fat cherry tomatoes. No sense letting this go to waste.

"Charity is something we can all afford to give, no matter how much we have." For a few minutes, neither spoke, both busy with the food. Chris watched him eat with a pleased smile. "There's a bathroom here if you want to wash up when you're done. It has a shower."

Bobby had to cough to keep himself from choking at how that struck him. "Do I really look that rough around the edges?"

Chris smiled kindly. "A little, yes. You mostly look like you've had a rough break recently."

"I ain't really that bad off, not really. I mean, it ain't no picnic, but I ain't starving or nothing."

"What happened?"

He wanted to help. Bobby had somehow managed to stumble across another of what he'd always thought to be a rare breed: people who see others in need and try to do something about it. This Pastor had nothing in common with the one he'd grown up listening to. Pastor Adam talked about how God punished fags with diseases. When a girl he knew got knocked up, Pastor Adam spent a sermon pointing at her and calling her a slut in league with the Devil. He said she got pregnant as a punishment from The Lord.

That man presided over holiday charity events, but the few times Bobby volunteered to help, the Pastor never showed up and the church ladies took care of everything. Thinking back on everything Pastor Adam did and said, he couldn't recall any personal acts of charity the man did. Everyone sinned and needed to repent by giving him money. His church had stained glass windows and mahogany pews.

Bobby sighed and stared at his water glass. He'd already gotten tired of explaining about the superpowers, and still had to do it several times. Still, other things weighed on his mind, and a priest could maybe help with that. This particular pastor seemed suited to it, anyway. "Do you think stuff happens the way it's gonna happen, and nothing we can do about it, or are we really running our own lives for ourselves?"

Pastor Chris's brow popped up in surprise. He took half a minute to finish the bite in his mouth, chewing slowly enough that Bobby suspected him to be stalling for time while he decided how to answer. "God did give us free will, making it a struggle to do the right thing when we could do what's easy or convenient instead.

That's why faith is important, it shows us the right path."

Poking his fork into the lasagna, Bobby frowned. "What if there's more'n one right path, or all of 'em suck? What if what I'm choosing is 'tween saving this guy or that guy? How does a body pick at times like that?"

"The road to Heaven isn't achieved through perfection, it's through doing the best that you can with what you have, and helping those who are less fortunate than yourself. Some will tell you it means following God's laws like they're the only things that matter, but I say, listen to your heart. It knows what's right. Do unto others as you'd have them do unto you. We're all in this world together and should act like it."

His frown growing deeper, Bobby said, "You sound kinda like a Democrat."

Chris laughed quietly, covering his mouth with his napkin. "I rather think I sound like a decent human being, but everyone is entitled to his own opinion."

"God's got a plan, though, right? They always say that."

"The only thing I'm truly certain of is that I feel Christ in my heart, there to guide me when I feel weak, warm me when I'm cold. Whether there's actually a plan or not…" He shrugged. "We are to God like ants are to men. Comprehending something on such a vastly different scale is chancy, at best. Use the mind He gave you, the heart He gave you, the hands He gave you. Think, listen, act. Preferably more or less in that order."

Bobby smirked. "If Pastor Adam heard you say all that, he'd call you a blasphemer."

"Not everyone interprets his pastoral duties the same way."

Nodding, Bobby stuffed the last bite of lasagna in his mouth. He broke the biscuit apart and used the pieces to mop up the last of the sauce before eating them. No matter how weird Chris might be, he offered up a good meal, and Bobby leaned back in his chair to tell him so. The door opening with a soft chime interrupted him.

In walked a man, wearing jeans and a hoodie, the hood pulled up and covering his face. He hopped out of the sunlight while the door closed and shook his hand with a hiss of pain. "I need gloves," the newcomer muttered.

Chris smiled at this person. "I'll see if I can find some, Stephen. There's a box of winter clothes in the basement."

Bobby narrowed his eyes at Chris, knowing he'd been snookered. "Why'n heckbiscuits didn't you just say he'd show here?"

Stephen pulled his hood down, revealing pale skin and short platinum-blonde hair. As expected, he had the icy blue eyes. One of his nearly invisible eyebrows arched up in mild amusement. "'Heck biscuits'?"

"You looked like you needed a friendly ear," Chris said with a restrained grin. "I'll let you two talk." He gathered up the plates and cups, taking them to the kitchen on his tray.

"What do you want from me?" He had a very mild Southern twang, much lighter than Bobby's. His one hand nearly glowed with a lobster red sunburn.

"I got a story to tell you. Might as well have a seat. It'll take a few minutes." When Stephen shrugged and obliged, Bobby told him the whole thing, from start to end. At this point, he could tell it without getting sidetracked or winding up on tangents. It took him about five minutes to lay everything out for Stephen.

"About a month ago, I woke up like you said." Stephen frowned as he spoke, looking down at his hands. The sunburn had faded to a light pink. "It was… I had this crazy thirst, like nothing I'd ever felt before. I spent that night with my girlfriend, and when I looked at her right then, I wanted her so bad I could taste it. I reached out to mess around and she was light as a feather." He paused and Bobby watched his face contort while he grappled with something, maybe whatever happened next. "I'm a vampire."

"Seriously?"

"Yeah. I drink blood, I'm unusually strong, I can fly, heal myself, the whole thing."

"Dang." Bobby lifted his hand and finally got to the demonstration part, letting his hand fall into dragons. "Don't look like holy ground bothers you. How about garlic?"

Stephen stared at the dragons. One landed on his hand and walked across it, sniffing his flesh. "No, nothing repels me that didn't already before. I never really liked garlic much, though. How many of these are there?"

"Lots. More'n I could count." Bobby sat back in his chair and watched the dragons, too. He never left them to their own devices. The bunch of them flitted around and investigated everything with curiosity and wonder. They stuck together for the most part, not straying more than a foot or so from the nearest other dragon, but otherwise spread out and got into everything nearby. "You leave behind fang marks?"

"No." Stephen kept watching the dragon on his hand as it ducked its head up his sleeve and chirped. "My saliva somehow removes the minor injury. It also seems to be a sort of aphrodisiac, or maybe just overloads the brain. Where do your clothes go?"

"No clue. The girl what can turn into a squirrel, hers go with her, too. One second, there's a fully clothed girl standing there. Next, a fuzzy little squirrel." Bobby shrugged. He couldn't think of any other questions for the moment. "You gonna head to Colorado?" So Stephen couldn't use the dragons as a distraction to evade the question, he called them back. They obeyed without hesitation.

Stephen tapped his thumb on the table a few times. "Seems I wasn't very hard to find."

"Not really, no."

"Unless you want some company, yeah, I guess so."

Leaning back, Bobby recalled Hannah suggesting that very thing. It sounded like a good idea then, and still did now. His back might not need watching as much as some other folks, but he could use the company. "How fast can you fly?"

"About a hundred miles an hour, give or take. You?"

"Same. Yeah, come with me, that's cool." He scratched his beard. "It's kinda late on for tonight, though, you maybe want to stop in and tell your family you're okay? Your momma was pretty upset."

Stephen sighed and raked a hand through his hair. "I left to protect them. From me. I don't want to accidentally kill one of them. They're better off without me around, at least until I can get some kind of reliable control over this."

Bobby pulled his phone out and set it on the table. "Least give 'em a call."

Reaching out, Stephen put two fingers on the phone and pulled it closer. He stared at it for several long seconds, then pushed it away again. "Not now."

"Don't wait too long."

Stephen hung his head. "Next pay phone I see."

"Speaking of pay phones, your momma gave me this." Bobby pulled out the wad of cash, trading it for the phone.

The stack sat for three or four seconds with Stephen peered at it suspiciously. He huffed and swiped the money, then flipped through the bills. "Christ, this is four hundred dollars. What did you tell her?"

Dang. "She asked if I was your brother, and I said yes."

"Ah." He peeled off the outer two twenties and left them on the table for Pastor Chris. "She must have assumed you were in the house I was taken out of when she adopted me. I can see how that might make her feel guilty enough to shove this at you." Standing up, he nodded for Bobby to come with him into the kitchen. Pastor Chris stood washing dishes in the industrial kitchen. "Bobby's staying in the basement with me tonight, we're leaving in the morning. Neither of us will be back."

"Are you sure? Because you know you're always welcome here."

"He's like me."

Chris's brow flew up. "You're a vampire, too?"

Bobby cracked a grin. "No, I ain't. But I ain't all human, neither, just the same as Stephen. If'n you don't mind, I'd rather keep what I can do to myself."

"Of course." Chris nodded and gestured for them to use the door Stephen headed for. "Whatever it is, don't let it be a burden so heavy you can only look down at your own feet."

Unable to think of a response, Bobby nodded and followed Stephen downstairs. The basement had boxes stacked in groups, all of them neatly labeled. This bunch had Christmas decorations, that bunch had pageant costumes, Easter stuff, and some with donated clothes. It also had a couch with blankets and a pillow on it, and two easy chairs that looked squishy and comfy.

"So, you sleep still, huh? Wasn't expecting that."

Stephen snorted. "Yes, I still sleep."

Chuckling, Bobby settled himself into one of the chairs. It had a lever that he cranked to stretch out with a footrest. Yeah, he could sleep here. "Hey, it's a fair question. What about sunlight? I saw your hand before."

Stephen threw a blanket at Bobby and sank down on the couch. He held up the burned hand, now as pale as the rest of him. "I've always burned easily, it's much worse now. A quick flash of full sunlight turns my skin red, a full minute in it makes me blister. I don't want to know what longer than that does. Sunblock still works, though."

"Why're you walking around in daylight and sleeping at night, then?"

Stephen shrugged. "It's what I'm used to, I guess. A lot of businesses are only open during the day. Besides, it's easier to meet prey that isn't skanky whores."

Bobby stared at him, trying to decide if he wanted to get into the 'prey' issue or not. No, he didn't. "Maybe we ought to go at dusk, then, get as far as we can before sunup tomorrow."

"Suits me. Dusk is in about four hours. Where are we going, anyway?"

Pulling out his list, Bobby checked. He hadn't read it enough times to memorize it yet. "Austin first, then Phoenix."

Stephen gave a low whistle. "Austin to Phoenix is a long haul. We might want to stop somewhere between. El Paso, maybe. At least for a meal."

"I gotta stop to eat every few hours anyway."

Chapter 10

Comfortable and safe, Bobby fell asleep within seconds of closing his eyes. At dusk, Stephen shook him awake, ready to go with a pack on his back. On the way out, Bobby paused in the kitchen to grab two bananas and stuff them in his pocket. His belly stayed quiet for now, so he put off eating in favor of getting to Austin as soon as possible. He'd eat there.

The swarm streamed up into the air and Stephen followed. He floated upwards with his body limp. When they reached an altitude high enough to pass over skyscrapers, he shifted to being hunched over in what appeared to be relaxed comfort. He had the dragons surround the vampire to make sure he didn't wander off course by not looking.

Less than two hours later, Stephen touched back down the same way he took off. The second he re-formed, Bobby gave him a funny look. "Why d'you fly like that? It looks…weird."

"How should I fly?" Stephen cracked a half-grin. "With my arms out, like Superman? Or maybe I should flap my arms." He demonstrated, proving it looked stupid.

"Don't you gotta do nothing to fly?"

"Like what?"

“I dunno,” Bobby shrugged, “something.”

Stephen barked out a laugh. “No, it’s a lot like making myself run. Just have to want to do it.”

“Huh.” Bobby shrugged and dropped the subject. “I usually find a gas station, they always got maps.” He snorted. “Listen to me. ‘Usually’, like this is something I do all the time.”

Clapping him on the back, Stephen chuckled. “Don’t worry about it, Bobby. Let’s just destroy Christopher’s life and get our asses to Phoenix to keep spreading the love.”

Bobby rolled his eyes. “Yeah, I think that’s a gas station up there.”

Half an hour later, Stephen rang the doorbell for the upper of two apartments over an ‘adult toy’ store. “I could get used to living with a location like this.” He nodded to indicate a bar across the street, and a nightclub next door to it. “Target rich environment.”

“I can’t see no reason to complain much, neither.” They heard footsteps inside. Bobby pulled out a banana and stuffed his face with it.

One of theirs opened the door. He had the swarthy complexion of Hispanic heritage, with dark hair. In good shape, he stood taller than Bobby, but not quite up to Stephen’s 6 foot 2. “Can I help you gentlemen?” The guy had a queer, girly-sounding voice, and he looked them both over the same way Bobby had been known to check out a shapely girl.

“Uh, yeah.” Bobby heard someplace that about ten percent of all people turned out gay. It still never occurred to him that members of their group would be. All his life, he’d been told gays were gross and an abomination. Christopher instantly repulsed him. At the same time, they might be half-brothers or cousins, which meant family. Nothing in the world meant more than family. He had no idea what to think or feel.

Christopher's eyes went flat and he pursed his lips. "My mistake," he told Stephen, turning his shoulder to deliberately snub Bobby. "There's only one gentleman here."

Mouth open to say something, Bobby stopped because Stephen elbowed him in the side. "We came to warn you that someone may be interested in abducting you because of the unusual abilities all of us with these unusual eyes have." Stephen tapped his temple.

Christopher sniffed. "Take your jokes someplace else." He slammed the door shut.

"Way to go, genius."

"What?" Confused by the exchange, Bobby looked from Stephen to his half-eaten banana. "I didn't say nothing."

Stephen's mouth twitched with amusement. "What do you want to do? I got the impression leaving people behind was out of the question until they understand the risk they're taking by doing so."

"Yeah. I dunno. Nobody never slammed the door in my face before." Food had none of these complications, so Bobby finished the banana, tossing the peel into the open dumpster below them. One look inside it and he had no interest in checking it for food.

"You know, you didn't actually say anything. He reacted kind of strongly for just the comical expression on your face."

"Gee, thanks."

"I'm just saying," Stephen grinned, "that maybe he can read minds or something. I sometimes get weird little bursts of inspiration about my prey—"

"Do you have to say 'prey'?"

Stephen ignored him. "I just suddenly know the name of a person they care about, or what they do for a living, or other little bits of information."

"Your point?"

"It's completely possible he saw something in your head, only he isn't aware it's happening."

"Great." Bobby harrumphed and gripped the handrail of the stairs, staring out at nothing in particular. "Maybe you should just talk to him, then. All I can think about when I see a fag is how gross it all is."

Stephen rubbed his chin in silence for several seconds. Finally, he said, "I know a lot of people who think that. It's really normal down here. Well, not in Austin so much, so I've heard, but yeah. Still, he's one of us, and that doesn't change just because he happens to like guys."

Bobby grunted in annoyance. "'S'not like I'm standing here calling him a pervert or nothing. Just something I was taught ain't right, and I was keeping it to myself."

"Go do something for fifteen minutes." Stephen waved vaguely towards the street. "I'll meet you out front."

"Yeah." Bobby sighed and hopped down the steps. He knew very well that gay people were still people. Pastor Adam used to say they perverted God's will. He called them dirty all the time and railed about the stories of Sodom and Gomorrah. The first time Bobby remembered him explaining gay sex, he'd been eleven, and the pictures disturbed him. Without that last part, Bobby thought he'd care about it roughly as much as he cared about the supposed damnation premarital sex insured. Now he thought about it, though, Pastor Adam focused on men and ignored the idea of lesbians, which struck him as weird.

Whatever. So long as he didn't have to think about it, he didn't care. Having a guy right there in his face made him think about it. He leaned against the wall of the building with his hands in his pants pockets, watching people walk past. A few people walking by looked him over suspiciously. A few minutes later, an ordinary guy in a rumpled suit stopped a few feet away.

"Um, hi." He glanced around nervously. "I've, uh, never done this before." The guy stuffed his hands in his pockets and wouldn't look Bobby in the eye.

After looking around a little to be sure he was the one the guy was talking to, Bobby blinked a couple of times. "Done what?"

"Um, are you a cop?"

"No." Was this guy—?

The guy's shoulders relaxed "Oh, good. Because that would just be—" He chuckled apprehensively. "Yeah. Um, so." His eyes roved down Bobby's body. When Christopher did it, Bobby got the impression he'd been appraised and found pleasant to look at. When this guy did it, he felt more like a slab of meat being judged for a meal. "Is a hundred bucks enough?"

Hot damn. Compared to Christopher, this guy made him want to take a shower forever. If this was how girls felt when he leered at them, he'd never, ever do it again. Putting his hands up, he stepped away from the building and noticed the display he'd been standing in front of. This store didn't hide its light under a bushel. Combined with his own appearance right now, he knew he'd brought this on himself. Punching this guy in the face would be downright rude. "Man, if you gotta pay to get laid, you need to seriously rethink things about your life. I ain't selling what you're trying to buy."

"Oh my gosh." The guy blushed so hard it was almost funny. "I'm so sorry."

Bobby grunted with disinterest and noticed a black SUV over the guy's shoulder, parked across the street. He peered at it and thought the license plate seemed weird, but it was too far away to get a good look.

"What?" Bobby watched two men in dark suits get out of the car, then saw they wore sunglasses despite the darkness. He waved the guy off. "No, go on and git. I ain't selling nothing." When he saw two more suits step out of the SUV, he knew something had to be up. Guys in suits showing up to Christopher's neighborhood couldn't be a coincidence.

"Nobody just stands around here." The guy didn't seem nervous anymore.

Bobby waved the guy off and walked around the corner of the building, intending to hurry up the stairs to Christopher's door.

"Stop." The unmistakable sound of a gun cocking got Bobby's attention.

Raising his hands, he stopped and turned around. "I ain't selling nothing, really."

"Who do you work for?"

"What? I don't work for nobody. Who'n heckbiscuits you think I am?"

The guy gave him a flat, unimpressed look. "I'm the one asking questions."

"I don't got time for this." Bobby had no interest in finding out what getting shot felt like. He burst into a cloud of dragons and sent them streaking upward, looking for a way inside Christopher's apartment. That guy's mouth fell open and he gawped, which Bobby considered to be better than shooting or screaming. The swarm noticed the suits huddled in a small group. One of them pointed to the porn shop, so he knew they had to hurry.

Desperate to get inside, the dragons found an open window. The horde destroyed the screen and poured through. He re-formed from the feet up in the room where Stephen and Christopher sat at a small table, talking. "Suits coming, out on the street. We gotta git, now. Sorry about the screen."

Christopher's mouth fell open, gaping at Bobby.

Stephen nodded. "We have five minutes for him to pack a

bag?"

"Nope. More like one for him to grab his wallet. Can you fly him out the window or something?" Bobby checked out the window and saw the suits hurrying across the street. "They're here, right down there."

"Christopher, you have sixty seconds to grab whatever you need, then were leaving. Don't bring your phone." When Christopher didn't move, Stephen slammed his hand on the table. "This is life and death."

Christopher jumped with a squeak and scrambled to his feet. "Right. Money, I guess." He hurried out of the room.

Bobby pulled the torn screen out of the window. "Can you get through this? You got them shoulders."

"Yeah, I think so."

"Can you grab some stuff outta the fridge for me? I ain't got nowhere to stick it, and I'm already hungry."

Stephen grimaced in distaste, but sighed and went into the kitchen. "What do you want to do with him? He doesn't have any powers he's aware of. I think its mental, but whatever it might be, he definitely can't fly."

"Christopher, you got a car someplace aside from right here?"

"Yes, I keep it at my parents' house. Parking around here is a bitch." He emerged from the bedroom with a small pack and frowned at Stephen rifling through his fridge. The doorbell rang. Bobby put himself between Christopher and the door.

"Ignore it. Where's your folks' place? Far?"

"A few miles."

"We can take you that far." Stephen slung his own pack, then he slipped in behind Christopher and grabbed him around the waist.

Christopher squeaked and his eyes popped wide and scared as Stephen lifted him off the ground and hauled him through the window. The swarm followed along behind them both.

"I feel like Lois Lane!"

"I'm more Dracula than Superman."

"Whatever!"

Chapter 11

When they landed at a nice house in the suburbs, Bobby gave Christopher the directions to the place in Colorado. He avoided touching the other man and tried not to think about gay sex. In return, Christopher wrinkled his nose and took notes without commenting. He and Stephen kept the drop-off short, taking off again as soon as they could.

They struck for El Paso, figuring to stop for the day so Stephen could hide from the daylight. While he could turn his body to avoid burning, they had to worry about being seen. High enough to be invisible from the ground probably meant high enough to be seen from an airplane or helicopter. Best to play it safe.

"Dang, I'm starving." These words spilled out of Bobby's mouth the second he re- formed in an alley. They'd stopped once in the middle of nowhere so Bobby could devour the food Stephen swiped from Christopher's fridge. By now, the sun had been up for nearly an hour, and he did his best to keep them in the shade of buildings as they walked through the city.

"I suppose it seems ridiculous," Stephen said as he adjusted the hood of his sweatshirt, "but I'm incredibly jealous of your… ability."

Bobby plucked a half rotten apple out of a garbage can and looked it over. The other half was fine. "Says the guy able to carry a backpack."

"To the guy who can eat regular food." Stephen's eyes tracked a woman passing not far away. She wasn't especially attractive, as far as Bobby thought, but the other man wasn't looking at her ass, or her chest. "I need to feed. I also need to not be charged with rape or any other form of assault."

Bobby took a bite from the good side of the apple and followed Stephen's gaze to a heavy-set middle aged lady. She pulled a wheeled basket of full cloth shopping bags behind her. Either Stephen had different tastes in women, or appearance didn't matter much. Given this was about food, the latter struck him as more likely. "How 'bout chomping on a guy?"

Stephen sneered with distaste. "It's too much like sex."

Bobby's chewing faltered. "Oh."

"And now you see my dilemma." Stephen snorted. "No offense, but having you with me isn't going to make this easier. We should make a plan to meet someplace later."

"I'm gonna look for the crappiest part of town and bunk down with the homeless folk. Maybe hit a soup kitchen if'n I can find one."

Stephen grimaced. "You want to stay with people who may very well rob you in your sleep?"

Bobby snorted. "So long as I don't show I got any money, all of 'em got more'n I look like I do. You might have trouble there on account of the pack, but not if it's clear we're running together. Risking two guys ain't worth it."

"Were you homeless?" Stephen put his hands up. "You just seem like you know how they think and operate."

Shrugging, Bobby said, "I had some friends in school that

were. Parents lost their jobs, and they didn't have no place to go."

"Ah. I'll find you there, then." They shook hands and Stephen jogged across the street, chasing after that woman. Bobby kept walking, grazing on what he found in garbage cans along the way. He checked with a couple in raggedy clothes under a highway bridge, and they pointed him in the right direction. The houses got progressively shabbier until he found a wide alley with weathered, beaten faces, shopping carts, and mounds of rags.

At the other end of the alley, he found an abandoned warehouse lot with shanties made of cardboard and garbage leaning against the building. Shopping carts full of stuff had been parked here and there, and they had barrels scattered around. Bobby guessed the cops left them alone so long as they didn't squat inside the building.

He walked through the gauntlet, head down and hands in his pockets, listening to them try to ward him off. There were no drugs here, they said, no hookers, and no social services. Kids didn't belong here. Get out while you still can. Go find a job, a girl, a life. If only things could be that simple again.

"You need a place to sit for a little bit, kid?"

Bobby looked up, expecting to find a man with disturbing, greedy eyes. Instead, the speaker turned out to be a thin, grizzled old man, bundled up in multiple blankets despite the warm weather. If he hoped for someone to take advantage of, it didn't show. Besides, he'd get a lot more than he bargained for if he tried that with Bobby, or Stephen when he showed up. "Yeah, thanks."

"You're kind of young for a place like this." He set out a ratty old cushion and gestured to it. As he withdrew his hand, he coughed and tried to cover his mouth with his elbow. Bobby saw a gob of blood on the sleeve when he pulled it away from his mouth.

"Just passing through." Bobby shrugged and sat down. "Ain't

got enough money to stay someplace fancy. You know, with showers and beds." He flashed the old man a friendly smile.

The man chuckled. It turned into more coughing and he hacked a dark gobbet of crap off to the side. "You have a name, kid? Mine's Kurt."

"Bobby. That's a nasty cough you got, Kurt."

"Yeah, it'll kill me someday." Kurt chuckled. "Where you headed for that you're just passing through?"

Unwilling to reveal anything about his plans, Bobby shrugged. "Someplace else."

"Mmhmm." He offered Bobby a small packet of peanut butter, one with the seal still intact. "You've got unusual eyes."

Figuring that refusing a gift would be taken poorly, Bobby accepted the packet and opened it. "Yeah, I guess. So folks tell me, anyhow."

Kurt nodded and went quiet, his eyes glazing over. A commotion at the other end of the shantytown broke the silence. Bobby looked up and saw Stephen with his gloves on and hood pulled up, stalking down the line, a swagger to his steps. It made him look like a seriously bad dude who stepped out of a comic book and any second now, he'd pull a sword to start battling ninjas or werewolves. The locals reacted like scared puppies.

Bobby stood up and got Stephen's attention with a two-handed wave. "Where'd you learn to walk like that?"

Stephen smirked. "Nightmares."

With a short and a shake of his head, Bobby gestured for Stephen to sit with him. "This is Kurt, he's being decent."

"Hi, Kurt, I'm Stephen."

Kurt nodded absently, still staring at nothing. His head kept bobbing until he watched Stephen sit down and focused on him. "I've seen eyes like yours before." His voice sounded misty and distant.

"Oh yeah? Where was that?" Odd that he hadn't mentioned it before, but Bobby figured he might as well see where this led. The guy probably saw a poster with elves on it and had lost enough marbles to believe it had been real.

Kurt shook his head violently and started coughing again. More blood smeared onto his sleeve. "Top secret. They'll fire me if I tell you, Aaron. I want to tell you, but I just can't."

Stephen and Bobby both blinked in surprise at the response and looked at each other. Covering his mouth to shield it from Kurt's view, Stephen whispered, "Keep going, sounds worth pursuing."

Keep going, he said. Bobby rubbed his face and tried to think about how they did this kind of thing on TV. "Can't you even say what kind of work it is?"

Kurt shook his head and looked pained. "Someday, you'll understand. They have to keep it a secret, son. Sometimes, the government keeps a secret to protect us, because the knowledge would get people killed, a lot of people."

"I wouldn't ever tell anyone, you know that. I just…I want—" Bobby paused, forcing himself not to fill the space with 'um' and 'uh'. He took a flying leap and guessed that when Kurt said 'son', he meant Aaron had been his actual son's name. "I want to know about what you do, about who you are."

Tears formed in Kurt's eyes, his face filled with pride. "I know you do, just— When you're older— If you really want to know about this, you'll have to get yourself into the Army and be able to get the highest possible security clearance. The project is called Maze Beset, remember that, but don't ask for it by name. Tell them you want to work on the same program as your old man, they'll understand."

Glancing over at Stephen, Bobby saw the vampire's mouth hanging open in shock. His own seemed to be doing the same thing, and he snapped it shut. Kurt worked on a secret military program where he saw eyes like theirs, a long time ago. How long ago? It couldn't have been recent. He reached over and shook Kurt's shoulder gently. "Kurt, wake up, man, you kinda drifted off there."

"What?" More coughing produced a little splat of black stuff on the ground. "Huh?"

"How long you been out here, Kurt?"

Kurt took a deep breath and shook his head. "Years and years."

"You sound like a pretty smart guy, though. How'd you wind up on the streets?"

Kurt hunched in on himself and said nothing for several long seconds. "It was a car accident," he whispered. "Belinda— My wife. She didn't usually drive, but it was my retirement party. I drank more than I should have. They said so long as I kept my mouth shut, everything would be fine. I could just be with my wife, we could do the things we never got to do because of my job. We were going to travel, see the world. But she was dead, they killed her. It should have been me. I ran for it, ran for my life. Such a coward."

Bobby put his hand on Kurt's shoulder, trying to be friendly and supportive. "How long?"

"I don't know." Tears spilled down his cheeks and he coughed more. "I was sixty. Twenty years ago, maybe."

Twenty years on the streets would wear anybody down to nothing, even someone fifty years younger. Bobby frowned and thought about Kurt's son, a man whose mother died and father disappeared. "What about Aaron? Where's he?"

Kurt shook his head, too busy crying and coughing to answer the question. Bobby put his arm around Kurt's shoulder, wondering if the hand of God sent him to this particular man at this particular time.

"Kurt," Stephen said gently, "can you just tell us your last name?"

He managed to rasp out "Donner". Another minute or so later, he said, "God forgive me, I see her eyes in my nightmares. Your eyes." An especially harsh coughing fit wracked his body and Bobby held on. He and Stephen looked at each other behind his back. From his taut expression, Bobby figured they must be thinking the same thing: 'her eyes'. Were they all siblings after all? Could 'she' be their mother, their real mother?

They sat with Kurt while he slowly calmed down and fell asleep, probably exhausted by the memories and coughing. Bobby felt ready to collapse himself, from watching and from not sleeping enough last night. "I'm about to fall over, too."

Stephen yawned. "Yeah, I at least need a nap." The two of them, neither talking about what they just learned, moved Kurt under his crude little shelter in case the weather soured. He had enough space so long as neither of them stretched out, so both stayed under it with him, falling asleep without issue.

When Stephen woke Bobby up later, Kurt lay dead.

Chapter 12

"That's Camellia's place." Stephen gave a jerk of his head to indicate the tiny beige faux-adobe house with the flat roof as they approached it. The tiny front yard had rocks instead of grass, some scraggly weeds and cacti poking through it here and there. All the houses on this block had the same small income, southwestern feel. No garages here—some of the driveways had beat up old cars in them, but hers didn't.

"It's dark."

"Some people sleep at night. It's after ten."

Bobby's stomach growled. "No wonder I'm hungry."

"You're always hungry."

"So're you."

"Touché."

Stephen rang the doorbell and knocked, tamping down the grin Bobby provoked. Neither had anything in particular to say while they waited, so they stood there in silence for a solid minute. Stephen hit the doorbell again, and they waited another minute or so.

"Don't think she's there."

Stephen peered in through the front window. He rattled the doorknob and found it locked. "We should break in and take a look around."

"What?" Bobby's brow jumped up in shocked surprise. "We can't do that. It's her house."

"How else are we going to be sure she hasn't been grabbed already?"

"But—"

Stephen cut him off with a roll of his eyes and a wave of his hand. "If she's there but just sleeps like the dead, we apologize and explain we were concerned she'd been grabbed. If she's not there, but there's no sign of anything nefarious, we wait for her to get home and do the same. Honestly, Bobby, did you really think you'd manage to always find people at home when you happen to get there?"

Bobby opened his mouth to protest again. Given their purpose here, what Stephen said made sense. He shut his mouth. Momma was pretty clear about messing with another person's house. Sure, he'd broken a few laws in his youth. It'd all been about spray paint and messing around, not stealing or smashing things, or hurting people. Except…he stole a car a few days ago, along with a radio, a baton, and a few other things. As far as lines to not be crossed were concerned, this horse had already run out of the barn at full speed. "Okay, fine," he sighed. "I don't know nothing about breaking into a house, though."

"Are you implying that I do?" Stephen chuckled. "Well check for an open window, and if there isn't one…" He shrugged and paced around the house without finishing the statement.

If there wasn't one, they were screwed, because he didn't have the first clue how to pick a lock. Bobby stayed by the door, looking up and down the street to check if any neighboring curtains twitched. All the other houses had the lights off, except two with the gentle glow of television bleeding around the drapes. He saw no sign of movement.

Half a minute later, Stephen came around the other side of the house. "Nothing. She doesn't have very many windows. It's even smaller than it looks, too. From what I saw, it's a bedroom, a bathroom, and the rest is all one space. Mom would have a fit at the sight of the kitchen. It's smaller than her closet."

Bobby snorted. "Okay, smart guy, so how do we get in, then?"

His eyes still on the house, scanning up and down it, Stephen paused and pointed up. "Can you get a dragon into that?"

His finger directed Bobby's attention to a vent on the roof with small openings, and he instantly felt stupid for not thinking of it first. "Let's find out." One dragon popped off his thumb and flew up there. Since he wasn't sure what would happen or how much they could handle autonomously, he focused on it. His mind slid into it. He became the dragon and its little mind served as his co-pilot. Or maybe the other way around, because it knew how to move the body around a lot better than he did.

The vent had a screen inside it, but the dragon knew what to do about that from Christopher's place. His dragon chewed open a hole in the screen, doing real damage faster than Bobby could realize Camellia might not appreciate that. The vent connected to a metal tube that went to the swamp cooler, which the dragon squeezed past.

Inside the house, the dragon flew around, orienting itself, then located the front door. Bobby set it to the task of unlocking the knob, noting the deadbolt wasn't thrown, then let the dragon go to get it done without his interference. Back in his own body, he blinked and noticed Stephen watching him. "What's it look like when I do that?"

"It's adorable." Stephen grinned broadly. "You look like you're thinking very hard. Either that, or taking a dump."

Unamused, Bobby smacked Stephen in the arm. "I'll get a second opinion." His dragon got excited, which he took to mean that it got the job done. He reached over and opened the door.

"Excellent. I'll turn you into a ne'er-do-well yet."

Bobby snorted and took his dragon back into himself as they paced inside. While Stephen walked through the main room, looking around, Bobby poked his head into the bedroom. "She ain't here."

"There's a few things tossed around, but that could be from her hurrying. Hey, she's cute. There's some pics on the fridge."

Moving into the bedroom, Bobby checked the closet and under the bed, finding two empty suitcases and no sign of anything missing. "She's got a computer in here." A laptop perched on her minimalist black plastic desk, screen flipped open and plugged in. A tiny green light glowed steady, though the screen was dark. On the off chance it might be turned on, he pressed the spacebar.

"She's got plenty of food, so she wasn't planning on going anyplace. Woman must know how to cook, there's no doggie bags."

The laptop's fan whirred into action and the screen blinked on. He saw an image of himself, as seen by the built-in camera. Given the angle and his height, Bobby noticed a stain on his left pants pocket. "She seem like the type to be careless enough to leave her laptop running?"

A beat passed before Stephen answered, "Not really. If I assume the small signs of disturbance are from someone else intruding, then no, not at all. She's got her leftovers labeled and dated."

"Yeah, her bed is made, her desk is neat, it's all tidy and stuff. You know how to use computers? I'm not really all that up on this stuff. I didn't even have a cellphone."

"Barbarian," Stephen said with a sniff of disdain as he walked in and shooed Bobby out of the way. "So, using the webcam, were we, Camellia? What were you taking pictures of?" He sat down in her chair.

"You do that, I'm gonna eat." Without waiting for a response, Bobby went out and poked through the fridge. God bless labels and microwaves. As he slid something labeled 'turkey vegetable tetrazzini' in dainty handwriting into the nuke-o-matic, Stephen called out.

"I think she was taken by suits."

"Oh yeah, why'zat?" He punched buttons on the microwave and started it.

"She got a picture of one."

Bobby blinked and rushed into the bedroom. "Seriously?" He peered at the the screen. Sitting in the same chair Stephen now occupied, he saw the girl in the pictures on the fridge, a perky brunette with blond streaks in her shoulder-length hair, the same icy blue eyes, a cute little nose, and a big smile. She showed off a tattoo on her shoulder blade, of a rose.

Behind her, in the doorway, a man in a dark suit and sunglasses held a syringe ready to use. The guy's face looked blank, impassive, uninterested. Just another day at the office. More chilling, Bobby recognized that jaw from the group that showed up at Christopher's apartment. Camellia had no idea what was about to happen to her, and he reached out to touch the screen, wanting to warn her.

Stephen looked up at Bobby. "The image timestamp is from today, about five hours ago. They've only had her that long. We only missed her by that much."

If only they'd…what? Not slept? Not paused in El Paso? Not met Kurt? "Weren't nothing we could do to get here faster'n we did."

"Yeah." Stephen nodded in grim agreement, turned back to the laptop. "You eat, I'm going to see if there's anything to tell if her power is active or not and what it might be."

Chapter 13

Phoenix lit a fire under Bobby and Stephen to get to LA as quickly as possible, and they arrived before nightfall. The city of angels was home to three different members of their group, so they split up to each grab one and meet back up at the third. Bobby met Tiana, a zoologist working at the zoo who could talk to animals with her mind. She had to be the most attractive black woman he'd ever met, and he took another moment to boggle at how pretty everyone on the list had turned out to be so far.

"Tiana didn't want to leave her job," Bobby told Stephen as they walked to the front door of Matthew Garrison's apartment, "but I told her we'd have a ton of wild animals at the new place, and she said she'd think about it. Also, we can crash at her place tonight if we need to. You? "

"Javier was so eager to go along he almost tried to jump on my back so I could fly him away," Stephen snorted. "I could see why, too. His girlfriend is a bitch. She's knocked up and pals with his mom. Could hear her screeching from a block away. I did him a favor and bit her to take the edge off her temper. He'll get himself out there if he has to walk." He reached up and knocked on the door. "Hopefully without her."

Bobby snorted, though he wasn't so sure one of them abandoning a pregnant girlfriend should be hoped for. They waited about three minutes for someone to answer the door. "Shoot, I guess we gotta do this the hard way."

Stephen sighed and nodded for Bobby to get on with it.

Four dragons came off his hand and flew around the place, looking for any way in they could find. A neighbor opened their door and they dove in, looking for air vents to go through the ductwork. About ten minutes later, while Stephen and Bobby stood around trying to look innocent and harmless, the locks on the door clicked open. Bobby opened the door and walked in, the dragons reattaching to him. "I gotta say, until you had the idea in Phoenix, I never woulda thought to do that on my own."

"You just have to think like a rapist."

"I'm gonna pretend you didn't just say something that messed up."

With a light sigh, Stephen said, "Sorry. It's hard to get sex off my mind since this happened. A lot of what I can do is wrapped up in it. When I get really desperate for blood, my mind conjures up—Let's just say some of what goes on in here," he tapped his head with a finger as they looked around the apartment, "isn't about cute little bunnies and fuzzy duckies."

"Message received and understood," Bobby replied absently. He flipped through the mail sitting on the counter, then checked the fridge. Since he was there and could use a bite, he grabbed a swiftly spoiling banana to eat it.

"There's a messy serial killer in LA," Stephen noted as he picked up a newspaper and looked it over. "Funny, this is from a week ago. And it's only the front page section. This next one is from two weeks ago." He flipped through the stack on the table. "Offhand, I'd say either Matthew is the killer, or he's pals with a victim."

Looking up, he rolled his eyes to see Bobby drinking milk from a cup. "Must you always eat in front of me?"

"I'm hungry. Flying all over the place like that takes a lot of energy, it don't just come from nowhere." He chugged down the rest of what was in the glass and rinsed it out in the sink, then put it in the dishwasher with the other dirty dishes there. "If he's killing people, that makes this more complicated."

Stephen waved dismissively. "Let's find out a little more about who our boy actually is before we decide who he might be. I'm just saying that him collecting these particular papers is suggestive."

"Yeah, yeah." Bobby started looking through drawers and cabinets. He saw a box of cereal and started munching on it while he kept looking around. Half an hour later, they knew he'd been discharged from the military about six months ago. He'd been having trouble holding down a job, his bills were all late, and he had a girlfriend. It looked like the girlfriend might be dead. There apartment had evidence of a woman living in it, but also not. Nothing in the bathroom looked like it belonged to a woman, but decorations around the place that pointed to a feminine hand. The fridge had bachelor food in it, but the cabinets had stuff that didn't match up.

At least they knew they had the right guy. A picture of the two of them in a classy frame hung on the wall. They were a cute couple, both good looking and happy.

"I think our guy has some problems." Stephen walked out of the bathroom carrying two different prescription pill bottles. "I'm guessing he didn't leave the Marines just because his tour was up. I have no idea what these drugs are, but they can't be for anything shiny or happy. The names are too long."

"D'you get the feeling like he just crashes here and that's it?"

Looking around, Stephen shrugged. "Maybe he's just a neat

freak."

Bobby sighed in frustration. "None of this really tells us where to find him."

"We could just wait until he comes home. Everything points to him sleeping here regularly."

"I s'pose. If he's out there killing folks, though, are we a little guilty for not finding him and stopping him?" Bobby looked in the fridge again and grabbed a box of Chinese takeout, sniffed it, and started eating it cold with his fingers. He dropped himself into a chair with that.

Stephen grimaced in utter disgust and sat down where he wouldn't have to watch Bobby eat. Both would be in sight of anyone opening the door. "No. I feel no guilt whatsoever for not being psychic or an experienced investigator."

Before answering. Bobby finishing chewing his mouthful of lo mein. "Fair enough. What about sending him to all the others if he's a serial killer?"

"I would feel some amount of guilt about him killing them, yes, I will admit that."

"I meant, maybe we shouldn't send him there."

Stephen steepled his fingers. "No. Regular cops won't be able to stop him, if they can even find him. Depending upon what his superpowers are, anyway. If I was out killing people, they'd likely never find me unless I chose my victims based upon a personal connection to me. If it was you, the same, and I'm sure for many of the others, as well. If you really want to stop him from killing people, sending him there is likely the only way it'll happen. Just call ahead and warn them."

Bobby nodded while he ate, seeing the point, and the wisdom. "We are kinda dangerous, ain't we. Nobody could stop me if'n I wanted to rob houses and stuff."

"I would make an unstoppable serial killer," Stephen agreed.

The memory of that one suit's brains splattered on the wall and floor surfaced, and Bobby set the empty food box aside. Alice's episode came to mind soon after, then the ease with which Ai stole what she needed. His mind wandered down the worst case scenario of the ones he knew about, and he saw bodies and destruction and looting. He let out a somber sigh.

"Yes, it is a little disturbing to realize the only thing really preventing you from taking whatever you want is your own commitment to morality."

Bobby nodded, finding the statement close enough to his thoughts to be the same. "If he won't go, there ain't a whole lot we can do about that."

"Untrue. I can take him forcibly. You can go on to the rest on your own."

"I s'pose that's the best option." He was going to say something else, but the sound of someone unlocking the door interrupted him, and they both went still. The door opened, someone slipped inside, plastered himself against the door like he was afraid something would open it to get him.

Bobby recognized Matthew from the photos. He wore jeans and nothing else. Blood had been smeared and splashed across his chest and arms, and his eyes stared out, wide and horrified. It took him a moment to notice them. In the space of perhaps two seconds, the jeans disappeared, his body grew muscles and fur and claws, and his head reshaped with a fanged snout. He shot upwards to nine feet tall, turning into the scariest damn werewolf Bobby had ever seen.

While Bobby blew out into dragons, terrified this thing would maul him, Stephen remained sitting with his legs crossed and hands laced together in his lap. "How apropos that a vampire and a werewolf should fight this close to Hollywood. With dragons, to boot. I wonder if we'll attract any orcs or fairies."

Matthew made a snarling, barking noise and jumped at Stephen. The vampire surged up to meet the werewolf. Bobby, unable to get into it much without causing a problem for Stephen, got the dragons to open the door a crack so ten could slip out and keep watch. If someone came to this door, he wanted to know about it before they arrived and got involved.

Stephen and Matthew seemed an even match, each strong enough to hold the other back. To try to help the odds, the dragons went in for the werewolf's legs. His little critters scratched and scraped against Matthew's furry flesh, finding it tougher than anything they'd encountered before. With them so ineffectual, he pulled the dragons out to keep them safe.

Furniture flew and fists smashed into the wall. Stephen threw the werewolf into the fridge, rocking it back and denting the wall. Matthew returned the favor by tossing the vampire through an inner wall, putting Stephen in the bedroom. They did what Bobby thought of as wrasslin', except for the fangs and claws and superhuman strength. It carried them back through the apartment, wrecking it as they went, until Stephen got thrown through a window and Matthew chased after, like a dog going after a stick.

With it now public, they stood a very real chance of this scrap getting noticed by the neighbors. If the noise hadn't already prompted a call to the cops, looking out a window and seeing this spectacle surely would. He could almost imagine the call to the police. 'Officer, there's two costumed freaks wrasslin' around outside, making a heckuva ruckus!' Or however the locals would say that. The swarm followed them out, keeping a watch all around.

Matthew filled the air with giant angry dog noises. Stephen hissed, reminding Bobby of a riled-up cat. Claws flew and fangs crunched. With every injury inflicted, each of them healed over. In

Stephen's case, the wounds knitting seemed to take something out of him, tiring him, or depleting something. Despite that, every time the werewolf tossed him, he righted himself and plowed back in, pushing Mathew back towards the apartment.

A police car screamed onto the scene, brakes screeching as it halted sideways to block their passage farther down the street. Bobby saw it coming and couldn't think of anything to do about it. As helpless as any other bystander, he watched and hoped the situation might clear enough for him to see a way to interject himself. This feeling reminded him of how he felt when that needle went into his leg at Jasmine's apartment, except that this just kept going on and he didn't get the luxury of blacking out for any part of it.

Jumping out of the cruiser, a cop held his gun out and shouted for the two men to freeze and get on the ground. The command drew Matthew's attention. He threw Stephen again and bounded for the flashing lights of the police car. Bobby couldn't let the cop get hurt just for being the one to show up. He dove at the officer and re-formed right in front of him, willing to take the hit. Matthew slammed into him claws first.The impact made his body disperse into dragons again, and Matthew fell forward, splaying on the ground at the cop's feet.

Dragons dove in and buzzed Matthew's head. Although it kept him from being able to see any other targets, it made him freak out more, and he scraped at the air around his head. This distraction gave Stephen a chance to grab the cop and toss him out of the way. The cop stumbled aside and fired into the fray, emptying his clip at the impossible scene. Stephen twisted and dropped to his knees. Still on the ground, Matthew's body jumped as bullets slammed into it.

The werewolf stopped fighting to lie on the ground panting. On all fours now, Stephen coughed and spat out a mouthful of blood. Bobby panicked. One of his dragons had been crushed by a bullet—

he could see it over there. What would happen when he re-formed? He had no idea, and didn't know what to do. He couldn't stay in the swarm forever; he needed to sleep and eat, and he couldn't do either as all dragons. Would he just not have a fingertip anymore? Would there be a bullet hole in a random place on his body?

Part of the swarm noticed the cop changing his clip and moving forward to threaten Stephen. The rest focused on the broken body of the little dragon on the ground several feet away. He heard Stephen say, "You moron, you have no idea what you've just involved yourself in." Did he mean to convince the cop he'd stumbled into some kind of secret vampire-werewolf war?

Dozens of dragons surrounded the broken one—and it was broken, he saw, not injured—to pick it up and… Eat it? Part of him rebelled at the notion of his dragons being cannibals. The rest freaked out about the 'broken' part. He was made of robots, tiny robots shaped like dragons. Tiny robots shaped like dragons that ate metal and each other. What did that make him? Was he even human anymore? Had he ever been?

The cop's voice, shaky and shocky, called for an ambulance, presumably over his radio. He ejected the clip from his gun and slammed a fresh on in. "I really don't care about whatever crazy thing you're doing out here, lie down on the ground and put your hands behind your head."

"Like that's going to happen." Stephen sat up on his feet and spat a bullet at the cop. It bounced and rolled to the cop's shoe. "You want to shoot me again?" Spreading his arms out wide in invitation, he gave the cop a wide-eyed glare, his nostrils flared. "Go ahead and shoot me."

Another cop car screamed into sight, snapping Bobby out of his panic. They had bigger problems than his confusion about himself. He re-formed and dropped down next to Matthew, checking him over. “He’s alive.” He had to clench his jaw to deal with agony in his hand. “I think he’s healing.” A quick check of himself revealed no missing parts and no holes or other injuries. The loss of a dragon seemed to have translated into sharp pain in his left hand and nothing else.

“Lovely.” Stephen spat out another bullet at the cop, who looked about ready to actually put another clip of bullets into Stephen.

Slapping his second hand onto his gun to steady it, the cop’s mouth dropped open and he took labored breaths. “What are you?”

Matthew’s eyes snapped open and he focused on Bobby. His clawed hand shot up to grab him by the neck, but he exploded into dragons again to avoid the problem. Growling, the werewolf picked up the nearby cop car and tossed it, sending it rolling down the street.

The second cop car switched into reverse to speed away from Matthew. It drew his attention, and he turned to chase it.

“I’m going to call him unwilling, Bobby. You should get out of here and I’ll handle this. And yes, I’m sure.” Stephen lurched to his feet, smacking the first cop aside hard enough to knock him for a loop. He jumped onto Matthew’s back before he reached the second cop car and sank his fangs into the werewolf’s neck.

Matthew flailed about to dislodge him, with no success. They lifted off the ground, moving upwards under Stephen’s power, and Matthew’s struggles weakened as they rose beyond the range of the street lights.

At that point, with one cop senseless and the other staring up, slack-jawed, Bobby took off. Stephen would get Matthew to their new base, and they’d handle him one way or another. These two cops would have to figure out what to put into a report. Good luck to them. Bobby had no intention of sticking around long enough to be questioned or charged with anything.

Thank God Stephen had been here, because Bobby couldn't have contained Matthew on his own, nor could he have picked him up and carried him away. He offered a quiet prayer to never find himself in that position without someone like Stephen around. People could get hurt or killed. No one deserved that.

Chapter 14

Bobby flew an hour north, then found a hole to curl up in near the coast. He slept until the garbage truck woke him up around dawn by picking up the dumpster he slept against. Before he had a chance to take in his surroundings, it slammed back down into him, sending dragons scattering. Half a block away, he re-formed and called Hannah while foraging for food.

"Good to hear from you. How are things going?"

"Sorry I ain't called since El Paso. Camellia in Phoenix got took. There's Javier and Tiana headed your way. Also, Stephen from Dallas is coming back with Matthew who didn't rightly want to go, exactly. I dunno, maybe he will when he wakes up. We hadta beat him into submission. Two cops and a buncha folks saw us, I think. Stephen and Matthew had a fight on the street."

"They…what?"

"It weren't our fault." Bobby could hear himself whining and made an effort to stop that. "There's something wrong with Matthew, we think he's been killing people and he's got meds and stuff. Andrew might want to keep a close eye on him when they get there."

"I see. So you know, the others have found four more gone missing in the past week, and we lost contact with Jasmine and Will.

Are you alright?"

"Me? Yeah, sure." He frowned at the news. Of the group, Jasmine seemed the nicest, and he hated to think of her locked up somehow. "Got a rude wakeup call this morning, but I'm fine. Looking to head out to Honolulu soon as I find a map so I'm sure I'm going the right way."

Actually, can you go north first? Ai is having some trouble in Portland. So, can you pop up to San Jose first?"

One sigh later, Bobby found himself nodding. "Yeah, sure. It ain't that much outta my way, I guess."

"It's about three hundred miles north. Follow the coast, or there's a highway that goes up the middle of the state. And thanks, Bobby, you're a champ. We'll have a bed waiting for you when you get here, promise."

"That's something, I s'pose, though I'd rather have a good meal."

"I'll see what we can do."

"Yeah. Stephen's got some news about a Kurt Donner. Don't let him forget to tell you." Bobby hung up, sorry he'd called. Not really, but a little. Now he had to think about Jasmine trussed up and getting tortured, in addition to knowing he'd have to go farther before seeing his new home and being able to rest in safety for a few nights.

Maybe he'd get lucky and this Lily would be able to fly to Hawaii with him, to keep it from being boring. Anything could happen, right? Depending on how far Hawaii actually was, maybe he could crash at her place and get an actual good night of sleep first. Eat a good meal, too. The dumpster-diving diet featured awful lot of bread and not much meat, and he missed fresh food, a lot. A nice, crisp, whole apple would really hit the spot right now, so would some medium-well steak with mashed potatoes and gravy.

Before he could get caught up in food fantasies, Bobby reminded himself that he had money. If he wanted to, he could eat a real meal every day. It seemed wise to not do that and hold onto it, in case of some kind of emergency. Like...he had no idea, but something could come up that required money and put him in a world of hurt without.

Setting the notion aside, he blew out into the swarm and flew north at top speed. He followed the coast from several thousand feet up and watched the sun climb upwards. By the time he reached San Jose and found a map, a clock in the convenience store told him the trip had taken about three hours.

Lily lived in a nice neighborhood, so far as he could see. It reminded him of Stephen's momma's house, only more green. It had that same upper middle class, homeowner's association, everybody uses the same guys to cut the grass feel to it. Either Lily still lived with her folks, or she did pretty darn well for herself.

Trying not to feel grossly out of place, he found a place to land and re-form, then walked up her street. Curtains twitched as he passed them. When he turned up the stone path to her front door, it felt like a hundred people must be watching him. He knocked and stuck his hands in his pockets, hoping no one called the cops while he waited. Nobody answered. This place probably had an alarm system, so he peered in through the window instead of sending dragons to break in for him. He saw nice living room furniture with toddler toys strewn about. If that kid's momma turned out to be Lily, she wasn't coming to Hawaii with him, even if she could snap her fingers and be there.

"Who are you?"

Caught in the act of peeking in, Bobby turned around and held up his hands. The woman standing there with two toddlers peeking out from behind her legs couldn't be Lily. The little boy, though, had to be her son. Cute little thing had a mop of brown hair and the icy blue eyes. Funny, he hadn't really thought to wonder if the eyes would get passed on as-is to their kids. Apparently, they would.

"I'm looking for Lily. Was hoping she'd be home, but life don't seem to work out the way I'd like most of the time." He noticed the woman's eyes flicking to his own, then she put a hand protectively on the boy's head. The boy gave him a shy little smile.

"If you actually knew her, you'd know she's working today."

He pulled out the 'aw shucks', getting the impression this might be Lily's sister or close friend. "I didn't say I know her, ma'am, it's just real important I talk to her as soon as possible. Where's she work?"

The woman backed away, pushing the two toddlers along behind her. "You must be crazy if you think I'm going to tell you that."

"I ain't here to hurt nobody." Bobby took a step after her. When she flinched, he stopped and stuffed his hands into his pockets. "I ain't crazy, neither. You seen the eyes. We're related somehow, and part of why I'm here is to figure that out." He almost asked after the boy, but thought that would probably make her run and call the police, maybe with a screech. "My name's Bobby. I just want to talk to her, nothing else, I swear on my daddy's grave."

She frowned and looked down at the boy. He nodded to her, so she sighed and nodded, too. "She works at the Wislen Garden Center."

"Thank you kindly, ma'am. I appreciate it." He, of course, had no clue where that was. Asking directions seemed like pushing her a little too far. Besides, he saw a gas station around the corner where he could ask anyway.

To his surprise, when he started walking, she said, "It's that way." When he looked back, she pointed in the opposite direction that he'd chosen to walk. He tipped an imaginary hat to her in thanks and turned that way, moving at a brisk walk. A block away, he dove behind a tree and burst into dragons to get a higher vantage point.

The Wislen family business wasn't hard to find. He walked into the place and looked around at the plants and decorative pots and things. Momma would like to be able to wander around and buy stuff here. The yard ornaments weren't so much her thing, but they had flowers he never saw before that he knew she'd like. Those big red ones the size of dinner plates would catch her eye for sure.

"Can I help you?"

He looked up to find the owner of that soft, sweet voice and found himself face to face with icy blue eyes. Long brown hair framed a delicate, pretty face, and she took his breath away. None of the other women had done that, and he couldn't explain why she did. For a long few moments, he stood and stared at her, gawping like an idiot.

Her pleasant smile dimmed. It shook him out of his stupor. "Lily Wislen, I need to talk to you."

The smile dropped away completely, and he wanted to punch himself for doing that to her. "Thatcher."

Oh. She was married. He blinked and scratched the back of his neck. Disappointment crushed him back to reality. "Sorry, ma'am. Mrs. Thatcher. I still gotta talk to you." He tapped on his temple to indicate his eyes. "It's important. No joke."

She reached up with a slim hand and brushed her hair back. For Bobby, the world slowed down and the pink polish on her nails flashed in the sunshine. Her gaze swept the area, then she pointed discreetly to the front gate. "I'll meet you out there in a few minutes. I just need to tell my boss I'm taking a break."

"Yeah, sure." He bobbed his head and watched her turn

around and walk away. Out of all the women he met on this wild ride so far, only she pushed all his buttons at once, making it hard to think. Naturally, she was married, probably happily. She'd have a tall, strong, handsome guy. He'd be a really great person, the kind of guy Bobby could never hate or measure up to. He might even be that guy over there, talking to a couple by the rosebushes.

Shaking his head to knock the stupid out, he ambled to the front gate, finding a curb to sit his butt on while he waited however long she decided to make him wait. For all he knew, she would go about her job for another hour before actually coming out to talk to him. Heck, she might just dismiss him entirely so he'd be still sitting out here after the place closed, not realizing she'd slipped out the back to get rescued by her Mr. Thatcher around the corner. The thought put a sour frown on his face, right up until she walked out and sat next to him five minutes later.

"You have fifteen minutes."

Pleasantly surprised by her joining him so quickly, Bobby nodded his understanding. He pulled his much crumpled list from his pocket and offered it to her. "About a week ago, me and three others got grabbed and shoved into a lab where we were experimented on. We escaped and found this list on the way out. We're going across the country, looking up everyone on that list to tell 'em you're in danger. Far as I know, seven of 'em gone missing in the past few days, we think they got took by government agents, and are right now being experimented on just like the four of us were. I don't know if they're for sure gonna come for you, but I'm here to warn you and offer a place to go where it should be safe. Even if they find us there, we're all willing to fight together to stay free and safe."

Lily listened to him. She found her own name on the list and ran her finger over it. Leaning close, she whispered to him, "Why are they doing it?"

"Not rightly sure, but all of us have these eyes, and so far, most of us have some kind of weird and crazy ability, like a super power. Not gonna pull mine out here in broad daylight, but if you got something you can do, you're not crazy, promise."

She sagged against him with relief. "Oh, thank God." Her head rested on his shoulder.

As much as he wanted her to lean on him, he coughed. "Ain't your husband gonna get a little tetchy if'n you do that?"

"I doubt it." She lifted her head back up with a sigh anyway. "He's been dead for a little over two years. I have a son. If I can't bring him, I won't go anywhere."

Oh. That changed things. He tried to hide how his heart swelled. "You can bring him, sure. I haven't been to the place we're taking up yet, so I can't say what we got for amenities yet, but yeah, bring him. He's got the eyes, right? They'd take him, so you should bring him."

She sat bolt upright, her body tensed and ready to run. "When are they coming?"

"I got no clue." Wanting to reassure her, he put a hand on her arm. It bolstered his resolve when she didn't pull away or brush him off. "The one in Phoenix was gone already when I got there a coupla days ago, but all three in LA were still there. No idea how they're deciding who to take in what order."

"They can't take him, I won't let them." She stood up and hurried back in through the gate.

Bobby stood up and stretched. His work was mostly done here. This momma had protective tiger written all over her now, and she'd take her cub to a promise of safety. As much as he wanted to stay and get to know her, he had to give her directions and get his own to Hawaii. Maybe on that flight, he could think about why he reacted to her so strongly.

She jogged out with her keys two minutes later, and her blue sedan got them back to her house in ten minutes. He saw no black SUVs or cops, or anything. She ran to the house next door anyway, and came out about ten minutes later carrying the little boy Bobby saw earlier. Holding him possessively and protectively, she squeezed him they'd been parted for a week or a month instead of a few hours. It made him want to call Momma.

"This is my friend Bobby," Lily told the boy. "Bobby, this is Sebastian."

"Nice to meetcha all proper-like," Bobby said with a wave.

"Bobby scared Auntie Allie," Sebastian announced, his small voice grave and accusing.

"Hum. I didn't mean to. Was just looking for your momma." He had a thought to leave it at that while Lily unlocked the front door of her house and led him inside, but he wanted Sebastian on his side. Besides, he had a cousin with a boy that reminded him of this kid. "Some bad men want to hurt your momma, and I'm trying to protect her from them."

His little eyes went wide. "Are you a policeman?"

Bobby grinned. "Nope, I'm a superhero."

The boy's mouth made a little 'o' of delight. Lily, on the other hand, rolled her eyes at him. The corners of her mouth tugged upwards, though, so she didn't think too poorly of him for it. "Bobby is going to help us pack up some things in Mommy's car so we can take a trip to a place where the bad men won't find us. You know what would be a big help?" She set the boy down on the stairs. "If you could go pull your most favorite clothes out of your dresser and your most favorite toys out of your bin, and put them all in a pile, that would help a lot."

"Okay, Mommy!" Sebastian raced up the stairs, using his hands and feet.

Watching the little boy move with such enthusiasm and determination made Bobby grin. “How old is he? ”

“I’d love to chat and do the whole ‘get to know you’ routine,” she said as she bustled into the kitchen, “but maybe that could wait until we’re in the car?”

He followed her, his eyes drifting downwards. “Oh, I ain’t coming in the car.” And that was a damned shame. Driving that far with her might mean being able to snuggle up overnight, and he’d liked the feel of her head on his shoulder. He’d liked that a lot. “I got another stop to make before I get to go to the farm. I was wondering if I could get you to look up on the internet how far it from here to Hawaii, though, because I gotta get my scrawny butt there next.”

Lily turned from pulling food out of the cabinets, probably meant for the trip. “It’s over two thousand miles from here. We went there once when I was a kid, it’s like a five hour flight.”

Bobby’s mouth slipped open, then he shut it. On maps, they always put it right below the 48 states, so he never thought of it as far away. He figured it would be maybe four or five hundred miles, a thousand at the most. At his speed, it would take him an entire day to get there, and he’d be so tired and hungry when he got there, he’d fall flat on his face.

“Dangit.” At that moment, he realized he hadn’t yet shown her his ability, so he held out his hand and let five dragons detach. “I was gonna fly there,” he explained, “but that’s too far for me. I can only go about a hundred miles an hour.”

She sucked in a surprised breath and stared. One of the dragons decided to walk on the counter, sniffing it, and she put her hand out next to it. The dragon sniffed her hand, then climbed up on it and walked all over it as she turned it around. “Wow. This is nothing like what I can do.”

“Yeah, I ain’t seen nobody else with anything quite like this yet. They kinda got their own minds, but they're me, too. It's hard to explain."

She chuckled. "If that's the best you can do, it must be."

By focusing down on that one dragon, Bobby got to vicariously explore her hand, noting the wedding ring still on it, the dirt under her short fingernails, the softness of her skin, a few freckles, and how delicate her fingers really were. "Yeah. Um, maybe I could find the number of the one out there and call before I find a way to get myself out there. Make sure she ain't abducted, too."

"Um." She pulled her hand to herself, and Bobby, sensing her sudden discomfort, got the dragon to hop off. "I can boot up a computer for you to use, I guess."

"Thanks, I'd appreciate that." Any idiot could look a person up on the internet, right? He called his dragons back and sat down where she pointed to try to find Maisie Polape. Weird sounding name, so maybe not too common. After finding a browser, he tried very hard to ignore the attractive woman in the room so he could punch the name into the search bar. It came back with only a few results. Halfway down the page, the hits only had one name or the other.

The first link went to the Honolulu Star-Advertiser, the paper out that way. It had an article about how Maisie Polape went missing last night. A leaden feeling settled in his gut, making him sit and read the whole thing. She'd been out with her boyfriend, it said, and he got hit from behind. When he came to, Maisie was gone. He saw nothing. The police were already investigating it as an abduction.

Why were the cops looking into it if the government snatched her? Maybe they did that as a cover, and they'd 'investigate' for a little while, give up and call it a cold case. Still, why not just arrest her? Then again, none of the other missing people had been arrested so far as the families knew. These people had enough skill to abduct a person without leaving witnesses, and either no connection to the police, or no interest in keeping the cops out of it.

"I think you should hurry," he said. Getting out of the chair, he found the kitchen empty. A plastic box full of food sat on the counter, and Lily must've left while he read the article and panicked. At least he now knew he had no need to figure out how to get to Hawaii and back. On reflection, he probably could have taken a plane out there and back, depending upon how much it cost. Or, heck, maybe he could fly in the baggage compartment if he stayed in the swarm the whole time. He shut down the computer and pulled out his phone to let Hannah know about Maisie while looking around the house for Lily.

As he passed the front door, he noticed movement on the wall, a shadow tracking across it. Hannah picked up the phone as he hurried to the front window and peered out around the side. The sight made him pale and pull back quickly, hoping the two guys in suits hadn't seen him. Two long heartbeats later, the doorbell rang.

"Hannah," he murmured into the phone, "there's guys in suits here, I'm at Lily's place." He took the stairs two at a time to go intercept Lily on her way to answer the door. "Maisie got took last night, according to the paper. It's so far, I decided to check first. If you don't hear from me again today, it's cause I'm took." Without giving her a chance to respond, he snapped the phone shut and stopped short of colliding with Lily. "It's them, they're here, now, to grab you up. What's your power?"

To her credit, she blanched without panicking. "I can make things, out of nothing. Simple things, like hand tools, toys, that sort of thing."

Nothing leaped to mind for how to make that useful in this situation. "You stay here, keep packing up, keep Sebastian close. I'm gonna see if'n I can get rid of them, one way or another. Make up a bag of what you gotta take if you gotta go with just one bag, keep that close, but keep working anyway, just in case." He took her hand and pressed the phone into it. "Hannah is speed dial one."

She nodded and ran to her son. He hurried down the steps to answer the door. Halfway down, the door smashed open. Two men in suits stepped inside with guns out and ready, sweeping them around the room. He had no Stephen or Jayce around to handle this kind of thing, so he'd have to do it himself. Lily could help, except she needed to keep Sebastian safe. Who knew how many men these guys actually had. They could send someone to circle around back and swipe the kid while these guys in the front kept them busy. Not acceptable.

In sight of the door, Bobby put his hands up rather than bothering to hide and draw them upstairs. Both suits pointed their handguns straight at him. Not a lot of choices presented themselves. He picked the best thing he could think of an committed to it. "I sent her away already, you're too late."

Then what are you doing here?" It bothered him a tiny bit that these suits had normal voices. With the sunglasses hiding their identities so much, they ought to have creepy voices, or say crazy stuff, or something.

Bobby shrugged. "Packing some of her crap, using the bathroom, that kinda thing. Y'all made it so I ain't exactly got lots of funding and all."

"What's your name?" Presented with an obvious target, they both focused on him. Good.

"That's a kinda personal question. How's about you tell me who you're working for, and I'll tell my name."

"Are you going to come quietly, or are we going to have to shoot you?"

He took a moment to think about that, and made sure they

could tell he thought about it. “You know, I ain’t rightly sure. Last time I got shot, it bruised up my hand something fierce, so I’d say it ain’t much fun, but I don’t rightly think it’s gonna kill me like it would you guys.” Saying that out loud gave him more confidence. He took the steps down slowly, keeping his hands up. “That kinda leaves me with not so much of a need to avoid it as a regular person might. A regular person such as yourself. I mean, you’re hunting us with guns? Really? Didn’t we make it pretty clear that ain’t gonna cut it?”

“Mitchell,” the second suit said into his sleeve, probably into a microphone of some kind. “It’s Mitchell.”

“Shoot, you figured out who I am.” He needed to make sure any bullets that got fired went nowhere near Lily and Sebastian. If he acted cocky, it might draw them out. Outside, he might be able to figure out a way to knock them down for a while. An old-fashioned fist to the face might work. “Well, I guess I ain’t got nothing left to bargain with. ‘Course, I know where they went, but you probably don’t care about that.”

“You’re lying.”

Bobby shrugged and forced himself to keep going down the stairs. They couldn’t hurt him, not really. This fear bubbling in his belly came from what their masters had done to him. Knowing that didn’t really slow his heart down. It kept beating a million miles a minute, ready to back him up the second he needed to fly into an adrenaline fueled frenzy. “Suit yourself.” Did adrenaline affect the dragons? Interesting question.

He pushed past the first suit, shoving him aside with his shoulder. Stepping past that man put him between the two of them. It felt stupid and crazy and vulnerable. The other suit holstered his gun, too. Behind him, he noticed movement, too late to do anything about it. The first suit jammed something into his back, and it buzzed and clicked.

A hot poker drove into his lower back. His body tightened, voltage sending him into spasms. His hands burst into dragons. His arms followed as he tried to scream and made only a weird whining noise. As more dragons fought their way free, the swarm flew into a blind rage. Stuck in a dizzying fog of pain, Bobby had no control over them. An eternity later, the swarm calmed down and let him re-form, his hands burning with agony.

Both men lay limp on the floor, covered with scorchmarks, and tiny bites and scratches. Their clothes had been shredded, with the damage focused around their hands and less frenzied across the rest of their bodies. Their faces hadn't been spared at all, and their eyes— He covered his mouth with a hand, tasting bile. He did this, not Alice or Jayce or Stephen. His dragons, which were him, killed two men. They wanted to hurt him and others, so he'd done it in self-defense, but he still killed them.

Scrambling to get away from them, he stumbled into the nearest bathroom and splashed water on his face. Both his hands hurt even worse than last night, and he wondered how badly the dragons had been damaged by the jolt. Like any other bathroom, this one had a mirror over the sink, and he stared at himself in it.

"I did that." He gripped the sink with both hands and groaned from the pain. "It was me, no one else. I gotta live with it. It was my fault." Just like killing those homeless people had been Alice's fault. "You dumbass. It had to happen eventually, but you just kept going, like you're invincible and perfect and all that, but you're not. You're just a guy with a gun who ain't figured out how to use it yet."

He splashed more water on his face and grabbed a towel, drying his face as he hurried back to the stairs. One foot on the bottom step, he froze at the sound of a car door slamming shut, then an engine roaring. Out the door in a second, he caught sight of a black SUV peeling away, another suit in the driver's seat. This one, he recognized. Austin, Phoenix, now San Jose, that guy got around, and fast. Though he wore sunglasses, Bobby thought it likely the suit saw him, too.

Part of him wanted to chase that guy down and demand to know where Jasmine had been taken. Terrified he'd kill that one, too, he ran back into the house. They had to get out of here. Would the suit call for backup or just let them go? How long would it take him to get backup? What would they bring?

Heckbiscuits, they had two dead bodies lying on the floor. As soon as anyone else walked through that door, they'd freak and call the cops. Taking the stairs two at a time, he ran up and called out. "Lily, they're…I— Um. It's safe for now. You don't want to let Sebastian see, though. I…it was kinda an accident."

The door cracked open and Lily peeked out. "Are you okay?"

"More or less, yeah. They had a taser, it stings, but I'm okay. They really…uh, they ain't getting up."

She nodded and let out a tiny sigh of relief, then her face clouded. "We should pack up the car and go, then, before they're missed."

"Yeah, uh, too late for that. We gotta move. Is it okay if I come with you after all? I don't need to go to Hawaii, as it turns out."

As a response, she opened the door and hugged him. It came as a surprise, one he needed badly. He wrapped his arms around her and held on tight. "Thank you," she whispered. "If you hadn't been here, they would've taken us."

The apology he intended to deliver for doing something so horrible as killing two people in her house died under the weight of her gratitude. "Nah, you'da done alright." With her this close, he wanted to kiss her. While he thought about that, trying to decide if he ought to or not, she pulled away. To cover up his disappointment, he crouched down to Sebastian's level.

"Hey, buddy, we gotta load up the car and go away, right? There's something at the bottom of the stairs, though, and I don't want you to see it. There's a..." He faltered, trying to figure out how to explain without explaining. "Here, just lemme carry you down the stairs and out to the car, okay?"

Sebastian looked to his mother, who paused for a second, then nodded. He put out his arms and let Bobby pick him up, and Bobby turned the boy's head into his neck, then covered the one angle he might be able to still see from. Lily followed behind him as he carried the boy down the stairs and stepped over the bodies. He heard her sharp intake of breath, then they both reached the car. Sebastian's car seat had already been strapped down in the back seat, so he settled the boy inside it.

"I'll bring stuff out, just tell me what to grab." Ten minutes or so later, she started the car and the three of them set out. With the one suit knowing exactly what had happened here, Bobby decided not to waste time trying to hide the bodies. He shoved them aside so he shut the front door and left it at that. His hands hurt. He did it all anyway, without complaint. Instead, he clenched his jaw and soldiered through it. His daddy would be proud.

Chapter 15

Once they reached the freeway, Lily turned on some soft jazz for Sebastian's amusement. Bobby hadn't had nearly enough good sleep over the past few days to resist that assault. Secure, warm, and comfortable enough, he passed out. He woke up to Lily shaking his shoulder.

"I hate to wake you, but I had to stop for Sebastian. We're just south of Stockton." She left him in the car and hurried around to Sebastian's door to let him out of his seat.

Blinking and rubbing his eyes, Bobby got out and stood up. "Dang, I was really wiped."

"Sebastian didn't want to wake you up or we would have stopped sooner." Lily held the boy's hand to walk him to the building. "He needs to use the bathroom."

"Sounds like a plan to me. I can take him into the men's room if you like."

"Sebastian, do you want to go into the boy's room with Bobby, or the girl's room with me? "

The boy looked from one to the other and said, "Mama, please."

Bobby cracked a grin. "Ain't nothing like the honesty of a

little kid." In the bathroom, he took the time to run his head under the faucet, the closest he'd gotten to a shower since being arrested. As he walked back to the car with a handful of spare paper towels, he remembered he hadn't called Hannah back yet. She must be worried to all heck. First Jasmine, now him. He groped around for his phone, started to panic, then recalled handing it over to Lily. At the time, he'd done it in case the suits managed to grab him somehow.

He found Lily making peanut butter and jelly sandwiches, a little one for Sebastian, and a full size one for him. He took his with reverent gratitude. "You got no idea how much I need this." He took the first bite with unfeigned and unrestrained joy at the simple pleasure of fresh food prepared specifically for him. Though he wanted to use the phone, he wanted to eat much more. Five more minutes wouldn't break Hannah. He sat down on the curb nearby and watched Lily make a sandwich for herself.

Sebastian sat next to him, enjoying his own sandwich. "Mama is pretty."

"Ayup." He nodded while he swallowed his bite. His gaze traveled from her feet up to her hips and he sighed with contentment. "She sure is."

Lily glanced over her shoulder as she screwed the lid back on the peanut butter. Knowing he'd been caught staring at her behind, Bobby looked down at his sandwich.

"Bobby's eyes are like my eyes, like Mama's eyes."

"Ayup, they sure are. That's why I'm here, kinda."

"Bobby talks funny."

Bobby snorted. "I'm from Georgia. This is how we talk down thataway. You talk funny from where I'm sitting."

Sebastian giggled and managed to smear peanut butter on his nose. Like he knew it would, a paper towel came in handy. Bobby used one to wipe the kid's face off, managing despite him squirming and blowing raspberries.

"Aw, quit yer grousing, boy." Bobby wasn't rough, and he chuckled as he said it. "You do that to my Momma, and she'd tan your hide. How old are you, anyway?"

"Two and a half." He held up three fingers.

Lily sat down with her sandwich, putting Sebastian between her and Bobby. "Not until September. His birthday is in March."

"You don't seem old enough to have a boy his age."

"I got pregnant right after I graduated high school." Lily sighed. "Got married then, too. His father enlisted, though, and was killed in action about a month before Sebastian was born."

Stunned, Bobby gaped at her. "He had a wife like you, and a baby on the way, and he enlisted?"

She stared off at nothing. "We didn't know there was a baby on the way when he did it. He thought if we were married, I'd be able to live near him easier. Then they sent him to Afghanistan, and he never came back." Her thumb fiddled with her wedding ring. "Besides that, though, he just had to do it. He wanted to…he said he felt like he had something to prove, to himself and to his own father."

He nodded, because he understood. He didn't share it, because he didn't feel like going off to die would make his father proud, but he understood it. "My daddy was a Marine. He died in Afghanistan, too, when I was twelve." He had nothing else to offer on the subject and couldn't figure out how to feel about her story. Plain as day, she still loved the guy. That might not leave much room for anyone else.

For several minutes, nobody said anything. Bobby polished off his sandwich and wiped his hands. "That really did hit the spot." He stood and stretched his arms up.

"You didn't say where we're actually going, just Colorado. Do you have more specific directions than that?"

"Yes, ma'am, but I think Sebastian here needs to be rambunctious. He's a boy, after all. I'll go take care of that." He picked the boy up and carted him to a grassy space, where he chased Sebastian around and threw him up in the air. They wrestled around on the ground enough to get the boy shrieking with joy while stopping short of how making him puke his food back up.

When they'd gotten back on the road, he picked up his phone where Lily left it for him and made the call. "Sorry I didn't call sooner, it was complicated and then I fell asleep."

"We were about ready to write you and Lily off."

"We're both fine. On the road to you right now. I…um, those two suits, they—" Bobby frowned, not wanting to admit what he did.

"Did you have to kill them?"

He sighed heavily. "Yeah."

"Jayce had to take two down, also."

"They're gonna come for us with big guns, you know that, don'tcha?"

"It's been on our minds, yes."

"Did Stephen get there yet?"

"No. Where are you? How long do you think it'll be until you get here?"

"I dunno. Lily has a little kid. We gotta stop a lot for him, probably. Just leaving Stockton right now."

Hannah left a long pause. "She has a kid?"

"Yeah, he has the eyes. Cute as a button, too."

"That's really interesting."

"If'n you say so. Do you want me to check in again before we get there?"

"No, just call if anything goes wrong."

"Alrighty. See ya soon." He hung up and watched the scenery go by.

Several quiet seconds later, Lily asked, “Who’s Stephen?”

“He’s a vampire.” That sounded all kinds of wrong, so he quickly added, “Not a real vampire. I mean, he doesn’t much like sunlight, drinks blood now instead of eating, is mighty strong, heals real fast, and can fly, maybe can do a few other things. But it’s not like there’s a lot of them out there and he was infected or turned or whatever, he’s like us. There’s a guy that’s basically a werewolf, too.”

“And Hannah?”

“She can make a shield with her mind, sort of like what you can do, only with blue stuff that I think is pure energy.”

“How many people are on that list?”

“Thirty-five. At least seven have been nabbed by guys like those two suits, we think. No idea who they are or who they’re working for. Why they want us, though, that seems pretty clear.”

Lily’s eyes flicked up to her rear-view mirror, giving her a view of her son. He cheerfully scribbled with crayons all over a coloring book from the box of toys and snacks next to his seat. “They can’t do that to Sebastian. I won’t let them.”

In that moment, hearing her steely determination, he wanted to reach over and put a hand on her leg. Wary of her husband’s ghost, he didn’t do it. “Neither will I. Ain’t right for nobody, doubly so for a little kid, triply so on account I like this particular one.”

“Thank you for playing with him like that. His uncle tries, but he’s got daughters. He’s kind of restrained.”

“No problem. I remember needing that sorta thing when I was little. Was that the guy I saw at the garden place? His uncle, I mean.”

“My big brother, yeah. He lives next door with his wife and three daughters.”

“That musta been the lady I met when I went to your house first.”

"Auntie Allie and Kaitlin," Sebastian supplied, proving he'd been listening.

"And we just left them all behind." Lily sighed again. "My parents, too. They've been really great about Sebastian, and his father. I feel like crap for just leaving like that."

"The alternative was waiting around to see how long it took them to send more goons with bigger guns." Bobby shut his mouth and watched the world go by, trying not to think too hard about how the dragons went out of his control, or what actually happened to his consciousness. Until then, he'd thought they were under his control unless he let them loose.

Now he knew they had enough autonomy to shut him out. One small point stuck out to keep him feeling sane: they had to all go into a rage for it to happen. He knew, somehow, that they'd still obey him so long as the majority of the swarm had no driving need to do anything in particular. Now that he thought about it, they couldn't force him into the swarm, either. He'd burst into it every time either because he wanted to, or to save his life.

With those moderately cheering thoughts, he settled back and let the radio blank his mind. The landscape shifted from one kind of farm to another, with towns planted here and there. At some point, that gave way to hills and trees, then mountains. They passed a sign announcing a turn for Lake Tahoe.

"Mama, I wanna stop."

"Okay, little man, we'll go for the next rest stop, but I don't know how long it'll be." She flashed Bobby a pleading look.

He nodded and turned enough to see the boy. "You know what, buddy, I got a cousin just about your age, and he likes dinosaurs. D'you like dinosaurs?"

"Rawr!" Sebastian made claws with both his hands.

"I'll take that as a yes." Where Sebastian couldn't see, he

popped one dragon off his thumb. It flew back to entertain the boy. "This here is a dragon, which is a lot like a dinosaur. You gotta be careful, though, because it's only a little bitty one. A big one, you could smack it all you wanted, and nothing would happen, but this one, it's real easy to hurt 'cause it's so small."

Sebastian watched it fly around him with delight, then land on his pudgy little hand and flex its tiny wings for him. "Baby dinosaur!" The dragon played for and with Sebastian, keeping him distracted. When the novelty started to wear off, he sent a second and a third in as reinforcements. They kept the boy from needing to stop for another hour. By then, Bobby wanted to stop, too, and so did Lily.

Bobby needed the roughhousing at least as much as Sebastian did, and the little boy's shrieks of laughter and joy buoyed his own spirits. After a dinner of bananas, granola bars, and more peanut butter and jelly sandwiches, Bobby drove. They had to stop one more time before Sebastian fell asleep in his chair and Bobby focused on getting them there in one piece. When he noticed himself nodding off, he pulled off the road and let himself sleep. Lily barely woke when he shut off the engine.

He woke up when his phone rang. Grabbing it, he rolled out of the car as fast as he could to let Lily and Sebastian sleep. While he intended to say 'hello', it came out as "Ungha?"

"Where are you?" Hannah's voice struck his foggy brain as urgent and concerned.

Rubbing his eyes with a thumb and finger, he yawned and collected his wits. "Um, just past the border into Utah from Nevada, on…" He'd seen so many signs with so many numbers, he had to think about it. "I-80, I think. The one that goes through Reno."

"Really? How fast do you think you can get back to Reno?"

"What'n heckbiscuits for?" He finally opened his eyes and

saw the bare hint of orangey-pink in the east, and knew he couldn't have had more than four or five hours of sleep.

"Ai went to get her pickup in Reno. She got there about ten minutes ago, just as two suits were hauling Anita into a black SUV, probably unconscious. She tried to intervene, but they got away and are now on 80, headed straight towards you."

"Seriously?"

"Yeah."

"Damn, we coulda stopped there last night."

Hannah sighed. "But you didn't, so move on. Can you go back and maybe ambush the SUV or something? Ai is following them, but can't really do anything to stop the car while she's running at that speed. She can, apparently, talk on the phone, but that's about all she can spare concentration for."

"Just a sec." Bobby pulled in a deep breath and rubbed his face. This meant he had to leave Lily and Sebastian, because he couldn't put the boy into that kind of situation. It burned to let them go. If Ai needed his help, though, then that had to come first. "Yeah, okay. Can somebody there do some math and get me an idea where to stop and wait? I go about 100 miles per hour."

"I'll check. Hang on."

While he waited, Bobby peered back into the car. In the dim light, he saw Lily rubbing her eyes and Sebastian stretching his little arms out. He opened the door and ducked his head in. "I gotta go help another one of us, so you'll have to go on from here without me."

"Are they okay?"

"We'll see. Hey, buddy, you sleep okay?"

The boy made some inarticulate noises, then strained against his seat, trying to get out. His struggles prompted Lily to get out of the car and unbuckle him. "Mama, I gotta potty."

"Bobby," Hannah said into his ear, "best guess is to make for Elko and intercept them there."

At the same time, Lily looked around. "There's no bathroom here, can you hold it?"

"Got it," Bobby told Hannah, then he snapped the phone shut. She'd call Ai and set that up, because none of them had anybody else's numbers. Stuffing the phone away, he paced around the car to Sebastian. "I'll take him off the side of the road here."

Lily grimaced in distaste. "There could be a rest area just up the road."

Sebastian hesitated, then he took Bobby's and walked with him down the shoulder. For miles around in all directions, he saw nothing but flat, boring desert. He would have preferred a corn field or some bushes to screen them. They had to take what they could get, and the sun hadn't really lit up the sky yet, so Bobby just turned his back on Lily and the car. He took heart that the boy followed along with him this time, not refusing in favor of his mother.

"Using a bathroom is better, of course," he told the boy as they paced back to the car. "When you gotta go, you gotta go." He crouched down to talk to Sebastian at his eye level. "I gotta go help somebody else, so it's just you and your momma for the next while. Remember that all this driving is about getting away from bad guys who want to do bad things to her. It ain't fun to go this far without stopping much, but when you get to where you're going, you'll have time to run around like crazy, okay?"

Sebastian nodded, then threw his arms around Bobby's neck, almost knocking him off balance. "Okay. Be careful."

Bobby squeezed him tightly, sorry to have to leave them both. "I surely will." He let go and gave the boy a solemn nod. "I'll see you again soon." Standing up, he tousled the boy's hair and turned to find Lily right beside him. "Um, yeah, so." Should he hug her, too? Shake her hand? He'd punch a guy in the arm.

She solved the problem for him by stepping in and wrapping her arms around him. "Thank you for everything. We wouldn't have gotten this far without you." Only a few inches shorter than him, her cheek rested on his shoulder.

Her body warmed him, and a powerful urge to kiss her bubbled up. He pushed it aside, knowing they both needed to get going. In opposite directions. "Just doing my part. Keep it no more'n five over the limit, and remember not to use a credit or debit card. You got cash for gas?" Reaching back, he opened the door for Sebastian.

"A little, probably not enough." Her eyes watched his mouth. Or he might have imagined that.

He put his arm around her shoulders and walked her to the driver's side door. Digging into his coat pocket, Bobby produced the money his momma gave him way back in Atlanta. "Here, take this. Should see you there."

She flipped through the bills. "Bobby, this is two hundred dollars, I don't need this much."

Dang, Momma gave him two hundred dollars? Why in heckbiscuits did she have that much lying around? Was she expecting him to break out and need cash to run for it? "It's fine." He waved it off and opened the door for her. "I been alright with nothing so far." He pulled out his list and the written directions for how to get to the base site and handed them over. "Don't need these no more, so you take 'em."

For a long moment, she stood there, looking at him. A light breeze lifted her hair, and the floating wisps glowed in the early morning sunshine. He had trouble catching his breath and caught himself leaning in. They still had no time for that. Before his mouth could say anything stupid, he stepped back and hurried around to buckle Sebastian in. "Take good care of your Momma, and be good, buddy."

The boy gave him a high five. Bobby shut the door and watched Lily signal, speed up, get back on the highway, and drive off. If he stood there, this road ran so straight and flat he'd probably be able to see her for a long time. Wondering if he'd made the right choice with Lily, he turned away and burst into the swarm. They had to reach Elko before that SUV did.

Two hours later, he stopped in Elko and wandered from dumpster to dumpster. Nothing he found came close to the meals Lily set him up with, despite the fact he found half a roast beef sandwich. Woman had a way with peanut butter. Something about her made simple, plain food taste better and go down easier.

Hannah hadn't called, and the SUV didn't show up, so he burst into the swarm again and looked for a good place to set up an ambush along the road. Traffic ran light on the highway this morning. He dropped down to the southwest of the city, where the westbound lanes separated from the eastbound with a berm between. As he settled, he noticed the dragons nudging about food.

To keep them quiet, he re-formed and sat on the side of the road. He pulled a banana out of his pocket and ate that. It made him think of Lily again. When she'd handed him that banana yesterday, he noticed the softness of her skin. Something about her flipped all his switches. Having her there made it easy to forget about the two dead—

Nope, now he thought about the men he killed. The dragons, which were him, but not, took control when some of them got seriously hurt. His hands still ached from it, and driving yesterday had been rough because of it. He pushed through that to get things done, but they still hurt. The part where they ate the broken dragon still bothered him, too.

Here he sat, waiting for more men to come and be killed by him. Was he actually planning to kill them? It seemed more like he intended to hurt them in a way they could recover from. That explained why he chose a spot this far from the nearest city, so they'd have to wait a while before any actual help would arrive when they called. Realistically, though, he came out here to kill them, and should admit it to himself. These men were doing something wrong, whether they knew it or not, and he had to stop them, one way or another.

Where did they even get this many guys in suits? Goons R Us? For that matter, who was 'they'? Some part of the government, certainly. Kurt said it was military, but that happened a long time ago. It could be anybody now. If the FBI actually knew about all of this, would they try to stop it? What about the President or Congress?

He hopped to his feet and paced, thoughts swirling around in circles. Too many questions to think about popped in his head, but at least they took his mind off the fact he killed people and planned to do it again. What if he took one of these guys prisoner and questioned him? He and Ai and the one from Reno could hold him down and demand answers. If either suit knew anything, they could probably force him to cough it up.

What was he willing to do to get that information? Thinking back to movies he'd seen that showed or hinted at things that could be done to a person, he scratched the back of his neck. They always had assorted sizes and shapes of small blades, plus scary-looking things with purposes he could only guess at. Would just smacking him around be enough? What if they had tasers?

His phone ringing provided a welcome interruption. "Yeah?"

"Ai just passed exit 261. Are you in Elko yet?"

"I'm west of it, waiting by the side of the road. A bit past exit

271. Ten miles means about ten minutes, yeah? I'll be ready." Snapping the phone shut, he peered down the road. No way would he see something ten miles off here, not with the way the road followed around the hills. He popped one dragon off and sent it up to keep an eye out.

One car whipped past him, then another and another. The dragon got his attention, and he saw a black SUV coming up the road with a cloud of dirt kicked up along the side of the road in its wake. The dirt had to be Ai. He dipped his hands in his trenchcoat pockets and pulled out two handfuls of broken glass he'd gathered in Elko, then tossed it all onto the road. In case that didn't work, he blew out into the swarm so he could follow it.

The car sped over the glass and none of the tires blew out. His next tactic had the dragons diving under the vehicle. They grabbed the undercarriage and wriggled around, looking for parts to eat or break or poke holes into. Half the swarm got its fill of metal, and one clump of dragons punched a hole into the gas tank. The liquid splashed out, leaving a line on the road and spraying over at least a quarter of the little critters.

The vehicle sputtered and died, then coasted off to the side of the road. It rolled to a stop on the shoulder, and Bobby let the dragons keep wriggling through the innards, eating what they wanted. With this snack, they'd staved off hunger for a while.

He heard a car door open. One foot in a dress shoe, connected to a leg wearing suit pants, stepped out of the passenger side and crunched on the loose gravel. Rushing air kicked dirt up into a cloud and a male voice grunted in surprised pain. Bobby called the dragons out, sending them streaming out of the exhaust pipe, the front grille, and the undercarriage. Part of the swarm immediately surrounded a man in a suit.

If he did nothing, the dragons would boil into a rage and

murder all four of these men. He panicked, grasping to keep them from pushing him away. Their tug-of-war took time, and the suits spent it zapping and smashing dragons. Though he felt no pain like this, he suspected re-forming would beat the heckbiscuits out of him.

Bobby felt like he only had two choices. Either he let them keep going and the dragons all got smashed, or he re-formed and kept control and hoped Ai could handle this. He did want to live, thank you very much—he wanted to at least live long enough to find out what he could have with Lily, if anything. Living to watch Sebastian grow up would be kind of nice, too.

He re-formed kneeling on the ground beside the car, bruised, battered, and beaten. Everything hurt, from head to toe, and his left arm ended at his wrist. The suit with the net dropped it to the ground and stomped on the struggling bunch of them before letting them go to rejoin Bobby. Several struggled to fly, hopping along the ground with wings too damaged for proper flight.

Blood trickled down from his nose, and the nearest suit slammed the baseball bat into his head. It hit with a crack, the dragons too scared of being crushed to fly apart again. Lying on the ground, unable to get up but still conscious, Bobby heard tasers sparking all around. He saw Ai crumple nearby, twitching.

"And Dazai," another agent sneered.

Something else hit him in the back of the head and everything went black.

Chapter 16

"You're quite a troublemaker, Mitchell. Where have you been sending everyone? Where are Hannah and Alice?"

Feeling like crap all over, Bobby tried to move his hands without success. Something held them down, and it hurt too much to struggle against it. He opened his eyes and cringed away from the too bright light in his face. "Go to Hell." He wanted to go swarm, even though they probably all needed time to recover as much as he did. Nothing happened. He figured the suits had pushed him past the point where he could do it.

"I heard Georgia boys were polite. I guess that's just another stereotype."

Something touched his side, then explosive pain rocked his body hard enough to make him scream. The crackle of electricity registered after the fact. He lay there, gulping air and now realizing his feet had been tied down, too. In the back of his mind, a tickle told him he had one dragon loose, on dragon watching this being done to him and gripped with enough angry terror to fill a bucket.

"Where are the others, Mitchell?"

"Go to Hell," he ground out between gritted teeth.

"Well, we have Dazai, too. She'll probably tell us whatever we want to know when we're through with her."

Bobby's eyes snapped open to glare at the suit. The light stabbed his head with spikes of agony, but he ignored that to focus on delivering his message. "Keep your hands off her," he growled.

"Put three patriotic men in a room with a female terror suspect, and you never know what might happen." The suit's mouth curled into a cruel smirk of satisfaction. "You've been injected with a muscle relaxant. We have reason to believe it will prevent you from using your freak ability, so you get to lie here and listen." The suit stood up and opened the door of what must be a bedroom in a house. He had no idea how they found a house, set it up, and got here fast enough for him to wake up and still feel this awful.

With the door open, he could hear someone whimpering and sniffling. It had to be Ai or the other girl. Either way, he wanted to kill these four men for causing it.

"The thing about Miss Dazai is that once she's tied down, she isn't going anywhere." The suit nodded to someone outside the room, then he crossed his arms leaned against the door frame.

"Get away from me," Ai said, a warble of fear in her voice. She whimpered and Bobby heard cloth ripping. "Stop," she begged, "please don't." She sucked in a breath, and it sounded like she'd begun to cry.

"Don't you dare touch her!" Bobby shouted with all he had, straining to free himself. He could feel the dragons still under his skin, but none could break free.

"Just answer the questions, and this all stops."

This couldn't be happening. No one really did this kind of thing, not in the States. Bobby stared at the suit, torn between disbelief and rage. "Let her go. She don't know nothing. It's all me, I'm the only one what knows. You let her go, and I'll tell you anything you want to know."

"No!" Ai cried. "Bobby, don't tell them anything."

How could he lie here and listen to that? He liked Ai, she was nice and friendly and a decent person. She didn't deserve anything like this. No one did. Had he really thought about doing it to someone else not so long ago? Listening to her crying and begging for them to stop, those men disgusted him. That he wanted to return the favor disgusted him more.

He shut his eyes and breathed deeply, trying to push away Ai's voice. It would give him nightmares later. No, he wouldn't torture any of these men, not even for a minute. "I'm going to kill you. All of you."

The suit snorted. "I seriously doubt that, Mitchell."

Something still held his dragons in check, frustrating him and forcing tears of sympathy out of his eyes. He stopped trying to ignore the noises and let them in to fuel his anger. If he couldn't take it in her stead, he would listen. For being unable to stop it, he'd have memories of her screams and tears as penance.

"You sick fucks," a new female voice snarled.

Bobby's eyes snapped open and he strained to see the person he guessed must be the Reno girl, Anita. He watched the suit in the doorway turn in surprise and pull out a gun and saw little else.

Something crashed in the other room and the suit fired his gun. He kept firing and ran to the side. Whatever Anita could do, he doubted she could dodge bullets, leaving Bobby with little hope for rescue. Heavy things scraped across the floor, wood cracked, men grunted and groaned, and gunshots rang out. A nightstand sailed past the door, giving Bobby an idea of what happened out there.

With one last crash, the gunfire stopped, leaving Bobby's ears ringing. "Come on," Anita said, barely loud enough for him to hear, "we've got to get out of here before they wake up."

"We can't leave Bobby."

Anita growled in the back of her throat. "Fine, I'll get him. Stay here." A Hispanic woman with the eyes appeared in the doorway. She hurried in and bent to unbuckling the straps holding him down.

"Anita?" He sagged to make freeing him easier. "What'd they do to her?"

Anita clenched her jaw. "Why didn't you save her?"

"They drugged me." With one hand now free, so he reached for the strap on his other wrist. Clumsy and stupid, his fingers fumbled with the buckle. Not willing to go to Ai unprepared, he persisted. "What'd they do to her?"

She stopped and glared at him, her nostrils flaring. "They didn't have time to rape her yet, but were going in that direction. She's mostly cut up some. You let it happen."

As if he didn't have enough guilt banging around inside his head already. She had to go and add an extra pile to the heap. He already knew he let this happen. It had been his idea to attack the car there, and his choice to attack it the way he did. Bobby growled at her. "You wanna blame me, fine. Get her out and I'll make my own way from here."

"Fine." She tossed open the strap on his right foot and shot to her feet, then stormed out.

"What about Bobby?" Ai whimpered and hiccuped.

"He'll catch up when he's ready to be a man," Anita sneered. "You need medical attention, let's go."

What did she expect him to do? Was it not clear he would have smashed skulls if he could have? Every inch of his body ached, especially his head, and he couldn't even manage to free his hand. Sagging back to take a short breather, he called out, "Take care of yourself, Ai. You're strong, remember that."

He heard a faraway door open and shut. If he called the one

loose dragon back, would the drugs make it reattach? Probably, so he couldn't chance it. He returned to freeing himself and managed to slide his hand free when he heard someone groan in the other room. Sitting up, he attacked the strap on his ankle. His hands still refused to do what he wanted, and he had to slow down to accomplish anything.

A suit staggered into the doorway. This one had been the driver at Lily's house. "Left you behind, huh?" Small cuts on his face oozed blood, and he held his side with one hand, a gun pointed at the floor with the other. "Still going to be loyal to those bitches?"

"Least I ain't a rapist." He kept working on the cuff around his ankle.

"It's a fine line, you know. But really, none of you are actually human. We can do whatever we want to all of you."

"I'm still an American citizen. So is she." Stupid, stupid fingers took far too long.

"Technicality. Cats and dogs aren't citizens, even though they live here. You just are because you look human enough to pass for one"

"I ain't a cat nor a dog."

"Close enough."

The buckle came loose and he looked up into the barrel of that gun. In his current condition, a BB gun could probably kill him. He froze and gulped.

"Think you're faster than a bullet, Mitchell?"

His dragons still wouldn't come out to play. "If'n you don't think I'm human, why d'you keep using my last name? That's my daddy's name."

The suit chuckled. "Cute. Hands up or you get shot."

With another gulp, Bobby slowly raised his hands. For now, he'd have to do what this guy said. Why did he have to mouth off at

Anita? Oh, right, because she blamed him for what these assholes did to Ai. His eyes danced from the gun to the man and back again as he thought about taking the chance. Another voice groaned out there. Two guys with guns sounded like way more than he could handle right now. Besides, the hospitality here sucked.

Adrenaline pumped through him, easing the pain all over his body. Ducking to one side, he swung an arm out to push the gun aside. It went off. He lunged. They scuffled over the gun, both in equally bad shape. Bobby heard another gunshot. Something stabbed him in the side and he felt himself go pale. No matter how much he wanted to keep going, to keep fighting, his body wouldn't let him. It had been beaten, battered, and now broken, and it couldn't take any more.

Staggering back, Bobby grunted as the suit shot him again. He collapsed and felt unconsciousness creeping up over him, so he reached out to the one lone dragon that managed to stay apart. It perched outside the window, claws around the upper edge and dangling down to watch. Somehow, he found himself in there with it, and he watched the suit nudge his body with a shoe, watching himself not react. This beat everything else he'd ever done or seen for weird, no contest.

The suit holstered his gun under his jacket and knelt beside Bobby's body. He tucked two fingers under his chin to check for a pulse, then ripped Bobby's shirt off. His muffled voice called out for the others and he covered the two the injuries he just inflicted, applying pressure to both. So, they wanted him alive. Had to appreciate the guy not putting a bullet in his brain and leaving it at that.

Hannah needed to know what happened here. His current assets: one tiny robot dragon with no ability to speak. It could, instead, make cute little dragon noises. Now that he paid attention, this tiny robot dragon had enough rage to kill someone fifty times over. Its claws had dug into the metal it held onto so hard they punched holes in it. In fairness, he had a powerful urge to gut these four men, too.

Getting a message to Hannah felt remote and impossible under these conditions. Freeing himself had to be his next best option. Thinking of it that way confused him, so he settled on thinking of it as freeing his body. The dragon preferred to do that, and let its rage simmer down to a manageable level to help.

From this vantage point, he watched another suit hurry in with a medical kit. Together, they worked on keeping his body from bleeding to death. Neither of them tried to pull the bullets out or sew anything up. Instead, they focused on using powders and applying gauze and bandages.

The problem of freeing his body occupied his mind while they worked. Actually, freeing it now would be stupid. He'd be unconscious, unable to accomplish anything and at their mercy. Waiting until it got real treatment and woke up struck him as a better plan, since he couldn't go swarm until that happened. In the meantime, he would keep track of it, listen in, and try to find a way to contact Hannah. This plan sucked. It was still a plan, and better than no plan.

For this plan to work, he needed to be able to hear what they said. Thankfully, the dragon understood it needed to stay apart from the swarm for now, so he could count on its help. Never mind the weirdness of that. This was not the time to be dealing with the absurdity his life had become. This was the time to be dealing with the crap in front of him. He directed the dragon to fly all around the house and find a way inside.

As soon as they saw the tiny dragon, they'd recognize it. If even one of them noticed the weird shape of his finger, they knew he had a dragon loose. There would be no element of surprise here, and no hiding in plain sight. This dragon had to stay out of sight, and had to do it where he could listen in and follow them. The possibility existed that they wouldn't think he could have his mind in the one missing dragon, which gave him a slight advantage.

The dragon found a vent in the eaves of the two-story house and crawled inside, then flew through it and found the dryer vent with no dryer connected to it. The laundry room had no washer, either. That meant no one lived in this house. How did they get here? Where was 'here'? The questions gnawed at his brain. Mind. Whatever. They gnawed. He flitted through the house from ledge to shelf, keeping track of the best hiding spots.

All the action had taken place upstairs, so he stopped on the moulding at the top of the doorway closest to the bottom of the stairs. Unless a suit shone a light up here, they should remain unnoticed. With so little furniture and decoration, the voices carried, so he heard the suits talking. In fact, it had such a small amount of anything, he wondered where Anita had found anything to throw around.

"Why did you even shoot him a second time? You could have just pistol whipped him." Bobby decided to call this voice Suit One, it being the first one he heard well enough to make out the words. He spoke in a clean baritone with no obvious accent.

"You saw the pictures from San Jose." As already noted from his brief conversation earlier, Suit Two also had no accent. Did they train these guys that way? "They didn't do his handiwork justice."

"He was doped up and couldn't do that right now. Christ, that's why we aren't dead now."

"Just call it in and get us another ride."

"You think the girls took the car?"

Suit Two snorted. "Of course they did. They'd be stupid not

to. These things may not be human, but they aren't stupid. If we've learned anything by now, it's that underestimating them will get us all killed. We're just lucky Martinez only beat the crap out of us."

Another voice groaned and debris shifted.

Digital tones announced an outgoing phone call. Suit One spoke. "Dazai and Martinez got away. Mitchell is in custody, but seriously injured. He's been shot twice. … Yes, sir, but Dazai and Martinez took our vehicle. … No, sir. … He's stable for the moment, but we need to move. This location has been compromised. We could all use some medical attention, we didn't let them go quietly or anything. … Yes, sir. … Understood."

"Did anybody get the number of that Mack truck?" Suit Three, also accent-free, joined the conversation as a pained tenor. "Jesus, I think she broke my goddamned arm."

"Barnes is still out," Suit Two said. "Check on him."

"Someone will be here in half an hour," Suit One said. "Privek is pissed."

Was that FBI Special Agent Steve Privek? The one that originally arrested Bobby a million years ago, on the other side of the world? Privek apparently had been slumming it by picking Bobby up, or maybe got a promotion from doing it with whatever freaky organization they all worked for. It couldn't really be the FBI. The country his daddy fought and died for wouldn't let the FBI do things like this. He hoped not, anyway.

"No shit," Suit Two growled. "We'll be lucky if it isn't a cleaning crew."

"Barnes is dead," Suit One announced. "We should blame him."

"Seconded." Suit Three grunted with pain.

Suit Two said, "Agreed. He was in charge of keeping Martinez subdued. His judgment on the subject allowed her to get free, and that's how she overpowered us and got away."

"Shooting Mitchell twice is all on you, though," Suit One snapped.

"Whatever. He was still a threat. At least we have him."

"Assuming he lives," Suit One snapped.

"He'll live." Along with Suit Two's voice, Bobby heard the sound of latex snapping, probably him pulling off gloves. "He'll never be a quarterback, but he'll live."

They moved on to tending Suit Three, who Bobby learned had a name of 'Walker' when Suit Two told him to stop whining. Whatever injuries he had, they seriously hurt. Bobby figured these guys had one thing in common with his daddy: they didn't bitch and moan about minor injuries. If they made noise, it damned well hurt. Walker made a lot of noise.

It took them fifteen minutes to get Bobby's and Barnes's bodies down the stairs and within easy reach of the garage. Walker had to go slow and cradled his arm. After that, Suit Two walked around the house, dousing it with clear liquid from a large canister they must have brought along with them.

At the same time, Suit One went through Barnes's coat in the kitchen, where Bobby could see it. He pulled out four different badges from four different agencies, checking each one and setting them in a stack. When he 'd checked all the pockets, he slid them in an already half-full bag, along with a set of keys, a pack of gum, and a few other small items. Bobby's own trenchcoat could be in the bag, though he doubted it.

With that done, Suit Two pulled Bobby's cheap cellphone out of a pocket and futzed with it. It had only one number in memory and the call log, and he punched a button to dial it. If only he could warn Hannah somehow, or at least hear the other end.

"Yeah, I got clear, sorry to make you worry." Suit Two did a reasonably good impression of Bobby's voice. He listened in disgust, praying for Hannah to see through the ruse before she revealed anything. "I'm pretty messed up, but I'll heal. Are the girls okay? … Good, good." He stood there for several seconds without saying anything. "Hello?" He growled in the back of his throat and snapped the phone shut. "She hung up on me."

Bobby would have breathed a sigh of relief if he could have. The dragon kept its head and didn't let him make any noise.

Suit Two showed the phone to Suit One. "Trace the number down. It looks like he's called it plenty of times. We should be able to get a fix on it."

Suit One pulled out his own smartphone and tapped on it several times while checking the number on the flip phone. "Assuming they don't smash it. Someone just pointed out they aren't stupid not too long ago."

A thumping noise cut off the conversation and made both suits look up. "Our ride is here," Suit Two said, snapping the phone shut and tossing it into the bag. The two of them headed to the front door. Bobby followed along, doing his best to stay out of sight.

Completely out of place in this nice, normal neighborhood, a sizable cargo helicopter landed in the middle of the street. Since they clearly intended to load his body into it, Bobby turned his attention to the task of getting into it unseen and finding a hiding place for the flight. Men in military camouflage hopped out and left the door open, and everyone kept their heads down, making his job easy. The dragon fought the wind from the rotors to come around the other side and swoop in over the top.

From his perch under the pilot's seat, the dragon could see part of the instrument panel. Bobby had no idea what any of the knobs, dials, and gauges meant. He did, however, figure out that one near the middle was a clock. Their flight lasted fifteen minutes and thirty-five seconds. It landed at some kind of military facility, one with hangars and an airfield, and some really enormous mountains in the distance.

This was not Elko. No one would be stupid enough to put an airport along a road that wound through the mountains, and these particular mountains didn't look like anything he saw flying over and near Elko. Until he got a better view or saw a sign, he had no guess for his location, other than 'not Elko'. That meant he might have been unconscious longer than he thought.

Soldiers hefted his body onto a stretcher, then into a building. He sent the dragon slipping in through the doors. From the way they shouted and gestured wildly, he gathered the medical facility and personnel only rarely saw gunshot wounds. They carried Walker in right behind him. Strangely, the soldiers accepted the suits without challenge, referring to them as 'sir'. He might have missed them flashing badges.

How in the heckbiscuits could he possibly escape this place? After surgery, they'd keep him so pumped full of drugs he couldn't burst into the swarm until the suits came and took him again. That meant he needed to get away on foot. From a military base. With suits on site. Assuming he ever woke up before they found a better way to restrain him.

He shelved that problem in favor of getting more information. There might be a way to get a message out. Besides, if the suits stayed more than another day at that facility in Virginia, he'd eat his boot. Knowing the four of them got out, they'd be sugar frosted stupid to keep using it. That meant the others they'd nabbed could be here. Jasmine could be in the basement.

Two hours later, the dragon had flown through the entire duct system of the building with nothing of interest to report. When he found his body again, a doctor was still working on him. The next time he went swarm, this would get translated into generic pain. They, of course, didn't know that. Even if they did, they wanted him unable to go swarm anyway. What did they even want him for at this point? They already spent five days doing whatever they wanted, and had plenty of his blood and whatever else they decided to take while he wasn't conscious. Why not kill him?

The dragon settled in at the vent over the surgical suite. He watched the doctor pull a lump of bloody lead out of his shoulder and drop it with a clang into a metal pan. It bothered him to wonder what purpose they possibly could have for him now. Thinking about it made the dragon surly, so he stopped. At least, he noted with some small satisfaction, they hadn't removed his jeans or boots. When he left here, it wouldn't have to be in a hospital gown.

When both wounds had been taken care of, the doctor let a soldier come in and wheel his body out. The surgeon followed at first, talking to the nurse. Because he wanted to hear what the man said, Bobby had the dragon follow along in the ducts, rushing from vent to vent. The nurse nodded in a bored, disinterested way at his instructions until he used numbers and words Bobby had never heard before, which he assumed to be drugs and dosages.

Along the way, they ran into Suit One and Two. The doctor sighed when he saw them and stopped while the gurney kept going. With the dragon confident it could find his body no matter what, Bobby also stopped to listen.

"Just the man we were looking for." Suit Two smiled, reminding Bobby of a viper. "What's the prognosis?"

Doc nodded. "He'll be fine, eventually. Nothing major damaged, just muscle and a rib."

"Excellent news. How long until we can have him back?"

"At least twenty-four hours," Doc said. "Mind, I'm saying 'at least'. If anything goes wrong before then, he's staying longer. We'll know more with certainty when he wakes up."

The two suits exchanged looks, their eyebrows raising up over their sunglasses. "We want him kept sedated." At this point, he had no doubt Suit Two wore the pants for his team.

"That's not in his best interests—"

Suit One gave the doctor a winning smile as he cut him off. "We're more concerned about the best interests of the US government. If he escapes, that would be...bad."

"He's in the middle of an Air Force base." Doc rolled his eyes. "We'll post a guard outside his door, he won't get away in his condition."

"I can appreciate your position, doctor, I really can." Suit Two's voice grated for how syrupy sweet he slathered on the sugar. "That man has already killed three of our agents when he should have been easy to subdue, and is a known terrorist." Three? They put Anita's handiwork on him? "We're much more concerned about the safety of everyone else here at the base than we are about his best interests. So long as he can be interrogated, that's all that matters."

Doc sighed and raked his surgical cap off to reveal short, graying black hair. "Fine." He crumpled the cap and jabbed a finger at Suit Two's chest. "But in twenty-four hours, we're waking him up, at least for an hour, to see what condition he's really in."

Suit Two shrugged, unmoved. "No problem. We'll be back in twenty-four hours, then."

Doc glared at their backs as they turned and walked away. Bobby had to decide which to follow. He wanted to hear what Doc said to the nurse, but he also wanted to know what the suits would say outside. If only he had two dragons, then he could listen to both. Before he made a decision, the dragon chose to follow the suits. They left the building, and he followed them out the top of the door, tail whipping out as it closed. The suits moved away from the door, finding a spot between buildings where Suit Two lit up a cigarette. Bobby perched in a nearby shrub to listen.

"I'll make sure he's dosed, you set up transport to the depot." Suit Two checked his watch. "It's just after one now, so I'll want to slip the stuff into his IV around noon tomorrow. I'll stop in on the way to lunch."

"Sounds like a plan," Suit One nodded. "Man, Mitchell better be worth the trouble. He's a serious pain in the ass, not easy like Milani was."

"Tell me about it. This time tomorrow, though, he'll be down for the count and hopefully on his way to being tucked in with the rest of them."

Suit One turned his gaze out to the airfield and stuck his hands in his pockets. "Playing them off each other might have been a mistake."

"No, that was the right way to go. Martinez just wasn't secured well enough. Mitchell would've broken when Dazai was actually raped. They still think they're human."

Suit One grunted in assent. "You hungry?"

"Starving."

Uninterested in watching them eat, Bobby let them walk off without following. The dragon's claws had crunched the small branch it perched on, and he found its anger difficult to separate from his own. Yeah, he still thought of himself as human. He'd grown up human and so had the rest of them. Whatever they'd become, they still deserved to be treated like people, not animals.

Thinking about this got him nowhere. In twenty-three hours, his body would be dosed with something, probably the drug that inhibited his ability to break into the swarm. He needed to prevent that. At the same time, his body needed to rest and heal. So, he needed to figure out how to do that, then kill some time.

His dragon noted it had gotten hungry, so he added finding something for it to eat to his to-do list. Knowing he prioritized that, it flew off in search of food. It sniffed around and found some spare parts in a hangar to devour. As he flitted around the base, he passed a sign marked 'Hill Air Force Base'. He'd never heard of it. Most Marine bases, he'd recognize, but not Air Force.

Before he could come up with any better ideas, he needed to know where he was. He and the dragon climbed into the sky to get an aerial view. The base sat on the north side of a large city, one with a major highway running through the middle of it. Huge mountains to the east and a giant lake to the west gave him a strong suspicion for his location.

They dove into the city, looking for signs. Sure enough, he passed one confirming he'd been taken close to Salt Lake City. If he remembered geography right, Utah was next to Colorado. Could he reach home base and get back in about twenty hours? Even if he could, would it be worth going? What would he do, have the dragon pantomime everything or try to hold a pencil three times its size?

He had to try. If he never tried, he'd never know what might've been. Besides, he'd be able to find his body again even if he got back late. Maybe he'd miss this chance, but there would be another one. At some point, his body would wind up in a position where one dragon could manage to free it. He had to believe that. Otherwise, he might as well give up and die now.

Turning east, they went up and beat those little wings as fast as they could handle. It flew high enough to go over the mountains that must be the Rockies. From that vantage point, he saw the ribbon of Interstate 80 winding along. He kept it to his left. Understanding the importance of this trip, the dragon pushed itself as hard as it could, and Bobby had no idea how fast it managed to go.

Up here, with nothing and no one around and the dragon

doing all the work, Bobby's mind wandered. He started with watching puffs of cloud, moved to tracing the contours of the land, and wound up hoping Momma wasn't worrying about him too much. She deserved better than him for a son. All his life, he'd given her a hard time. Maybe he did it because deep down, he knew he didn't belong to her.

He had weird eyes. He could turn into tiny robot dragons. The suits made it clear they thought that made him something other than human. What if they were right? Did that mean he had no right to call himself a citizen? They took his blood and did tests. Did they find some proof? God, if he wasn't human, what was he? What were they all?

The dragon didn't actually say 'shut up, I'm concentrating', but the impulse came through loud and clear. Bobby quit thinking so hard and watched the land slide by underneath. To think, he spent his time moping over Mandy not too long ago. He wasn't even sure how long had passed since then. Two weeks, maybe. He'd liked her, sure. Compared to everything that happened since Privek arrested him, she meant nothing. That thought threatened to spiral into those same topics he already annoyed the dragon with, so he cut it all off again and made an effort to just be and enjoy the scenery.

Chapter 17

Bobby guessed it took four or five hours to fly from Salt Lake City, Utah to their plot of land south and east of Fort Morgan, Colorado. When he got close, they had to follow the roads, using the directions he'd memorized to find the right place. They zoomed up a tree-lined driveway to find a decrepit farmhouse in the middle of renovations. The barn off to the side looked much worse than the one in the picture had. He had no doubts, though, that he came to the right place.

Matthew unloaded boxes from a van, straining with the effort. Despite not seeing him much without his fur, he recognized the werewolf immediately. Until the moment he saw a familiar face, he had no idea how much he needed one. Matthew, though, couldn't help him right now. Bobby needed someone who would instantly recognize the dragon as being part of him. The werewolf had been focused on Stephen the whole time.

With no real idea about the layout or where anyone in particular might be, Bobby let the dragon wander. Eventually, he'd find someone that could help. It took a slow, lazy circle around the house. In the back, some Asian guy sat on the ground, eyes closed and hands in the dirt. Dan and Lizzie, hands all over each other, slipped into the woods surrounding the house. They'd be no help, and he had no interest in watching them get naked and sweaty together.

Voices came from inside the house, promising better results that way. As he neared the closest window, the back door slammed open. A little boy barreled out, naked and shrieking with glee. The sight made him want to laugh. Even better, Lily would be along shortly to collect Sebastian. He chased the boy down and dropped into his sight. Sebastian stopped and recognized it, then put out his little hand. The dragon landed and chirped a greeting at him.

"Bobby! Mama, Bobby is here!" Sebastian turned around and ran back to his mother. Even with a red bandanna over her hair, she took Bobby's breath away. If he could have one wish right now, it would be to climb out of this dragon and be there to take her in his arms. He'd wrangle the boy for her, too.

She peered all around. "Where? I don't see him." When her son presented the dragon, she bent down and wrapped an arm around the boy to prevent him from getting away again. "Bobby?"

The dragon trilled, trying to get her attention. She kept twisting around, waiting for him to come walking around the corner. A minute later, she shrugged and picked Sebastian up. The boy squirmed and wriggled, and she had to abandon the search in favor of handling him. He did have to admit that getting the naked kid into clothes rated higher than him. Sort of.

"Hannah," she called out as she opened the farmhouse door, "one of Bobby's dragons is here," The inside of the building had more to recommend it than the outside. They'd put up a fresh coat of paint and scrubbed the floors so far.

"I'm in the meeting room," Hannah's voice called out.

The dragon leaped off Sebastian's had to follow her voice up the hallway. It passed a large kitchen with a picnic table and Andrew stirring a large pot hanging over an actual fire.

"I've got Seb—" Lily stopped and smiled. "Oh, it's heading for you."

Bobby had to give them all a lot of credit for what they'd done so far with a place that must have been a real dump. They didn't seem to have electricity yet, and still managed to get the place well on its way to livable in a short time. Lots of hands willing to help at least part of the time made a big impact.

Another hall branched from the first one, and he kept going until he found a large space. A wall running across the middle of it had been half smashed, and a thin layer of white dust covered everything. Stephen yanked a sledgehammer out of the plaster and drywall with a grin on his face. Good to see him able to help out in a way that amused him. Hannah stood near the door, using her force field to catch the debris he pulled away. They had an ancient, rust covered wheelbarrow she dumped it all into.

"Just one of his dragons?" Stephen set the sledge aside and wiped dust and plaster off his face with his gray shirt. "He won't be able to talk through it. We'll have to ask it yes/no questions. Oy, dragon!"

Thank God. Bobby nudged the dragon to land on Stephen's hand. It danced in a circle and trilled at him. Much to Bobby's surprise, it also belched out a tiny puff of fire.

Stephen flinched away and put his other hand up. "Okay, okay, you got my attention. Christ, don't do that again." He smirked. "Okay, Lassie. What is it, girl? Is Timmy down a well?"

The dragon stuck its tongue out at Stephen, then nodded. Bobby had no idea these things even had tongues. Also, he appreciated that it translated what he thought the best it could.

A grin flashed on Stephen's face, then he schooled his face into a frown. "Is Bobby in trouble? " Nod. "Is he hurt?" Nod. "Damn.

How are we going to figure out where he is?"

"A map? I'll see what I've got." Hannah hurried out of the room.

"Can you lead us to him?" Nod. "How many hours did it take you to fly here, little guy? Can you tell me that with fingers or claws or whatever?"

Without knowing the time, Bobby had no clue how long it took. He saw Stepehen's watch on his other wrist and had the dragon walk to where it would be. There, it sniffed and prodded until Stephen got the hint and held up his other hand so the dragon could see the watch face. At his direction, the little dragon held up four claws, curling the thumb partway under.

"More than four but less than five?" Nod. "Okay. Bobby can go about the same speed as me, that'll put him someplace between four and five hundred miles away, give or take. Is there a time limit? Is Bobby going to be moved in some amount of time?" Nod. "Hm. If you have any ideas about how to express that, I'm paying attention here."

How should he explain noon? It took Bobby a few seconds of furious thought to come up with something. The dragon rolled onto its back and showed him twelve little claws.

Stephen's lips moved while he counted. "Twelve? Midnight or noon? Er, is it midnight?" Shake. "Noon tomorrow?" Nod. "I can get that far by then. Violet can, too. Actually, we could drive that far. Is Jasmine there?" Shake. Stephen sighed and shook his own head. "We'll find them, all of them."

"I hope he's still in America." Hannah rushed in with a simple map of the country, showing only state borders and capitals.

"Four to five hundred miles away, so yeah, he should be."

"Huh." She crouched down and set the map on the floor so the dragon could walk on it.

He jumped down and scurried to Salt Lake City, tapping north of it with a claw.

"Salt Lake. Okay. If we had internet, we could get more specific, but that's close enough for right now. Let's see, we need to make sure there's at least one person with defensive ability here, and we're not taking anyone who can't handle a fight. I wish Jayce was here already."

"We smashed all the phones," Stephen explained to Bobby. "A suit called with yours. Er, Bobby's. Hell," he turned his attention to Hannah, "I don't even know if he's in there or it's just the dragon. Anyway. You stay here, I'll take Lizzie and Dan, Violet, and—"

"Not Violet, she has no idea how to fight. All she can do that we know of is fly."

"I'll go." Matthew stood in the doorway. He had a quieter, more intense voice than Bobby expected from listening to him roar.

Stephen pursed his lips. "No offense, but I'm not so sure that's a good idea."

"None taken, and I agree, but I'm going. If there's going to be a fight, I should be there."

Hannah frowned and stood. "I'll go talk to Andrew."

"Wait." Stephen put out a hand to prevent her from getting up. His eyes stayed on Matthew. "I can handle it."

"This is going to be messy enough already." Hannah sighed and rubbed her neck. "At least bring an insurance policy."

Bobby saw Matthew and Stephen exchange tiny nods. Seemed like they'd connected on the trip up here. From his perch, that seemed a good thing. "I'm enough of an insurance policy. We'll be fine. No need to put Andrew in harm's way. He can't fight, either."

"Oh, whatever." Hannah rolled her eyes. "I'll go find Alice, then, and Lizzie and Dan. Anyone else?"

"Andrea," both men said at the same time.

Hannah sighed. “Please don’t kill any more people than you have to. That’s all I’m going to say.” She left the room without waiting for a response.

“People are going to die.” Matthew said it flatly, as a statement of fact.

“Yeah.” Stephen nodded. “We’ll wait here so we don’t have to wait around there too long. Let’s see.” He turned to the map and ran his finger over the basic route despite the lack of roads on the page. “This drive will probably be, what? Eight or nine hours? Be ready to leave at midnight. Let’s push it a little, but not cut it too close.”

“Twelve hours to make a nine hour drive?” Matthew fiddled with his watch. “Sounds reasonable.” The two men shared a look, and Bobby thought something else passed between them. With a curt nod, Matthew left the room.

Bobby stuck with Stephen as he explained what they knew to Lizzie, Dan, Alice, and Andrea. Andrea reminded him of an underwear model, with frothy brown curls and cinnamon skin. It might have had something to do with the tight little shorts she wore. Even so, despite getting an eyeful of three different attractive women at once, Bobby’s thoughts still strayed to Lily. He wanted to curl up with her and never let her go.

Stephen watched the four of them go to prepare and sighed. “I will never get tired of watching that,” he muttered, his eyes firmly on Andrea’s backside.

Bobby had to admit the view could be much worse. The dragon trilled his agreement, provoking a smirk from Stephen.

“Hey, you have a minute?” A girl with a ton of freckles and straight red hair in a bob cut poked her head around the corner. Her ears had five hundred piercings filled with different colored studs. Back home, Bobby called a girl like that ‘freaky’. He’d since developed a whole new definition of that word, and chose instead ‘different’.

Stephen saw her and smiled. "Sure, Kaitlin, what's up?"

She stepped into the room, showing off an outfit that hurt Bobby's head: orange and pink striped tights, a black pleated miniskirt, fuzzy purple slippers, an orange tank top, and a gray hoodie with the zipper halfway undone. 'Different' definitely covered Kaitlin.

"I heard Hannah saying some of you are going out to rescue Bobby?" As she got closer, Bobby put her height at about five foot nothing.

"Yeah." He quirked an eyebrow at her. "You want to come?"

"Hell no." She waved her hand, dismissing the idea as crazy or stupid. "I just thought you might want some guidance. Oh, hey, is that one of his dragons? Can I hold it?"

"That's kind of up to it, not me." How true. "And yeah, that would be great. Thanks."

Bobby urged the dragon over to another girl who wanted to touch the cute dragon. She held him up high enough so the dragon could touch her nose, then shut her eyes. Figuring she might be using a power, he sat patiently, tail wrapped around the dragon's feet. A minute or so later, her eyes snapped open.

"Don't speed on 80 in Wyoming. He's on a military base with planes. Don't expect him to be able to help. Jayce will be here just after ten tonight and you should bring him. Don't take Hannah's van. There are three suits, don't let any of them get away." She offered Stephen the dragon back, then paused with her other hand up, finger extended to make him wait. "Don't go through the front gate, and watch out for the little girl inside the building: pigtails, red shoes, red dress. Protect her at all costs."

While the dragon hopped back to Stephen's shoulder, he repeated everything back to her, and she corrected him when he made a mistake. "Will do. I just love saving little girls." The words came out creepy, leaving Bobby—and Kaitlin, probably—with the impression that he meant to add 'for snacking' on the end.

"She's important." Kaitlin grabbed his arm and yanked him closer, her whole expression steely and daring him to try something. "Really important. She has to live and see you guys as big damn heroes."

All traces of humor gone in an instant, he nodded. "I get it."

"Okay." She let go and gave him a satisfied smile. "Good luck."

He tipped an imaginary hat at her and left the room. Bobby watched him stuff a change of clothes in a bag, studiously avoid the kitchen, field a few questions from the others, then return to the work of smashing through that interior wall. Just when he thought he'd have to figure out how to pass the time without his mind buzzing or distracting Lily from her boy too much, the dragon settled on a shelf and shut down. Everything went black.

The dragon came awake again. Surprised to find himself still in the dragon, Bobby accidentally made it yawn and stretch. It tumbled and brushed on something, revealing it had been scooped up by a hand. He found himself eye to eye with Stephen. "Are we ready to go?"

Bobby trilled and stamped, then flared his wings and jumped into the air.

"We didn't get all dressed up for nothing," Jayce said with a smirk.

Warm relief flooded through Bobby at his voice. Nothing like hearing the rock-steady sound of someone he knew and trusted. He flitted to Stephen's shoulder and chirped a greeting for Jayce.

"Is that Bobby in there, or just the dragon?" Jayce flashed him a confident grin and climbed into a van.

Stephen slid into the driver's seat. "I don't know, and actually, I'm not sure I want to know. I mean, thinking about that is a little mind-blowing. Sure, we all defy the laws of physics already, but that's just going way, way past logic and into crazy."

Jayce chuckled. The rest of the van gave up a few snorts and chortles. "Because getting your nourishment from blood isn't way past logic and into crazy."

"It's only crazy," Andrea's light Tennessee drawl said, "when it hasn't been written about in umpteen books already."

Bobby checked the rest of the passengers and smiled when he saw Alice. No matter how big a pain she'd been, familiar faces made everything seem better. Noticing him, she gave the dragon a wave and a pleasant smile. He lifted a claw and waved back.

Lizzie sat across Dan's lap, both of the refusing to use seat belts. Andrea, sitting beside Alice, now wore black leggings and leaned against the window. Matthew lounged across the back, arms crossed and eyes shut. When Stephen started the engine, he faced front again.

Lily ran out the front door in a green flannel robe she clutched shut. Standing on the front stoop, she waved, her hair mussed and eyes drooping. She must have gone to bed already, but made sure to wake up for this. Through Stephen's open window, he heard her say, "Be careful and bring him back safe! "

Stephen gave her a thumbs-up out the window, and she smiled. It held enough worry to crush Bobby for doing that to her.

"Awww." Lizzie's rough alto voice crooned from the back. "She's so cute. Probably jump him the second he gets back."

Bobby ignored her. Sort of. Aside from the guilt, seeing her make a special effort for him… He didn't get warm or flush or blush or sigh, but he felt like if he had his body, he'd definitely do at least one of those. He'd also follow through on all the other impulses by taking her in his arms and finally kissing her.

Alice sighed. "Doesn't it bother you the slightest bit that we might all be siblings?"

Dan grinned. It bothered Bobby how much he and Dan looked alike. It crossed his mind that the two of them might have the same real parents, making them full brothers. "Honey, we grew up as brother and sister. Mom had me and adopted Lizzie two years later. She called us a matched pair." He kissed Lizzie's neck. "We so totally are."

"And if we are related by blood, who cares?" Lizzie raked her fingernails across his scalp to brush his hair behind his ear. "It's not like we're planning on having kids and a white picket fence."

"I want a dog, though. I like dogs." Dan grinned and kissed Lizzie hungrily. The rest of the group, aside from Matthew who seemed to be asleep, either rolled their eyes or grimaced.

Leaning forward, Andrea said, "I dunno. I mean, no offense to you two, but I'm just not that interested in any of the guys at the farm. Oh, sure, you're all pretty. Being at the farm is a lot like living in one of those weird perfume commercials and all. But nobody's a spark for me. I need a spark, a pop, razzle-dazzle."

"None taken," Jayce said with an amiable smile. "I'm not particularly interested, either. Nice to look at, but not interested."

Stephen, Bobby noticed, kept his mouth shut and his eyes firmly on the road. His knuckles, already normally quite pale, had gone white from his grip on the steering wheel. Odds seemed high he had one of those cute little bunnies and fuzzy duckies moments going on in his head. At least he knew those things were wrong and actively avoided following through with any of them.

With that, and Dan and Lizzie not bothering to stay quiet, the chatter in the car died. Jayce turned the radio on, flipping between stations until he found one that Andrea danced in her seat to. The pop songs blurred into each other, broken up only by commercials.

Bobby couldn't stop thinking about Lily. If she turned out to be his sister, half or full, nothing would change. Like Lizzie said, he had no plans for kids of his own. Sebastian did make him think he might be a passable daddy. That didn't mean he felt ready to raise his own from the ground up. Anyway, their problems started and ended with her dead husband.

The dragon found this line of thought annoying and stupid. It hopped down and settled in the ashtray, shut down before Bobby could protest. It opened its eyes twice when they were switching drivers, first to Alice, then to Jayce. The third time, the car stopped because they didn't know where exactly to go. It was daylight by then. Jayce hopped out, checked with the guy manning the gas station, and came back with some snacks for everyone.

"There are two bases in Utah, Hill and Dugway. Hill is just north of here, Dugway is pretty much the western half of the state."

Stephen was in back now, sitting with Matthew and huddling under his hoodie. "Kaitlin said it had planes, and the dragon pointed to Salt Lake City."

"Probably Hill, then." Jayce looked down at the dragon. "Is it Hill?" Nod. "We should have a plan of some kind. We can try walking in the front door and asking politely, but I'm going to go ahead and guess that won't work."

Dan and Lizzie came back, disrupting the discussion. They settled onto the same bench seat again and Bobby wondered how either of them ever managed to accomplish anything. Then again, their house had been in need of enough repair that he would've been ashamed to let his Momma see it.

"Kaitlin specifically said not to use the front gate. If I fly in, I can probably find a way to get everyone else in quietly. Biggest problem, though, is the damned sun." Stephen scowled.

"I can help." Lizzie held up a black bondage mask for him. Her dress, so far as Bobby could tell, had no pockets, and he hadn't seen her reach into their bag. With a moment of reflection, he realized he'd be better off not knowing why she had it in hand.

Stephen stared at her for a long moment. His lip twitched, showing one fang. Reaching back, he grabbed it and muttered, "Thanks."

Lizzie grinned and blew him a kiss. "Can't we just blast our way in? That would be a good diversion."

Andrea rolled her eyes and shook her head. "How public do we want to get? That kind of thing is a line. Once we cross it, we can't really go back."

Alice shrugged. "It's a military base, we won't get a lot of press from it. Mostly what will happen is the suits will know that a bunch of us are working together and get an idea of how well we do that, plus they'll learn about the powers the rest of you have."

"And—" Matthew, now sitting in the front passenger seat, had to cough and clear his throat before finishing the thought. "And we'll be telling them that we'll go to the mat and pull out the stops for one of our own. They'll be more ready for us the next time it happens."

"They might also step up the effort to find us in this region, because they'll have a time frame to work with." Jayce checked the roads on the map, following them with his finger. "Since they know how long Bobby has been here, they know how far away we can't be. Maybe we should wait until the last minute to keep as much area in their search pattern as possible."

"Why did Kaitlin say not to take Hannah's van?" Stephen fiddled with the mask, giving it a dirty look. "That's the one thing she said I didn't really see the need for." He finally put it on, getting familiar with the zippers and snaps and figuring out how to make it fit best.

Everyone went quiet and Jayce started the engine. Bobby figured that since the suits knew she'd come with them, Hannah's plates had some kind of alert on them. Not only that, she had Pennsylvania plates, which would stick out in these parts. The Montana plates this van sported wouldn't get a second look.

Dan broke the silence. "We should swipe some local plates for this van, just keep 'em long enough to do this job and toss 'em on our way outta state."

Almost three hours later, after another stop and another close look at the map, Jayce parked the van in a residential neighborhood. Everyone piled out to walk the rest of the way. The dragon perched on Stephen's shoulder and saw him check his watch, noting the time as 11:15. With his dark hoodie, creepy mask, leather gloves, and nondescript jeans and sneakers, he looked like a serial killer. Without them to keep him sane, he could be one.

They moved in a disjointed group, Stephen keeping Jayce and Matthew between him and the few people they passed by. A few blocks later, they reached the last row of houses before the razor-wire topped chain link fence providing a wide buffer for the base. The dragon pointed at the cluster of buildings in the distance, making sure they knew not to go looking in the hangars.

"We'll see you on the other side." Stephen tipped an imaginary hat and grabbed Dan under the armpits. They flew up and over the fence, landing on the other side. Lizzie blew Dan a kiss and Stephen flashed a peace sign back at the group, then the two of them dashed across the open space to the nearest hangar. Anyone paying attention to this section of the perimeter would see them, no question. Bobby doubted anyone watched it all the time.

Getting into that building required pushing a button and being buzzed in, which would be harder. Security might be lax around the edges, given this base sat in the middle of the country and had a barrier against casual trespassers and dumbass kids. The actual buildings, so far as he saw before, told a different story.

Knowing what would happen in a minute or so to help defeat that security, the two men put their backs to the building Bobby pointed out for them and waited in the shade. Right on cue, an enormous, billowing bale of fire exploded at the spot where they'd left the others behind. Lizzie certainly did have a flair for the dramatic. He barely knew her, but could easily imagine her dancing around in the flames like a giddy schoolgirl in a shower of confetti.

"That's my girl," Dan murmured. He smiled as a second huge plume of fire erupted near the first.

Stephen pulled the mask off while they waited and stuffed it into a pocket. "Damn, that thing is hard to breathe through. You're sure you can make someone push a button?"

"Yeah, I'm sure."

"I should mention that I'm hungry."

"Awesome." Dan grinned, showing no sign of squeamishness. "You take down whoever gets in the way, I'll grab Bobby."

Vehicles raced across the base in time to see a third fireball explode. So far, only a few scraggly shrubs had caught fire, presenting no real threat to the base or the neighborhood around it. Andrea or Jayce would be standing next to Lizzie, reminding her not to kill anyone. Hopefully, she'd listen.

"Lizzie isn't a patient woman."

"Yeah, my girl is more of the instant gratification type."

Stephen checked his watch. "We'll give them a couple of minutes to muster everything that's going to get mustered."

"Burn, baby, burn," Dan chuckled, his eyes lit up glee. They watched as more and more vehicles streamed off in that direction and more and more fire shot into the sky. Any of those blasts hitting a building could demolish it. They had to be that big to attract enough attention and cause enough chaos.

Stephen tugged his hood up and patted Dan's shoulder. They

rolled around the corner, slipping up to the front door. He pushed through the outer door of an enclosed entry with ease. The inner door, on the other hand, had a place to swipe a key card and a button to press to get someone to open it for them. He tapped the glass to check how solid it was, then pressed the buzzer to get someone to show themselves.

Dan scowled as no one popped into view. "It's a camera system. Sorry, can't use that."

"No problem. We can do it the hard way instead." Stephen took three steps back, then threw himself at the glass, hitting it with his shoulder. The glass cracked.

"Awesome." Dan flicked a finger at the MP stepping out into view as he drew his gun. The guy shot the glass four times. He turned the gun on himself and shot his own leg.

Stephen hit the glass with his shoulder again and smashed through it. He stopped a few feet inside the door and shook off glass.

Dan followed him through the hole and picked up the dropped weapon. He clucked his tongue at the guard's whimpers of pain. "Don't bitch, buddy, I coulda made you point it at your head."

When a second MP jumped into the hallway, Stephen grabbed him by the neck and threw him at the wall with enough force to leave a dent. "Lead the way, dragon." He pulled out his nightmare swagger and stalked up the corridor.

The plan Bobby heard discussed outside neglected to mention mayhem inside the building. These two seemed to have intended to do it all along anyway. On the bright side, Dan was right, he could have had the man shoot himself someplace fatal. The dragon flitted forward, trying not to think too hard about the angry path these two men had decided to carve through the staff here. Dan's gun barked several times along the way. Not one of the shots hit anything vital on anyone, suggesting he was either a lousy shot or a fantastic one, and he only aimed at men.

Less selective in his targets and methods, Stephen also avoided killing people. Some hid fast enough, the rest got his fist in their face or thrown into a wall. "If I'd known it would be this easy, I would've just come by myself." He smirked as he ignored a doorway to a room full of scared people. Several had phones out, taking pictures or tapping away.

"That wouldn't be fair, to keep all this fun to yourself." Dan tossed his empty gun and caught the one that a surprised guard lobbed to him. That guard turned and punched the guy next to him in the gut. "Do we care if anyone besides the base takes pictures of us?"

"A little." Stephen backhanded a guy not quick enough to get out of his way. Bobby took a look back at the groaning bodies and debris littering the hall and realized the vampire had lost most of his control. He breezed through, treating this like a party. The guy needed cake.

Dan stopped at a doorway and stared into the room beyond it with a feral grin. The sound of several people smashing their cellphones put a bounce in his step as he moved on to the next group. More gunshots rang out and they hit the stairwell.

Damn, these two men scared the heckbiscuits out of Bobby. This seemed like a good idea up until now. He should have found a way to free himself. There would have been a window, he could have figured something out. But no, he had to go for help. The blame for all of this belonged on his shoulders. When the suits came looking for the group with a nuke, it would be his fault. If anyone got killed, that was on him.

Chapter 18

The dragon fluttered against the door to his room, then landed on the knob. Seeing that, Stephen grabbed the nearest nurse and put her in standard hostage headlock position. Dan opened the door and shut it behind Stephen and his guest. He held his latest gun ready to fire at anyone else coming through it.

There he lay on a gurney, wires and tubes monitoring him and keeping him alive. His body still wore those jeans and boots. Funny how they never bothered to remove either. No sheet covered his torso, leaving all his injuries available to be seen. Bandages covered the stitches, with purple bruising peeking out from underneath. His wrists had less severe bruises, and angry red burns marked where he'd been repeatedly tasered.

"Damn, you got messed up," Stephen breathed. Adjusting his grip on the nurse, he pushed her forward. "Unhook him, now."

Bobby wanted to stay out here and watch while he woke up. The dragon didn't care about that. It dove at his body and merged back with the swarm. Everything went black again. The next thing he knew, someone patted the side of his face.

"Wake up, sleeping beauty." Dan had picked up a penlight and shone it into Bobby's eyes. "Welcome back, Bobby."

Flinching away from the light, he tried to talk. "Nguh." His tongue refused to work. A moan of ecstasy attracted his attention, and he turned his head to see Stephen with his mouth locked on the nurse's neck from behind. Her eyes fluttered and her mouth hung open. Not wanting to watch that, he tried to lift his arms and found them uncooperative.

"Yeah, Kaitlin said you'd be useless. Anything burning important you want to tell us?" Dan had tucked his gun into the front of his jeans for the moment. He put an arm around Bobby's shoulders and tried to help him sit up.

Squeezing his eyes shut, he tried to think around the vampire porn happening in the corner. "Suits." It took a lot of effort to push that word out.

Failing to make much progress with getting Bobby vertical, Dan gave up. "Three, like Kaitlin said? "

The woman slumped in Stephen's arms and he let go of her neck. He licked the last smear of blood off her flesh, then set her aside and adjusted his jeans. "I needed that. I really, really needed that."

Bobby blinked repeatedly, trying to focus. "Yeah." In the movies, the drug cloud always lifted pretty fast. He could feel the edges perking up, at least. It might not be too long before he could help.

"He's a big lump."

Stephen stretched, standing up and reaching until his fingertips brushed the ceiling. "Muuuuuuuch better." He breathed deeply and cracked his neck. "Push him out on the bed and watch for a wheelchair. I'll plow the road."

"Pig." Bobby had a take a breath between the two halves of the word. "Tails."

At the door, Stephen looked back, one eyebrow quirked. "You

were in the dragon all along."

"Yeah."

Stephen looked away and rolled his shoulders in a squirm. "I'm not going to think about that right now. And I've been watching for the girl all along. Give me a minute to check the hall." He opened the door and slipped out, shutting it behind himself.

"I'm with him on this one, Bobby. Thinking about how your mind got crammed into a little bitty dragon while your brain was here the whole time… Nope, don't want to go there. Crazy enough I can control other people's bodies and he drinks blood. You're just out and out off the scale."

Shutting his eyes and hoping the drugs would fade quickly, Bobby mumbled, "Thanks."

"No offense."

Bobby grunted. They heard crashing outside and a handful of gunshots. Dan pulled his gun again and pointed it at the door. Stephen's voice roared in rage through the muffled door. Bobby noticed Dan relaxing, the tension draining out of him. Either the vampire's anger or the prospect of doing more violence calmed him. Nothing like having a deranged psychopath on his team. Like Matthew, though, no one else could hope to control Dan. If this counted as 'control'.

"C'mon and try it," Dan breathed. Suit One threw the door open, gun up and ready to shoot. Dan took one beat to check him over, then he squeezed the trigger and put a bullet between the suit's eyes. "Too slow." He grinned as the body crumpled and kept the gun pointed at the open doorway. Someone flew past the door to crash into something loud and clattering.

Stephen stormed past, putting a hand up for their benefit. "I got this, get moving."

Dan smirked and saluted him with the gun. He shoved the

corpse out of the doorway, then reached inside and yanked the wheeled bed through. Bobby turned his head to the side and watched Stephen bear down on Walker, aka Suit Three. The man had one arm in a cast, yet still held a gun after being tossed for distance.

Stephen grabbed the gun and flipped it aside, not bothering to use it. The two men scuffled, though Walker had no chance against Stephen in a 'fair' fight. Dan kept going, kicking debris side and dragging the bed to the elevator at the other end of the hall.

"There's more." His mouth felt a little less stupid, so Bobby pushed out a few more words. "Another suit. Four, 'Nita killed one, hurt one. Boss left."

Dan grinned wide enough to seem manic. "Awesome, a boss fight. Time for the big guns."

As the elevator doors opened, Stephen caught up with them, swooping in and holding his side with a scowl. "That sonofabitch tased me."

"You kill him?" Dan asked, eyes alight with interest.

"Yes. I gather there's another suit. Five bucks says one of us will have to shield the pigtail girl from him shooting her."

"No bet," Bobby grunted. He rolled onto his side while the elevator carried them down two floors. It took a lot of effort, and his eyes went wide as he saw something unexpected in the corner. Unable to keep himself there, he slumped onto his back again. "Guys. Pigtails. Right here."

Both men turned to look. The little girl with the red dress and shoes, her blonde hair in pigtails, sat curled up in the corner. Maybe eight or nine years old, she clutched a teddy bear and stared up at them in terror with wide, icy blue eyes. Hers were otherwise normal, lacking the odd tilt all of theirs had. At a glance, though, she could be easily mistaken for one of them.

Stephen rubbed his forehead and mouthed a curse. He

breathed deeply and crouched down to her level. “Don’t worry, we’ll protect you. I swear on my father’s grave that I won’t let anyone hurt you. We’re not going to take you away from whoever you’re here with, either.”

“We ain’t the bad guys, I swear.” Bobby licked his lips and prayed for Dan to keep his mouth shut. “There’s gonna be shooting, though, so stay small.”

The girl nodded and hid her face, pushing herself closer to the corner.

Stephen stood and put himself in the middle of the doors. Dan braced himself between the back of the elevator and the bed. The doors opened. Four soldiers pointed guns at Stephen and fired. Stephen grunted as the bullets hit him. He reached over and pushed the button to shut the doors. Bullets clanged as they hit the metal and dimpled it inward.

He flipped the emergency switch so the doors would stay shut, making an annoying bell ring. “Dammit, I’m going to have to feed again soon.”

“Maybe it wouldn’t creep you out so much if’n you called it ‘eating’ ‘stead of ‘feeding.’” Here he lay, taking all of this in stride. He could freak out instead, except that wouldn’t help anything. Bobby took a deep breath and lifted a hand, flexing his fingers. “The drugs’re wearing off.”

“What are you?” The little girl’s voice managed to reach him despite the bell.

Bobby smiled at her, hoping for the best. “Superheroes. Misunderstood superheroes.”

“Like Wolverine?”

“Yes.” Stephen reached over again to the elevator panel, meeting Bobby’s eyes and asking without words if he was ready to try again. “Exactly like that.”

Bobby offered the girl his hand and inwardly groaned at the words he intended to say to her. “Come with me if you want to live.”

She blinked, sniffled, and nodded. Surging to her feet, she grabbed his hand and jumped to get onto the gurney with him. Ignoring how much he hurt he curled his body around her protectively. Nestled in his arms, she asked, “Is my Mom okay?”

“We made an effort not to hurt anyone too much,” Dan reassured her. “Except the as— er, guys that want to lock us up and treat us like lab rats. Them, no mercy.”

“Are we ready to do this?” At the affirmatives from Bobby and Dan, Stephen flipped the emergency switch off and let the doors open. He spat the bullets out, causing the eight soldiers now waiting for them to stare with varying degrees of disbelief. “Would you like to shoot me again?” He took a step forward and lifted his hoodie and shirt to show them his intact chest. “I can do this all day, really.”

One man turned his gun on the one next to him and shot him in the leg. Another soldier decked the one with the gun and took a bullet in the shoulder for it. Dan’s handiwork, no doubt. At the other end of the line, another soldier shot a different man in the leg.

Stephen reached the group of men and backhanded one of them so hard he spun around. “Shame to ruin my clothes, but hey.” Grabbing two by the collars, he smacked their heads together and flung them in opposite directions. “The things we do for friends.” He threw a punch that sent the last man standing to the floor.

“You’re a goddamned showboater,” Dan snorted. “It’s fun to watch.” He wheeled Bobby and the girl out while Stephen cleared a path for them.

Glancing back over his shoulder, Stephen grinned. “It’s not like any of these guys can—”

A gunshot cut him off. Stephen jerked and twisted, a bullet punching out through his neck. He collapsed in front of the gurney.

The second shot hit Dan in the shoulder, missing his head because he ducked. With no ability to regenerate or deflect anything, Dan dropped to the floor, wheezing in pain.

"Animals, every last one of you," Suit Two snarled. He stood between them and freedom, feet apart and gun held in both hands. "Rabid dogs that need to be put down." Stepping calmly over debris to reach them, he let go of the gun with his left hand to retrieve a syringe from his jacket.

Bobby's heart stopped. That's what it felt like, anyway. Were they still alive? He didn't know, couldn't see either of them. "I got you," Bobby whispered to the girl, then he looked at the suit. The girl turned to look, then buried her face in Bobby's chest again. That gun wasn't going to hurt him, he could feel the swarm building with incoherent rage inside him, but the girl was another story. "I said I was gonna kill you for trying to rape my friend. I meant it."

Suit Two's eyes narrowed, focusing on the girl. She must have looked much younger to his eyes, terrified and huddling for safety. His gun twitched so it pointed more at her than him. "There aren't any children in the program anymore. Which one of you does she belong to?"

"What program? Where's Jasmine? Did you kill Mr. Peterson to set me up?"

Suit Two's nostrils flared and he sneered. "Never mind that. I won't bother trying to injure this time, Mitchell. There's a level of acceptable risk, and we're past it now. Hand over the girl and come quietly or die."

It seemed to Bobby that the suit figured he must still be harmless, since he still laid on the bed. In fairness, he did feel pretty useless right now. The swarm had so much rage, it took every drop of effort he had to hold it back. His dragons hated this man, so much. No matter what, Suit Two would not leave this building alive. Bobby would let them loose already, except Kaitlin said the girl needed to understand, and to see the whole picture. "I don't really like those choices. Is there a third option?"

Suit Two's mouth curled into a disdainful smirk and everything slowed down for Bobby. The gun fired and he saw the bullet spin out of the barrel. He burst into the swarm and let it have its way, so long as it protected the girl. The dragons noted three different innocent people watching him. Stephen got up on his hands and knees, gasping for breath. Dan, pale and bloody, clutched his shoulder.

Three dragons dove at the bullet, all willing to sacrifice themselves to keep the girl safe. One let it rip its wing off, the second bounced off it, and the third threw its body in the way. Their efforts knocked it far enough to the side to hit the bed instead of the terrified girl.

The rest of the swarm went for Suit Two. They pushed Bobby aside while they converged and destroyed him with claws and fangs and fire. Suit Two screamed and shrieked until they tore his throat out. His arms flailed for another half a minute, then he stopped and sagged, held in place by the swarm refusing to let him fall.

When he felt certain the suit had to be dead, Bobby mustered everything he had and forced the swarm to let the corpse go. They stopped and buzzed about for a few seconds, then swooped to the gurney and picked up the three damaged dragons. The corpse of Suit Two collapsed to the floor.

Bobby re-formed standing next to the bed in his jeans and boots, bandages gone. His hands and arms hurt all the way to his neck. He took a deep breath and averted his eyes from the gory pile his swarm made. The air carried the awful stench of fresh and burned meat. This little girl needed to get away from that.

Stephen breathed deeply and stood up. He looked at the girl, who watched his neck heal over with her mouth hanging open. "We're not full of sunshine and daises, but we aren't sadistic monsters, either."

Bobby saw her gulp and nod. He gritted his teeth and picked her up. He'd hefted appliances heavier than her on his own, though not when he felt this awful. "Don't you look at that thing on the floor. I'm gonna give you to one of these folks who works here. Soon as you can, you go find your Momma and tell her all about what you saw."

She clung to him, wrapping her legs around his waist. "He tried to shoot me," she breathed.

He grunted and stepped over debris to reach a side room with awe-struck people hiding inside it. "I think it was more about me, but yeah."

"You saved me." She kissed him on the cheek when he set her down and waved as he backed out. Both things taken together went a long way towards making him feel better about this whole episode.

"You have a fan," Dan croaked out from the floor.

"I thought I was supposed to save the girl. I'm the vampire, I should get the girl." Stephen smirked as he bent to help Dan.

Bobby rolled his eyes and returned the girl's wave. Part of him wanted to ask her name. The rest noticed people peering timidly out through doorways. Choosing one at random, he pointed to a man who stared up at him with his hands up in surrender. "More of these suit-wearing guys are going to show up here on our trail. You tell 'em something for me," he said, watching the man nod and gulp. "They mess with one of us, they mess with all of us. We're coming for the rest of ours, and we ain't playing around."

Stephen pulled Dan to his feet and supported him to he could walk. Bobby turned and strode out through the front door, holding it open for them. This part had no real plan. Everyone needed to get back to the van without getting caught, killed, or followed. Back in his body, with the pleasantly warm midday sun shining down on him and all three of those suits dead, he felt invincible. How hard could it really be to get out of a military base?

Surveying the chaos, he sighed. Lizzie had gone hog wild. The entire end of the base they came in through burned. She'd set a handful of vehicles on fire, and one hangar had gotten engulfed. Multiple types of trucks circled in that area, with more still heading that way. Lines of soldiers streamed that way, and Bobby thought maybe they ought to have had her set the distraction up on the other side of the base.

Jets firing up their engines momentarily drowned out the gunfire filling the air. That whoosh and boom sounded more likely to from a rocket launcher than Lizzie. She'd started a small war, one they needed to get out of before somebody got the bright idea to use satellites for spot-targeting them with smart bombs or space lasers, or whatever they had. "Stephen, you need to get Dan outta here. I'll see if I can get the others going."

"I suggest no one tells Lizzie I been shot so long as it can be avoided." Dan panted, dark circles forming under his eyes. Sweat beaded on his forehead, and his one arm dangled, useless.

Agreeing completely, Bobby nodded. Lizzie did all this just to have fun. He shuddered to imagine what she could do if when she got angry. "Yeah, you just go straight for the van. Get it started up and ready to move." Because it would be faster and safer, he burst into the swarm and headed for the center of the mayhem. That's where Lizzie would be, and everyone else should be nearby.

Chapter 19

From his new vantage point, Bobby saw Stephen carrying Dan out to and over the fence. Sunlight glinting on metal pointed him at Jayce. Several squads of soldiers hoofed it towards him. These Air Force folks probably never saw anything like this before, and he felt sorry for them. Screaming distracted him. Nowhere near Jayce, an exploding fireball threw three soldiers for distance. One might have been lucky enough to survive.

The werewolf ran out and pounced on that soldier, ripping him in half. Bobby revised his opinion of the definition of 'lucky'. Another soldier on the run emptied his weapon at the werewolf. Although he failed to hit Matthew in the chaos, the soldier got his attention.

Jayce could take care of himself. Matthew needed to be lured out, now. The swarm dove with all the speed his dragons could muster. He watched in horror as Matthew, to quick for Bobby to prevent it, pounced on the shooter and tore his arms off. The swarm surged in and buzzed around his head, belching fire out to singe his fur and tugging on his ears. Matthew swatted at them, catching and crunching four.

Rage bubbled up in the swarm, pushing him away. The

dragons wanted to deal with this, their way. Bobby held them off. Matthew needed help, not death. No matter what he did, no matter how low he sank, he still deserved a chance to figure out how to control this side of himself. Everyone else got that small favor. It looked like Matthew left the building when he sprouted fur. So did Bobby, when the swarm got angry. How could he look himself in the mirror if he judged Matthew for something he'd done himself?

He had to flee. The swarm flowed off the werewolf and towards the fence, taunting Matthew by staying just out of reach. Movement distracted him, so Bobby sent a handful into his face to goad him. Another dragon got crunched. The rest of that group hauled it out of reach with them, devouring it on the way.

At the chain-link fence, the dragons streamed through. Matthew stopped. Too many targets on his side of the fence gave him no incentive to try to climb out and chase the swarm down. Bobby re-formed and clenched his jaw against the pain. "C'mon, buddy, I ain't leaving you behind, no matter how many of my dragons you swat." God, he hurt worse than he had before. At this point, his arms hurt from one end to the other, and his feet ached up to his knees. If he kept going, he'd be a walking ball of agony in no time flat.

Matthew roared at him, grabbing the fence and shaking it violently. Right now, they needed Stephen or Jayce. Either of them could take what Matthew could dish out. Bobby wanted to be able to, but he couldn't, not even at his best. If he stayed here and kept trying to pull Matthew out, he'd only succeed in getting himself killed. Considering this operation was entirely about rescuing him, that would be pretty rude, not to mention counterproductive.

Getting away from Matthew became his top priority. He whisked out into the swarm again and, steering clear of the angry werewolf, poured back through the fence. Despite worries about what Matthew would manage to do in his absence, Bobby streamed away to find Jayce. Fortunately, that turned out to be easy. There he stood, glinting in the sunshine next to with Lizzie, Andrea, and Alice. Ice formed a high wall around them in a horseshoe shape with Jayce at the mouth. Alice had to be working hard to maintain it against all the incoming gunfire, and her skin had turned blue again.

Landing and re-forming in their midst he immediately punched Jayce good-naturedly in the arm. "Hey, you can retreat now. Somebody's gotta get Matthew, though. I tried, but my way ain't working."

"Good to know. Alice, you shield them out. Andrea, set up an obstacle course for anyone following you. Lizzie, time to stop and run for the van. I'll go get Matthew. If I'm not back before you see Stephen, send him to help." He took off in the direction Bobby pointed, running at full speed.

Bobby breathed a sigh of relief at his words. Jayce not only accepted responsibility for the werewolf problem without argument, he also chose not to punch him back with that big metal fist. Lizzie pouted, of course. Alice pushed a wall of ice out around them and forced Lizzie and Andrea to rush for the fence. Irregular craters blew out with a shower of dust in their wake, which he assumed to be Andrea's power at work. These women truly terrified him.

"I should mention I saw fighter planes taking off. Also, I'm going swarm." Pain went away for the swarm. He might have considered that weird, except everything else about his power fit that definition, too. One more thing hardly rated notice.

"Oh!" Lizzie squealed with glee. "I've never blown up a plane before."

"And you're not going to start now," Andrea said, her voice strained by concentration. "We're trying not to kill people, remember?"

Lizzie pouted. "It would just be one guy."

"That really doesn't make it okay."

"Spoilsport." Lizzie reminded him of a kid called in from the playground by her momma. "Maybe I should just go off on my own."

"Go ahead. Just keep in mind you're not immune to bullets and Dan is back at the van now."

Lizzie heaved a sigh Bobby considered meoldramatic. How in heckbiscuits had she managed to make it this long without getting herself killed or thrown in jail? She probably had one of those stories that winds up in a crime show, telling the woeful tale of how a rotten childhood can turn a body into a monster. Maybe someday, he'd be forced to listen to it.

Bobby flew along with the girls, staying low to avoid catching lead. The dragons noticed something coming from the side and he focused in that direction to see a missile streaking in ahead of a jet. Flabbergasted, he directed the dragons around Andrea to roar and point as a group. She could stop it. Right? After everything that happened so far, getting obliterated by a missile would be unfair.

Andrea flung her hand out and grimaced with effort. It closed in fast, then appeared to hit a wall that reduced it to find dust. "Christ on a cross," she breathed. "I can't do that too many times."

"Guys, I'm getting tired." Alice slurred words, and she panted and stumbled. "I can't keep this up forever."

"There's the fence!" Lizzie sprinted for it, sending a huge ball of fire out in front of her. Immune to its effect, she plunged in and out of sight.

"I really wish she'd stop doing that." Andrea blasted another hole in the ground behind them, then scanned the skies.

Bobby re-formed next to Alice and grabbed her arm. She radiated enough cold to make it a special form of torture. He still tossed her arm over his shoulders. "Lean on me, Alice, I got you." He grunted in both pain and surprise when she collapsed onto him.

Scooping her up into his arms, he gritted his teeth and ran as fast as he could manage.

Andrea's eyes widened as she ran along with him. "I can't disintegrate everything coming at us. Just so you know." When a bullet whizzed between them, she glanced back and squeaked.

"Great." Adrenaline helped Bobby push past the pain to get this done. The flames had died down, so they plunged through the gap in the fence together.

Alice passed out in his arms and the ice stopped flowing. Her limp arm fell forward, and her body shifted. It knocked him off balance and he pitched forward. Curling around her protectively, he cried out at the agony of hitting the ground and rolling. More dust hit them, attesting to Andrea sticking close enough to help.

Part of him wanted to lie down and die rather than keep going. Glancing the way they'd come, he saw the soldiers hanging back. They stopped shooting, taking up defensive positions a few dozen feet inside the fence. Maybe they figured out their tactics didn't work. Took them long enough. "Help Alice," he grunted at Andrea.

"Not leaving you behind, dumbass, that's how we got into this mess in the first place." Andrea grabbed the waist of his jeans in back and hauled him to his feet.

"Jesus, woman," he growled.

She ignored him and took Alice by the wrists, dragging her across the grass to the street.

Her actions gave him what he needed to keep going, which meant he had nothing to complain about. He caught up and grabbed Alice's ankles to suspend her between them. Something about those soldiers staying back bugged him, niggling at the back of his mind. It could be they'd decided to defend against Matthew on his way out, he supposed.

Then again, they had the planes go past once already. He looked up and saw dots in the sky. With the missiles having failed already, possibly twice, they'd probably try something else. "Fighter jets have regular big guns, right?"

Andrea's mouth fell open, her eyes wide with panic. She gulped and nodded. "I don't think I can stop those. I have to target things specifically, that's why bullets are hard."

"How in heckbiscuits are we gonna get outta here? I mean, even once we reach the van." The dark blur of Stephen zoomed over the fence and into the base. That meant Lizzie had reached the van, which meant she knew about Dan. Would she fawn over him, or come for the group? Within a second of the thought crossing his mind, the van screamed around the corner and screeched to a stop in front of them. Lizzie at the wheel sounded pretty scary to him. He had no ability to drive right now, though, and maybe crazy would turn out to be the best way out of this.

At the end of the street, two puffs of dirt and debris plumed into the air. Bobby and Andrea dove for the van and threw Alice into the back seat. More pairs of plumes marched up the street to greet them. Lizzie slammed on the gas and launched the van sideways, out of the strafing line, then managed to get the vehicle turned around. She floored it towards the plane, which seemed crazy until they screamed down the next street without getting shot up.

Flanked by houses, Bobby thought they might be safe for the moment. If those planes were willing to strafe through the houses here, they had bigger problems than he thought. Peering out the back window, he saw no more plumes, and figured the planes must have diverted to go after Jayce, Stephen, and Matthew.

"We need radios," Bobby croaked, in fresh agony. When the van had turned, he, Andrea, and Alice had all tumbled around, and now both lay on top of him.

Andrea levered herself up and into the front passenger seat. She buckled herself in. "Probably not, but I bet they noticed the color."

"Stop someplace and I'll send a dragon to show the guys the way to us." He shoved Alice off himself, wishing he could protect her from whatever else Lizzie might do. At the moment, he could barely protect himself. The swarm could get him up into a seat. It couldn't help him get Alice into one. Besides, they refused to touch her skin when it went frosty blue. He didn't like that either, but could suck it up if he had to. Raising himself up on his arms made him whimper.

Lizzie slammed on the brakes, throwing him into the front seats and pulling a sharp, short scream out of him. He heard Dan hiss in pain from the cargo area in the back, too. "Don't do that again, baby, it really hurt." He sounded like heckbiscuits, and they had eight hours of driving ahead of them.

"Dan," Bobby groaned, "you get bandaged up yet?"

"Not really."

"Great." He gave up trying to move. "We're gonna have to stop someplace and get him some genuine medical attention. 'Less one of you ladies has some experience pulling bullets outta shoulders."

"I could try?" Andrea looked back and patted Bobby's arm, which made him wince. "I don't *think* I can disintegrate living matter."

The van had stopped moving. Bobby said he'd do something. It took him another second, then he popped off a dragon and sent it out the window Lizzie lowered. He sent it on a mission to find Stephen and lead him back to the van, wherever it wound up. "We can't go far, on account of Jayce. He'll have to run to catch up. Maybe drive around the neighborhood some? Park in a driveway?"

"No offense, Andrea, but I don't want to be your guinea pig

only to have my shoulder disintegrated."

"None taken, and I don't want that, either."

"Is it still in there? You sure about that?"

"Yeah." Dan groaned as Lizzie hit the gas again. "It didn't come out the other side."

Bobby groaned, too. They drove around, both men making pained protest every time Lizzie turned a corner. As he lay there, trying to brace without hurting himself, something occurred to Bobby. He hated it, but a solution was a solution, and if he turned his nose up at weird, he'd be in a world of confusion. "You think it might be small enough for one of my dragons to crawl in?"

A few seconds of silence passed before Andrea finally said, "Ew."

"Maybe?" Dan sounded more hoarse and less clear.

"Nothing for it but to try." Deciding not to worry about the state of his body, Bobby popped ten dragons off and chose one to send his mind into. The small swarm zipped to where Dan, ashen and panting, lay on the floor of the van with one hand barely holding a wad of bloody cloth to his shoulder.

"This is gonna hurt, isn't it." His hand shook as he pulled the cloth away, revealing a ragged hole in his flesh. Blood glurped out in time with his heartbeat.

Bobby felt confident the answer would be 'yes'. The dragons converged on Dan's shoulder. Neither Bobby nor the dragons wanted to do this. What if he made things worse? He could cause more problems than he solved. He could kill Dan by accident. One dragon chirped, and he agreed they either had to do it or give up and figure something else out.

Five dragons gripped the sides of the wound and forced it open, eliciting a whimper from Dan. Two watched, and the last two grabbed a corner of the cloth and daubed at the blood. Bobby's dragon folded its wings down flat and crept into the injury. Warm and squishy, the hole felt gross. Bobby and the dragon both wanted to get this over with as fast as possible.

Dan's whimpers turned into screams. The dragons didn't like that at all, and Bobby pushed his to wriggle faster. He found the bullet lodged in a bone and had to grab and yank, yank, yank to pop it out, making Dan shriek. Worse, it had mushroomed enough to cause more damage on the way out.

If he had teeth, he'd have gritted them. Bobby maneuvered around the bullet, knowing it made things worse, and pushed the bullet as hard as he could. Another dragon reached in and grabbed from the other side. Together, they tore the bullet out. Dan had gone past the point of screaming, now shaking so hard his teeth rattled and his whimpers sounded like a tiny helicopter rotor. When Bobby pushed out of the wound, awash in fresh blood, he saw Matthew's face looming over him.

"That's freaky." Haggard and wiped out, Matthew reached down and put pressure on the wound, using the already sacrificed wad of cloth. "Anybody got a needle and thread? Some alcohol? I won't lie, Dan, whatever we do, it's going to hurt, at least as much as that did."

Bobby saw that Dan had a pen in his mouth, keeping his teeth apart. Those two dragons thought to get that. The ten of them lifted out of the way, his work there done. On their flight back to his body, they bathed each other with fire, burning the blood off. He left them to that, returning to his body now sitting upright in a seat. Jayce stretched the seat belt across him and clicked it. Stephen sat between the two front seats, murmuring to Lizzie, probably keeping her calm while Dan made all that noise.

"Welcome back." Jayce sat back and the metallic sheen faded from his skin.

"Yeah, you, too." Bobby lifted his missing fingers to rub his face. The dragons arrived and re- formed them.

"I have some dental floss in my purse," Andrea offered. She rifled through the glove compartment. "There's duct tape, and a wad of napkins."

"He really needs actual medical care," Matthew said, shaking his head. "I only have basic first aid training."

"Can't." Bobby winced as the van went over a bump. "What d'you need to do the best job you can?"

"The duct tape should work well enough, but I'll need something to clean the wound. If we can stop at a drugstore, we can get rubbing alcohol and gauze."

"Does anyone have any money?" Bobby's question got him a couple of head shakes.

Stephen shrugged. "I have money, but it's for gas."

"Well, heckbiscuits, we can push the van if we gotta. Lizzie, you see a drugstore, you stop. Hey, did anybody think to swap out the van's plates yet?"

"No, but it's a good idea, and we can do that when we stop." Stephen pointed to a place, then directed Lizzie to a place to park. It put them out of obvious sight so they could swap the plates and still not have to walk far to get into the store. The second she shut the engine off, Lizzie darted out with tear streaks down her cheeks and went to Dan. Stephen nodded for Andrea to drive while Jayce headed into the store. "Bobby, give me a hand."

Although he knew what Stephen meant, he let his hand fall into dragons and sent that group out with the vampire. More conventional assistance required him to be less chewed up and spit out.

Stephen snorted. "Smartass."

"Starving smartass," Bobby corrected.

Andrea grabbed the cooler and shoved it at Bobby. "Take whatever you want. Andrew packed plenty." She watched him wince and open it. Without paying much attention to the contents, he grabbed a sandwich and stuffed it into his face. "It's nice to meet you, Bobby. Don't take this wrong, but I hope you were worth it."

His mouth full already, he glanced around the car. Matthew and Lizzie both tended to Dan. Alice lay slumped on the other seat. These people had all gone to bat for him, and most of them almost died, himself included. "Yeah." He swallowed the bite and sighed. "Me, too. There any leads on Jasmine or the others?"

"Not yet, no. That name you and Stephen got, we can't find him, either. It's like he doesn't exist. His son, too. Both of them are ghosts."

The sandwich tasted like sawdust. Bobby still chewed mechanically, but they'd hit a dead end. "We'll figure something out." Inside, he fretted over what kind of torture Jasmine had to be enduring right now. With what he knew they'd done to him and Ai, it made his stomach churn.

"Eleven of us were taken, everyone else is accounted for. There was some talk of going back to the site you woke up in, but Sam found a news blurb saying it was burned to the ground, two days after you escaped."

Later, when he might care more, he'd ask who Sam was. "Not a big shock, that."

"Whoever 'they' are, they're pretty good at cleaning up after themselves."

Bobby nodded, forcing himself to take another bite. "We just weren't what they expected."

"Best guess is you have a higher metabolism than they could have predicted. Stephen says you eat like a horse, and the times you've been dosed, it didn't affect you very long."

His mouth full, Bobby grunted. He turned to stare out the window, not wanting to hear any more bad news. If he could sleep on the way home, that would be a small mercy. If the place could actually be a home for him, that'd be a greater one.

Chapter 20

Either they somehow missed the roadblocks or checkpoints, or none were set up. Bobby dozed off early in the ride. He woke in the dark, finding the van quiet and Stephen driving. He felt much better for having slept, with the pain in his arms and legs much more manageable. Hungry again, he rummaged through the cooler for more food and bolted it. Filling his belly improved his mood more and he unbuckled to roll forward and perch between the front seats.

"How much farther?"

"We're almost there, maybe fifteen minutes."

Bobby nodded and looked up through the front windshield at the stars. "Thanks. For coming after me. And bringing food."

Stephen glanced down at him, smirking. "It didn't seem possible they would be feeding you as much as you can pack away."

"Not even close," Bobby confirmed, a grin forming, then fading away. "However it works out, I'm going when we find out where Jasmine is."

Stephen nodded. "So am I, and I expect Jayce and Andrea will want to, also."

"Means while the brains are working on it, we ought to train together."

"Good idea. We'll start tomorrow. Most of us have barely discovered what we can really do."

Reaching up, Bobby scratched at his chin, reminding himself he had plenty of beard. The act hurt his fingers, so he stopped. "Man, I ain't had a shower in…I don't even know how long."

"There's hot water at the farm." Stephen grinned. "I'm sure Lily will be happy to help you shave."

Bobby coughed and looked away. He and Lily hadn't even talked much yet. "Shut up."

Stephen chuckled. It sounded like he suppressed a much louder belly laugh. "Would you like a lecture about safe sex?"

"From a vampire?" Bobby snorted. Part of him wanted to punch Stephen in the face for talking that way about Lily. He told it to shut up. "No, I think I got it covered, thanks."

Covering his mouth, Stephen shook with the need to laugh. A few minutes later, he pointed at a red reflector on the side of the road. "There's our turn."

The rest of the van woke up when they turned down the bumpy, tree-lined dirt road. Bobby had every intention of helping to carry Dan or Alice inside, but Stephen scooped Dan up effortlessly and Jayce had no trouble picking Alice up. Matthew gave Lizzie his shoulder to lean on, which she only took because she'd just woken up. Andrea didn't need or want help, either.

Someone must have heard the van, because the door opened when Jayce got to it. Ai held it open for everyone to troop through. When she saw Bobby, the last of the short parade, she gave him a conflicted, pained smile. "I'm glad you're okay," she said softly.

Well heckbiscuits, this had all kinds of awkward all over it. What was he supposed to say? 'Even though you left me behind, I still managed alright, except I had to be rescued on account I couldn't escape on my own. By the way, I got shot twice.' He had no reason to get into it right now. Unable to come up with anything else, Bobby shrugged. "Yeah, me too, for you."

She didn't meet his eyes and shut the door behind him. "Um, are you tired? Hungry?"

"I dunno." He shrugged again, watching the parade keep going deeper into the house. When he'd been here in the dragon, he hadn't paid much attention to the layout. Even if he had, no one showed him to whatever he'd use for a bed. "Guess I ought to try to get some sl—"

"Bobby!" Lily ran into him and wrapped her arms around him. "You're here, you're safe."

He grunted in surprise and pain. "Yeah." His arms slid around her to return the hug, and it felt damned good. He noticed Ai scuttle away and closed his eyes with a sigh. Lily's body pressed close to his bare chest, warm and soft, and wiped away all the pain and confusion and distraction. If he could stay like this for a while, he'd be a happy man.

The second she shifted, it broke the spell and he let her go. She stepped away and tucked some hair behind an ear, looking at the floor. "Sebastian will be really happy to see you in the morning. He keeps asking about you, even more since your dragon showed up yesterday."

"Oh. I like him, too." It almost sounded like she meant the boy liked him and she didn't. That confused him, because her hug felt welcoming enough. "Uh, I kinda need to rest and heal up. If'n he's gonna expect me to wrassle with him, I mean. I ain't in no right shape for that just now."

Okay, here, I'll show you to your room." She tossed a thumb over her shoulder and smiled at him, bright enough to melt him into a puddle. "It's just down the hall from ours. They're small, but it's a bed and a roof."

Bobby nodded and followed her, watching her hips sway. He should've kissed her. She stood there, in his arms, and he let the moment slip by. All kinds of excuses welled up in his head. Only one of them mattered: he couldn't force himself to piss on her husband's memory. She'd be ready to move on when she decided to be ready to move on. He had no right to force it.

"This is it." She stopped and pointed into a tiny room. It had enough space for the twin bed already inside it, and not much else. Good thing he had almost no clothes. "I guess I'll make sure Sebastian doesn't run in and wake you up."

"I'd appreciate that, thanks." He stood in the doorway and stared at the bed. In his head, he turned, pulled her close again and kissed her.

She patted his arm, forcing him to bite back a tiny yelp and disrupting his ideas. "Good night, Bobby. Welcome home." She walked away.

"Yeah. Night." Stepping inside the room, he rubbed his arm and shut the door. In the van, he thought he still needed to sleep. Here, having fumbled that with Lily, he needed something else entirely. He couldn't get it by wandering around the house or out in the dark. Sitting on the edge of the bed, he unlaced his boots and considered running himself through a shower.

Soon, they'd find something, some kind of lead on Jasmine. He'd be the first one out the door. Not because he wanted to spend time away from Lily. Now that he had those experiences to reflect on, he thought he could do this stuff. Yes, he'd gotten captured. He'd been naïve. He knew better now.

He'd learned his lessons and itched to take the test. As soon as he knew where to find it, he would, and he'd finally get a grade worth showing his Momma.

INTERLUDE AT THE FARM

A Night On the Town

Bobby

The warm afternoon shade under a cluster of tall pine trees reminded Bobby of home. This time of year, he'd sit on the front porch, sipping a cold beer and watching the shadow of his small house in the Atlanta suburbs creep across the brown grass and cracked sidewalk. His momma would come home from work, tired but still smiling after her walk from the bus stop, and lie down on the couch under the ceiling fan.

He wanted to take Lily there, to meet his momma. They'd get along. Momma would be charmed by Lily's little boy, Sebastian. They'd cook together, or do whatever else women did. He only had to get up the gumption to say something to Lily. He took a drink of his beer, wishing he didn't have to compete with the memory of her dead husband.

Something sharp struck the back of his head. From the neck up, he instinctively burst into silver dragons, each the size of a quarter, to absorb the impact and protect him from harm. His hand still held his beer, splashing it over the little dragons, the weirdly precise end of his neck, and the front of his shirt.

Before he could think too hard about whether his body would continue to act without his brain, Bobby ordered the dragons to re-form his head. They merged into his flesh again and he hopped out of his beach chair to the sound of Matthew laughing in the next chair over.

Bobby glared behind them at Stephen, the tall vampire. "Man, what in heckbiscuits you do that for? " Bobby's Georgia drawl draped over the words, heavy and thick.

"To see what would happen." Stephen's icy blue eyes, the same as everyone else's around here, crinkled at their canted corners. He floated six inches off the ground as he approached, but still moved his body as if he walked.

"What happened is you spilled beer. That ain't right. Wasting beer is criminal."

"Bah. You aren't even old enough to drink anyway." Stephen snatched the bottle away from Bobby and held it up. "Ought to report you for contributing to the delinquency of a minor, Rover."

Matthew snorted and brushed droplets of beer off his Marine Corps desert camouflage pants. "He's not a minor, he's nineteen."

"Close enough."

Bobby huffed, knowing Stephen was bored. "Whatever. Gimme the beer back."

Stephen handed the bottle back and adjusted the hood of his sweatshirt. "What are you guys doing over here, anyway? All the work is happening inside the house." He pointed at the nearby rundown farmhouse undergoing renovations so it could be used as their base. It sat in the middle of nowhere, eastern Colorado, where they hoped no one else would ever find it.

"I needed a break," Matthew said, his amusement fading. "If I let myself get too exhausted, I can't hold the wolf back. It's better for everyone if I don't push too hard."

Bobby ignored the question, but Stephen stared at him so hard he thought the vampire might develop laser vision to burn holes in him. He sighed and wished he could get away with escaping under the pretense of changing his shirt. "I just needed a break is all."

"Of course." Stephen picked up the rock he'd thrown at Bobby and tossed it into the woods. His superhuman strength sent it sailing into the distance. "I'm sure it has nothing at all to do with a certain pair of shapely hips attached to a certain—"

"Hey now," Bobby spat. "Don't you be talking about Lily like that."

Stephen grinned, dark and mischievous. "Oh, were we talking about Lily?"

Bobby scowled and considered tossing his beer at Stephen's pasty white face. "Shut up."

"Ease off," Matthew said with a dismissive wave.

"Damn, both of you need to lighten up." Stephen let his feet touch the ground and gazed off into the distance. "I'm hungry and none of the woman here will let me tap a pint. I'm going out to find food tonight. Come along for the ride. We can make a night of it."

Bobby looked to Matthew, who shrugged. "Sure, I guess. Ain't got nothing better to do."

Hours later, after the sun set, the trio met in the woods and took off. Bobby's dragon swarm re- formed his body in a dark alley after a half-hour flight. Stephen landed beside him. Matthew, who'd ridden Stephen piggyback, jumped to the ground, his combat boots splashing unknown liquid from a suspicious puddle onto Bobby's jeans and sneakers.

Bobby grimaced and shook his leg, hoping the stuff didn't stain. He only had two pairs of jeans and one pair of shoes. Getting new clothes after fleeing terrorism charges a few weeks ago had proved challenging with his face plastered all over the news.

Matthew stepped to the mouth of the alley and patted his hip where a gun holster would normally sit. He spat a curse and took a deep breath. "I'm calm," he murmured. "I'm fine. God in Heaven, let me not kill anyone tonight."

"Relax, Fluffy," Stephen said with a smirk, his dark eyes glittering in the light of a distant streetlamp. "If anybody's going to accidentally kill someone tonight, it's much more likely to be me."

"Ain't nobody needs to be killing nobody," Bobby said. "Don't joke about that." He stood at the mouth of the alley, checking the street. "Ain't right."

"Listen to the Voice of Morality, Matthew. He knows what's right."

"Shut up," Bobby snapped. "We done came here to have a good time."

"And by God," Stephen said with his right hand raised, "we will do so. Hey, did you hear that? I said 'God' and didn't burst into flames."

Matthew shoved him, though nothing happened. Without the superhuman strength granted by his werewolf shape, he couldn't budge the floating vampire. "That's because you're not a real vampire, dumbass. You're a science experiment gone wrong."

"That hurts, Spot. Right here in the feels." Stephen tapped his sternum. "C'mon, guys, let's find some fresh blood." He strode out of the alley with a swagger that would have been more impressive had he been wearing a trenchcoat or cloak.

Bobby stuffed his hands in his pockets and followed Stephen. They walked past a boarded-up video store and a man lying in the gutter. This already felt like a bad idea waiting to get worse. All three of them had government markers on their hides and they decided to go out for a night on the town? He tried and failed to remember why he'd agreed to do something this stupid.

Matthew kept pace beside him, his hands in the pockets of his Marines desert fatigues. "We could've picked a better part of town."

Scantily clad women in high heels tottered up and down the street. Garbage cans overflowed. Iron bars covered every window and garish neon advertised sex, drugs, and rock n' roll. Bobby avoided making eye contact with anyone loitering near them. He had no idea what kind of guy trolled a shady street like this looking for hookers, but they must come because this street had plenty of them.

Stephen sniffed the air as he pretended to walk. He passed several women before heading straight for a young one in a pink miniskirt with bleached blonde hair up in a peacock spray Bobby thought had gone out of style before he was born. Heavy makeup reminded him of the drama club girls getting ready for a show back in high school.

Bobby stopped and tried not to look like he came to pay for sex, though he didn't quite know how to do that. He saw Matthew sigh and cross his arms over his chest. The man did a good job of projecting impatience. His approach wouldn't work for Bobby, though.

The girl giggled at something Stephen murmured into her ear. Wrapping an arm around her waist, Stephen turned the girl away from the street and tucked a twenty dollar bill down the front of her too-tight shirt.

"Hey baby, you looking for a date?"

"No," Matthew said with cool stare. "He's not."

"How about you, sugar? Military discount."

Bobby felt dirty just listening to her. "Man, I don't need this." He saw Stephen leading the girl around the corner of the convenience store they all loitered in front of. His belly rumbled and he thought about bursting into dragons to go find a snack. That would mean leaving Matthew behind with Stephen, which would be a jerk move.

"You know what I do need?" He asked the girl. "Something to eat. There anyplace with decent, cheap food around here?"

The girl huffed at him. "Amy's Diner, a few blocks up."

Headlights strafed over them, making everyone turn away, hiding their faces from any cops in the area. Bobby followed suit. So did Matthew. They drifted past the store with a silent agreement to move slowly enough so Stephen could catch up when he finished with the girl.

Stephen's hissing voice buzzed in Bobby's ear. "Bobby, Matthew, c'mere."

Bobby rolled his eyes, figuring the vampire had a cheap joke he wanted to play. Matthew shrugged and gestured for him to go first. They reached the corner and found the girl limp in Stephen's arms. A dribble of blood ran down his chin.

"I think I killed her," he whispered in a panic.

"Heckbiscuits," Bobby spat. "I told you not to joke about that."

Matthew helped Stephen lower her to the ground and held a hand in front of her mouth and nose. "No, she's still breathing. You drained her unconscious, you idiot."

"Kimmy, you okay back there?" a woman asked.

Bobby gulped. They needed attention like they needed extra holes in their heads. "Yes, ma'am, she's fine."

The woman wobbled toward them, her stiletto heels catching on the broken asphalt of the weed-infested parking lot. "She can tell me herself then. Kimmy?"

"Get her out of here," Matthew growled. "Take her to a damned hospital before she really does die."

The incoming streetwalker screamed.

Bobby gulped. "Ssh! It ain't nothing." He reached for her.

She stumbled back. Her heel caught and she fell. "You killed Kimmy!"

Matthew stepped toward the streetwalker, hands held out to try to calm her down. "I swear she's not dead."

"She's only unconscious," Stephen said. "It was an accident."

The woman's eyes went wide at the sight of Stephen. "Is that…blood? On…on your…were you *drinking her blood*?"

Bobby winced as she shouted the last three words. "We gotta get outta here."

Stephen tossed the girl over his shoulder and flew down the alley, not bothering to pretend to run. Matthew swore and sprinted after him. Bobby gulped. He faced a dozen angry hookers and had no idea what to do about it. If these people got the cops riled up, the government agents chasing them might notice a report about a guy drinking blood. They'd be able to narrow down the search for the whole group to this part of the country. After that, finding their base would only be a matter of time.

He held up his hands. "It ain't like what it looks."

"Kimmy is one of my girls," a big man in a dark coat said. He cracked his knuckles and flexed his thick biceps. "Bring her back."

Bobby knew a fight brewing when someone slapped him in the face with one. He took a step back. His dragons could kill people. They'd do it if someone riled him up enough, no matter what he wanted. "I don't want no trouble."

The man punched him in the face. Bobby's head exploded into the dragons and the rest of his body burst into the swarm. Hundreds of tiny dragons swirled, light glinting off their silver skin. Half the crowd screamed while the other half bolted.

His mind floating in the middle of the swarm, Bobby put

every bit of effort he could into pulling the dragons away so no one got hurt. Through their tiny eyes, he saw Matthew abort a charge into the fray. He beckoned for the dragons to follow him and darted up the alley again.

At the next street, Matthew ducked around the front of a bowling alley to lean against the wall. "Christ, Bobby. What were you thinking? Stephen's on the roof."

Bobby flew the swarm up to Stephen and re-formed his body next to the vampire patting the girl's cheek. "Shouldn't you get her to an emergency room already?"

"Sure. I'll just fly over, drop into the front door, and walk away. What could possibly go wrong?" Stephen sighed. "I didn't mean to take this much from her. She just tasted so good and I was so hungry."

"You can stop saying creepy things like that right now."

"I drink blood," Stephen intoned like he'd practiced explaining this a hundred times. "I need it to live. It's not my fault."

Bobby rubbed his face and touched the girl's cheek. "She looks awful young."

"Back off," Matthew snapped, still down on the street. "She's not dead. He took her to the hospital."

"I don't see no car pulling away," the big man said. "You rich white boys think you can just come down here and kill these girls because we won't go to the cops? You got the wrong bunch, white bread."

"I said back off," Matthew snarled.

"She was the only one that smelled healthy and clean," Stephen muttered.

"Again with the creepy." Bobby noticed the small purse across her body and unzipped it, checking for her ID.

"The real one is probably in a side pocket."

"How in heckbiscuits you know that?"

"Do you honestly believe this is the first time I've hired a hooker to drink blood?"

Bobby stared at him. A man's scream cut the silence. They left the girl behind and dashed to the roof's edge. Below, they saw Matthew, now in his terrifying nine-foot werewolf shape complete with thick claws and yellowed fangs, throw his furry head back and howl. The big man bolted back up the alley.

Stephen spat a curse and jumped off the building. Bobby wondered how this night could get worse. He watched the vampire snag the werewolf's arm and distract him from his fleeing prey. Matthew flung Stephen aside, throwing him across the street. Unable to recover and prevent it, Stephen slammed into the bars over a storefront window, denting them and cracking the glass behind.

Bobby smacked his forehead, now knowing how it could get worse. Those two would be at it until Matthew wore down enough to get control over himself and change back. He sighed and hoped they got away before cops showed up. Turning away from the spectacle, he saw the girl, still lying on the roof. Someone had to get her to safety, and the roof didn't count.

He checked her purse again and found a driver's license for an eighteen year old woman. In the side pouch, he found a folded note with a different name and a phone number.

"I guess Beth must be your real name." He brushed her cheek and tried not to listen to the snarling, hissing, and smashing on the street below. Stephen's twenty dollar bill had fallen to the roof. He picked it up and tucked it into her purse. Poor girl deserved at least that much. If he had a phone, he'd call the number and tell them she was okay.

Flashing red and blue lights strobed across her skin and Bobby cringed. Somehow, he, Stephen, and Matthew had to get out of here and take care of this girl without the cops reporting that dragons, a vampire, and a werewolf had terrorized the city. Proving Beth still lived might help, and it might distract the cops from the fight moving up the street. At least Stephen had the sense to goad Matthew out of the area instead of deeper into it.

Bobby's body dissolved into dragons and the entire swarm wriggled underneath Beth's body. They all flew up at once, lifting her into the air. He didn't want to be seen as dragons, so he had the swarm carry her to the ground at the end of the alley, then he re-formed and picked her up. She seemed so light and fragile as he carried her back to the convenience store.

"Stop where you are!"

Light shone in Bobby's face, blinding him. He squinted and stopped. "Hi there," he said, trying to sound harmless. "I think—"

"He's the one that's made of flying metal!"

"I saw it too!"

"Quiet!" a man snapped. "Is the girl okay?"

Bobby took another step. "She's unconscious."

"The vampire sucked her blood out!"

"C'mon, lady, really? Ain't no such thing as vampires. I think she maybe needs to go to a hospital, though." He breathed a sigh of relief when the light dropped from his face to the girl.

The owner of the flashlight, a uniformed police officer, approached Bobby. "These people seem to think you and two friends tried to abduct this girl."

"They did!"

"Naw." Bobby ducked his head, hoping the cop would fall for the guilty-but-not routine his momma learned to see through years ago. "Shoot, my friend done, well, you know, he shouldn't oughta done nothing, but he, you know, did, and then she passed out. He didn't even do nothing, but he panicked and run off anyway. I figured we shouldn't oughta leave her lying on the ground."

The cop held up a hand and Bobby knew he'd at least confused the man enough to have to think things through. "Just set the girl down. No sudden moves."

"Here? Ain't there a better place? More comfy-like?"

"There is fine." He touched the radio clipped to his shirt and called for an ambulance.

As he bent to lay Beth on the cracked asphalt, Bobby noticed the crowd dispersing. With an ambulance coming in, they probably expected more cops to show up. Bobby didn't want to be here for that either. He laid her on the ground as gently as he could, taking care with her head. Then he stepped back with his hands up.

"C'mere, kid," the officer said. He pointed to the space next to him.

"What for?" Bobby stayed still, resisting the powerful urge to glance behind him. "I ain't done nothing wrong. Just trying to help."

"Don't make me pull my weapon." The cop rested his hand on his holstered pistol.

"No good deed goes unpunished, huh?" Imagining himself getting fingerprinted, photographed, identified, and filed, Bobby blanched. Next would come men in dark suits. They might even have some nearby. "I swear I didn't do nothing."

The cop scowled and approached. "Kid, you're coming down to the station with me for questioning."

Bobby backed up. "Ain't it—" His voice cracked. He coughed and tried again. "Ain't it more important to make sure the girl is okay?"

"An ambulance is on its way. Stay where you are, kid."

Trying not to panic, Bobby took a deep breath. He only hoped Momma would forgive him for using her like this. "If'n my momma finds out I been out, she's gonna whip me but good. I sure don't need more stripes up my back."

The cop sighed and took his hand off his gun. "Fine, just tell me your friend's name, then you can go."

Bobby tried not to let his relief show too much. Except he couldn't tell a cop any of their real names. He cracked into smile to buy time and tried to think of a harmless name, someone who would neither lead the agents to them or get into trouble. "Brian." When the cop gave him a raised eyebrow, he tacked on a random last name. "Walters."

"I don't want to see you or Brian around this part of town again."

"Yessir." Not trusting his luck to hold, Bobby turned and bolted up the alley. As soon as it seemed dark enough, he burst into dragons and they shot upward. Through the dragons' eyes, he saw the cop shake his head and return to Beth's side. With that handled, the swarm turned to darting up the street to find Stephen and Matthew.

Ahead, Stephen rocketed up with the werewolf in hand, then tossed Matthew higher and got out of the way. As Bobby reached the spot, Matthew slammed into the street below, cracking the asphalt. The werewolf shrank back into Matthew, who groaned as his injuries healed themselves.

Stephen dropped to the ground and crouched beside him in the light of a nearby streetlamp. Bobby touched down next to them as he re-formed.

"Oh, yeah," he spat, still reeling from his police encounter. "We'll just hop on over to the big city. Nothing bad'll happen."

"I never said nothing bad would happen." Stephen smirked. "I said we could make a night of it."

"Made a mess of it is more like."

Matthew grunted and propped himself up on his elbows. "We

should probably get out of here."

"I'm still hungry. Especially after dealing with Fido here."

Bobby rubbed his face. "Great. Just great."

"Seconded." Matthew rolled to his feet and took a deep breath. "Maybe we should try a bar or cafe this time. You know, a place where your intent isn't illegal to begin with?"

Bobby followed Matthew away from the crater he'd left in the street. "Maybe you could go for not near-killing the girl this time too. Since that was actually the problem and all."

"This is why I should eat more often. Daily is preferable. Can't I just kidnap some woman and take her home to feed from?"

Bobby rolled his eyes. "You're kinda messed up in the head."

"Yes! I need at least two or three. Then they can entertain each other. Do some light housework…and probably plot together to kill me in my sleep. You're right, this is a bad plan." Stephen went quiet while they bypassed the area now drawing cops in swarms.

"I suppose one good thing came out of this disaster," Matthew said.

"Oh yeah? What in heckbiscuits is that?"

"I'm not really thinking about my own problems. Thinking about his instead."

Bobby laughed and hoped the rest of the night turned out less eventful.

Stars and Stripes

Matthew

The moon hung fat and full in an impossibly starry sky. Matthew remembered sights like this in Afghanistan. His unit had spent nights dug in, waiting, in awe of the sky he never seen in LA or Camp Schwab. He now lay on a section of roof he'd spent all day repairing with some of the others. It seemed like a good place to avoid people. When he had a weird urge to run like a maniac, howling at that big round thing in the sky, he felt confident he should stay away from people.

Not that the moon held any true sway over him. He had a feeling the urge came more from his expectations of werewolves than anything else. At least he could say he had things in common with fictional werewolves. He also had some things in common with the Marine he used to be. Not control, though. He'd lost any semblance of that.

"Mind if I share the roof?"

Matthew glanced to the side and saw only a dark shape

blotting out stars. He knew the voice, though. "Knock yourself out."

Stephen landed an arm's length away and stretched out over the roof. "I'd never seen the stars until the trip out here with you."

Matthew grunted to show he'd heard and had a thought to leave it there. For some reason, though, he wanted to poke at his scars. "I took Beth to the planetarium once, but I didn't pay any attention to the show. She did, despite my best efforts. She said she didn't want to go back with me unless I promised to keep my hands to myself. Because we could do that without paying to get into some public place."

"Sounds practical."

"She was going to be a nurse."

"Must've been smart too. My last girlfriend was undeclared. Since leaving her, I've thought over the six months I spent with her. In retrospect, I think her major was actually about finding a husband to support her."

"Not my Beth." Matthew chuckled. "She said she let me stay at her place because I was nice to look at and picked up after myself. I guess she knew I was an overglorified dog before I did."

Stephen let a companionable silence hang between them for a while. "How did you meet her?"

Memories bubbled up that Matthew didn't want to deal with. He scraped at the scabs anyway. "Ninth grade history class. We sat in alphabetical order. Bethany Gale, Matthew Garrison. I spent an entire year staring at her hair and learning nothing. Took me another year to grow the balls to ask her out. And that was only because her cousin and I sat together in art class. He talked me into doing it."

If he asked Hannah, she'd probably give him some funds to pick up art supplies. Some of the VA guys swore by art as therapy. He hadn't drawn anything since he got back, though. The things that might show up on a blank page scared the hell out of him.

"Art class? Big, bad Marine werewolf did art class?"

Matthew growled. "What? You think the only thing I know how to do is kill people?" He spat the last few words.

Stephen left a long pause before he sighed. "No. That's not what I meant. Sorry."

Rubbing his eyes, Matthew clamped his mouth shut to avoid saying anything else stupid. Obviously, Stephen hadn't meant it that way. "I'm just really damned good at it. Too good at it. I'm so good at it I'm a fucking serial killer." Then, the thing he'd been thinking since he got here spilled out. "That makes me a shitty Marine."

"You were trained to kill people, though. I mean, that's what Marines do. Rifle, handgun, knife, claws—it's all the same idea."

Hearing it put that way made Matthew scowl. Stephen didn't understand. He'd never been through military training or in a war zone. He'd never seen a guy's brains blown apart. He'd never—

"Get your damned fool head down, Garrison!"

Matthew sighted down his scope, waiting for the right moment. He didn't care about the incoming fire. Beth's picture rested inside his helmet, right in front of his brainpan, protecting him. His world shrank to his target, sealing away the rest of the world. Dirt puffed into the air, probably from a bullet hitting nearby.

His target dropped something. The man stopped and bent to pick it up. Matthew exhaled, pulled the trigger, and finally ducked under cover.

"Target eliminated," he reported.

But Sergeant Ackers didn't answer. His body lay in a heap with too much blood staining his fatigues.

"—not a war zone, Matt!" Stephen hovered over him, shaking his shoulders. "Snap out of it. You're halfway to furball."

Raising his hands, Matthew found long claws where his fingers should be. He swore and took several deep breaths. The metallic tang of blood left his mouth and the werewolf receded with the memory. Of course that one would trigger the wolf inside. After that moment, he'd been on his own for five long, bloody minutes. His CO promoted him for those twelve enemy kills.

"You're not a murderer, an animal, or, for that matter, a shitty Marine," Stephen snapped. He let go and drifted to the roof again. "You can control that. If I can handle my inner asshole, you can handle yours. You just need more practice."

Matthew rubbed his face again. "I'm fine. For certain definitions of 'fine,' anyway." He breathed deeply several times. "How do you handle yours?"

"With blood. Mine gets bad when I'm hungry. Even then, though, I've had lots of practice holding him back now. Willpower."

He only had to want it to stay in the box until he needed it. Easy as pie. Matthew stared up at the sky for a while, wondering if he'd ever find peace with those memories. "She was furious with me for enlisting. Said it was the stupidest thing I'd ever done. My dad, though. He was a Marine. His boy was going to be a Marine too, goddammit. I wanted to go to art school. Beth waited for me. When I got back… Dammit, I miss her every day. It like those sonsabitches stabbed me in the chest and ripped out everything they could get their hands on."

"And you killed them," Stephen said.

"And I killed them. With my bare fucking hands. Claws. Whatever."

"And it didn't bring her back."

Matthew shook his head. "No." Revenge hadn't made anything better at all. "When I think about what they did-"

"Stop thinking about it."

"Sure," Matthew scoffed, "just like that." He snapped his fingers.

"You can't change what happened. None of it. Remember her laugh, or her body, or the sex, or whatever else works for you. Not the bad stuff, just the good stuff."

Forget the bad stuff and focus on the good stuff. Stephen sounded like…Beth. She had a thing about silver linings. Matthew pictured her face first thing in the morning, when she had no makeup on and her hair stuck out every which way. The woman had horrific morning breath and he didn't care.

"I took her camping once, after I got back. It rained, a snake scared her half to death, some dog kept barking on and off all night. Ground was too hard for her to get comfortable. I slept alright, but she barely did. Went home in the morning because she wanted to. She slept for hours when we got back. While she was asleep, I went out and finally bought the ring I'd been saving for. Cheap piece of glass in silver.

"I made her lunch in bed. Used the ring to hold a rolled-up paper napkin. She said yes before I had a chance to ask. Best lunch I've ever had. Later, she told me she knew it was a piece of crap ring, but she didn't care if it came from a cereal box. I'd planned to get her a real one someday. Like for an anniversary."

"Sounds like a pretty good day. When did the nightmares and flashbacks start?"

Matthew scowled as the new question chased away pleasant memories. He needed to talk about it, though. "When I woke up in a hospital bed. Took some shrapnel. Nothing major or vital hit, just lost a lot of blood and had to heal up. I could've gone back into the sandbox if that stuff hadn't started up. I even tried to talk them into letting me go back until the time I woke up screaming.

"They shipped me home and the soft bed made it worse. But every time I woke up, she was there. She did whatever it took. My personal nurse. They'd faded away for the most part. I had maybe one a week, and I wasn't having trouble getting back to sleep. Had a steady job. Kept up with my share of the bills. I even laughed. We saw movies without me freaking. On the fourth of July, I didn't panic."

"She was holding you together."

"No." Matthew groped for the right word. Since those assholes took her from him, he felt adrift, lost. He had no home base anymore. "She was my anchor."

"When you found out what happened to her, all the horrors she was holding back shook loose and you lost it."

"Yeah. I was kind of there when I killed those guys that did it to her, but not really. All I could see was enemies that needed to be terminated, and I didn't have my rifle. I mean, I knew they were the guys who did it to her, but…" He hesitated, not sure how to explain.

"When I get hungry, it's like there's another person in my head, one that has a very different opinion of right and wrong. He looks at women and sees talking cows. Except it's worse than that, because you don't have sex with cows. He has some pretty screwed up ideas about sex, too. I think he might even like—" Stephen stopped himself with a cough. "What I'm saying is, it's someone inside me, a part of me that I have to conquer and force into submission. Those thoughts are my thoughts. The difference is, I know that part of me is wrong. Which is why I look at it as a separate guy who needs a leash around his neck."

Matthew could roll with thinking of the wolf as something to conquer and force into submission. Looking at it that way made the task seem possible. He was a goddamned fucking Marine, and Marines don't quit. No except, no until, no nothing, just no quitting. "Yeah. That makes sense. Thanks. And I guess I never thanked you for— For the other stuff."

"It's cool. Some of the others think we might be siblings. That's the kind of thing brothers do for each other."

Another Night on the Town

Stephen

Summer sucked. Stephen stood in the shade of the farmhouse, wishing the damned sun would set already. He got up an hour ago, having slept most of the daylight hours away in the basement of the farmhouse. Two weeks ago, he showed up here and Hannah pressed him into work, knocking down walls and moving heavy things. So long as he could avoid deadly sunshine while doing it, he found the work helpful in keeping his mind busy.

He missed his girlfriend. The first time he woke up as a vampire, he almost killed Marie with his Hunger. When he dropped her off at the hospital, her body too light and cold, he walked away forever, certain he'd never be able to look her in the eye again. She'd always been good at handling him, though. Certainly, he missed the regular sex. Much more, he missed the smell of her favorite perfume mingling with her musk at the nape of her neck.

Lizzie sashayed past him, Dan following with a guiding—and possessive—hand on her hip. She saw Stephen and smirked. Her hands ran through her thick, red hair and lifted it so he got an eyeful of her neck. Only his respect for Dan's claim on her...*heart* kept him from darting to her side and sinking his fangs into her smooth flesh. His Hunger flared, making it an effort.

Tugging on his hoodie distracted him. He turned to find Hannah had snuck up behind him. She stood in the shade with him, her blue shirt and blonde ponytail leaving her tanned neck exposed. With nothing in plain sight to stop him, he clenched his hands into fists to prevent himself from closing the distance and feasting on her blood.

Chirping sounds distracted him enough to tear his eyes away from his favorite part of a woman. The noise had been Hannah saying something, and her expression prompted him to answer.

"What?"

Her smile faltered. "I asked how you're feeling."

He closed his eyes and wished she'd sent Jayce or Matthew to ask instead. Even better, she could have less interest in his feelings. "I'm hungry." The words came out with more of a growl than he intended.

"It's really great that you can control it like this. I knew you could do it. It's three days now, right?"

"Four." Four torturously long days ago, after a disastrous visit to Denver, the committee of everyone else here asked him not to leave to feed. He'd agreed without realizing none of the women would let him drink their blood. Clenching his jaws together, he sucked in a deep breath through his nose. It carried her scent, making him regret doing it. "If I don't feed soon, I'm going to attack someone."

"Don't threaten me."

His eyes snapped open and he gave her a flat stare. "I'm not threatening anyone. I'm stating a fact. I'm going out tonight."

She sighed and let her head lean to one side in disappointment. "If you could just try for one more day…"

Her voice faded under the thump of her heartbeat. He stepped closer to her, unable to see anything but the angle of her shoulder and the blood pulsing under her skin. The hot ambrosia would spurt into his mouth. She'd gasp and sag in his arms. He'd drink and drink and drink.

His face bounced off something blue. Blinking, he saw her force field shimmering between them and rubbed his nose. "Sorry."

"Have you…considered trying the goats? Tiana says she won't object so long as you don't kill them."

Curling his lip in distaste, he shook his head. "I need human blood. Asking me to drink from animals is like asking you to eat raw sewage."

She pursed her lips and threw a handful of money on the ground between them. "If you have to go, be careful." Her force field stayed active until she escaped around the corner of the farmhouse.

He scooped up the bills and counted them, finding sixty dollars. At least she hadn't asked him to pick up groceries.

The well-lit block he picked had women in flattering little dresses and men pretending not to stare at them. They roved in clumps and pairs. He walked up the street, hoping he fit in well enough to be ignored. Pulsing beats from five different nightclubs thumped in opposition to each other, brief snatches of music pouring out every time someone opened a door. A cheer rang out from the sports bar nestled between them, announcing the home team had scored.

Part of him wished for a dark trenchcoat to flutter around him as he swaggered down the street. Add black boots and tight pants and he would attract bouncy coeds looking for a one-night stand with the bad boy strutting through the clubs. Sixty bucks wouldn't cover that kind of makeover. Especially not in this neighborhood. A hoodie and jeans would have to do.

Amid the hot spots, a trendy café boasted hip young people sitting at tables with colorful mugs, a clothing boutique offered low quality for high prices, and a drugstore with muted lighting promised a safe haven. He slowed to stare through the window of a shop with tiny, bite-sized cubes of cake. Once, he would've stared at the confections instead of the patrons and staff. He missed chocolate. More to the point, he missed having easy access to different flavors. Maybe he could find a cow willing to try eating different things to see if it had any impact on her blood for him.

Reflected in the window, he saw a gaggle of women and turned to get a better look. Ten cows huddled in a clump outside a club, assessing their choices. One in the center seemed drunk and appeared to be in charge. The rest ran the gamut from apprehensive to amused. In his experience, this kind of group had to be a birthday party or a bachelorette outing. So long as he steered clear of the sloppy drunk one, he'd be fine.

The redhead caught his eye. Unlike her friends, she wore a suit skirt with a vest and blouse, her hair tied up in a tight bun. Her mild frown spoke of annoyance and a desire to leave. He guessed she might have been snatched directly after work and dragged along. The other cows probably told her she needed to lighten up or let her hair down for a night.

When they flowed into the club, he hurried across the street to follow them in. Reaching it in time to catch the door for the last few, he smiled at the blonde in the rear who flashed him a toothsome come-hither. If he couldn't have the redhead, he'd go for this one. He wanted the redhead, though.

The bouncer checked IDs and collected cover charges for the girls. Though he hated to do it to a guy, Stephen grabbed the burly man's hand and licked it. While the guy's eyes unfocused in bliss for a few seconds, Stephen stamped his own hand and moved on. The guy would only remember a brief dizzy spell. Given his size and muscle tone, he'd probably find it embarrassing and keep his mouth shut.

Inside, the pounding music beat in his chest. Flashing lights hit a disco ball and threw colored spots everywhere. The party princess grabbed his redhead's sleeve and slurred something at her then shoved her toward the bar. His redhead stumbled into a table and he growled when another man reached out and offered her a steadying hand.

She gave that interloper a grateful smile and let him set her on her feet. Only a few steps away, Stephen tracked them to the bar where the guy settled his hand on his redhead's butt. In this miasma of humanity, Stephen couldn't smell if her smile at the guy was strained or genuine. She shifted away from him, though, and he thought he might get the opportunity to swoop in and rescue her.

As much as he wanted to rise up and watch from a perch out of sight, he couldn't see any way to do it with no one noticing. The club's corners had dim lighting, not darkness. He settled for leaning against the bar a few spots away and keeping track of her. To assuage the bartender, he ordered a cheap drink and handled it without drinking.

His redhead had trouble getting the bartender's attention

until the guy with her waved a twenty in his direction. She flashed him a fake smile and spent at least a minute placing a long order. The guy ducked to nuzzle at her neck and she squirmed away with a smile that grew more fixed and forced by the second.

Though he still smelled too much and felt too many heartbeats, Stephen suspected his redhead's evening might take a turn for the worse any moment. He stepped away from the bar and caught sight of the guy's hand as it reached much too low for a stranger's fingers to probe. Stephen stumbled into him on purpose, sloshing his drink all over the guy's pants and shoving him against the bar.

Grinning like a drunk fool, he laughed and shouted a cheap apology. His redhead escaped while Stephen slapped the guy on the shoulder hard enough to force him into the next person down. That next person happened to be a large, muscular gentleman with tattoos, and Stephen ducked away to let his redhead's tormentor handle the situation on his own.

She stormed to the bathrooms. The back hallway had too much light for Stephen's tastes. He slipped to the side, waiting for her out of sight. When it seemed like a long time had passed, he tapped a waitress on the arm.

"Hey, my girlfriend went into the bathroom like ten minutes ago. Can you check if she's okay? Redhead in a suit with no jacket. Don't tell her, though. She gets mad when I check up on her."

The brunette cow snorted and nodded, then bustled off to the ladies' room. She breezed back out half a minute later wearing a smirk. "Your girl is gone. Probably went out the back door."

He frowned and dove down the hallway. Slamming the back door open, he stepped into a dark alley thick with the stench of rotting food and wondered what idiocy had prompted her to choose this over clustering with her friends. Maybe he'd chosen the wrong girl. Dumb cows would wind up dead cows, and disposing of a body would be a major hassle.

With a sigh, he caught the door before it shut and slipped inside again. That blonde would be fine. He stopped only two steps in when his redhead blocked his passage with a cool stare and crossed arms. The stern set of her shoulders drew his eye to her neck.

"Why are you following me?"

Stephen smiled, hoping it made him seem harmless. "Because you're five steps above the garden-variety club bimbos lurking around here."

She shifted her hands to her hips. "You think my friends are bimbos?"

"I haven't met any of your friends. I *have* met a lot of girls who hang out at clubs, though. A fair number of them are only looking for guys who'll buy them diamonds and horses." He took a step towards her so the door could shut behind him. "The rest, an elite few, are worth meeting and getting to know."

Her mouth quirked into a smirk. "But you don't think too highly of yourself or anything."

Now that he'd heard her talk for half a minute, he found her irresistible. "My mother always told me that women appreciate confidence in a man."

"You do everything your mommy tells you?"

"No, but I listen to her advice." He offered her a hand. "Can I buy you an obligation- free cup of coffee in a public place, or are you having too much fun with your friends? It's not like they dragged you out kicking and screaming, right?"

She glanced back and her arms hung loose, signaling her interest. "Yeah, let's get out of here."

He smiled, pleased by her acceptance. "I'm Stephen."

"Kris."

"Pleased to meet you, Kris." He escorted her through the club to let her pick up her purse. In silence, they walked to the trendy café and he bought her a cup of hot chocolate. To keep up appearances, he got himself the cheapest tea they had. Both found the place too loud with chatter to have a conversation and stepped out to walk down the street with their drinks.

"I'm guessing you have some kind of professional job."

Kris nodded. "I'm a personal assistant for a jerk in an office. You?"

Usually, he told anyone who asked that he attended a nearby college. The lie stuck in his throat. Something about Kris made him want to tell the truth. He knew the rest of the team needed him to keep his mouth shut and ignored that inconvenient fact. "I'm a vampire."

She let out a rich, rolling laugh that drew his attention to her mouth and kept it there. "Is that code for 'stripper'?"

Wanting to show her for some reason, he took her hand and pulled her around a corner. Tossing his tea, he wrapped his arms around her and flew up until he felt confident no one would see them.

Her mouth fell open and her eyes went wide. She dropped her coffee to wrap her arms around his neck and cling to him. What she didn't do, thankfully, was scream.

"No," he said with a grin, "I'm actually a vampire."

"Jesus Christ." Peering down, she shook her head. "This is unbelievable. Did you actually spike my coffee somehow and now I'm having a really crazy dream?"

"Sorry, no. This is real. You're not afraid of heights, are you?"

"Not really, but damn." Meeting his gaze again, she gulped. "Can we land someplace anyway? I'm afraid I'm going to lose my shoes. Or maybe my dinner."

He checked the area and picked a building. Setting down on a tall, flat roof, he let go and watched her stumble a few steps away. "I wasn't lying. I'm attracted to you. That's why I bumped into that guy to distract him."

Taking deep breaths, she rubbed her cheeks. Her blood pumped through her body loud enough to be distracting. She closed her eyes, and he figured it was to help herself think. "Okay. So, you're a vampire. You can fly. Do you drink blood?"

"Yes."

"Of course. Because if you didn't, you wouldn't be a vampire."

"That's kind of how it works, yeah."

She opened her eyes and met his gaze. Though she showed no fear, her scent gave him a hefty dose of it. Under it, he smelled arousal. "Does it hurt?"

"No. As far as I can tell, it feels pretty good."

She gulped. "Did you pick me up because you, er, need some blood right now?"

Holding up both hands in surrender, he smiled. "Only if you're willing. I wouldn't force myself on anyone."

Her head bobbed in a nod, then she stopped and peered at him suspiciously. "Wait a minute. How often do you drink blood?"

"Every day, if I can."

"So you pick up different women all the time and suck on them and move on? Is that why you grabbed me? To have a…a… really weird one night stand?"

He didn't need her scent to pick up on her spiking anger. Every way he could think of to phrase his answer sounded awful in his head, so he paced to the edge of the roof and stared out, hoping for something better to fall out of his mouth. "I'm tired of the one night stands. It's a really intimate thing, to drink someone's blood. It's a lot like making love. I keep doing it with strangers, and it's flat and stale and fake."

Turning to face her, he sighed. At least he could tell her anger had faded. "I don't even know why I didn't just pretend to be a regular guy trying to get to know a girl. Something about you…I don't know. I didn't want to start with a lie, I guess."

Her expression softened. "That's a pretty good pickup line."

"If it was a line, I would've said 'Honesty is the only path a true hero can take.' " He puffed out his chest and put his fists on his hips in his best Superman impression. When she laughed, he closed the distance between them to offer her his hand. "I'm just looking for the same thing everyone else is: someone I can connect with."

She looked at his hand. "Yeah. Me too." Slipping hers into his, she smiled. "Worst case, we hate each other, right?"

"Something like that." He pulled her in close and lifted her off the ground. "What do you want to do for our first date?"

Wrapping her arms around his neck, she grinned. "Let's go flying."

He scooped her up. "I thought you'd never ask."

Barnyard Explosions

Albert

"Awesome." Pushing up his safety goggles, Greg looked up from his current project to watch Jayce, currently shiny silver, set down five cardboard boxes, all full of the things he'd asked for.

"If you need anything else, there're a few hardware stores relatively nearby, but most of it was pretty hard to find." With a tip of an imaginary hat, Jayce left the barn. He had other heavy things to lift and move.

"Is it Christmas?" Albert sat with his laptop, transcribing Greg's notes for him.

"Better. This day doesn't rely on religion for existence, just science." Greg grinned and waggled his eyebrows.

Albert snorted. "And what will science be bringing us today?" The question would, he knew, keep his inventor talking for at least five minutes.

"A plane. I'm building a plane that will run on a second generator, just like the one we're using." He went on for several minutes, talking about drag and coefficients and sonic booms.

Most of it went over Albert's head, as he'd known it would. He'd asked the question to fill the barn with the pleasant sound of Greg's voice while he chattered about some part of his favorite subject: applied science. Nothing beat the way his eyes lit up when he explained physics and electrical engineering.

As Greg spoke, he wielded a soldering iron with practised expertise, tiny wisps of smoke dispersed by a small fan whirring on the edge of the table. Eventually, he sat up and rolled his shoulders. "Which all mostly just means it'll be a really fast jet airplane capable of flying indefinitely and evading modern detection capabilities."

"Sounds useful." Albert finished his work and saved the document, then sent it to Greg's tablet so he could refer to it. The man could build a supersonic stealth jet from spare parts in a rundown barn, but he couldn't open his email without help. He grabbed the tablet to make sure the document went where he wanted it to.

"It'll take a couple of months to build, which kind of sucks, but we don't happen to have a chassis to gut. That would make it go faster."

"I'll see what I can do." Albert's stomach rumbled. "I'm going to get lunch. Hungry?"

"Not quite yet. Bring me back something?"

Setting the tablet aside, Albert nodded. He expected little in the way of attention while Greg worked. Once, he'd set a project in process aside in favor of Albert. It had taken the University of Wisconsin six months to rebuild that lab. Everyone appreciated that the insurance company decided to call it an accident.

"Sure." He squeezed Greg's shoulder and stepped out from under the tarp tent protecting the workshop. The farmhouse had higher priority for repairs, which made sense given how many people slept there. He and Greg could live with a leaky roof until people had time to fix it.

Albert strolled in dappled sunshine past John's garden and to the back door. He'd never lived outside of a city before, and all the trees made this feel like a bizarre camping adventure. In many ways, that described it perfectly.

He saw Owen, shirtless and muscular and delicious, handing a sheet of plywood up to Matthew on the farmhouse roof, also shirtless and muscular and delicious. Violet, hovering several feet above the ground, guided it for them. Jayce walked around the corner, still silver from head to toe, carrying a stack of cement blocks.

Lizzie sashayed away from the house as she ran her fingers through her hair and lifted it off her neck. Such a gross vamping display had to be meant for Dan, who followed her into the woods with a hand on her hip. Albert caught John's eye as he straightened from picking tomatoes and they shared a moment of incredulity at her.

This place definitely fit the word "bizarre."

Inside, he headed straight for the large kitchen. Aside from the appliances and plenty of counterspace, it held two picnic tables. Sam and Ai sat around a large platter full of sandwiches with Lisa and her husband, Clive. As a fellow hanger-on for all these superpowered people, Albert felt like he ought to be able to befriend Clive. It seemed, so far, that they had nothing else in common and Clive preferred to spend his time with Lisa. Albert could hardly cast stones on that count.

"Hello, ladies," Albert said with a cheerful wave. "And gentleman."

Ai waved him over and patted the spot beside her. The slim Japanese woman had been the one to bring him and Greg here. He had yet to decide if he truly felt grateful for that. "By yourself?"

Albert sat and let Sam put a sandwich on a plate for him. She added a pile of cut vegetables and a cup of ranch dip. "Boy Genius is hard at work. I'll need something to take for him."

Ai filled a cup with water from a pitcher for him. "How's the barn working out for you guys? "

"Oh, it's a little drafty, but we've got plenty of body heat to spare. John said he'd put up some shrubs or something to help block the wind." He took a bite of his sandwich and chewed it up. "Is that rosemary in the mayo?"

Sam nodded and ducked her head. "It's my dad's recipe."

"It's delicious. I'm not sure—" A minor earthquake rocked the building, followed by a boom Albert felt in his chest. His heart stopped. He dropped his sandwich and sprinted for the door. The most likely source—and victim—of an explosion here was Greg.

Black smoke belched from the barn in every direction and Greg stumbled out of the dark cloud, coughing and waving his gloved hands in front of his face. He bent over and sucked in clean air, punctuated by more coughing.

"Are you okay?" Albert ducked to avoid the miasma as he hurried to Greg's side.

Nodding, Greg let himself be pulled farther from the smoke. When he could straighten, he pulled his gloves off and pushed his safety goggles up. "All fingers, toes, and limbs accounted for." Though his words came out coherent, his voice had a dazed quality. "Eyes and ears functioning within normal parameters. I seem to be okay."

Albert hugged him, forcing another spate of coughing. "What happened?"

"Oh, you know. The usual." Greg sighed with contentment. "Science."

With a roll of his eyes, Albert pushed him away and looked

him over. "You're filthy. Did you roll around in ashes?" He saw no signs of burns or scratches, which filled him with relief.

Greg chuckled without coughing. "Yes. I know how much you love that. Thought it would be a special treat."

"It's special, all right." Furious he'd done something to make him worry, Albert thumped him in the arm. Then he grabbed Greg and hugged him again. "Remind me again why I put up with this?"

Greg tilted his soot covered face down and brushed his lips across Albert's. The last time he'd done that where other people might see had been in Madison, at a dinner party with their gay friends. Afraid of being targeted for it, they barely touched in public.

Eyes watering, Albert straightened and smoothed Greg's leather apron. "Of course, silly me. I forgot. It's for the sex." He noticed a crowd had gathered, making that tiny kiss all the sweeter.

"And you like programming my phone and tablet for me."

Albert gave him a watery smile. Movement made his eyes flick over Greg's shoulder and he watched Lizzie strut by with a sour frown.

"There's no fire," she whined.

Out of reflex, Greg and Albert each took a small step apart.

Lizzie smirked. "Don't stop on my account."

Albert rolled his eyes. "Is there anything you need to do to stop the smoke?"

"Nah, it'll run itself out in a minute or two." Greg straightened his shoulders and took Albert's hand. Such a deliberate statement in front of others made Albert want to cry. "I guess it's time for a lunch break."

"If you ask me," Lizzie said as she walked away, "it's more time for shower sex."

Afraid of what might come out, Albert covered his mouth. He agreed but had no intention of saying so out loud.

Greg coughed awkwardly and squeezed his hand. Setting off for the house, he tugged Albert along.

Albert swallowed past the lump in his throat and sniffled. "She, ah, does have a point. Look at my hand. I'm almost as dirty as you are."

"I think it's safe to say that, between the two of us, you're definitely the dirtier one." Greg opened the door and smirked at him.

"I've just read more porn than you. Really, though, we should at least wash our hands before using them to eat." Albert tugged him toward the nearest bathroom.

Looking himself over, Greg nodded. "You and your sensible ideas. Let's go do that."

After three years together, Albert knew the look Greg got in his eyes. The gears in that colossal brain whirred and clicked. His mind jumped back onto the Science train, chugging along to some destination only Greg understood. His boyfriend had a woman on the side—a distressingly needy woman. Nothing he could do would ever pry her claws out of Greg's side, and he'd be unhappy if he ever found a way. Without his obsession, Greg wouldn't be the man Albert fell in love with in the first place.

He stepped inside the bathroom and turned on the water. Greg shut the door with his hip and stuck his hands in the stream. Albert picked up the soap and rubbed it over Greg's skin, gently washing the soot and dirt and grease away. His eyes flicked up to the mirror to see Greg smiling at him.

"Was it a major setback?"

Greg blinked and seemed to come out of a trance. Science, of course. "Hm?"

Albert sighed. "The explosion. Do we need to get replacement parts because of it?"

"Oh. Nah. I've got plenty of all that."

Albert shut off the water and noticed Greg smiling at him again. He wrapped his Brainiac's hands in a towel and patted them dry. To his surprise, Greg tossed the towel aside to cup his cheeks and kiss him. It felt less hungry and demanding than what usually followed an explosion.

When he broke it off, Greg stared into his eyes. "We should get married."

His heart stopped again. Albert held his breath, wishing with all his might that he hadn't imagined those words coming from Greg's mouth. "What?"

"I love you. Marry me."

Albert's eyes burned and tears slid down his cheeks. "We're on the run from the government and you want to go file paperwork with it?"

Greg's hopeful smile faded. "We can…go to Canada? They do it there, don't they? "

A noise halfway between a laugh and a sob burst out of Albert and he wrapped his arms around Greg's neck. "I don't think that's feasible right now, but yes, if there's a chance, of course I will."

Greg held him close and kissed his cheek. "Good. For a minute there, I thought you were turning me down. I know I'm a pain in the ass sometimes, but I didn't think I was *that* bad."

"You're awful."

Chuckling, Greg squeezed him and let go. "Damn. I made a mess all over you." He brushed at soot on Albert's shirt, but gave up after only two swipes. "I'm making it worse. Come on, we should hurry up and eat so we only have to clean up once."

Wiping his face, Albert swatted playfully at Greg's arm. "You say that like cleaning up is a bad thing." He shoved Greg away and turned to the mirror, despairing at the streaks on his face and red in his eyes. "You go ahead, I'll catch up."

"You look fine." Greg put a hand on Albert's shoulder. "No one cares, especially not me."

Albert huffed. "*I* care." Shooing Greg out, he pretended to be affronted.

"Well, fine. If it matters to you, then I can pretend to care." Greg grabbed Albert's hand and kissed it, then left the room with a smile.

Albert splashed some water on his face, hoping it would help him stop crying. "He asked me to marry him," he whispered as he stared into the sink basin. "He's never even joked about it before. Does that mean we're engaged? That's how it works, isn't it?" None of their gay friends had considered marriage before they left, so he had no role models for the etiquette. Several of their straight friends and relatives had tied the knot, of course, but he had no idea if the rules worked the same.

Should he ask for a piece of jewelry? For Christmas last year, Greg gave him a pair of diamond stud earrings made in his own lab and personalized with a blue tint to match Greg's eyes.

He toweled off his face and checked himself in the mirror. Greg's mother would be a nightmare about the whole thing. She'd already offered to let Albert rifle through her closet. No doubt she'd pull out her old wedding dress to make him try it on. His protestations that he had no interest in wearing dresses or skirts fell on deaf ears. Just because everybody—including Albert and Greg—knew he'd be the wife in this relationship didn't mean wanted to pretend to be a woman.

With a sigh, he resigned himself to red, weepy eyes. At least his Chinese ancestry meant he avoided the unpleasantness of blotchy cheeks. After splashing water on his face and toweling it off, he left the bathroom to find Greg sitting next to Ai in the kitchen, grinning while she filled a cup with water for him. Since boobs held no appeal for Boy Genius, he didn't care. Still, Albert slipped in beside his man and took over the duty of making sure he ate.

"It's not a major setback, I don't think," Greg said. "I'll know more when I go back in, after the smoke clears. We should have a plane at our disposal in a few months, I think."

"You guys are really cute together," Ai said with a dreamy smile. Albert knew that look. It was the look of a girl who fantasized about romance. "How did you meet?"

"College." Albert gestured with a carrot stick. "I was Greg's English tutor. The poor boy didn't even know what a dangling participle was."

Greg waggled his eyebrows. "That was a fun lesson."

"Yes," Albert smacked him playfully on the arm, "yes it was."

Ai giggled. "Was that your first date?"

"Dangling participles?" Albert thought back to their first date, getting his own wistful expression. "No, it was about two months after."

"I didn't really realize I was gay then. The idea of going out with a guy kind of confused me a little, but I really liked Albert, so I figured I should give it a shot and see what happened."

Albert sniggered. "I used my gay predator wiles to woo him over to the dark side. Such an impressionable young boy, all ripe and eager to please." A light blush colored Greg's cheeks, letting Albert know he was going a little too far. "But we mostly just went out to a few places as friends at first, because it was so painfully obvious he didn't really know what he wanted. It helped a lot that his mother is really great."

Greg shook his head in amusement. "My mom figured it out before I did, I think. I mean, I dated a few girls in high school, and it was always…off, I guess. I figured I wasn't as interested in them as I was in physics, but it turns out they didn't do much for me because they were girls."

"You're disgusting." Tony stepped into the room with a revolted sneer on his face. The Cubano walked up and snatched a sandwich from the part of the stack as far from them as possible.

Albert rolled his eyes. He'd lived with that sort of thing for years and it didn't bother him. Much. Knowing how it still hurt Greg, though, he reached over and put his hand on his boyfr—fiancee's thigh.

Ai, though, gave Tony an unfriendly look. "Greg is one of us."

"So? That doesn't make him any less a fag."

"I'll just go back to the barn." Greg picked up his half-finished sandwich and left the room.

"That's where the animals belong."

Albert picked up extra food to follow Greg with. Out of pique, he tapped the rest of the visible sandwiches with his upraised pinky. He had no doubt this exchange would leave him with no appetite at all, but that didn't mean he no longer needed to eat. "You know what's really disgusting? Blind hate. How you can still cleave to your idea of God in the face of all this is beyond me, but you're welcome to keep it to yourself. Especially if you enjoy electricity and internet access."

As he left the room with his bundle, he heard Ai say, "You can always leave if you don't like relying on a gay man for anything."

Finding Greg right now would actually be harder than it seemed on first blush. Back at school, whenever he got upset for one reason or another, Greg always went to the same place: the back stoop of their apartment. Here, it hadn't happened yet, so Albert hadn't the first clue where to find him. On the off chance it would turn out to be the barn, he checked there first.

He found the source of the explosion, now sitting inert on a table. Tools and other parts and things were scattered around from the blast. Judging by the minimal damage, the blast itself had been small. Breezing through, he checked the old horse stall they used for a bedroom and climbed the ladder to peek into the rickety loft above it.

With no sign of Greg anywhere, he went outside and walked around the entire building. He found Greg around the back, sitting on an old tree stump. Slipping up behind him, Albert laid his hands on the younger man's shoulders and swirled his thumbs around his spine. The usual tension caused by hunching over his work seemed multiplied.

Greg sighed and let him work for several minutes before saying anything. "I wasn't expecting that."

"I wasn't, either. We've all been here for a few weeks now. I figured if it was going to happen, it would have been right away, at the beginning. I guess he's finally comfortable enough to spend his time being judgmental."

Greg nodded and looked down at his own hands. "I don't know how you can listen to people say things like that. I don't feel like it'll ever not bother me."

Albert shrugged. He knew Greg didn't mean that the way it sounded. "I'm just more used to it. There's a reason I never wanted take you home with me."

"Yeah." Greg took in a deep breath and let it out slowly then put a hand on one of Albert's. "I love you."

"I love you, too. Nothing anyone else says can change that."

Tomatoes and Zucchini

John

So many vegetables, so little time. John prodded a tomato plant, causing a small fruit to expand to the size of his fist and turn red. Andrew asked for a tomato to use for making lunch, so he'd get a tomato. Plucking the mature fruit, he offered the plant some general nurturing, a thing he'd been doing on a rotation with all of them since he started the garden a few weeks ago. So far, he had beans, corn, tomatoes, a few types of quash, several varieties of berry, and carrots. The property had come with a pre-existing apple orchard, a patch of mixed grains, and a wild herb garden. He'd coaxed all three into submission already.

The list of seeds he wanted grew every day, but at this point, they'd survive with what they had. Until he could get someone rig cold frames for him, he needed nothing else. On the other hand, he'd give his right arm for some lettuce or broccoli. More variety. Of course, all of it had to be preserved for the coming winter, so maybe waiting would turn out better.

"Hey, John." Hannah's voice made him look up on his way back to the house. The pretty blonde smiled at him.

"Hi, Hannah. How's the basement project coming along?" He held up the tomato as an explanation for his current destination.

"Actually, I have some questions about it. Can you come with me down there? Looking for some guidance on space and storage and that sort of thing."

"Of course. I just need to drop this off."

She followed him to the back door. "How are the plants?"

"We'll have a large harvest over the next few weeks. I'll give each variety a week off, then force them through it again. I'll be busy, but that's alright. We should have our first apple harvest in a month. The grains have been my lowest priority because we don't really have the equipment to harvest and process them efficiently."

"Good. What do you think you'll be able to do over the winter?"

John shrugged. "I can grow some things indoors in pots, I suppose, but we don't really have any pots."

"Is there any way you can, I don't know, winterize the crops? I mean, you can change the plants, right, not just make them grow and mature?"

He opened his mouth to refuse, then he shut it. Could he do that? "I have no idea. It doesn't seem like a good plan to rely on it."

"Fair enough. Work on it and let me know. In the meantime, what can you do to extend the shelf life of the vegetables we will have?"

"It depends." He frowned, working through what he knew he could do and what he only guessed. When he opened the door, still thinking, he noticed someone approaching.

"Hey, Ai. Do you have a minute?" Hannah pushed the door open wider. "I'll be right back, John."

Hearing the name of the other person, John's cheeks flared with heat and he blinked at Ai. The willowy Japanese woman smiled, her icy blue eyes crinkling at the canted corners and making his brain churn to a stop. Today, she wore her long, black hair in a loose braid. It bounced as she moved.

"Sure," Ai said, her voice drifting on the air like dandelion seeds.

When Hannah stepped past John and let go of the door, the spring snapped it shut. John stumbled forward a step and blushed harder. He ducked his head and hid his face as he darted into the nearby kitchen while Hannah and Ai walked out. Thankfully, Andrew didn't care and took the tomato without a word.

Andrew sniffed the fruit while John faced the counter and knocked his forehead on a cabinet. "Smells good. Thanks, John."

"Right. Yes. Good. Brilliant." If he could die, maybe that would fix everything.

"How is it that so many of you guys get so caught up with the women here?" Tony's light Hispanic accent held blunt disapproval. "They're our sisters."

"We don't know that," Andrew said, his heavy Creole accent marking him as a proper chef.

"What else makes sense? That we all just happen to have the same eyes by some freak coincidence? "

"We could be cousins."

"And that makes it all okay?"

Not paying much attention to them, John stepped to the side to watch Hannah and Ai through the window. Ai tucked an errant wisp of hair behind her ear. Hard work must have tousled it free and an errant breeze made it tickle her cheek. He imagined her with all that coiled on top of her head like a Chinese princess from the stories his mother used to tell him as a child. A small spray of baby's breath and miniature roses would complement her well.

"Are you even listening?" Tony shoved John's arm.

"What?" John blinked at the Cubano man and shook his head. He'd lost the thread of his thoughts and wanted to punch Tony for making it happen. Afraid of the consequences, he shook his head. "I needed to do something in the basement."

Andrew grinned as he slid the diced tomato off his cutting board and into his stock pot.

Tony rolled his eyes. "You all make me sick," he grumbled as he stalked out of the kitchen.

"Ignore him," Andrew suggested. "He's probably just cranky because none of them will sleep with him."

John shrugged and went for the basement door. "He does have a point, I just don't care that much. It's hard to get upset about it when we were all science experiments to begin with."

"Sure. How about zucchini for tomorrow? Say, ten foot-longs."

"Yeah. No problem." John trekked down the stairs into the cool air of the basement. They'd covered the bare earth floor with rug remnants and sheets of broken plywood rejected for the renovations upstairs.

Columns held up the floor above in the gloomy space. One lone washing machine churned laundry in the corner with a freezer beside it. They had nothing else down here now. After spending the first two weeks here, enough bedrooms had been finished upstairs for everyone to get their own slice of privacy.

The boards creaked as Hannah walked down the stairs. "So, as you can see, not much has happened down here."

"What are you looking for from me? I realize I have spatial planning skills, but…" John shrugged.

"You're the one who's going to be producing the things we

need to store down here. I'm looking for your thoughts on how to set this space up to accommodate that."

"Ah." He surveyed the room without seeing it. "We'll need shelves and bins, mostly, some racks might be helpful, but not necessary. Shelf paper would be good, I suppose. I really don't have a good idea about how much of that will be necessary, though. After the first round of the rolling harvest, I should have a better idea. For now, just cram as many shelves as possible down here while people are still working on everything else."

"Do you think we'll eventually need to have this whole space filled with your shelves and bins? "

"Probably. For now, though, we can use a single dresser, about six feet long, and a standard bookshelf. I'll have a lot, but we'll go through it pretty fast. And we'll need a ton of jars for all the pickling and preserving and all that. That's what the bookshelf is mostly for."

Hannah nodded her satisfaction. "That's pretty much what I needed to know. Thanks, John." She gave him a grateful smile.

"I'm glad I can help." He failed to see how she couldn't have figured that out for herself, but shrugged and followed her upstairs again. Maybe she just had too much to do. While she plunged back into the organizational fray, he checked the window and saw Ai walking among his flowers. He gulped and headed to his room.

His tiny bedroom had enough space for a bed, a closet, a nightstand, and some shelves. Three plants in pots grew on his windowsill. One, the bamboo, reminded him of his mother. The aloe had a soothing presence and the ivy felt like a jolt of caffeine when he touched it first thing in the morning.

While he stood in the doorway, breathing in the aloe scent on the breeze, someone brushed past him.

"Hi, John."

He noticed Ai waving at him out of the corner of his eye and turned in time to catch her smile and look away. Too late for her to see, he smiled and waved. And felt like an idiot. Before he figured out how to say something, she stepped inside her own room and shut the door.

He banged his head on his door. If only women could be as easy to deal with as plants.

"Goodness gracious." Christopher, the resident Tejano empath, tsked as he approached. He patted John on the shoulder. "Oh dear," he said with an exaggerated sigh and pity in his eyes.

John considered shutting the door in Chris's face rather than figuring out how to deal with him. But that would be rude. "What?"

"You know, she will never find out you like her if you don't say something."

Rolling his eyes, John took a step into his room. "Yeah. Thanks."

"No, wait! Wait. I wanted to ask you for something." Chris pressed his palms together in front of his chest. "I know you have a ton to do and you don't want to talk to me, but please, please, pretty please? I'm on a mission."

John sighed. "What do you need?"

"Do you have any daisies growing out there right now?

"No, there's feverfew, but no daisies."

"Oh, poop. Can you grow some?"

"Out of nothing?" John snorted. "No. I need a seed or a cutting that's still alive. Get me that and I can grow anything."

"Okay. I can do that. Thanks, John!" Chris waved and glided up the hall.

"Sure. Whatever." John shut his door and kicked off his dirt-stained sneakers. He needed garden clogs. Looking down at his jeans, he decided they were too dirty to keep wearing and shucked them.

His t-shirt, too. Weariness rolled over him. Using his power took a lot out of him, and he'd been doing it almost nonstop since he got here. Sitting in just his boxers, he reflected that he should have grabbed a sandwich.

Too tired to bother getting one now, and also thinking he needed to get a bathrobe, he lay down and relaxed. As he drifted on the edge of a nap, someone knocked on the door. His eyes snapped open and his heart jolted. He had to pant to catch his breath. Whoever decided to disturb him could go to hell.

"John?" Ai called through the door. "I'm sorry to bother you —" Before she finished the sentiment, leaped to his feet and yanked the door open. She looked at him and binked, then turned away with a blush and a giggle. "Oh, wow, um, yeah."

He remembered his state of undress. "Oh, crap." Pulling the door partway closed, he hid behind it. "Sorry. Not really as awake as I could be, I guess."

"Um, yeah. It's okay."

Much too embarrassed to look at her now, his gaze stayed on the floor, the wall, the door, the doorframe, anything but her. "So, um."

"Yeah. Um."

"Uh, did you, um, want something?"

"Oh! Right. I wanted to ask you if I could help with the harvest. I mean, I can go pretty fast, and it's not just my legs, it's all over."

Mention of her legs drew his gaze to them. She wore shorts today, leaving her shapely calves and knees bare. He let his gaze meander up her thighs until he remembered she'd asked him a question. Snapping his gaze to her face, he gulped and hoped she didn't notice how long it took. Another second later, he grasped the question. "Um, yeah, that would be great. It'll go a lot faster, especially the grains."

If he considered it from a particular point of view, this would be a lot like a date. Exactly like a date, in fact, except without date-style activities, a set day and time, and dignity. "I'm not sure how soon that'll be, but I'll let you know…I guess the day before."

"Okay, cool. Are you alright?"

"Yeah, I was just…" He waved into the room, trying to recall the word for trying to sleep. "Um."

"Oh." Her eyes went wide. "Ooooohhhhh. Okay, I am really, really sorry for bugging you, then." She took a step back.

He blinked once. A beat passed. The way she covered her mouth and grinned made him realize what she thought he must have been doing. "Wait, no, that's not what I meant."

"It's okay, it's cool." She waved him off and took another step. "You're a guy. No big deal."

"Well, yeah, but I'd much rather do it with you." It took a moment for his brain to catch up, notice, and be completely mortified. "Um, nap. Tired. Sorry." He shut the door, hoping she didn't knock again. Or ever talk to or see him again.

Can't UnSee

Kaitlin

"Don't even."

Jayce stopped and blinked, hands raised to show he meant no harm. "I only came—"

"Ssht." Kaitlin flicked her hand at him in irritation. Had she let him come one step closer, she knew he would've knocked the table with her glass, spilling water all over her laptop. "Don't care. Go away."

"Fine." Jayce huffed and left.

Already ignoring him, she switched focus on her web browser from her favorite stock ticker to her broker's online portal. Based upon the vision she had five minutes ago, she needed to sell three stocks before the end of business today and buy four more. Tomorrow, she'd sell those four and make a killing.

Of course, since her precognitive power allowed her to play the stock market, she already had over a million dollars. Five weeks ago, her power went active and she started with two hundred bucks and a freebie online trading account. Now she had a personal broker—selected by her visions—to do her bidding. He made a ton off her in commissions. Most of it went to pay outrageous medical bills for his daughter.

"Kaitlin?"

Glancing up, Kaitlin saw one of the many interchangeable female blonde residents of this superhero safe house. "What?"

"I don't mean to bother you. I can come back." The woman wrung her hands and bit her lip.

"Too late." Kaitlin tapped on her keyboard, waiting for the request. She finished typing orders to her broker and the woman still stood in silence. Apparently, she couldn't handle blurting out her problems. "What do you want?"

"I was wondering…" She glanced to the side and blushed. "The thing is, I think I might be pregnant."

"And this has what to do with me?"

"Clive and I were going to drive to the nearest town and pick up a test, but I thought maybe…?"

Kaitlin gave her a long, slow blink. She'd never been used as a pregnancy test before. The novelty amused her as much as it annoyed her. "Sure. Why not? Saves time, right?" As an added bonus, no one ran the risk of being seen or tracked because of a silly errand. Shifting her laptop to the side, she held her hand out.

The woman tensed and stared at the hand.

After several long beats, Kaitlin arched an eyebrow. "Are you going to let me touch you or what? I barely know you and this has nothing to do with my future. If you want me to read this, you gotta take my hand."

"Oh. Sorry." Moving with enough tension to coil a rusty spring, she touched Kaitlin's finger.

With a roll of her eyes, Kaitlin snatched her hand. She closed her eyes, expecting a vision instead of an impulse or information delivered straight to her consciousness. Two deep breaths later, she focused on the knowledge she wanted and mentally pushed the button to make her power activate.

The imagery rolled over her in a tidal wave. Bullets, blood, water, ash. An elevator dinged. Acid sizzled. Chunks of stone and masonry blew apart.

Kaitlin snatched her hand back before anything became clear. She covered her mouth against the impulse to throw up.

"Oh my gosh, are you okay?" The woman crouched and reached for Kaitlin's face.

"Don't touch me," Kaitlin snapped. "Get out. I can't help you."

Letting out a startled gasp, the woman stumbled backward. "I'm sorry. I didn't mean to hurt you."

"You didn't." Kaitlin turned her attention to her laptop, expecting it to soothe away her nausea. As the woman reached the doorway, Kaitlin realized why she felt like barfing. "Stop," she called out. "Yes. You're pregnant."

"Thank you."

"Whatever," Kaitlin muttered at her laptop. "Never touching her again."

Weapons

Lily

Sebastian chased the tiny silver dragon in the sunshine. It lured him away from the herb garden, away from the cars, and away from Lily. She sat on a tree stump, practicing with her power. Bobby stood beside her, watching her son with his hands in his pockets. His command of his dragons did nothing to boost Lily's confidence with her own power.

To make this effort useful, she focused on creating a new blanket for Sebastian. Everyone said they'd get snow here this winter. She and Sebastian would experience that for the first time together. Only five minutes after she heard someone say that, she realized snow only happened in the cold. This place would need more blankets.

Her hands itched for half a second while she activated her power. A white nimbus outlined her fingers and flowed into solid material. More and more slid out of her until she had a one foot square. The solid, inflexible sheet of thick, white material had nothing in common with the fuzzy blue blanket she wanted.

With a heavy sigh, she tossed it onto the stack of her previous failed attempts, now numbering ten. It hit with a wood-like clunk. The stack rattled again as the bottom failure dissipated.

"I'm useless."

"Naw." Bobby flashed her an encouraging smile. "Just ain't what your power is good at, is all. If'n you can make it permanent, you'd be real good for building materials. Could probably redo the barn in a snap if'n you can make it all one piece."

"But that's so…" She sighed again, not sure how to explain. Bobby's power let him do nearly anything. The same was true for so many of them. Even Lizzie could use her fire in umpteen ways, including somehow powering the water heater even in her absence. Lily's own ability seemed so limited and pointless. She could make building materials and tools that lasted half an hour.

"Maybe you just gotta relax. You seem kinda tense."

"Maybe I'd just be better off without an audience," she snapped.

Bobby held up his hands in surrender and backed away. "No problem. I'll go wrangle the boy."

Lily watched him go. As soon as he left her sight, she regretted her sharpness. She'd finally found someone capable of helping her put Sebastian's father behind her. The day someone showed up at her door to tell her he'd been killed in action remained the worst of her life. In second place? The day he told her he'd enlisted. To make his father proud.

Brooding over Sebastian, Sr. accomplished nothing. Lily closed her eyes and forced herself to think about a fuzzy blanket. Since everything she'd made so far had been white, she abandoned the need for blue. The thing didn't even need to be fuzzy if she could just get something that behaved like cloth. She opened her eyes to find another square plate and tossed it on the pile. Trying again, she waved her fingers to see if that made any difference and discovered she could produce a hard plate with ridges like a crinkle- cut potato chip.

She tossed the new failure and rubbed her face. Her power had to be useful for something besides avoiding the need for a tool box.

"Hey, chica. What's the matter?" Javier draped an arm around her shoulder.

Both surprised and repulsed by him, Lily jerked away and jumped to her feet. "Nothing." Her cheeks burned and she had no idea why.

"I doesn't look like nothing." His smile held what seemed like genuine sympathy. He spread his arms wide, offering to hug her.

Something about him set her on edge. Maybe it was the fact she knew he'd abandoned his pregnant girlfriend to come here. Or maybe it had to do with the way he'd smacked her butt the first time they met. "I'm fine. Thank you." She raised a hand to stop him. "I came over here to avoid distractions."

"Okay, okay. I get it." He trudged into the trees, shoulders slumped, making her feel both greasy and bitchy.

"Um. You're working on the roof, right?"

He paused at the treeline and turned back, a hopeful gleam in his eyes. "No, we're done." He leaned against the trunk and she saw his gaze rove down her body. "They're getting materials together, then we're gonna work on the barn. I got nothing to do until then."

"Oh." After his ogling, she no longer felt bitchy. "The leaks are all fixed, then. That's good to know. Thanks."

"No problem, chica. You want me to keep you up to date on the news around here?" He grinned.

She got the impression he'd take a positive as an invitation to bother her anytime. "No, thank you. I should get back to work." Turning her back on him, she returned to the stump and prayed for him to leave.

"You know—"

"I'm fine. Just need to concentrate now. Thank you."

It seemed like a long time passed before she heard twigs snapping and leaves crunching to announce him walking away. A shiver worked its way down Lily's spine as she tried to forget that encounter. She needed something to ground herself.

Sunlight caught her plain gold wedding ring. He'd been dead for two years, eight months, and twelve days. Not once had she considered taking the ring off until she left Bobby on the side of the road in Utah. He hadn't stayed long after she drove away with Sebastian, but for the rest of the trip here, she'd seen him every time she checked the rearview mirror.

Shaking her head, she made an effort to stop thinking about men. Sebastian—the little boy—needed a new blanket. End of statement. Her power produced another stiff board. She stood and flung it into the trees as hard as she could. With another flick of her power, she made a white hammer and held it up to examine it.

Apparently, fate wanted her to supply transient tools and nothing else. She dropped it and made a screwdriver, then a pickaxe, a hatchet, a crowbar, and five things she'd seen before without learning their names. Then she made a brick. This would never serve anyone as a tool. Since it only lasted a short time, it couldn't be used for building. That made it a weapon.

She dredged up memories from her husband's favorite movies and made a throwing star, then a throwing knife. In another few minutes, she'd created a pile of swords, axes, and similar weapons. Nudging the pile with her shoe, she had no idea what to do with any of it.

Her entire upbringing had centered around her parents' gardening business. She knew how to identify and take care of plants, had some skill with landscape design, and could run a cash register. If someone asked her how to handle slugs, she knew which products to suggest and could explain the differences between them. Everything else she knew revolved around raising a sweet little boy.

And here she sat with a pile of weapons at her feet. Nothing in her life had prepared her for this, with the possible exception of marrying a man hell-bent on joining the Army. With that realization, she noticed she'd avoided creating one particular type of weapon. Lifting her hands, she couldn't decide if she wanted to succeed or fail.

The white nimbus surrounded her hands and created a gun. Sebastian had been proud of his marksmanship, but the pistol felt strange in her hands. At once, she wanted to drop it and cling to it. This thing, if it worked properly, had so much potential to harm her son, and she didn't only mean if he accidentally shot himself with it.

"Lily? Are you okay?" Jayce, his flesh made of something silver, carried a load of old, rotting wood to the forest, probably to dump it there. He stopped, his gaze flicking from her to the gun to the pile of weapons.

Numb until now, Lily felt her eyes burn with tears. "Not really?"

"Is that loaded?"

"I don't know," she whispered, horror creeping deeper into her.

Jayce blinked, then he tossed his armload aside. His normal brown fleshtone rippled across his face and arms as he approached. "Where did you get this?" Stepping to her side, he covered the gun with his hand and took it from her.

"I made it." She wiped her cheeks, not sure whether it upset her more to have made a gun so effortlessly or to not know what to do with it.

"Ah." He popped it apart with practiced motions. "I'm guessing you don't know much about handguns. This is a non-functional revolver. It lacks some of the internal parts necessary to actually shoot a bullet."

"Oh, thank God." She held up a hand and made a bullet like ones she'd seen on TV. It took no real effort or thought. "Here I was worried it was really this easy."

Jayce cocked his head and took the bullet. "This is for a rifle. It won't fit." He dropped the gun on the pile and held the bullet up to examine it. "But it looks like it might have all the right parts. If I brought you an example, do you think you could reproduce it?"

Lily whimpered. "I hope not."

He tossed the bullet onto the pile. "You know, there's nothing inherently evil about guns. They just have a rather singular purpose and that purpose isn't about cute little duckies and fuzzy bunnies."

She nodded and wiped her face again. "They took his father away from me."

"Which hurt. And you're afraid they'll also take him."

He'd hit the nail too hard on the head for her. She covered her face and cried.

"Lily. If you don't want to make guns, you don't have to make guns. Or bullets. Or any of this. No one will ever force anyone to leave this farm and go fight for us. You just want to be Sebastian's mother, and that's perfectly fine. Just because you have a superpower doesn't mean you have to use it, especially if it makes you this uncomfortable.

"But if you ever want to work on it, I can help you make a real gun and real bullets. I can teach you to shoot and show you how to keep yourself and your son safe. I also know how to fight hand-to-hand. Matthew is another good resource for this kind of training. All you ever have to do is ask and we'll teach you. And if you never ask, we won't pressure you. I promise."

"Why's Mommy sad?"

Lily swiped her sleeve across her face and flashed Jayce a smile. "Thank you," she whispered to him. "Hey, little man," she said louder, forcing as much cheer as she could into it. "I'm not sad." Hopping off the stump, she scooped him into her arms.

Bobby jogged into sight and took in the scene. He gave Jayce a half-hearted dirty look. "You making her cry?"

"No. It's fine. I'm fine."

Jayce rolled his eyes and waved Bobby off. "How long will all this stuff be here?" He pointed to the pile of weapons.

Shifting Sebastian to her hip, Lily frowned. "Not long, but we should play somewhere else." She carried carried her son into the trees, in a different direction than Javier had gone.

"Mommy be happy!" Sebastian hugged her neck.

"I'm fine, kiddo."

"Mommy. You're lying." He kissed her cheek and rested his head on her shoulder.

"You're too smart for your own good." Noise behind them made her turn to see Bobby following. She stopped to wait for him.

Sebastian raised his head with a bright smile when he saw Bobby. "I know! Mommy needs tickles." He wriggled and squirmed until he could reach her belly and strained to tickle her. His efforts made her want to laugh, but not because of his fingers.

Bobby caught up with a grin. "Can't argue with that logic." He darted a hand in and brushed his fingertips over her side.

Lily giggled and blushed. Once she started, Sebastian had her doubled over, laughing. She set the boy on the ground as she shied away from more tickling, unable to stop. Both Bobby and Sebastian chased her around a tree until she wound up with her back to the trunk, out of breath and facing Bobby.

"Okay, buddy." Bobby, also laughing, set a hand on the boy's head. "That's enough. Let your momma breathe."

"Laughing is good," Sebastian said.

"So's breathing." Bobby pushed the boy aside, getting him out of reach. The movement put his body closer to Lily's, warming her and making her blush again. "It's kinda important and all." He faced her again and seemed surprised to find her so close. "I…um." His gaze dropped to her mouth.

Lily touched his chest, feeling his heartbeat. She'd seen how he treated her son and how he tried so hard to do the right thing. He'd saved their lives and she knew he'd do it again without a second thought. If he had to, he'd sacrifice himself for either of them. Just like Sebastian's father.

He hesitated. She kissed him. After a moment of surprise, he wrapped his arms around her.

"What are you doing?" Sebastian asked, his small voice thick with suspicion.

Bobby pulled away far enough to look her in the eyes. "Falling for your momma."

Sebastian picked up a rock, losing interest in them. "Mommy with catch you. Or she'll kiss the boo-boo and make it all better."

"I can live with that."

Lily grinned and slid her arms around Bobby's neck. Behind his back, she tugged off the wedding ring.

Common Ground

Anita

With a sandwich and a glass of milk in hand, Anita stepped into the backyard. She strode past John, ignoring his garden, and paused at the unexpected sight of a pile of white weapons. Lifting her glass telekinetically, she bent and picked up a sword. It reminded her of her big brother. He played the king's guard for some medieval dinner show in her hometown.

Since the entire reason for carrying her late lunch out here had been avoiding people, she took the sword into the trees. Out of sight of the house, she swished the sword around, knowing she had no skill with it. After half a minute, she transferred it to her telekinesis and ate her lunch while the sword slashed through the undergrowth.

"Hola, chica." Javier dropped out of a nearby tree and landed in a ridiculous three-point superhero crouch. He straightened and puffed out his chest, looking pleased with himself.

Anita rolled her eyes. "What do you want?"

"Ouch." He pretended to flinch, meeting all the expectations he created with his East LA accent. She could easily picture him stealing a car or knocking over a gas station with his homie gangbangers. "I didn't even do nothing yet, chica."

She swept the sword around to point at him, making it hover inches from his neck. "You think you're going to do something?"

He gulped and raised his hands. "Nope. I don't got nothing here for you if you don't want it." Nervous gaze on the blade, he grinned. "If you do want it, though, I got you covered, chica."

"Stop calling me that," she snapped.

"*¿Quieres que te llame 'mujer'?*"

Anita scowled and let the sword fall. Having it there tempted her to use it too much. "I don't speak Spanish, you dumbshit."

Javier's brow shot up. "You didn't even learn your parents' language? That's sad."

"My parents are black, asshole. I'm adopted."

"Oh. Huh." Javier crossed his arms and averted his eyes. Then he shrugged. "I guess I don't know if my mama is really my mama."

Wanting Javier to go away, Anita sneered. "You know your own kid is really your kid."

He laughed. "Only if you think my girlfriend never slept around. I guess we'll find out when it's born."

Suddenly, Javier seemed a lot less disgusting to her. One little fact changed everything. She reflected on that and wondered if maybe she'd been too hard on Bobby. "Would you go back if it's your kid?"

"I dunno. I mean, I guess if it's my kid, he'll probably have powers someday. So he should be here with us. I'd have to go talk to Renata." He grimaced. "I can't think of anything I want to do less. She likes to hit me with a baseball bat. She's not real strong, so it doesn't hurt much, but she's such a *puta*. A bitch. I liked it at first, then my mama met her and decided I needed that to keep me straight. She thought I'd wind up working in a chop shop."

She watched him lean against the nearby tree and wondered if he realized how relaxed he seemed. For the first time, she noticed how his shoulders always bunched up and he moved with just a hint of stiffness. In this moment, all that faded away and he stood with his head up and a pensive expression.

"I worked in a casino, as a pit boss. My parents work there. They got me the job." Anita sighed and wished she could make the hurt inside stop. "Some of the men I worked for, they…don't really understand the concept of 'no.' " She had no idea why she told Javier that. Most of the women here would understand if she told them. Out of all the men, Javier struck her as the most likely to rape someone. Yet, she picked him to tell.

For several long, tense moments, Javier remained quiet. "I know a lot of girls who got knocked up in high school. They act like they wanted it, but sometimes, you can see it in their eyes how much they really didn't. Some guys, they see it like it's how you prove you're a man. Some girls, they think it's the only thing a guy wants from them, ever. It's all kinda messed up."

"Yeah." Maybe East LA and Reno had more in common than Anita thought. "Peace?"

Javier smiled at her. "Yeah. Peace. You and me, nobody really likes either of us. But maybe one person here is a start."

Maybe all she needed was to sit down with some of the people here and really talk to them. If she could make a friend out of Javier, of all people, she ought to be able to handle anyone. "You ever need to talk to someone, I guess I'm here."

"Me too, chica. Me too."

Meddling

Chris

With every step closer to the farmhouse, Chris felt a headache building. So many people in such a small space meant a lot of emotions packed together and rubbing against each other. This place had far too many dysfunctional relationships. He kept trying to help, but that had made him about as popular as Javier or Anita, so he gave up. Sort of.

Right now, the blob of distress in the vegetable garden would drive him insane if he did nothing. Chris marched over, finding John brooding among the sunflowers. In only a few weeks, John had grown them from seed to towering six foot stalks with giant flowers bigger than Chris's head. Chris thought they might also be bigger than Tony's ego. Maybe.

"Didn't I say you needed to tell her?" Chris stopped in front of John and planted his fists on his hips.

"What?" John frowned up at him, then shook his head and rubbed his face. "She thinks she caught me jerking off."

"Oh dear." Chris sighed. "Did she?"

"What? No!" Embarrassment rolled off John in waves.

"I was just asking. No need to be snippy." Crossing his arms, Chris pondered how to fix the problem. John and Ai obviously belonged together, at least temporarily. "Would you like me to talk to her for you?"

John shrank away from him. "No. I'll figure it out."

"Before or after you give me a stress headache?" Chris rubbed his temple. "Because, honey, you're damned distracting. All knotted up and emoting all over the place. If you don't deal with it soon, I might have to get Jayce to knock you out so I can sleep."

Shame bubbled to the surface. John mumbled too quiet for Chris to hear.

"Was that a yes? Because I can't hear you."

"Yes, fine. Do whatever."

"Oh, thank gawd." Ignoring the rest of John's mumbles, Chris hurried inside. He flashed a cheerful smile at all the pretty boys as he passed the kitchen. As usual, discomfort colored Bobby's otherwise inoffensive feelings, but no one else's. He pinpointed Tony elsewhere in the house—alone and grumpy—and turned a corner to avoid the biggest homophobe in the group.

He reached a workroom and opened the door to find Ai, Lily, Alice, and Lisa all attacking various cloth mending projects. He recognized curtains, socks, and a blanket between them. All four smiled at him and waved him inside.

"Ladies."

"Did you come to help?" Ai patted a chair beside herself.

"Oh, goodness, no. I'm horrible with this sort of thing." Chris sat and let Lisa drape a blanket over his lap to make her job easier. "I came to gossip."

Ai giggled. Lily and Lisa both blushed and looked in different directions. Alice's smile faltered.

"Do we have to?" Alice closed a hole in a sock with dainty, even stitches. The woman would have made a capable surgeon.

"Yes. It's absolutely imperative. There are too many people here not to." Chris nudged Ai with his shoulder. "This young lady, for example, is driving someone completely nuts. Besides me, I mean."

"What happened" Lisa asked, her voice hushed.

Ai rolled her eyes. "It's not a big deal."

"I have it on good authority he's mortified. You should jump him. If you wait until he girds his loins, nothing will happen before you're both sixty." He noticed the other women smirking and pointed at Lily. "Don't think I don't know what you've been up to, missy. Rolling around in the bushes with Bobby."

Ai gasped in surprise. "Really? Oh my gosh!"

Lily blushed again, bright pink. "It wasn't rolling. He kissed me. That's all."

"You can't just stand around waiting for boys to kiss you," Chris said with a huff. "Seize the initiative! Grab them by the shirt and throw them down." As much as he'd like to do that with his particular daydream, he couldn't. Jayce was friendly and sweet, but straight as an arrow.

Ai paused in her stitching and straightened. "You're right, Chris." She set the curtain aside and stood up. "If he's fantasizing about me, I might as well give him a try."

"Good for you." Chris watched her leave the room, then tracked her adorable determination as she marched outside. Something curious happened when she passed the mass of boys in the kitchen. Bobby flared with guilt. Chris had never noticed that before, probably because he avoided spending a lot of time around everyone. Everyone knew about what happened between Bobby, Ai and Anita, of course, but why Bobby felt guilty was beyond him.

Anita screwed that pooch, the poor dear, not him.

"Lily? Have Ai and Bobby chatted since he got back?"

"Oh. Hm." Lily gazed off at the wall. "No, I don't think so. He's been spending his time with Sebastian and the guys."

"Oh dear." Chris sighed and shook his head. "I think it's high time they fixed that. I'm not going to touch the matter with Anita, but those two? They need to figure things out. Sooner, not later. I refuse to stand idly by while they emote at each other in secret and fail to talk it out."

"You're such a meddling bitch," Alice groused, though Chris could tell she meant it more fondly than it sounded. "Just let them get to it when they get to it."

Feeling melodramatic, Chris heaved a long-suffering sigh and jumped to his feet. Lisa's blanket fell to the floor, dragging Lisa's needle and thread with it. "If I didn't have to feel everything all of you do all the time, I wouldn't care in the slightest. Since I do, I want harmony, dammit. And I'm not above 'meddling' to make it happen!" He pretended to flip his short hair in a saucy toss, then stormed out.

Behind him, two of three women tittered. Lily touched his shoulder. "Wait."

Chris stopped and turned in the hallway to see her still holding the sock she'd been working on. "I can tolerate a lot, but only so much."

Lily smiled, open and honest. "I don't want to stop you. I want to help you."

"Oh!" Delighted, Chris draped an arm over her shoulder. "We have to machinate to get them into the same room with no good reason to escape."

"Does it have to be like that? Can't we just tell them both to deal with it?"

"Do you think that would work with Bobby?"

Lily paused and pursed her lips. After a long few beats, she said, "No. Probably not. You're right, we'll have to scheme." Looping her arm through his, she tugged him back inside the workroom. "What's the best way to force Bobby and Ai to talk without an audience?"

Alice shrugged. "Those two? Give them both a job they have to do side-by-side that neither would abandon. So, something kind of important, but stationary. Nobody else can be available to do it. But don't tell either of them they'll be working together. They show up, endure the awkward until one breaks, then they figure it out."

"We can use Sebastian," Lily said. "Bobby would do anything for him."

Lisa shook her head. "It doesn't take two people to watch him. What about assembling something for Sebastian? Oh, wait! Hannah said we need to put together bins and things for the basement, to hold food. Bobby eats a ton and Ai would probably do about anything for John."

"Brilliant!" Chris noticed the pair outside only interacted briefly, then Ai left. "Let's set them up for tomorrow morning, after breakfast. Lily, you tell Bobby. Alice, please tell Ai to show up. I'll ask Jayce to bring some raw materials." He waggled his eyebrows and waved goodbye, then found a place to lie in wait so he could ambush Jayce and his delicious abs.

Uncomfortable Apology

Ai

Stacks of wood, a box of nails, and Bobby sat in the shade beside the barn. Jayce crouched beside him, laughing at something. Ai paused before they noticed her and tried to figure out how to approach the situation. Alice had said Hannah asked her to help John out with vegetable storage. She thought that meant she and John would be working together. Apparently not.

Jayce glanced up and smiled at her, making escape impossible. He beckoned her over. Her feet forced her to join them.

"Hi." She hoped it didn't sound as awkward as it felt.

"And now that you have company, I should get back to work." Jayce stood and tipped an imaginary hat at Ai then he walked away.

Bobby turned and saw Ai. His face fell. He picked up a piece of wood, some nails, and a white hammer, giving it his full attention. "Hey," he said, the one word curt and clipped.

Ai considered leaving him to work by himself. They'd both probably be happier. Except she'd have to face Hannah knowing she backed out of helping with a task her power could be useful for. She sighed and sat with the pile of wood between them.

The silence hung thick and stifling, ugly and tense. Groping for something inoffensive to talk about, Ai picked two pieces of wood and fitted them together. She grabbed nails and realized they had only one hammer. Leaving to go find one appealed, but she couldn't guarantee she'd come back.

She watched him hit a nail without supporting both boards enough. He needed a third hand. A fourth would help a lot. Without a word, she moved closer and held the two boards together so he could use the hammer. They ought to trade tasks, because Ai could do the repetitive job a thousand times faster.

Deciding someone had to start someplace, Ai fell back on stranger chitchat. "The weather's been nice."

"Sure." The thunk of wood against metal echoed in the small clearing.

"Hasn't rained in a while."

"Nope."

"I guess that means it'll rain now."

"I s'pose."

With him unwilling to participate, Ai decided she'd amuse herself. "The bunnies are boinking."

"Uh-huh."

"I saw a giant hedgehog ramming the barn yesterday."

"Right." He paused in mid-swing and squinted at her. "What?"

Though she'd been trying to provoke him into talking, now that she had his attention, Ai didn't want it. "Nothing. Just saying stuff."

He stared at her for several seconds, then he sighed and pounded on the nail again. This time, he slammed it into his thumb, releasing three dragons. "Heckbiscuits," he snarled as he watched them scatter.

"Are you okay?" Ai took his hand and looked it over. The stump of his thumb, with its abrupt, non-bleeding end, made her uncomfortable. She tossed his hand at him. "Yeah, I guess you are. You always are." To her surprise, she sounded bitter about that.

Bobby hung his head and let the hammer fall to the ground. He raked a hand through his hair and squirmed. "I'm sorry. If'n Anita hadn't never done did what she done, you woulda been—"

"No, it's okay!" Ai coughed and covered her mouth, heat flaring in her cheeks. Now he'd started the conversation, she knew they had to see it through and finish it. "I mean, I know you did everything you could. I'm the one who should be apologizing. I never should have let her leave you behind."

He shrugged and looked away. "I don't blame you for nothing. Weren't your fault."

"But if I hadn't left, you wouldn't have been shot."

"That ain't on you." He glanced to the side and sighed again.

Ai followed his gaze and saw Anita carrying a pile of debris with her telekinesis. "Never mind her. She's not worth hating. Or even thinking about much."

Shaking his head, Bobby wouldn't meet her gaze. "I ain't really mad, Ai. Not at you nor her."

"Really?"

He rubbed the back of his neck and squirmed again. After a long pause, during which she thought he made some difficult decisions, he said, "I sure don't appreciate her choices, but hate is an awful strong word. If she'd'a done it to you too, just shucked herself out without looking back, then, yeah, I think I would, but she took you with her, and if'n I was in a little better shape, I'd'a been right behind you. It ain't your nor her fault I got shot, not really, and some folks ain't used to doing the whole 'team' thing. Can't fault her for that."

Ai stared at him for several beats, amazed by how reasonably and rationally he approached the whole thing. In his place, she thought she'd want to throttle Anita and herself. That very fear had prevented her from broaching the subject sooner.

"I, uh, wow. I thought you'd be really upset."

"Well." He smirked. "In fairness, I done gave it a whole lotta thought. And it's hard to stay angry for real around Sebastian and Lily. I don't want no hardship 'tween any of us if'n I can help it. Ain't no telling when stuff'll happen, and if'n something's the last word, it oughta be a good one."

Knocking the wood aside, Ai draped her arms around Bobby's shoulders. For a moment, he stiffened, then he relaxed and hugged her back.

"I'm so sorry, Bobby. I'll never, ever leave you behind again. I promise. No matter what."

"I don't think it's something I can promise that I'll never let you get strung up in that sorta situation again. Don't seem reasonable. But I won't leave you behind, neither, Ai. Nor nobody else if'n I can help it. I promise that much."

Ai heard someone sniffle, and it wasn't Bobby. They both let go and found Christopher standing in the shade nearby, fanning his eyes with one hand.

"Oh my gosh. You two," Chris warbled. With that, he hurried away.

Bobby grinned. Ai giggled. They both laughed and got to work.

Winter Forecast

Violet

Violet flew over the ratty old barn roof, wondering why Greg and Albert consented to live in such a wretched dump. She ducked through a gaping hole to inspect it from the underside and saw no reason to change her opinion. They'd have to replace the entire structure. For now, tarps formed a large tent below, sheltering the boys' workshop and living space.

She poked at a loose slat. With a loud crack, it crumbled, and she had to scramble to catch all the pieces before they hit the tarps. A curse slipped out as she wished she could fly back to college in Montgomery, Alabama. Her tiny apartment had been nicer than anything here. Then Will and Jasmine showed up. By then, her power had already gone active, of course.

Pulling her sweater tighter around her body, she decided to be grateful she had pants. With an ability like flight, skirts had become impractical. The first time she rose into the air here, Javier looked up. After that, she'd worn shorts or these yoga pants she had for working out. Never once had she needed to wear pants outside in her whole life. Until now. Whenever she had time, she had to go shopping.

With her inspection complete, she drifted to the ground. Smoke roiled in a thin wisp from the table where Greg worked. Albert sat to the side, tapping on his laptop. Neither looked up when she landed. Rather, she stopped an inch above the ground and hovered. None of her shoes suited this environment, so she wore fuzzy blue slippers. Like Stephen, she had no need to ever touch the ground and avoided doing it whenever possible.

"Excuse me, honey." Violet sat next to Albert, her power supporting her without a chair.

Albert smiled at her. "What's the verdict?"

"I'm hardly an expert, but the whole thing needs to be torn down and replaced. Even if we replace the roof, these walls won't hold it up for long."

Albert pouted. "We're already roughing it out here."

"I know it, honey. Maybe you can get John to do some plant magic."

"I've already asked him about it. He said he's not up to that level of manipulation yet. He could give us six foot walls from the shrubs all around, but that's the best he can manage for now. Which isn't really good enough for the workshop. We need a high ceiling to manage smoke."

"Well, we know how to replace the walls now, at least. Had to do it for the farmhouse already. I think some of those boys like using the nail gun. Maybe a little more than they should."

Laughing, Albert waved at Greg. "You should see him with an arc welder."

"I heard that." Greg pointed at him with a soldering iron. "We don't need the whole structure replaced. I've got plans for the workshop, I just have a dozen other projects to finish first. We only need to make it through the winter in this thing, so don't waste a lot of money or effort on fixing it."

She smiled at him and straightened. "Sure thing, honey. I'll make sure it gets taken care of."

"Thank you," Greg said. He returned to his work.

Albert flashed her a smile as she floated outside. Not for the first time, she wondered what winter here entailed. Several people had already mentioned preparing for it, but she had no idea what that meant. Back home, her mom paid attention to the weather and covered some plants for occasional overnight dips below freezing. Nobody with any sense went out in that kind of cold.

She rounded the corner of the farmhouse and found Jayce sitting in the sunshine with Owen, both drinking out of brown bottles with their shirts off. For a few moments, she had to pause and admire them. Each had a sheen of sweat on his muscular chest. Owen's red beard and hair, not to mention his physique, reminded her of a lumberjack from the cover of a romance novel.

Owen noticed her and grinned as he waved her over with his bottle. "Would you like a beer? We have more."

"No, thank you, sugar." She floated closer. "We need to come up with a way to protect Greg and Albert from the winter without rebuilding the barn. I think a stiff wind might blow that thing down as it is right now."

"Hm." Jayce leaned back and checked what he could see of the barn towering over the farmhouse.

"We could maybe set them up with just an insulated sleeping space for now," Owen said. "But those tarps won't cut it in the snow, so we should look into something more sturdy."

Violet nodded along until she realized what he'd said. "Wait a minute. Snow? What're you talking about?"

Owen paused with the bottle halfway to his mouth. "Uh, frozen water falling from the sky in crystalline patterns?"

"It doesn't really snow here, though. Not much. Right?" She glanced at Jayce and found him grinning so hard he might hurt something.

"Well. Um." Owen coughed. "It snows a fair amount here."

Violet glared at him. "You're joking just to mess with me. It doesn't really. Right? How do you even know? You're not from around here any more than I am."

"I'm from Denver," Owen said. "Which isn't very far from here. Maybe an hour and a half by car. So yes, I *am* from around here more than you are. We'll probably get two to three feet over the course of the winter, maybe more. Starting sometime in November."

Violet tried to imagine living with snow. She saw herself curled up with a blanket and hot cocoa, sitting in the window and watching it. But that would get boring after a while. "What do you even do when it snows?"

"Plow it and get on with life?"

"Do we have a plowing thing here?"

"I seriously doubt it. The stores should have them out in October." Owen's grin faded and he set his bottle aside. "It's really not that big a deal. We won't see anything like Minnesota or Alaska, not here. We're not going to have any serious survival issues. We'll be fine."

"But…snow is…*cold*!"

Owen chuckled. "Yes. Snow is cold."

"How cold are we talking here?"

"Here? It probably doesn't go lower than ten below."

Violet blinked rapidly, trying to translate that. "Ten below? Below what? Zero? Are you crazy? Why do people even live here? Coming here is the first time I've ever left Alabama, and it's for some kind of frozen wasteland hellscape!"

"That's a little harsh," Jayce said.

"No, below zero degrees is harsh." Violet jabbed a finger at him, more upset by his grin than the weather.

"You know what we do in Vegas when it gets cold?" Jayce waggled his eyebrows.

Tossing her arms up, Violet grunted in disgust. "Honestly. Men. Doesn't matter what the question is, the answer is always sex. Too hot? Sex. Too cold? Sex. Tired? Sex. Can't sleep? Sex. Cranky? Sex. Happy? Sex. Hungry? Food sex." She turned to storm away. Instead, she stopped and stared at the bearded man staggering up the drive.

His backpack had seen better days and crusty mud spattered his clothes. Duct tape held his shoes together. He looked up and saw her, then he collapsed. Though she didn't recognize him, Violet darted to his side.

"Violet," he rasped, "thank God I found you."

"Will?" She pushed his shaggy brown hair aside and gaped at the state of him. "What happened to you, honey?"

"I've been walking forever. I don't even know how long." He held her arm, his grip weak. "They got Jasmine. I didn't know what else to do or where else to go."

Jayce and Owen reached them. "You did the right thing," Jayce said. "Let's get you inside and cleaned up. Then you can tell us everything."

"I don't know where she is. There's not much more to tell."

Violet watched while Jayce picked up Will and carried him inside. "Jasmine, honey," she whispered, "We'll find you. I swear on my Grannie's grave. Whatever it takes, we'll find a way to get you free."

DRAGONS IN CHAINS

Prologue — Maisie

Summer in Honolulu meant work, from morning to night. Maisie didn't mind. Though exhausting, her job was fun. At the moment, she sat wit the other girls in the show, rubbing her feet and grabbing what rest she could in the half hour break between performances. Normally, she stayed in costume all day. After an incident during the last show, she wore only her bikini and leafy wrist- and ankle-band, with flowers woven into her black hair.

"Maisie, what happened?" Dave, the stage manager, leaned in and scowled at her.

"Talk to Rob," she snapped.

"I did. He said you flubbed the sequence."

Her nostrils flared with irritation and she narrowed her eyes. "He's a damned liar. He missed a step and I tripped over him. That ass is just lucky I was able to recover without falling on my butt."

"I saw it," Linda confirmed, nodding. She'd been directly behind them both as part of the chorus. "It was Rob's fault."

"When you go back and tell him we said so," Maisie sneered, "you can let him know I'm still not going to sleep with him, no matter how many times he asks."

Dave rolled his eyes. "You guys need to keep the personal

stuff off the stage."

"Tell him, not me." Maisie stood up and jabbed a finger in the air. "I don't want any 'personal stuff' with him. Just because he gets to grab my ass on stage doesn't mean he gets access to it any other time."

Dave shook his head and huffed the sigh of a man who doesn't care but has to deal with it anyway. "You're not making my job any easier."

"I'm not the one causing a problem, Dave, he is." She held up her grass skirt so he could see the damage to the side. Two inches of leaves had been ripped. No amount of shimmying could hide that. "You want to do something about that, go right ahead. I'd be happy to break in a new partner. Right now, though, I need a new skirt because Rob stepped on it." At least they wore swimsuits under these things. Otherwise, she would have been flashing the audience the whole time. A quarter of them probably wouldn't have minded, but it was a family show: bikinis for Dad, shirtless men for Mom, fire and drums for the kids.

Dave held up his empty hand—the other had a clipboard—in a placating gesture. "Fine, fine, whatever. Just— Whatever." He waved it off and left quickly.

"Rob needs to get fired," Linda said. "He's such an asshole."

Maisie threw her damaged skirt in the bin for that purpose. Someone would try to salvage it later. Fortunately, she had a backup skirt, and pulled it out of her locker. "No argument here."

"He's cute, though." Amy sighed, a dreamy look in her eyes.

Maisie snorted. "You're welcome to him."

"Hey, do you want to go to the beach tomorrow, Maisie?"

Looking over at Linda, Maisie shrugged. "Sure, I guess. Not like I have anything better planned."

"You know he's only asking you out because you keep turning

him down." Amy still had that look. It would be annoying if she wasn't nice.

Maisie snorted. "Meaning what? I should just sleep with him and get it over with? No thanks. He is so very much not what I'm looking for. Like I said, he's all yours."

"What's the matter, Maisie?" Bunny's voice held a generous dollop of fake mocking. "Don't you like a guy who's full of himself?" The group of women fell into amused giggles and laughter. They all knew the break would be over before they knew it, though, and set to the task of adjusting costumes and makeup and hair. Chatter turned to plans for tomorrow. Maisie and Linda would hit up one of the tourist beaches and spend the day prowling for beefcake to watch.

Soon enough, they moved out to assemble for the show in the garden setting, around and on an artificial pond. Maisie was the star attraction: the best dancer of the group, and the one Hawaiian girl with icy blue eyes that made her a bird of paradise among the hibiscus. As for the men, none of them stood out among the muscles and six-packs. Rob stepped up beside her, ready to heft her onto his shoulders as soon as the announcer introduced their act.

"Bitch. That was your fault."

"It was not, and you know it, asshole. Watch your damned feet this time or I'll improvise kicking you into the water."

"Whatever."

"Go to hell." She had more to say, but Rob grabbed her and she forced herself to smile. He picked her up and carried her out on his shoulder, both of them playing the part of lovers for the audience. While she shimmied her hips and swung various props to show off her flexibility and skill, the other women danced around her. Three men banged sticks on drums. Another five danced with fire. Rob spotted her on jumps and flips, and lifted her and carried her around.

The last show of the day started in the twilight hours, making the fires flung around by the men more dramatic. Maisie always liked the ones in the dark and near-dark better—it felt magical. When it ended, everyone shucked their costumes and makeup to get out quick. Much to her annoyance, Rob stood by her bicycle where she'd left it locked up for the day, under a freestanding fake tiki torch. She could get a car, but then she'd have to figure out where to park it and pay for the gas. The buses didn't go close enough to her parents' house to be worth it.

"I guess 'beat it, asshole' isn't explicit enough?" The way he stood blocked access to her bike, but only from one side. She stifled a gulp and went around him to unlock the chain.

He scowled with his arms crossed over his chest. "What's your problem?"

Glancing around, she thought she caught sight of a security guard walking past the alley. It made the stabs of apprehension in her gut ease a tiny bit. "My problem? I'm not the one with the problem. Let go of my bike."

Rob spent all day, five days a week, supporting her weight, lifting her, and throwing her around. She had no chance of breaking the grip he had on the top tube of her bike. "Not until you agree to go out with me."

Those words made her blood run cold. She stared at him, knowing she looked scared, and could see in his face that he knew it, too. And he liked it. "Is this seriously the only way you can get a date?" It came out much less scornful and much more breathless than she wanted it to.

Smirking, he grabbed her arm with his other hand, gripping it tightly. "I'll take that as a yes. Let's go."

Stunned by the idea he intended to haul her off whether she wanted to go or not, her mind blanked. He yanked her away from the bike. It took her three stumbling steps to finally form the coherent thought that he wouldn't stop. Something stupid popped into her head as she glanced back, and she said it. "Someone's going to steal my bike, asshole."

He glanced back and dismissed the matter. "I'll buy you a new one."

There had to be a way to get him to let go for a second so she could run for it. Her panicked thoughts chased themselves until the answer stared her in the face. Maisie opened her mouth and screamed. Instead of letting go, he pulled her close and covered her mouth. She bit his finger and jabbed her elbow at his ribs. He still didn't let go. Why didn't he let go? She kicked and squirmed and made as much noise as she could through his hand. Someone would hear it. Someone would stop him, or at least call the cops.

When he reached the car, he thumped her against it, making sure to hit her head. "Shut up," he snarled. "Jesus, just shut up already."

The impact knocked her senseless long enough for him to let go and hit her across the face. Her head snapped to the side with the sharp blow and she crumpled to the ground, curling up to protect herself from more and whimpering. More would come, she knew it, and if she tried to crawl away, it would be worse. After a few seconds of tense waiting, she looked up to see Rob lying limp on the ground, face down, two white men in dark suits standing nearby like sentinels. A third crouched down and checking him over. The fourth stepped close and crouched beside her.

"Are you alright, miss?" They all wore sunglasses, and she saw the little cord going down from his ear and into his collar. He offered her a hand.

For a moment, she stared at it in shock. "More or less?"

"Is he your boyfriend?"

Shaking as she rose to her unsteady feet, she gripped his hand for support. "No." He'd shoved a syringe full of clear liquid into her upper arm and pushed the plunger down. She blinked, suddenly dizzy.

"Good." She saw him pull the syringe out and felt numbness seeping across her body. Before she could cry out again, she collapsed into his arms and everything went black.

Chapter 1

"Remind me why I thought this was a good idea."

"You never said it was a good idea, you just agreed to do it."

Bobby snorted and shook his head. "Least I know my expectations been met."

Stephen chuckled. "The plan is going swimmingly so far."

"That's for sure." Bobby looked around the holding cell they occupied, not remotely afraid of the four punks they shared it with. A month or so ago, he would've been sitting on the edge of the bench, worried about offending or annoying guys like that. Now, they couldn't hurt him even if they all had guns stuffed in their pants. If they tried anyway, the vampire sitting next to him wouldn't let them. "How long you reckon before a suit shows?"

One of the punks stood up and cracked his knuckles, radiating menace. His Chicago accent sounded weird to Bobby, even after being around so many different people from so many different places; Bobby's own Southern drawl would always be what sounded 'normal' to him. "Nobody cares about your stupid plan or whatever."

Two of the others egged him on with guttural noises of approval. The fourth guy sat apart and huddled on himself, watching with keen interest.

Bobby and Stephen both turned to look at the guy, neither of them impressed. His black tank top showed off muscles and tattoos, probably from gang affiliation. The guy's baggy jeans had a studded leather belt holding them lower than Bobby liked to wear his, but at least covering most of his dingy white boxers. The guy's hair was slicked back with a black and white pattern bandanna wrapped around his brow.

"Bobby, would it be a problem to add assault to the charges against us?" Stephen addressed him without looking away from the punk.

"So long as you don't kill him," Bobby shrugged, "don't see why."

"I'm not afraid of you," the punk said with a jut of his chin. He took another step forward and held his fists up.

Since Bobby could only see the back of Stephen's head, he had no idea what the punk saw on his face. Whatever it was, the guy paled and gulped. So did the other two. "Your survival instincts are a little dull."

"Oh yeah?" The punk gulped again. He took one step back and lowered his hands, yet kept the defiant stance. "You talk tough, but I bet you got nothing."

"Wrong answer." Bobby sighed, because it didn't have to be like this. He turned away so he only had to hear the thump and crack as Stephen pursued some small violence. "Don't hurt him bad, neither," he chided. "Cops'll forgive a little scrapping, but they ain't so kind when somebody needs to go to the hospital."

Stephen sat back down beside him, no sign of anything having happened from him. The two other guys, though, had to pick their bold friend up off the floor. "It's not my fault the floor is bare concrete."

"That there is an excuse."

"Excuse, explanation, tomayto, tomahto, whatever."

"If'n this weren't a jail cell, I'd be real disappointed, but they probably got something coming to them."

Stephen laughed again. "I expect we'll see a suit in no more than four hours from when they processed us," he peered up at the clock out of reach beyond the bars, "so anytime now."

Bobby glanced up at the clock, too, wondering what Lily was doing right now. Half past midnight in Chicago meant half past eleven in Colorado. She ought to be asleep. Unless, of course, he decided to be an ass of an idiot who ran off without a word or note to be a stupid hero. At least he was doing something. Jasmine and ten others were still prisoners, and he meant to find them and free them. No matter how stupid this idea might be, it was better than sitting around at the farmhouse, waiting for a clue or something they'd never get.

The door into the area opened, and Stephen smirked. "Right on time."

Bobby turned to see two suits, both looking straight at him and led by the black lady cop that stuck the two of them in here. The one in front paused and said something into his cuff while the other one kept going. "Mitchell and Cant, on your feet, give me your hands. What happened to Ibanez?" No one said anything. Stephen and Bobby dutifully presented their hands and got them slapped with cuffs. "Mmhmm," she said with narrowed eyes.

"It's nice to finally meet you, Mitchell." The suit grabbed Bobby roughly by the arm.

"Am I famous or something? Would you like a signed photograph?"

"I'd like one," Stephen said cheerfully. The other suit grabbed him and hustled him out right behind Bobby.

As they reached the front door of the station, Bobby lifted his hands. “Guys, you know as well as we do the cuffs are kinda silly. If’n we wanted to get gone, we wouldn’t be here, don’t act like you don’t know that. It’s insulting.”

The suit glanced at his partner, then they nodded to each other. They took the cuffs off and tossed them off to the side without bothering to try to aim for a cop. “What do you want?” Bobby’s suit asked as they pushed through the door and into the Chicago night, his hand still firmly gripping Bobby’s bicep.

“We’re tired of running, of the bickering and stuff.”

“Whatever it is about us, it must make the women especially bitchy. It was fine at first. But the girls,” Stephen said with a roll of his eyes, “it’s like trying to deal with angry cats.”

“Seriously not worth it.” Bobby nodded his agreement. “You don’t stick us with nothing, we come willingly, somebody on your team gets to pitch us a deal for what y’all want. We don’t like it, we walk away, we leave y’all alone so long as you leave us alone. That’s the deal.”

The suits stared at them with identical blank expressions. Several long seconds later, one jerked a thumb at the standard issue black SUV illegally parked in front of the station. “We’ll have to clear that first. In the meantime, get in the car.”

“One of us could just talk to your handlers directly,” Stephen offered. “It would save time.”

“Fat chance,” his suit snorted. “Get in the car.”

They got in the car while both suits stayed outside to use their phones. “I ain’t sure whether to be insulted or not that they only sent two guys to pick us up.” Bobby popped a single dragon off his thumb. It zoomed around the car, looking for anyone hidden in the shadows of the back. It found nothing and returned to him.

“Here’s hoping they don’t just stick us with something and shoot us in the head.”

"D'ya think that would kill you?"

"No idea. Not keen to find out." Stephen sat back casually, adopting the relaxed persona of a Very Important Person waiting to be driven by his chauffeur.

Bobby tapped the buckle of the seatbelt, trying to decide if wanted to put it on or not. "You reckon they figure it don't matter how many they send?"

"Probably. Why risk four when you can risk just two and get the same result?" Stephen shrugged. "I think they're just goons anyway."

"Should we ask about that old guy?"

"As soon as we mention the name, they'll know we know something and stop treating us like dumb but dangerous kids. We'll become smart dangerous kids, which is kind of a scary thing to old white guys used to being in control."

"Yeah, I guess."

Stephen rolled his shoulders again. "We're here to be agreeable because we're tired of running and tired of bitches telling us what to do. Just remember that and we'll be golden."

Bobby nodded. That was the plan, along with hoping they'd be taken wherever the others could be found and freed, or someplace they could find records to tell them where that might be. As plans went, it lacked subtlety, nuance, and greatness. He'd gotten tired of waiting for a better one.

The suits opened the doors and climbed into the front seats. "Your terms are acceptable." The one in the driver's seat started the car.

His statement relaxed tension in Bobby's shoulders he hadn't previously been aware of. "Where we going, then? I hope it ain't Salt Lake City." He ignored Stephen's small cough and elbow nudge.

"No. We'll meet someone in Indianapolis. It's about a three

hour drive, give or take."

Bobby let out his own tiny cough, hoping to cover his surprise. How many locations did these guys have? More importantly, these suits didn't need to know how fast the two of them could fly, and didn't need to know how interested both of them were in the location. "Don't suppose we could stop for a bite to eat on the way? I'm starving."

Stephen snorted. "You're always starving."

"I'm a growing boy." Bobby grinned. "I ain't picky, neither. Anything's fine."

"I, on the other hand, am extremely picky."

The suit in the passenger seat turned around with a blank face, the sunglasses keeping the movements of his eyes a mystery. "Define 'picky.'"

"I prefer redheads, between ten and five inches shorter than me, clean and sober, in heels."

Passenger Suit's mouth puckered up in annoyed distaste. "We can hit up a drive-through."

"I 'preciate that." Bobby rolled his eyes and shoved Stephen.

"It's the truth," Stephen said, sounding wounded. He looked back at Passenger Suit. "Nothing for me. Get him enough to feed a small army."

Bobby snorted and watched the suit face forward again. With nothing left to do now but sit back and wait, he wound up staring out the window, watching the highway go by. About an hour later, they paused long enough to get some food. His belly full of cheeseburgers and fries, Bobby dozed off for the rest of the trip.

He woke to Stephen jabbing him in the side with an elbow as the SUV rolled through the streets of Indianapolis. The suits kept quiet until they pulled into the well-lit parking lot for a two-story office building. Light peeked through the blinds of three windows on the second floor. They parked next to an identical black SUV.

"This is it," Driver Suit said as he shut off the car.

"Ain't exactly what I was expecting," Bobby said, peering at the building. Nothing about it held any interest, from the blank, whitish walls to the squared shrubs. He thought the place where these guys did their business should have some kind of sinister feel to it. This reminded him of nothing worse than his dentist's office.

"Your expectations aren't really our concern." Passenger Suit hopped out and opened the door for Stephen.

"Do they surgically remove your sense of humor before you're allowed to wear the sunglasses?" Stephen asked.

"Yes," Driver Suit deadpanned as he opened the door on Bobby's side.

Bobby chuckled. "I reckon that actually means no." He chose not to resist when Driver Suit grabbed his arm.

"People keep telling me that no means no, and yes means 'probably.'" Stephen let Passenger Suit grip his arm, too.

Feeling a surge of mild paranoia about this too-quiet spot, Bobby let his free arm dangle and popped a dragon off his thumb without comment. If nothing happened, great. If something happened, he'd still have a dragon on the outside.

The suits marched them in through an unlocked door, then up the stairs. On the second floor, Driver Suit knocked on the door for Suite 204, and another suit opened it.

"How many guys in suits y'all got, anyway? Seems like an unlimited supply."

The new suit's mouth went thin, and he slapped Bobby across the face. He tried to, at least. His hand connected with Bobby's face, but he burst into the swarm with the impact, so the suit's hand went right through his head. Hundreds of tiny robot dragons, all outraged that this man dared to hit Bobby, converged on that hand to destroy it.

Surprised, Bobby took a moment to absorb what happened as his mind hovered in the center of the swarm. If he didn't stop them, the dragons would shred the suit's hand and move on to engulf his whole body. They'd kill the suit and this whole trip would be for nothing. Also, a man would be dead, which was a Very Bad Thing, for more reasons than the obvious one.

Stephen shoved the suit to the side while Bobby clamped down on the swarm. "Get a grip," the vampire snarled at the new suit. "We can kill all three of you faster than you can pull out syringes and use them. Remember that."

Aside — Paul

"What do you think?"

Paul watched the minor scuffle through a tinted window, the kind that allowed a person to observe out of sight so long as the light stayed off. One agent gripped his hand in real pain. The two newcomers glared at the agents and moved with the wariness of cobras facing a mongoose. They sat in the chairs suggested by the remaining two agents and seemed to have divided the responsibility for watching the agents by unspoken accord.

He hadn't expected them to look so…normal. The taller one was too pale, but otherwise reminded him of an average college student. Paul could easily picture the guy on his own home campus of Seattle University, and, he noted with a small bite of jealousy, with coeds on both muscled arms. Raymond had that, too.

The other one had about a week's worth of light brown beard to match his shaggy hair, and wore jeans with a blank t-shirt. In the footage he'd seen of the incident at Hill Air Force Base, these two men struck him as monsters. Here, now, they seemed more like earthy movie stars, the kind of men people would meet and comment about how nice and friendly they'd been. Although he didn't appear to qualify as the kind of classically handsome that the girls went ga-ga for, he could imagine this shorter one with a girl-next-door in his arms.

"I can't read anything at all off Cant," he told the other man in the room with him. "He's blank. But he looks like he's not afraid of anything he can see coming, and doesn't have much respect for authority. Mitchell, on the other hand... There's a lot to read from him, too much. It's like he's got—" Struggling under the weight of so much input, he frowned. "Like each individual thread of thought occupies a different part of his mind, and they all crash around together. I think maybe it's the dragons I'm sensing, somehow."

"You think each dragon has some part of his mind?"

"I don't know." Paul shook his head. "Maybe if I could read just one dragon, separate from all the others, I could answer the question."

"So your talent is useless with these two."

"I guess so." Disappointed with this truth, Paul sighed. He wanted to help. "Maybe if I was in the room with them—"

"No." The other man pulled his sunglasses out of the breast pocket of his suit jacket. "They don't know any of you are working with us yet. I'd like to keep it that way for as long as possible."

Paul nodded and put his hand on the glass. This close, his icy blue, almond shaped eyes were reflected back at him, but he was more interested in the two men on the other side of the glass. "Are we really related?"

"Blood tests have confirmed you all share one parent, yes."

"How did they wind up being such cold killers, then?" It bothered him, a lot, that he had half siblings who could murder people.

"Everyone reacts to power differently."

Nodding, Paul sighed. He knew that, he studied psychology, it just seemed more disturbing when it hit so close to home, so to speak. “What are you going to do?”

“Offer them a job.”

“What?”

“What kind of prison could hold them? It would be better to have them on our team, with some kind of control on them, than to try to find some way to stuff them in a box. They’ve already proven they’re willing to kill to get free, and capable of a fair amount of mayhem. Besides, if we can flip them, they know where we can find the rest.” He covered his ordinary hazel eyes with the sunglasses. “Put your earbud in. I want your opinions as I talk to them.”

Paul nodded again and pulled the small device out of his pocket, then stuck it in his ear. “Is this thing working?”

“Yes. Since you can’t get anything from their minds, just pay attention to body language and tell me if you feel strongly they’re lying or obfuscating.”

“Right. Got it.” Paul watched while he opened the door and walked into the other room, hoping he’d be able to read these guys well enough. Lives might depend on it, maybe even his own.

Chapter 2

"Gentlemen." That voice sounded oddly familiar, and Bobby turned to see who walked in through the side door. The sunglasses did a lot to make him just another anonymous suit, but that chin tugged on his memory. He'd seen this one before and recognized him. Realizing his identity took him about the same amount of time as it took the guy to pace in and sit down behind the desk, looking like he owned it.

At the time, he'd been FBI Special Agent Steve Privek. Had he actually been an FBI agent then? Bobby reached up without thinking and rubbed his jaw where the man had socked him a good one about six weeks ago. "You're kinda far from Atlanta."

Privek smirked. "So are you, Mitchell."

"You're the one what made me leave in the first place."

"The situation was, perhaps, mishandled in some ways."

Bobby glared at Privek. "'Mishandled in some ways'? Are you joking? You framed me for a murder and chained me up like a dog."

"I'm sure that's how you see it." Privek laced his hands together on the desk and leaned forward. "I'm prepared to offer you a deal. Are you here to listen or to address past grievances? "

Stephen reached over and put a restraining hand on Bobby's

arm. "We're listening."

This wasn't the time to blow up at Privek and Bobby knew it. The dragons hated this situation and it made him crankier than he ought to be. The contact with Stephen reminded him why he sat in this office, and he snapped his mouth shut, leaning back in the chair with a glower. He could listen, but he didn't have to be happy about it.

"Good. What I have to offer you is a chance to work for the betterment of your country by applying your unique abilities to problems we find difficult to solve with current manpower and technology."

"Is that what you were gonna offer when—" Stephen's hand squeezed his arm painfully, making Bobby stop. A little harder and it would have become dragons.

"What he means is that we're concerned about petty things like bodily autonomy and right of refusal for requests we find objectionable."

One of Privek's eyebrows arched up over the sunglasses. "You'll have to prove we can trust you. After what happened in Salt Lake, we're a little hesitant to just give you whatever you want."

"Being shot kinda makes a guy get surly."

"You wouldn't have been shot if you hadn't already killed three of our men."

"Which was only 'cause—"

Stephen cut him off again. "Bobby. You're not helping."

Nodding, Bobby shut his mouth again. He had to remember that he'd come here for Jasmine, not for himself. Every time he opened his mouth here, he put himself before her, and she didn't deserve that. Worse, he put himself before all of them. While they had a few he didn't much mind doing that to, most of them ought to get better from him.

"I won't speak for Bobby, but I'm definitely interested. What could I expect for the first twenty- four hours?"

"We'll want to run you through a full physical and take some samples for testing."

"What kind of testing?" Stephen frowned. "I'm not interested in being anyone's lab rat."

Privek nodded his understanding. "Just drawing some blood and taking a swab of DNA for examination. After that, we'll want a full explanation of everything you know about that makes you different from a normal person, then we'll assign you missions based upon your abilities. From what we already know of what you can each do, you'd both be well suited to war zone duties."

"I ain't no soldier." Bobby shifted in his seat, annoyed that the idea of actually doing soldiery things made him wonder if Lily would be more attracted to him for it.

"I understand that," Privek said curtly, "but what you can do would be useful to other soldiers. This is about saving lives, gentlemen. A small army of people with your type of capabilities could end most wars with very little loss of life, on both sides."

Bobby sat and glared at the desk. Stephen, though, leaned in and seemed very interested. "I'm not sure how useful I can be in a desert environment, but I'm willing to do what I can to help soldiers come home. Can this be provisional, with the sample-taking after the first mission? I'm hesitant to just give that up right now. It feels violating on some level. I want to know I'm on the right side of the line before I go all in."

Privek pursed his lips and furrowed his brow. After a long pause, he finally said, "Very well. We don't need anything from Mitchell anyway. Hagen will take you to your next destination, where you'll be looked over and questioned about your capabilities."

"If it ain't too much trouble, we'd rather work together than apart."

"I'll make a note." Privek stood up and gave them each a nod without offering his hand to shake. "I hope this is the start of a long partnership, and that we can put all the messy business from before behind us."

Stephen stood with an echoing nod. "So do I."

Bobby stood and grunted his unenthusiastic assent, not caring if that bothered Privek or not. He watched the agent leave the room and turned his mild glower on Stephen. They probably had some kind of setup to listen to whatever they might say in here, so he kept his mouth shut. The vampire wordlessly headed for the other door, the one they used before. Having nothing better to do, Bobby followed. Passenger Suit stood waiting for them alone, checking his phone. At least they didn't get stuck with Touchy Suit.

"I'm Hagen," Passenger Suit said as he looked up. "We'll be heading east. If either of you need to use the bathroom, this is a good time."

"I don't have such petty mortal concerns." Stephen smirked, his humor slipping back on.

Bobby rolled his eyes and headed for the door Hagen pointed out. He needed to settle down. They took a job working for Privek. The dragons seethed inside about it. Heckbiscuits, he seethed inside about it. If he found out Privek had only been an FBI agent following orders before, he might decide to be more charitable about the whole thing. Until then, he wanted to do things to the man that would horrify Momma.

Speaking of Momma, why didn't he think to ask that surveillance be taken off of her house? They might do it anyway, given they had him here now. He still should have asked. Maybe he should teach people how to be as lousy at negotiation as him. Hannah would've handled all this much better. Lizzie could probably have gotten more, too. On second thought, her idea would be to blow stuff up until she got what she wanted, which might not really qualify as 'better'.

At least this mission thing should help people, even if it meant knowing Privek officially pulled his strings. How did that saying go? Good done in the name of Evil is still Good. He splashed some water on his face and stared at himself in the mirror. "You sure you wanna do this?" Thankfully, his reflection didn't answer. The question did galvanize the dragons, though, reminding them why he'd just given up his autonomy to Privek. They had to do something. This qualified as 'something'.

He toweled his face off and took a deep breath. "Just don't forget this is all for them," he told his reflection. "Just don't forget about them, no matter what."

Chapter 3

Ten hours later, Bobby and Stephen sat on a couch in the living room of a big old house. Hagen had disappeared to get some sleep after the long drive, and they now faced a man in a normal suit and holding a clipboard. He'd diligently scribbled down their names and now waited patiently for them to explain their superpowers.

Instead of using words, Bobby popped one dragon off his hand. Its fingertip disappeared, the end of the knuckle smooth as if it had originally grown that way. The dragon swooped around the room, chirping its annoyance at this whole process. "My whole body's made of 'em," he told the guy. "Hundreds, maybe over a thousand." It landed on Stephen's shoulder and quieted.

"They eat gears and stuff, I still need to eat, too. One gets smashed or shot or blown up or whatever, the others eat it and I get a sore spot for a bit. They do what I tell 'em to, but can do simple stuff themselves. If'n they get mighty angry, they can blow fire, but I ain't sure they can just do that whenever. Not real good at killing, but the swarm can take a guy down if'n we gotta."

The guy nodded and wrote on his clipboard. Bobby suspected they had cameras recording this interview, too. "Are the dragons 'they' or 'we'?"

Bobby shrugged. "Yes."

He looked up gave Bobby a hard, frowning stare. "What's that supposed to mean?"

"Dunno. If'n I figure a way to tell you, I will." Bobby shrugged again.

Stephen snickered. "I, on the other hand, am easier to explain."

After smoothing his expression and flipping a page over the top of the clipboard, the guy said, "Go ahead."

"I'm a fairly classical vampire, though I have no issues with garlic or holy symbols. I'm very sensitive to sunlight and burn easily, more than a person with fair skin. I couldn't say if I catch fire under prolonged exposure, and am not interested in learning the truth of that. Other than that, I have the superhuman strength, can fly, regenerate, and drink blood. I have no capability to handle food or other liquids and no longer have need of a bathroom. What happens to the blood in my digestive tract is a mystery I cannot explain, and again, I'm not especially interested in solving it."

The suit nodded and scribbled. "Does sunblock work?"

"Briefly. I tried SPF 70 once on the back of my hand, it started to redden in five minutes instead of five seconds. Clothing works just fine, anything that ordinarily protects from sunburn."

"Ya know, technically, you do have a problem with garlic," Bobby pointed out.

Stephen smirked. "Yes, well, it's not really confined to garlic. All food is problematic. It doesn't repel me is the point, nothing does."

The suit didn't find that funny. "From what I saw you're both perfectly fine with killing? "

"No, not really." Bobby shook his head.

Stephen pursed his lips and looked off at the wall. "It's not something I prefer to do. Drinking blood is fairly primal, though. The instincts are there, and can be difficult to suppress."

Bobby squirmed. "I only did take down three of your guys. Them first two, the dragons were kinda…" He shifted again. "I lost control of the swarm, they went berserk on account of what was done to me up to then. That third one, he tried to shoot me and a kid, and it didn't look like he was gonna stop. I don't got a whole lotta control over that—once they're looking to kill, they're looking to kill."

The guy huffed and wrote something else down. With one brow arched, he glanced from Bobby to Stephen and back. "If you were asked to kill someone, like an assassination, would you be able or willing to do that?"

Bobby looked at Stephen, who shrugged. He scratched at his beard and frowned. "I guess if'n it was a bad guy who done things what ain't right, then maybe, yeah. Call it a case-by-case sorta thing, but it ain't neither of us's first choice. I'm good at scouting, and getting in and outta places."

"My talents seem obvious to me," Stephen said, "but put bluntly, I am good at being very difficult to kill, and incapacitating those who block my passage."

The suit nodded. "Alright, this is good enough for now. I'm pretty sure they'll want to send you to a war zone to try to put a dent in the insurgency, but we'll see." He stood to leave the room. "Can I get you anything while you wait? It might be a few hours."

"I am kinda hungry," Bobby nodded. "Whatever's lying around is fine."

Stephen rolled his neck to the side, cracking it. "If you have any females willing to take one for the team, I could use a few pints."

"I'll…" The guy frowned again and tucked the clipboard under one arm. "I'll see what I can do." He walked out, leaving them sitting in silence.

On the way here Bobby saw the road signs, so he knew they'd come to Virginia. This wasn't the same place he woke up in that lab a month ago. He knew nothing else about it so far. It seemed unlikely this house played a major role in Privek's operation. He'd be stupid to send them to a location with strategic value.

"Basement," Stephen said after the door clicked shut.

"Yeah, that's my guess, too. Otherwise, they'd have more security for the ground floor."

Stephen stood and stretched. They'd both slept on the drive here, and hadn't had a chance to walk around much since arriving in mid-morning. "I wonder how long they'll keep us waiting."

Tired of sitting, Bobby followed suit and paced to the window. He pushed the gauzy white curtain aside and peered out. Hagen's black SUV sat parked outside, no other vehicles in sight. "I wonder where they put the rest of the cars. Round the back, maybe, so it don't look like there's folks here so much."

"Makes sense to me. I suppose they'd get a little annoyed if we went snooping around."

"Probably." Bobby shrugged. "Reckon they're gonna ask us to take out terrorists? "

"Yes. I also expect they'll use a very broad, overly inclusive definition of the word 'terrorist.'"

Sighing heavily, Bobby kept looking out the window. He'd seen the trees screening the house from the highway on the way in and watched the leaves sway in a breeze. "Yeah, I reckon."

"More interesting to me is what they'll do about my nutritional needs."

"You just ate last night. I thought you could go a coupla days between."

"I can," Stephen nodded, "but I don't like to. It's best if I get at least a few pints every twelve hours, or a good, heavy meal once a day. That blonde was too skinny to take much from her. Before that, my last real feed was two days before that. It's getting a little dark in here." Without any further explanation, Bobby knew Stephen referred to his Hunger taking over, bit by bit.

"Maybe you oughta been a little more upfront about that."

"Group like this probably has a bunch of people who'll do anything to keep their jobs. The suits strike me as zealots."

They both heard footsteps coming their way and went quiet. When the door opened, a brunette with dusky olive skin and brown eyes walked in. She wore a forest green suit with black pumps. Her eyes immediately went to Stephen's, then Bobby's, a flicker of recognition lighting them up. "Hablas español o parlez-vous français?"

She had a smooth voice, one that rolled around in Bobby's head and made him want to like her. If he had to guess, he'd say she was Spanish or Mexican, because he understood the first two words well enough, and recognized the accent. "No, ma'am, sorry."

Stephen also shook his head, and offered her his hand. "This both complicates and simplifies things," he muttered with a smirk. "Stephen," he said, gesturing to himself.

"Elena. English little. You…" She trailed off with a frown.

Raising a hand solemnly, Stephen gave her a small, gallant bow. "No harm to you, I promise. Sit? " He pointed to the couch.

Though he didn't really want to watch, Bobby had only seen Stephen feed once. At the time, other things had been going on and he hadn't been all there. Curiosity made him half-watch from the side while still standing at the window.

Elena perched on the edge of the couch, facing him and watching Stephen. She glanced at Bobby and back to Stephen. Bobby thought he'd be nervous in her position, too. Her boss sent her into a room with two unknown men she had no real way to communicate with, probably without telling her exactly what to expect.

"Relax," Stephen said softly, slipping onto the couch beside her. "Five minutes." Holding up his hand with all five fingers out, he used it to distract her while he seized her arm and licked her wrist. Elena's eyes went wide and she gasped. Stephen brushed her thick hair away from her neck and plunged his fangs in.

Elena moaned and grabbed Stephen's jeans. The small sounds of arousal sounded like "Liam" a few times. Her body pushed back against him. Suddenly, Bobby felt like a voyeur, watching his buddy have sex with a random girl, and he turned away from it.

Worse, the scene reminded him of kissing Lily a few days ago. Not only did he regret not leaving her note, he couldn't wipe away the memory. He'd managed to get a few minutes alone with her in the woods around the farm. The second he touched the small of her back under her shirt, she used the pet name for her dead husband. Everything got awkward in a hurry.

"Much better." Distracted from his thoughts, Bobby saw Stephen licking his lips, Elena draped across him. His eyes snapped open and he slipped out from behind her. When he'd settled her on the couch, he adjusted his jeans. "That'll keep me for a day or two."

"She alright?"

"She'll be fine." He reached down and checked her pulse chin with two fingers. "Mmm, I maybe took a little more than I ought to have."

"She ain't dead, I hope."

"No, just weak. She won't be down for long, though. Probably." Stephen shrugged. "All I know for sure is Kris bounces right back with just a night of sleep."

Bobby snorted. Stephen's new girlfriend may or may not be real, but the vampire definitely had a steady source of blood keeping him away from the farmhouse. “What’d you tell her, anyway?”

“I said I needed to do a thing for my brother and couldn’t say how long I’d be gone. If I get a chance, I’ll call her.” He waved the subject off. “I suppose we ought to let them know she’s out cold.” He paced over to the door and peered out. Someone must have been standing right there, because Bobby heard Stephen say, “I’m done. She probably needs the rest of the day off.”

The way he said it made Bobby feel dirtier than he had a moment before, like he’d helped Stephen rape the woman. He looked back out the window and shook it off. The guy needed to eat to live and not be a depraved monster, after all. Behind him, someone walked in and carried Elena out without a word.

Outside, he saw a dark blue sedan pull in and park. A man in a brown military uniform stepped out of the driver’s door, then opened the rear door for what Bobby assumed must be a military officer of some kind. Since he knew what Marines looked like, he knew this man wasn’t one. Navy wore white, he thought, and he knew Air Force used blue, so the tan uniform had to mean an Army guy. Given Lizzie blew up half of that base in Utah, he decided to be glad they hadn’t brought an Air Force guy.

“I’m thinking they want us to work for the Army.”

Stephen paced over and peered out over Bobby’s head. “Apparently. I guess this means we get to kill terrorists and find land mines.”

“I ain’t sure how I feel about that.”

Dropping himself back on the couch, Stephen shrugged. “If they’re going to send soldiers to do this stuff anyway, we might as well do it and keep those guys from getting shot or blown up. Maybe we can even put the fear of Allah into them enough to make them tell us stuff.”

“I don’t speak no Arab.”

The door opened and the Army officer they saw outside walked in with his hat under his arm and a brown folder in his hand. His name tag read 'Delane'. Bobby had no idea what all the colored bits and rank bobs meant, other than this guy had more of them than his Daddy had. Hagen escorted him in. As they walked in, Delane nodded to something Hagen must have said moment before.

"Boys." Delane had the kind of stern voice that commanded attention and demanded obedience. "I'm Lieutenant Colonel Delane, US Army. I understand you have some unusual talents and would like to use them to serve your country as quietly as possible."

Every time he thought he understood what was going on with the suits, something came up that destroyed Bobby's notions. He didn't understand how guys who pretended to be FBI, CIA, and who knows what else would have a genuine Army officer guy here to recruit them. Were these guys actually part of some legitimate government agency that somehow, nobody actually knew about? "Yeah, that's a fair way to put it."

"Mitchell, right?" Bobby nodded and Delane opened his folder to read from it. "I understand your father was an excellent Marine."

"Didn't stop him from getting killed." If they wanted to bring his Daddy into this, he had no reason not to tell it like he saw it.

Delane barely reacted, giving Bobby only a tiny jut of his chin in response. The man probably dealt with unhappy families all the time. He turned his attention to Stephen. "Allen Cant was a good soldier, too."

"Happily," Stephen sneered, "my older brother is still alive and no longer in harm's way." It might be a challenge for both of them to avoid mentioning Matthew and his PTSD issues. They had to, for everyone's sake.

"If you two are willing, maybe we can do something to keep

more of our military men and women alive and unharmed."

"Sounds like a plan," Bobby said hurriedly, wanting to avoid a discussion that would reveal more than they wanted to. "We ain't real keen to be doing assassinations, though."

"I told him that," Hagen said.

"And I understand. It takes a certain kind of person to handle that kind of mission, and there's no shame in not being one." Delane took the chair and gestured for Bobby to sit on the couch beside Stephen. "It seems to me you'd be best used as a team, accomplishing objectives we'd ordinarily send a larger group to handle. Assaulting strongholds, retrieving prisoners, clearing the way for demolitions and other experts, that sort of thing."

"We agreed to take on one mission and evaluate whether we want to work for you after that."

Delane nodded. "That's fine. We'll need you to run through some basic training, just so you're familiar with how things work, and some routine survival training. It won't take long, considering your unusual abilities. We'll get you some uniforms, too, and all in all, you can be out in the field in three or four days, depending on when we can schedule the flight to get you out there. We'll give you a few objectives, and when those are complete, if you're not willing to continue out there, that'll be that."

The only thing Bobby didn't like about this plan had to do with remaining out of communication with the farm. They knew that might be a problem when they left, and decided to chance it. He should have left a note. Matthew knew. He wanted to come along. They'd turned him down for two reasons: he had no control over his shapeshifting and he couldn't fly.

It had taken the pair of them about nine hours to fly to Chicago. Driving would've taken at least fifteen, and they would've needed to take someone else's car. Bobby wished they could've brought him along, if only so he didn't have to face the rest of the group when they discovered Bobby and Stephen missing. The memory of Matthew ripping arms off at Hill made him certain they'd chosen wisely on that front.

He could hardly wait to find out how they all reacted to the two of them taking matters into their own hands. It probably depended a lot on how successful they were and how long it took to get that success. As long as Lily stopped short of hating him for this, he could probably live with it. "Might as well get started, then." Bobby hopped to his feet and did his best to seem eager to be on his way to glory for God and country.

Less eager, Stephen stood and offered Delane his hand to shake. "Yes, I think we're your men."

Taking the hand and shaking it, Delane stood, too, and then shook hands with Bobby. "Just so we're clear, it's my understanding this will all be done in a classified fashion. That is, only those who absolutely must know who you are and what you're doing will."

Chapter 4

"These are my clothes." Bobby said it again, for the hundredth time, as he and Stephen walked off the plane depositing them at some base in Afghanistan. They'd been shoved onto a flight to Germany, then another one to someplace in Turkey, and now here, to the country where both Lily's husband and Bobby's father were killed. Would either she or Momma be proud of him for doing this? Doubtful. His Daddy would be, though.

Stephen huddled in on himself, shrinking down in the harsh light. Though they both wore hats and sunglasses and combat boots and full Army desert camouflage BDUs, the sunshine beat down and reflected off everything. The vampire also wore gloves and a balaclava. With every square inch of flesh covered, he had to look like he ought to be sweating his skin off. As for Bobby, the heat didn't bother him much. The dryness of the air, on the other hand, took his breath away and instantly made him thirsty.

It took them twenty minutes and a Corporal to find the guy they'd been instructed to report to. He couldn't be military, because he wore a suit with no jacket. Everyone around him dressed the same, in business attire with jackets slung across the backs of chairs. It seemed likely these folks were civilians in Intelligence, which made their being directed to him make sense. Sort of.

"Mitchell, Cant, I'm Klein." Shaking hands with them, Klein brought them to a table with an unattended laptop sitting open. He had that average white guy look to him. If Bobby saw this guy walking down the street, he'd just assume he was an upstanding citizen with a professional job, then not think anything else about him at all.

"I've been told you're a two man team of specialists capable of doing things I'm not allowed to ask about, and can handle objectives that ordinarily take a squad or two." Klein looked to both of them for confirmation. They both nodded. "Okay. I've got a couple of missions that you might be able to handle." He tapped on the laptop, bringing up photographs. "Three different ones, see if any of them sound doable to you.

"One: a town too far north for us to do anything but airstrikes that we suspect is a weapons stockpile but can't prove it without sending in a ground unit. Two: a warlord working against us holed up in a secure compound surrounded by civilians. Three: a cave system that needs to be explored. We think it's mined and there might be an easy ambush against us in it."

"Yeah, we can probably handle those," Bobby nodded, fiddling with his sunglasses.

"Shouldn't be a problem. We'll need maps and..." Stephen had his sunglasses off, too, and he scanned the room. Pointing to a brunette that happened to be the most attractive woman in the room, the corners of his mouth curled up. "Can you spare her for the rest of the day?"

"What? Wait, back up." Klein furrowed his brow. "Which mission?"

"They ain't too far apart, looks like," Bobby said with a shrug. "All three."

"Uh, okay." Klein followed the line of Stephen's gaze. "Then what do you need Jenny for? She's a secretary."

Though he didn't want to, Bobby shoved aside his squeamishness. "Pretty sure you just said you weren't s'posed to ask questions."

By this point, Jenny had noticed the interest in her and joined the three men. "Did you need something, Pete?" She had a pretty, open face, and Bobby knew he'd be interested in her if he hadn't met Lily.

"I'm in need of assistance, Jenny, please, this way." Stephen sounded so gallant and gentlemanly. She glanced at Klein, who sighed and nodded. The pair of them disappeared out of the tent.

"He ain't gonna rape her or nothing." At least, Bobby hoped he wouldn't. The vampire's morality on the subject had been left somewhat vague, and Bobby had no idea how devoted he'd really become to Kris in the few weeks he'd allegedly known her.

Klein's frown deepened, and he sighed again. "She's my responsibility."

"She ain't being hurt. You got my word. He's just got a peculiar…uh…" Giving up, Bobby shrugged. "I got no idea how to explain, so never mind. Gimme all what we need to know, 'specially about this warlord guy and what he done to deserve killing, and we'll leave soon as he's— Soon."

Ten minutes later, Bobby had three maps with dots on them and understood the three missions well enough to get them done. When Stephen joined him, coming from the medical tent, he said, "Klein's a mite worried about Jenny."

"She'll be fine. I was careful not to knock her out. They," he jerked a thumb over his shoulder, "think she's dehydrated, which is more or less accurate."

Deciding to take what Stephen said at face value, Bobby

handed a few things over. "I got maps and a headset for ya. They'll have someone who can interpret standing by starting two hours from now. I just wanna stop and grab some food and water, and then we can get going, 'less you want to wait for nightfall. Looks like it'll take us about two hours to get to the weapon place, the other two are in that same region, maybe a half hour to the caves, another fifteen to twenty to the warlord."

"What time is it here?"

Checking his nice new watch, courtesy of Hagen, Bobby said, "It's just past three in the afternoon. Klein said it'll get dark a little after six."

Stephen looked around, though Bobby could only tell because he actually turned his head. "Get what you need then let's get going. I'm covered up, we might as well travel. We can wait there just as easily as here."

Bobby nodded and clapped him on the arm. "Meet me on the north end. I'll be quick as I can." Without waiting for a response, he jogged off to find supplies. With the First Lieutenant rank insignias they'd been loaned, he had no trouble requisitioning as much food and water as he could stuff into his pockets and a small pack.

Twenty minutes later, he found Stephen on the north end of the base, looking over the maps in the shade of a tent structure. Bobby passed the pack over because he wouldn't be able to carry it himself, and they took to the air. They went up high and fast enough to not be a spectacle for people on the ground, then headed to the first site.

For the next two hours, Bobby had nothing to do but fly and think. The dragons hated it when he thought a lot. With no distractions, it happened anyway. Everything came back to Lily. She called him 'Bas' out of habit. She'd never kissed anyone but her late husband. Knowing that didn't lessen the sting.

He genuinely liked her, and told her so, and she seemed to feel the same. Then she slipped and made it clear she considered him a stand-in for a dead man, allowed into her arms as a replacement. Sure, he'd more or less stepped into the Dad role for her son, but that didn't mean he wanted to be Sebastian Thatcher, Sr., Part Two. He wanted to be a whole new movie.

He'd have to beg for her forgiveness. Often, probably. Why were they even out here, doing this? Was this what the suits were having the eleven they grabbed doing? Why did they torture him if they wanted supersoldiers? Maybe they were stupid and thought… something stupid.

What if he figured wrong? Those guys could've constructed the circumstances he woke up under. He imagined how it might have turned out if he woke up with someone 'rescuing' him from that. Until given a reason not to, he would've trusted that person implicitly.

Privek said "mistakes were made". Bobby had assumed he meant the framing, the arrest, and that part. What if the 'mistake' had been more about not having everything ready when he woke up? They probably learned from that mistake. His thoughts turned to Jasmine and how that could be applied to her.

As much as he liked her, Jasmine wasn't the brightest bulb in the box. A scenario took shape, where she woke up and found suits telling her things she believed, then showing her the footage from Hill. She'd nod along and agree that kind of destruction needed to be prevented in the future. They'd find a way to use Will's unknown whereabouts to motivate her.

efore he managed to follow these ideas to more concrete suspicions and conclusions, Stephen angled downward. With the sun setting, they chose a spot in the craggy hills outside the small town they planned to assault first. The cluster of buildings surrounded on three sides by barren, rocky inclines would be rough to reach on foot or by vehicle. The fourth side must be what they used to actually come and go—it was open ground and the approach could be seen for miles.

"We'll wait for true darkness, then drop in from above."

Bobby re-formed and pulled out an MRE, leaning back against a rock. "Stephen, I'm starting to wonder if we're actually working for the bad guys."

Stephen kept his eyes on the village. He didn't answer immediately. Bobby waited in silence, figuring he'd been thinking about other things for the past two hours. "I have a feeling that we'll discover this isn't about black and white so much as it is about methods and ideology. We've attacked and killed for our freedom. They've attacked and tried to kill for what seems to be a desire for control over us. It's a pretty classic type of conflict, really—it happens over and over again throughout history. My guess is they generally see us as weapons, and the more we act like that, the more likely they are to assert we aren't human, aren't citizens, aren't deserving of basic rights."

If he wasn't sure of it before, Bobby now knew without a doubt that Stephen had more brains than him. "I got the feeling when Privek said they made mistakes, he meant something different from what it sounded like."

Stephen nodded. "That's probably true. Some part of me wonders why they kept that list in that file cabinet. From what you described, it seemed like a serendipitous event, Ai finding it, but I just have to wonder if it was left there for a reason. Maybe you were supposed to find it. Maybe every file cabinet had several copies of that list distributed through the folders. Your escape could have been part of someone's larger plan. To what end, I don't know, but it's a thing to consider."

His mouth being full gave Bobby the chance to temper his initial reaction without saying something dumb. "I ain't sure I'm up for tinfoil hat theories yet."

Stephen grinned. "Yes, it does seem a little overly Machiavellian, doesn't it?"

"I never heard that word before, but if it means complicated and creepy, sure." Taking the canteen from where Stephen set it for him, he downed a few swallows of water to wash the food down. His garbage went back into the pocket he pulled the thing from in the first place. "I'm good, and it's pretty close to dark."

Still grinning, Stephen pointed vaguely towards the village. "How do you want to do this?"

"Well," Bobby shrugged, "I figure I can dragon through and see what there is to see. If'n we find anything, I tell you and we go blow it all up."

"Seems reasonable to me. I'll see if I can come up with anything more detailed for the 'blow it all up' part. Given that neither of us is really exceptional at that sort of mayhem."

"Yeah, we're kinda more people mayhem than stuff mayhem."

"Agreed. A shame we couldn't bring Matthew. But, c'est la vie. I'll come hang out over the village and wait for you there."

"La vee." Bobby blew into the swarm and flew with Stephen to the village. The vampire stayed a few hundred yards up while the dragons dove into the buildings, flying through in whatever way seemed least likely to get them noticed. He couldn't micromanage them all, so he had to rely on them understanding his demand to avoid being seen.

This was the first time he'd ever dispersed the swarm so much that no central glob of dragons remained. To his surprise, his 'mind' didn't automatically hitch a ride with any particular one or grouping so much as float in the center of them all.

Pushing that oddity aside, Bobby watched through their eyes, able to handle getting all of it at once. They dove in through windows and zoomed under doors, all on the lookout for any of the things Bobby considered 'a pile of weapons'. Room after room of house after house, they kept going and going, sometimes stopping to peer at things. Half an hour later, the swarm came together around Stephen and urged him back to where they initially landed. He reformed and immediately shrugged.

"'Less they got a different definition of 'weapon' than I do, there ain't nothing here. I mean, every house's got at least one military looking gun, but ain't none of 'em with more'n two or three. That don't seem like a 'stockpile' to me."

"You sure there aren't any caves or tunnels where they might be stashed?"

"If'n they got anything like that, it's hid pretty good. Didn't see nothing weird, neither. These folks don't even got 'lectricity and running water, let alone stuff to make chemicals and stuff."

Putting his hand up to his earpiece, Stephen said, "Cant and Mitchell reporting in at the suspected weapons depot." He paused for a moment and rolled his eyes. "If you wanted to have some sort of code, you should have set it up before we left. … These people have personal arms, but no stockpiles or armory. They've actually got goats they're actually herding. …

"That seems a bit extreme. What they do have wouldn't even raise an eyebrow in Texas. In fact, some of them might be accused of being pussies for having so few firearms." Stephen's face slowly went annoyed, until he looked more or less like he'd swallowed a lemon. "I believe I have a duty under the Geneva Convention to tell you to go fuck yourself, Klein. Unless you can give me some actual reason why we should attack an obviously non-military target posing no apparent threat, you can farm that job out to someone else. We don't murder civilians for no reason."

Bobby glanced back towards the village, able to guess what Klein wanted them to do. "I could take another look, to make sure. Or we could let them capture us." The idea of allowing himself be taken prisoner to work the place from the inside while he was in the middle of doing the same thing with the suits gave him a humorless smirk.

Stephen sighed. "We'll go back in and take another look around to see if we missed anything. I'll contact you when we've finished that." He pulled the earpiece out and stuck it in his pocket. "Did either of us say something to suggest we were interested in spree killings?"

"Nope. You wanna just stay here?"

"Nah, let's go see if there's a welcome wagon for visitors new to town."

"Here's hoping they got somebody what speaks English."

He was already halfway into the swarm as Stephen said, "Anything is possible." They flew together to the nearest edge of the village, where Bobby reformed next to Stephen as he landed. From there, they walked among the buildings, looking around like anyone in a new place would. From his earlier foray, Bobby knew the layout and guided Stephen to the center. There, a ring of rocks marked the edge of a round hole in the ground filled with water.

A woman in a blue dress with a black headscarf, carrying a jug likely intended to hold water, stopped at the edge of the small empty space around the well and took in a surprised breath. She said something that sounded alarmed and confused.

"Ma'am, any chance you speak English?" Bobby figured he might as well try. He pronounced the words slowly and carefully.

Instead of answering, she shouted, her intent clear enough: calling for help. Within seconds, doors all around slammed open and out came men with those assault rifles Bobby saw earlier. Both he and Stephen put their hands up, but that didn't stop some of them interposing themselves between the two men and the woman. She scurried off. The men stayed.

"Good evening," Stephen said, sounding friendly and polite. "Do any of you speak English?"

"I do, some." One man nodded to call attention to himself. He had a thick accent. "What you want, Americans?"

Bobby looked at Stephen, who returned it, they both shrugged, and Stephen indicated him with a jerk of his chin. Bobby sighed—elected spokesperson again. "We're lost. Our boss thinks there's a bunch of weapons lying around somewhere near here, but we can't find 'em."

Stephen almost managed to stifle down a chuckle. "We have no intention of harming anyone here, so long as you don't shoot first."

The man stared at them skeptically. "You come to poison well, to murder women and children? "

"No, sir. Ain't got no reason to hurt folk what're just doing what you can to survive out here. Must be tough, on account you all got weapons like that in easy reach. Folks come out here all the time just to harass y'all?"

"You are here."

Man had a point. Bobby grinned. "Ain't that the truth. We ain't here to cause no trouble, though."

"This is silly." Stephen put his hands down. "Are you aware of any reason why anyone might want to destroy your village? Because we were sent here to look for weapons you obviously don't have, and when we reported back that fact, we were ordered to kill you all anyway, something we don't particularly want to do."

The man took a few seconds to think about that, then he

spoke rapidly with the other men. Bobby followed Stephen's example and put his hands down while the locals chatted. After a few minutes, during which Bobby wondered if they'd made a mistake, the lead man said, "Come, we show."

Bobby and Stephen shared a surprised look, then both shrugged and followed the man. Only three of the men escorted them, plus their interpreter, and all kept guns handy. They went to the edge of the village, the same one they arrived through. "Taliban come here," the man explained as they walked. "We give them one girl and metal, or they kill two men. Americans come to war, Taliban want more, but we have no more girls to give. They take goats, food, cloth, and metal. Americans give us weapons for metal, we fight back. Taliban not come anymore."

He pulled up what was apparently a fake shrub anchored by some kind of plaster brick and scraped dirt away from a wooden trap door. It had an iron ring he grabbed and yanked on to open the door. "You go down, look, see."

Not expecting anything like this, Bobby blinked a few times, then realized he was supposed to be delving down into that hole. He pulled out his little flashlight and clicked it on, then crouched down beside the hole and shone the beam around in there. "I reckon somebody done mixed some papers up or something." It had no ladder or stairs. They'd have no problems getting in and out. "That sounds kinda familiar."

He jumped down and stumbled at the bottom. Looking up, he guessed the ceiling had to be about ten feet high. "It's fair sized, come on down," he called up for Stephen.

"Thank you for showing us this," he heard Stephen say, then the vampire also jumped in, making it look like gravity actually affected him.

"Ain't this a surprise." Bobby swept his light around, revealing wooden shelves and large metal cases, the dull green type that always had rocket launchers and that sort of thing in the movies. The yellow letters stamped on the sides in English indicated they held ammunition, grenades, and similar things. Several of the shelves had large silvery lumps of irregular material. They looked like mined ingots of raw metal. A tunnel led out of the chamber, running under the village. Shining the light down that way, it resembled an old mine shaft, the kind in abandoned gold mines in the movies.

Shining his light back on the metal cases, Bobby shrugged, "Reckon we oughta look through them all? "

"Yes. That seems like a very good idea." Stephen paced over and helped Bobby open them all, checking each one and finding most still had at least some of what the outside indicated they should. One was still completely full of explosives.

"Huh." Bobby straightened from the last case and shone his light down the tunnel again.

"You can say that again." Shutting and latching the last case again, Stephen also stood up. "At a guess, they found this ore and started mining it. When they sold it, someone decided it would be easier to just take it from them. Then our guys come in and find out they're using this metal and don't like the bad guys, so they trade for the metal and give them weapons to help them fight the good fight. Now someone wants to go back on that deal and just blast the town out of existence to take the metal."

"Yeah. You think telling Klein we found the stash on the second pass and destroyed it would work? "

"No, they'll just send troops in or do an air strike or something. Because it's got to be all about the metal ore."

This was a tough nut to crack, for sure. Metal would probably survive a bombing, so they had no incentive not to do it. Unless—"We could tell 'em we destroyed the weapons and found one little ingot of metal." He pointed to the smallest rock on the shelves, one only about the size of his fist. "They done got a tunnel and we followed it to the end and it's all exhausted of the metal, there ain't nothing here."

Stephen rubbed his chin thoughtfully, picked up the small rock. "It's heavy." It didn't burden him in any way. "Or we could tell Klein the truth, that they have this metal and are willing to sell it."

Bobby paced back to the hole. "Gimme a boost, we'll figure it out there. No reason to completely wreck these folks' evening."

Chuckling, Stephen paced over, rock securely in hand, and pretended to give Bobby a boost while actually tossing him up. In return, Bobby turned around and reached down to give Stephen an unnecessary hand to get out. "We'll do what we can to prevent other Americans from coming here and being unreasonable," Stephen told the one man. "No one deserves to die over this." He lifted the one rock. "This may help us do that, is it alright if we take it?"

"Yes. Good." The interpreter shook hands with both of them. "Allah watch you."

Chapter 5

Stephen cracked his neck and pulled the headset out of his ear again. "I'm pretty sure they aren't going to torch the site." He stared at the rock, still in his hand. "I'll have to hand this over as proof. Klein seems like a decent guy who wants to get it right."

Bobby spent those five minutes chewing mechanically through another protein bar. "Seemed to me like a guy what's got overseers breathing down his neck, looking for results with not enough time to provide."

Nodding his agreement, Stephen pocketed the rock. "Let's move on to the second site. What do we need to do there?"

"Warlord," Bobby said with his mouth still half full. He swallowed the last bite before elaborating. "We're s'posed to scout his compound well enough to draw a map, check the security, and generally provide enough intel for a team to go in and take the guy out."

"Listen to you," Stephen smirked, "using grown-up military words like 'intel.'"

Bobby snorted and stuffed his garbage away in a pocket. "Klein done said that if we got a good chance, and are okay doing it, we should just take the guy out, but I done told him to stuff that."

"Well," Stephen said thoughtfully, staring off into the darkness, "we'll see. If we catch him raping a twelve year old or something, I won't have a problem killing him."

One short hop later, they reached a city more modern in appearance than Bobby had expected to find in a constantly war-torn region. "What d'ya think?" They crouched behind some juniper bushes a block away from the compound, in the shadows of a smaller house. Neither of them was hidden terribly well, but anyone walking by would have to specifically look to see them.

"It's too easy."

"'Course it's easy. Nobody expects the Vampire-Dragon Inquisition."

Stephen blinked once and stared at Bobby. "I never would have figured you for a Monty Python fan."

"I got no idea what that's got to do with snakes, but I ain't 'specially keen on 'em."

"Okay." Stephen blinked again, shook that off, then went back to the matter at hand. "But, I what mean is, there isn't enough security for it to be what they said it is. They can't possibly think we're stupid enough to just go in, poke around, and hand over everything needed to kill a man."

Bobby shrugged, not sure he saw how Stephen reached that conclusion. "Maybe we played dumb better'n we thought."

The vampire raised an eyebrow and quirked one corner of his mouth up into a grin. "Perhaps. If we don't do this for them, though, they'll just go in without the quality information we could get them, and probably several people will get killed, including this man who may or may not be in need of killing."

"Well, okay. So now what?"

"I don't know."

Sighing lightly, Bobby rubbed his face. "I got an idea, but it ain't a good one."

Stephen snorted. "Where have I heard that before?"

"C'mon." Bobby chuckled. He tapped Stephen's shoulder as he stood and they walked together up to the front door.

"This is your brilliant plan?"

"Worked last time, didn't it?" They walked through the courtyard outside the house, past cameras that tracked them. Bobby resisted the urge to wave. When they reached the front door, he used the knocker shaped like a lion's head. "If somebody shoots first, we eat them."

"I am amenable to your plan."

"If'n that means you're up for it, then okay, good."

A dusky skinned man in a black suit opened the door and looked down his nose at them. "Can I help you?" He looked and sounded certain the answer would be 'No, sorry to bother you'. He also had a British accent, suggesting where he learned the language.

"We're looking to have a chat with Mr. Hanamidi, please."

The man looked at Bobby like he was a very strange creature, indeed. "Why do American soldiers want to speak with Mr. Hanamidi?"

"On account our boss says we gotta. You can tell him if he don't talk to us, a SEAL team'll probably be here sometime in the next few days to talk with bullets 'stead of words." In an effort to show his earnestness, he lifted his hands and unbuttoned his jacket to show he had no gun or explosives. With a light jab from his elbow, Stephen did the same.

The man looked them both over skeptically. "Wait here." He shut the door.

Bobby turned and waved at the cameras, and pulled his jacket off so they could see without a doubt that he had no weapon. "C'mon, play nice."

Stephen heaved a long suffering sigh and followed suit. "If they want us to pull down our pants, I'm going to be very unhappy."

"Me too." Grabbing a protein bar out of a pocket, Bobby ripped the package open and chomped it. "These things're awful."

"And yet, you eat them."

Looking down at the bar, he sighed, then swallowed the bite as quickly as possible. "Yeah. I s'pose it's better than a half-rotten apple from a dumpster."

"I've seen you eat those, too."

Nodding, Bobby took another bite. Just as he finished that and was about to stuff the rest of the bar into his mouth, the door opened again. The man in the suit gestured for them to come inside. "Mr. Hanamidi will see you." They followed him, Bobby tucking his 'food' into a pocket for later. It wasn't as nice on the inside as it seemed like it should be from the outside. Compared to that little village, though, this was a palace. It had hardwood floors, white walls and ceiling, and decent wood and metal furniture.

The butler led them a short way in and gestured to a small room with one couch and two chairs, some knickknacks on a coffee table, and bookshelves full of books along the walls. The person who must be Mr. Hanamidi stood at a bar on one end of the room, pouring amber liquid into a glass. "Would either of you like a drink?" He looked like the locals, with the proper dark olive skin tone, graying black hair and beard, and dark eyes, yet he sounded American. At a guess, Bobby would peg him as being in his 60s, maybe a well-aged 70.

"No, thanks," Bobby said as he sat down on the couch. Stephen shook his head and paced nonchalantly to a bookcase, where he started examining the contents. "I appreciate you seeing us, Mr. Hanamidi."

"The way you phrased your request was convincing." He

waved to the butler and the man left them, pulling the door shut to give them privacy. Mr. Hanamidi brought his glass to one of the chairs opposite Bobby and sat down. At this point, he noticed Bobby's unusual icy blue, almond shaped eyes, and looked a bit longer than would generally be considered polite. He glanced at Stephen, but the vampire had his back to them. "I'm not surprised to know someone in the military wants to kill me, but I *am* surprised you both would warn me about it."

Stephen stepped to the next bookcase, still examining the titles. "As it turns out, their duly appointed assassins aren't really of a mind to just kill people for no reason."

"We noticed you ain't got a whole lotta security, and were kinda wondering if you might be able to tell us why the folks pulling our strings think you're a warlord what oughta be dead."

Hanamidi laughed. "Is that really what they told you?" Shaking his head with amusement, he snorted. "How pathetic it took them this long to find me. I assume you know nothing, then?"

"You assume correctly," Stephen said. "We'd like to learn."

"Mmm. Knowledge. It's a double-edged sword, often." Hanamidi took a sip of his drink and regarded it. "Do either of you know much about physics and the Theory of Relativity?"

"Nope, nothing." Bobby shrugged.

Stephen turned to regard Hanamidi, his brow raised. "Is this about time travel?"

"No, not exactly." Hanamidi looked at Bobby, apparently intending to direct the explaining at him. "My parents were Afghan, they wound up in Russia before I was born, where they both became scientists. When I was ten, they defected to America. It was a popular thing to do then, in certain circles. I studied physics, like my father, and went into government service, where I was tapped for a very sensitive project that had been going on for a long time already, some forty years. It was called Maze Beset."

Surprised by this unexpected connection, Bobby leaned in and nodded along. Stephen stopped pretending he had any interest in the books and stared openly at Hanamidi.

"Ah, so you know something more than nothing, then. What have you heard of the project?"

"We ran into Kurt Donner," Bobby explained, remembering the homeless man in El Paso. "He didn't tell us nothing more than the name. Then he keeled right over and died."

Shaking his head, Hanamidi said, "I don't know that name. He might have worked there at a different time or in a different part of the project. I was in Sierra Tango Alpha, STA, the Space-Time Anomaly section. The whole thing was so hush-hush that I only knew my partners. I saw other people around, but wasn't told anything about the other sections. They had data from what they asserted was an anomalous space-time event that occurred over Roswell, New Mexico in 1947. Our task was to recreate it somehow."

Stephen snorted. "Seriously? Roswell?"

"Yes, seriously." Hanamidi shrugged. "A weather balloon really did crash, but it wasn't the only thing to happen that day. I know very little about that—it was need to know and we were told we didn't need to know. What I do know is that the data I was working with was…" He took another drink, this one more than just a sip. "It made no sense in some ways. We were able to reproduce one part or another part, but never all at once. It was highly suggestive, though, of things that hadn't even been dreamed of when it first happened." His eyes lit up with interest. "So much of what we know now, in astrophysics specifically, and other branches of physics generally, came from the research done there, the experiments, the attempts."

"I don't know nothing about none of that," Bobby said slowly, frowning. "You recognize us a little, though, don't you? You kinda looked at the eyes."

Hanamidi took another swallow of his drink and sighed with nostalgia. "I saw a picture once. I wasn't supposed to see it. She was a beautiful creature, even in a black and white photo, but so sad. It was in a folder that a woman dropped and scattered the papers all over. I picked up the photo and she snatched it out of my hands without an explanation." His eyes unfocused. "Such haunting—and haunted—eyes."

"What'd they look like?" The answer seemed obvious, but Bobby had to ask the question, especially since Hanamidi didn't seem like he was going to snap out of his reverie any time soon without help.

Another tiny sigh escaped him and Hanamidi looked down at his rapidly depleting drink. "Just like yours." His gaze went to Stephen first, then Bobby. "Exactly like them, in fact. I'm not sure what color hers were, but I expect it was the same as yours, or quite similar to it. Her face was more angular, and the one ear I could see had a point at the top corner, but your eyes, they're hers. I have no idea who she was, but she must have had something to do with the Anomaly."

Stephen frowned through all of this, then finally shook his head. "She sounds like an elf."

Hanamidi chuckled. "I've seen some of the fantasy art. Yes, that is generally what she looked like: an elf. Less humanish than is typically portrayed, though." He shrugged. "In '95, they decided I was ready to retire and be replaced by a younger scientist who they could pay less. Someone tipped me off that my ability to enjoy my retirement would be rather shorter than I would like, so I fled back to my parents' homeland, knowing I could hide effectively here. Who knew the US would decide you could succeed where the Russians failed? Not I, certainly. And now, here you are at my door, telling me I have been found."

Bobby sighed heavily and rubbed his forehead with one hand. "I ain't here to kill nobody what I ain't gotta."

"We could just report back that we've done it and let you leave on your own."

"Don't be foolish," Hanamidi snorted. "They aren't stupid enough to let me walk out of here alive now that they know where I am. It's possible they sent you to flush me out, expecting you to let me go but hoping you'll be too stupid or thick to ask questions. After all, I'm an Afghan in Afghanistan who they labeled a 'warlord'; that should be enough for any red-blooded American boy to mindlessly kill me."

Uncomfortable with that statement, Bobby shifted in his seat and rubbed his face again, trying to figure a way out of this without anyone having to die. "We could get you out of here without anyone seeing it if the lights are turned off."

Hanamidi sighed and stared off at the wall again. Perhaps half a minute passed in silence, with Bobby and Stephen sharing a glance, then watching the other man. What might be going through his mind, Bobby had no idea. "Perhaps." He said it like someone asked him a question. His gaze snapped back to Bobby, intense and piercing. "If I give you some papers, would you swear to get them to my daughter? "

It was a weird question, and Bobby blinked, but also nodded. "Um, sure, soon as I could, yeah."

The scientist stood up abruptly. "Give me…ten minutes should be enough. Too much longer and they'll start to question what you were doing in here all this time." Without giving either of them a chance to respond, he left the room, his stride swift and purposeful.

Bobby watched him go, bewildered. "What in heckbiscuits was that?"

His mouth sliding downward into a grimace of distaste, Stephen shook his head. "Not sure, but I have a guess. Ten minutes strikes me as about enough time to put together a packet for his daughter to claim his assets, if his affairs are already in order, as they say."

Understanding what Stephen just hinted around the edges about took Bobby a minute. "You think he's going to tell us to kill him."

"Sometimes," Stephen sighed, "the best way to deal with something like this is to let it happen."

"That's—It ain't right is what it is." Bobby stood and wanted to throw something. Instead, he tucked his hands into his armpits and paced, kicking the couch as he went by. "I ain't no killer." The moment it left his mouth, he knew he'd just lied; he'd killed three men. Clinging to that made him a damned hypocrite. "I mean, not like this, not a-purpose-like, not because somebody told me to. Them, I killed because they were gonna do stuff to me or somebody else. This guy, he ain't doing nothing to nobody."

"Relax." Stephen sank into his chair, grimace turning to disgust. "You don't need to stain your hands, I'll do it. He won't even feel any pain."

Bobby froze and faced Stephen. "Shoot, I didn't mean it like that."

"No," Stephen smiled darkly, "I didn't think you did. But, the fact remains that I can do this and you don't have to."

"We could still sneak him out some—"

"It won't work. No matter how much you want it to, Bobby, it won't." Stephen snorted. "He's right: they're probably watching, they know we walked in through the front door, and once we report it's done, they'll find a way to make sure we weren't lying. That means there needs to be a body, and it needs to be his. Since neither of us has any way to generate a fake body, we need the real one."

"This is—" Kicking the couch again, Bobby couldn't settle on any one word to fit best there.

"Demented? Yes, but life is like that. Remember how I said this isn't going to be about right and wrong? Welcome to that world. We have to make choices and live with them. Our choice, the one to do their dirty work in the hopes we'd be able to get to Jasmine, set us up for this choice, and now we have to deal with it."

Jasmine's name felt like a slap in the face, and Bobby turned away to not have to look at Stephen's determination and gods-be-damned calm. This wasn't right, no matter how it got sliced or diced or blended. Noticing his belly rumbling again, he pulled out the last of that crappy bar and jammed it into his mouth. Really, he couldn't decide which thing bothered him most: that they were talking about killing someone, that Stephen was so unfazed by the idea, that he found himself hungry while talking about it, or that not killing Hanamidi might be worse overall than killing him.

"This sucks."

"I agree completely."

Someday, Bobby would be able to sit his ass down on a porch again and not have to deal with all this crazy crap. He'd drink a beer and watch the world drift by, knowing no one waited on his decision to save or damn them. Today wasn't that day. Tomorrow didn't look promising, either. "I guess maybe I oughta scrap with some of his people while you're…doing that."

He couldn't find it in himself to look at Stephen, so he just heard the vampire say, "That sounds like a good plan."

The door opened again, and Hanamidi walked in with determination written across every inch of his being. He offered

Bobby a large envelope. "I'm not sure how to ask this. You've both been decent and reasonable."

Scowling, Bobby took the envelope. Tidy yet hasty letters on the manila paper gave them a destination in Albuquerque.

"Ah, I see you've figured it out, then." Hanamidi moved stiffly to the bar. "To you who are young, this probably seems strange, but I'm seventy-three and my wife passed a few years ago, I haven't seen my children since we fled without them. I don't even know how many grandchildren I have, if any. Living here, it's like half of a life." Shaking his head, he huffed out a not-quite-amused breath. "You know, I've thought a few times about saving everyone a lot of time, effort, and money by eating a bullet." He poured himself another glass of amber liquid and drank it down.

Stephen crossed the room with small, slow steps. "At least this way we were able to learn something that may eventually help us discover who we really are. If it helps to know, there will be no pain."

"I appreciate that."

Unwilling to stand there helplessly and watch, Bobby fled the room. He saw the butler standing in the hallway, leaning against the wall and staring, his face pale. "I've been with him since he got here," the man said. "He's a good man, a good employer. Like a brother."

Bobby squirmed as he walked over. This was not fair, it was not fun, and it was not right. He was going to do it anyway. "I gotta rough you up some," he said apologetically. "I ain't gonna do nothing that won't heal."

The butler looked up at Bobby and nodded. "That's a small mercy, I suppose, but I expect anyone who comes to verify his death will kill me. I'm too big a risk to be left alive."

Blanching, Bobby thought very hard about turning around and just walking away from this whole mess. "I ain't gonna do that. We could help you run for it, get you out far enough anyone watching can't just cut you down. A good shiner'd probably be a good idea still, though."

Much relieved, the butler nodded. "Yes, that might work. Thank you."

Tasting bile, Bobby scowled again as he made a fist with his right hand. "Dammit, don't thank me for doing this."

Chapter 6

Stephen reported in to Klein as they left the house, his face dark and brooding but a bounce in his step. They flew away, the vampire carrying the unconscious butler, and left him in an alley a few blocks away where the man claimed he should be safe enough for a few hours, long as they covered him with garbage. Bobby clenched his jaw the whole time they spent tending to the task in silence.

The pair took back to the air and went looking for the cave entrance. It was only a short hop, giving Bobby barely enough time to even deal with the facts of everything that just happened, let alone how he felt about it. Frequent glances at Stephen kept him from saying anything about it, worried, the vampire might need the silence.

They returned to the ground about a mile from the dot on the map, neither of them ready to tackle this situation. Bobby re-formed and shoved protein bars into his mouth to keep it busy while Stephen sat and stared into the darkness. Glancing at Stephen's watch, he saw the time: 11:32pm. Not even midnight, and they'd already finished two-thirds of their to-do list.

Bobby chewed and stared and stared and chewed. He hadn't done anything, except stand by and let his friend murder a man, and beat up another one for no reason. He listened to dry leaves scraping across the hard- packed earth in a light breeze and wondered if he'd left a piece of his soul behind in that house.

Beside him, Stephen pulled the envelope out of his pack and turned it over in his hands. He ran his fingers over the lettering on the front, then found it unsealed and peered inside. Sliding the thick stack of papers out, he held them so Bobby could see, too.

The top page began Hanamidi's last will. Several pages under that appeared to be legal documents of one kind or another. Next, they found pictures, both loose and mounted on scrapbook pages. Stephen flipped through them, showing all family and kids' school pictures. The rest of the papers had scribbled notes in Arabic with drawn diagrams. Some boasted coffee stains.

Tucking the stack back into the envelope, Stephen said, "I wonder what kind of space-time anomaly it was."

"I wonder if anyone at the farm'll be able to understand any of this stuff."

"I also wonder how long it'll be before we can get back there, and if we'll be relieved of all these documents before then."

Pleased to discuss anything other than what happened to Hanamidi, Bobby scratched at the few days of beard on his chin. "Maybe we oughta mail 'em."

"Maybe. That would mean a mailman would have to go there, though, which might be counter- productive."

Bobby grunted to concede the point. If only Hannah had a Post Office box set up someplace, but why would they do that? To make sure they could get lingerie catalogs? "We could mail it to Kris."

"We could mail it to Adesha," Stephen tapped the address already on the envelope.

"I dunno." As good as the idea sounded, Bobby figured there had to be a downside, even if he couldn't think of it. "If mailing something to her was all what needed to be done, Hanamidi coulda done that anytime."

Stephen grunted to acknowledge the point. "I don't want to involve Kris in anything she can't back out of yet."

"I guess the best choice right now is to hold onto it all. S'pose if'n we gotta, we could stash it someplace and come back later."

Nodding, Stephen tucked the envelope into his pack again. For several seconds, they sat in silence again. "It felt really good."

Bobby shifted with discomfort. He looked down at his hand and made a fist, remembering the satisfaction he felt for a flash when it connected with that man's face. "Mmm." He wanted to deny it until it went away. Stephen deserved better from him. Covering his mouth, he coughed. "It was kinda scary how much I really needed to beat the crap outta someone."

Stephen picked up a dead leaf and crumpled it in his hand, then let it fall to the ground. "I've fed before, plenty of times, but I've never killed anyone doing it. Gotten close, but never all the way to death. Killing Hanamidi, it was like really great sex, and part of me wants to do it again. Not right this minute. I'm completely sated right now, but I can feel how it'll be harder to stop myself the next time I feed. It's like…"

He stared out at the darkness, breathing slow and even and deep. "Like having chocolate for the first time. You've had ice cream, cake, maybe cookies before that, but then you get to have chocolate, pure and perfect, and nothing else is ever as good."

Bobby didn't have that kind of feeling towards any particular kind of food. He got the idea anyway. "You don't know that."

"Yes, I do. It's the same difference as between having a little snack and draining them to unconsciousness. I can stop, but why should I? Every pint past the first tastes better than the one before, and that last one, when I had to suck it out instead of letting it dribble into my mouth, it was like pure fucking ambrosia. If I hadn't felt it coming on, I would've made a mess of my pants."

That kind of admission had to be tough to make. Bobby couldn't relate to it. Sure, he got a rush out of beating that guy up. For him, it had been nothing more than a way to exorcise some frustration, and had nothing to do with sex or pleasure. On top of that, he'd felt… It confused him, because he went out of control, but while it happened, he'd thought he had total control.

He flexed his hand and wondered if some of that came from the dragons. "Thanks for stopping me. Sorry I couldn't do the same for you."

Stephen nodded, still staring off at nothing. "We were so worried about Matthew. We're just as dangerous as he is."

Sitting around brooding got them exactly two places: no and where. Bobby breathed in deeply, wanting to shake off the impulse to be horrified at the pair of them. What could he do about that? Not be himself anymore? Somehow kill Stephen? "We just gotta do what we can to fight it." The absurdity of his statement made him huff. "C'mon, though. Night ain't getting longer."

"Yeah." Stephen rubbed his eyes and got up by virtue of floating until he could unfold and put his feet on the ground. "I can control this. I'm the one in control, not the Hunger. It can go fuck itself off a short pier with a dead armadillo." He set off across the rocky steppe, paying attention to his footing.

obby struggled with that mental picture, then shook it off as unimportant and flowed into the swarm to avoid tripping over anything. A handful of dragons landed on Stephen's shoulders and the rest swirled around behind him.

A quick glance to one side then the other made Stephen smirk and murmur, "Exit light, enter night. Take my hand, off to never-never land." Bobby didn't recognize the tune or the words, but the dragons didn't get brushed off, so he left them there. They seemed to like Stephen, in a different way than they liked Sebastian. Maybe a better word for it was 'respect'. He thought the kind of respect a body gave to a tiger was more appropriate, but he didn't have much say over what they thought. Which was demented, of course, since they were him and he was them.

Despite efforts made to camouflage it, Stephen easily found the entrance to the cave they'd come looking for. A few shrubs and creative door placement didn't defeat the vampire's senses. "There are definitely people in there someplace," he said softly. "I can…tell." That wasn't at all the word he was going to say at first.

Right then, for the first time, he wondered if he could re-form only enough of himself to speak, and what that would look like, and how it would feel. He imagined a disembodied mouth being held up by a bunch of dragons. If he could shudder at the thought, he would have.

Stephen took the disguised handle and gave it a little yank. Two animal hides had been lashed together in a wood frame decorated by sprigs of plant material. When it had opened a tiny crack, Bobby heard a jangling noise like a bunch of small metal things hitting each other came from the inside, and Stephen swore under his breath. "So much for the element of surprise," he muttered. Ripping the door off because he could, he tossed it for distance and strode inside. "Time for Plan B. Go ahead and scout the place in clumps, confuse whoever you find, and lead me to whatever I need to deal with."

This plan sounded a lot like all their other plans so far, giving Bobby no reason to object. He sent the dragons inside, choosing to see this as an opportunity to get more comfortable with his ability. The swarm flowed around Stephen, then down the earthen tunnel. It had just enough space for one person to walk, two if they were really friendly. It twisted and turned, and within half a minute, Bobby found the small room where the door chime must have been before Stephen pulled it out, along with the door.

Two men lurched to their feet from crate chairs with woven blankets falling to the floor from their laps. They looked how he expected terrorist-types to look, which reminded him of those folks in that first village. Those men had been ordinary folks, doing what they could to protect and feed their families. He saw one major difference: those people lived above ground, and these people lived under it. Otherwise, they all had the same clothes, the same weapons, and the same general appearance.

That village turned out alright, giving him pause. Klein had called Hanamidi a warlord, and he'd said that village needed to be wiped out. Both had been one hundred percent wrong. Without any evidence of these people doing something they oughtn't to, attacking them struck Bobby as fulfilling the monster label. He wanted to grumble, because he had no idea how to tell the good guys from the bad guys if everybody looked the same.

Stephen would react to whatever those two men did, and Bobby had no particular reason to interfere. He could spook them, in the hopes they'd take pause and not get violent the second they saw him. The swarm spilled into the room, spreading out and filling it. The two men freaked in a foreign language and tried to bat away the dragons. Fortunately, neither had a taser or anything like it, and neither tried to shoot the swarm. It meant Bobby could keep the dragons from hurting the two men.

"I'll take it from here, Bobby, keep going." Stephen appeared in the tunnel mouth and shooed the swarm away. The dragons withdrew, and as they did, Stephen moved in and beat on the two men, putting them down without killing them. It may have happened by accident, but the vampire didn't rip anyone's body parts off or throw them too hard. He did, however, pick up a rifle and look it over.

One dragon stayed behind and perched on his shoulder again. Bobby figured he could use it to lead him when he had a reason to. The rest of the swarm found branches off the main tunnel and explored them. He found other men along the way and avoided them by flying fast and along the ceiling.

He flowed through a labyrinth of curves and unexpected drops and ladders into upper chambers, all lit at irregular intervals with bare light bulbs on what might be a continuous wire. Evidence of human effort in the digging out was minimal, mostly limited to rounding corners or enlarging individual chambers, and perhaps joining a few here and there. Some had generators chugging away, the wires from the lights connected to them, small holes shooting out from those spots to the outside. He found a few computers and plenty of weapons caches.

It felt big enough that fully exploring it would take months. He had the dragons splinter again and again to follow the various tunnels until they flitted about in groups of nine or ten. His mind floated around between them, getting the input from all their tiny eyes at once and painting a picture of a female-free zone focused on survival above anything else.

In one deep, dark, dank chamber, a group of dragons freaked out until he focused on one and found five men in partial US military uniforms, all hog tied, gagged, and lying on the floor. He quashed his first impulse: getting the dragon on Stephen's shoulder to goad him into trashing the place to reach them. Until he knew whether these soldiers still lived or not, he saw no point to rushing through.

Instead, he flowed his mind into one of the dragons there and looked around. One guard sat nearby, smoking a cigarette with a paperback book and a gun. The book had characters on the cover that Bobby assumed must be Arabic, though he'd never seen text of it before. As he watched the guard turn a page, obviously absorbed by the text, it occurred to him that dead bodies didn't need guards.

He flew the dragons down, avoiding getting into the guard's peripheral vision, and landed on the man farthest from the guard. His skin felt warm and his chest moved in the even rhythm of sleep or unconsciousness. This close, he could make out the others breathing, too.

With only five dragons—the number currently present—Bobby had no confidence he could handle a single guard on his own. If he could free these men, though, and they were capable enough, that would give him time to bring down the rest of the swarm, then these men could follow him as they fought their way back to meeting up with Stephen. He'd had worse ideas.

While the swarm changed direction to converge on the spot, these five dragons landed on the one soldier's legs and arms. They chomped on the rope bindings, using their sharp little teeth to saw the fibers away. The last few strands snapped and the soldier slumped, making Bobby freeze. When nothing happened, they moved to the next one.

This soldier, who appeared to be about Bobby's age, had no major, grievous injuries. On the way to the next, he had his one dragon fly up and down his body, checking, and he found a black eye, a split lip, and some purplish bruises on his bare feet. His plain gray shirt had smears of dried blood and minor rips with older bruises showing through. His camouflage pants appeared to be intact, aside from the mud and blood staining them.

All four of the others had received similar treatment. The oldest one by Bobby's estimation had cuts and bruises on the bottoms of his swollen feet. At a guess, he'd been tortured, maybe for being the highest ranking man among them, or just the one who resisted the most.

Rage simmered in the dragons. Though soldiers had been the enemy at Hill, he still considered them overall to be the good guys, especially here. Seeing them treated this way pissed him off. Whatever his feelings on the subject, though, he sternly reminded the dragons that five couldn't do anything useful to that guard, because they wanted to go rip him to bits. Freeing the rest of these men should at least distract them long enough for the swarm to gather.

None of the soldiers woke while he worked. All five had been freed by the time the swarm converged on the dark, empty space between the open doorway and the ladder up. He had the five dragons slip around to the rest of the swarm and re-formed, concerned about them going berserk. Without using them, though, he only had the element of surprise.

He took a deep breath, then rushed the guy. Unafraid of hurting himself, he slammed his body into the guard's and knocked him against the wall. The guard took the impact with a grunt, his eyes bulging. Both the book and the nearby assault rifle fell to the floor with a clatter. Bobby threw a solid punch across his jaw, kicked him in the gut, and stomped on his head.

Before he could get carried away this time, the dragons burst out of their own accord and fell upon the man, little claws scraping, little mouths blasting tiny jets of fire. The guard rasped and gurgled and mewled, all of it goading the swarm into a frenzy. When they finished killing the guy, Bobby got control back and re-formed standing beside the grisly corpse.

Staring down at what his swarm had done, Bobby swallowed down the urge to throw up. This time, he'd done it on purpose, except that he'd really done it to save those soldiers. That guard deserved to die for whatever part he'd had in cutting up the one soldier's feet. He nodded to himself, sure in the truth of it.

When he looked up, he found five pairs of eyes staring at him. Though he could see all around as the swarm, they'd been so focused on the guard that he hadn't noticed them waking up. For a few beats, he stood there with no idea what to say. The weight of their eyes made him squirm, so he raised a hand and cut through the air with it in an unenthusiastic wave.

"Hi. I'll be your rescue today."

All five had cloth gags Bobby hadn't messed with. The one in the back discovered they'd been freed and reached up to pull his gag out. "What *are* you, man?"

Bobby pursed his lips and dropped his gaze to the ground. That left him looking at the mangled body. He frowned, then he shrugged. Right now, they needed to get out of here, and him fussing about the state of his immortal soul wouldn't accomplish that. "The guy what's getting you out of here, that's what." He offered the nearest man a hand to help him to his feet. "You guys hurt, or just roughed up a bit? "

The man with the cut up feet recovered from the shock of Bobby first. He pulled his gag out and hefted a foot to take a look at it. "I don't think I can walk." He kept his voice low, yet Bobby could hear command in it, that certain something his daddy always had that made other people listen. "We're all that's left of our unit, the ones that weren't hurt or killed in the initial skirmish. Don't know what they did with the rest."

Nodding along as the man spoke, Bobby backed off and went to the doorway to see if he'd attracted any attention. No one had popped their head down or called out, so he turned back. They rubbed their wrists and ankles, and generally needed some vacation. "Y'all look like hell. I ain't much with a gun, so you guys should grab whatever he's got," he jerked a thumb at the dead guard, "but let me and my buddy do most of the work." At this point, he had the one loose dragon lead Stephen in.

"'Your buddy'? Is that a freaky way to refer to…um—"

"No. That'd be a 'them', not a 'he'. I mean I ain't alone. Brought me a vampire to help out." Rather than take the time to explain that, he sent a handful of dragons to scout it ahead. Behind him, the five men quietly freed themselves the rest of the way, searched the guard, and figured out how to get the one injured man out of here. Paying more attention to his scouts than the soldiers, he didn't hear if they said anything about him or a vampire, but figured they'd probably decided he must be insane.

Whatever they thought, these guys had their heads screwed on right. Two men hefted the injured one up and the other two had the guard's two guns between them. With their faces set in grim determination, these men obviously would do whatever it took to get out, and Bobby knew he had to take the same attitude if he wanted them all to survive.

"I'm gonna do whatever I can to keep you from having to use those to get outta here. Just so you know." Taking the lead, he approached the ladder and wondered at the best way to get the injured man up it.

The dragons wanted to dive in and take more of these men down with a disturbing level of eagerness. Bobby pressed on his forehead, trying to make them understand that one scream would make this much harder, and so would gunfire. Getting shot wouldn't help, either, and neither would senseless rampaging.

His solo dragon let him know that Stephen waltzed through the place, leaving a trail of bodies in his wake. They might be unconscious. Bobby watched the vampire grab two men and smash their heads together as he breezed past. They might have survived that, and he chose not to have his one dragon investigate. Some things, he figured, should be left unknown as long as possible.

Bobby peered up the ladder, knowing they'd find men up there, playing cards. His handful of dragons reported that nothing had changed. He held up a hand, put a finger to his lips, pointed up, and showed five fingers. They could wait for Stephen here, though it felt cheap and cowardly.

While he concentrated on what the dragons saw, one of the soldiers tapped him on the shoulder and leaned in to whisper to him. "We can lure one or two down here and ambush them. I speak the language."

Finding the plan better than anything he'd come up with so far, Bobby nodded. "The other choices are waiting for my partner to reach us, or making lots of noise."

The soldier frowned at that and flicked his eyes back to the rest of the group. He nodded and led Bobby to the huddled group. They welcomed him to join with only a sidelong glance or two. "Sarge, we can set up an ambush, wait for cavalry, or go guns blazing."

Sarge was apparently the one with the cut up feet. "Ambush for as long as we can, then switch to guns blazing. We're here, we should take advantage of that fact to take this base out."

"That ain't really my mission." The moment the words came out of his mouth, he knew them to be a complete lie. Klein said it would be full of traps. He never used words out loud that demanded the deaths of everyone inside. His meaning had been clear, though, and Bobby had been stupid not to realize the true purpose of the mission. Obviously, they had been sent to verify the cave was full of bad guys, then kill them or make it easier for someone else to kill them.

He wasn't cut out for this stuff. For the first time, with his eyes on Sarge, Bobby realized that his daddy's job had been, more or less, killing people and not being bothered by it. How so many managed to handle it seemed more unbelievable than how many fell apart like Matthew. Clenching his jaw, Bobby nodded. "But let's do this. Call up for them whenever you're ready and I'll take care of it." He broke apart into the swarm and surrounded the ladder hole, spread out in the darkness and ready to engulf whoever dropped down into the trap.

The soldier called out with a request of some kind. Bobby heard the men upstairs mutter to each other. A chair scraped on the floor and one squatted beside the ladder hole. He called out in response and the soldier answered him. The man grumbled and climbed down the ladder.

Bobby waited until he had reached the ground and taken two steps away from the ladder. Dragons flung themselves at his face, intending to do tiny acts of violence to his eyes and neck. The man opened his mouth and one dove inside, shooting down his throat to shut him up. It reminded Bobby of digging around in Dan's shoulder to get that bullet out back in Salt Lake.

Killing a man happened to be easier from the inside than the outside. Bobby didn't want to re-form after the dragon on the inside burst out through the man's chest, mostly because he feared he'd throw up, which wouldn't help anything right now. The dragons, though, found the new knowledge invigorating. They shoved Bobby aside to get the job done, surging through the hole and diving at all four men at the table at once.

Streaking back through the place, the dragons went wild, gleefully forcing themselves down throats in small groups and bursting out through chests and stomachs. They found Stephen, who watched dragons explode out of two men with a stony expression, one he couldn't read. Not that he cared. Bobby managed to wrest control back and re-formed on all fours, violently heaving up what little had been in his stomach.

"I see you found something worthy of killing all these men," Stephen said as he crouched down beside Bobby, offering the canteen. His words came out gentle, without judgment.

Taking the water, Bobby spat out bile, then sat back up on his heels. His mouth tasted horrible. A mouthful of water swished around and spat out helped that. "They were holding some soldiers, five. Back thataway." He jerked a thumb to indicate the direction.

Stephen nodded. "Give me a dragon to lead me, and I'll meet you outside."

"All them on the way here dead already?"

The vampire's mouth went thin. "Yes. I assumed the dragon getting all excited meant I should."

"Yeah. Okay." He popped a dragon off his thumb, and it whirred off with instructions to show Stephen where to find the soldiers. Bobby got up and stumbled to the entrance, hand on the wall to steady himself and trying not to look as much as possible. He kept going until the cool air outside slapped him aside. Falling to his knees, he clutched his face with both hands. "What'd I do?"

He could feel them, the weight of their tiny minds pressing on his. They didn't understand. "A life is a life," he said aloud, trying to explain to them because he knew they could hear it, and he didn't feel coherent trying to think it at them. "I ain't saying these guys didn't deserve to die, but we ain't s'posed to be judge, jury, and executioner all at once. It ain't right to just take it all in our hands. Claws."

He pushed his hands up and through his hair, winding up with them grabbing the hair at the nape of his neck and tugging on it. "I'm the one in charge, you hear? Y'all are part of me, I ain't just another bit of you! I'm made of dragons, you're parts of me. You do what I tell you, not whatever you want."

His arms dropped to his sides and he stared up at the impossibly starry sky. It looked about the same here as at the farm. Maybe it was different, but not enough that he could tell. Right now, he should be there, not here. No one there would ask him to kill anyone. Not only would they not think he would in the first place, but if they did, they'd actually ask him not to kill anybody. How many men did he murder in that cave? He had no idea, and no intention of going back to count.

How was he supposed to look anyone in the face now, most especially himself? He had to remember that he came here for Jasmine, for all eleven of the ones they couldn't save. This was for them, because he and Stephen were sure if they could just get the damned suits to trust them, they could find out where those eleven had been taken and get them out. There wasn't supposed to be all this killing, wasn't supposed to be anything like this. When Privek said they'd be doing missions, he thought it would be a lot of spying, watching people and reporting back and not thinking. So stupid, he was so stupid. Both of them were monsters. Privek saw that and deployed them accordingly.

"I gotta be in control. I'm the person here. Y'all are just little pieces of me, and ought to act like it. Nobody else dies on account of me 'less I say so, and that's that." Until he could be sure they'd listen to him, he was a danger to anyone around him, even those soldiers, but he had no idea what to do about that. He heaved a heavy, despairing sigh and got to his feet, keeping his back to the cave entrance.

"I should report in," he heard Stephen say as they stepped outside. Bobby's dragon trilled and zoomed over to reattach to his thumb. "Can I get your names and ranks to let them know who we have? "

"Buffalo Soldiers Sergeant Riker and Privates Hansen, Carson, Platt, and Hegi. Tell them like that. The rest of our unit is dead, so far as we know." Bobby recognized Sarge's voice.

Feet slapping the earth filled the silence that must have been Stephen putting on and activating the earpiece. "Cant and Mitchell reporting in. The cave has been cleared, we found five men." He relayed the names, as Riker told him to, then paused. Bobby glanced back to see Stephen carrying Riker on his back. The other four looked around, maybe just happy to be outside, maybe trying to unsee all those gruesome dead bodies. None of them looked at him, he could tell that much for sure. "Yes, Riker is injured, they're all beat up and probably dehydrated. We don't have enough water to walk through this come daylight, but we'll get as far south as we can."

"You heard the man," Riker barked. "Move out."

"Bobby, let's go."

He sighed again and stayed staring off into the darkness. "I'm thinking maybe I shouldn't oughta go back."

"I will admit the cave is nice and cozy, but the decorating isn't to my taste, and it's definitely a fixer-upper." Stephen left a short pause, then dropped the jovial tone. "At least walk with us, Bobby. We can talk later."

Rubbing his chin, Bobby nodded. "Yeah, I reckon." He turned and followed along behind the others, trying not to think much. His belly started to rumble angrily within a minute, and he bolted two of those gross protein bars without tasting them. As he stuffed the second wrapper in his pocket, it occurred to him that he maybe ought to offer the other bars to these guys. Then again, they seemed alright, and it would probably be better for them to get real food instead of this crap.

"Is it okay to ask…" One of the four Privates said it tentatively, and the statement hung there without him finishing it.

"No, it's really best if you don't," Stephen answered. "It would be even better if you forget we exist. Because we don't. We're figments of your imagination to be redacted from any retelling of this event that only sort of happened."

"Understood," Riker said. "Whatever happened in that little base, we didn't see it. Hansen wasn't tied up very well and managed to free himself, at which point we discovered we were clear to leave. Anyone have a problem with that?"

"Why's it gotta be Hansen?"

"I got double jointed thumbs." Hansen held up his hands and demonstrated the unusual way he could bend his thumbs. "All of you owe me your freedom," he grinned, "because without me, you'd have all starved to death down there."

From there, they fell to joking. Bobby listened in and couldn't figure out how they could see all that and move on so effortlessly. Maybe it had to do with their lack of involvement in the... butchering. They'd probably seen a ton of gruesome bodies before. Beyond that, freedom had to taste plenty good enough to ignore it all. As he'd done several times already, he rubbed his face with both hands. Imagining what Momma would say about all this didn't help in the slightest. Substituting Lily in there made things worse.

The thp-thp-thp of a helicopter nearing jarred him out of brooding and he looked up to see the lit up bird dropping down nearby. The soldiers rushed while Bobby slowed. He stopped dead a good forty paces away, watching two of the men climb in and help Stephen get Riker up and strapped in. Stephen turned and noticed Bobby. The vampire rolled his eyes and nodded to get Bobby to join them.

That look, the one that suggested Stephen considered it stupid for him to hang back, made him move. He couldn't say why, exactly, but his feet jogged over and he grabbed on. The helicopter lifted off without waiting for him to sit down or strap in. That was fine. If he fell, he'd just fly alongside. In a lot of ways, hanging out felt good, like someone blasted him with sand to scour away a layer of him, the layer that couldn't handle it all.

Did he want to be that guy? The one who could do something like that and move on? Was it enough that they deserved it? Did they 'deserve' it? What right did he have to judge something like that? He could only wonder if men like Klein thought about all the lives they ordered others to take for some greater good, if he wondering whether he'd done the right thing kept him awake at night.

About an hour later, the bird set down in a smaller camp than Klein's. It had most of the same features, and Bobby forced himself to follow his nose to the food. He ate mechanically until his belly filled, then found a rock to sit on and stare at nothing. Orange and pink announced the impending sunrise, and he watched it climb up over the horizon.

By all rights, he ought to be tired. His mind buzzed with the things he'd seen and done in that cave, from the first corpse to the last, and all their innards. Some of those things, he'd never wanted to know what they actually looked like, because they belonged on the inside. Of course, that bothered him a lot less than the rest of it.

"Do you want to talk about it?" Stephen's voice, muffled by the cloth protecting his face from the sunshine, came from behind him.

"I ain't even got any blood on me. I oughta have a little, a few smudges or something."

"I expect all the stains are on the inside."

Bobby had no answer for that. He scratched his chin, the stubble rasping against his fingertips.

"I reported in, Klein is ecstatic. As part of the report, I informed him we aren't interested in continuing to pursue these sorts of missions. He pouted, but said he'd pass that along."

"How d'ya know he pouted?"

Stephen chuckled lightly. "Don't tell me you've never heard anyone pout over the phone."

The slight change of subject brought out a bare hint of a smirk. "Can't say as I have. Had girls roll their eyes at me over the phone, though."

"This is sort of like that, only more amusing to listen to." The vampire let silence hang between them as he moved closer and sat on the next rock. "I won't lie to you, Bobby. You scare the crap out of me. I can kill people pretty easily, but only one, maybe two at a time. Right now, I'm wondering if you could kill me by crawling down my throat and ripping your way out. A massive amount of damage? I might not be able to heal that before I bleed out. I'm not actually afraid of you, though, because I know you'd never try it unless I needed to be put down."

Nodding, Bobby tried not to take it as a stinging indictment. "Did those men need to be put down? "

"I really don't know. I'm fairly certain that, if given the chance, they would've tried to kill us. They would've failed, though, so I can't say where the balance there is. Is it justified to kill someone who shoots me? What if he only points the gun? How about if I only know he would but kill him before he can? Does that really make either of us any better than paranoid serial killers? I just have no idea."

He paused and took a deep breath, letting it out slowly. "I do know this is a war zone, and in war, it's us against them. No matter who's right or just more right, we have to pick a side. Staying neutral back home is fine, but staying neutral out here isn't possible. We chose us, so they want to kill us, and out here, that means we kill them first so they can't kill any of us. It sucks, but that's war."

That did pretty well sum up the whole situation. "You think I'm being a whiny pansy-ass twit."

"No," Stephen laughed, "I think you're being human. But then, we aren't really human, are we?"

No, they sure weren't human. If this whole thing didn't show him that, nothing could. "We back out now and they're gonna come after us."

"Probably. I propose that if our request to be utilized differently is refused, we make for Albuquerque to meet Hanamidi's daughter. From there, Roswell is probably the next stop."

"We should go back to the farm and get reinforcements for Roswell."

"Or send someone else, yes, good point."

"There probably ain't nothing in Roswell, though." Glad for the true change of subject, Bobby thought about it. "I mean, they got tourist stuff there. It'd be kinda dumb to keep a secret base or whatever in a place what gets so much traffic."

"Yes," Stephen nodded thoughtfully, "it's more likely to be in some kind of Area 51."

Huffing out a light snort, Bobby shook his head and grinned. "That ain't really real, is it? "

Also amused, Stephen smirked. "It's probably not called that, but yes, I assume we have at least one secret installation somewhere that pursues projects best kept away from public opinion." Gloved fingers of one of his hands drummed idly on his knee. "You know, I'm curious why they decided to put us out in the real world instead of doing this whole thing as a controlled experiment. It would have been easier to get us to do whatever they want if we were all raised to just be soldiers."

That notion hadn't coherently occurred to Bobby, but now Stephen said it out loud, he agreed. "Momma said she was part of a program, they helped her clean herself up. Lots of women were in it, though, and she was the only one what got knocked up that she knew of. Maybe…" The gears turned in his head as things fell into place and made more sense than they had before. "She said it was still a new process then. What if that was the best way they could think of to try lots of times? I mean, look, we're all from all over the country, right?

"Momma was born and raised in Atlanta, she ain't never left much, and didn't say nothing about going far away for that testing stuff. I got the feeling Lizzie and Dan ain't never been outta Arkansas, Javier and Tiana was from LA, Alice was from San Francisco, and on and on. So, say they done did this in lots of places, hid it as a 'social program' on account they were helping women. Heck, it mighta even been part of the war on drugs stuff. Momma said they offered to get me adopted, but she said no. Maybe the ones what the momma decided to keep 'em, they couldn't do nothing about. Maybe it weren't something they thought about before starting the program.

"But more, what if they didn't have no idea what we'd turn into? If they didn't know if it would rightly work, maybe they didn't know what would happen when it did work. Momma also said they told her to watch for 'anything unusual'. She thought they meant sickness. *Maybe they did mean sickness, and this was a big surprise.* Ain't none of us got picked up until recent-like, and all of us started having superpowers around the same time. What if…what if they picked the four of us—me, Jayce, Alice, and Ai—by random offa that list because one of us what got their superpower came to their attention already by then?"

Stephen kept his mouth shut, letting Bobby ramble until he finished. "We're all in a small age range, eighteen to twenty-two. They may have had to cut something because of funding issues, and chosen our program, viewing it as a failure. This is all just guessing, though, Bobby. It could be a lot more sinister than you think."

He had a point. Bobby shook his head anyway. "You know, I didn't do so hot in school or nothing, but it seems to me that most of the time in the real world when science gets used like this, it's less 'I wanna take over the world' and more 'I wanna see what happens.'"

"Fair point. But where did they get the DNA they crossed with human to wind up with us?"

"No clue." He shrugged and snorted. "Maybe there really were aliens in Roswell."

"Anything is possible, I suppose, though I wonder how it really got here. If there was actually a spacecraft, I would expect our space program to be a little farther along by now." Cocking his head to one side, Stephen held up a hand to stop the conversation and touched his ear to activate the mic. "Yes, Klein, I'm here." He listened, then sighed. "Just a minute, let me confer with Bobby." He turned off the mic again and shook his head. "We were so efficient, they want to appeal to our desire to be patriotic Americans and to save the lives of more soldiers by pursuing other dangerous missions that would likely involve a lot of killing."

Unsurprised, Bobby scratched the back of his neck and stretched. Riker and his men had probably been written off as killed in action before he and Stephen rescued them. That whole cave now held dead bodies instead of presumed terrorists. Hanamidi was dead. A suspected weapons cache had been emptied. They did their job well, and Uncle Sam liked soldiers who did their job well. Really, he couldn't blame them. Weapons like them changed the course of history. "They ain't never gonna let us leave until this thing is done here. We wanna stay and end this damned war, this here's our chance."

Stephen shrugged. "I have to admit there's some allure to that.

A lot of good people have died here." He paused and turned to fix Bobby with a stare, though his sunglasses made that unclear. "We should decide together, though, not separately. I have a feeling that there will come a point when I don't remember why it matters anymore. All this blood and death will drag me down into a pit until I become the monster inside and nothing more. Having someone here with me should help prevent that."

"But you wanna stay?" Bile rose up in Bobby's throat. He swallowed hard to push it back down where it belonged.

"Not exactly. I like knowing that Riker, if he has a brother or a sister, a wife, whatever, they didn't lose him. Because of me."

"Hm." The question, then, was how much he, Bobby, could stomach. If he looked at it as saving American lives, could he be okay with taking some Afghan kid's big brother or dad away instead? Both of them stared out at the nothing, as if the rocks and scrub would have answers. "Tell 'em… Shoot, I dunno. Right and wrong is all screwed up out here. Which is more important—saving soldiers' lives or finding the missing eleven?"

"Yeah, I don't know, either." Stephen hung his head and shrugged. "If we save twenty lives, is that worth those eleven? I'm not used to tackling truly difficult moral issues. Up to know, I've been going based on killing and rape being bad, the Hunger's wishes notwithstanding. I didn't really need more nuance than that."

One of them had to make a decision. "Tell 'em—" Bobby rubbed his face again and sighed. "Tell 'em we're on board. Privek ain't gonna trust us with nothing if we bail now. We gotta at least try. If'n it means we gotta kill more, then, well, I guess." He rubbed his eyes, finally tired enough to sleep.

Nodding his agreement, Stephen moved his hand to talk to Klein again. "I can live with that. Can you?"

Bobby grimaced. "I already got forty-some bodies on my tab.

What's forty more?"

"Maybe we should get some sleep, because that actually sounded funny."

"A-damned-men."

Aside — Liam

Liam hated his job. Nothing else could be worse and he had no choice. Three weeks of this crap so far. Three weeks since Elena disappeared. Three weeks since his world fell apart. They'd find her. He only needed to do something in return, so they could justify the man-hours. Oh, sure, he tried to pay them off. His father had more than enough money to cover those salaries. That bastard Privek wanted something else.

Gritting his teeth, he laid a hand on the unconscious soldier's bare thigh. At the ankle, this leg ended in a mass of blood-stained gauze. Under that, he knew he'd find a ragged end, treated enough to prevent the victim from bleeding out. No one told him what happened to his patients, and he didn't ask because he didn't want to know.

Doing this meant serving his country, he'd been told, as if that would make everything better. He took a deep breath and braced himself. With a twist and a pull someplace inside, he did the impossible and clamped down on a scream as the injury transferred from the soldier's leg to his own. Blood gushed out of Liam's ankle and flesh wrapped itself around the soldier's.

His thrice-damned power created miracles at the cost of his

sanity.

An eternity of agony later, the soldier still had no foot, but his leg ended in a smooth, healed and rounded stump. They'd be able to fit him with a fake foot now, there would be no oozing and weeping and pus, and the guy could avoid the potential problem of addiction to pain meds. Liam glared at the man for the crime of putting him through a few minutes of hell.

Reaching down, he swiped the blood off his already regenerated foot with a towel. The second he'd seen the injury, he'd pulled his combat boot and sock off and set them aside. His assistant swooped in with her mop and sloshed the blood off the plastic under him for the thousandth time since he got here. She'd gotten good at it, and took only two swishes before she wordlessly wheeled the soldier's gurney out. He'd wake up later and be confused, and someone would tell him to thank God, or his lucky stars, or whatever, and to not ask questions. He'd be walking again by nightfall if they had any prosthetics handy.

Before he had a chance to put his sock back on, two soldiers carried a third in. Another pair peered inside the tent. All five—curiously barefoot and stained, bloodied, and half-dressed by camp standards—had been banged up, but Liam didn't treat bruises and cut lips. He dealt with serious injuries. His patients either avoided months to years of surgeries and rehab, or they went back out into the field as a result of his ministrations.

He might have shooed them out, except the man they carried had serious foot injuries. They'd been cut and smashed and generally mistreated to the point of uselessness. Torture did things like that, he supposed. If this guy wound up being able to walk after it healed normally, he'd have pain for the rest of his life. For whatever reason, they hadn't cut off any of his toes. Maybe he'd escaped or been rescued before they got that far.

Standing with a sigh, he vacated his stool and gestured for them to set the injured man on it. Since both feet had been hurt, he stooped to remove his other boot. Once he'd set it aside, he looked up at the other soldiers, intending to tell them to get out.

"Hey, your eyes." The one with the cut up feet said it, staring at Liam's icy blue, almond shaped eyes. The other four snapped their attention to him.

He knew he had unusual eyes. In his social circles, people noticed and considered him exotic for them, and thus more desirable. Before he met Elena, he'd played on it to get what he wanted, often. These men staring at him, however, pushed outside his comfort zone. "Yes, they're unusual," he said curtly. "Privacy, please."

No one moved. "Are you a faith healer?" Despite the fact none of these men wore any rank insignia, he guessed this one to be higher than the rest.

Liam snorted. "No." He pointed to the silver bar on his uniform shirt collar. He'd been given the Lieutenant rank to make his life smoother in the camp, though he hadn't actually been inducted into the Army. The General who'd handed him the insignia had gotten short with him when he'd insisted upon making that clear. "I believe I gave an order, gentlemen."

"Then what can you do? Is it anything like turning into a scad of itty bitty dragons?"

Two things annoyed Liam right now: these men refused to obey him, and he hated explaining this. A surge of raw, icy panic surged in his gut, eclipsing both things. "What? Where did you see dragons?" His hand shook as he reached up to check the man's temperature. His skin felt no warmer or cooler than anyone else's, which meant he had no easy excuse to discount anything he said.

"His name's Bobby. He said we shouldn't talk about him, but

if you're one of them, it probably doesn't matter as much. Right?" The other four nodded slowly as the injured man spoke.

Liam paled. Bobby could only be Mitchell, the one responsible for all that footage he saw of that apocalypse-level chaos in Salt Lake City. Privek called him dangerous, and the footage backed him up. On top of that, Mitchell had most likely been behind Elena's abduction. He tried not to gulp too hard. "Did he do this to your feet?"

"No." The injured man raised an eyebrow and snorted. "He rescued us. Him and the vampire one."

"Stephen," one of the others supplied. "We'd still be POWs getting tortured for information if they didn't show up."

Liam had no idea what to do with that information. Stephen the vampire must be Cant. The report said he might have drank blood from one of the nurses, but she couldn't really remember. By all accounts, Cant might be worse than Mitchell. Liam had been warned to watch out for them trying to lure him into a life of crime, or something along those lines. "Oh. I'm…glad to hear that. I, ah, do something like faith healing, but without the faith part."

He healed the man's feet and sent the soldiers on their way. "I need a break," he told his assistant.

She handed him another towel. "You just started an hour ago."

"Yeah," he snapped, "and now I need a break." He wiped off his feet and pulled his socks and boots back on. "I'll be back in a few minutes. Just need some air." Fleeing the tent, he sucked in a lungful of dry, warm air and let the morning sun bake him for a few minutes.

The monsters in the images he'd seen wouldn't have rescued soldiers. They would've killed everyone and moved on. More importantly, he had no idea why those two would come all the way here to kill people. They could go berserk in the States without the bother of traveling. He wondered if they'd come here to kill or abduct someone specific and rescued those soldiers by accident.

Maybe he should find them. Men able to empathize with imprisoned soldiers might listen to reason and be persuaded to release Elena. If he played his cards right, he could even talk them into working for Privek. As much as he hated the situation that agent had put him into, Privek clearly wanted the best outcome for all of them. Besides, they probably wouldn't attack him because of their common parent.

Hurrying through the camp, he peered around tents and vehicles until he spotted Mitchell with another man, both wearing desert camouflage. They sat on rocks at the perimeter, chatting. Cant had to be the second man. He'd been told the man had a sensitivity to sunlight, and he wore too much clothing for the heat. Cant reached over and shoved Mitchell playfully in the arm, Mitchell laughed and shook his head. They seemed so normal.

He took one step toward them, then froze. What if there was a reason—a very good reason—why he shouldn't walk over there and introduce himself? They wore uniforms and appeared to belong, making him wonder why. His hand found the bar on his own collar and he rubbed it between a finger and thumb.

Privek could be using them, or working his own angle for converting them. If he walked over there and said the wrong thing, he could ruin a lot of work. It would be easy to get huffy with Elena on the line, and his head full of people having their arms ripped off by their werewolf buddy. No, he needed to stay away from them. Elena needed him to do what he promised he'd do.

He took one last look before turning away and hoping his choice meant Elena would be back in his arms soon.

Chapter 7

"And they're sure these guys got some of our guys?"

Stephen snorted. "Only as sure as they were of that weapons cache."

Frowning, Bobby looked down at the asphalt under his boots. Airstrikes had smashed the buildings on either side of it to rubble, yet left the road intact. Though only about half of it had been demolished, the entire town had been abandoned, and Klein said a Taliban unit had moved in. According to him, they had "reason to believe" at least three American soldiers could be found imprisoned here. Three men maybe held someplace wasn't enough to justify a conventional rescue operation.

"I reckon some scouting's in order, then."

"I agree. I'll wait overhead." Stephen went up without further discussion, leaving Bobby alone in the dark.

"Yeah," he muttered. Stephen's presence had more to do now with giving Bobby someone to talk to and a second brain to chew on things than anything else. Otherwise, the vampire had, more or less, become excess baggage and they both knew it. Bobby let the dragons peel away, sending them in to check out the town. It spread out, darting around and through the rubble, then into the intact buildings.

By the time they finished, they'd found three buildings they couldn't get into without Bobby specifically directing them. The swarm came back together and he set them on the task of breaking into the first one. Its appearance and size suggested a warehouse. Dragons found their way in through one of his favorite access points, an air vent. The place had been set up as an ambush, with tripwires, explosives, even simple stakes and stairs rigged to collapse.

At first, he couldn't understand why they thought anyone would fall for this, or why they'd enter it at all. Then he found the odd little devices clipped to the power lines. Aside from the surprise of finding power out here, he had no idea what to make of the devices. Several dragons fell on the boxes to figure out what they were.

The devices had no buttons or dials, switches or levers. The cord appeared to be a standard three-prong power cable, with no extra wires. It had no antennas, and emitted no sounds or signals he could pick up. They did give off heat, like any other electronic gadget. It seemed to be their sole purpose, which made no sense to him. In a place already hotter'n heckbiscuits this time of year, they had a series of tiny space heaters.

His dragons poked and prodded at the things until they noticed the devices emitted not heat, but a *specific temperature*. The surrounding air matched what the dragons knew to be his own natural body temperature. It took him another minute to think of a reason anyone might want that.

These things had to be intended to fool detection methods that searched for body heat. For a moment, he admired the ingenuity of whoever came up with them. If a normal military unit came in to rescue those men, they'd be lured to a building full of death. Riding on the heels of this realization, seething rage threatened to overpower him. The swarm wanted to find whoever created these death traps and rip them apart from the inside out.

The second building proved to be empty. When he breached the third building, he figured he'd find people, and meant to scout it and return to Stephen to plan. In the first room they found, the dragons saw men sitting around a table, playing cards and speaking some kind of Arabic-type language. They bore a strong resemblance to the men in that cave system. Before he realized he needed to restrain them, the dragons poured out and attacked, flooding the room and diving into the throats of the surprised men.

Bobby watched the men thrash and gurgle, watched them claw at their throats and chests. They exploded, dragons bursting out in enough places to rip their chests and backs and bellies apart. In seconds, his swarm reduced four men to shredded meat and sprayed blood and gore everywhere. Dragon fire sparked all around as they cleaned each other off, and he pulled them in to re-form and survey their handiwork with his own eyes.

Fresh meat, blood, bile: they mixed together in a horrible stench. They had died so fast, with so much awful violence. He would never have to worry about dying like that. What did that mean? Anything at all? He covered his mouth and swallowed bile. Turning on his heel, he slipped and grabbed the bloody doorknob to steady himself.

He shut the door behind himself and sagged against it, breathing in the dirt and sweat and dust of the hallway. No matter how many times he wiped his hand on his pants, it refused to feel clean, and he swiped his hat off to wipe his sleeve across his brow. He'd come here to scout, not to slaughter.

Somewhere else in the hallway, a door opened and shut. It goaded him to stagger away from the door and move. His boots clomped on the thin, industrial carpet and he used the wall for support. As he passed it, a door opened, smacking into his side. The man behind it stared, wide-eyed, then he raised his assault rifle and pointed it at Bobby's chest. He said something.

The dragons yearned to be freed. Bobby clamped them down and raised his hands. "I only speak English," he informed the man, which earned him a rough nudge in the arm with the gun.

"Go," the man said with a thick accent.

Bobby let himself be shoved along, too numb and distracted to resist. As he went, the guy shoved the gun barrel into his back on one side or the other at random intervals, and it got so annoying that Bobby recovered his wits. He could get away at any moment, but this guy seemed to have a destination in mind, and it could turn out to be where the prisoners were kept. That would make everything faster and simpler.

They went down three flights of metal stairs, two more than necessary to reach the ground. Finally, they passed through a door and down another hallway. Bobby got shoved into an empty room with a bare earth floor and walls. The door clanged shut and his host jangled keys, then he said something that sounded like a sarcastic welcome and walked away. Though the dragons wanted to stream out the window with the bars across it to destroy that man, Bobby wanted to wait and learn more first.

"Hey," he called out. Moving over to the door, he grabbed the bars and stood on his toes. He managed to get high enough to peer out, doing it for the sake of appearances."Hey, is anybody out there?"

"Yeah," a male voice croaked. "Save your strength." He had a Bronx accent, and sounded tired and defeated. "They'll be down for you soon enough."

"What'd they do to you?" He hated to ask and would have preferred never to know. Someone in his position would ask. Besides, better to hear about it before seeing it.

"Doesn't matter. Not getting out of here no matter what."

Bobby took a deep breath and forced the dragons to stay put. "Anybody else down here?"

"Yeah. You make eight. If Turtle's still alive."

"I'm here," a voice called out, reedy and in obvious and extreme pain. "Sort of."

Great, just great. Bobby leaned his forehead against the door, trying to cool the rage in the dragons. His own anger worked against him. Before he went on another murdering spree, though, he wanted to be able to say they'd deserved it beyond a shadow of a doubt. "Why ain't they just killed ya?"

The first voice huffed out what might have been a laugh if he had more energy for it. "I think these sonsabitches just like torturing us. They ask questions, but it doesn't matter what we answer. Might as well be asking what time it is for all they seem to care about the answers. Face facts, kid, you're in for a long, slow, painful wait for the day when they finally decide to let you die."

"Butler got out." This voice came from a cell deeper down the hallway, and had a mild East LA accent

"Butler killed himself," the first guy snorted.

"How long you guys been down here?"

"Who the fuck knows." The first guy coughed, it sounded wet and unpleasant. "Shit, I'm spitting blood again."

Now, he'd heard enough. The swarm burst violently out and poured through the window. Dragons attacked the other doors, pulling, pushing, burning, and scraping. They ripped apart hinges and handles, and the doors fell into the hallway with clangs that had to echo up the stairs. Men would come, soon, to investigate the noise. The swarm flowed to the only exit—the stairs he'd been brought down—to ravage whoever came down. He had enough presence of mind to send five dragons to get Stephen.

Frothing, burning rage carried the dragons through the entire building, spreading out to make sure no one escaped. They churned through every human in the building, except those seven prisoners, and Bobby let them do it without reservation. Whatever had happened to those men down there, it had been gratuitous and cruel and unnecessary. What happened to Riker and his men almost seemed reasonable and justifiable in comparison.

When Bobby re-formed in the middle of the worst of it on the ground floor, he could hear Stephen outside the door, probably there to get better reception for his earpiece.

"Cant and Mitchell reporting in. There are seven wounded men here. The building has been cleared. So far as we can tell, there's no one else in this town. None of these men can walk on their own, so we need on-site evac and it'd be best if you send at least one medic to bundle them up for travel...I didn't get names. Some of them can't talk in their current condition, and the ones that can aren't in good shape. It's questionable whether they'll all actually survive until you can get someone here...You maybe want to inform the evac people that the site is—" He coughed. "They should be prepared for carnage."

Bobby stared at his handiwork, empty inside. "Carnage", Stephen called it. This time, he had no urge to throw up and no idea what that meant. Maybe he'd been born for this, designed by those scientists to be an unstoppable killing machine. Up until this trip, he'd thought of the dragons as scouts, not machines of death. Now he knew better.

"We'll do what we can," Stephen said, still talking to Klein, "but we aren't medics and have no idea what will make things worse. In fact, it might be in our bests interests to leave before anyone gets here. They're in the basement." He stepped back inside. Bobby heard more than saw him. "Are you okay?"

Yeah, he was all full of peaches and sunshine. Bobby's expression went sour as he noticed his stomach growling. At a time like this, surrounded by bodies destroyed by his dragons, he was hungry. "No."

"Maybe you should get some air." Stephen headed for the stairs. "I'm going to do what I can to make sure these guys last until help gets here, but then we should go."

He could turn his back on all of this and put it behind him. No one expected him to do more than he already had, not even Stephen. He rubbed his face with both hands and heard his daddy's voice in his head, telling him to stop being a weak, lazy lump. Fleeing now would be just that: fleeing. Momma didn't raise a coward, and he could face this.

He stepped over a charred pile of shredded meat and pulled a protein bar out of his pocket. "I want to see them."

"Didn't you see them already?"

"No, we weren't looking. Kinda focused on bad guys."

Stephen glanced over as they took the stairs down together, his eyes flicking from food to face. He said nothing, though. They reached the bottom and the vampire pointed at one door."That one's the worst."

Nodding his understanding, Bobby stopped before he could see inside any of the doors and let Stephen go ahead. Despite his certainty upstairs, he hesitated now. The vampire continued on and disappeared into one of the cells, unruffled by any of this. It seemed that he had no problem stomaching anything he hadn't caused himself.

Bobby frowned at the ground, trying to figure out what bothered him more about the men down here than what he'd done upstairs. He didn't do any of this. He couldn't have prevented it. He hadn't failed to act. Someone did, someone could have, someone had, but not him. What, then, was he afraid of? He stood there, trying to figure it out and listened to Stephen talking to one of the men.

"They're on their way. No idea how long it will take. I think you're in decent enough condition I could move you, but I'm not sure it's wise."

"It'll probably hurt a lot." The other voice was that Bronx guy. "Then the medics will come and do more. Yeah, maybe I should just stay put. How's Turtle?"

"Turtle's screwed, that's how he is." Turtle sounded worse now, as if his condition had deteriorated since Bobby last heard him. His breaths came out ragged and labored, and every word cost him something to force out. "Would you guys tell my mom I'm sorry I didn't listen to her when she begged me not to join?"

"Tell her yourself," Bronx called back.

Turtle made a noise that could have been a strained laugh or a stifled sob. "Not likely."

Either Stephen or Bronx muttered something too low to be understood, then the vampire paced out of that first room. He paused in the hallway and looked over Bobby questioningly. He opened his mouth to say something, but stopped and closed it, then shook his head with a sigh and went for the next room.

Whatever his intention with that, the gesture made Bobby's feet take him to the first room, where he looked in and saw a cell no different from the one he'd been tossed into. Bronx wore a pair of khaki pants ripped off at the knees and nothing else. He sat with his back against the far wall, covered in dried blood and dirt. His left foot—Bobby knew was no other word for it than "mangled". If he had to guess how it'd been done, he'd say someone shoved it into a meat grinder, then let it heal that way. Strangely shaped burn marks and acid scars covered his chest. They chopped three fingers off his right hand and split the big toe on his right foot in half. Bobby's brain refused to figure out what had happened to the man's right knee, but it looked wrong.

That didn't even qualify as the worst. "Hey," he said to Bronx, because the man noticed him there. "I'm, uh, the guy what was in that cell." The dragons wanted to burst out and kill those men all over again. And again and again, until nothing remained but pulpy piles of sludge.

"You busted us out?"

Now, he wanted to throw up. Swallowing bile back down, he gave a vague little nod of his head with a shrug of his shoulders. "Yeah, with Stephen. It was kinda an unplanned jailbreak kinda thing. I weren't rightly expecting what I done found here."

Bronx's mouth lifted in a strained, lopsided smile. "Thanks, man. I dunno how you did it, but you did."

Looking down at the floor, Bobby scuffed a boot and tried not to show what he actually felt. The damage done to this guy's body repulsed him, and hated himself for it. Pity filled him for what he'd go through starting tomorrow, and he hated himself for that, too. Worse, he couldn't figure out what to say. Everything that came to mind seemed stupid or pointless. "Wish I'd'a been here six months ago."

"You and me both." Bronx coughed. It might have been a laugh. "I figure I'll be in a wheelchair when I get home, but hey, at least I won't be here or dead, right?"

"Yeah, that's something."

"It's okay, man, I know it's hard to look at. I been living with it for a while and I don't want to look, either."

"There anything I can get you?"

Someone else called out, "You got a girl in your pocket?"

Bobby got a ghost of a smile. "Nah, sorry. If it makes you feel any better, though, I ain't got laid in a while, neither." He cringed, not sure if that was an okay thing to joke about, not sure if it even came off as one.

Bronx cough-chuckled. "Big damn hero like you doesn't have 'em lined up around the corner? Must be doing something wrong." Bobby also heard a few pain-spiced sounds of amusement from the other rooms.

"Yeah, I reckon so. Guess I gotta brag more or something. Any of you got girls back home already? " Was this helping? Talking to them about stupid crap—did that help, or make things worse? He had no clue, but at least, he supposed, he had them thinking about something besides their own misery.

"I got a wife," a new voice said, strained and kind of soft. "She was pregnant when I left. I have a little girl I've never met. I guess I'll get to spend some quality time with my girls now."

"I had a girlfriend," Hispanic said, and he sighed. "I expect she's long gone by now."

"I got a girl back home, but she's..." Bobby paused and breathed, trying to get the anger to drain down. None of that was for Lily, he only had frustration about her. "Man, it don't matter. I don't think it's gonna work out anyway."

"Oh, come on," Bronx cajoled. "What'd she do? Bite your dick? Sleep around? Get pissy about you joining up?" A few of the others echoed his interest, trying to get Bobby to open up and tell them what happened.

It made no sense to him. Why did they want to hear about his love life? All that seemed stupid and petty compared to what they'd lived with for the past few months and would deal with for the rest of their lives. Enough of them piped up and urged him, though, that he told them. "She was married right outta high school, the guy was some kinda bigger damn hero than me. He come over here in the Army, I think, got himself killed a few years ago. She's got his little boy, and she's still in love with him. Last time I saw her, she called me by his name. Ring ain't there, but it is, you know? Private First Class Thatcher, might as well be Saint Sebastian for her."

"Thatcher?" Hispanic asked. "The wife is a hot brunette with these kinda funny blue eyes?"

Bobby blinked a few times. Bronx beat him to answering. "From the look on his face, I'd say that's a 'yeah.'"

"Huh, small goddamned world. Thatcher was in my unit when I first got here. We were both green as shit. He had a picture of her he kept in his helmet. Didn't even know the baby was going to be a boy. Good guy. He got off easy. Pushed me out of the way and took the hit that shoulda taken me out. No idea why. If I had a girl like that back home, I wouldn't have done that."

Now he knew how the guy died, and it made things worse. He was a real hero, the kind Bobby wasn't and would never be. "Thanks, I feel tons better now," he grumbled. Rubbing his face with a hand, he sighed heavily and tried not to think about her. It didn't work.

Bronx cough-chuckled again. "I think you done a little better than saving one guy."

"I guess that depends on how you look at it." Bobby glanced at Bronx and shook his head. "Pretty sure she ain't taking me back after I left like how I did."

Several of them laughed at him, and he decided they'd more than earned the right to do it. It all faded away into coughing and then quiet until he could hear Stephen murmuring to Turtle in that second room. Bobby had a thought to try another subject to keep them entertained. When he opened his mouth, Stephen's voice rang out.

"I'd really appreciate if you guys could convince Turtle he wants to live."

The request forced Bobby to move, bring him to the doorway where Stephen sat with his back against the wall, unhappy and exasperated. The other guy's body had been broken in so many ways Bobby couldn't even comprehend what they did to him to make it happen, or how he'd managed to survive this long. A long list of thing that guy could never hope to do again filled his head, starting with walking and rolling through everything imaginable that would be fun. In his opinion, the man ought to be allowed to die if he wanted to.

"Turtle," Bronx called out, "you still got your mind. Whatever they did to your body, they never took away what's in your head."

Whatever happened to a man's body, it didn't have to happen to his head. Bobby stood there and thought about that, wondering if it rightly applied to him. Was he still the same guy as before? No, not at all. A month and a half ago, he had a decent job and didn't cause any— Except for how he went over and punched Mr. Peterson in the face for what he did to Momma. If he had the dragons then, would he have killed the man? Did he blame the dragons for his own anger? If all they did was make it more obvious and easier to give in to, what did that really mean?

Vaguely, he heard Turtle respond. "Like none of us has nightmares every night, like any of us is ever going to be okay. I'm not— I'm not strong enough for this."

He opened his mouth for Stephen's sake, not Turtle's. "I ain't rightly sure what comes after. I been raised to think it's Heaven, that we all get to see folks we lost and be happy all the time and all that. More I see and do, though, more I wonder if'n that's true. There's lots of things that're just as likely as what the preacher done told me, including nothing. I know you done suffered a lot, and I don't think nobody'd really blame you for wanting that to end.

"Thing is, what if there's a girl waiting to meet you, maybe in the hospital or something, or a doctor what needs to see what happened to you to make some kinda leap in logic or something to make a new kinda thing for a kid what needs help? What if you're stronger than you think and it ain't a nightmare ahead of you?"

He felt cheap and slimy for trying to talk Turtle into living. The guy was crippled, wouldn't have a real life ever again, and Bobby plain didn't have to ever consider the prospect of facing that. If he got mangled up like that, he'd go swarm and re-form and everything would be put back. He had no right to try to guilt someone else into living with something he'd never have to.

Turtle didn't answer. Stephen looked up at Bobby in surprise. It was in his expression; he could tell Bobby only said all that to try to spare him, and couldn't decide how to feel about that. The vampire looked back at Turtle and sighed heavily. "It's your life, your choice."

Unwilling to watch the guy choose, Bobby walked away and peered into the next door. He paused and nodded to the guy there, then moved on to the next one and continued until he reached the last one. Most of them had similar problems as Bronx. One of them lay unconscious, breathing with a wet raspy sound to it. He might never wake up.

"Somebody tell my mom this isn't her fault," Turtle rasped.

Bronx answered, voice shaky, "Yeah, I will. Rest well, buddy."

A gasp came from Turtle's room, then a little moan with no pain in it. "Thank you," he whispered.

Bobby hurried for the stairs to get away from that. He and Stephen needed to get the heckbiscuits out of here and move on to the next mission. That one would be simpler, and they'd handle it and move on, and it would only take a few more until Privek would let them in. They'd find Jasmine and free her and go home.

Outside the door, he leaned against the wall and closed his eyes, wishing he could unsee everything inside. The dragons still wanted to destroy people, or was that him? Either way, he only held them back because they'd already killed everyone here.

Stephen stormed out a few minutes later, throwing the door open hard enough to tear it off the hinges and send it flying several feet away. He didn't want to talk. It seemed to Bobby that he needed a trenchcoat billowing out around him to go with that angry swagger. The vampire took to the air and Bobby followed him as dragons, keeping them all out of arm's reach, just in case. For both their sakes.

Chapter 8

The flight to the next target lasted long enough for Bobby to get frustrated by his failure to collect his thoughts into true coherence. He wanted to specifically not think about what had happened at that warehouse. More than that, he needed to exact revenge for it, yet all those responsible had already been killed. That minor detail irritated him, and he flicked it aside.

Of course, all these people, the ones who lived here and thought the same way and looked the same and followed the same religion should be held responsible. They hadn't prevented it, they hadn't stopped it, they hadn't condemned it. The only way to save more lives, the lives that mattered, would be to kill them all. None of them deserved to live, and all of them had to die to protect Jasmine and Liam and Paul and the rest.

They descended on an armed compound. Neither Bobby nor Stephen cared about double-checking on the mission. Not this time. Both had frustration and anger to vent, and nothing could stop them. Since all of these people bore guilt, Bobby wasted no time with scouting.

Stephen started on one side, and Bobby went from the other. They moved through it and slaughtered everyone, meeting in the middle. Bobby re-formed in time to watch the dragons that made up his hands burst out through the chests of three different men, all of them screaming as they fell to the ground.

It didn't bother him. These men had tortured Bronx and Turtle and Riker by proxy. Given the chance, they'd do the same thing to someone else. The fact they found no American soldiers here meant only that they hadn't managed to capture any for whatever reason, or the ones they captured were already dead and the bodies disposed of. These people had blood on their hands, he knew it.

Stephen pushed his way out of the small room off to the side, wiping blood off his chin with one hand while he tucked his shirt into his pants with the other. His expression mirrored how Bobby felt as he stood there, finishing off a chicken leg he picked up off a table: pleased, sated, and righteous. He tossed the bone over his shoulder and stepped over bodies to join the vampire.

This place had also sated and pleased the dragons. They'd stopped pressing to break free, stopped pushing him to do something. He felt pretty good, too. They'd done something important, something worth doing. This scum had to be wiped off the face of the Earth, and he and Stephen were just the right tools for that job. Admittedly, he didn't need Stephen all that much. For just cleansing this plague, he could handle that on his own.

They landed inside the small forward base nearest to where they'd been busy tonight. "Cant and Mitchell reporting in," Stephen told his earpiece. "Mission complete, we're stopping for tonight. I'll call back in before dusk again." They strode through the base together, Bobby having no idea of their destination. "Understood." Stephen pulled the earpiece out again. "The unconscious guy didn't survive being loaded for transport. The rest are either on the table or otherwise stable. So, five made it."

Bobby nodded and tried to ignore the flashes of fresh memory. “Maybe we oughta split up. Get more done at once.”

Stephen stopped and put a hand out to grab Bobby’s arm, making him stop, too. “What are you talking about? We’re not here to get as much done as possible, we’re here to get Privek to trust us. Bobby, this isn’t about killing people, this is about getting closer to finding the others. Did you forget that already? ”

Scowling, Bobby looked away. “I didn’t forget nothing.”

The vampire pulled his hand away and crossed his arms, also looking off at nothing in particular. “We were going to stick together for a reason. After what happened last night, I don’t think…” He sighed and shifted uncomfortably. “You didn’t want to deal with those soldiers. Someone had to. What would you do if you wound up in that situation again?”

He knew the vampire was right. It changed nothing. “I ain’t helpless or nothing.”

“I’m not your dad.” Stephen snorted. “If you want to go it alone, it’s not like I can stop you. But, you don’t have one of these,” he held up the earpiece he used to contact Klein, “and I’m not giving you this one, because I need it, too.” Before Bobby considered swiping it, Stephen tucked the device back into his pocket. “I’m going to get some sleep. Which is your cue to eat. See you later.”

Annoyed, Bobby shrugged it off and gave Stephen a curt, unenthusiastic nod. His stomach growled with the mention of food, so he sniffed the air and headed for the mess tent in a sulk. He didn’t need Stephen, not to do this stuff. The vampire was smarter than him, he knew that. Stephen didn’t know everything, and these missions had nothing to do with brains. Out here, no one had that stupid drug, and none of those suits lay in wait. No one could stop him, and he had no need for someone to watch his back.

Brooding at his food tray, he shoveled food into his mouth

without tasting it, a tactic that served him well out here. Whether Stephen wanted to admit it or not, this mission only needed killing, and he now had the best way ever conceived to do that. His entire body was made of hundreds of little assassins. Stephen didn't think he could handle himself on his own. No one ever did. He could, and he would.

Of course, that did nothing to dispel the ghost of Saint Sebastian lingering at his back. Bobby had no idea how the guy's voice sounded, but he could hear it anyway, telling him how he didn't stand a chance, how Lily could see right through him. Sebastian would always be the better man, because he'd sacrificed everything to be a hero.

Bobby sacrificed nothing. He could kill everyone in the country—no, everyone in the world—without suffering so much as a paper cut. Sebastian had been a normal guy, rising above his human limitations. Bobby had no limitations to rise above.

Before now, he hadn't dwelt on how thoroughly unstoppable he'd become. The suits stopped him by catching him off guard, in his human costume. What would happen if someone chopped his head off while he was drugged and couldn't go swarm? That was an experiment he'd rather not try. Like Stephen, he preferred to just not know the extent of his nigh-immortality. But, out here, no one had that drug. The sooner he killed all these terrorists, the sooner Privek would declare the mission complete. He ought to get on with it.

Resolved to end this war on his own, he crammed the rest of his meal into his mouth and hurried out of there. He didn't know where exactly to go, but how hard could it be to find people that wanted to kill American soldiers when he looked like one? Not hard at all. At the edge of the camp, he broke into the swarm and flew up and away. So far, all the missions took them to the north part of the country, so he went that way.

Landing just outside a small town an hour or so later, he walked boldly down the road. A stone wall about five feet high all the way around the low, squat buildings all squished together in a clump. Four men loitered with assault rifles in front of the wooden gate, watching and pointing at Bobby as he got close. Considering nothing else had probably happened near them in a while, he took no offense at the pointing.

Going by looks alone, these men needed killing. They looked the same as those other men, the ones he knew deserved the unpleasant deaths he gave them. But he couldn't be completely sure everyone here needed that kind of judgment passed on them, and thought he ought to give them a chance before meting it out.

Approaching the four men, he held up his hands and let them take a good look. He stopped twenty feet away and turned around to prove he had no weapons. Their actions would decide how this went, not his.

Two pointed their guns at Bobby, one held his more casually, and the fourth rested his against his shoulder, looking unconcerned with this foreigner on his turf. He was the biggest, taller than Bobby and more muscular, and stood with his feet apart enough to be intimidating with his confidence. Intimidating to someone actually worried about death or debilitating injury, anyway. Bobby gave the guy some respect for show.

"Hi there," he called out. "Don't s'pose any of ya speak English?"

Confident Man nodded. "Some. What you want, American?"

Bobby suddenly realized he needed a story. It had to be something where they'd feel free to treat him however they wanted, instead of how he wanted them to based upon a gun to their heads. "I got separated from my unit, and kinda need to use a phone or something. If'n you can spare it, a drink of water'd be appreciated, too."

Confident Man turned enough to speak to the others, using another language, and chuckling at some grand joke. Casual Rifle Guy grinned and replied, jerking his chin to indicate Bobby. Confident Man eyed Bobby up like a predator checking out potential food. "Come, phone."

Anyone else would have been six kinds of stupid to follow that man. Someone genuinely in the situation he pretended to would be better off wandering around in hopes of bumping into Americans. Bobby, though, smiled. "Thank you kindly." He ambled after the man, acting like a stupid hick. Stephen would probably tell him that he came to the role naturally, and he'd be right.

As expected, Casual Rifle Guy tried to use the butt of his rifle to hit Bobby in the back of the head. Instead of the impact the guy hoped for, Bobby burst into dragons and let them run wild. It took them half an hour to spread through the town and kill all the men. Women and children, he left alone. Without pausing to examine his handiwork in human shape, he put the town behind him and moved on.

That term, "human shape", covered it. He wasn't human, he had a shape that appeared human. In reality, he was a great big bunch of dragons all linked together. His life up until he discovered that had been pretend, or maybe learning how to blend in. Considering it that way, he didn't deserve to be considered a murderer. Instead, he ought to be thought of a janitor. They should to thank him, even, for cleaning up their stupid messes. They weren't even worth getting fussed up over, anyway. Anything that could die so easily couldn't have much value.

He let the landscape go by under the swarm, only stopping when he saw another town. This time, as soon as he saw the men who looked exactly like those other ones, he let the swarm go without bothering to pause and check them out. Because they didn't matter to him, he let the dragons kill whoever they wanted without paying attention. Instead, he floated in the middle of the bloodbath, trying to figure himself out.

If he was a big pile of dragons, what *was* the Bobby part of him, this overall mind? He remembered seeing a TV show once where a bunch of little things that were dumb individually got smart when they all came together. That seemed to kind of fit, though he couldn't imagine how it must work. Loosed from a physical shell, it didn't make any sense that his consciousness actually came from his brain, though when he tried to move the part that he knew to specifically be Bobby, nothing happened. He was as chained to the dragons as they were to him.

The thought kept him busy until swarmed together again, burning the blood off of each others' tiny bodies. Letting them do what they wanted to these people took no effort on his part, and even felt good, like relaxing a muscle he hadn't noticed was tense.

In the next town, the dragons went through and killed everyone, then he found an empty bed in a room with no bodies or gore and lay down to grab himself some rest. He fell asleep easily. When he woke, vague impressions of unpleasant dreams sat on his shoulders. Standing and stretching brushed them away.

The sun set while he rummaged through the kitchen. He found crackers, raw vegetables that tasted fine, and some pastes and sauces he liked. One tub in the fridge had some chicken with lentils he devoured with gusto.

"Bobby, are you still here?" Stephen's voice drifted through the window from the street below.

How did the vampire find him? He scratched his cheek and figured that ignoring Stephen would be childish. Instead of shouting out the window, he went dragon and poured out of the house, re-forming on the street a few feet away from Stephen. "Yeah, I'm here." The stench of death—raw and rotting meat, blood, urine, feces, bile—hung heavy here, and flies buzzed everywhere.

Stephen held an arm up to shield his nose. "I see you've been busy."

"Ain't no sense in waiting."

The vampire pulled his arm down and rested both hands on his hips. "No? Am I slowing you down by giving a shot at trying to determine if people we kill actually need to be killed or not?"

This sounded like the start of a lecture. Bobby's eyes narrowed and he scowled. "If'n you got something to say, then say it."

Instead of answering, Stephen pointed. Bobby's eyes followed the line of the gloved finger until he saw it. A little boy lay surrounded by his own gore, dead eyes staring up at the sky. Next to him was a woman that might be his mother, also dead. She held an infant in her arms, also ripped apart. The handiwork was obviously his own; no one else came and did this while he slept, but he didn't remember doing it. He hadn't been paying attention while the dragons exercised their freedom.

Bobby turned away from that horror and found himself looking at another two young children, faces twisted in terror. He'd casually murdered children whose only possible crime was being born here instead of someplace else. By not caring enough to keep track of the dragons, by feeding their blind rage, he killed these kids, that mother, that baby. He could live with killing grown men who took up arms to fight. Little kids, though…

Bending over, he put his hands on his knees and threw up into the street. Everything he ate came back up, most of it still recognizable. Stephen stood by in silence, only moving a foot to stay clear of the new mess. When he had nothing left inside, Bobby suffered through a few dry heaves, then took a drink from the canteen Stephen offered him and spat it out.

"I thought maybe you'd had a psychotic break." Stephen took the canteen back and tucked it away in a pocket.

"What did I do," Bobby breathed, eyes wide and staring. "What did I do?"

"That's an excellent question. Offhand, it looks like you decided to pass judgment on a few thousand people, if you count the ones in the other two places you went through." Stephen's voice held no emotion, only detached curiosity. "Which is interesting, since you're so disturbed by my drinking blood, something I am forced to do to continue living and which does not require the death of my victim. As I recall, it also disturbed you when I discovered how much I enjoy killing someone when I do it."

Bobby stumbled back a few steps, tripped over something, and landed on his backside in congealed blood mixed with other things. His mouth moved, but no sound came out. He killed these kids and that baby, and others like them. What was he doing when the dragons forced their way into these little mouths? Pondering his existence? Thinking. When he should have been acting, when he should have been in control, he'd been thinking about life, about his invincibility, about his superiority.

Stepping gingerly to Bobby's side, Stephen offered him a hand. "We need to get you out of here, Bobby. I thought I was the one that would have trouble with all this, but it's you."

"What did I do?" Bobby stared at Stephen's hand, not sure what to do with it, not sure if he deserved it.

"Only you can answer that question." Stephen reached down and took Bobby's hand, pulling him to his feet. "Let's go ponder it someplace else. The ambiance here hasn't been improved by adding your breakfast to it."

Afraid to let the dragons out, Bobby stood there, his mind

gone blank. Stephen solved the problem by hefting him in a fireman's carry and flying upwards. Slung there like a sack of potatoes, Bobby chased circles in his head. Those people died because failed to prevent the dragons from killing them. He'd spent time worrying about himself and ignoring the rest of the world, and those people all paid the price for it.

Stephen flew for a while in the darkness, then touched down in a spot with nothing around for miles. He dumped Bobby into a pile of wild grass where he got an unobstructed view of the star-filled sky. No light pollution spoiled the view, and he stared up at the impossibly full, moonless night.

All those millions of sparkly dots burned with heat so intense his dragons wouldn't withstand it. They stared down at him, not giving a crap about his problems or confusions or wonderings. Once upon a time, he might have prayed to God for forgiveness, but had had no idea if that would help now. It didn't feel like that mattered much.

Several minutes later, he said, "The dragons, they're me and I'm them." He left it there for a bit, feeling small and insignificant compared to the sky. A few minutes later, he he opened his mouth again, not sure what would tumble out of it. "I keep thinking of them as something else, but they're me. I'm all little bitty parts jammed together into one bigger piece. What they want, it's what I want. They did all that while I wasn't paying attention, only I was, because they're me. I knew what they were doing."

"They controlled you instead of you controlling them," Stephen murmured into the darkness.

"Yeah. And no. And yeah." Nothing had changed since he killed those two suits, other than efficiency. Then, he'd been surprised they could do such a thing at all. Now…he didn't want to think about it something this confusing and disturbing. "I gotta get outta here, afore I ain't nothing left worth having."

For a few minutes, Stephen said nothing. He stood nearby, also staring up at the sky with his hands in his pockets. "Agreed. Let's get moving. If we're lucky, we can get a fair distance before anyone notices we've gone."

Bobby let the dragons peel off, ready to carry his own weight again, at least for traveling. It would be unfair to expect Stephen to haul him any further. Not that fair had a seat at his table right now, but if he wanted to take control back, he had to start someplace. "What about Privek?"

"Screw Privek. None of those eleven would want you to sacrifice your sanity, to become a monster just to get them free."

Uncertain how to take that, Bobby nodded before his head dispersed into dragons and had the swarm follow Stephen. They flew all night, pausing a few times to let Bobby eat, then went to ground for the day in some rural area Stephen thought might be in Turkey. As little as he liked them, Bobby choked down more of those stupid protein bars to keep his stomach under control.

"We're going to discuss what happened," Stephen said as he leaned against the rock of a shallow cave. The direction the mouth faced meant he could expect to be in the shade for most of the day.

"I ain't got nothing to say 'bout that." He sounded childish and knew it, and didn't care.

"Fine, then. You can listen." Stephen pulled his hat, sunglasses, and balaclava off, setting them aside and moving on to his gloves. He looked tired, which came as no surprise. Bobby suspected the vampire wouldn't take any crap from anyone right now. "To me, humans are basically over-glorified cows. Walking, talking food. It's really difficult to actually care about them as people. Yet, I grew up thinking I was one of them. Sure, I always suspected I wasn't quite as normal as everyone around me was, but I was human as a child and had a family that cared about me. My parents are good people, so are my brother and sister. Pastor Chris is a good man.

"And yet, here I am, looking at people like that Elena chick and thinking 'food'." Stephen stared directly at Bobby, the weight of it so intense Bobby had to look away, down at the ground. "Since I've had a fair amount of time to think about this, it seems to me that is entirely because people are now food for me. At first, I bit my girlfriend during sex. Didn't even realize why I was doing it, I just did it. She didn't remember me doing it, and the sex was great. As women do, though, she got her period. She didn't like sex during that, said she felt too crappy. Which is fine, I could live for a week without sex. I still needed to eat, though.

"I didn't feel comfortable looking for a whore at the time, partly because of the stigma and partly because that would be cheating on Marie, and wasn't sure where to go for that anyway. I also didn't feel like I could go to anyone I knew, because it was so crazy and demented. So I found a few homeless people and paid them ten bucks each to let me bite them. It was nothing like as great as sex and food together, but that was how I came to the understanding that drinking blood is an intimate thing, something inextricably linked with sex. Biting men bothered me because I'm not attracted to them.

"But, my point is that they're food. If I wanted to let that rule me, I could. There's no shame in slaughtering food animals, so long as you're actually eating them, and I've never managed to feel 'full', so I know I can drink more than one person dry at a time. Which, of course, means that I could pick people out and eat them and feel nothing, because they're just cows." He stopped there, still staring at him.

Bobby scowled at his feet, having a feeling he knew what the point might be. "But you ain't doing it," he mumbled to the dirt.

"No, I'm not. I could, and I already know what it feels like to do it—it's amazing and intense and I want that, badly. But I'm not doing it."

"And you think I'm an asshole for giving in."

Stephen arched an eyebrow up. "No, I think you allowed the dragons to become your scapegoat. Whatever they do, it's them, not you, and you can be disgusted by it without feeling responsible because they're not under your control. In reality, they're little pieces of you, Bobby, and you're completely responsible for everything they do. In the same way that my hunger for blood feels like a separate thing, a demon possessing me, if you will. I could blame it for whatever depraved things I do, but that's a lie, a bald lie. It's not some other entity, it's nothing more or less than my deepest, darkest desires, made more palpable for what I have to do to survive. This is about taking responsibility for what you are and can do. I understand you didn't quite realize what they're capable of, but now you do." He smirked. "If you keep letting them do it, *then* you're an asshole."

Bobby huffed out a very mild snort, but also nodded his understanding. They sat in silence for a few minutes while he chased his thoughts around to form them into coherence. "I ain't rightly sure what actually happens when I'm dragons. To me, I mean. I tried to see what I could do while they were— I let 'em go to just do whatever they wanted, and they flipped out at folks what look like those guys in the cave. In that first town, one tried to smack me upside the head with his rifle, and I let 'em loose, but we only done killed the men."

Thinking back, he replayed it, trying to figure out where things went wrong. But then, it had actually been before that. Maybe a lot before that. He never killed anyone until that day at Lily's house. Those two suits came in and the dragons surprised the heckbiscuits out of him by attacking. They killed those two men. Because—because he was angry at the suits for what they did. At that point, though, they hadn't really done much. "I think—I think maybe I got lotta anger in me, and I just don't feel it so much because they do."

Several seconds passed before Stephen offered, "Maybe you should ask yourself why you have all that anger."

"Shoot, I dunno. I always been the scrawny kid, the one what got beat on, not the one what done the beating."

"You were bullied as a kid and you can't imagine why you might be angry as an adult?"

Bobby opened his mouth to respond, but realized he had no intelligent words to put there, so he shut it and looked off into the distance, making a little hmm noise. "I reckon maybe I gotta stew on this stuff."

"Probably wise." Stephen picked his hat back up and used it to mostly cover his face. "Don't forget I changed two months before you met me. Also, I had therapy when I was young."

Chapter 9

If anyone noticed them perched on the top of this cruise ship, Bobby would eat his boot. He sat next to Stephen in a t-shirt and boxers, working on a plate piled high with food. This was the best meal he'd had in a while—fried chicken, buttered corn on the cob, mashed potatoes slathered in gravy, thick biscuits, and a beer. His camouflage clothes lay in a rumpled pile nearby, where he'd shucked them to blend with the natives and enjoy the sunshine.

"This is the way to travel." He loosed a mighty burp. "They don't even ask nothing, cause ain't nobody should be on the boat without a ticket at this point. I said I forgot my ID and they just gave me the beer anyway without no hassle."

"I hate watching you eat." Stephen, still lying where he'd been asleep until a few minutes ago, grumbled from behind his balaclava. "It's like watching your best friend screw a gorgeous redhead while you're chained to a chair on the other side of a window."

Bobby choked on the comparison, thumping his chest to get the food clear. His neck separated into dragons, a chunk of chicken fell into his lap, and it all re-formed too fast for his head to fall apart. "I could eat it down there, but it don't seem rightly like a good plan, since someone might actually notice I ain't wearing proper shorts."

"Take some."

"I ain't seen a good opportunity to. Nobody walks around with spare clothes in their pockets. It's all in their rooms."

Stephen snorted. "Since when does that stop you?"

"I don't need it, it ain't right to take something when you don't need it."

"Seriously? You're still going to cling to that morality?"

"'S'only one I got." The food suddenly tasted bitter for Stephen hinting to All Of That. Bobby sighed and resolved to think of everything that happened in Afghanistan as staying in Afghanistan. Like Vegas, only a lot less fun. He hadn't had any nightmares, at least. Not yet, anyway. "You gonna grab a meal tonight before we take off?"

"Yes, I am. If I don't, I may well get hungry enough to chomp on you."

"Shoot, that's pretty gosh-darned hungry. Don't worry, though, I don't think I'll ever get hungry enough to try to eat you."

"That's neighborly of you." Stephen sat up and went quiet while Bobby stuffed his face. "Man, I can smell them all. It's like the ship is one giant buffet."

Since he thought the same thing, Bobby chuckled. "You wanna stay on the boat until tomorrow night or fly on after you eat?"

"You said it's headed in the right direction, but it's so damned slow." Stephen huffed out a mildly annoyed breath. "While I'm prowling, check their maps to see if leaving now is potentially committing suicide. More than fourteen hundred miles is probably too much to go before your next meal."

"Good point." Nodding, Bobby shoveled the last bite of potatoes into his mouth and set the plate aside to finish his beer. "We might be screwed."

"Nonsense. The worst that happens is we wind up on some stupid little island in the middle of nowhere, eating raw fish and sleeping out in the open."

"So we might be screwed, then." Bobby grinned and felt like laughing for the first time since All Of That.

Stephen snorted. "Yes, we might. If it's too far, we can always go back to land and catch a flight. You and I can both ride in a cargo compartment, and I seriously doubt we'll have any trouble sneaking into one."

"Fair point, but maybe we can find another cruise ship after this one. I kinda like it."

"Imagine that. I'm shocked, I tell you. Shocked."

Bobby followed Stephen's gaze as he turned his head west. The sun had slipped down to the horizon, throwing brilliant orange and pink light across the sky. It drifted down, disappearing from sight.

"I will not kill anyone on this ship." Stephen unlaced his boots, ready to pull them off the second he wouldn't burn for doing so.

"Me neither, and I know you won't. Maybe you should graze a bit here and there to make it easier to resist."

"Yes, that's a good idea. I'm not sure I like this ship business as much as you do. No hookers, no slums, and too many people who'll ask questions."

"I bet they got hookers, just not the cheap kind you mean."

Stephen reached over and gave him a playful shove, the first time he'd done it since All of That. Then the sun disappeared and he shucked his clothes, down to the same shirt and boxers as Bobby. Breathing in the sea air, he wiggled his toes and stretched. "Don't wait up."

"Don't s'pose you'd drop off my dishes? It was kinda a pain to get them up here without being noticed."

"Yeah, I can do that." Stephen took them and stepped off the side of their perch.

"Don't do nothing stupid."

Stephen grinned broadly. "No, that's your job."

"Damn straight." With the vampire gone, Bobby lay back and popped off a single dragon. He tossed his mind into it and flew all around the ship, scouting. Plenty of people milled about and sat on the open air decks, some of them enjoying the buffet he'd collected his dinner from. Kids ran and shrieked, and this boat even had a pool.

He dove through the first door he found open at the right time. From sitting on it all day, they knew it headed west, but had no idea where to. At a guess, it would head halfway across the Atlantic to some island paradise, then go back to wherever it came from in Europe or North Africa. They could fly on from that pit stop and probably be okay. The ocean couldn't be *that* big.

He thought a map would be difficult to find, until he discovered the part with all the shops. A screen dominated one wall, showing the ship and its route. This boat started in Lisbon, Portugal, and had a destination of Ponta Delgada, a tiny island somewhere in the middle of the Atlantic. It had reached halfway between the two ports already, and had no stops listed between them. Instead of mileage, the route had been marked by days and hours. Three days from now, it would reach the island, which might be a good place to rest and stock up on supplies before crossing the rest of the ocean on their own.

The shops sold most anything a body could want on a trip like this, and he found himself contemplating how best to take a pair of shorts without it being noticed. Out through the back of the shop would probably work. He summoned five more dragons and had them perpetrate a small heist of shorts, a shirt, and flip-flops. It was all necessary to fit in, because he intended to vote for sticking with the boat at least until tomorrow night.

Something started to annoy the dragons, and he had to land out of sight and focus to figure it out. They wanted to eat. When was the last time he let them eat? He couldn't remember, which meant it'd been too long. They messed up that car outside Elko, then…nothing. That happened two weeks ago. Dammit, he could've gone to Fort Morgan or Denver any time during that week before they went to Chicago. But no, he spent all his time with Lily and Sebastian, afraid of missing something with them. Stupid, stupid, stupid.

Right now, he could do nothing about this. Whatever might be found on the ship, he suspected letting them eat it might damage the engine or other important parts, stranding all these people out here. What would happen when they got really, really hungry? It seemed like maybe he'd find out, depending on how long it took them to get to that point. Hopefully, they could last three or four days. This island place probably had nothing for them, which meant they'd have to wait until he got back stateside.

On the way back to his body, he spotted Stephen, now somehow wearing a pair of shorts and an unbuttoned Hawaiian shirt. The vampire sat with a rather attractive blonde, talking to her about something. They both laughed. It must be nice to have that easy a time with seducing women. He said and did all the right things.

Then again, maybe he only knew how to pick the ones that would be receptive to a one night stand. He watched Stephen lean in and whisper something in the girl's ear that surprised her and made her cover her mouth. When he pulled back with a predatory smile, she gulped and nodded, nervously eager. They stood up and walked away, Stephen smug enough to peel a grape. Damn.

Chapter 10

"Bobby, I have to stop someplace, soon. I can't just go forever."

The dragons responded with chirps of acknowledgment so Stephen knew he'd been heard. They'd left Ponta Delgada at dusk yesterday and hadn't found a place to touch down for even five seconds since then. Twenty- four hours later, Bobby could hear the exhaustion in the vampire's voice.

The vast size of the Atlantic surprised him. He worried they might be flying in giant circles, they could have turned toward Antarctica by accident. While they had both the sun and stars to go by, he'd never navigated that way before and had no idea if they'd managed to stay on a due west course. He'd expected to find dinky islands dotting the ocean, at the least.

It'd been so long since they last stopped, he had no idea what to expect for the condition of his body. He'd never gone a full day without pausing to eat before. Worse, the dragons were cranky now, hungry enough to not give a crap about what he wanted. The second they found food, they'd devour it, no matter how much he wanted to stop them. Stephen would probably feel the same way by then, too.

What would happen when his body wanted to shut down for

lack of food? What about the dragons? Was he slowly killing himself right now? Contemplating the possibility of accidentally starving himself to death gutted his morale, so he stopped doing that. He tried to, anyway.

"I think I'll be okay with blood, but I need to sleep." Stephen's voice did a much better job of breaking his downward panic spiral than Bobby's resolution to make it stop. "I'm not sure if I can drown or not, and don't really want to find out. Can you spread out to look for a place to land? Even just a little fishing boat would be enough."

Certain he could handle that, Bobby had the dragons trill. A third of the swarm streaked north, a third headed south, and the rest stayed with Stephen. Fortunately, they understood that food required land and cooperated with him.

Half an hour later, still with nothing in sight, the vampire slid downward. The dragons screamed at him. He woke up and held his head in both hands. "I'm just not up for two all-nighters in a row, Bobby, not without something more interesting to look at or do. Maybe I can float on my back? The water's pretty calm."

Great. Stephen would float on the current while Bobby did what? Keep going? Float with him? The dragons could keep going forever, so far as he could tell. Their little minds, though, had become consumed with hunger. He felt like hundreds of toddlers saying "why?" over and over again had camped in his head.

"What I wouldn't give for some caffeine right about now," Stephen mumbled. His body bobbed up and down as he fought to stay conscious. Thankfully, the dragons could see the value of keeping the vampire going, and did what they could to help: chirping in his ears when he started to fall. Even so, they gradually drifted downwards. When they reached a few feet above the surface, Stephen finally fell in. Hitting the water only woke him up enough to roll onto his back, then he passed out again.

The dragons converged on him, no longer watching for anything in particular, and struggled to keep him from sinking under the surface. It overrode their hunger. Briefly. They came together, re-forming his body against his will, and Bobby realized with horror that he'd pushed them too far for too long. Usually, he did that fast enough to not consider the process. This time, it took them about a minute to do it, and he registered the exact point when his mind snapped into his head.

He slipped underwater and struggled to break the surface again, then thrashed about to reach and grab hold of Stephen. An all-consuming hunger hijacked his head as he did do, twisting his insides into knots of agony. His eyes drooped and his leaden limbs refused to cooperate. The dragons could go without sleep, but Bobby couldn't. The next time they did this, they'd take a plane, dammit. Because there would be a next time. Somehow, despite his gross stupidity, they'd survive this. Somehow.

Sputtering on salt water that he kept swallowing when his will to remain conscious wavered, he tried to relax with his arm looped through Stephen's. He blinked and caught himself coughing again. Any minute now, he'd slip under the surface for the last time, too weak to push his way back up. Karma caused this, he figured. For his crimes, he'd drown in the middle of the Atlantic, which he'd failed to grasp the vastness of.

In the middle of a disjointed prayer for God to watch over his Momma, he caught some kind of strange sound chugging closer. In his current state, he couldn't comprehend it well enough to attach a label to it. Momma shouted, saying something about water. He thought he blinked, then he fell onto something hard. Faces swam in his vision. Momma told him to wake up and spit the water out. Rolling to his side, he coughed and thought he saw Stephen. Either he'd died or he'd been pulled onto something that would keep him from drowning. Assured the matter had been settled one way or the other, he closed his eyes.

When he opened them again, he groaned. His belly had wrapped itself around his spine and squeezed, making everything hurt. "I died," he gasped. His body curled into a ball of its own accord.

"Take it easy, Bobby, we're relatively safe. There's some fish, it's cooked. I can feed you, but you have to help me out a little."

"Where?" Without opening his eyes, he opened his mouth. A forkful of food pushed in, and he marshaled every ounce of willpower he had to take the time to chew it up before swallowing. Nothing had ever tasted so good as that bite of fish, a food he usually avoided.

Stephen fed him several more bites before answering."A private yacht. The owners fished us out of the water and are headed back to port. The boat isn't very fast, though, and they were a fair distance from land. I've only had a short nap. When I woke up, I met them both and told them I didn't remember how we got where we were. I suggest you go with that, too. They think we're Army, I haven't tried to correct that."

"They call?"

"No. They were out in international waters and didn't want to deal with whatever the military might send out. Besides that, they were apparently headed back anyway, something about running low on food and water. It's a very nice older couple. We're in one of the bedrooms on their very nice boat. They sometimes bring their grandkids out with them."

The fish put a dent into Bobby's hunger. Not a very big dent, but a dent all the same. It let him relax and think about other things. "Dragons won't come out 'less there's food for 'em. They done starved, too."

"Understood. We'll have to be careful, then." He sighed wearily. "I need to get some more sleep before we hit land, Bobby. There's a bowl of oatmeal here, an apple, and a glass of juice. Also, the envelope is mostly okay. There's some water damage, but it's still all as legible as it was before."

"'Kay." Finally opening his eyes as the bed shifted under Stephen's weight, Bobby found himself in a bedroom. Everything had a nautical theme with a dark blue background. Their uniforms had been draped over every available surface to dry. He mustered the energy to sit up and finish off the fish and devour the rest of the food. It gave him enough to feel a more normal level of hunger. Given the choice between finding more food or getting more sleep, though, sleep won.

A knock on the door woke both of them. Stephen sat up as the door opened. It was a woman with white hair up in a bun, wearing a light blue shirt and white pants. Bobby rubbed his eyes and propped himself up on one elbow, thinking she must be sixty or so. "Boys, we're about twenty minutes out from the marina, it's just past noon in Myrtle Beach. Denis is wondering if you might be up to helping us dock? It's just holding ropes and that sort of thing." Her light Southern accent made Bobby feel like he'd come home.

Stephen smiled. "Yes, ma'am, we'd be happy to as soon as we're dressed."

"I'm glad you're both okay."

"Thank you kindly, ma'am," Bobby managed to get out. "We're pretty happy about that, too."

She chuckled. "I'm sure you are. Just come on up when you're decent." Backing out, she shut the door again.

"Ma'am," Bobby muttered, "I ain't been decent for near on a week already."

"It's been a lot longer for me." Stephen grabbed clothes and pulled them on.

Rubbing his face, Bobby sat up and ignored his belly rumbling. “Did we make the right choice, leaving instead of staying?”

Stephen sat back down to get his socks on. “How many bodies did you pile up again?”

“Yeah, you got a point.” Scratching what had become a full beard while he'd been busy, Bobby sighed. “One good thing about this whole stupid flying across the ocean thing: it feels like that happened a million years ago.”

“I hear you. I know I said otherwise at the time, but that cruise ship was a good idea. Made for some pleasant detox. And we didn't even kill anyone.” He said it with a grin. Dark brooding lurked underneath. “Thankfully, Joan there isn't really enticing to me, so I haven't had to worry too much about the Hunger taking over. I'll need to hit something before we go too far, though.”

“You can do that while I hit a junkyard.”

“Yeah, good deal. I'm sure we'll be able to find one not far from here. I can carry you there.”

“From there, we head for…did we decide?”

Stephen tucked Hanamidi's envelope into his coat and buttoned it up. “Not really. Either Albuquerque or the farm. I suggest we hitch on a plane.”

“I'm good for that. Let's do Albuquerque and figure from there.”

Chapter 11

Myrtle Beach didn't have a junkyard, but another town just up the road did. Stephen dropped him off inside, then went off to find his own food. The dragons descended on that place like a plague of locusts, tearing through it with delight and fervor. They spent a full hour diving in and under and through, chomping and chowing. Poor guy who owned the place got ripped off something fierce. One more pile of crap on his soul, if he even had one.

They met back up and flew to Columbia, where Bobby grazed on dumpsters before they sneaked onto a plane bound for Dallas. He stayed in the swarm for the flight in the cargo compartment. Stephen stretched out on the luggage and took a nap. The next plane to Albuquerque kept them waiting for a few hours.

Another hour after their second flight landed, they stood in front of Adesha Wahiz's house. The neighborhood made Bobby smirk. Half the houses all looked the same and the other half were really, really different. It'd probably been built a while back by folks with all different ideas about what a house ought to look like. Then, some time recently, other folks came through and bought some of them, knocked them down, and replaced them with faux adobe, "properly Southwestern" houses.

Adesha lived in a faux adobe one, of a not-quite-peach color. It had cacti and rocks for a front yard and a small courtyard space in front of the door. Keenly aware they still wore in military uniforms, Bobby opened the gate and led Stephen to that door without hesitation, where he rang the doorbell. At least they didn't have guns. That would probably send a much worse wrong message.

All the way here, neither broached the subject of how to handle this conversation. Bobby pondered it briefly, only able to think of the worst possible way: "Hi, we killed your dad, and he wanted you to have this!" He glanced at Stephen while they waited for someone to answer the door. They'd crossed into shade, so he pulled his headgear off, and Bobby snatched his hat and sunglasses off, too.

The door cracked open, the woman inside holding it open while bracing it with her body. She looked them over, her brow furrowed and eyes suspicious. Bobby could see Hanamidi in the straightness of her nose, and a little around the chin. The woman in the pictures he figured for her mother showed a lot more.

He threw on the most pleasant, friendly smile he could manage. "Howdy, ma'am. We're looking for Ms. Adesha Wahiz."

She let go of the door enough to cross her arms defensively. "That's me. What do you want?" For some reason, he'd expected her to sound Afghan like her father. Instead, she had a hint of a Southwestern twang.

"Well, I'm not sure how to paint this nice. I'm sorry to inform you that your father passed a few days ago."

Adesha narrowed her eyes. "Is this some kind of scam? He's been dead for years."

Bobby glanced at Stephen, who shrugged and produced the envelope from inside his coat. "Welp, he put your name on this here packet, at this address. We just figured you must be his daughter."

Maybe he'd faked his own death? Bobby shrugged and pressed on. "At any rate, this is addressed to you, and we were kinda hoping you might be willing to tell us what the notes are about."

She took the envelope, expression clouding over as she ran her fingers over the writing on the front. "You looked through it? "

"It wasn't sealed," Stephen said. "And everything got wet on its journey here. We made an effort to dry the papers for you."

Tapping a finger on the envelope, she looked them both over again, then opened the door wider. "Come in and sit down while I look it over. If I can tell you anything, I will."

"Thank you kindly, ma'am, we appreciate it." They followed her inside the well-appointed and clean house to sit on plush couches, both choosing to perch on the edge rather than sink in and get comfortable. Watching her pull the papers, Bobby found himself fidgeting, like her opinion or reaction or something mattered more than anything else.

"This is his will, this is my father's name." Adesha sat down across from them in a matching armchair, confused and upset. "Where did you find this? Are you sure he died just a few days ago? "

"Yes, ma'am, it was found in a town in Afghanistan, along with him." He wanted to tell her the truth, as much of it as possible. If anything happened to his Momma, he'd want that courtesy.

Shaking her head in disbelief, she said, "I thought he was already dead. Nothing from him for years. What about my mother? Was she there?"

"I'm sorry, ma'am, we got reason to believe she passed a few years ago."

"Huh." Adesha frowned as she leafed through the pages. When she found the pictures, she flipped through them and stopped at one. "He was a scientist, worked on some top secret government thing. We used to ask him what he did, and he'd tell us silly things like ‘looking for worms.’” She set the pictures aside and scanned the notes.

Bobby scoured all the corners of his being for every scrap of patience he could muster. The woman needed to take her time and deal with this stuff. At the same time, he hoped she took forever. Once they got what they needed from her, they’d go back to the farm. Screaming and yelling probably awaited them, then lectures and cold shoulders.

“I guess he wasn’t lying.” Adesha sounded both amused and surprised as she looked up, papers in her lap and hand and the arm of the chair. “This is about wormholes. Unless I’m mistaken, he was working on the idea of interdimensional travel. He calls it out as an absolute possibility, starts from that basis. There was an event that convinced him it was possible, and he had data he was trying to use to re- create the event. He never succeeded, but thought he was getting close when he finally gave up and retired.”

Stephen leaned in, looking more keenly interested than Bobby felt. They already knew this part, after all. If they acted like they knew it already, though, she might clam up. “Why did you think he was dead? ”

She sighed and slumped her shoulders. “They lived in Alamogordo. He worked at White Sands Missile Range, so too far to see all the time. I used to talk to my mother a few times a week. One day, she just stopped calling and didn’t answer her phone.

“My husband and I drove out there to check on them that weekend, and we found the place trashed, like someone went through everything. The police investigated, or said they did, and never found any evidence of what actually happened to them. After a few months, we assumed they were taken and killed. That was years ago.”

Bobby shared a glance with Stephen and knew he thought the

same thing: if he worked at White Sands, maybe the project was still there. Also, Hanamidi's bosses didn't mess around, so they needed to be careful poking around this stuff. Kurt Donner had, more or less, suffered the same fate, after all. This sort of thing happening two separate times suggested some unpleasant things.

"That's a crappy thing to have to deal with, ma'am, I'm real sorry you had to go through that."

Adesha nodded. "Do you know how he died?"

"It was quick and painless." Thank goodness Stephen answered right away, because Bobby would have sat there looking guilty and probably given the whole thing away. "We don't know anything about your mother." He stood up, apparently convinced they had all the new information they were going to get.

Taking the cue, Bobby stood, too. "What're you gonna do with them notes?"

She looked down at the pages. "He wanted me to put them on the internet. I guess I'll do that."

"Be real sure before you do that. There's folks what might not appreciate it."

Nodding, she set the papers aside and also stood. "Yes. I'll talk it over with my husband first. Thank you for bringing this to me. If for no other reason than so I have the pictures."

"Thanks for taking the time," Bobby nodded. Adesha showed them out, and neither said anything until they'd turned up another street and lost sight of her house. "We were gonna head for the farm now."

"We're really close to the missile range, though. It's just south of here."

"Yeah." They both stopped. Stephen leaned against a lamp post. Bobby crossed his arms and scuffed his boot on the sidewalk. "I ain't keen to go back."

Stephen snorted. "I keep thinking about how much we're going to be bitched at for having done this."

"That pretty much covers it. If'n we go back now, though, we can maybe have a better chance at White Sands, on account there'll be more talents to choose from."

"There may also be more chances for things to go wrong because of more people being involved." The vampire sighed and stared off at nothing in particular.

"Maybe we oughta just go back and get the tongue-lashing done with. At least we got something to show for it." It seemed to Bobby like both choices sucked. "I guess there's something else to consider, which is that the suits gotta know we bailed by now. They might be expecting to see us at White Sands. It's been near on a week since we left already, and that's plenty of time to set up for us here, just in case."

Stephen sighed heavily and straightened away from the post. "Fine, fine, we should just go back. I suppose it's not that far anyway. I want to see Kris before I deal with the rest, though."

"Coward." Bobby gave the vampire a flat look, because he knew that meant he would go back first, by himself. "After I done pulled your ass outta the fire, and you did it back, more'n once, you're gonna bail because of a little social pressure?"

The vampire made a little whiny noise. "I don't like dealing with angry women."

Bobby snorted and started to laugh. He couldn't help it. "Big, bad vampire is scared of girls yelling at you? Really? Mr. I Am The Monster In The Shadows don't wanna get bitchslapped."

Stephen scowled. "Oh, shut up."

He gave Stephen a mock glare. "If'n you think I'm gonna let you go off to get laid in Denver while I face the firing squad, you're nuts."

"Fine, fine, let's just go before I decide to try and eat you."

"Yeah, it'll be 'trying'. Let's see them fangs work on metal." Still chuckling, Bobby broke apart into dragons spiraling upward.

Aside — Camellia

When the two men got far enough away to not notice her even if they looked back, Camellia stepped away from the wall she'd been leaning against and let her body's camouflage fade away. She pulled out her phone and hit the speed dial on the way back to her rental car.

"It's Camellia. You were right, they came here."

"What did they do?" Privek sounded like he always did: sharp, focused, crisp.

"They went inside and talked to Adesha for maybe ten or fifteen minutes, then left."

"Did you hear anything?"

"Yeah." She took a deep breath and hoped she hadn't joined the wrong team. Privek and his people rescued her from those suits, but all she had to go on was the video and what he said. Whether Mitchell and Cant and the others really did all that damage for the reasons Privek said they did, she had no idea. Still, they were obviously capable of causing plenty of harm. That made them a particular kind of dangerous, no matter what.

"They're going to someplace they called 'the farm', and expecting to be yelled at. They're also planning to go to White Sands

Missile Range, but not until they go back to that farm place."

"Did you get any impression for where this farm is?"

"Kind of. They went north, and said it wasn't far. Mitchell mentioned Denver, but like it's nearby, not where they are." She decided not to pass on the name Kris, on the off chance Privek would tear Denver apart and ruin all kinds of normal lives to find her. Even if it would help, she'd be pissed if he harassed her friends, and assumed they'd feel the same. "What do you want me to do?"

For several seconds, she heard something tapping. Maybe he fiddled with a pen or pencil while he thought. "Was it due north?"

"I'm not a compass, Privek, I'm a chameleon." She went ahead and gave the car an annoyed glare even though he couldn't see it. At least he could probably hear it.

"Could you follow them if you left now?"

Shading her eyes, she peered at the last place she saw them in the sky. That dark spot and collection of glinting flashes around it was probably them. She wondered if they followed roads to navigate, or had some weird, innate sense of direction. Chelsea said she could always somehow tell north. "I doubt it, they're pretty fast and I don't know the roads very well."

Another pause let her hear clicking noises might be him tapping keys on a computer. "Go to White Sands. Wait inside the base. Whoever shows up, follow them around and try to hitch a ride back with them. If you can't, call me when they're gone."

She unlocked the car and slid into the driver's seat. "Will I be on the access list, or do I have to sneak inside?"

"You'll be on the list. If you're not, tell the gate guard to call his supervisor."

"Understood." The impulse to chuck all this and go home lurked in the back of her mind as she hung up the phone. In six or seven hours, she could be back home in Phoenix. Now that she had this weird superpower, no one would find her if she didn't want them to. Her brother missed her, and she missed his stupid puns.

She started the car and thought again of the footage she'd seen in her mind's eye. Soldiers had shot themselves, things had spontaneously blown up, people had had arms ripped off. Men as dangerous as those two and their friends needed to be stopped. Normal people had no chance against them. She'd agreed to do her part to take them down because she believed it needed to be done. With a heavy sigh, she checked her purse and pulled out enough money to grab something to eat. At least she could get authentic Mexican food around here.

Chapter 12

Bobby and Stephen landed together at the far end of the driveway. The sun had gone behind the mountains in the distance about five minutes ago, putting them in twilight. Stephen pulled off his balaclava, hat, gloves, and sunglasses, stuffing all of it into pockets. Bobby tucked his own sunglasses into his breast pocket. They set a slow, unenthusiastic pace up the long drive.

"I'd suggest sneaking in, but I'm starving." Bobby's belly rumbled to punctuate the statement as truth.

"Damn you and your stomach," Stephen smirked. "Someday, it'll get us both killed."

"Got close already, not sure I wanna test if it can do the job proper-like."

"Do you have any brilliant idea for what to tell them?"

This last flight took nearly four hours. Both of them had had plenty of time to think about it. Bobby had ignored that in favor of enjoying the flying. After starving the dragons by being stupid, he thought they deserved a little time with his head not annoying them. "I'm thinking we should go real light on details. They don't gotta know what all we done, just the important parts."

"Agreed. They especially don't need to know about Hanamidi

or the caves. Or anything else after that, really."

"No, they surely don't." Bobby nodded emphatically. "If'n I could think of a way to put it, I'd say they don't need to know we was in that country at all. Not rightly sure how to explain the uniforms without that part, though."

Stephen sighed. "No, we'd have to lie to do that, and I don't think we should do that, not to them."

"Ayup."

They reached the house far sooner than he wanted to. All the cars sat parked in a row, and the front porch light shone in the gathering darkness. Bobby stopped where the two parallel lines of trees flanking the drive ended. So did Stephen.

"Look, whatever happens in there, I think we done the right thing more'n we done the wrong thing. Ain't nobody was doing nothing, and we done something. It didn't work out as great as we hoped, but we got something, which is more'n nothing."

Nodding, Stephen clapped him on the arm. "Well said." From the way a grin lurked around the edges of his mouth, Bobby suspected he meant the opposite and rolled his eyes.

As they stood there, stalling, Andrew stepped out the door and immediately lit a cigarette. The Creole had a book under one arm, but was definitely more interested in smoking just now than reading. He didn't notice either of them.

"Guess we might as well get this going." Bobby reluctantly forced his legs to move.

Andrew's eyes snapped open and he peered around. "Who's there?" He called it out loud enough for anyone to hear him through the nearby open window.

"No one of consequence," Stephen responded.

Movement on the roof attracted Bobby's attention. "Thank God you guys are back." Matthew flipped himself down to the ground, landing with a soft thump. He paced over quickly and gave Stephen a brotherly embrace, then clapped Bobby on the shoulder. "They've been harping on me since I spilled, and that was the morning after you left. It's like having a bunch of cats watching you all the time."

Bobby chuckled. Stephen snorted. Andrew approached, smirking as he flicked ashes off his cigarette. "Did you boys at least get something worthwhile?"

"Yeah. Where's Hannah?"

"Meeting room." Andrew pointed with his lit cigarette. "With Alice and Violet. Kaitlin's in there, too. Lily's not. Everyone else is either out in the woods or screwing. You hungry? Soon as I'm done here I can warm up some leftovers for you."

"Starving," Bobby nodded gratefully. "That'd be great, thanks."

Andrew took a step back to blow his smoke away from them. "Sure thing, Bobby. Just watch yourself, don't talk stupid."

Matthew grimaced. "I'll stay out here. Already taken enough, thanks."

"I'll be up after," Stephen nodded to the werewolf.

"Right. Time to go get ass-whupped." Squaring his shoulders, Bobby marched himself to the front door and walked in without knocking. Voices buzzed from different parts of the house, too quiet to be understood. Pulling off his hat as a form of contrition, he stepped into the doorway of the meeting room and put on his best smile.

Hannah, Kaitlin, Alice, and Violet all looked up from their separate seats. They must've heard Andrew, at least, but all four seemed surprised to see him. Maybe they expected an encyclopedia salesman or something.

"Hi," he said with an uncertain wave. He scratched the back of his neck awkwardly.

Behind him, Stephen also stepped into the room. "Not interrupting anything important, I hope?" He sounded about as fake with cheer as Bobby felt.

"Bobby! Oh my god!" Alice jumped up and threw her arms around him, giving him a firm squeeze of a hug.

Kaitlin shrugged and returned her attention to her laptop. Hannah and Violet both stood and scowled. The former put a hand on her hip and the latter crossed her arms.

Alice let go and slapped him hard enough to knock his head aside. "You ass! What were you thinking? "

Stephen coughed. It sounded like a stifled laugh. "Matthew explained?"

"Yes," Hannah snapped. "Nice leaving him here to carry your water."

Bobby rubbed his face. He could live with Alice slapping him. "We got some stuff, at least. It weren't a waste."

"You're not Head Cowboy here, Bobby." Hannah glared at him. "It was your idea in the first place that we shouldn't go off and just do whatever without the rest of the group agreeing to it. I mean, really, I can understand Stephen haring off, but I would've thought you'd be against something like that."

Glancing back, Bobby got the distinct feeling the vampire decided not to be offended by that in favor of not getting blamed for this. At least he'd come along, but still. Coward. "It weren't like that." Even to him, he sounded whiny. Time to cut that out. "Look, do you want to know what we got, or don't ya? 'Cause we can spend an hour telling Bobby how he's a dumbass, or we can go straight to how it weren't a disaster."

"I think they should apologize to everyone." Violet reminded him of Momma. Maybe it was just her heavy Alabama accent, or maybe it had more to do with that stern, no-nonsense tone. He could almost imagine her saying 'don't you sass me, boy'. "For being arrogant, self-righteous dicks."

"Sure," Stephen said, "but that can wait."

"Yeah, we got a place to go." No, Bobby did not want to stand in front of the whole group and beg for forgiveness. If that would let everyone move on and get to work on more important things, he'd do it.

Hannah quirked an eyebrow. "Is that it?"

"We coulda just gone there and maybe had more, but figured maybe y'all'd like to know about it and maybe some come along. It's White Sands Missile Range. The Maze Beset project was there, or at least part of it was, and might still be. There was more'n one project under the name, all separate parts."

"Alright." Hannah's glare softened. "Come in and sit down, spill it."

"What's with the camo?" Kaitlin spoke without taking her attention away from her laptop.

Alice hugged Bobby again, then shoved him towards a couch. "They both look good in it, at least."

Bobby cracked half a grin and dropped down on the couch. "We were kinda in the Army for a few days, but that ain't important. They don't know nothing they didn't know before. We did a few missions for 'em, and run across a guy what knew some stuff." He explained what Hanamidi had told them, using the man's words. When he finished with that, he added his own thoughts and ideas from his discussions with Stephen.

"At this point," Stephen said, "it seems clear that we were created with alien DNA. It's a bit of a leap, but the evidence is piling up."

Bobby nodded. "I really do think somebody oughta break in at White Sands and see what there is to see, but it's got some risk."

"By 'somebody,'" Hannah said dryly, "you naturally mean you two."

"We are fairly good at this sort of thing at this point." Stephen must have figured the worst had passed, because he leaned back into the couch and appeared to have relaxed.

"It don't gotta be us, but we're willing and got the skills and uniforms now."

"Hannah, I'm done—"

Bobby froze at that voice. He'd wanted to have a chance to change into regular clothes before she saw him. Turning to look, he found her staring at him in surprise, sliding into horror. Her eyes had gone wide and her mouth hung open, and she still took his breath away.

He gulped. "Hi, Lily." His eyes traced the lines of her face, wanting to etch them into his memory so well he never lost hope or his sanity again.

The room held its breath while she stared at him. Then she blinked and broke the spell, looking away to focus on Hannah. "I'm done with the towels, they're hanging in the basement. I'm going to bed. Good night." She turned on her heel and marched away.

His butt left the couch in a flash. As he reached the door, he heard Hannah say, "We'll figure this out in the morning."

Nothing else mattered except that when he hurried into the hallway, he saw her back. "Wait, Lily." He tried not to beg and knew he'd failed.

The words made her stop, giving him a chance to take a few steps closer. She crossed her arms and looked over her shoulder. "You could have left me a note."

"I know. I'm sorry."

"It's not just about me, Bobby, I had to explain to Sebastian. He thought you weren't coming back, and I didn't know if I should tell him otherwise."

He closed the distance and touched her arms, hoping for the best. "I didn't mean to make things hard on you." He'd told Momma that a thousand times, too. Somehow, he always managed to find himself needing to say it again.

He'd expected her to flinch, to haul off and slap him, to melt into his arms, to do something. Instead, he stood there and did nothing. "I'm tired, Bobby." His stomach chose that moment to rumble. "Go eat," she said wearily, walking out of his hands and away from him.

This time, he watched her go, wondering if he'd done worse than she could forgive. He took heart from her not slamming her door for half a second. Then he realized Sebastian must be sleeping already. Hanging his head, he sighed and trudged to the kitchen. He found Andrew setting a plate heaped with food on one of the picnic tables.

"She'll be happier to see you in the morning," Andrew said

Bobby dropped onto the bench and shoveled food into his mouth. What had he expected? That she'd run and jump into his arms? Yes, actually. As stupid as that seemed now, he'd genuinely hoped she'd do exactly that. Obviously, he'd been a dick to leave without a word. Then he showed up in a uniform, probably reminding her of Sebastian, Sr. and how he never came home after putting his own uniform on. Dumbass. Stupid, stupid dumbass. Yesterday, this was the only place he wanted to be, and today, this was the only place he didn't want to be.

"Sulking is bad for digestion, Bobby." Andrew brought a glass of milk over for him. "I don't care if you eat that without tasting it, but you might. Best to pull your head out of your ass and pay attention to it."

"How long you reckon before she forgives me for being a

dumbass?"

Andrew smirked. "Probably about as long as it takes for you to do something else stupid."

"So, just a day or two." It could have been a joke, but Bobby grumbled it, glaring at his food.

"Give or take, sure." Taking some pans to the sink, Andrew turned on the water and scrubbed them. "So long as you can accept it's your fault, I'm sure it'll turn out alright."

Bobby grunted and forced himself to slow down. The food, simple and bursting with fresh vegetables, surpassed everything he'd eaten lately. "Thanks."

"No problem." Andrew set one pan aside and moved on to the next. "My advice would be to ask John for some flowers to give to her. Not all women appreciate that, but she would. Best wait for morning on that, though. Far as I know, he's in bed already. Here's hoping it's with Ai, because I swear those two are driving me nuts with the looks and awkward conversations."

Though he found that funny, he couldn't muster more than a hint of a smirk. "I'll wash my plate and stuff."

"Don't worry about it, just leave it in the sink." He turned to go, but stopped and fixed Bobby with a particularly piercing stare. "Was it bad?"

"You could say that, yeah."

Andrew nodded. "Get plenty of sleep, then."

It was good advice. Bobby lifted a forkful in acknowledgment and farewell as the Creole left the kitchen. Not wanting to brood over food, he forced himself to stare at a knot in the table rather than think as he finished it. In his own room, he stripped the uniform off slowly, each piece feeling like a heavy load he could finally pull off and discard. With it, he was Mitchell, the freak who killed all those people for God and country. Without it, he was just Bobby. Was that how his daddy handled it when he came home between tours? The uniform did it, not him.

He balled up his shirt and threw it at the wall. That felt right, so he hefted a boot and hurled it as hard as he could. The other one followed, and within minutes, he crouched naked on the floor. Choking, gurgling noises filled his head and he grabbed his hair, trying to yank the death gasps out.

Had expecting her approval been the one thing holding him together? He bounced back up to his feet and paced back and forth across the tiny room. The walls closed in around him, too confining to breathe. Lashing out in frustration, he hit the wall with enough force that it exploded into dragons. Rather than pulling them back in, he flew apart.

The swarm surged to the window, yanked the screen out, and poured outside, spreading out and flying around like that would solve everything. He saw Stephen sitting on the roof with Matthew, talking. Light from the barn suggested Greg hadn't gone to bed yet. He might find Tiana or John out in the trees. But he didn't want other people, he wanted… He wanted Lily. After everything he did and saw and went through, he'd expected the hero's welcome and got the scapegrace's one instead.

He noticed Stephen give Matthew a hearty handshake, then take off straight up and head off to the southwest, probably for Denver. What he really needed was to exhaust himself, to make himself so tired he couldn't see straight. Alternately, he could beat his head against a tree trunk until he lost consciousness—that would work, too. It occurred to him that alcohol might also work, but he'd never been the type to drink that much at once.

Mad to get away from everyone and everything, he fled for the edge of the property. There, he landed and re-formed, and let out a primal scream, then another. A third croaked out with less force.

Nothing changed, except his throat hurt and he had less of an urge to fly apart.

Standing there, he took in several deep breaths, letting them out slowly, just trying to calm down, to force away the memories, to get a grip. Maybe ten minutes later, he realized her come out here buck naked and broke apart into dragons again. It reminded him of the first few days after he discovered his power.

Having spent the last week or so on a sleep cycle that kept him awake at night, he had no interest in sleeping now and let the dragons loose to do whatever they wanted rather than try to deny he needed to settle. Some of them zipped through the trees, playing a weird game of chase, some dug around in the dirt, some hunted around in the trees, some found whatever surface they fancied and walked or rolled around on it. He'd never just let them do as they pleased outside of killing, and it surprised him to discover that they had different preferences.

"Welcome back, Bobby." Tiana's voice had him direct a clump to trill at her. "If you don't mind, the goats actually like to eat those plants you're digging up." The tall, slender black woman picked her way through the undergrowth towards him. Her hair, usually up in a tight bun, hung straight and loose with twigs and leaves stuck in it. The look suited her.

Bobby pulled the dragons up from the ground and figured she'd probably want to actually talk to him. If he could sigh, he would. Instead, he called the dragons back to re-form his body on the other side of a tree, out of respect for her more than any real sense of modesty on his part. "Thanks. And sorry. Here I thought I might go a full day before screwing something up again."

Her rich, rolling laugh invited him to join her. "Aw, I'm not all twisted up about you haring off like a half-cocked idiot. Otherwise known as 'being male'. Truth be told, I'm surprised you guys were the only two that ran off to do something. I would've thought Jayce would get a bee in his bonnet well before you two did. I guess he's got enough to keep him busy with lifting and moving things for Greg."

Grinning, Bobby huffed an amused not-quite-snort. "Yeah, well, he don't strike me as the type to come up with dumbass plans."

"No, I suppose he doesn't." She leaned against the same tree he'd squatted on the other side of. "Is there any particular reason you're naked and chewing up nature?"

With that question, all traces of amusement fled. "Stuff." He waved a hand vaguely, hoping she'd leave it alone.

"You want to talk about it?"

"No."

"Mmhmm." She stood there in silence for a few minutes. Neither of them said anything at all and neither of them went anywhere. It was kind of nice, having someone there without asking or telling or demanding or needing or wanting or judging. Stephen could do that. Stephen had gone off to get laid.

For some reason, thinking of the vampire made him think about All of That, and he discovered he had to say something. "We killed some folk, and it weren't real clear if'n we oughta or not. We done it on account Privek sent us to work with the Army. Saved some lives and all, but it's kinda messed up how saving lives can mean taking others away."

"You've killed people before, Bobby. Why were these different?"

"I didn't have to kill them. I coulda…just—" That felt like a lie. It was true in the same way that saying 'the sky is blue' is true: sure, it's blue, but 'blue' covers a lot of colors. "No, it's really not so much that I killed them, or how many, or the ones what didn't deserve it. It's *how.* The dragons went all rage-monster and— We found some soldiers, our guys, being held prisoner, and they'd been beat up and tortured some. It pissed me off, and the dragons too. We…ah…found a new way to kill. A few dragons climb down into a body's mouth, fly down, and punch their way out through the middle parts. No screaming, just funny gurgling noises and a little hacking."

"Wow."

"I ain't never seen lungs from the inside before, or a heart up close. I don't even know what all the parts I saw from in there were. And I can do a bunch at once, with hardly no noise. I throwed up after I done it to some three dozen guys in maybe ten to fifteen minutes." He peeked around the tree at her, afraid of what he'd see there. "After that, there was more, it was less…justified and stuff."

He saw her in profile, staring out at the trees with her mouth pursed up and eyebrows halfway up her forehead. "Damn, Bobby, that's…efficient. Something to be careful with. Do they know you can do that?"

His shoulders relaxed when she failed to freak out. "I don't think so. Them rescued soldiers mighta said something, but I doubt it."

"I wouldn't advertise it if I were you."

"No, that ain't gonna be my first choice for chitchat, never." He let out a breath he didn't truly realize he'd been holding. "The dragons, they…they're—I dunno how to explain this. They're me. Like a part of me what's wild and angry."

Tiana nodded thoughtfully. "You're not, though. You don't strike me as angry all the time. Maybe it's less you and more them than you think. You could try talking to them directly, explain your beliefs and that sort of thing. If they're part of your caveman brain, that might help."

"I dunno." He shrugged. "I never been scared of myself before."

"You're not a monster, Bobby. None of us are monsters. Some

of us struggle with our humanity, but that doesn't make us beasts. The key is never to give up and stop struggling. So, it bothers you that you did something icky. Good. It should bother you. When the horrible things you do stop bothering you, that's when you've fallen off the cliff."

Put like that, he had to agree. "Making peace with it is my own damned problem, though."

"More or less." She paused and turned to look in the direction they both knew the house lay in, despite acres of trees between them and it. "Maybe you should talk to Matthew about it. He has less control over his killing, but he knows what it's like to have those kinds of awful regrets."

"Maybe." He sat down on his bare butt and leaned against the tree, staring up. "I had a girlfriend not too long ago what knew all the constellations and a bunch of star names. Looking at them now makes me think of Lily, though."

"Fair enough. Thanks."

"Next time you want to talk, I'd prefer if you come looking for me instead of ripping up the woods."

"Yes, ma'am." Bobby let the dragons out again, directing the swarm back to his room. He grabbed a towel and got himself a shower, standing under the hot water longer than he normally would. More than dirt and sweat and salt sluiced away down the drain. Being clean improved his mood considerably, and he changed into shorts and a t-shirt, then went to Lily's room and knocked softly on the door.

Half a minute went by, leaving him wondering if she'd fallen asleep. Then she opened the door, her eyes red and cheeks blotchy. What he really noticed more, though, was how her shoulder-length hair framed her face, and how the nightshirt she wore hit her at mid-thigh and hung off her just right to hint at her figure. Her regular clothes were revealed more for fitting better, yet this somehow stirred his blood more.

Her eyes flicked from him to the door. He put a hand on it to keep her from shutting it in his face. "Just gimme a minute" he whispered. "Please?"

She sighed and stepped into the hallway with him. "I don't want to deal with you right now, Bobby. I'm tired."

He reached up to touch her face, stopping when she flinched. Letting his hand fall again, he said, "You could wallop me a good one. It might make you feel better."

In a blur of motion, her hand flew. She slapped him so hard his head exploded into dragons. "No," she spat, "it's really not that satisfying." While his head reassembled, she ducked back inside.

"I'm glad we sorted that out," he told the door, trying not to be annoyed with her. The jerk stood on this side of the door; she'd reacted to him. Maybe Andrew had the right idea after all. Plodding back to his room, he dropped onto his bed and tried not to think about anything.

Chapter 13

"I really appreciate this, John." Bobby took a fistful of flowers from the Chinese guy who force grew them with his power, right in front of his eyes. He couldn't think of any way for John's power over plants to be used offensively (or defensively, for that matter), and kind of envied the other man for it. Obviously, if his dragons couldn't kill anyone, he wouldn't be in exactly this position.

John shrugged. "I'm still working on the whole 'figuring out women' thing myself."

With a heavy sigh, Bobby said, "I ain't rightly sure that's ever a thing you get to stop trying to figure out."

"Don't tell me that," John grimaced.

"Sorry. Um, how 'bout it's a thing you just get used to? I dunno." Bobby stifled a yawn and scratched the back of his neck. When the stupid birds started chirping this morning, he tried to roll over and go back to sleep. It didn't work. "I'm pretty much throwing everything I got at the wall and hoping something sticks."

"I'm sure they are." Bobby realized he only kept talking to stall, so he raised the flowers and walked away. "Anyway, thanks."

John waved him off and turned back to his herb garden. "Good luck."

"Yeah." At least some folks here had decided not to hate him. He chose to consider that a win. Cracking the back door open, he listened to figure out who he might run across. It opened into the kitchen, from which he heard limited noise. Andrew hummed and talked to himself while he cooked, so he guessed it must be Sam making breakfast.

Judging the area safe, he walked in and found Sam stirring something that smelled like apples and cinnamon in a huge stock pot. Out of all the women in their group, she happened to be the one he wouldn't call 'gorgeous'. Though she had a tall, thin supermodel's body, he thought maybe her nose had been broken at some point and hadn't healed quite right, her blonde hair always laid flat, and a scattering of white chickenpox scars decorated her cheeks. Even with all of that, she still blew away any normal girl, like all the rest of their kind did.

"Hey, Sam," Bobby said as he paced in, peering around to make sure he wasn't missing someone at the table. It was empty, though.

She glanced over, did a double-take, then smiled at him. "Oh, hi, Bobby. When did you get back? "

"Last night. Can I get something to put these in?" He held out the flowers.

"Sure." She went to a cabinet and pulled down a metal cup, the kind used with a drink mixer. "This is about the right height, and it isn't really much use without the mixer."

"You ain't mad, then?"

Filling the cup with water, she shrugged. "Did you tell them where we are, or not take a chance to free the others?"

"No, I surely did not."

She smiled more and took the flowers from him, stuck them in the cup. "Then no, I don't really see a reason to be angry. I hope she likes them."

Taking the cup, Bobby nodded and returned the smile. "Yeah, me too." He stood and watched Sam return to her pot. "Smells good."

"It's just oatmeal." She paused and stirred. "You're stalling."

"I'm hungry, though. Eating first won't hurt nothing." For once, his belly rumbling happened at an opportune moment.

Sam glanced at him, a bemused smirk turning up half her mouth. She said nothing, though, as she scooped him up a bowl and handed it over with a spoon. He sat down, set the flowers where he'd have to stare at them the whole time, and started shoveling.

"Bobby." He knew that voice well enough, and froze in mid-bite, bracing for a hard slap on his back. It hit with almost enough force on his shoulder to knock him into dragons. "I can't believe you didn't even ask me to come along."

Bobby swallowed and grinned up at Jayce as he got his own bowl. "Well, you know. I'm Head Cowboy, Hannah says so. Must be true."

"Mm. Cowboys and Injuns do not mix." The Native American man could out-hulk Stephen, and did so without the creepiness. He nudged Bobby with an elbow as he sat beside him. "You might have asked, though. Said something. Communicated your plan. Gotten feedback."

"Waited for committee assignments."

"I seem to remember *you* being the one—"

Bobby waved a hand to cut Jayce off. "Yeah, yeah, Hannah already done said her piece and she's probably still pissed enough to spit housecats."

Jayce chuckled. "I will never get used to the colorful ways you have of putting things. Just when I think I've heard them all, out comes another one." He pointed at Bobby with his spoon. "None of this cowboy stuff next time."

"Yeah, yeah. I just done said I already got the lecture."

"I can hurt you."

"Not really." He smirked and got one in return. "Maybe a little. I can hurt you back, though, so we're even."

Bobby thought he heard Sam mutter, "Boys."

Jayce's eyes flicked to her, proving he hadn't imagined it.

"We gotta sneak into White Sands Missile Range next. I done turned over that whole thing to Hannah. She can figure who's going and who's not and what all." He burned to be in on that, wanting answers to his questions firsthand. The dragons, though might not behave well there.

"If it's all about sneaking, you're probably the only one who can do it. Maybe Tony." Jayce turned to his oatmeal and shrugged. "I wonder if the missing eleven all have sneaky infiltration powers, because a lot of us do pretty full frontal destruction." Jayce gestured with the back of his hand at the cup of flowers. "Trying to make up with Lily?"

"Something like that."

"I expect Sebastian will have her up shortly."

"Yeah." Bobby inhaled the last two bites of food and stared at the flowers, working up the nerve to try again.

Jayce waited two beats before he snorted. "Suck it up and do it, dumbass."

Bobby stuck out his tongue and grabbed the flowers, then stalked out of the room. While he would have preferred to keep stalling, now that Jayce knew, he had his pride on the line. Standing outside her door, he listened for the sounds of the boy, and heard nothing. In a flash of brilliance, he popped a dragon off his thumb and sent it inside to check if he'd be waking them or not.

The dragon flitted down to the cheap carpet, flattening itself as much as it could. It wriggled under the door, wings flat. One wing got stuck, causing it to struggle and then tumble out to lie flat on its back. He looked out through its eyes, and found her in the middle of changing her clothes.

He had a view straight up her sleep shirt as she pulled it off. That left her in lacy blue panties and nothing else. It'd been a while since he got to see any girl in this state of undress, let alone the one he wanted more than anything. Tiny dragons eyes traced the contours of her body, noting silvery lines around her abdomen and on the sides of her breasts that he guessed must be old stretchmarks. Her left hip had a brown mole. A spray of freckles graced her lower back.

Suddenly, she seemed so much more *real*. The imperfections made him want her more. He wanted to touch the lines and count the spots and kiss her everywhere and make her smile and gasp. Thoughts of walking and pulling her down onto that bed danced in his head until the dragon panicked and scrambled. The movement fouled his view and something forcibly snapped him back into his own head. He had to put a hand on the wall to keep himself from falling over.

She yanked open the door, face contorted with rage, and sleep shirt clutched over her chest. From the way she pulled up short, she hadn't expected to find him there. It did nothing to assuage her anger. Kicking the little crunched dragon out of her room, she shoved an accusing finger in his face. "If I ever catch you spying on me again," she growled, "I will never speak to you again." Her eyes flicked to the flowers and she shoved the cup so the water splashed him in the face and down his shirt.

His wits came back with the drenching. "Wait, that wasn't..." But she'd already shut the door. Yes, he was an incredible dumbass. Why did he not realize that was stupid *before* he did it? He could have just knocked. He *should* have just knocked. And he thought she was mad before. Now she had an even better reason to hate him. Yes, this relationship ended before it got anywhere. Maybe he was too dumb to handle a real woman.

He wiped the water off his face and let a handful dragons off to eat the crunched one. Three flowers had landed on the floor and he picked them up. Instead of going for a towel, he shucked his shirt and mopped up the small puddle on the floor. Jaw clenched in frustration, he retreated to his own room, two doors up. At the time Hannah offered it him, she'd done it out of kindness so he could be close to Lily. Just now, he saw it as a wicked form of accidental revenge.

Inside, he threw his shirt at the wall and used his towel in jerky, rough motions. When he pulled a new shirt on, he popped a seam, so he flung that one away, too, and just went without. As a sort of demented punishment for himself, he put the dropped flowers back into the cup and set that on his windowsill. It would stay there until he managed to accept that no matter how well he got along with Sebastian, he had no chance with the boy's momma. They lived in the same place and would have to deal with each other, and that's all they'd ever have.

On his way out the door to go find something physical to do, he walked into Christopher, who'd been about to knock on his door. "What d'you want?" he snarled.

"Honey, you're stinking up the whole place with how hurt and angry and just plain unhappy you are. I can help, if you let me." Chris's mild lisp and preference other men made Bobby uncomfortable. The man's empathy made Bobby even more uncomfortable.

"Get offa me," Bobby snapped, aware he'd caused them to get tangled up in the first place. He pushed past the other man and stormed away, stomping out into the trees. Once he felt secure he'd been swallowed up by the forest, he picked a tree and smashed his fist into it. The pain from his crunched dragon compounded with this as he punched it, over and over. When it hurt enough to make him balk, he hit it one more time. His steam spent, he sat at its base and leaned against it.

Things could get worse, he knew it. Somehow.

"There you are," Hannah's voice accused.

"Yeah, here my dumb ass is. If'n you want to sling it for something, go right on ahead. I won't dodge or nothing."

She stepped into view. Since he kept his glare directed at the ground, he saw her feet in flip-flops. "I think we're going to send Lisa and Tony to the base. They should be able to handle sneaking around."

"Yeah, sure, whatever."

After a long pause, she stepped in front of him and crouched down. "Look Bobby, you broke your word and I don't trust you anymore. It's nothing more complicated than that. I didn't really trust Stephen in the first place, so nothing much has changed with him. But you, I trusted you. To have a level head, to put the whole group first, to not hide things from the rest of us. You broke all of that, every part. How am I supposed to send you to do this job when I don't even know if I can send you to fetch a book without turning it into a disaster?"

"Fine." He wanted to protest. She ought to give him a second chance. His skills would handle the job best. Nothing would get screwed up this time. The words never got far enough for him to open his mouth. Flicking his hand, he dismissed the issue, telling her without words that he wouldn't argue about it. No matter how wrong that seemed, he knew she had the best interests of the whole group in mind. Better that someone else handle it. He'd turned into a walking damned time bomb, or a killing machine, or something like that, and had no other use.

For a long minute, she watched him in silence. He picked at his jeans. Finally, she asked, “What kicked you in the balls?”

The question took him off-guard, and his mouth tossed out the answer before his brain caught up. “Lily.”

“Ah.”

He scowled. “I done it to myself.”

“I see.” She sounded amused, which annoyed him. “Why didn’t you even tell anyone what you were going off to do?”

“I dunno.” He shrugged and rubbed a fold of his jeans between his thumb and finger. “Everyone was just settling into a routine, like this is it, this is all what matters. Like having a place for us what didn’t get scooped up is the whole thing. Even with Will here, coming back the way he did, it just didn’t feel like nobody was even thinking about it no more. I guess I wanted to do something, and didn’t want everyone to tell me it was too dumb or too risky or whatever.”

She sat on the ground, crossing her legs in front of her. “Maybe you missed the freedom of being out there on your own, doing something that mattered.”

“Maybe, I guess.” That sounded very reasonable to him, and likely. He shrugged again, feeling that he must seem incredibly juvenile. “I wanna go down to the base, Hannah. I done a lot, and I ain’t much good for sitting around no more. Ain’t nobody here makes a better spy than me, and you know it, ‘specially inside a building.”

Nodding, she looked off into the distance. “I was thinking about your theories, and I agree with them. Which would make us some kind of government property, in a sense.”

“Which means there’s someone out there what thinks we belong to them and oughta be collected up.”

"Probably." She patted him on the arm. "Pick someone to be your driver and take Tony and Sam down to White Sands. Add Lisa in if you want. I'd prefer if you pick somebody other than Stephen. Get whatever you can, but it's more important to go unnoticed than to get files or anything. Everything's probably electronic, so you might be able to carry it all on a thumb drive or something."

He finally met her eyes and gave her a muted smile. "Thanks."

"Good luck." She squeezed his shoulder and walked away.

Purpose rushed through his veins, a more potent drug than anything he'd ever tasted before. Hopping to his feet, he hurried inside, already certain about who he wanted to drive. He asked Sam to pack up a bunch of food, and would have done little more than grab a change of clothes if Kaitlin hadn't joined Sam in the kitchen. She said with a bowl of pasta salad, picking out olives and artichoke hearts to eat them and leaving the rest of it alone.

It had been stupid not to come to her before he and Stephen left. It might have even been stupider than not leaving Lily a note. As much as he found her power creepy, she hadn't steered any of them wrong yet. This time, he had no intention of making the same mistake.

She, it seemed, felt the same way, because she waved him over and grabbed his hand when he held it out for her. "Blech, what a load of mush."

"Why're you eating them if you don't like them?"

She rolled her eyes and threw his hand back at him. "The future, dumbass, not the food. All I've got is 'mike'. I don't even know if it's a name, a microphone or something else."

"Anything we're s'posed to do or not do with it?"

"It's a positive thing, but I don't know how or why." She stuck her hand into the bowl and pulled out another olive.

"That's something, I guess."

"I get what I get, and that's all I got." She shrugged and ignored him in favor of the olive.

Getting up, he couldn't help but compare this prediction to the last. That one had been oddly specific. This one couldn't have been more vague, and he couldn't imagine how it would turn out to be useful. He left the two women with a wave and went to pack a change of clothes or two. Less than half an hour later, Jayce pulled their chosen car onto the highway. Bobby sat in front with him, and Tony, Lisa, and Sam shared the back.

Tony hailed from Miami, a Cubano who could shapeshift his body into a variety of inanimate objects, like tables and chairs and boxes and things. Sam came from New York City and could access computers and electronic things with her brain. Lisa was from Portland, a kindergarten teacher. Her superpower allowed her to access some kind of invisible space and store things in it, including herself. Someone else could carry it for her, which sounded plain weird to Bobby. As if he had room to talk on that front, though.

"It only took Stephen and me about four hours to fly from Albuquerque."

"You didn't have to follow roads or speed limits," Jayce answered amiably. "And we're going a bit farther than that."

"I s'pose it's for the best it'll be dark when we get there."

"Do we have a plan?" Tony had a light accent, one that hinted around the edges at his upbringing.

"Not really. Get in quiet-like, find whatever we can about Maze Beset or MB-02, get back out without being noticed, with or without hard evidence. I ain't never been there, though, so I ain't rightly sure how to set up a more specific plan than that. If'n one a'you has…" Bobby looked from one face to another, and all of them shook their heads. "So, I can do a scouting run when we get close, and we can figure something from there."

Sam ducked her head under her hoodie. "I found out I can… um…be inside an electronic device. If you can carry a thumb drive, I can go in without being seen."

"Good to know." Bobby looked to Lisa, who seemed very nervous.

"Clive—" Lisa's husband had proven himself capable by doing his fair share of work around the farm without complaint. "—says I'm about five pounds when I'm in the pocket."

"Dragons can handle five pounds, and a thumb drive. How about you?" He looked at Tony.

Tony shrugged. "I can't shift into something any smaller than half my size." The guy stood a few inches taller than Bobby and had about the same muscle mass. "A particularly large tumbleweed could get me to the building. I might be able to be a cart and get pushed inside, if we can just figure out which building to go into."

"I'll be in the car," Jayce smirked. "Bobby, maybe since you only have to carry a little bit, you can leave some of your dragons in the car. If I'm going to need to provide a fast getaway, that would be good to know before you all come tearing out with an angry, armed escort in hot pursuit."

"Ayup, I can do that. Not sure how many it'll take to hold up five pounds, but I can leave the rest here. Best not send in more'n I gotta anyway, just to avoid being seen."

Watching the scenery go by, Sam said, "I can sense you, like you're some kind of giant, busy device."

"Um." Bobby had no idea how to respond to that. "Okay. I guess we can experiment a little?" He popped five dragons off, and they flew to Sam, landing on her hand. As she stared at them, all five got really excited and looked up at her like she was a wonderful thing, and extremely interesting. Interested in what went on inside their little heads, Bobby threw his mind into one of them and found himself thrown into a conversation.

"—just doing what he feels is right."

"Sam, can you hear me? It's Bobby, inside one of the dragons."

"Yes, I can." She looked at his body and nodded, though Bobby couldn't see out of his own eyes right now.

"Good to know. We'll be able to talk, then." Jumping back out of the dragon, Bobby called his five back. "I can't hear nothing you tell them if'n I ain't in one of them. They're kinda all separate even though they're not."

"Yeah," Sam nodded, "I think I finally understand what you mean when you try to explain this."

"At least somebody does." Bobby turned around and settled in for the ride. A few times, he opened his mouth to try to start a conversation, but couldn't figure out what to say that wouldn't annoy one or more of them. His mouth shut again each time without a word, and the inside of the car felt tense to him.

They took turns driving to break the monotony. Bobby had a snack every time they stopped to switch. Jayce wound up behind the wheel again as the sun set and they passed a sign for Alamogordo. He picked a gas station and Bobby filled the tank while Jayce chatted up the girl working inside. When he finished pumping gas, Bobby dug into the cooler of sandwiches and polished off two before Jayce returned.

Inside the car, he opened a map he'd just purchased with the gas and held it up for everyone to see. "We can go into the National Monument here. You can fly across to it from there. Or we can take this road north and just claim we're lost when we reach the first person who wants to see some ID."

Sam pointed to some numbers written on the side in blue ink. "What's that?"

"The cashier's phone number."

Bobby leaned out and peered at the girl, judging her pretty in a normal sort of way. "You were in there for ten minutes and you got her phone number?"

Jayce shrugged. "It happens."

"Hmph." Bobby rolled his eyes.

Tony chuckled. "Man can't help it if he's got what the ladies want."

Lisa cleared her throat. "It looks like both choices are about the same distance from here? "

"I suggest the park." Tony tapped the monument on the map. "If we try to fake being lost, they may write down the car's plate number. Me getting out and walking around won't be strange, either."

"Sounds like as good a reason as any." Bobby shrugged. "Works for me. If'n you can't find a way through, on account of a fence or something, just go back to Jayce and wait in the car. I'll send one dragon with you, and if'n you need to turn around and go back, I'll know and it won't be no big deal."

"Good idea. I'll park as close as I can." Jayce pored over the local map.

"My dragons can always find each other, so it ain't no big deal where you're gonna park. I can have that lone one with Tony lead him if'n he needs it."

With that possibility accounted for, they drove into the National Monument. As soon as Lisa pointed out the sign declaring a per person fee for entry, Sam disappeared into her thumb drive, Lisa climbed into her pocket, Bobby dissolved into dragons and hid them all around the car, and Tony became a large piece of luggage. Jayce looked around the "empty" car and chuckled to himself.

Pulling up to the ranger booth, he rolled the window down and flashed a brilliant smile at the woman inside it. "I'm sorry, sir, but the park is closed for today."

His smile faltered. "Are you sure? I'm on my way through, and I really just want to do the drive and get to Las Cruces for the night. I don't know when I'll be along here again. Please, I've heard it's really something to see. The preview is impressive," he gestured to the heaps of white sand on either side of the road that could easily be mistaken for snow.

She sighed.

He held up the cash and begged with his eyes.

The ranger blushed. "Well, okay." Taking the bills, she pointed into the park. "Just take the drive, though. I'll get into trouble if you go through the rest of it or get out of the car. Be out by forty-five minutes from now."

"I have no wish to cause you trouble," Jayce said gallantly. If he could have, Bobby knew he would've bowed. "Thank you for your indulgence. I won't waste it." The car trundled past her booth and he rolled up the window. "Well, that was fun. Maybe I can pick her up on the way out. Bobby, you wouldn't mind getting in the trunk, would you?" He grinned broadly while Bobby re-formed.

Unable to be truly annoyed in the face of that grin, Bobby snerked at him. "I ain't got nothing against you getting laid, but that kinda defeats the purpose of most of me staying in the car."

"Damn, I knew there was a flaw in this plan."

Chapter 14

After thinking about it more, Bobby did climb into the trunk and leave one dragon in the car with Jayce. The alternative meant that ranger possibly giving Jayce extra notice for the extra guy in the car with him on the way out. If she took a closer look, she'd notice his semi-conscious state and missing hand, and things would only get worse from there.

One dragon went with Tony. It took fifteen to hold up Lisa's invisible pocket and another one to carry Sam's thumb drive. Tony became a giant tumbleweed and rolled across the white dunes. Much faster than him, the rest of the dragons streaked ahead. He picked one of that group to hold his mind so he could talk to Sam as soon as they arrived somewhere interesting.

A fence marked the boundary between the monument and the missile range. Since it had no lights or cameras or patrolling guards nearby, Tony would be able to climb it and keep going. Rather than waiting in case that turned out not to be true, Bobby plunged onward over the weirdly white sand that reflected moonlight.

Two or three hundred feet into the base, the sand diminished, making Bobby think of water frozen in the act of sliding down a plain. Once he left the sand behind, he had trouble making out the contours of the landscape and stayed high to avoid hitting anything. Lights blazed in the distance, marking a cluster of buildings that he headed for.

As he approached, he saw that a handful of roads snaked out from the central hub, heading in all different directions. It had tank tracks alongside some of them, too. Considering how much secrecy surrounded the Maze Beset project, he suspected they housed it in a building flung out by itself. It would take hours to find the right one in the dark, even if he knew what to look for from the outside.

This middle part had the feel of a proper military base, and he picked the tallest building to land on top of, hoping they'd be able to find a map or overhear something, or randomly stumble across a useful person. He set both the pocket and drive down, then backed the small semi-swarm off and had them chirp all at once.

Lisa stepped out of nothing. Her fingers appeared, then her head, and she wriggled out. Sam's drive wobbled and spat out a stream of weird, silent lightning. The lightning outline Sam's shape, then she solidified on the spot. Between the two, Sam's made more sense to Bobby.

"What do you think?" Lisa did something with her hands, like folding a piece of paper, then she brushed them on her capri pants.

Sam covered her mouth and belched. "I think I hate doing that."

Lisa patted Sam's shoulder. "I don't really know anything about scouting."

"Sam, we're going to look around. I'll be back shortly."

"Okay, Bobby, don't forget about us." Though still green around the gills, Sam smiled faintly at him.

"I'll leave one behind in case you need to move." He picked one dragon and sent it to Sam's shoulder. It danced around happily there.

The rest of them spread out and flew through buildings, looking for anything worth investigating further. Having done this before, and with no expectation of finding anyone who fit the dragons' idea of a "terrorist" around, Bobby felt confident they could be loosed to search for information on their own.

He found himself distracted by the dragon back with Jayce. It wanted his attention with something that confused it. Focused on the sight of the dragon he inhabited now, he tried to dismiss its concerns as something that could wait until later. When it grew insistent, he checked what that one could see and immediately wished he hadn't.

This poor dragon had no basis from his own life to understand what it saw inside the car. From its perspective, Jayce could have been in danger. It hesitated in defending him because that cute park ranger had been nice and friendly. Bobby wanted to smack his forehead. He settled for assuring the dragon that it had nothing to worry about. None of those moans had anything to do with pain and he could let the ranger be unless she pulled out a knife or other weapon. Later, when he wasn't trying to infiltrate a military base with only sixteen dragons, he'd explain. He could only hope that he'd get to demonstrate instead.

That handled, Bobby returned his attention to the more pressing problem of finding something useful and determining the security scheme. The ventilation system, as usual, gave him a personal key to every room, closet, nook, and cranny. The dragons flitted through the main base, noting minimal and sparse security. He feared the trip might have been a waste of time until he found a computer room with no one inside and only one camera that he felt confident he could turn enough to avoid it picking them up.

He brought the girls into it through the vents and moved the camera. Sam commandeered a computer and let her fingers fly across the keyboard. The screen did things faster than her fingers moved, leaving Bobby wondering why she bothered touching it at all. Habit, maybe. In a few minutes, she'd cut through the security.

"There's a map here," she pulled it up to display on the screen and tapped it with a finger to indicate two of the outbuildings. "This one is MB-STA, this one is MB-02."

Bobby peered at the screen, fixing the layout in his mind. *"STA means 'Space-Time Anomaly'. We already know what that's about, and we ain't gonna find the others there. We want 02. Are you sure it's current?"*

"The file was last modified two weeks ago."

"Then let's go. Tony is on his way, he should be there shortly."

Orienting in the dark from the map he saw for only half a minute took Bobby a short time, then the semi- swarm plunged into the darkness with both women. It bothered him that this seemed easy, too easy. Privek had to know they'd wind up here eventually, one way or another. The agent could even have set them up to meet Hanamidi so he'd have someplace to aim the gun, which would be right here. Wouldn't it?

The dragons found the building with Tony only a short distance away. Rather than waiting, they dove into the vents to see about unlocking the front door. For a location with a top secret project, it had little security: no cameras, no motion detectors, no guards, no fancy locks. He set the drive and pocket down and chirped. By the time Lisa opened the door, Tony had returned to his human shape. He slipped inside, Lisa shut the door, and they filled Tony in.

"This is weird," Sam said, sitting with her back to a wall and her hand on her belly. "There's almost nothing here." The rooms they'd found so far had empty desks, clear tables, and blank shelves.

"Maybe they just haven't gotten around to reusing the building yet, so they leave the old designation on the map." Tony opened an interior door and poked his head through it.

Lisa rubbed her arms. "I'd hate to have gone through all of this for nothing."

"We should explore the building."

Sam nodded. "Bobby's right. Let's split up and look around. There's obviously no one here. Maybe they left a computer behind, or some files or something."

The dragons fanned out, searching for anything of use. After spending at least an hour in the place, Bobby found nothing—no computers, no files left behind, nothing. Did he and Stephen really go through all of that for nothing more than some new theories?

"Maybe we should check that STA building after all."

Sam called out and the four of them gathered back in that front room, showing all the nothing they had found to each other. "Bobby wants to check out the other MB building."

Tony shrugged. "You go, Bobby. If it's as empty as this one, no sense in all of us breaking in."

The dragon chirped his agreement and Bobby took thirteen of his dragons with him, leaving behind one for each shoulder in case they got separated. As his group darted out through the venting, he saw them leave the building and lock the door behind themselves. The other building also had minimal security. This one, though, had computers and books and papers and used coffee mugs. Bobby got his dragons to lead the others to him, then his dragons fanned out to search the site.

By the time the others arrived, he'd unlocked the door and explored most of it. Sam sat down with the first computer she found while Tony and Lisa poked through the other rooms. Bobby sent half the swarm with Tony while he and the other half followed Lisa, keeping watch in case he'd missed someone buried under paperwork in the back.

"Who're you?" He squinted at her, his mouth tugging down into a frown. She wore black leggings and a navy tunic shirt belted at her waist with navy flats. She'd done her best at fulfilling his off-the-cuff suggestion of "ninja expedition suit".

She paused a beat too long before answering. "I'm Lisa?" Her voice shook. "Who are you? " Then she offered her hand to shake with him.

His eyes flicked to her hand, her chest, her face, and her waist. "Where's your ID?"

Bobby had no interest in hurting this guy, let alone killing him. He had no gun and presented no physical threat. No one deserved to die for the crime of working late. When Lisa hesitated and shrank, he knew she couldn't handle this situation. He had to take control, dragon-style. The sub-swarm darted out from behind Lisa and into view, surrounding her head as a weird sort of halo.

The man's eyes bulged and he stumbled backwards, sloshing coffee onto his shirt. "Oh my God. *What* are you?"

Lisa looked from side to side and covered her face. "Oh my gosh," she whispered, mortified. "Bobby, what are you doing?"

The man's eyes bulged and he stumbled backwards, sloshing coffee onto his shirt.

"Sam!" Bobby called out as forcefully as he could.

"What happened?"

Relieved he wouldn't have to go find her, Bobby tried to figure how to sum up the situation without sounding like a complete ass. *"There's a guy in the break room and Lisa needs help."*

Tony ran in. He looked around, blinked several times, and chose to grab Lisa and pull her out of the room. Fat lot of help either of them were.

Sam showed up, panting from the sprinting, and almost ran into the wall. She caught herself on the doorframe, and Bobby hoped that only happened because she'd gone too fast to stop properly. Instead of leaping in to do whatever she could, she scanned the room and stood there, staring.

Bobby wanted to smack his forehead again. *"Tell him to sit and calm down or the dragons will eat him. Hands out in plain sight."*

He saw her gulp and nod. "The dragons won't hurt you if you take a seat and keep your hands where I can see them."

Thank goodness she only needed to be prodded. The dragons backed off, giving him room to breathe and follow her directions. They stayed close enough to dive in and do unpleasant things if he chose not to. *"You'll need to ask him about the Space Time Anomaly and MB-02. I'll help if'n you need it."*

The guy, his eyes darting from Sam to the dragons and back several times, put his hands up. "Don't hurt me." He edged to the seat and dropped down into it. "I'm just a software engineer, not a spy or anything. I probably don't know anything about whatever you want."

Sitting in the other chair, Sam rested her forearms on the table and leaned on them. "We know this project is about trying to reproduce a space-time event. What do you know about the original event? "

Bobby landed on the table, and the rest of his dragons followed suit. They formed a line in the middle, ready to defend Sam at any moment.

The guy gulped. "Almost nothing. My job is about data analysis and extrapolation. I don't have access to the raw data, just an exemplar set for formatting and ranges."

Frowning, Sam nodded. "Then can you tell us anything about the MB-02 project?"

"Sorry, never heard of it. I saw that's on the new map they distributed a couple of weeks ago. That building was empty before that so far as I know. I figured it was some new project thing they haven't set up yet."

Bobby currently had no stomach for the bottom to drop out of, nor did he have blood to run cold. *"This is a trap. We gotta git."*

"Okay. Just one other thing." Sam took a deep breath and fixed him with a piercing stare. It had to be the most bold thing he'd ever seen Sam do. "Have you ever seen anyone, even in a photograph, with eyes like mine before?"

The guy blinked and stared at her eyes. "No. No one, ever. They're..." The intensity of her gaze must have bothered him, because ducked his head and looked away. "Um, you have nice eyes. Nice to look at, I mean."

"Thanks. We'll go. I hope you don't get into trouble over this."

"Damn, me too. I guess if we all just keep quiet, everything will be fine."

"We didn't take anything," Sam said with a small, shy smile, "so there's no evidence if you don't tell."

The guy echoed her smile. If he had regular eyes instead of robotic dragon ones, Bobby would have goggled at the fact these two geeks tiptoed on the edge of flirting at a time like this. *"Sam, we gotta go. Sooner, not later."*

"Right." She ducked her head and shuffled out of the room. The dragons took off and followed her.

"Wait, um, wow, this is weird and awkward, huh? I'm Mike."

Despite the insanity of this encounter, his name made Bobby pause. Given what Kaitlin said, they could at least expect him to not say anything. Still, they needed to get out of here before the trap sprang. The dragons trilled at Sam and flowed around her, hoping she'd hurry up.

"Sam," she told the guy, then paused at the doorway. "It was nice to meet you. Sorry for the scare and trouble."

"Yeah. It's okay."

More dragon trills goaded Sam into moving again. With a last glance back at Mike, she hurried to the front door. Tony and Lisa stepped outside a few steps ahead of her and she pulled the door shut behind herself.

Too frustrated to be civil, Bobby had exactly nothing to say to any of this crew. Lisa stepped into her pocket and dragons picked it up. Tony's body twisted and squished into a giant tumbleweed and he rolled east. One dragon followed it.

Sam, though, stopped with the thumb drive in her hand and checked the door. It opened and Mike popped his head out, smiling like an idiot when he saw her. "Hey, um, can I give you a lift someplace?"

"Tell me you ain't seriously considering that."

A dumb smile of her own sprouted on Sam's face. "Yeah, that'd be great." *"Maybe he knows more and I can get him to open up."*

Bobby the dragon hovered and stared at her in disbelief. *"And maybe he's one of them and'll stuff you in the trunk if'n he gets half a chance."* When she didn't respond to that but did take Mike's hand, Bobby's dragon rolled its eyes. *"Fine, but I ain't letting you go alone. Drop the drive and I'll bring it along, so we can have a getaway if'n it goes all wrong."*

She scuffed a shoe to cover the sound as she dropped the drive. Bobby scooped it up and watched her walk away from the small puddle of light outside the building with a random guy. He decided his mood would only get worse if he had to listen to them being nerdy at each other. The thumb drive in his claws, he landed on the back bumper of Mike's dark blue sedan and held on.

Aside — Camellia

Privek had said they would come here, and they did, which made Camellia wonder how much he'd held back about these people. Probably a lot. Privek struck her as a guy who kept lots of secrets and rarely parted with one willingly. That, of course didn't matter now.

They traveled in a highly unexpected way, and she had no idea how to follow them. Sure, she'd entertained the possibility it would be Mitchell and Cant again. They certainly knew how to get things done and weren't afraid to do it. Based on what they'd said in Albuquerque, though, she figured they'd be benched in favor of others who'd need a vehicle to get here.

It surprised her more that they went to the second building. Privek said to expect them at the first building, and to follow them out of it. He'd never mentioned a second site, not even as a vague possibility. She had no idea why they came to the base in the first place, let alone why they'd trooped from one building to another.

While they'd been inside, she'd considered calling him, except she had nothing to report. This qualified as a wrinkle, not earth-shattering news. Wrinkles needed to be ironed out at the time and dealt with. Her mission involved one thing and one thing only: finding a way to follow them to their compound so Privek could use the GPS in her phone to pinpoint it.

They spent a lot more time in this building. Her jaw dropped when the employee offered the last one a ride. Those two obviously had some sort of something going on between them, even with only an hour or two spent building it up. Did men ever think with anything besides their dicks?

She watched them walk to his car, parked in darkness, and realized she owed that guy's libido her thanks, because he made it possible for her to follow them. Hurrying over, she noticed the dragon landing on the bumper. It carried…a USB drive? Interesting. Why didn't the woman just take that? For that matter, why not carry the dragon in her pocket or purse?

Never mind. The rear lights came on and she let the car back up past her, then hopped on when she thought the occupants and dragon wouldn't notice over the bump between the tiny parking lot and the road. Holding onto the spoiler, she made sure to keep her head away from the dragon so it wouldn't hear her breathing.

Chapter 15

Bobby had no interest at all in listening to Mike and Sam together. The guy somehow forgot the fact that he'd run into her while she'd been breaking into his workplace, and might be in control of a small quantity of tiny robot dragons. Didn't he have to get a security clearance to work on a part of the Maze Beset project? This completely explained every time he'd ever heard about governmental incompetence.

When they got out of the car, Bobby flew into Sam's pocket. If anything happened to her, he'd be there to help get her out of it. He settled in, worried about five hundred things going sideways, only to find himself listening to them using words he'd never heard before. They may as well have been speaking Swahili for all he understood.

He did understand when they ordered coffee and sandwiches, at least. From the noise level in the place, he figured they'd be here for a while. Any unpleasant surprises Mike meant to spring would likely come after the meal, which meant he could settle back and ignore them. Since he had nothing better to do, he threw himself back at his body to fill Jayce in.

For the first time, he felt something during the brief moments between dragon and body. It reminded him of falling, then he woke up in his body, in the darkness of the trunk. The distance must have affected him, since he hadn't tried it from so far away before.

After checking with the dragon in the car for nearby witnesses or the park ranger, he pulled the release to open the hood and climbed out to find himself in the back of a nearly abandoned big store parking lot. Jayce had picked the one spot with a malfunctioning light, or he might have climbed up somehow and smashed it.

He shut the trunk and stretched. Jayce stepped out of the car, holding a bag of food out. "Aw, you shouldn't have," Bobby said with a smirk, finding a fat foot-long sandwich inside.

"I know, but I'm a nice guy."

"Mmhmm." With only one hand, getting the sandwich out, peeling the paper away, and holding onto all of it proved a challenge. For food, he could make an extra effort. "This ain't gonna make me forget having to deal with a dragon what didn't know heads nor tails about you getting some with that ranger."

Jayce blinked in surprise, then laughed. "Huh. Sorry about that. She asked me." His grin turned decidedly smug.

"You expect me to believe that after you talked her into letting us through the gate, when you left, she asked to jump you?"

"Of course not." Jayce snorted. "That's ridiculous. She asked me out to dinner. I just got creative regarding what 'dinner' entailed."

"And I got to watch," Bobby grumbled. "You know, I can't actually turn it off. I can ignore it, more or less, but I can't just not see it. Especially when the dragon wants to know if that lady is trying to kill you because you're making funny noises it thinks might be on account of pain. You're lucky it didn't just attack first and ask never."

Lisa returned, sparing him the indignity of being laughed at for several minutes. He got most of his hand back when that clump of dragons returned, too, and he attacked the sandwich with fervor.

After checking around for anyone else and not finding them, Lisa bit her lip and asked, "Is Sam okay?"

"Yeah," Bobby gave a little amused huff, "she and that Mike guy are geeking all over each other."

"Is that what they call it in Atlanta?"

Reaching out, Bobby punched Jayce in the arm. It hurt, because even though Jayce had his own flesh for now, he still had more muscles in his wrist than Bobby had in his thigh. "I mean they're talking about computers and stuff. It was boring. She's hoping to get him to reveal he knows something else accidentally, but this whole thing was pretty much a big damned waste of time. Soon as Tony gets back, we should head to where she is."

"Sounds like a plan."

Lisa pulled a box of crackers out of her nowhere pocket and nibbled on them. "They updated that map two weeks ago. It's too bad we didn't look up a map from two weeks ago to see what they changed."

Bobby shrugged. "I got a feeling this was a trap of some kind, but it's a weird trap. I mean, ain't nothing been sprung I can see. We came, we left. What in heckbiscuits they hope to accomplish by having us do that?"

Jayce rubbed his chin. "They could already have the location of the farm. This might have been intended to lure some of us out so they could attack while we're gone."

Halfway through a bite, Bobby stopped and looked down at his sandwich. If the suits were assaulting the farm right now…he could do exactly nothing about it. It would take him at least five hours to fly up there, by which time it would be over and done. Besides, they left capable people behind, and Kaitlin should be able to warn them about anything major. Right?

Lisa blanched and put her crackers back away. "Clive is still there. They wouldn't hurt him, would they?"

"I doubt it." Jayce shrugged. "They've been more or less going out of their way not to hurt anyone but us. But they might take him to use as leverage against you."

"Oh, God. We have to go back."

"Yeah," Bobby said with a sigh, knowing exactly how she felt. "But not until Tony gets back and we pick up Sam." Resolved he could do nothing at the moment, he stuffed more sandwich into his face. The dragon accompanying Tony escorted him to the car a few minutes later.

"I guess it's time to get moving," Bobby said as his dragon reattached to his hand. "I can lead us thataway, and I'll go into that dragon when we get close to see how she wants to play it."

"Are you sure she's okay?"

Her bright, earnest concern made Bobby wanted to pinch Lisa's cheek or pat her on the head. "If'n she weren't, the dragon in her pocket would let me know. If'n it couldn't, I'd know that, too." He gave her an encouraging smile. "I promise."

The drive took them to the other side of the town. When Jayce parked across the street from the little strip mall, Bobby flung himself back into the dragon and found the pair still talking about stuff he didn't understand.

"Sam, we gotta get going. Starting to think this was a setup to get us outta the way for an assault. Car is across the street."

He saw her tuck some hair behind her ear and incidentally look at her watch. "Oh, my gosh, the time. I need to get going."

"Oh." Mike's face fell. "Here's my email address, and this is my username, we should meet up in game sometime."

"I'd like that. Thanks for the nice time, Mike, I really enjoyed it."

"Yeah, me too. Can I give you a lift someplace else?"

"Nah, I'm just going to disappear into the ether." She laughed as she said it. Mike laughed, too.

"I sure hope that weren't the biggest mistake ever."

"So do I, but it was worth it. Now I have a contact inside the project."

Unconvinced but unwilling to belabor the point, Bobby went quiet. He noticed the trunk pop open and up for no apparent reason and sent some dragons to check it out. They found nothing, so he hopped out and tugged on the release handle in case it had gotten stuck. Slamming it shut gave him a tiny vent for his worry and frustration. He really needed a much bigger one.

He wanted to yell. Because he had no cause to sit up on a high horse with these people, he kept quiet until they hit the freeway. "Did you look up everything there is to look up on that guy?"

"His name is Mike." Sam pulled her hood up and shrank into it. "And no, not yet. I have his email address now so I can get into everything, I just need anonymous wifi to do it. I'll check him out when we get home."

"If there's a home to get to," Lisa said with a light edge of panic.

"The drive back will be just as long as the drive there," Jayce said. "We'll be lucky to get back before noon. Everyone should try to get some sleep so we don't have to stop on the way."

Bobby stared out the window. Jayce was right, of course, though that did nothing to make him tired. As much as he didn't want to think about what happened in Afghanistan, the place had a strange sort of certainty to it that didn't apply here. Klein pointed him at bad guys, and he killed them.

Granted, the "bad guy" label had caused some problems, and he'd peered into the deep end of the pool there. Aside from that, the whole thing was really straightforward: identify, kill, move on.

Stephen got professional about it, too. None of this fraternizing with the enemy stuff, not unless the enemy wasn't really an enemy. Or something like that. His own discontent confused him, yet again, and he let out a heavy sigh.

"Bobby." Lisa's voice startled him out of what had become a good brood.

"Hm?" He rubbed his face to wipe away all the thoughts bouncing around inside.

"Why did you throw all the dragons in him?"

Bobby bit back the impulse to snap at her. "Because he's a normal and coulda went for a phone to call security or somesuch."

"But he wasn't doing that. He was just standing there. You scared the petals out of him."

The odd turn of phrase made him stare at her while he figured out what she meant. "Uh, you can't just react to everything, sometimes you gotta do something before they do it first. Life ain't about sitting around and waiting for it to hand you some eggs so you can make an omelet, you gotta go find the chicken yourself and take them."

Lisa nodded meekly and turned away.

Tony, though, eyed Bobby. "Everyone was all surprised by how you took off." He gestured to Jayce. "They all said you were cool and relaxed, and it must have been that Stephen talked you into it. But they were wrong, weren't they?"

"You got something to say, come out and say it. It ain't like Hannah ain't already said it, I'm sure."

Tony snorted. "You're an arrogant brat."

"Fuck you." Bobby glared out the window.

"Well," Tony chuckled wickedly, "at least we know they're right when they say you aren't the sharpest tool in the shed."

"I can kill you." For once, when he said that, Bobby actually meant it.

Another scoffing huff came out of Tony. "Yes, a true gentleman and oh so concerned about the rest of us."

"Stop it," Lisa snapped. "We're all in this together. We should act like it."

"Tell him," Tony sneered, pointing at Bobby.

"Shut it," Jayce said cheerfully, "or I'll shut it for you. Bobby knows he screwed up. He doesn't need everyone reminding him over and over again. You'd be surly, too. Talk about something else."

The car went silent and Bobby glowered at the glass beside him until he nodded off. He woke with a start after a nightmare that left him with nothing but a deep sense of unease. The sky glowed with early morning light and Sam was driving. Afraid he'd startle her and cause an accident, he stayed quiet and still.

After a minute or so, she said, "There's still food in the cooler. It should be in reach."

The suddenness of her statement made him jump, waking him up better than a splash of cold water. "Thanks." He rummaged through the cooler and pulled some fruit salad and a regular sandwich out. "Wasn't sure if I was really awake or not."

"Sure." It sounded like she believed him. "I saw Lily before we left."

"I don't wanna talk about that." He grabbed a banana and an unmarked sandwich. Thank God for sandwiches.

"Okay."

This sandwich had lots of vegetables and some kind of paste in it. It tasted alright, and he had no cause to be picky. He bolted the food, trying to ignore the thoughts Sam's small statement had dredged up. He'd been an utter dumbass, and he knew it, and anyone she told probably thought worse about him than before. Given where he started, that almost seemed like an accomplishment, of sorts.

He licked his fingers and sighed. Sam had given him an opening to explain, and he needed to take it if he wanted to fix this. "It weren't like I was just trying to see her naked or nothing. If'n that's all I wanted, I woulda done it proper-like, with asking and groping and stuff."

"Why did you do it, then?"

"I didn't want to wake her up if she weren't already, and kinda got distracted when she turned out to be up and getting undressed already." He stared out the window to avoid seeing Sam's reaction. "It made sense at the time."

She choked down a laugh. "You're kind of an idiot, Bobby."

"Yeah."

"I'm sure if you explain, she'll forgive you. Eventually."

He shrugged. "I ain't." That hurt had only hit him yesterday, not even a full day ago, yet it already felt distant and faded. Leaving for this had done some good, at least. The hard part would be keeping it from affecting Sebastian. He liked the kid, liked playing with him and teaching him things. Liked his momma, too, but couldn't have her. Heckbiscuits, maybe that was even for the best. Dating a half-sibling sounded bad. Even if they never had any kids together, it would still always weird. "Don't matter."

"Sure it does. We all live in the same place, Bobby, we're a community whether we want to be or not. All of us feel the friction between people. Tony's a strident homophobe, which makes Greg stay away from the common spaces, even just to eat. We're all missing out on talking to him, and he's a pretty interesting guy. Plus, he's missing out on talking to everyone else. He now interfaces with the group through Albert instead of in his own right, just because being treated with such blatant, blind hate upsets him. In turn, I don't want to deal with Tony, either, so we wind up out here together, and maybe I took a risk I shouldn't have, just because I was annoyed with Tony, even though he hasn't done anything specifically annoying on this trip."

Bobby slouched in the seat, unhappy with how complicated everything had to be. "It's like high school all over again," he groaned.

"It's worse than high school." She grinned. "It's *superhero* high school."

"I don't wanna deal with that kinda crap."

"Then why did you come back? You could have just stayed with the Army and kept doing their missions. If you stayed out there, you could probably end the war completely, one way or another. Or you could run off someplace else. With your superpower, you can probably get anything you want, and never need to work another day in your life. But instead, you came back. Even though you knew everyone would be angry, you came back. Why?"

"'Cause Lily." The moment he said it, the hurt came crashing right back down. It had been held back by a fragile dam of denial before. Also, though, he realized the truth had more to it. "And Stephen, and Jayce, and having folks what I can trust my back to and understand."

Sam patted his arm. "Yes, that's exactly it. The farm is still pretty new. Give it a chance. And talk to Lily. Maybe wait until tomorrow, though, when you've had a good night's sleep."

Bobby grunted noncommittally. He'd have to think about how to say what needed to be said. Because she was right, and he needed to admit he wasn't ready to let go of Lily, not even close. "I'll take a turn driving."

Aside — Maisie

"What's important here," Privek told the group over their headsets, "is that these people are dangerous. No matter how harmless any individual might seem, they all need to be contained. Our methods aren't foolproof, but should give us enough time with each of them safely under control to at least find out if they can be reasoned with."

"What about my Will? What if he's there?" Jasmine's legs bounced nervously and her empty hands fidgeted.

"Yes, there may be a few innocent bystanders among them, so be careful. Brewer's husband went missing with her, for one. There may be others we don't know about. We assume they've all been brainwashed, so don't be surprised if they don't want to come quietly, just be careful not to hurt them. Use only tasers on anyone who doesn't have the eyes, and when in doubt. Alpha Leader is in charge on the ground. We'll be dropping you a mile out from the property to avoid detection."

"Are we sure they're really there?" Dianna sat placidly, her dark face smooth and neutral.

"Yes. Camellia is already on site. She arrived when Mitchell and a few others came back earlier today."

Maisie didn't want to do this at all. Not even a little. Did anyone care? No. This had to be done. They had no other choice. The footage from Hill and the pictures from that cave horrified her enough to throw up. These people had no decency or empathy. That broken infant haunted her nightmares, and she'd only seen a picture of it. How could anyone live with himself after *doing* that?

The worst part seemed to be the idea they could stand up to that kind of firepower. Beyond the babies and kids, these monsters had taken out squads of armed men. The second helicopter held ten SWAT guys from Homeland Security. She thought they'd need ten thousand to have a chance. Privek said the element of surprise, combined with tranq guns and tasers, would be enough.

The gun still felt awkward in her hands, even after two weeks of training with it. The barrel held one shot at a time, and used the four darts strapped to her hip, plus the one already loaded. She'd practiced reloading it until she could do it in five seconds. Everyone else here had done the same except Jasmine. She'd be a squirrel the whole time, and seemed flighty enough that a gun in her hands would probably be a bad idea anyway. At least Liam and Paul looked as awkward with it as she did. Everyone else seemed fine with it.

They landed on a two lane road surrounded by miles and miles of farmland. She snapped off the headset and climbed out behind Raymond to look around. A pinprick of light shone in the distance, but someone pointed in the opposite direction. That way lay a dark splotch of doom, the jagged shapes of giant trees hinted at by the starlight.

She'd been given flares, a flashlight, carabiners, zipties, a lighter, and twenty other things that fit into the tac vest she had to wear to mark herself as 'friendly'. Straightening it gave her something to do with her hands besides awkwardly fondling the gun while waiting for someone to tell her what to do.

Alpha Leader gestured for everyone to gather around while the two helicopters lifted off again. He took a knee in the center and waited for the noise to die away. "Okay, everyone, this is it. We all know what we're in for. Hopefully, they'll all be asleep, but if they aren't, it's their home base, so they shouldn't want to blow it up. Moore," he pointed to Liam, "you stay with Alpha Seven. You'll hang back, but not so far you can't do anything. O'Malley," he pointed to Chelsea, the girl with giant feathery angel wings, "and Jackson," he pointed to Dianna, who could control the wind, "go in topside, in case anyone is overhead or on the roof. The skies are up to you. The rest of you stay with me, say something if you see something or have any brilliant ideas. Stealth is our friend here, if you can't hack it, move to the back."

Like everyone else, Maisie nodded and stepped away. She took a deep breath and gulped. No longer did she have one more day to train, one more day to think about it, one more day to hope someone else would take care of this for her. Air whipped around as Chelsea's wings beat to get her off the ground and Dianna summoned up the wind to pull her into the sky. Maisie's hands itched. She wanted to get this over with, and also wanted to stay here forever.

They kicked into an easy jog along the side of the road, gear jangling and her hands finding the gun to keep it from shooting her own foot. "I, um, should be able to get us across anything out in the open," she said uncertainly. The earpiece didn't have a microphone stick going to her mouth, and she felt self-conscious talking without knowing for sure she'd be heard.

"Don't worry," Liam said, patting her shoulder from behind. "If one of them starts trying to hurt you, just pop away to behind Beller. I'll certainly be hiding behind him if I need to."

Raymond chuckled. "Yeah, you can hide behind me and my

shield, I don't mind." The muscular black man made the metal shape appear on his arm, in its kite shield form. All the times she'd seen it before, it had been a drab gray color. This time, he'd made it so black it almost sucked light in. She knew it could be as big as a ten foot square and as small as a six inch circle.

"You should be trying to herd them towards me." Brian sounded much more nervous than he looked. His voice quavered, yet his feet moved with rock-solid surety. "Especially Westbrook. I can take what he can dish out."

"I'll do what I can," Paul broke in, "but if any of the rest of them have closed-off minds like Cant or chaotic ones like Mitchell, I won't be much help. I might be able to distract them, but that's about it." From the way he moved, he desperately wanted to holster his gun-thing. The weapons came only with a clip for their vest so they couldn't fall and be lost. Their trainer had told them to avoid doing that, as the stupid things could accidentally go off. Whoever designed it needed a swift kick in the rear for that one.

Kevin stayed quiet, which made sense. He could turn invisible, and it seemed to extend to his personality. Jasmine made excited chirpy noises as she bounced along, her ponytail bobbing and swishing.

Maisie nodded to all the chatter, not sure how to respond other than to hope they didn't all die tonight. "Um, Alpha Leader?" Referring to a human being like that made her feel stupid. "Can you run over the goals part again?" She wanted to remind him that until a few weeks ago, dodging flowers when they fell off the costumes had been one of her biggest problems.

"Sure." He didn't sound annoyed, but had to be. These guys normally dealt with trained operatives, not random kids with superpowers. "Goal one is to find the house and re-acquire Androvitch. Goal two is to gain stealth entry into the building. Goal three is to acquire all twenty-four targets without harming an unknown number of civilians. Lethal force is not sanctioned without imminent threat."

"Thanks."

"It's normal to be nervous about something like this." At least Alpha Leader wasn't a dick. He also didn't push them too hard, setting a pace they could all keep up with. It took about ten minutes to reach the driveway, and Camellia stood up as they reached it, her camouflage fading away.

She took an earpiece from Alpha Two and tucked her phone away in a pocket. "I haven't been able to check out the whole property, but I'm pretty sure there are only two buildings. The farmhouse is where most of them spend their time and live. The barn has two guys living in it, one of us and his boyfriend. I get the impression that one is some kind of inventor; he tinkers with stuff a lot. The farmhouse is big, it's been expanded from its original size. Two doors, one in front, one in the back. Also, plenty of windows. Each bedroom has a window, and the kitchen and their big common room. The basement has casement windows, too."

One of the other Alphas—Maisie hadn't managed to learn all their voices yet—asked, "What're they using the basement for?"

"Storage, so far as I can tell. No one living down there."

"Sounds like a possible entry point. Alpha Three and Four, you're on it, take Androvitch. Five, Six, and Astrid, target the barn. Subdue, wrap up, and rejoin. Two and Nine with Beller, check the front door. Ten with me on the back door. Arralt, pick a spot you like not too far from the building, and everyone else work on a funnel to get them to him. "

Maisie nodded even though no one would see it and tried to think of how she could help with funneling. Nothing came to mind. In fact, she thought she'd be much more useful trying to get inside.

"Alpha Leader, it's Polape. If I can look in through a window, I can throw a portal inside."

"Hm. Alright, new plan. Five, Six, and Astrid, still on the barn. Three and Four, spike the back door as quietly as you can, then join Arralt with Two. Put yourself in the line of fire for the front door, but try to be out of sight from inside. The rest of us are going in through the basement. Stealth is highest priority. If they wake up and start fighting back, everyone gets out as quick as you can. We have orders not to kill, they don't."

"Permission to set annoyance traps?" a different Alpha asked.

"Granted, but keep them away from the door. If we've got to run out, we need to not trip them."

"Understood."

"It's Chelsea. Um, O'Malley, I mean. We've done a sweep of the whole property. There doesn't appear to be anyone outside. They've got animals, though. We saw some chickens and goats. We're over the house now, and can't see anyone."

"Good work, O'Malley. Keep your eyes open and assist as needed. Jackson, do what you can to pick up anyone who comes out through anything other than the front door, or if Arralt and Pearson look like they're getting overwhelmed."

"Yeah, okay," Dianna said. She sounded annoyed, maybe bored.

Lined by a row of stately trees with a wild tangle of younger trees, shrubs, and grasses beyond it, the driveway kept going and going and going. Isolated and overgrown, this property seemed perfect for this purpose. From the highway, no one would expect to find people living here, other than maybe rural hillbillies best left undisturbed.

The driveway ended at a wide empty space with the ground churned up. Alphas shone flashlights around to reveal a bunch of cars and vans parked in a line in front of the one-story house. It seemed normal from the front, with a small porch and dark windows. Camellia's description seemed off-base.

Alpha Leader held up an arm before they crossed the open space. Everyone halted. Paul doubled over to catch his breath. Everyone else, including Maisie, seemed fine. "Two, this is a good place to set up. Seven, stay a good thirty feet back or so. Androvitch, where's the barn?"

Camellia pointed off to the right. "There's a lot of tarps. The two men are in a converted horse stall. And probably naked."

"Let's all go that way," Alpha Leader said quietly, using another hand gesture to get everyone moving. "Lights on the ground, people."

Maisie figured the instruction had been intended for her and pointed her flashlight down. She paid close attention to the ground, avoiding dead leaves and twigs, and small rocks that wanted to trip her.

"If I'm needed, someone will have to tell me," Liam said. "I won't see anything in this."

"Anyone who needs medical, either get yourself there or call 'Medic' and give your position. Whoever's closest goes to pull them out and to Moore. We don't want to expose him if we can help it."

"From the bottom of my heart, Alpha Leader, I sincerely appreciate that."

Alpha Leader snorted. "No more chatter."

With that, the earpiece in Maisie's ear went silent and they padded across the way to find a window. The house extended much farther than she expected, and this wall had to be new construction. Big, leafy shrubs grew next to it, which confused her. Plants couldn't grow that fast and they hadn't been cut back on the one side. How did they get the shrubs to grow this big this close to what were obviously new outer walls? With flowers.

Someone took the time to get these bushes blooming with pretty flowers. She didn't expect to see flowers. Maybe creepy weird flowers, or wild ones growing wherever. She mostly only knew Hawaiian flowers, so she couldn't say what kind these might be, but she liked them. The delicate pink and white ruffly petals reminded her of the wads of jasmine her aunt grew.

Seeing that made her wonder how much of what Privek told them was really true, and how much he finessed to manipulate them. Surely, he couldn't lie to Paul, though. Paul could poke through people's minds and see their thoughts. Unless Privek didn't know the whole story. They could be pawns and never know it.

Privek had rescued her personally from the men who abducted her in Honolulu. Since she woke up to his face, she hadn't come across any reason to doubt him. The video of what happened at Hill Air Force Base had cemented her trust.

Of course, demented freaks could like flowers. No rule forbade that. Maisie shook off her confusion. Distractions could get someone killed here. Halfway around the side, the barn guys peeled off to handle that and Maisie saw the first window. "Alpha Leader," she whispered, "window." Her attention on the pane of glass, she laid flat on the ground to get a look inside.

Shining her flashlight into the darkness, Maisie saw nothing special: shelves, baskets, and a washing machine. One washer for this many people almost seemed criminal. Satisfied it had plenty of space, though, she flicked the fingers of her right hand out, causing a swirling blue oval to spring into existence on the nearest wall she could see. She stood up, brushed herself off, and flicked her left hand out, an orange oval appearing on the wall in front of them. Instead of swirling orange and black in the middle, it offered a view into the dark basement, through the blue oval.

Wordlessly, Alpha Leader hopped through The rest of the Alphas followed him, then the rest of them. They didn't have designations. She didn't want one. It would, however, make referring to them collectively less weird. So far, in her head, she called them all "freaks". Some of them seemed like the type to take offense at that, so she never said it out loud.

"We're in," Alpha Leader muttered.

Maisie pulled the blue portal back into her right hand, leaving the orange one in case she needed a quick exit. It made a soft metallic *whum* noise that cycled endlessly like a sine wave, only noticeable within a foot or so. In fact, she suspected the noise might actually only be in her head. At some point, they'd all be able to discuss their powers together and figure out those sorts of details. To this point, Privek and Alpha Leader had kept them training too hard for that.

Alpha Leader lead the team up the stairs. "Fourteen of us, at least twenty-six of them. Split up and take different doors. Dose and move on. Say something if you need help or one gets away."

Maisie gulped and hoped she didn't get into trouble here. If it came to a fight, she'd lose. Paul tapped her on the shoulder. She turned to see him tap his forehead, then reach over and tap hers. She blinked blankly at him, having no idea what he meant by that. For good measure, since he didn't seem to be getting her confusion, she shrugged.

"I can speak directly into your mind. Is that okay?"

Maisie squeaked with surprise, then clapped a hand over her mouth.

"What happened?" Alpha Leader asked.

"Nothing," Maisie hissed, embarrassed. "Stubbed my toe." She saw him turn and glare at her, then heard him sigh and move on.

"Sorry. I have no idea how to do that more gently."

Staring at Paul, Maisie gulped again and nodded. *"Do I have to do something special? "*

"No, just think what you want to say to me. I don't think I can do this with more than one person at a time, though. You just seemed really nervous, so I thought maybe it would help if you had someone to talk to."

"Uh, thanks. Yeah, this is really a thing, and I'm really scared I'm going to screw it up."

"Me, too, actually. I really wish we didn't have to have these gun things."

She agreed, and didn't need to coherently say so for him to get it. But they had more important things to worry about. Alpha Leader turned up a hallway and gestured for the group to split up. Maisie found herself at the end of the line, so she went the other way. Alpha Nine assigned her to a door by pointing. He gave Paul the next door up and sent her some wordless encouragement, which she needed.

Her hand on the knob, she turned it as slowly as she could to avoid making a noise, then inched it open. She found a tiny little bedroom, the floor space only enough to swing the door open. The bed took up most of the room, along with a dresser and small table. A second door inside suggested a closet. The most important thing in the room, though, was the man asleep on the bed. She knew him immediately, recognizing him from the video. Out of all these people, she had to be the one to get Mitchell. One of the dangerous ones, he'd killed people. Lots of people. Privek had said he might be indestructible.

"I'm scared I'll mess this up."

"Do it fast. Don't hesitate, just do it. It'll be okay."

Maisie lifted the awkward gun and crept into the room. A light breeze tumbled in through the open window and stirred the half-drawn curtains. The screen looked battered; maybe it was old, or maybe he beat on it like a wild animal. She could do this. So long as he didn't wake up before the drug took effect, he couldn't do anything to her. Pointing her gun at his chest, she took a deep breath to try to calm her stomach. It didn't work. Fine. She just needed to do it, like Paul said.

She stared into his confused, frightened icy blue eyes and saw her own. She'd just shot her brother. Her hands shook. Bile threatened to crawl up her throat. His mouth opened and he made a confused, gurgling noise instead of words. He thrashed around, maybe trying to sit up.

Stumbling away from him, her fingers fumbled to reload the gun, snatching the next dart and shoving it into the chamber. Her leg bumped into the table and she dropped the gun. It went off and shattered against the floor, splashing clear, viscous liquid onto her shoe.

Covering her face in embarrassment and horror, she tried to block out the sounds coming from the bed. Because it sounded like pain, like despair, like death. "Mitchell is down," she croaked.

Someone male swore violently into her ear. Then she heard the loudest noise imaginable, a scream that filled her whole being with terror and agony, and threatened to deafen her ear. Pawing at her ear, she yanked the device out and dropped it so she could clap her hands over her ears.

Chapter 16

The impact woke him. By the time he understood what was happening, the drug had already been delivered into his body. All of Bobby's will focused on getting as many dragons away as he could. They resisted, wanting to sleep and stay put. He kept pushing, throwing everything he had at them. At least one had to be able to get away.

One little dragon crawled sluggishly off his foot, taking the small toe as the drug surged through his system. The edges of his vision blurred, pulling him down into unconsciousness. With one last, desperate effort, he tossed his mind into that one dragon.

It looked around, trying to understand what had happened. A girl in SWAT gear stood over him with a weird-looking gun, then she backed up, her face screwed up in panic. She reloaded her gun with a dart and it went off, hitting the floor.

Owen's super-voice rang out. The girl pulled something out of her ear and dropped it. Her eyes screwed shut and her hands covered her ears. Somehow filtered or muted by the dragon, Bobby found the noise a nuisance. Elsewhere in the house, he heard shouting voices.

The dragon dove to the floor and grabbed the thing she dropped, then flew out of the room. All kinds of people in the same tactical gear filled the house. Lily's door hung open and he wanted to go check on her and Sebastian.

Everyone's doors hung open, he noticed. A man stepped out of Alice's, his next door neighbor, holding his ears. Bobby caught sight of the guy's eyes and saw his own staring back at him. The sight took him one beat, then another, to register, and he suddenly felt stupid and betrayed. All this time, he'd been trying to save that guy, only to have him come here and assault them.

Owen's voice stopped, maybe because of a dart to the chest. He heard a familiar squeal in the sudden silence. "Will! I knew you'd be here!"

Now he had no idea what to think. Jasmine came to assault the farm? He needed to find Stephen. His only recourse here would be killing people, and he had no desire to harm any of them. Not yet. Not until he understood all of this.

It would take him about an hour to get to Denver, then…he'd have to find one girl named Kris, or some variation of it. Stephen hadn't even told him which part of Denver she lived in. For all he knew, her place could be in one of the suburbs, and he had no last name to search for.

No, that was stupid. Stephen would come back before dawn to catch some sleep here. He could wait outside and intercept him before he reached the house, or be here if these people all left by then. That option sucked. It also happened to be the best one available with his body down for the count.

The dragon flitted through the house, darting from hiding spot to hiding spot in a desperate dash to avoid being seen. So long as no one knew he'd gotten one dragon free, he could accomplish something. He could follow them back to their base and free everyone and wreak all kinds of havoc there.

Jayce had managed to get up and change his flesh to steel. The big man roared with defiance and threw a person across the room while darts smashed into him. They'd have a heckuva time putting him down, if they figured out some way to do it.

Bobby would've given a lot to be able to tell Jayce that he had a dragon free, and no matter what, he'd come for them. But he couldn't do anything of the kind without giving himself away. Now he heard Sebastian screaming for his momma, then saw a guy in tac gear carrying him as the boy reached back for Lily. The sight crushed a piece of him. How could a man do that to a little boy? He wanted to do horrible things to that man and only didn't because he knew these men were just following orders.

Privek. He did this. Bobby and Stephen would find him and eat him for breakfast. This time, they'd take that sonofabitch to some hellhole, throw him in, and beat the shit out of him until he told them everything. Or maybe they'd tie him up and do obscene things to him until he begged to die. Or something. No matter what, he'd suffer.

The dragon found a perch in a tall tree and watched, even though it hurt to not be able to do anything about it. Sebastian wailed as the guy carried him away from the house. Jayce burst out of the house and tripped on something as he charged after that guy. Something Bobby couldn't make out in the darkness smashed him to the ground and kept him from getting up again.

Through the earpiece in the dragon's claws, he finally heard voices again.

"This is Alpha Leader. Is anyone back on the channel yet?"

"Nine here, with Polape. She lost her earpiece, but she's fine. This section is cleared."

"Seven here, no issues. Mezilis and the civvie are here with me and Moore."

"Two reporting in. Eight needs a medic, so does Androvitch. We're in the second wing. Need backup."

"Ten on my way."

"Four on my way."

"Party on Two's Six."

"Three here, I've got the kid. He's not calming down. Don't suppose one you is good with toddlers? "

"Suck it up, Three." He recognized Alpha Leader's voice again.

"Everything topside is good." This voice didn't identify itself, but was notable for being female.

"I have my Will!" Bobby recognized Jasmine's voice without issue.

This one spoke through gritted teeth, under serious strain. "Westbrook is contained out here, but he's still putting up a hell of a fight. Paul, get your mindfuck on already."

"I'm trying! He's resisting me."

The strained voice spoke again. "Maybe we should just call him fucking Superman."

"Jesus," Alpha Leader grunted, "anybody got a sledgehammer?"

"I can help if you let him go, Brian." Another female voice spoke. Bobby saw something dropping out of the sky to land gently next to Jayce. So, they had people who could fly. How many of the others did they have on this raid? All eleven? What did Privek tell them?

"Okay, on three, I'm letting him go. One, two, three." For three seconds, he heard nothing over the earpiece. He watched while Jayce, lit up by several flashlights, struggled to push himself up, his face twisted in a rage unlike anything Bobby ever saw him wearing before. He growled and it grew into a roar. Finally, his expression went slack and he slumped to the ground. His skin shimmered to normal flesh tone.

"Holy fucking Christ. Westbrook is down." Someone walked up and shot him with a dart. "And now contained."

"That's that, then," Alpha Leader said. "If anyone else is

resisting, they're doing it by hiding and not fighting. Police these bodies outside by Seven for pickup. Seven, keep a count, we need to know if we missed anyone. Nine, get Polape to set us up with a shorter walk."

Bobby flew farther away and wanted to ditch the earpiece. Watching and listening to this hurt enough that he questioned his decision not to kill anyone. The dragon hefted the earbud to toss it for distance so he could stop hearing the awful words.

He stopped it. If they mentioned anything that could help him, he needed to hear it. Not only that, but Stephen might be able to use it against them. Settling on a branch out of sight, he resigned himself to monitoring the cleanup.

They chattered about hoofing bodies, some of which happened to be naked. At least a few demanded they be covered with blankets, and the Alpha Leader agreed. They rooted through Greg's stuff, taking anything that seemed worth the effort. No one realized what his generator did, though, and they left it running.

Eventually, they counted their victims. They had twenty-two "targets", three civilians, and Sebastian. No one knew how to categorize the little boy. That meant someone else besides Stephen was still loose. Only a few got identified by name, so going by what he'd heard and seen, it couldn't be Jayce, Alice, Ai, Greg, Owen, Lily, or Lizzie. Given the quiet, he figured it wouldn't be Dan, either. Someone had been able to hide, like Lisa and Sam could.

"Helicopters are inbound," he heard Alpha leader announce. "That means we're done with the tac channel. Alpha Two, police up the earbuds."

"What about those two missing targets?"

"One of them is Cant, he's probably off hunting. Unless he doesn't live here, he'll be back at some point. The file said he's averse to sunlight, so it'll probably be by dawn. So long as you tag him before he gets close, there shouldn't be any problems. No armored skin or anything like that in the file. The other one, we can't confirm the identity of without pictures to compare to our bundles."

"Orders, Boss?"

"Nine, Ten, stay behind and grab Cant when he returns. We'll have a bird standing by, waiting for your call. Just in case it goes sideways, Arralt, stay with them. See if you can find our mystery number twenty-four, but don't sweat it. Probably not here, might even be off on their own."

"Understood."

Bobby watched them all hand in their earbuds. Helicopters took his family away. He wished he couldn't see how stupid it would be to fly into the engines and blow one up. He wished he could find Privek right this minute and rip him apart. Most of all, he wished Stephen had been around to hear all of that so he wouldn't have to find a way to explain it through a dragon, without words.

This shouldn't have happened. They relied on secrecy for security, when they should have done something active to make the place safe. Was it the trip to Alamogordo, or Stephen's forays into Denver, or Kaitlin using her money? Who knew, and who cared. They should've been paranoid. They should've expected this to happen eventually and planned for it. Their priorities had been all wrong. Knowing changed nothing right now.

Dropping the earbud as useless now, he flew a circuit of the property, checking for anyone who might have hunkered down on the edges or chosen to sleep outside tonight. He saw goats and chickens, but no people. Tony could've turned himself into a plant and be hiding in plain sight. Sam could be in the house wiring, Lisa could be in her pocket, Violet could have flown somewhere, John could have encased himself in a tree. He held onto hope that he'd be able to find another ally after Stephen took care of Nine, Ten, and Arralt.

When he returned to the farmhouse, he saw the three men left behind. Two of them gave off a military vibe as they crouched on the ground, futzing with something. That made the other one Arralt, a brother willing to work for Privek for some reason. He scribbled license plate numbers on a notepad.

That girl who shot Bobby seemed so scared and unwilling. He wondered what story Privek spewed to get them all to believe they needed to come here, wreck the house, and tie up their brothers and sisters like dogs. Did he have some leverage over them, like blackmail? Did he learn from the mistakes with him and Jayce and Ai and Alice to manipulate those others better?

Avoiding the three men, Bobby slipped back inside the house and flew from room to room. The dragon let out a soft trill wherever he thought the men outside might not overhear, hoping to find someone tucked away. It wound up in Lily's room, and he had to turn away to get Sebastian's screams to stop echoing in his head.

The place had been wrecked. They'd smashed furniture, ripped down doors, and punched giant holes in the walls. Bobby saw broken picture frames in bedrooms. Plants lay in piles of dirt, surrounded by shards of pottery. Tiana's cat had been shot with a dart that had ripped fatally through its small body, staining the ground with its blood.

Finally, a closet door opened in response to his trill. Kaitlin stuck her tinfoil-wrapped head out, clutching her laptop to her chest "Is it safe?" she whispered, peering around.

He swooped in and wished he could hug her. The dragon sat on her knee and held up three claws. Asking about the tinfoil seemed too hard, so he ignored it.

"There are three of us, or three of them?"

Both questions technically had the same answer. He nodded. In an attempt to explain to her about Stephen, the dragon put two claws up by its mouth like fangs, doing its best Dracula impersonation.

"Stephen wasn't here, he's off with his girlfriend?" The dragon nodded. "Is that you in there, Bobby?" Nod. "Because they got you?" Nod. "And there are three of them outside waiting for Stephen to come back?" Nod. "Well, shit." She rubbed her forehead. "We're kind of fucked." Nod. "Thanks for agreeing," she said sarcastically. "I feel so much better now."

The dragon put up the claw-fangs again, pointed to itself, then pointed outside. Kaitlin nodded. "Yeah, good idea. You go wait for Stephen, intercept him. I can keep myself clear." She held out a finger to rub the dragon's belly, which it liked more than he expected it to. "Sorry I couldn't save anyone else. I didn't understand what I was seeing until it was too late."

Hoping she wouldn't spend much time beating herself up over that, he patted her knee and took off. She deserved zero blame for any of this. He, on the other hand, needed to have his ass kicked. That trip down to White Sands had to be the way they found the farmhouse. The timing hit too close for coincidence. Maybe someone found the car while Jayce had been banging that park ranger and slipped some… thing… Actually, now that he thought about it, the trunk had popped open randomly when they picked Sam up. Considering their varied abilities, one of them could've hit the release while they were all distracted and jumped in or thrown in a tracking device.

The assault on the farm had been his fault. Chicago had been his idea. Afghanistan had been his call. Albuquerque had been his plan. Everyone else suffered for it. Sebastian's screams echoed in his head again, and some part of his mind helpfully replayed the memory of seeing him hauled away, terrified.

This hiding crap ended now. No matter how it fell out when they got free, there would be no more hiding, no more huddling together for anything other than kinship and camaraderie. He'd stand up and tell the whole world what he could do and how little he cared what they thought about it. The bunch of them would do what they wanted to do, not what other people wanted them to do.

Perched in a tree again, the dragon sat and stared out at the sky, expecting Stephen to come from the southwest. He'd fly in a straight line, and should pass by this point to reach the house. Hopefully, he actually would come back this morning. If they all had to wait a couple of days while he got laid and fed a few times, there might be a problem.

Trying avoid thinking, Bobby dozed and wondered about the condition of his body. Would they try to reason with him, or judge him too dangerous and unreasonable to bother? If he hadn't managed to get a dragon off, they could've set him up to be drugged into unconsciousness for the rest of his life. Finding that depressing, he forced himself to think about something else.

His mind latched onto Will, the one person here whose situation seemed weirder than his own. He could easily imagine how they got Jasmine confused enough to actually believe she was doing the right thing. Now they'd have to convince Will, a guy smart enough to become a genuine veterinarian. Either that, or they'd have to tread a line between threats and action to get him to play along without alienating Jasmine.

That led him to wondering about the others. Arralt seemed to think he'd picked the right side. That girl in his room seemed conflicted about hurting him, so they hadn't been turned into assassins or monsters. Unlike himself, a tiny voice reminded him. Stephen probably had the right of it: nothing was as simple as he wanted it to be.

With dawn, Bobby saw a dark spot appear in the sky. The dragon leaped into the air to intercept him. Fortunately, Stephen happened to be the one person who, upon being accosted by a single dragon, knew to accept it and start asking simple questions. He looked good, well fed and sated. Bobby caught up with him near the edge of their property. The vampire had already pulled his gloves on and settled his balaclava into place. "One dragon? Bobby, are you in there?" Nod. "Something happened, then." Nod. "Are you in there because your body is in trouble?" Nod. "Is this all an epic joke you're helping to play on me as penance for our trip?"

Stunned and stung by the accusation, it took Bobby a few seconds to come up with an answer. The dragon shook its head fervently.

Stephen snorted. "Sure, right. I believe you." Rolling his eyes as turned to face away from the sun, he continued at full speed to the farmhouse.

Unwilling to give up, the dragon grabbed his coat and clung, chirping madly to get his attention. Dammit, if he could just talk!

"Cut it out, Bobby, seriously. I get they're all pissed at us, but you're trying too hard." He landed in the clearing in front of the house.

Bobby saw a dart thump into the vampire's chest, a few inches away from the dragon. The dragon trilled out the curses he wanted to shout and he let go to watch Stephen blink stupidly at the dart, drop to his knees, and collapse.

Something wrapped around the dragon, encasing him in a world of distorted light. It pressed close, then it crushed him and everything went black.

Epilogue — Brian

"Damn, I didn't mean to crunch it." Brian pulled his hand back. It returned to normal from its liquid state with a smashed dragon in his palm. "I hope that didn't kill him."

"Call it in, Ten." Nine nudged Cant with a boot.

Ten pulled out his phone and made the call. "Alpha Base, this is Alpha Ten, we have Cant."

Poking the little metal corpse, Brian sighed. "Ask them who the last missing one is, and if Mitchell is okay. I just crunched one of his dragons."

Ten relayed the questions for him while Nine used zipties to secure Cant. Ending the call, Ten said, "Base reports Mitchell's vitals are clear. The last one is Kaitlin Tremont, abilities unknown. None of the captures are awake yet to interrogate. Orders are to sweep the house and property one more time, then call for pickup. Here's a picture. She's cute."

Brian rolled his eyes. All the girls were cute, or hot, or had plenty of potential. "I'll check the woods. You guys check the house."

"Copy that." Nine dragged Cant into the shade and left him by a tree trunk. "Watch your six."

"Yeah, you too." Brian's entire body liquefied, becoming a

mass of water with an outer membrane stronger than steel. Some day, he wanted to understand how what they could all do didn't violate every law of physics. For now, he sloshed through the trees and shrubs faster than a person could run, his ability to see somehow spread across his entire outer skin. Everything about his superpower was weird, much like Mitchell's. He really hoped the guy was actually okay, because out of all of them, he really wanted to talk to Mitchell. About being this level of crazy weird, mostly.

DRAGONS IN FLIGHT

Prologue

This moment needed to last, as long as possible. Will couldn't help but let a few tears free with his arms around Jasmine and face buried in her neck. Even if they were in a helicopter piled with the sedated bodies of everyone he'd come to trust, he had her. Finally, after so long without her, they were together again and he could smell her scent. He had no idea what was going on. That didn't matter right now.

"Will, you're squeezing too hard," Jasmine shouted over the noise of the helicopter.

As little as he wanted to loosen his grip, he did, though he still held her close. "I missed you." He didn't really care if she heard it or not, but her ears were sharp, and the way she rubbed her cheek on his told him she probably did.

The ride felt excruciatingly long and unbelievably short at the same time. As soon as it landed, he'd have to let go so she could walk. Also, they'd be able to find quiet and have time to talk. Hopefully. When the helicopter touched down and he was ushered out with Jasmine, the gun pointed at him made that hope seem foolish. Obviously, they wouldn't want him to ruin whatever they told her to get her to work for them.

Before anyone could rip them apart, Jasmine stopped and wrapped herself around him, kissing him again with joy and lust and longing. It might be the last time he got to do that for a while, so he returned it with everything he had. For a few minutes, he forgot where he was and how he got there and why.

As such things always must, it ended. Someone tapped him on the shoulder. "C'mon, we gotta get you in for a debrief."

Will stared into Jasmine's eyes, the part of her he'd been initially attracted to years ago when she brought Walnut the injured wild squirrel into his practice. The rest of her, from mind to toe, was a delight, and she kept him sane and alive, but her eyes—icy blue and so exotic—made him ask her out the first time. He put a light kiss on the tip of her nose, still oblivious to nearly everything going on around them.

"No, really. Let's go, loverboy." The soldier stepped behind Jasmine where Will could see him easily and gave him an unamused, impatient glare.

Granted, that guy had a really big gun, but he had a squirrel-girl. "I'm not going anywhere without her."

Jasmine smiled up at him brightly and squeezed him. "No, never again. No more being apart."

The soldier, a square-jawed muscle man, glared at Will, brown eyes hard and unfriendly. "That's not how this is going to work. Boss says you come alone, so you come alone. Milani can grab a bunk and wait for you."

Will clenched his jaw. "No, I'm not playing that way. If you want to haul me off at gunpoint, then Jasmine," he turned his gaze back to her, giving her a look he hoped she would understand, "is going to run for it and you'll never see her again." The guy had orders, Will knew that. He didn't care. "Tell you what, though. If you let it go until morning, I'll come willingl and, tell them whatever they want to know without a fuss."

The soldier growled in the back of his throat, eyes narrowed and mouth a thin line. "I'll see if I can get authorization for that," he grunted. A gesture got some other soldier to hold a gun on them both and he trotted away.

Jasmine wanted to be hugged more, so he pulled her close again and held her there. He shut his eyes against the sight of people he knew and cared about being carried past unconscious on stretchers. He had no superpowers, unless being a licensed veterinarian counted. What could he possibly hope to do about all of this? If he got a chance to help them, he'd do it. Jasmine could only do so much, too.

"Nope, your offer was refused. Let's go." Hands grabbed him and dragged him away.

"Jasmine, run!" Hands grabbed him and dragged him away. He opened his eyes to see Jasmine blinking in shock. "RUN!" He saw her blink one more time, then she shrank down into her squirrel shape and took off faster than the eye could track. The men around him swore. Several fired guns at her. All of them missed.

"I ought to shoot you right now for that." The soldier pressed the barrel of a pistol to his temple and cocked it. "Give me one good reason why I shouldn't."

Will had never been seriously threatened with a gun before. The feel of the metal on his flesh scrambled his brains with panic. "I warned you," he whimpered. One thought sustained him: Jasmine got away. If he couldn't stop hyperventilating, though, it wouldn't matter much.

"Might as well take me in to be questioned at this point, or duping Jasmine was all for nothing. It isn't like she won't know it if you kill me." Hopefully, that quaver in his voice wouldn't undermine the message.

The soldier restraining him coughed. “Sergeant, we should just take him in. Those are the orders.”

Sergeant grunted in the back of his throat.

Will squeaked in panic, cringing away from the gun. If he had to die right here, right now, at least he knew Jasmine was safe. Thoughts about how she would manage without him flooded his mind. She’d been fine before he met her, but did so much better with him than without. He imagined her weeping over his grave and consoling herself by binge eating mixed nuts.

An eternity later, the gun left his temple and Sergeant clicked the safety on. “Get him out of here,” he snarled.

“Oh, thank God.” Will sucked in a lungful of air, grateful for whatever made this man not kill him.

“We’ll see how you feel in an hour.”

Chapter 1

He wriggled down a tight, dark, slimy tunnel with squishy sides. It meant he couldn't go as fast as he wanted and couldn't fly. That mattered because he was a dragon, and dragons had wings. It wasn't important, though, because he had a mission, and he'd be there soon. Another few steps and he reached it.

Blowing fire at the tunnel floor made it weak and he punched his sharp claws and face through it, then launched himself forward. More fire made the gunk he found shrivel up. Soon, he punched out into open air and could finally fly.

He turned to see what he'd ripped his way out of to find a flat chest with a faded red shirt covering it, the gory hole spraying blood up at him. The girl had dusky skin and big brown eyes, wide with shock. She couldn't be more than five years old and clutched a fuzzy brown bear in one hand. Her hair was swept up out of her face in twin pigtails.

While he watched impassively, she fell to the ground in slow motion, reaching out her hand to touch him. Her eyes went rigid and glassy, yet they still stared at him with silent damnation. "Why did you kill me?" Her mouth didn't move; the words came out of nowhere.

"I don't know." Bobby's voice was cold, wrong. "I just did."

"I died for nothing?"

"Yeah." He looked around and saw more of his dragons bursting out of the chests of more children. They surrounded him, a circle of babies and toddlers and kids. All of their dead eyes stared at him and he felt nothing. The dragons came together, burning the blood and gore off each others' bodies. These were just foreign kids, they didn't matter.

One little white boy stood in the middle of all the carnage, looking around with his icy blue eyes. "What happened?"

Bobby the dragon flew toward Sebastian. The boy didn't need to see this kind of thing. Before he could reach the spot, Lily stepped out of nowhere and grabbed Sebastian up. "Stay away from us, Bobby." That hate-filled glare, he knew it too well.

"Wait, it was an accident!"

"Everything is always an accident or a mistake with you, Bobby. We won't be your next mistakes."

"Come on, hurry up and wake up." The voice didn't fit her this time. It belonged to someone male that he vaguely recognized. All of a sudden, a bright light flared in his face and something patted his cheek.

He tried to pull his claws up or turn his neck. Everything refused to obey him. "What in heckbiscuits?" His speech came out slurred, sounding like himself. No more of that cold, flat stuff.

"We don't have time for this. They said you have some kind of super-metabolism."

Bobby groaned and blinked repeatedly. Though he tried to roll to his side, something held him in place. In reaction to that, he struggled to get free, to no avail.

"Quit it. You're tied down. All I want is answers."

"Turn down the lights or something. I can't see nothing."

Something got between him and the source of the light. He blinked a few more times to see icy blue eyes looking down at him. Two pairs. Both belonged to men about the same age as him, so nineteen or maybe a year or two older. One was taller than the other and in better shape, and he had short, light brown hair in a messy-on-purpose sort of style. The other one had shorter red hair and lots of freckles. Brown Hair looked angry, specifically at Bobby. "Where's Elena?"

Bobby wished he could rub his eyes. Instead, he kept blinking. "Who? I don't know no Elena."

"Don't lie." Brown Hair turned to Redhead. "Is he lying?"

"I have no idea." Redhead shrugged. "I told you I couldn't read him."

He didn't understand any of this. They were talking gibberish or something. "Read me? What in heckbiscuits is that s'posed to mean? I ain't lying, I ain't never met no—" He frowned. Actually, now he thought about it, that name did sound familiar. Sort of. "Wait. She about five and a half feet tall, long hair, nice rack, don't speak no English, Mexican looking?"

Brown Hair's nostrils flared with annoyance and his eyes narrowed. "Spanish. She's from Spain. And yes, that's her. It's nice to know you can't be bothered to remember names. Now, what have you done with her?"

"Whoa, wait a minute." If he could put up his hands to ward the guy off, Bobby would. "I ain't done nothing to, with, over or under her. I met her is all." This didn't make any sense. "Why don't you just ask your buddy Privek? He knows where she is."

"I don't think he's lying," Redhead said. "It's hard to tell, but I don't think he's lying."

Brown Hair reached up and ran a hand through that messy hair in frustration. He paced out of and back into Bobby's sight. "He said you took her, you and Cant."

"Stephen didn't do…well, it weren't like he—" Bobby frowned and struggled fruitlessly against his bindings again. He couldn't lie there and not want to be free. "What I mean is, we didn't grab her or nothing. She was working for Privek when we met her."

"What?" Brown Hair hurried back to Bobby's side and looked down at him with a face full of disbelief. "What do you mean? Why would she be working for him?"

"That there's a question I'd like to ask you, turns out. On account ain't nothing good never happened around him."

Redhead frowned down at Bobby. "You're not getting out, the drug is still in your system and the bindings are secure. But, more importantly, I'm a telepath. If Privek was jerking us around, I'd know."

A telepath? Bobby stopped squirming and looked up at Redhead. He knew what that meant, the guy could rifle through a body's head and read everything there. "He had a guy killed and framed me for it. He had me trussed up in a lab and experimented on. He had me shot, he sent goons after me, he's been abducting everybody like us, across the country, and you think he's an okay guy? Where in heckbiscuits your head get shoved up?"

"Hang on," Brown Hair said.

Bobby cut him off. He knew getting cranky didn't help anything from his perspective, but he was the one tied up on the damned slab. "Look, either you're gonna let me go and we're gonna figure this stuff out together, or you're gonna throw me back under whatever rock I done got shoved. Make up your damned mind and get to it already."

"Fat chance," Brown Hair snorted. "We've seen what you can do. We'd have to be stupid to just let you go."

Scowling, Bobby could easily imagine what kinds of things

Privek showed them and told them. "Lemme guess. I'm dangerous and gotta be contained or whatever until I can be talked into sense or something? Privek show you stuff from Hill?" Redhead nodded. Brown Hair watched him, his expression slowly changing from skeptical to thoughtful. "He bother telling you why all that happened?"

Redhead jumped in to explain with all the eagerness of a brown-nosing pupil. "You killed people, they managed to detain you, and you broke out."

Bobby laughed. He couldn't help it. As much as he expected it, the answer still surprised him. They both watched him, Redhead with some alarm, and Brown Hair getting more calculating. "I kinda figured he'd leave out details and all. That's the only way to explain you lot working for him. Them two men I done killed, they were trying to abduct Lily and her boy. I didn't even mean to kill 'em, that were an accident. One of 'em tased me afore I did anything to them, and the dragons got mighty angry about that.

"They managed to get the drop on me, sure, and two girls, too. Took us all to some house, pumped me full up of these drugs. When I woke up, they wanted me to talk, so they started—" Just thinking about that made him angry, really angry. "Let's just say it was all guys in them suits and they were using a female prisoner against me and leave it at that." Honestly, he didn't know if they would've actually raped Ai without Anita intervening, but he was mightily glad he didn't have to find out.

"The other girl managed to get free and them two escaped, but I didn't. I got shot, they took me to Hill for medical attention. All that mayhem there was the rest of us doing what best they could trying to rescue me from their custody. Killed a guy there, yeah, but only because he was trying to kill me first."

Redhead blinked and looked up at Brown Hair. "I could

actually tell he was being honest with all of that. It's hard to explain, but he's not lying."

Brown Hair nodded to show he understood. "What about Afghanistan? I saw pictures. They were a lot more…disturbing."

It would be nice if he could turn away and look at something else. Bobby settled for shutting his eyes. The girl from his dream stared back at him. "I…ain't rightly proud of what all I done there. Some of it weren't a'purpose or even needful. All I got to say in defense is it were mostly what Privek told me to. Stephen and I was trying to get him to trust us so we could find Jasmine and the rest of you to break you outta wherever he had you stashed. Weren't no reason to think he weren't doing to you what he done to me, Jayce, Alice, and Ai. I got stains on me, sure as heckbiscuits, but it ain't on account I'm just a rabid dog or nothing."

"What's a 'heckbiscuit'?" Redhead squinted at him.

Bobby shrugged and looked up at Redhead again. He tried to, anyway. "Something Momma says. Ain't polite to use stronger language 'round folks you don't know."

"What will you do if we let you go?" Brown Hair seemed to be taking all of this at face value, which was good, because he would obviously be the one who to the decision.

He didn't even have to think about it to answer that question. Bobby locked his gaze on Brown Hair, who didn't flinch away from the intensity. "Bust as many out of here as wants to come, go back to the farmhouse, and get as many as I can to go public so they can't do this crap to us again."

Brown Hair grimaced in distaste. "I don't want to be public. With what I can do, I don't ever want people to know about it without my telling them on purpose."

"I can respect that, but it ain't gonna work for us all to keep quiet." Bobby heaved a sigh. "I don't especially want to be DragonBoy or whatever, but if that's what I gotta do to keep anyone from being able to use Sebastian for a test subject, then I'll be the first one in line, I'll answer every stupid question I gotta, I'll go on TV and make a damned fool outta myself. Ain't right what I saw, taking a boy from his momma like that. Didn't you hear him screaming? 'Cause I sure did."

Redhead's eyes went wide. Brown Hair took a step back, looking like he wanted to think. "How did you hear that?" Redhead asked. "You were the first one down."

"I got one dragon off and tried to warn Stephen, but it didn't work. Something smashed it when they shot him."

Redhead looked up at Brown Hair, who Bobby couldn't see anymore. "I think—" He cut himself off, probably in response to a gesture by Brown Hair, and looked chastised. They stood in silence for maybe half a minute.

Brown Hair came back into view, moving so he could look Bobby in the eyes, face to face. "We're going to let you out, and we'll even help you free everyone else, but," he raised a finger in warning, "you have to prove it first. Privek has been nothing but professional with me and has repeatedly asserted you're a dangerous maniac. Paul has never sensed any duplicity from him. Your assertions are believable, but you need to prove them."

Man, this guy used a lot of big words. Bobby had to actually think to understand what the guy said. "What's 'duplicity' mean?"

Redhead got an amused half grin. "I've spoken with him several times, and I've never sensed him lying to me. If what you're saying is true, I should have picked up something, something to tip me off he was omitting details or plain lying. But I never have. How someone might do that, I have no idea."

"But, in spite of that," Brown Hair smirked, "you seem more reasonable than he gave you credit for, and I know you rescued several soldiers in Afghanistan when you didn't need to. So, we're going to give you the benefit of the doubt. Just you, though. Everyone else stays here until we're sure. Just in case you're thinking about killing us to eliminate us as an obstacle, I have some more of the drug that makes you unable to use your powers."

Bobby narrowed his eyes at Brown Hair, mildly annoyed by the threat and the implication. "How d'you know about them soldiers?" It seemed like something Privek would want kept as quiet as possible.

"I healed them." Brown Hair bent to the task of undoing the straps.

"Huh." The guy could heal, that was pretty handy. Well, not for him, he didn't need that, but not many of them could heal themselves. "Are you sure it ain't okay to grab one other person?" He turned his head, and that felt like Heaven.

"I think it's in our best interest to only have one of you to keep track of. Besides, it's going to be hard enough to get you out quietly."

Oh, his arms, yes, and his chest. Finally, he could sit up. His head still felt a little woozy, probably from the drugs, but freedom was heavenly. "How long I been trussed up?"

"A couple of days." Brown Hair stood back and let Bobby finish undoing the restraints himself.

Clumsy hands fumbled over the straps, bringing back the memory of Anita leaving him behind, but this wasn't that, and these guys weren't her. When it became clear he needed help with the releases, Redhead stepped up and clicked them open for him. "Where are we? Like, what state, I mean."

"We're in Washington, DC."

"You guys got names? Everyone calls me Bobby." He needed help to get down to the floor, too, and his legs were unsteady.

Redhead yanked a tube out of his arm.

"Liam," Brown Hair said, then he pointed at Redhead. "Paul. We'll see if it's actually nice to meet you or not."

Bobby snorted. "Your girl was in Virginia last I knew. Was paying attention when we got close, figured we'd want to go back there again." He gave a shot at popping off a dragon. It didn't work. "I guess we'll need a car or something. How we getting outta here?"

This room reminded him of a TV show morgue. It had a bank of drawers the right size, and looked sterile and easy to clean. The bed he just got up from was a sliding cot. Paul shoved it back into the drawer it belonged to. This bank of drawers had nine of them, which wasn't nearly enough to house everyone. Maybe only the ones they were really scared of wound up in here. He'd give a lot to be able to check who was in them, but didn't think Paul and Liam would just stand by and let him do it.

"Leave it to me," Paul said with steely determination. He went for the door.

Behind his back, Liam grinned like Paul was possibly the most amusing thing he'd ever seen. "Lean on me, I'll help you out." The guy stood at least four or five inches taller than Bobby, definitely over six feet. Paul was about his own height, five foot nine. All three of them had a similar compact build, not broad shouldered or hulking. Of the three, Bobby had the most muscle, but Liam was no slouch. Paul probably never did any kind of hard work in his life with anything but his brain. "We'll have to take your car," he added to Paul. "Mine doesn't have a backseat."

One arm over Liam's shoulders, he looked around, taking in details. They left the small room. The place felt very institutional with cement walls painted white and some kind of stone flooring in red flecked gray, fluorescent panel lighting overhead. A guard sat at a desk just outside the room, but the man ignored the trio completely for some reason, his eyes glued firmly to some papers in front of him.

Much to his surprise, they took the elevator at the end of the hall. An escape seemed to Bobby to be a window or stairwell thing. According to the row of buttons, they were in the second and lowest basement of a building with seven floors above ground. Paul actually looked nervous and stressed now—his eyes darted around as if he could see through the ceiling, and this did nothing to inspire confidence.

"You guys sure about this exit plan?"

Liam coughed lightly. "Let's not distract the telepath while he uses his mind to clear a path for us."

"Ain't that creepy as heckbiscuits."

"A little, yes."

"Can I ask you, how'd those guys turn out after you healed 'em? The ones that were really messed up."

Liam frowned and looked down. "There's only so much I can do."

"Meaning what?" Bobby wasn't harsh with the statement, he just wanted to know. "Look, I done seen 'em beforehand. One of 'em didn't want to live, another one died on the way to you, I'm just wondering how the ones what survived are doing. I mean, you said you saw pictures of what happened out there. It's on account of what got done to them more'n anything else."

Huffing out another breath that spoke of discomfort with the subject, Liam nodded. "I can't replace lost parts. As for the rest," he cringed, "we had to cause some damage to heal what was wrong. Each of them had something that healed up horribly in the time they were there. None of them walked away whole again, but they're all in much better shape than modern medicine could have done. "

That was both a terrible thing to know and a great relief. "I'm glad to hear that. None of those guys deserved to live crippled up like they been made. Heckbiscuits, nobody does."

Liam glanced at him, measuring and weighing. "You're a dangerous man, Bobby." The elevator doors opened on the ground floor and they walked out into a nearly empty lobby. He didn't give Bobby a chance to ask what he meant by that. "Keep quiet until we get to the car."

It made no sense to Bobby at all, given he only wore his pajama pants and still needed the help Liam provided, but no one even gave them a second glance. The guards here—actual uniformed police officers of some variety—looked, then their eyes slid right over the trio and ignored them. They walked boldly out the front door and into sunlight too bright for Bobby's mood. He didn't like leaving all the others behind. How he would explain that he did it without everyone assuming he'd gotten back up on the Head Cowboy horse?

They reached the car, a little four-door piece of crap. At a guess, it probably had more years on it than any of them. As soon as Paul shifted his attention away from the building to the car, he froze in the act of pulling out his keys. "Guys, there's…some…thing in the car already."

Bobby looked up and saw a person sitting in the back seat. Liam must have been mostly watching the ground as they went too, because he stopped, just as surprised. She turned her head right then, and Bobby recognized her. "Oh, It's Kaitlin. No worries, then. She's one of us."

"Kaitlin? Kaitlin Tremont? What's she doing in my car?"

"Obviously," Liam muttered so Paul wouldn't hear, "it's because she has no taste."

Bobby snorted and moved to get Liam to go again. "She sees the future and stuff. Creepy, a little cranky, but harmless." Before he could reach the car and knock on the window, she saw him and waved with a mildly amused smile. Of course, the doors weren't locked. Paul probably forgot to do it, since she didn't have any special car boosting skills he knew of. Then again, he didn't really know Kaitlin all that well. Maybe she could break into one with her eyes closed. Didn't seem likely, but it was possible. He reached out and opened the back door while Paul fumbled with his keys.

"Don't panic," Kaitlin said with a grin. She wore red, black, and gray in the form of a hoodie, miniskirt, leggings, and chucks, and sat there calmly with an orange and pink striped backpack on her lap, like this wasn't a clever, daring escape from that giant, unmarked institutional building.

Bobby smirked and tipped an imaginary hat to her as he bent to get into the back seat with her. She scooted over so he could. "Kaitlin, what're you—" Stupid question. "Never mind. I'm real glad to see you got outta the farm alright. This here's Liam." He jabbed a thumb at his rescuer.

"There's something in the car," Paul announced again, this time with an edge of panic to his voice.

"That's Paul." Bobby leaned back out and glared at the other guy. "She ain't a 'something', she's a 'someone'." He wasn't inclined to explain anything else right now and just wanted to get out of here.

"Where are we going?" She watched Paul and Liam stand there beside the car and have a whispered conversation.

"If'n I can get Liam his girl back from wherever Privek's got her stashed, them two're gonna help get to the bottom of all this and get us all free."

"Ah." Leaning forward over Bobby's lap, she stuck her head out through the door. "Gentlemen, Agent Privek is coming back from lunch in about five minutes. If you want to conveniently miss him, we should get going."

This pronouncement made both men stare at her. Bobby sat back with a bemused smirk and watched them take a few seconds to come to some kind of realization, then hurry to get into the car. Both kept glancing back at her without saying anything.

Paul navigated them away from the building, waiting until traffic forced them to sit at a light to turn around and look her over with narrowed eyes. "Your mind is weird."

She shrugged. "So is your nose, but I wasn't going to say anything. Because it would be rude."

Paul's mouth opened and shut twice, then he faced forward, staring out the front windshield. "I meant it isn't like a normal person's mind," he said with a kind of sulk to it.

"Same goes for your nose," Kaitlin retorted.

"You know, they're actually helping. You ain't gotta be difficult."

Liam, who ignored the exchange up to then, turned around and said pleasantly, "What does that mean, you can see the future?"

"Precognition, the real deal." Kaitlin shrugged again. "I make a killing on the stock market. I also wind up in the strangest places, sent there by stuff I see. It's a double-edged sort of thing. I knew you were going to haul Bobby out and take this car, and that it would be unlocked already. So, here I am."

Liam nodded, his mouth drawing down into that same thoughtful, calculating quirk as before. It struck Bobby as funny how this wasn't the first time he sat in a car with three others of his kind, escaping Privek and his Suits, off to do whatever it took to get the others to safety. He'd give a lot to have Jayce, Alice, and Ai—or Stephen and Matthew—here with him instead. He knew them and trusted them. These three would have to do.

"Which part of Virginia?" Paul pointed at a sign with too many numbers and unfamiliar names for Bobby to know how to direct him.

"Southeast of Culpeper on Route 3." Bobby watched Liam pull out his phone and tap on it to get a map. It looked like a fancy one, with all the bells and whistles. His clothes were nice, too, though Bobby wasn't much of a judge of that kind of thing: slacks and a crisp shirt, a slick watch, nice shoes. Paul, on the other hand, wore jeans and some band's t-shirt with a soft plaid button down shirt hanging open over it. They got to keep all their own stuff. Must be nice.

"I don't want to be a pain, but is there any way I could get some clothes?"

Kaitlin shoved her backpack at him. "I brought some of your stuff from the farmhouse."

"Oh, thanks." Bobby opened up the pack and fished around in it.

"You were at the farmhouse?" Paul frowned and glanced back. "How come we didn't catch you? Wait, how come I didn't notice your mind there?"

Exaggerating her enunciation and drawing it out like she was saying it for a stupid person, Kaitlin said, "Pre-cog-ni-tion."

"Why is the car making that noise?" Liam looked over at Paul, probably referring to how the engine knocked. It might have been a question only asked to distract him from that discussion.

Paul blushed. "It's an old car. It does that sometimes."

"What d'you drive, Liam?" Bless Kaitlin, she brought him jeans and a t-shirt.

"Something newer than this," he answered smoothly.

Kaitlin rolled her eyes. "Instead of talking about cars, why don't you all just pull down your pants and compare already?"

Cracking into a broad grin, Bobby chuckled. "Yeah, yeah. We're all on the same team here, ain't no reason to get touchy about nothing. Any chance that noise is any different than it ought to be,

Paul? 'Cause I'm pretty sure one of you eleven folks climbed into the car while we was at White Sands, and that's how you found the farmhouse."

Paul gulping audibly and Liam shifting in his seat confirmed that theory. "Maybe we should stop to check. It might be bugged."

Liam shrugged. "In which case we're already screwed and they already know where we're going. Stopping now to check would only delay us further and give them more time to prepare."

"When you know there's a trap, charge in to take 'em off guard. My kinda tactical approach."

"Look," Liam turned around, annoyance on his face loud and clear, "I gather this is all very entertaining to you, but Elena is my— She's—" He made a frustrated noise and turned back around. "She's very important to me."

Taken aback, Bobby blinked a few times. "Ease back, I don't mean nothing by it. I get it, you're in love with the girl, it's cool. We're gonna rescue her." He knew a thing or two about being willing to do whatever it took for a woman.

Liam rubbed his face and didn't answer. Kaitlin watched Bobby, her expression thoughtful. "While you were gone, people talked about you a lot more than they normally do. No one really thinks very highly of your brains. They all figured Stephen talked you into taking off. But he didn't, did he? It was your idea, to go ride on the fancy white horse, wearing the white hat. You were expecting to come back a big damned hero."

Bobby sighed and looked out his window, not wanting to admit the truth in front of Liam and Paul. Not out loud, anyway. "It don't matter." Tony had figured the same thing out, and he hadn't liked it then, either.

"Uh-huh." Kaitlin crossed her arms and stopped watching him. "I could have told you it was going to be a disaster."

"Yeah, well, I can tell you it woulda been stuck in committee for a month," he snapped. There was no reason to get testy with her, though. She had every right to be annoyed and prod him. "Look, yeah, I know, all this is my fault, okay? I get that. Been said, don't need a refresher."

She snorted. "It's not your fault, Bobby. That's like saying it was Tarkin's fault Alderaan got blown up. Technically true, but Palpatine was really to blame for that."

"What?" Bobby had no idea what she was talking about. Those names meant nothing to him. Actually, that last one maybe sounded a little familiar, but he couldn't place it.

Kaitlin rolled her eyes. "Never mind. I'm just saying that everything's connected. You can take responsibility for your choices, but it's not really your fault we're all in this situation. Liam, why are you working for Privek?"

Liam slumped against his seat. "We were at the airport, going through customs. Homeland Security was giving me a hard time, they separated us. When I got it straightened out, she was just gone. Elena, I mean. She disappeared. They had no idea where she went or when, and when I got them to check the security footage, there was nothing to see. Privek showed up, said he was leading a special task force to deal with us. He said he'd help me find her if I work for him. I tried to just pay him off, but he didn't want money, he wanted me to use my…ability for him."

Kaitlin nodded like that matched her expectations. "See? Privek. So, he takes Elena and says these dangerous mutants or whatever stole her, and if you work for them, he'll get 'his people' to find her. Classic bad guy tactic."

Even though he didn't quite follow the logic, Bobby shrugged. "I guess we should just be grateful they only managed to get eleven of us."

"Why do you keep saying eleven?" Paul looked at him in the rearview mirror, genuinely confused. "There's only ten of us on our side."

Bobby took a long, slow blink, and stared back at Paul through the mirror. "What d'you mean there's only ten? We checked every name on the list, and Privek got ten, plus Jasmine." He'd read that stupid list so many times he had it partially memorized. It was in alphabetical order by their last names, though he could only recite the first names down pat. "Brian, Kevin, Raymond, Dianna, William, Chelsea, Kanik, Paul, and Maisie. Them's all the ones what got took before we found 'em. Jasmine got took later."

"William is me, I go by Liam, but I don't know any Kanik."

"Yeah, I'm obviously Paul, and I recognize the other names, but not Kanik."

Bobby looked at Kaitlin, who he figured had to be thinking something smarter than him. "Ain't that a broke pickle."

"Whatever that means," Kaitlin said, then she shook her head. "This Kanik guy is maybe someone we should be interested in talking to."

Liam asked, "Where did you get the list? We never saw one, Privek just had all your names somehow."

"It were in the place we done broke outta that first time. Privek said 'mistakes were made'. Stephen and me kinda figured he meant that they didn't expect me to wake up like that, so they weren't set up for us yet. Ai picked it up on the way out. Though, in fairness, Stephen also has an alternate theory that we was supposed to break out and that list was planted all over the place to make sure we got it. I just can't figure that angle out, on account it don't go square with everything that happened."

"I remember him saying that," Paul said thoughtfully.

"How in heckbiscuits d'you remember that?"

Sheepish and blushing again, Paul hunched down as much as driving would allow him to. "I was there, when you met with him. In the next office over. Privek wanted me to read your thoughts. Only, I couldn't, because you're too… I pick up each of your dragons as a separate little mind, and they're all too tight and close to pick anything out. The only time I seem to be able to get anything from you, other than a highly confusing mess I can't really read, is when all the dragons seem to be thinking the same thing. I guess that doesn't happen much."

"Wait, right now? I'm a bundle of dragon minds right now?"

"Yeah. It's like you're made of bees. There might be a central, core part, but I can't see it."

Here Bobby thought the dragons didn't really exist unless he wanted them to. To find out they were really always there, just out of sight, shocked him so much it hit almost as a physical body blow. And he thought it was hard to explain his superpower before. Now, he didn't even understand it. Was he really just a weird hive mind effect? How did this make sense, given he wasn't made of dragons until he broke apart that first time? Or was he always this way, just with no instinct to guide him to let them loose?

"Stephen doesn't exist to my mind," Paul admitted, "and Kaitlin, you're…disturbing. Your mind is running backwards and forwards at the same time with an echo in both directions, and feels like it wants to burst out of you and eat me."

"Nice to know you can't read me," Kaitlin said cheerfully.

"I can, it's just difficult and unpleasant."

Bobby still sat there, stunned, while the conversation moved on around him. The drugs had to be out of his system by now, and he popped a dragon off his thumb. It sat on his palm, looking up at him as he looked down at it. Was it him or was he it? Was there any way to tell? Did it matter? Knowing that wouldn't bring back those kids he killed. Knowing that wouldn't get Sebastian out of whatever they were doing to him. Knowing that wouldn't fix what went wrong between him and Lily.

"I'm you and you're me," he told the little dragon softly. It nodded and chirped. The small silver critter walked across his hand to rub its head on his thumb affectionately. "Hey," he said, louder and to Paul. "If'n you see a place, I need to eat soon. Ain't picky. A junkyard'd be good, too. Dragons gotta eat separate."

"Yeah, I'm a little peckish, too," Paul said with a nod. "I'll keep an eye open for something."

"That makes no sense," Liam said. "Why do they need to eat separately?"

"I dunno. I almost done drowned on account of it once, though, so the why ain't nearly so important to me as the fact of it. They gotta eat, but it ain't urgent right now. Just can't let it go too long."

"It still makes no sense. When you eat, they should be fed, and the reverse."

Kaitlin laughed. "Yeah, because any of this makes sense. Don't even get me started about how what I can do jives with free will. You can't possibly tell me that out of all of us, Bobby's the only one that defies logic for you."

The car went quiet. Bobby stared at his dragon and didn't know what to think. Mostly, he didn't want to think at all. Sure, he spent some time trying to figure out what his mind really was, but that had more to do with knowing his limits, not understanding how it actually worked. In truth, he didn't want to know how it worked. On some level, he worried that the second he understood it, all of it would stop working, even though he knew that was stupid. He wasn't Wile E. Coyote.

After a while, he decided to find out what the other side

actually knew. “You guys all know where we come from?”

Liam and Paul shared a look. Liam shrugged. “We have theories. You?”

“Ayup, we got a theory. Starts with ‘half’ and ends with ‘alien.’”

Kaitlin snerked. “It’s not like Privek doesn’t already know we know things. We think the government has or had an alien locked up someplace, and spliced her DNA with human to make us, probably by harvesting her eggs and using human sperm. Presto, test tube babies. Someone is still working on how the alien got here.”

Both men reacted. Liam seemed to know how to keep himself more or less under wraps, but Paul had no such skill and Bobby could tell before he opened his mouth that he couldn’t believe what she’d said. “How did you figure all that out?”

Kaitlin snorted and said, again very slowly and with exaggerated pronunciation, “Precognition.”

Bobby laughed, hard. He hadn’t had much cause to in a while, and it felt good. “I know Privek thinks I’m stupid, that’s fine. But I ain’t. None of us is.”

“Privek did lead us to believe you aren’t,” Liam paused and spoke delicately, “precisely *talented* mentally.”

“Yeah, I bet.” Bobby stared out the window, trying not to take offense at that. It was what they wanted, him and Stephen, to be underestimated. It just kind of burned to know people talked about him that way. Time to change the subject again so he could stop thinking about it. “Why you on Privek’s team, Paul?”

The telepath blushed. “Agents showed up on my doorstep, saying my country needed me. I guess…I don’t know. It was stupid. My dad is a cop. He was actually proud of me for something for the first time.”

Since he looked embarrassed, Bobby just nodded. “That there’s some powerful motivation.”

Liam scowled. "If Privek took Elena specifically to manipulate me, he will regret it."

"I'm in," Bobby said cheerfully. "I'll hold him down, you open up a can of whupass."

Paul gripped the steering wheel until his knuckles turned white. "I just don't understand how he fooled me. That's not supposed to be possible."

"I fooled you by wrapping my head in tinfoil." Kaitlin shrugged. "At least, I assume that's why I did it. Maybe he's actually got some superpower or something."

That quieted the car again. Bobby could only guess what Paul and Liam might be thinking about it. For himself, he squirmed a bit about how much he and Kaitlin had shared compared to how little they got in return from Paul and Liam. But then, he figured they didn't have a lot of trust here and had to start someplace. Somebody had to give first, and he didn't mind being the one to do it. Especially if it meant they'd hold up their end of the deal.

Not long after, Liam turned on the radio and found a station playing inoffensive jazz. An hour later, they'd passed Culpeper and Bobby perked up, paying attention to where they were. "Seems like a bad idea to just drive right up to the front door and park in plain sight," he said as he noticed a familiar sign. "I suggest driving past and finding a place to park off the road what ain't too far away."

"Good plan," Liam nodded.

Kaitlin shrugged. "I'll wait in the car."

Looking her over, Bobby lifted an eyebrow. "That ain't 'cause you know something bad's gonna happen, right?"

She gave him a very fake innocent look. "Nope." Her face dropped into a more serious cast. "You don't need me to do this. I'll only be in the way and don't have anything like the skills needed to break into a place and infiltrate security and whatever else you're going to have to do. Besides, if Paul leaves the keys, I can bring the car around for a quick getaway."

"If anyone's gonna be able to do the whole quick getaway thing, I expect it's you," Bobby nodded. "Assuming that's okay with Paul?"

Paul gulped. "Maybe I should stay with the car, too."

Liam gave Paul a flat look. "How are we supposed to get in without your help? Should I heal them as a distraction?"

"I just—" Paul made a frustrated noise in the back of his throat.

Bobby laughed. "You don't trust Kaitlin not to drive away and leave you both stranded with rattlers."

"All three of us," Liam corrected.

"Naw," Bobby shrugged, "I ain't that easy to leave nowhere, seeing as how I can, ya know, fly. I ain't worried." He pointed out the window at a wall of shrubbery. "That's it, I swear on my Daddy's grave."

Kaitlin reached over and put her hand on Bobby's arm, her eyes unfocused. Paul squeaked. The car swerved and went into the ditch on the side of the road. Bobby burst into the swarm on impact and surrounded Kaitlin to protect her as the car flipped over and rolled a few times before landing upside-down in the field across the road from the target house. His intervention kept her conscious.

As soon as it stopped moving, Bobby re-formed and yanked the back door open, then hauled her out. "You okay?" He grabbed her by the shoulders and made her look at him.

She mumbled some swearwords, then shook her head to clear it. "More or less. What the hell happened?"

"I dunno. C'mon, we gotta get 'em out before anything blows up." How he wished for Jayce or Stephen, because either of them could rip the doors off. Both Paul and Liam had been knocked out cold. At least this beat up old piece of crap was made more of metal than plastic. It didn't look like either managed to get seriously hurt or would need to be wrenched out. Both still wore their seatbelts and probably had their bells rung.

"I didn't even see that coming," Kaitlin grumbled. She crawled to Paul's door and yanked on it. The door groaned and refused to budge.

Bobby tried Liam's door with the same result. "Just worry about getting them out." He scowled at the car, then remembered he had a small army of tiny claws at his disposal. Letting off a handful, he had the dragons zoom inside and cut the belts so they both thumped onto the ceiling of the car. From there, he and Kaitlin hauled them out through the broken windows.

"Someone heard that, they had to," Kaitlin said as she pushed one of Paul's eyelids up and peered at his eye. "We've got to get them away from here before anyone shows up."

"Are you people okay?"

"Too late," Bobby muttered as he looked Liam over for serious injuries. They were both incredibly lucky because they must have hit that ditch at fifty miles an hour. Someone crunching through the leaves made him turn to see the owner of those feet. And stare.

"Sergeant Riker?"

The soldier stopped and stood there, staring stupidly for a full second before hurrying over to put a knee down beside Liam. "What are you guys doing here? I figured you would've stayed in the Sandbox."

The last time Bobby saw Riker, he had injuries to his feet that meant he'd likely never walk right again, yet here he was with no sign of any kind of lingering debilitation at all. He even still wore in military gear: jungle BDUs. Riker looked over Liam, showing full recognition. Liam had said he healed soldiers. At the time, Bobby thought he only meant the really messed up ones in that warehouse. It hadn't crossed his mind that guys with lesser wounds might have gotten the benefit of his ability. Especially not this one.

"I…uh…long damned story, man."

"Yeah, same here. This guy," he patted Liam on the chest, "fixed me up right. I got shunted to this duty as a sort of reward, I guess, and to keep me quiet. All five of us are here, doing the most boring guard duty rotation imaginable. What are you up to?"

Bobby had a choice. He could be honest, or he could lie and try to play Riker. Which wasn't really a choice at all. "Looking to break into the facility you're guarding to relieve your new boss of something he stole away: Liam's girlfriend. Don't expect we got a whole ton of time to explain, so the short version is like this. There's a guy named Privek what's running all this, in charge of us with these superpowers, and he's been lying to us and using us against each other. We're looking to expose him and get some justice. Right this minute, I need to prove all that to these two, which is why we came for his girlfriend."

Riker frowned and nodded. "I have no way to evaluate that information, but you saved my life, and what was left of my squad, and Liam healed me up better than doctors could've done. There's no one named Privek here that I know of, but if his girlfriend is here, let's get her out."

Relieved by his response, Bobby gave him a grim smile. "You got any ideas, Sergeant?"

The Sergeant stood up and scratched at his clean-shaven chin. "I don't think it'd be a good idea for me to do your dirty work for you, but I can look the other way and report this as nothing."

"That'll do," Bobby nodded with a grim smile. He offered his hand to Riker, who shook it firmly. "I hope there's a chance to have out the long version of the story."

"Yeah, me too. Good luck." The soldier got a lopsided grin. "I didn't see anything. The noise must have been animals."

With a bemused snort, Bobby tipped an imaginary hat and broke apart into dragons. As the swarm streaked away, he heard Riker say, "Still a trip to see that." Kaitlin said something in return that he couldn't hear. His attention shifted to the simple task of getting into the house. Like most buildings, big or small, this one had vents and he sent the swarm in through one. From there, they flew around in the ductwork and stopped where they could see in. The ground floor remained as he remembered it: furnished like a house and barely used.

He remembered sitting in that room over there, watching Stephen drink Elena's blood. Stupid vampire. Damn fool would be free if he'd just given Bobby the benefit of the doubt instead of assuming he was playing a dumb joke. As if he would've done that after everything they went through together.

His dragons wanted him to focus on the job and get it done, and made that clear to him. The sooner they got Elena out, the sooner they could get to other, more important things. That stupid vampire was counting on him, not to mention all the others.

Bobby threw himself into one of the dragons and found a door he thought to be for the basement. It was in the kitchen, which they must use as a kind of break room. A coffee maker percolated away on the counter, dirty dishes sat in the sink, and the dishwasher ran. Would anyone notice if he dropped his whole body in here and swiped something to eat? Better question: was it worth it to risk being seen here just to fill his belly?

Thinking about it that way sent him to the door, where he landed on the deadbolt that locked from the other side. A keypad on the wall next to it had a card swiping thing, so he needed someone else to open the door for him. The downstairs probably had ventilation, finding its access would just take time.

Screw it, he needed to eat. Dragons poured into the room. He re-formed and went for the fridge with one hand missing and a rumbling belly. That other two dozen dragons spread out through the ductwork to find the right access point. Most of what he found in the fridge was in bags or reusable containers, lunches for the people here. If every person working here brought one of these things, then there were twenty. Hopefully, that included Riker and his men, so there would only be fifteen or so. He could evade that many people.

Nothing else in the fridge would feed him; ketchup and pickle relish sounded gross by themselves. He shut the door and scanned the room, noticing a bowl of fruit. Just as he stuffed a bite of banana in his mouth, the mysterious locked door beeped, the little light with the keypad flashed green, and it opened. Of course it happened then. Bobby made a start to flee for a hiding spot, but he didn't have enough time before the door opened all the way and an older woman with a severe bun stood there, looking at him with suspicion and confusion.

Jeans and a t-shirt probably didn't measure up to the dress code around here, given she wore a navy skirt suit with matching pumps. Add to that what must be a comical expression of surprise on his face, his icy blue eyes, and his missing hand…she had plenty of reasons to be suspicious and confused.

Bobby really did want to eat the banana. He wanted more for Privek not to know he'd been here. Dropping the fruit, he rushed her before the door could shut and clamped his one hand over her mouth. Her back and head thumped against the door frame and she squeaked without trying to bite or kick him.

"I ain't gonna hurt ya," he whispered into her ear, "if'n you don't give me a reason to." It worried him a bit that he couldn't be sure how much he meant those words. He saw her eyes go wide and scared, which made him feel a little dirty on the inside. He'd killed people indiscriminately and had more or less come to terms with that. It still bothered him to rough up some random woman. A real man didn't treat women like this.

She nodded and put her hands up in surrender. What did she do here? No idea. Could be nothing more than a pencil pusher, could be in charge of the place.

Swallowing back bile from his own behavior, Bobby nodded back. If only Stephen was here, he could do his vampire thing and get what they needed from her that way instead. "I'm gonna pull my hand away, on account I got some questions. You scream or shout for help and I'll kill you, we clear?" Would he really do that? No. Yes. Maybe. Hopefully not.

Again, she nodded and looked like she took that threat very seriously. When he pulled his hand away, moving his arm to keep her restrained, she sniffled. "Please don't hurt me," she whispered.

"There a girl named Elena here?" He remembered her introducing herself with that name, so he figured she must be using it with her co-workers. To be on the safe side, he rattled off a description of her.

The woman shook her head. "No, she was transferred two days ago."

Of course she was. Bobby bit back a few unfriendly words. "Where to?" The woman swallowed nervously, so he added, "It's important. Her family thinks she been kidnapped."

She blinked several times in surprise. "Oh. Um, I could… maybe find out?"

One of Bobby's eyebrows lurched up skeptically. "You think I'm gonna trust you to go back down there and not tell folks there's a guy up here what ain't supposed to be? I may not be a genius or nothing, but I ain't stupid, lady. Just tell me all the places she might be. You gotta know that, right?"

Nodding again, she took a deep breath. "White Sands, Groom Lake, or Adelphi. If there are any other facilities where she might be, I don't know about them."

"What about the one in DC?" Wouldn't it be funny if Liam had walked past her five times a day without realizing it? No, not really.

"No, she doesn't speak enough English. She has to be someplace where no one will ask questions."

That made sense to Bobby. "You know why she was here? Or why she was transferred?"

"Something about her boyfriend? Not really. Work here for a little while and you learn not to ask questions."

Bobby snorted, amused by that. "Sure. What you don't know is what you can't object to." The little growl on the edge of those words made the woman go still as her heartbeat raced. "You listen and listen good," he told her with quiet intensity in his voice. "I don't know what you think is going on here, but it ain't all it seems. Maybe you're doing some good, I don't know, but from where I'm standing, you're doing stuff where the ends justify the means, and that ain't never nothing good." If saying that made him an immense hypocrite, he could live with believing Privek had forced his hand.

"Point is," he continued, trying to be as dangerous looking and sounding as he could manage, "I aim to cause some ruckus for your bosses on account they done caused harm to a bunch of folks I care about, and if you tell them I was here and what I wanted to know, it's gonna make things harder for me. What d'you think I ought to do about that?"

She gulped. "I don't feel well all of a sudden," she said breathlessly, eyes even wider than before. "I think I might go home and sleep it off. Maybe I'll call in tomorrow, too."

Pleasantly surprised by her answer, Bobby nodded. He also understood: he had until the morning after tomorrow for sure, but past that, all bets were off. "Sounds like a plan to me." Letting go of her, he backed off. "I hope you ain't hurt." He scooped up the banana, because he didn't want to swarm in front of her. If she never saw him use his superpower, she couldn't tell Privek which one accosted her. Might as well finish the fruit he'd already peeled. And take an apple and an orange.

"No," she said meekly as she reached up to rub her head.

"Well, go on and git." He waved her off with his one banana-filled hand, trying not to call attention to how the other arm ended abruptly at the wrist.

She turned and scurried away, the sounds of her shoes moving swiftly down the hall punctuated by a door opening and shutting. As soon as it banged closed, he flowed into the swarm and got them to carry the fruit outside, where they met up with the rest of the dragons. From overhead, he saw Riker standing at what must be his post, watching the woman get into her car. Bobby stayed high enough to not attract attention, and slipped over to re-form on the ground next to Kaitlin.

The other two men had awakened. Paul looked perfectly fine, though annoyed. Kaitlin sat without a scrape on her, her whole body turned away from Paul. Liam, on the other hand, held his head gingerly and had several cuts and bruises.

"Ain't you a healer?" Bobby started munching on the apple the second he had a hand and mouth to facilitate it.

"I can't heal myself," Liam groaned, "only other people."

"Dang, that sucks."

"I was already aware of that, thank you. Since we're pointing out the obvious, you don't have Elena."

Bobby sighed as he finished his bite of apple. "Well, she ain't here. I got three possible places she might be and only today and tomorrow afore somebody probably realizes I been here. If'n we had more help, it'd be easier to get 'er done in that span."

"Forget it," Paul grumbled. "Not a chance we're letting anyone else free after Kaitlin made me crash the car."

"It's not my fault," Kaitlin snapped, "that you can't focus well enough to drive straight when my power goes active. Thanks to you, I didn't even get anything out of it."

"Great." Bobby stared off at something else, not really paying attention to the bickering. His mind moved on other things. Like how to get where they needed to go and do what they needed to do. "Is the car dead?"

"Yes. Kaitlin killed my car."

Kaitlin reached over and smacked Paul in the arm. "Whatever. It was already making a funny noise and probably older than you. Quit whining. The bigger problem is we have no transportation and a time limit. Why do we only have that long?"

Bobby shrugged, unwilling to get into it. "Life's like that. I can get me gone no problem, you lot are gonna have to walk until you find something." He crunched into the apple again and had another thought. "Or maybe see if Riker will give you a ride or something. Your phone," he said to Liam, "has bells and whistles, don't it? The places I got to try are White Sands, Groom Lake, and Adelphi. I know where the first one is, I been there. The other two, I got no idea."

Liam tapped on his phone. "Groom Lake is a military base in southern Nevada, also known as Area 51. Adelphi has too many options."

"Area 51 is real?" Paul peered at Liam, echoing Bobby's skepticism.

"Apparently." Offering his phone so Paul could see for himself, Liam went back to nursing what must be a headache of serious proportions.

"Where's White Sands?" Paul looked the map over, holding it so Kaitlin could see, too.

"New Mexico. Which ain't far from Nevada. You all could work the Adelphi angle while I get myself out west and check those places out."

"I don't think so," Liam growled. "You're not leaving my sight again."

Bobby huffed. "I came back, didn't I?"

"Doesn't matter. If you're going, so am I."

"You can't leave me alone with this." Paul indicated Kaitlin with a little jerk of his head.

Kaitlin rolled her eyes again. "Like I want to spend my time with you, either."

His hands too full to rub his face, Bobby sighed. "Look, I can fly. Can any of you? We don't got time to wait for whatever you can do to get a ride to someplace worth being. I coulda just took off and left you here, but I didn't. I came over to tell you what's up. I ain't your enemy, we're on the same side. All I want is all of us free and not being used against our will. Ain't no more complicated than that. Everything I done's been about that, whether it seemed like it or not."

Kaitlin got to her feet and picked up her bag from where it lay on the ground behind her. "You guys can keep me as a hostage against his word if that's what it takes."

"All it will take is one stupid phone call," Liam said irritably, taking his phone back from Paul, "and we'll be on our way as soon as a tow truck can get here."

Bobby lifted an eyebrow, wondering if he was the only one feeling like a healthy dose of paranoia would a good idea. "You planning on using your name and all, let Privek know you been here? I'm sure he won't notice, won't read nothing into it. Ain't nothing wrong with you going for a joyride and needing a tow truck out near Culpeper, where there just happens to be a facility Elena was in until two days ago."

"I hate you." Liam grumbled it with no real heat and stuffed his phone into his pocket.

Poor guy had to be in a lot of pain, and he even get his girl back yet. "Yeah, yeah." He waved that off and fixed Liam with a dead serious look. "We'll find her, man, I promise, and you'll get her back. Don't know how, but I got this far. Ain't gonna give up now."

Chapter 2

"So, there he goes. We're never going to see him again." Liam rubbed his aching head as he got to his feet with Paul's help.

"If there's any one person you can trust to stick to the mission of 'rescue the girl', it's Bobby." Kaitlin smirked and led the way back to the road, peering down the direction they'd come from.

"What are you looking for?" Liam had so many bumps and scrapes that he felt like a walking ache from head to toe. Some of it had healed when he took on Paul's injuries, but not much. His power sucked.

Kaitlin waved at someone and walked down the road in the other direction. "Traffic, duh."

"Why are we going this way? Culpeper is back that way."

Paul still scowled at her. "She saw something, just now. I can tell."

Kaitlin pursed her lips and waited a second or so before answering. "Yeah. I saw Riker, pointing this way. Across the road."

"But your mind went wonky for a second," Paul insisted. "What did you actually See? "

"Why, did it make you want to crash your legs?"

Paul growled under his breath. "If you hadn't killed my car, we wouldn't be in this situation."

"If you had the balls to handle the unexpected, your car would be fine."

These two might kill each other, unless he killed them both first. Liam took a deep breath to push aside all the pain so he could try to make some peace, or at least shut them up for five minutes. "It doesn't matter. What we need is to get back to DC, as soon as possible. Someone's going to notice Bobby's missing at some point, and if we're not accounted for, we're going to be the prime suspects. Did you see anything that will help us get there?"

"Yes." Kaitlin looked both ways before jogging across the road, beckoning them to follow. The driveway she went up belonged to the next property over. He followed her and so did Paul, figuring that getting anything more would to be similar to trying to get his mother to eat at a greasy spoon diner: close enough to impossible as to not be worth the effort.

She led them a short way past a gap in the wall of trees and shrubs to absolutely nothing, where they stopped and looked around. "Something is going to happen here, right?" Liam was starting to think he'd entrusted his fate to a lunatic.

This time, she skipped the sarcastic reply and only nodded. She stood there serenely, like everything was right with the world, and everything she expected to happen was happening. Liam couldn't see any reason not to, so he sat down and put his head in his hands, wishing the precog had the foresight to bring a bottle of aspirin. Seriously, if she knew so much, how come she didn't see that? She brought clothes for Bobby, after all. He also wished he could get his head to stop playing light jazz in the background, which it had been doing for a few minutes now.

"Liam, can you stop…thinking so much?" Paul stood with his hands crossed and a grumpy frown on his face.

"Given the alternative of being a blank, drooling moron, no, I don't think I can." He heard Kaitlin snort. "I think you need to work on your shielding. The crash must have jarred your concentration more than you think. I can hear music."

Paul blushed bright red and mumbled an embarrassed apology. Putting his hands on his head, he paced several steps away, then turned and came back.

After a minute of merciful quiet passed, a blue sedan pulled in and Riker leaned out the window. Bewildered by this turn of events, Liam stared stupidly as Kaitlin took the passenger seat, leaving the back for him and Paul.

Riker gave him an expectant look, which shook Liam awake. He got to his feet, hurried over, and got in. Mindful that his ability didn't really protect him from anything, he put his seatbelt on.

"What're you doing?"

"Helping." Riker backed the car out, choosing the direction Kaitlin pointed him in, away from Culpeper. "This is bullshit duty and I know it, so does the rest of my team. We know something's going on, and trust Bobby. Even if this means we get branded as traitors, we want to do what's right, not what we're told. Where are we going?"

"That way," Kaitlin said, pointing straight ahead.

Liam glanced back and saw another car falling into line behind them. The driver gave him a perfunctory wave. He waved back out of habit and settled into his seat, facing forward. Bobby was more dangerous than he thought. Not because he killed people—Riker did that for a living. Because he was so damned likeable and believable. He had that harmless good guy routine down pat, so sincere Liam thought the guy believed himself. "This is getting out of control."

"You healed me," Riker reminded him amiably. "I was given

an option to either keep my mouth shut about that or be charged with treason. Bobby and Stephen asked me politely to keep my mouth shut about them and what they did to free us. Guess which one I trust more."

Now he stood firmly on the other side. There wouldn't be any going back. He wanted proof and hadn't gotten it yet. He still switched sides anyway. Heaving a sigh, he rubbed his eyes. They ached as much as everything else. More than anything, he wanted Elena. He never knew how badly he needed someone until he had her, and then she was gone, disappeared so abruptly he worried he'd dreamed her up. For all he knew, he'd sent Bobby off on a wild goose chase, searching for a figment of his imagination, one that laughed and danced and made him willing to do nearly anything to get her back.

"We should go back." Even the stupid tree-lined road made him think of Elena, mostly because he wanted to watch her watching it. She'd love this, all the vibrant life streaming past. Who knew what she'd see in it that he didn't. "To the facility in DC, I mean. And by 'we', I mean Paul and I."

Paul made a small noise of discomfort beside him and pressed the heel of his hand to his forehead. Liam snapped his head to Kaitlin and watched tension seize her shoulders. Paul was a precognitive vision detector, apparently.

"No," Kaitlin said as she relaxed, "we don't want to go there. We need to go someplace else. Riker, does 'Adelphi' ring any bells for you?"

"That's where the Army Research Lab is based. A couple of the cars that come and go from this site have parking stickers for it."

"That must be it, then." Kaitlin turned around in her seat and fixed Liam with a square look. "She's there, I know it."

Dear God, he thought, let it be true and a lie. "What—" His

voice cracked enough that he had to cough to clear his throat and start over again. "Is she okay?"

"She's alive, I can say that much for sure. Her condition—" Kaitlin pursed her lips. "What I see, it's going to happen unless we change something, but there's no way to know if we're actually changing something or doing what will make the thing happen, not unless I can see a cause-effect chain with a link I can break. Like, I saw a car crash for Lisa once, so I told her not to get in the car, but I couldn't have said whether it mattered if she got in the car and chose a different destination, or left an hour later, or anything like that. All I could see was that if she got in the car, she was going to die."

Liam nodded. He tried not to think about the ramifications of someone having that kind of ability, because he wasn't interested in examining his beliefs and feelings about religion and predestination and the rest of it right now. Elena made him want to believe in God wholeheartedly, if only so he had someone to properly thank for nudging her into his life. "Just tell me. I need to know."

Kaitlin left a long pause—long enough to make him want to grab her and shake until the words fell out—before she said, "She's working for them, using a computer a lot. She's about to stumble across something she doesn't understand and take it to her boss. Whatever it is, he tries to get her to just ignore it, but she won't, because it has your name in it. He—" She turned away, settled back in her seat properly again. "It all goes downhill from there. In a bad way. But they aren't going to kill her."

Someone seized his heart and squeezed, trying to crush it. "Okay," Liam heard himself say in a strangely distant voice. Part of him panicked. The rest tried to think of a way to get around whatever awful thing Kaitlin had seen happening to her. "Then we should hurry. I can call someone, get reinforcements or other help."

"Who're you going to call? The Ghostbusters?" Kaitlin

snorted to further express her disdain for his idea. "We've got Riker and his guys, they can get us into the facility. Paul can do his thing. I'd rather not go in, but the alternative is standing around by myself, which probably isn't a good idea."

Paul put a hand on Liam's shoulder. "We'll get her out," he said softly. "We'll be in time. I'll do whatever we need to make sure it happens." Turning to Riker, he said, "Put the pedal to the metal. I'll handle any cops that take an interest."

He'd do anything to get her free—anything at all. If the rest of these people wanted to get dragged down with him, that was their choice. He wouldn't force them. He wouldn't turn them away or try to run off without them, either. Seriously, he was about to break into a military research facility. He needed all the help he could get.

Chapter 3

Bobby headed for White Sands, Liam's phone number on a slip of paper in his pocket. His gut said Groom Lake was more likely, but the Missile Range had unfinished business, of a sort, and he wanted to finish it. It was dark when he flew over the main clump of buildings at White Sands. The place had enough streetlights that the dragons could see just fine where to go, and they dove into the ventilation system. Just because he didn't have much ability with a computer didn't mean he couldn't find anything. This entire place would be checked over, inside and out, and nothing was going to stop him. If Elena was here, he'd find her.

The swarm spread out, as it had in those small towns in Afghanistan. Freaky nightmares aside, that felt like it happened a lifetime ago, even though only about two weeks had passed. Here, no space would be left unexplored with them on the job, and Bobby waited for them to get it done. The only things he cared about right now were finding Elena and not being noticed, though he did make a point to be really clear about how no one should be attacked or killed.

While they worked, he floated in the middle, trying not to let either the dead stares of those kids or Sebastian's wailing replay in his head. The first one he couldn't do anything about except deal with it. As for the second… He should have pushed harder for him and his momma to get freed, though he could well imagine they'd be under more intense security than him. After all, he'd only been a thorn in Privek's side. Lily had proved they could pass the eyes—and maybe their superpowers—on to children.

At least this time, he'd been awakened on purpose by someone without a grand plan beyond finding a girl. If Privek had set this up somehow, he'd done it to mess with Liam and Paul, not him. To heckbiscuits with Privek. No way he gave everyone at that house in Virginia instructions on how to deal with that kind of questioning just in case someone showed up and asked about Elena. Actually, now he thought about that, it was possible. Sounded like an awful lot of excessive paranoia, though. Privek hadn't displayed that before. Instead, he'd carried out plans and reacted.

His dragons found a lot of sleeping people, but none of them were pretty Spaniards. None of the awake people were Elena, either. The foray didn't take long, and he sent the swarm out to check on the outbuildings, several structures scattered about the rest of the base. Each of them was set up with a fair amount of security and intended for a different project. He knew this from his last visit.

For the sake of being thorough, he sent them through both the Maze Beset buildings, knowing he'd find one empty. The other one not only had been where they'd met Mike, but also housed a project trying to recreate some kind of space-time thingumbobbadoodle. Stephen and Sam understood it better than he did. Actually, probably everyone understood it better than he did.

Speaking of that Mike guy, one dragon found him. He sat in the break room with a sandwich, reading a book with no one else around. Guy must not have any friends. Maybe that was why he had been willing to follow Sam out instead of calling security to haul her off. Bobby figured introducing himself ranked low on the list of Intelligent Things To Do. Mike might know something, though, or hear something later and be willing to pass it along.

Bobby jumped into the dragon and landed it on the table. Engrossed in his book, Mike failed to notice it. He had the dragon tap a claw on the table, then chirp.

"What's…" Mike lowered his book. "Oh my God. Um, Sam? Are you here?" His eyes darted all around expectantly.

The swarm converged on the room while Mike watched, his mouth falling into an 'o' shape. Bobby re-formed and held up his hand in greeting, pointedly not smirking. The one dragon flew to him and merged onto the end of his thumb. "Hi there. Sam ain't here." Since Mike obviously thought of her, he decided to follow that bone. "She's in trouble, actually, which is why I'm here. I need your help."

Mike hesitated for only one second before he grabbed his book firmly and stood up straight and tall. Bobby got the feeling he'd march off to storm Fort Knox if he thought he'd find Sam trapped inside. The reaction seemed over the top, but who was he to judge what a guy would do for a girl after only meeting her once? "What happened? What can I do?"

"Can we talk private-like in here without worrying about nobody coming in?"

Mike scanned the room, as if he had to check for other people. "Yeah, everyone's gone for the day. I'm just running some test routines."

"Great." Bobby gestured and Mike sat down again with him. "My name's Bobby. I'm made of tiny little dragons. Sam's got a special ability, too. There's thirty-five of us in all, and there's somebody trying to mess with us. Doing a pretty good job of it, too. Sam and bunch of the others are locked up right now, and I'm working on getting 'em free. In order to do that, I gotta understand what all's going on."

He had Mike's rapt attention. "Were you all born like this?"

"That there is a pickle of a question. Suffice to say that we all been developing these abilities all sudden-like over the past few months. Don't rightly know why now. Don't much matter, neither. I gotta figure out the future, not the past. They're up to something, and I want to know what. You got any real idea what they're working on here?"

"Well, actually, I didn't know much until a couple of days ago." Mike stroked his chin thoughtfully. "The day before yesterday, there was a boom and the whole building rocked like an earthquake happened, then everyone was really excited. I really only work with data, inputs and outputs and manipulating it to do what they want. It wasn't ever necessary for me to understand the whole picture. Some of the project leads here were *so* excited by what happened, though, they started babbling about it. They've been trying to create a wormhole."

From the way Mike looked at him, Bobby got the impression this was a big deal, or at least interesting. His idea of wormholes involved worms making them in the dirt. This probably related to the stuff Hanamidi told them about. He didn't understand any of it then, either. "And that means…?"

"Okay." Taking Bobby's response in stride, Mike held up his book with one hand and fished his keys out of his pocket with the other. "Imagine the book is Earth and the keys are some other planet in the universe someplace." Mike took his keys to the counter and left them there, then returned with the book. "They're really far apart from each other. The distance is outside a human being's ability to actually comprehend. If you were to try to drive the distance in a car, it would take thousands of years."

"That's a long damned time."

"Yeah. Now, suppose you could somehow create a conduit between the book and the keys so that when something is put into it, it comes out the other end in just a few minutes. That would be pretty incredible, wouldn't it?"

"We're still talking about that thousands of years thing with the Earth and the other planet, right?"

Mike grinned. "Yeah. Essentially, on this scale, if I put my sandwich in the conduit, it would appear at the keys instantly."

"Okay, I got it. So, that's what they're trying to do. What happened day before yesterday? "

Mike retrieved his keys and sat back down. "They had a breakthrough. Apparently, there was some kind of event a long time ago where this wormhole opened and dropped some stuff on our side. Nobody knows if it was a freak natural occurrence or someone on the other end caused it somehow, or what, but they've been trying to reproduce it ever since. Really smart men have worked on it, like Einstein. No dice. They came up with all kinds of ideas, but nothing ever came close to working.

"Two days ago, they tried something and it was a partial success. They created a conduit through space." He paused. Bobby figured it was obvious he couldn't understand a technical explanation, so Mike needed to think about how to explain it in plain English. "Okay. Right. So, they made the tunnel. They dropped in a penny just to see what would happen, and it disappeared. A second later, the tunnel collapsed."

"That sounds kinda like a failure."

"If all you care about is the tunnel working," Mike shrugged, "then yeah, it is. They've never managed to get a stable tunnel for even a nanosecond before, though, and now they have tons of data to work with, so it's only a matter of time. Heh, so to speak."

Bobby sat there, not sure how knowing this helped him. It was interesting, and sounded exciting. He doubted it would help him with his current problems. This tunnel thing would have Elena, or anyone else he cared about, at the other end. "Alright. That's…real helpful." What was he going to do? Say it was useless information?

Mike brightened. "Good. Is there anything more concrete I can do to help Sam?"

Standing up, Bobby scratched the back of his head. "I don't rightly know. She's in a sort of a jail thing in DeeCee right now. I don't suppose you can get me into Area 51 so I can do a thing I gotta do there? "

"Seriously?"

Bobby chuckled at the comical amount of shock on Mike's face. "Yeah, I'm serious, but I think I can handle getting in on my own. Tell you what, though. Let me give you a phone number for a guy, name of Liam. He's trying to help me out, too. If'n a body can figure out how you can help, it'll be him. He's a pretty smart guy. I wouldn't call him from here, though."

Mike offered him a pen and Bobby scribbled the number down on a piece of paper. "I'll call him when I can. Is he like you?"

"Ayup, he's one of us." He offered his hand and Mike shook it. "You be careful. Folks been killed over this stuff."

"Really?" Mike gulped. "I'll, uh, not hop in my car and start driving, then."

"That's a good plan." Bobby couldn't think of anything else to say or do here, so he gave Mike an encouraging smile and broke apart into the swarm. As the dragons went for the ventilation system, he heard Mike gasp in wonder, a reaction he didn't mind at all. If he intended to be public like he kept saying he did, he'd need to get used to all sorts of reactions. But not now, not yet. It was too early. He still needed the element of surprise, and had no idea what Privek would do if he caught a video of dragons on TV. The agent had the others at his mercy right now, and he didn't dare take that kind of risk with their lives.

Outside, he reflected that coming here had almost been a waste of time. Closing the book on White Sands left him feeling accomplished, at least. It must have been a setup before, a way for Privek to get one of his people in with them so he could find their home. A home he could slip up to right now. The side trip would only take him about five hours. He'd likely hit Groom Lake in the middle of the day tomorrow, or he could wait until tomorrow night to hit the other base.

Except he did promise he'd be as fast as he could manage. Liam was counting on him to find her and free her. Though she didn't seem to be in much actual danger from Privek, the longer she stayed under his thumb, the longer everyone else did, too. Sebastian, Lily, Stephen, Jasmine, Hannah, Lily… All of them. He had thirty-four brothers and sisters and one nephew, and they all needed to be set free, even Liam and Paul. How fast or slow he sprang Elena dictated how fast or slow he sprang the rest.

He paused in Albuquerque long enough to graze on restaurant dumpsters and let the dragons strip a junkyard of what they wanted, then headed for Groom Lake. The scenery along the way, mostly empty desert, reminded him of fleeing Afghanistan and Turkey. He didn't want to think about any of that. The dragons didn't want him to think about any of that, either.

Chapter 4

The facility looked about how Liam expected it to look. His father's company did government contracting, it built things and had research divisions, and most of it looked a lot like this. The only notable difference was the soldier at the guard post taking Riker's ID and looking it over. Sitting beside him, Paul took deep breaths while concentrating, trying to manipulate the outcome of this brief encounter. For whatever reason, making a bunch of people ignore Bobby earlier had been easier than getting this one man to let them through.

"This isn't a scheduled visit," Riker told the guard. "Surprise inspection with civilian contractors."

Liam, busy dwelling on Kaitlin's words from two hours ago, perked up and realized he needed to play a part "Is there a problem?" He asked with an air of annoyance. He could do bored impatience, no problem.

"They usually put the names of anyone coming on my list, Sergeant." The guard's expression held a peculiar vagueness, and he kept twitching head. "This is a secure facility."

If only they had a clipboard. Liam pulled his phone out, hoping it would be good enough for the purpose, and pretended to take notes. In reality, he scrolled through his contacts to see if anyone could be useful here. Laurie owed him for fixing things up with her professor last fall, and her father happened to be an Admiral. He tried to imagine how to word what he needed, and couldn't come up with a way that didn't sound awful or go far beyond her debt to him. Also, he'd have to explain it out loud. The guard would catch on.

"Well, the security is clearly good, but it's not supposed to keep out people who should be here, only those who shouldn't be."

"He's resisting me," Paul muttered out of the side of his mouth.

"I'll just call it in," the guard said. "What name should I give?"

Liam seized the moment and ran with it. He gave the guard a sharp glare. "How about if I make a call instead, Private—" His eyes flicked to the name patch on the guard's uniform as he held up his phone. "—Hillson? Would you like to talk to General Hanstadt yourself, maybe make this go quicker?" He flicked his finger to scroll through his contacts list. The key was confidence, and Liam projected plenty of it.

Hillson swallowed and looked to Riker. Whatever expression the Sergeant gave him along with a curt nod, it convinced the guard. "Um, no, that's not necessary, sir. Sorry, Sergeant."

"It's okay, Hillson. Just doing your job."

"And doing it well," Liam added as he pretended to tap a note out on his phone. "Carry on."

The arm barring the way went up and Riker drove through. "Nice name drop," he told Liam as soon as the window rolled up.

Paul sighed. "His mind was too strong and alert, sorry."

"It worked out, nothing to apologize for." Liam noticed his hand shaking and gripped his leg to make it stop. He'd talked a lot of people into and out of things, but never anything with these kinds of stakes before. He took a deep breaths to calm himself.

When the car stopped, he was as ready as possible for the rest of this. "I think our best bet is if Riker and his men use their uniforms to get us through, and when that's not enough, I do the talking. You two back me up as needed. Okay?" He didn't really want to order them around. Kaitlin especially struck him as the type to dislike authority. Someone, though, had to step up, and this was his show. They came for him.

"Whatever." Kaitlin shrugged.

"Let's use channel four," Riker told his men. They all fiddled with something at their belts. "Hansen and Platt, you're our getaway drivers." He handed his car keys over to Platt. "We're not outfitted for a hostile entry, hopefully we won't need to be. If this thing goes fubar, aim to hurt, not kill. We're walking on the wild side here, but that doesn't mean we have to go all dark side."

The other four men nodded and two got into the cars while the other two fell in behind Paul and Kaitlin. Liam knew how to do this, leading a group of people through a facility as if he belonged there. Every other time he'd done it, he actually *did* belong there, because he'd been giving a tour of one of his father's company's buildings to Important People.

He still wished he had a clipboard. Especially when they greeted the first hurdle, the security right inside the front door. A soldier sat in a small booth on the other side of the door with glass between them and him. They could see the shiny, red button for opening the door, so close and yet so far away.

Riker knocked on the glass to get the guy's attention and stood there, staring at him like he ought to be expecting them and should just go ahead and let them in. "Surprise inspection," he barked, voice full of command.

The young soldier jumped and slapped the button. "Yes, Sergeant!"

Apparently, the guard held a lower rank than Riker. Liam didn't have much experience with such things and chose to be glad Riker obviously knew what he was doing. He grabbed the door as it buzzed and nodded his approval to the young man. Although tempted to praise the soldier's efficiency, he had a feeling that would cause problems and kept his mouth shut. Knowing when to *not* talk helped at least as much as knowing what to say.

"We're in," Riker muttered once they passed the guard post, presumably to let Hansen and Platt know.

"Take a left," Kaitlin murmured. They had no reason not to follow her directions, so Liam and Riker turned down the next hallway to the left. "Go in the next room on the right." This put them into a small office with minimalist furniture and no occupant. Kaitlin shut the door softly behind them all and stood there with her ear pressed to the door and a finger to her lips to shush them.

A glance at Paul confirmed for Liam that they did this for a reason—the telepath rubbed his temple and stood as far from Kaitlin as he could manage in such a small room. All his own aches and pains had faded into the background, completely overwhelmed by the rush of infiltrating a military facility pursuing secret research projects combined with the anticipation of seeing Elena again—finally—after a month apart.

He'd only met her two weeks before she was taken away from him. They'd been the most intense, wonderful two weeks of his life. After spending years chasing and being chased by skirts he had no real interest in and expecting his mother to find him a wife he'd have to settle for if he wanted to continue to live the lifestyle he'd become accustomed to, he'd fallen hard, in two weeks, for a woman he'd bumped into by accident. The thought terrified him and liberated him at the same time. But she was gone, and he'd done things he never would have otherwise to get her back. Like using his awful ability for total strangers, and breaking into a high-security military facility.

Would she still want him? He'd never been dumped in his life. His relationships—such as they'd been—always ended well, except for a few he had to get stern and unpleasant with. In those cases, it he'd done the dumping. The idea of Elena doing that to him crushed a piece of his soul, and he delicately avoided it. That she might be mad at him because of whatever Privek and his lackeys told her was fine, and he could live with it. Getting past those kinds of lies wouldn't be too hard. Dealing with the truth was always harder.

Kaitlin opened the door and walked out, beckoning for them to follow her. Liam let her lead without argument. She could, apparently, get them through this place without incident. For Paul's benefit, he spruced up his expression of blithe confidence as he followed Riker out. The telepath looked nervous and a little green around the gills.

"It's continuous right now," Paul breathed at him, staying by Liam's side. "She's walking around in the future or something. It feels like her mind is some kind of dragon that's going to pounce and eat me as soon as we both stand still."

Liam nodded to project more confidence than he felt. "It didn't happen in that room, so you should be safe. Stop fidgeting, it makes you look suspicious."

"First rule of not being noticed is to fly casual," Hegi murmured from behind them. "Act like you belong and aren't doing anything worth looking into."

"Easy for you to say," Paul grumbled.

Putting a hand comfortingly on Paul's shoulder, Liam leaned down and said, "Try imagining it's looking at something behind you it wants to protect you from."

The telepath blinked stupidly and whipped his head around.

Aside from nearly clocking Liam in the jaw, he found himself face to face with Carter, who managed to avoid walking into him. Liam rolled his eyes and shoved Paul to get him moving again.

Kaitlin ushered them all through a door with an admonition to be quiet again. This time, they crammed themselves into a janitor's closet. Unlike last time, they could all hear the muffled voices moving past the door.

"I can't believe they're doing another surprise inspection."

"Nobody can just trust us to do our jobs anymore, Jesus. It's like they *want* to find the stuff they don't want to know about."

"Where the hell *are* these people? We can't damned well keep them out of the black sections if we can't find them."

Black sections? Well, obviously, the government researched things they didn't want anyone to know about. He wondered if any of the experiments or programs related to them. It couldn't be a coincidence that Elena had been moved here. Well, okay, it could, but it would be exceptionally unfair if they couldn't kill two birds with one break-in. Besides, if he understood the very little Bobby had said, Privek's project managed this site, so it made sense to be related.

They'd been stuffed in so tightly that Liam half-tumbled out of the little room when Kaitlin opened the door. It almost felt like a madcap comedy, except he had no reason to laugh. Being in that tight space with five other people all worried about a hiccup or sneeze giving them away hadn't improved his already frayed nerves.

They kept going, down a flight of stairs, up a hallway, down more stairs, around and around in what seemed to be a giant circle, spiraling into the pit of Hell. The longer they walked, the more he wondered if this would turn out to be the biggest mistake of his life. Horrible things, the consequences of being caught down here without some kind of official authorization, danced through his head, getting progressively more unpleasant with every minute that passed.

Glancing at Paul, he noticed an obscene amount of tension in the other man's shoulders and a tight, pinched look on his face. Walking beside a frantic ball of worry probably made things worse for the telepath. He stopped himself from apologizing and instead groped for something else to focus on than how horrible this situation could become.

Elena, the reason for this whole disaster in the first place, came to mind. Instead of thinking about how much he missed her, or how much she panicked him overall, he thought about her face, her laugh, her smile. With her wide hips and strong nose, she would never qualify as conventionally pretty. To him, she stuck out as the most beautiful woman he'd ever met.

She'd be the first person to tell him to stop being stupid, and to stop worrying so much about something he had no control over. Her finger would lay over his mouth and shut him up, and she'd dance for him. With that thought came the memory of their first night together, spent in a grotto he never would've found without her.

The two of them lay on a bed of moss together, a gap in the rock overhead showing him more stars than he'd ever seen before. They huddled for warmth when the temperature dropped unexpectedly. Dazed by the incredible whirlwind that had fallen asleep in his arms, his heart swelled with the strange knowledge that he felt more connected to her without sex than he'd ever felt with any of the girls he'd jumped into bed with.

Somehow, the Spaniard who'd stopped randomly to ask him for help that morning had turned out to be everything he wanted. He stroked her hair and sighed. For once, he had no audience or expectations, and it allowed him to relax. That forgotten feeling surging through his veins was so strange that it took him several minutes to identify uncomplicated happiness.

Kaitlin stopped abruptly at a set of thick metal fire doors, jarring Liam out of his reverie. "From here, there's no evading anymore. Riker, you guys will just have to punch people. I don't see any way around that. There are cameras. I know how to shut them off, but that will bring people down here, expecting something's going on. We need to go into the third door on the left. That's not where Elena is. She's through the second door on the right. We'll have to grab her after. I'm not sure what's through the other door, just that we have to go in there. Maybe there's someone in with Elena that we need to avoid."

Everyone looked at Liam. He could tell. Taking a deep breath, he nodded. "Okay. You haven't led us wrong yet, I trust you."

"Good." Kaitlin gave him a firm nod. He wondered if she knew how to smile without it being a smirk. Probably not. "Because I'm not trying to screw with you, I just want to get out of here in one piece."

"Seconded," Riker said. "No shooting if we can avoid it down here. No telling what or who you might hit." He, Carter, and Hegi all switched over to their pistols, safeties on, letting their rifles hang from the straps across their bodies where they wouldn't get in the way.

Paul swallowed nervously as he watched them. "Didn't you just say 'no shooting'?"

Riker got a half grin. "They make good substitute brass knuckles in a pinch." The statement made Paul go pale, and Kaitlin smirked. For his part, Liam just nodded, because if he said anything, it would probably be a whimper or squeak.

"We'll follow you three in," Kaitlin said confidently. How did she manage to stay so calm? Did she know this would work out okay, making panic seem foolish? Maybe she just knew she'd be alright. That struck Liam as a lot more likely, given what he'd seen so far. "The panel to disable the cameras is on the other side of these doors. I'll take care of that."

Carter moved up and grabbed the handle for the fire doors, waited for the go ahead from Riker, then heaved it open. Riker and Hegi slipped inside. Carter followed right behind them. Kaitlin stopped Liam and Paul from following immediately. She counted to ten, then opened the door and darted inside. Liam looked at Paul, who happened to also look at him, and wondered if his own face held as much panic as the telepath's did. Hopefully not.

For a long moment, they both stood there. Then Liam, bolstered by the notion he'd find Elena through there, grabbed the door handle and yanked it open to see the three soldiers dragging bodies through the first door on the right while Kaitlin clicked a panel on the wall shut. "None of them are dead," Kaitlin whispered. "Come on, no dawdling, this'll be noticed pretty soon."

Liam held the door open for Paul, who came through it reluctantly. They followed Riker past the second door on the right. No one else so much as looked at it. Liam couldn't stop himself from staring, wondering, and stopping. The rest of them kept going while he put his ear to the door. He heard noises on the other side, too muffled to decipher. His heart beat so fast he thought he might explode. Right then, he knew that, no matter what he'd said, he could not leave this door, not even with a gun to his head.

Glancing up and down the hallway, he noted he hadn't been missed yet. Paul was probably too scared to keep track of him, and the others focused on what lay ahead, not behind. He grabbed the knob and threw the door open. There she was, like Kaitlin said she would be, only he couldn't have prepared for the incredible amount of anger tearing through him at what he saw.

The room resembled a doctor's office, with cabinets and a chair, and a rolling bed instead of a fixed exam table. The walls had even been painted a soothing light minty green color, with darker mint trim. Between himself and Elena, a man stood with his back to the door, wearing a lab coat that didn't hide the light bruising on his right hand knuckles. To complement them, an ugly purple splotch tainted Elena's dusky skin around her eye, blood stained her lower lip. She'd been knocked out cold, and her attacker held a needle. Once he profaned her hand with it, that needle would probably be attached to the IV bag at the head of the gurney.

The guy in the lab coat turned and frowned. "Who are you? You can't—" His eyes snapped to Liam's, then widened in surprise and horror. It might have had something to do with the pure rage unfurling in Liam's chest, because that had to be written across his face. Instead of backing away like a sane person should, the very average guy with glasses put up his hands and blocked Liam from coming in any further. "You shouldn't be here. Get out. She's not your concern."

How dare he. Liam had no need to assert his manhood and didn't feel he owned Elena. But he loved her, and seeing her like that, when this man obviously did it to her… And now he tried to shove Liam away, to get him to leave Elena behind. No damned chance.

Brawling didn't come naturally to Liam. He'd never had trouble defusing the sorts of situations he found himself in where such things might happen, and thus never had a need to learn to fight. Despite that, Liam threw his fist at the man's face. There would be no chitchat here.

So much adrenaline pumped through Liam's body he didn't feel the impact as anything more than a confirmation of a solid blow. He used his body to shoulder the man into the wall and hit him again, wanting to make him hurt a hundred times worse than what Elena felt from the blow she took. Idly, part of his brain noticed the sudden end to the dull throbbing he'd managed to push into the background during the car ride. The hundred little aches from the crash evaporated. He felt good, in fact, aside from wanting to kill this man.

The moment he realized he actually *could* kill this man, Liam stopped and let him fall to the floor, panting from the exertion. He was in good shape, but had never done anything like this before, ever. Elena's attacker crumpled to the floor in what seemed like slow motion, with cuts and bruises on his face that seemed oddly similar to the ones he himself had suffered in the crash. That little slice there was eerie. Liam reached up to touch his own face with smooth, perfect hands where his own slice should be, only to find more smooth, perfect skin.

He'd transferred his wounds to someone else. The thought made him go cold all over and stumble backwards until he bumped into Elena's gurney. He could take the wounds of others and regenerate the injuries, or he could take his own wounds and give them to someone else. God, that was scary. Worse, almost, than just healing people. Could he take someone else's wounds on himself and pass them on before he healed them? Could he bring someone back to life by killing someone else?

He didn't want to think about it. Turning, he let all that wash away at the sight of his girlfriend, lying unconscious with a bruise on her cheek. His fingers brushed that bruise lightly, pulling it out of her, along with the concussion keeping her down. His head split with a blinding ache for a few seconds. He'd gladly take it for an hour in exchange for seeing her eyes flutter open and her lips smile at him.

"Liam, what did you do?" Paul stood in the doorway, staring at the downed man in horror.

Scooping Elena up into his arms and holding her tightly, Liam heard himself say dully, "He hit Elena."

"Oh." Paul gulped and gave a weak chuckle. "Remind me never to say anything rude to her. We need to move, though. Before someone comes along and—"

"What's going—" Too late. A guy in a lab coat peered inside and blinked, then turned to run.

"I'll handle it," Paul said, sounding really glad to have something to distract him from the contents of the room. He turned away, leaving Liam and Elena alone again.

"They told me—" She barely spoke English and he barely spoke Spanish, so they used French. His mother had made him learn it, and he'd never been more appreciative of that than since he'd met Elena.

He put a finger on her lips. "It can be no worse than what they told me. They lied to us both." All his life, he'd chased blondes, women who looked like his mother. Sometimes he entertained a brunette or a redhead, but he couldn't ever get blondes out of his system. Now, he had the most lovely woman imaginable, and she had such dark hair, dusky skin, brown eyes. For those two weeks, he took her for granted, but after a month forcibly apart, he never would again.

"I worked for them." She held onto him as tightly as he held onto her.

"I know. We're going to make sure this never, ever happens again. We have to leave, though, and hurry." He had to force himself to let go of her, and only managed it because he could take her hand. They hurried out of the room together.

Chapter 5

Bobby skirted around the bright lights of Las Vegas until he found the installation he'd come looking for. They hadn't bothered trying to hide it from above. The airstrip even had its lights on tonight. As the swarm slipped up on the buildings, of which it had fewer than White Sands, he noticed a small plane-thing taxiing into position to take off. That explained the lights. The craft had a weird shape. They must've been doing a test flight of some fancy new aircraft. That explained the choice of night for the flight.

Nothing about this base from above, however, explained how much fervent conspiracy theory surrounded it. The installation appeared to be nothing more than an experimental aircraft testing facility. It had a few hangars, an air traffic control tower, emergency services, housing, and a few other buildings that probably served the other basic needs of the folks stationed here. Putting it out in the middle of nowhere meant less danger to regular folks if anything went really wrong, and their planes and stuff could stay out of normal commercial air traffic lanes.

Of course, he'd been created by a top secret cross-species breeding program, and had no idea what kind of facility the actual process had been carried out in. His mind supplied a darkened room full of men wearing glasses and surgical masks, playing with medical equipment and shipping the engineered embryos out for implantation in special orange coolers labeled *live organs* or *biohazard*, or whatever else would keep anyone from opening them up for inspection. In this fantasy, the room existed inside a decrepit old warehouse, one easy to ignore as another example of urban blight. Atlanta had places like that.

The dragons wanted him to quit it. Letting his imagination run with the idea distracted and irritated them. Time to focus on searching for Elena. He sent the swarm in to infiltrate the place, looking for her and for anything else interesting, though he had low expectations. It surprised him when one dragon vibrated with excitement.

He threw himself into that dragon to see what it found. It had buzzed into a site building. From the outside, it appeared to be an ordinary storage warehouse. Inside, as expected, it had rows of shelving full of boxes and crates. The dragon directed him to the back corner, where he found an elevator. Its housing had no room to go up, only down.

This certainly qualified as something interesting. Why didn't any of the other dragons find anything for an underground facility? It should have ventilation, their favorite way to get into places.

If it had originally been set up as a nuclear fallout shelter, something he remembered seeing crappy videos about in school, it might be sealed and not vent to the surface. Though he had no idea how that might work, it seemed plausible.

He grumbled, not sure how to breach such a place without being noticed. The elevator doors had a keypad next to them, which meant a code, and he had no way to guess, hack, or otherwise get around that. The dragons flew all around the housing for the elevator, looking for ways inside it without finding even so much as a tiny crack. There must be some way to service the thing, but he didn't see anything like an access panel.

So far as he could figure, he had two options. One, he could sit around and wait for someone to either come in or leave. The other involved a lot of trying to disguise himself and convince someone to escort him down there.

By the time he'd given up on the idea of faking his way in, the sun had crept up, making the waiting option seem perfectly reasonable. People working at a place like this probably got started pretty early in the morning. He remembered his Daddy—when he'd been stateside—having to be at work by six, so he got up much earlier than Momma did. Bobby sometimes got up early so he could spend five minutes with the man while he ate his breakfast and packed his lunch, then he'd watch him drive away and go back to bed.

Should he take the whole swarm, though, or just bring the one dragon? With one dragon, getting caught seemed less likely. On the downside, he wouldn't be able to talk to anyone. Though that might work in his favor, he had a feeling he might want to chat with Elena when he found her. At the very least, she'd recognize him as… the guy with that vampire who knocked her unconscious by drinking her blood. Suddenly, he felt confident this would go sideways no matter what he chose. Might as well drag the whole swarm down there, so he had as many options as possible when he got an opportunity.

It only took a few minutes for the swarm to converge, and he tried not to think too hard about how much he would like to have his Army desert camouflage uniform right now. He could have gone to the farm first and picked it up. But if he had, he wouldn't be here now, he'd be here at lunchtime instead. These folks might not leave until late in the day; who knew how dedicated they were to their jobs or when they actually all went down there.

A few minutes later, he appreciated his choice more, as a group of three men walked in and headed for the elevator. Two wore regular Air Force uniforms. At least, he thought they were Air Force. His Daddy was a Marine and he knew those uniforms. He sometimes got the other branches' uniforms mixed up.

As for the other guy, Bobby didn't consider himself a fashion expert, but he was pretty sure no one wore ties that wide anymore, and he thought slacks ought to reach all the way to your shoes. Light blue and blood red argyle socks clashed horribly with the brown of his suit. His graying dark hair hung long and loose and, combined with his somewhat scraggly beard and thick rimmed glasses, made him seem averse to the concept of a mirror, and of personal grooming in general.

All three men had ID cards on lanyards around their necks. When they reached the elevator, chatting about the weather forecast for the weekend, the guy in the suit punched a six digit code in, which made a panel slide to the side. He held up his ID card to the new black panel and bent enough to let it examine his eye. A little light went green, a little *bing* announced the arrival of the elevator, and the doors slid open.

He saw no space between the doors and the shaft, and he'd never get more than one or two into that elevator without them being noticed. So much for sending in the whole swarm. He picked one dragon, jumped into it, and flew it into the elevator. The rest got instructions to stay nearby and out of sight.

One of the two uniform guys stuck his hand out to stop the elevator doors from closing. "Did you see that?"

Bobby's dragon froze, hoping the carpet and brushed silver walls provided enough camouflage.

"See what?" The other man in uniform put his hand on the

gun belted at his waist and peered around.

The man in the suit looked serious as he asked, "Was it a UFO?" He barely managed to get the words out of his mouth before he cracked a grin.

First Uniform gave Ugly Suit a sour look. "I saw something flash in the light."

Second Uniform poked his head out through the doors and looked all around. "I didn't see anything, and I still don't."

Ugly Suit chuckled with a weird, snorting laugh. "Maybe it was nanobot aliens, trying desperately to communicate with us."

First Uniform let out an aggrieved sigh. "You know, Doctor, this is why no one likes you." He pulled his hand back and waved to Second Uniform, who shrugged and stepped back in, letting the doors shut. The elevator moved downwards without them doing anything else. It had buttons, but none of them got pushed or lit up. Likewise, it had a display over the door that showed nothing.

"Ouch, that's not a nice thing to say." Ugly Suit didn't seem perturbed, just amused. "Seriously, though, what could you possibly have seen that the scanner won't pick up?"

Scanner? Bobby didn't like the sound of that. If they scanned the elevator for anything, they'd probably notice him in this one dragon. Without knowing what it would actually scan for, he couldn't say if climbing onto the nearest pant leg would do him any good.

The only way out here might be sacrificing this one dragon. He wanted to avoid that. Aside from how the dragon wouldn't like it much, he'd be left with an aching hand and no way down. He got the dragon to slowly inch its way to where the doors would open in the hopes it would be able to zip out before anyone or anything noticed him.

First Uniform huffed, then shrugged and crossed his arms. Second Uniform rolled his eyes. Ugly Suit continued to smile cheerfully. The elevator trundled downwards in silence for over a minute. From his distance to the rest of the swarm, Bobby guessed they'd gone ten or twelve floors underground when it finally stopped and the doors slid open. The dragon grabbed the bottom of the door and rode it open. It waited for the three people to walk past, then grabbed the pant leg of Second Uniform and held on for the ride.

He couldn't think of anything else he could do to defeat an unknown scanner, especially without being able to open the door at the other end of this brightly lit, blank white corridor. This strange, short, empty hallway actually reminded him of some movies he'd seen. In them, the hallway or room had hidden cameras all over the place, and that's where the scanning equipment was. Someone on the other end of those would check the people over and be able to kill or stun an unwanted intruder.

"Barnes, there's something on your left ankle." The voice came from nowhere in particular, with a bit of distortion, enough to make it clear the owner used some kind of device to get it into the hallway.

Bobby focused on not panicking while the dragon let go, darted up to the man's belt, and grabbed the edge. Barnes bent down and checked the hem of his pants.

"It's moved to your belt," the voice said, "in the back."

Before the dragon could decide where to go next, a hand smacked it. "I've got something," Barnes said as he managed to grab the dragon and pulled it around in front of himself.

Afraid the dragon would be crushed, Bobby took over and refused to allow it to struggle, bite, or burn. Appearing harmless seemed like the best way to avoid disaster here. He hoped Barnes had kids or found himself around kids frequently. Under his orders, the dragon stayed still as Barnes used both hands to keep it contained. An eye peered inside the dark space.

"It looks kind of like a toy." Barnes sounded confused. "I have no idea how it got there."

"You'll have to be detained, Barnes. Put it in the box."

"Seriously? I really have no idea what this thing is, or where —"

The voice cut him off again. "You know the rules."

Barnes sighed heavily and dumped Bobby into some kind of glass or clear plastic box. It slid into the wall and a cover blocked out the light and his sight of Barnes. The box kept moving in the darkness. Bobby had the dragon knock on the side and scratch at it, finding it to be solid and stronger than he could affect.

The last time he'd felt this completely trapped had happened years ago, when some kids beat him up for no reason other than being scrawny. That time, he'd crawled away with two cracked ribs, more bruises than a body could shake a barrel of hissing cats at, and a bunch of bleeding cuts all over the place. He had a rather strong feeling the likely outcome of failing to escape this situation would be at least as unpleasant.

The box slid out on the other side, into a less harshly lit room with computers and screens and people with earpiece headsets. Peering at him through the box, he saw a slightly overweight man with glasses in uniform, the chunky kind of guy Bobby would peg as a computer geek.

"Well, well, what do we have here? Hey, guys, take a look at this thing." At his gesture, two other men, also in uniform, rolled their chairs over and peered at the dragon. Bobby kept it still, figuring performing for them would only earn this dragon a dissection. It was a little surprising he could hear them through the box—even though their voices were muffled, they were still perfectly understandable.

"A dragon bug? Freaky. And awesome."

"Why bother making it all detailed like that?"

"It looks more like a mini than a bug. What's a douche like Barnes doing with a mini?"

"Maybe it's supposed to throw us off."

"Crack it open and let's see if it's a bug or not."

The original geek appeared to weigh the options and shrugged. "I'm gonna go scan the bejeezus out of it." Geek Guy picked up the box and carted it elsewhere.

Bobby had no worries about where he'd wind up. What Geek Guy did with him when he got there mattered a lot more. He needed the box to get opened in a situation that allowed him to escape unnoticed.

Geek Guy stuck the box into a machine. For an eternity, Bobby saw lights of every color and heard a wide variety of sounds. He figured something on the other end would use whatever it collected from all that to decide what kind of animal, vegetable, or mineral the dragon should be categorized as. Though he doubted he'd understand any of it, he kind of wanted to see the readouts and reports.

Eventually, Geek Guy took the box out and set it on a table. Bending down, he peered at Bobby, his nose less than an inch away. "What are you, little dragon?" He shook his head and tapped the side of the box with one corner of his mouth quirked up in a smile. "Not giving you back, little dragon, but I don't think I'll turn you in, either. If you can keep a secret, so can I, and we'll just say you were destroyed."

It sounded like Bobby would get an opening to make a break for it at some point. It could wind up being long enough for his stomach to hate him. With the rest of the swarm up in that warehouse, though, he could easily go take care of himself. He only needed to have the dragon put into a situation where he'd have no reason to worry about it.

Geek Guy opened up the box and grabbed the dragon, which Bobby let him do, and stuffed it into his pants pocket. "It was nothing," Geek Guy told his coworkers as he returned to his post and sat down. The pocket got tight enough the dragon had to go flat to avoid potentially losing a wing, and couldn't wriggle out without alerting Geek Guy to its movement.

"Are you keeping it?"

"That would be against regulations."

"Uh-huh." The other guy sounded unconvinced, but didn't press the subject. From there, the conversation turned to their job, which apparently consisted of monitoring cameras and other things, as well as playing some sort of computer game involving shooting and blowing things up. It sounded positively boring to Bobby, so he left the dragon behind with instructions to stay still until he got back.

Returning to the swarm, he took stock of his options. This military base had nothing around it for miles and miles. He could either chance finding and not getting apprehended in the mess hall, or take off and leave his one dragon behind for a couple of hours.

He thought he remembered Jayce being from Las Vegas, which wasn't far from here. If he could find it, maybe Jayce's stuff would all still be at his place. Finding people hadn't been too hard when he'd done it before, and "Jayce Westbrook" sounded like an uncommon enough name to make it doable.

Determined, he left the base behind, flying up high enough to not be noticed, and spent the next hour heading for Las Vegas. There, he walked around, grabbing food out of the garbage and fending off weariness as he looked for a way to find Jayce's address. Once upon a time, he spent a few bucks to use an internet cafe for stuff like this. He didn't have a few bucks right now. He even checked all his pockets to make sure Kaitlin hadn't stuffed some money in them, anticipating his needs. She didn't see everything coming.

After spending a half hour walking around, he found himself in front of the Monte Carlo hotel and wandered inside in search of a drinking fountain and some relief from the heat. While there, he decided to try the "aw shucks" approach with an employee. No need to at being a hick, because he'd never seen a place as ritzy as this one before, and he naturally gawked all around at everything, from the marble floors to the glass chandeliers to the heavy wood and plush velvet furniture.

The front desk, made of polished dark wood, had him sticking his hands in his pockets to keep from accidentally touching and sullying it. It took him off guard that the cute girl standing behind it in the crisp uniform with her brown hair tied up neatly in some kind of bun smiled pleasantly at him, like he must be an honored guest. He guessed her to be about his age, probably a college student working her way through school.

"Hello and welcome to the Monte Carlo. Do you have a reservation?"

"Uh, no, I don't. Um, actually, I'm kinda lost. My buddy says to stop by if'n I'm ever in town, but I done lost my phone someplace 'tween home and here, and I ain't got no idea where to go. Any way you could maybe look up an address here in town for me? I'd bug someone else, but I got let out nearby and ain't got no clue where nothing else is."

Her polite smile crinkled, becoming more genuine. "Sure, I can do that." Leaning towards him, she lowered her voice. "Just don't tell anyone." She winked.

"I sure won't," he nodded with his own answering smile and echoing her volume, "and thank ya kindly. His name's Jayce Westbrook."

Her eyebrows jumped up. "Oh, you know Jayce?"

"Um, yeah," he answered warily, not expecting such a reaction. "That a bad thing 'round these parts?"

"No, not at all. He works here. Or, he did, anyway, until he got arrested. I'm supposed to call the police if anyone comes asking for him. But, you know, I don't really believe what they said, and…" She bit her lip. "You don't look like a terrorist."

Five hundred hotels in this town, and he managed to pick the one where Jayce had worked. "Huh. Weird. No, I ain't no terrorist. My Momma says I'm kinda a pain in the ass, though."

She flashed him a grin. "Sorry I have to be the one to tell you that."

"Yeah, it's okay. Guess I'm in Vegas with purt near nothing and knowing nobody." Why in the heckbiscuits was he hitting on this girl? He could feel himself putting on a kind of pout, trying to get a pity date. Lily did make it clear she wasn't interested. He still hoped and wished and wanted, and couldn't make himself give up yet. "I don't suppose you could look up his address anyway? If he done got out and just ain't ready to see about getting his job back yet, I can maybe still get a place to crash for the night."

"Well," she said with a sigh. "I don't need to." She grabbed a piece of paper, scribbled something on it, and offered it to him. "Look, if he's there, would you tell him—" She sighed again. "I know it was just a casual thing to him, but we had a really good time, and I thought maybe— I just— Would you ask him to call me?" Tapping her name tag, which read *Beverly*, she gave him a pleading look. "I'll listen, even if whatever happened while he was gone was really bad."

Bobby blinked and took the paper. Heck, even Greg managed better than him. Except Bobby, always except him. Everyone else got all the looks, everyone else smiled and got girls to shed clothes, everyone else didn't get into half as much trouble as he seemed to wander his damned fool head into. "Yeah, sure, I can tell him.

Beverly at the Monte Carlo says to get offa your ass and stop feeling sorry for yourself and give her a call. That about right?"

He successfully amused her again. "Yes, that's about right. Thanks. I hope he's okay."

"Me too." He used the slip of paper to wave at her, biting back the urge to ask if he could count on her as a backup option for tonight. He'd become a tomcat out on the prowl for some reason he couldn't put his finger on, and needed to stop that, right now. Maybe it only happened because he had nothing but a fight to look back on and nothing but more fights to look forward to.

HHurrying out of the place, he checked the paper. On it, she'd put directions with the address, to get from here to there. Next time he saw Jayce, he actually would tell him to give Beverly a call. She deserved that much, at least. Assuming he actually managed to find Elena so he actually could see Jayce again, which dawdling here didn't help in the slightest. He slipped behind a palm tree to cover himself breaking apart into the swarm, then swirling upwards to follow the directions from above.

Jayce had an apartment on the top floor of a decent four-story building. He got in without a problem to find it trashed. Someone went through it without much regard for his things, and Bobby got the distinct impression it had been the cops. His rent must have been paid up for a bit to keep the landlord from sweeping it all up into a dumpster.

Leaving the fridge alone seemed prudent—he couldn't imagine what might have survived this long in there, and had no desire to get a whiff of what didn't. In the cabinets, he found some cans and boxes of food. With a can of beans in one hand and fork in the other, he paced around the place, peering through the mess. He had nothing in particular to look for and only did it to not wonder later if he'd missed something by ignoring it.

The closet had dark suits and Bobby found a motorcycle helmet. Most of the debris came from magazines, mail, and the stuffing that had been ripped out of the couch and bed. His clothing drawers had been dumped out, too, along with a small collection of kitchen utensils. It interested Bobby that Jayce kept no knickknacks or other mementos, not even pictures stuck to the fridge or mirror. Then again, the cops might have taken some of it as evidence.

Until he headed into the bathroom to use it for its intended purpose, he thought he'd wasted his time coming here. That room had been taken apart like the rest of the place, but he found something unexpected along with the usual bathroom stuff. Sitting on the counter, someone had left a digital camera lying on its side, mostly covered by a towel. Had he found it in a different room, he would have dismissed it as unremarkable.

Leaving the can and fork behind in the sink, he picked up the camera and turned it on. The battery had plenty of charge left, and he fiddled with it until it showed him the contents of its memory card. The pictures went backwards in time, starting with a few of various things in the apartment when it was already mussed, then a handful of pictures from before they did anything, showing it all neat and tidy. After that, he found one in a very different location, of Jayce flanked by two suits in a room that reminded Bobby of the place he'd been interrogated when he'd first been picked up.

What struck Bobby about this picture was Jayce. He had a droopy and goofy look about him, one Bobby found weird and jarring on a man he'd never known to be a pushover or a heavy drinker. His posture entirely lack the solid, straight-backed professionalism the Native American man always had, even when he cracked jokes or batted his eyes at a pretty girl. Two suits flanked him, struggling under his weight without him resisting. One side of the frame had a sliver of another suit's arm.

As he stared at it, he noticed other details. That suit on the left had a familiar jawline, and had to be Privek. That guy showed up everywhere. How did he get from Vegas to Atlanta in time to pick them both up, and had he been there for Ai and Alice, too? He thought the one on the right might be Hagen, who seemed to be his favorite lackey.

In the new picture, Jayce stood with his back straight, glowering at the suit with his back to the camera. That suit had to be the one from the previous frame, this time captured with one arm raised, a hand reaching for Jayce's face. It took staring at the picture for nearly a minute for Bobby to decide the pose of the hand had nothing to do with slapping. The owner of that hand wanted to touch Jayce.

He also noticed something wrong with the hand, something weird about the skin. Where the shirt under the suit jacket ended, the skin tone almost matched Jayce's. It had some weird distortion, though. The camera had too small a screen to get detail beyond that.

No one with a hand like that had been there when Bobby got arrested. Privek grabbed him from the police station, took him to some other jail, made him change, then loaded him into a van for the most unpleasant and boring ride in his life. As far as he could tell, he could account for every minute of that journey except for the time spent sleeping. After he'd been stationed in that weird cell, he had missing time, yeah, but not before. At least, he didn't think so. Thinking back over the experience, though, he had to admit it had been a blur in some parts.

Jayce hadn't ever said anything about missing time or gaps in his memory. Did that mean it might have happened to Bobby without him realizing it? He did remember getting punched in the face by Privek. After that, he'd tried to talk to those suits, then he gave up. Maybe Jayce did more than wriggle a bit and try to chat them up, so they used a bigger gun. Or, maybe they saw him as a bigger threat to begin with because of his security guard background.

Bobby flipped through the last two pictures of Jayce as his normal self. Neither showed the mystery hand or its owner. He knew that person had to be important, somehow. Unable to come up with any brilliant ideas, he slipped the camera into his jeans pocket.

He'd discovered something, for sure. The trip to Vegas had been worth it. Now, he only needed to stuff his face enough to last however long he needed to in that one other dragons. Yawning, he gave the shredded bed a longing look. Later, he'd sleep. For now, he broke apart into the swarm, grateful it would keep him from noticing how much he needed to rest.

Chapter 6

His solo dragon had stayed in Geek Guy's pocket, stuck there. Bobby had good timing, though. After only a few minutes of listening to him lose at whatever video game they played on company time, Geek Guy announced he needed a break. Sitting around on his ass goofing off was, apparently, hard work. As soon as he got up, the dragon climbed up the pocket to stick its head out and look around.

The other two guys grunted. As absorbed as they seemed to be in their game, he chose not to take the risk they'd notice something small moving in their peripheral vision. This room wouldn't be the best place to get out and find the ventilation system anyway, since he couldn't see a vent.

Geek Guy used a different door than last time. This one opened into a hallway with other closed doors. At the end of the hallway, he went into a break room, a kitchen sort of space with a coffee machine and a fridge and a microwave. Bobby saw a vent near the ceiling and no other people, making it a perfect place to get out of the pocket and disappear.

The dragon flew behind Geek Guy's back and skimmed the ceiling to reach the vent, the wriggled through it. He flitted down the tunnels, checking every access point for anything worth seeing. The ductwork felt vast and cavernous, and the place had endless strings of offices and conference rooms.

Next, he found labs full of people in lab coats and face masks, all bent over glass tubes and big machines and microscopes. Nowhere did he find Elena. Until he checked the whole place, though, he wouldn't give up.

Which was why he found her. Not Elena—she definitely wasn't here. He found *her.* Slim and willowy, she sat in a floral print armchair, downcast and listless, folding a piece of colored paper carefully and delicately. Her skin looked almost translucent and her dull yellow hair hung limp and straight to her chin without bangs. They had her wearing a white t-shirt with an Air Force logo on the upper left, just above her minimal breast, and a pair of blue running pants.

He stopped and stared because of her eyes. The same as his own, as all of theirs, hers looked out from a face with high cheekbones and a more angular feel than any human he ever saw. Pointy ears just poked out of the curtain of hair. This woman had to be the one he'd been told about more than once, the one who started all of this.

His real mother.

Not only had he found her alive, he'd found her in the custody of the US military, as a prisoner. If he had to guess her age, he'd say somewhere in her twenties, though that made no sense. He'd been told they found her in Roswell, in the 40s or 50s. Had she been stuck in a prison since then?

Did this mean she had no unusual abilities, or did they keep her dosed up to prevent her from using them? Either way, he had to find a way to get her out of here. Even if he had nothing more in common with her than half his DNA and the military being interested in them both, he still felt that he owed her something. Blood is thicker than most anything, so the saying went, and if not for her, he wouldn't be. Besides, no one deserved to be stuck in a box just for being different.

He had one dragon to get her out. She wouldn't fit into the ducts, and even if she could, they didn't go anywhere useful that he'd found yet. As he'd suspected, this underground facility used some kind of closed system without a vent to the surface. It meant no way to get the rest of the swarm inside, which meant no way to actually break her loose. Nothing that he could think of, anyway. Leaving her here bothered him a lot, though.

Was this really any different from leaving the others behind? In fairness, he felt horrible about that, too, so it didn't really matter. If he could have, he would have grabbed them all and to heckbiscuits with Liam and his stupid girlfriend. But he wanted them all on the same team, he wanted not to have a rift between them all if he could help it. That led him to here, staring at his biological mother with no idea what to do about it.

He could get the swarm to bust into the place, but he couldn't carry a person that far, not up through that elevator shaft. No, he'd have to find a way to get someone to release her, or transfer her somewhere else, or something like that. Paul would be a big help. Or Sam—she could make fake electronically delivered orders. With the whole group, they could assault the place. Dammit, he needed backup.

No, he didn't. There had to be a way to get her out. Seeing her sitting there, like habit kept her going, like she'd forgotten the feel of the sun kissing her skin… It hurt him, someplace deep down. That kind of ache made no sense, yet he had it all the same.

Before he could eagerly drop to go meet her, the dragon noticed a pair of cameras in the corners. The next room had a sink, making it a bathroom. Odds were good they didn't let her have even a moment of privacy to use the shower, so whatever he decided to do, he needed to come up with a distraction to keep those three security guys busy watching elsewhere.

He went back to the next closest vent and found a soldier outside her cell—no matter how cushy the chairs, he considered it a prison—sitting at a table, reading a book. If she walked out, he'd stop her, so this guy needed a distraction, too. Checking the area over, he noticed a fire alarm on the wall and wondered how the base would react if he set it off. Would they evacuate her or focus on finding the nonexistent fire?

A real fire would cause more chaos, especially if he started several in different parts of the facility. He could do that. The dragon danced in lace, excited by the idea of actually accomplishing something and getting to her. Why did it care? Might as well ask why he cared, and he had no answer for that, either.

This place featured concrete, hard industrial floors, and fire retardant ceiling tiles. The furniture he saw everywhere but the cell had been made of metal and hard plastic. This guard had a paperback book, which made him think of paper, leading him to recall seeing garbage cans. They had more kitchen-style break rooms scattered across the place, too. He could probably find something flammable in those.

Now with a genuine plan, he zoomed around the base, randomly lighting up whatever would burn here and there and everywhere. Within thirty seconds of the first fire, alarms went off, then sprinklers made it rain inside. Despite the fires being small and put out almost as fast as he could start them, people shouted and screamed, grabbing up laptops and papers and running around. Since he didn't really want to destroy the whole place or cause a genuine fire, this was perfect. The security guys would have their hands full dealing with the chaos and panic, leaving them unable to do their real jobs adequately.

By the time he returned to her cell, he'd started more than twenty fires. The guard stationed outside set down his radio as Bobby arrived and hit the button to open the cell door. Bobby took a chance and swooped in behind him. "Asyllis, we're going to the bunker." He said "bunker" like it should have a capital letter. More importantly, it sounded like her name was Asyllis, which appealed to Bobby for no reason he could explain.

She took a spiritless breath deep enough to move her head. Her eyes blinked heavily. "No." The voice that made the one word was stale like cardboard, but he knew, somehow, that it could be musical and beautiful. It pissed him off that it wasn't.

The guard glared and made a fist. "It's kind of an emergency, and I'm not asking you. Get up, we're going. I'll use the stun stick if I have to." His other hand went to a baton on his belt with a button on the end of the handle.

Bobby refused to stand by and let the guard deliver on his threat, and he needed her to get up and leave the room. Only one solution came to mind: more fire. Dropping down fast enough to avoid notice, he blew fire at one of her chairs until it caught, and kept blowing at the chair until one of them noticed.

The guard made a wordless sound of unpleasant surprise, cuing Bobby to peer around the side. The dragon couldn't be hurt by fire, so he didn't care about the chair burning. Interestingly, it didn't seem that this room had any sort of fire suppression system. He watched the guard grab Asyllis by the arm and haul her out of the chair. She didn't resist. He wondered if she ever truly resisted anything at this point, aside from doing so to avoid moving.

Once on her feet, Asyllis stumbled after the guard while still watching the fire. A tiny flicker of fear crossed her face, so muted he thought she might be too dead inside to feel anything. Since the guard watched ahead, Bobby had the dragon fly out where she could see it. She stared at the tiny dragon, putting a hand out to let him land. Obliging her made the dragon happier than a biscuit in gravy. Recognition lit up in her face. Either she'd somehow seen one before, or guessed it would help her gain her freedom.

Nodding to the dragon, she closed her hand around it and moved more smoothly, like she decided to actually run with the guard instead of being dragged by him. "The Bunker is too far," she told him, "we should use the door, go to the surface. Who knows where the next fire will break out?"

he guard stopped running and Bobby heard them both panting. "You know you're not allowed up there."

"Please, Cander, I haven't seen the sun in so long, I've forgotten what it looks like. You did it for my safety, until the source of the mysterious fire could be determined. To protect the precious prize your superiors charged you with." The more she spoke, the more Bobby could hear her light accent. It was strange, foreign in a way he couldn't explain. Aside from the fact he figured she must be an alien, which completely explained it in every way. In light of that, she had a stellar command of English. Then again, she'd had a long time to learn it. With little else to do over several decades, he could probably master a language or five, too.

"I don't know, Asyllis. I could get into a lot of trouble. We should go to the Bunker." If he knew where it was, Bobby would take off and go set a fire in this Bunker to cross it off the list of Safe Places.

"I have no dignity left to shred for you, Cander. I beg you to just grant me this one small favor. Please." Bobby imagined her getting to the guy's personal space and trying her damnedest to appeal to his decency. He couldn't have resisted her even if he wanted to, and wished he could scream at Cander to give in already.

Cander didn't answer for one agonizing second that stretched into an eon. "Alright, but you have to stay close to me." They hurried on their way again.

"Thank you, Cander. Thank you."

"Don't thank me yet. For all I know, this'll make them think you're more trouble than you're worth."

No one accosted either of them as they moved swiftly through the halls. Bobby didn't feel like this might really work until they ran down that blank hallway and slid into the elevator. Apparently, he'd successfully managed to thoroughly distract the security guys, because they said nothing about Cander and Asyllis walking right out the front door with the strange dragon that had officially been destroyed and unofficially still sat in Geek Guy's pocket.

Bobby jumped back out of the dragon, certain it would stay there and be fine. No one else had evacuated to the surface, leaving Bobby free to re-form and walk right up to punch the soldier guarding Asyllis in the face. Too stunned to react, Cander stood there and let Bobby hit him again, then follow up with a third that knocked him down enough to keep him there for a short time.

"Asyllis, this here's a jailbreak."

She wasn't listening. She wasn't even standing there anymore when he turned to look. She'd walked out the door of the warehouse already, staring up at the sky. "It's so blue," she said softly.

He hurried to her side. "If'n you want to spend more'n a few minutes looking at it, we should grab a vehicle and get the heck outta Dodge. 'Less you can fly?"

"Fly?" She blinked and looked at him. "No, I can't fly." She stood at the same height as him, putting them eye to eye. Reaching for his face, she brushed her fingertips across his cheek. "Who are you?" To his joy, her voice gained more color and melody with every moment she spent in this patch of sunshine.

"This really ain't the time, but pretty sure I'm your son. If'n you got any special ways to get yourself away from here, you oughta pull it out, but if not, we gotta take care of that. Your other choice is going back inside." He jerked a thumb back towards the elevator.

She looked at Cander, still lying unconscious on the floor. "They won't let me go so easily."

"Yeah, that's what I thought about myself, but I done escaped. Ain't giving up now, not ever." Unsure how this would actually work, he offered her his hand.

Turning again, she gazed out over the base. "We may both be killed."

Was she trying to talk him out of it, or just making sure he understood the stakes? If anyone understood the situation, it was him. They were extremely lucky not to have sirens wailing already, and that the base hadn't yet been locked down with guys carting machine guns hoofing it all around. "Wouldn't you rather go down in the sun than waste away in the dark?"

A fierce grin transformed her into a warrior angel, a woman come down to kick some ass and not bother taking any names. She let go of the dragon and grabbed his hand, watching with wonder as it darted to his thumb and stuck back on. "You? You're the *drathiké*?"

Instead of answering, he ran, pulling her willingly along behind him. He already knew the layout of the base and took them to the motor pool. It had only a few vehicles, and a handful of dragons would have no trouble grabbing a set of keys. When they stood with their backs against the wall, waiting for his dragon scouts, he looked at her and nodded. "I'm them and they're me." It made no more sense now than it had before, but she had a word for them, which made him want to talk about it.

"How? How is that possible?" She touched the smooth stump of his wrist, running her fingers over it.

Why did he expect her to have all the answers? The question disappointed him. "No idea. I kinda thought you could tell me."

"Me? Why? I've never seen anything like this before. It's strange, bizarre. What are you?" The edge of disgust to her voice hurt to hear.

"I'm your son," he reminded her with a mild glare. "They done took your stuff and crossed it with human and made kids. There's thirty-five of us. None of us is your responsibility, but we are your kin."

"Why would they do such a thing?" She let go of him and sighed, staring off into the distance. "I had no idea. Not that I could've done anything if I did. I haven't been allowed outside since I was moved here, and I was drugged for that trip."

Whatever he expected, she failed to live up to it. He had to admit to himself that, fair or not, he thought she'd be a lot like his Momma. That noble woman accepted him immediately when he told her what he'd become. She also carried him and raised him and knew him. Asyllis, on the other hand, had nothing more than DNA in common with him. They were strangers.

"It kinda seemed like you cooperate with it all."

Before she came up with a way to respond, the dragons returned with a ring of keys. She watched his hand re-form with rapt attention. "Are the others like you?"

"Not exactly. But we gotta move now. There's a Humvee, I'll point to it. Move quick, just get right in and hopefully we'll be able to drive away before anyone realizes we shouldn't oughta."

They slipped through the cracked open door, moving low and quiet to avoid attracting the attention of the two soldiers inside. Bobby pointed to the vehicle he wanted Asyllis to get into.

A soldier jogged to the Humvee with a clipboard in hand. Bobby grabbed Asyllis before the soldier could notice them and pulled her down behind some barrels. The soldier hopped into the vehicle Bobby intended to take and did a bunch of things to start it up, scribbled something on his clipboard, then got out, leaving it running. That whole process took a couple of minutes. He watched the soldier just walk away from the running Humvee and frowned down at the keys in his hand, confused. Never mind. They'd never get a better opportunity than this.

Hauling Asyllis up, he practically threw her at the passenger door and ran around to the other side. Her door shutting must have echoed, because as he planted his butt in the driver's seat, a voice called out, "Hey, who're you?" Good thing he let the other guy start the Humvee up, because he saw nowhere to jam a key in, and it had all kinds of lights and switches and buttons. At least the shifter had labels, and he yanked on it, only to realize he had to push the button and twist the handle to make it move.

Despite the differences between the two vehicles, sitting in this seat reminded him of driving Lily's car, taking his turn to get her and her boy to the farm. He had things he needed to say to her, most of it an apology for being such a dumbass. If she gave him five minutes, he knew he could make things right with her. Probably. Maybe. So long as he didn't say or do anything else stupid. Probably not, then.

He needed to stop thinking about her. One of the soldiers came around the front of the vehicle with a gun out. Bobby did his best to not hit the guy as he slammed the gas pedal to the floor. "Hold on," he said. Asyllis already had her seat belt clicked in and she gripped the seat and door so tightly her knuckles went an odd shade of purple.

The reason for her distress probably involved the sight of the door ahead, only open about halfway and possibly not quite enough to get this thing through it. With the added obstacle of the soldier in the way, Bobby missed, slamming his side of the vehicle into the door. Unlike in the movies, the door failed to fly off. It did buckle enough to get through. The sound of metal scraping on metal grated enough that he clenched his jaw since he couldn't cover his ears. Somewhere in there, he started making noise to urge the Humvee on, as if him growling would make it go faster.

Gunshots announced the fact that the soldiers weren't going to just let them get away. Asyllis ducked down and covered her head with her hands like it would make a difference. Bobby swerved some, not sure if it helped, but at least they didn't hit the tires yet. This plan probably wasn't going to get them very far. He needed to think of something else to follow up with. Driving like this wasn't going to make that easy.

Glancing back to check on the soldiers, he caught sight of something wore: a small helicopter. He'd heard about drones, and guessed this one had either a camera or a gun. Both options sucked for them. Dragons could take care of it, but he kind of needed both hands to keep control of the Humvee.

"I'm not sure this is better than being locked up down there."

Bobby cranked the wheel and refused to give up.

Chapter 7

Another door down the hall stood open. Paul must have left it that way when he came looking for Liam. He pulled Elena through it, giving Paul space to muck around in that man's head. They slipped in behind the others, all staring through a pane of glass into a dim room.

"Hi, Elena," Kaitlin said offhandedly, only barely glancing back. "This is something, huh? Didn't see it coming, no idea what to make of it." She pointed at the glass, indicating the vast array of gurneys on the other side, most of them filled with people. There were at least two hundred of them, no more than ten or twelve empty. They held people of both genders and varying skin tones, though they seemed to all be in a particular age range: late teens to mid twenties. Each had a sheet for a covering and an IV bag going into a needle in their arm.

Elena blinked and waved uncertainly at Kaitlin's back. Liam squeezed her hand and tried not to be freaked out. "What are the chances this is actually of some interest to us?"

"I was sent here. There's got to be a reason." Kaitlin put a hand on the glass, her fingertips resting on it gently. She sighed and shook her head. "We have to free them."

Riker reached out to restrain her the second she started for the other door, the one that would let her into that room. "We don't know what's really going on here. If you go in there and just pull those IVs out, you could hurt them worse than leaving them there."

Kaitlin stared at him, then blinked. Paul whined behind Liam. "Dammit, does that have to keep happening, over and over?" He shivered and pressed a hand to his head.

"If we don't free them now, there will be blood shed over them. I'm not sure, but some of it might be theirs." Kaitlin put her hand back on the glass, only this time, she clearly did it to support herself. "This isn't exactly a goddamned picnic for me, either, Paul."

"Say we do free them." Liam tried not to look, because he knew that he shouldn't leave them behind while Elena got to walk free. He was selfish, and he knew it and had no intention of doing anything about it. When he'd insured her safety, then he'd look at the idea of freeing other people. "Then what? We're not prepared to get them out of here, and if any of them have medical conditions, we're not prepared to handle dealing with them. I don't want to leave them here any more than you do, but we aren't going to magically find a tour bus in the parking lot to evacuate them with, and even if we somehow did, we'd never be able to prevent some of them from getting hurt or killed in the escape."

"We could take one or two, Sergeant," Hegi offered. "But I don't know how you'd pick."

Riker grunted. "If they're out cold, we can stuff them in the trunk or something."

"That's my sister," Paul pushed his way to the glass, even though that put him next to Kaitlin. "She's been missing for weeks. We thought she ran away from home again, but she didn't come back. She always came back after a few days or a week, looking for a place to crash again and more money. Mom and Dad were ready to send her to a rehab place, then she disappeared again, but she didn't come back this time."

Only one thing about that made no sense to Liam. "And Privek didn't use her against you?"

"No." Paul still stared at the one girl, not shaking his head or otherwise moving. "I wouldn't have believed him anyway. When she didn't come back after two weeks, we figured she was dead. I mean, my parents didn't come out and say it, and neither did I, we just kind of all silently agreed."

Kaitlin crossed her arms and seemed to be having a contest of wills with Riker. "Is she one of us? "

"No, we were both adopted."

Riker rolled his eyes. "We can't afford to stand here and argue and chat. Hegi, you carry the sister. Carter, you go pick one out at random. We'll question them when they wake up, find out if there are any similarities in their stories. I'll take point with Kaitlin, Paul fall in behind us to handle whatever you need to. Liam, take the rear. You'll be able to maneuver better than these two."

While the others hurried into the room to grab two victims, Liam turned and explained what just happened to Elena as succinctly as he could. She didn't understand any of this, but thankfully, chose not to ask questions. They fell in behind Hegi. The soldier had a young, pale brunette girl wrapped in a sheet tossed over his shoulder like a sack of potatoes. She had more piercings than he considered flattering, making Liam wonder what she got up to when she disappeared.

With Kaitlin guiding them and Paul there in case anything went wrong, their exit seemed assured. Liam's phone rang. He pulled it out and frowned at the caller ID. Why was Privek calling him? He hadn't shirked any duties in particular that he knew of. "Hello?"

"Moore, where are you?" That was Privek: all business.

To help him feel an excuse he hoped the agent would swallow, he shrugged. “I went out for some air. Did you need something?” In this moment, he realized he wouldn’t be able to pull anything on Privek face-to-face anymore, not knowing what he knew now, not having rescued Elena like this.

“Some air. I see.” He heard Privek take a deep breath. “Yes, you’re wanted here. There’s been a development and I’d like all hands on deck. How soon can you get back?”

“Well, I took a drive and kind of got lost. The GPS can’t seem to connect to any satellites for some reason, so I really have no idea. At least an hour.”

“Mmhmm.” Liam had a sinking feeling that noise meant Privek didn’t buy it. “Call me when you reach the city again.” He hung up without giving Liam a chance to say anything else.

Liam stared at his phone, feeling like he’d missed something. That conversation went more or less fine, but it felt off, and he couldn’t— They’d taken Paul’s car. His own car sat in the parking lot. The bastard probably stood next to it when he called. Now Privek knew. As soon as he got reports about everything going wrong today, he’d blame Liam. For all of it, even whatever trouble Bobby managed to get himself into.

He cursed, then repeated it because he hadn’t meant to say it out loud in the first place. Their breathing room with Privek had evaporated, and they’d lost any chance at a surprise assault. Their exit from this building might even have just gotten more complicated.

Paul’s phone rang, giving Liam a sudden rush of panic. “Paul, it’s Privek. He’s going to ask where you are.”

Turning around with his phone already in hand, Paul paled. “What should I tell him?”

Liam’s brain froze, imagining all the horrible things that could happen to Elena. As a Spanish citizen and not an American, she could be detained, or deported, or worse.

"Tell him you're busy," Riker said, "there's a girl."

Why did he say he'd gone out in his car? He could've said he'd gone for a walk. Though he couldn't have claimed to be lost, he could still have said it would take him an hour to get back. Liam bit back another curse for his incredible stupidity.

Paul nodded and answered his phone. He said what Riker suggested, mumbling nervously. He hung up the phone and shook his head with a frown. "I don't think he believed anything I just said."

"Worry about this when we get to the car. We're not out of the building yet." Riker reached over and patted Paul on the shoulder encouragingly. "Nobody's perfect, we just do what we can with what we've got."

"How come you never say anything nice like that to me, Sarge?" Carter joked.

Riker turned back with a grin. "Because you're a thick-skull dumbass and only shouting gets through to you."

"Oh, right. I forgot." Carter chuckled and Hegi snorted.

The banter faded into the background for Liam. He glanced at Elena, hoping that what he and Paul just got her into was really worth it. No, he didn't mean that. Obviously, being free made her instantly better off than locked up, especially if he'd prevented her from being stuck in one of those beds. Just as obviously, he benefited from having her by his side. He worried, though, that he'd jumped into a rabbit hole without knowing whether she'd get hurt by following him or not.

Between the efforts of Paul and Kaitlin, they walked out the front door to find their cars waiting, engines already running. Liam wondered how long it would take Privek to hear about this and whether he'd connect them to it. He imagined the guards getting a call any second now, asking about suspicious or unexpected guests.

In his head, soldiers fired guns at them, tires squealed, someone got shot, and he had to watch Elena die because the bullet hit her between the eyes.

One thing kept him from falling apart: the precog. Paul wanted to stay as far away as possible from Kaitlin. Liam pushed Elena towards the car Kaitlin chose. They shared it with Riker, and Platt drove, with Kaitlin's random male damsel in distress draped across their laps in the back seat. As awkward as it felt, he suspected having Paul's teenage sister there instead would be worse.

"Where are we going?" Platt asked as he pulled the car away from the building. "I can figure out 'off the base' on my own. I mean after that."

Riker turned around to check with Kaitlin, who had the unknown man's head in her lap as she sat next to Elena. She leaned back against the seat with her eyes closed. "I don't know, stop looking at me. I'm kind of wiped from all that in there. It takes energy to do that, and I was doing it almost the whole time we were in there. I really need something to eat soon, and a nap."

Liam rubbed his eyes with one hand. The other refused to leave Elena's shoulders. "For now, head towards Chicago. Maybe something will come up before we get there and we can pick someplace else."

"That's what, ten, twelve hours away?"

"Something like that, yeah," Riker nodded. "We can't drive all the way there like this, though. Not with minimal cash and a body in the backseat."

Liam pulled his phone out of his pocket and stared at it. He didn't like paranoia. It always struck him as silly and stupid, the province of mentally unstable people. Yet, here he found himself pursuing the worst possible dark fantasies imaginable. "I'm concerned that Privek is tapping my phone or I could call my father and arrange to meet his plane at the airport."

Without missing a beat, Riker offered his phone. "Odds are pretty low he's tapping mine yet. That'll probably change when he's had a chance to look over the security footage. Might as well use it while we got it."

"Who is Privek, anyway?" Platt asked as Liam took the phone and dialed.

"He said he was NSA," Liam answered absently, "but I really don't know." The last time he spoke to his father had been before Afghanistan. His parents didn't even know he'd gone there. He hadn't told them about Elena yet, either. He'd intended to introduce her when he got home. Then Privek took her and he lost sight of everything except getting her back. The one time he spoke to them, he only said he'd miss his next semester at Harvard Business School. They expected so little of him that his father didn't even give him a hard time about it.

"Hello?" His father's voice, full of suspicion, jarred him out of his thoughts.

"It's Liam, I'm borrowing a friend's phone." He didn't need to explain. Robert would assume he'd let his phone's battery run dead, or he'd left it in some girl's purse. "Can you send the plane to DC for me?" As soon as the words left his mouth, it occurred to him that he should have made this request the way he usually did, by calling his father's secretary.

Robert left a pause. "Are you alright?"

The entirety of the last six weeks tried to push its way out of his mouth. From the joy of meeting Elena to being on the run right now, he burned to share it all. "Yeah," he heard himself say in a voice so easily controlled by years of practice in the fine art of keeping his parents happy that it happened with no effort. "I…I think I met someone."

"Ah. This is all about a girl." He sounded so relieved that he must have expected something devastating, something he'd dread explaining to his wife.

"Yeah, it kind of is. She's…" He turned and kissed Elena's temple. "Something special."

Robert chuckled. "Good to know. I'm glad you called. When you decided to blow off school, your mother got a little difficult, but I convinced her to give you your space. You're welcome for that."

"Yes, thank you, I appreciate it. Things have been, I don't know, crazy, I guess. I'll add Chicago to my list of places to take her soon."

"See that you do. I'm looking forward to meeting her."

Liam felt the urge to say goodbye and hang up. That's what the conversation demanded. How could he explain what he'd seen and done, what he'd become? How could he even ask about who he really was? He wanted to know and understand, yet he wanted to do it without causing a problem or driving a wedge into the middle of his family. "Dad, um." It must have sounded awful coming from him, something so inarticulate and needy it made Elena look up at him with concern.

"It sounds like you fell, hard, son," Robert chuckled again. "Don't let her use that against you too much. See you soon."

Liam pulled the phone away from his face and stared at it when his father hung up, caught between the shame of not being able to figure out how to ask a question, embarrassment at sounding like an idiot, and something tight in his chest he didn't have a name for. His father cut to the heart of things, guessing right while also guessing wrong. He did fall, and it was hard, and it was wonderful, and he loved her.

People tossed that word around in the circles he ran in, using it to mean "like" or "lust". He feared saying it out loud, worried it would cheapen what he felt. Worse, he had no idea what he'd do if she didn't feel the same things back. He had no fear of rejection, yet found the idea of *this* rejection terrifying. He could live if everyone else rejected him for the rest of his life, for everything, so long as Elena didn't.

Reaching back, Riker took his phone and pocketed it. "You think that hard for too long, you're gonna blow a gasket. We going to Reagan?"

"Yeah." Liam frowned. Elena had been taken from him there. He'd wanted to show her around the city for a couple of days before taking her home. With the still unconscious man laying across their laps and three other people in the car, he preferred not to make any grand displays of affection, yet he needed Elena's support now. He pulled her closer and leaned into her, brushing a finger down her cheek. "We'll probably beat the plane there."

"Gives us time to eat," Kaitlin said with a yawn. "We should go back to the farmhouse. It's kind of a mess, but no one will look for us there."

Liam thought about that. "Privek already knows where it is." Her logic, though, took no effort to follow. "But he'd never expect me to go there. Even if he thinks Bobby is with us, he wouldn't expect Bobby to go there, either, because that would be stupid. Going there makes no sense when the people we need to free are in DC."

"Sounds like a plan, then." Riker nodded his approval. "We go there, make an assault plan, meet up with Bobby, and prepare to hit them hard, where it counts."

They arrived at the airport with enough time to pick up food for everyone, then boarded the plane while the Moore family pilot took care of refueling. The middle aged retired Navy aviator said nothing about the number of people or the two still unconscious ones carried inside still only wrapped in sheets. He was a professional and worked for wealthy people. Although Liam didn't think any of them had ever done anything this strange, his father paid well enough for the man not to comment.

Liam pulled out spare clothes his parents left in the drawers for the times when a business meeting in another city went from a few hours to a few days and left them next to the still sleeping bodies. Paul sat with his sister on the bed in the back of the plane, holding her hand. Kaitlin took a nap on the couch. Liam and Elena sat together at one of the windows. The five soldiers played cards at the table. The other victim lay on the floor.

About two hours into the flight, the guy on the floor curled up in distress and mewled. He appeared to be having a seizure, or something similar.

From the back, Paul called out in a panicky voice, "Something's wrong. She's waking up, but something's wrong!"

Riker nodded towards the back. "Hegi, go check on the girl. Platt, this guy." The two men tossed their cards and followed orders.

Liam cringed, knowing he should do something and not wanting to. He much preferred to stay quietly by Elena's side and enjoy her presence. The piteous noises coming from the guy's mouth punched him in the guilt, and he left her to crouch beside the guy. The poor guy hurt so much that he twitched, and it sounded like Paul's sister had the same problem.

Hesitant to take on that level of pain, Liam rubbed his forehead nervously and took a deep breath. "I don't want to do this," he whined.

Platt gave him a sympathetic pat on the shoulder. "Nut up or shut up."

The abruptness and crudeness took him off guard; he expected some kind of short inspirational speech. Liam barked out a laugh and put his hand on the guy. Nothing happened. He could tell the man suffered. He could also tell his ability wouldn't fix it. All amusement disappeared and he frowned "I think…I don't know. It's like— His body is attacking itself, but that's not really the right way to explain. It's not like cancer, not a tumor. It's something different." ven he knew that made no sense.

Riker gathered up all the cards calmly. "Maybe they were being kept sedated so they didn't have to suffer through this, whatever it is."

"That makes sense," Liam agreed. "If I had to guess, I'd say he's mutating." That thought led to another, which made him want to know how Privek got all these people. "Okay. They've had blood from at least a few of us for months now. Assuming they have lots of money and access to lots of intelligent people they can keep under control one way or another, I'm going to guess that a facility connected to this whole thing was conducting research into our abilities."

"I'm with you," Riker nodded, "and I see where you're headed. They're trying to make more of you guys. They've got the resources to try it, and given secrecy level Ridiculous, they could pretty much do anything they wanted, including human testing."

Platt shrugged. "If we had some morphine or something, I could give it to him, but I don't see anything I can do or diagnose. What I don't get about that theory is where they got these people."

Riker shrugged and gave the guy a closer look. Liam did the same thing. He hadn't paid this one much attention before, thinking of him as nothing more than some guy in a sheet.

He was young, maybe twenty at most, with light brown hair and beard. He seemed decently fed but lean, without a lot of muscle mass. Something about him made Liam guess he'd had a hard life before he'd been grabbed, though he couldn't put his finger on what.

"Probably not military," Riker said with a shrug, "unless he's been in that facility for a while. Hair's too long. Beard only suggests a couple of weeks at most since he last paid attention to grooming. And the girl is obviously not—too young and pierced."

In the back, Liam heard Paul quietly begging Hegi to do something. He couldn't blame the guy. If it was his own sister or Elena, he'd probably feel the same way. He got up and put a hand on Paul's shoulder, hoping to distract him. "Come on. There's nothing we can do here, you need to stop looking. She'll come out of it eventually and we need to talk."

"You don't know that. She could be stuck like this! It could kill her." Paul looked up at Liam, naked helplessness on his face, crinkles of pain tightening it. "I can hear her screaming in my head. She doesn't even pause to take a breath in there."

"Paul." Gripping his shoulder more forcefully, Liam pushed him back. "You have more control than that. You can block it out. I know you can. Listening to that won't help her, it only makes it harder for you to do anything useful. As soon as we land, we'll try to get some kind of painkiller or sedative, or something, but we can't do that right now. There's nothing we can do, except try to figure things out. We need your help to do that."

Paul nodded and let go of his sister. He covered his head with both arms and cringed with agony. When he opened his eyes again, he averted them from the girl and stood up, following Liam away from her. "She's going to be fine," he said a few times, probably to himself.

They sat down in the two seats vacated by Platt and Hegi, who moved the unknown young man to lie on the bed beside Paul's sister and stayed with them both in case anything changed. "Paul," Liam said gently, knowing he was still upset, "you said your sister ran away from home. What's your best guess for what she would have been doing out there?"

The telepath rubbed his face with both hands. "I could find out, I'm sure it's there, under all the—" He finished the statement by waving his hand and slumping his shoulders.

"Just guess for now," Riker said in the same perfunctory tone he always used. "You know her, right? What do you *think* happened?"

Paul shrugged. "She was probably on the streets. Mom checked with all her friends and Dad looked for her. He's a cop. There are a lot of places a…someone like her can get lost."

It wouldn't help to suggest that Paul actually meant "a young, pretty girl" instead of "someone like her", so Liam politely refrained. "Seattle is a long way for these guys to go just to pick up a test subject."

Paul snorted. It managed to be depressed and amused at the same time. "They could have picked her up at the same time they picked me up for all I know. I mean, they lied to us about everything else. Why not this, too?" One hand gestured back at Elena, who sat looking out the window. "You remember how Maisie said she was picked up by guys in suits, then Privek and his guys rescued her? How can we think that was anything but a setup at this point? Camellia said something similar, so did some of the others."

"Yeah." Liam sat back and stared glumly at the table. They'd all been played, hard, and it annoyed him to discover he had such an obvious blind spot. All his life, he'd been able to finger the women who only wanted him for his money. Privek walked up and manipulated him effortlessly. Elena was his Achilles Heel and always would be. She'd been used against him so easily and effectively that he was ashamed of himself.

"I think maybe it's time for you guys to fill us in on the whole story, from front to back." Riker's voice startled him out of a brood. "We're here because we trust Bobby, for the most part, and I'm getting the basic picture, but if you could lay it all out, we can help more effectively."

"I don't think we know the whole picture," Liam admitted, sounding grumpy because he felt grumpy. "Not as much as Bobby does."

Sitting up and rubbing her eyes, Kaitlin yawned. "I know the whole picture, so listen up, kiddies. This is the bedtime story to end all bedtime stories. Roswell. There was really at least one alien. They got DNA from her, one way or another. In vitro fertilization comes along and some asshats say 'hey, what would happen if we crossed this alien DNA with human?' They try it through a program that looks like a social service organization, managing to actually impregnate thirty-five women across the country.

"The program loses funding, the kids all go on to grow up without knowing they were part of an experiment. Their parents don't know, either. One day, one of us gets a superpower, someone notices, government gets interested. Four of us get picked up by men in suits, of which Privek is one. Bobby was one of the ones they picked up. They fumble the whole thing and all four manage to escape after their superpowers become active. Led to believe they were part of some crazy experiment, they go across the country, with a list they conveniently happen to find while escaping, to try to convince the rest of the thirty-five to band together for the purpose of self-defense.

"We were going to try to work together to determine what to do, how to live in this human world without fucking it up for everyone and getting war declared on us for existing. Turns out, ten of us were actually taken by the other team," she gestured to indicate both Paul and Liam, "and convinced the rest of us are the bad guys and need to be stopped and locked up until we can be convinced not to cause trouble. You guys came in the middle of the night and ripped us out of our beds, shot us with tranquilizer darts like animals and bundled everyone off to freezer drawers.

"I only escaped because I just barely knew what was going to happen. Since then, we've learned there's another one of us we can't account for, Kanik Okpik, who must be the first one of us that got his power. He's got to be part of this whole thing, somehow, but whether Privek is using him or the other way around, we don't know yet. Looks now like they're experimenting, probably with the intent to create their own little army of supers. Who knows what their ultimate goal really is. Depends on how crazy they are."

Everyone stared at Kaitlin as she spoke. She met Liam's eyes the whole time. He wanted to look away, but felt that would be cowardly beyond even him. When she stopped, she smiled without even the tiniest trace of happiness. "We wanted to be left alone, and you fucks came and killed Tiana's cat. I buried it myself."

The moment she said that, Liam flushed with shame. Paul paled and covered his mouth with a hand. "We didn't know," Liam murmured. He regretted the words instantly.

"Yeah, no shit." Kaitlin snorted and shook her head. "I bet you all thought you were doing the right thing and deserved a fucking cookie and pat on the head for being such good boys and girls."

"Sounds like it's time to make amends," Carter said lightly, too lightly for the situation. "Can't take back the past, but you can own the future. We need a plan to break the others out of the freezer drawers, show the rest how they were played, and then what to do from there."

Riker nodded. "If all those people in those beds are going to have superpowers like you guys, good chance we'll have a war on our hands until we can convince them they're being used. Even if we can, it's possible they'll have someone with mind control, right? Have to plan for that."

"Bobby is good for riding to the rescue." Kaitlin stopped glaring at Liam, which had no effect on how much he felt like an asshole right now. "When we meet back up with him, he'll have ideas."

"His mind can't be controlled," Paul offered, his voice subdued. "He's in too many parts. And Cant's mind is shielded. Roulet's blocked from me, too."

Kaitlin shrugged. "I don't know anyone's last names."

"Um, Stephen and…Andrew?"

"Stephen is a vampire, he drinks blood, is super strong and can fly. Can't handle sunlight. Andrew can block anyone's power and make it not work. He's going to be a big help if we're up against others like us."

Riker nodded thoughtfully. "We'll need both of them on our team. Here's hoping our bad guy doesn't figure that out and shoot them in the head rather than risk facing them."

When the conversation stalled, Liam got up to try to ignore the guilt he now felt on top of his shame. She was right. He did all that for a cookie and a pat on the head, and didn't really stop to consider how he might be wrong, how they might all be wrong. It had been all for Elena. That failed at making it okay. Losing her shouldn't have prevented him from using his brain.

Dropping himself down next to her, he took her hand and reveled in how she smiled at him. He kissed her palm gently and explained all of that in French, bracing for her to hate him because of it. To his surprise, instead of showing any disappointment in him, she climbed onto his lap and hugged him tightly and told him, "I love you, too." After a pause she added, "I will try not to do anything that stupid to show it."

He didn't deserve her.

Chapter 8

"I need you to kinda take half the wheel, Asyllis. Can you do that? I gotta use dragons to get that tail offa our tail." Bobby aimed the Humvee at a place where the base had minimal fencing, probably only meant to separate military and public land. It'd keep the weirdo conspiracy guys out well enough, but wouldn't do much to keep a vehicle like this in.

"I don't see the connection between those two things."

"It's my hand and arm. I gotta let them off and I can't use it while they're gone."

"Why can't you just make your leg into dragons? You don't seem to be using that one."

Bobby blinked a few times. "Uh." The thought never occurred to him before. Every time he needed some, they popped off his hand, then his arm. A few times, he'd re-formed without a toe because of a dragon being missing, but he'd never tried it on purpose."I, uh, don't really got time for experimenting right now. Kinda need my attention for the road."

She sighed in resignation and offered her hand. "What do I do?"

Oh, heckbiscuits, she had no idea how to drive. Because she

spent her whole lifetime on Earth in a box. Great, just great. "Hold on here," he grabbed her hand and stuck it on the wheel. "Don't resist when I crank it around, just help me keep it straight while I ain't turning, okay?"

"I'll do my best."

Bobby had a powerful urge to quote a movie he liked, mocking the notion of "your best", but curbed it since she probably wouldn't get it. Her room hadn't had a TV, after all. Instead, he put his effort into pushing his whole right arm into dragons and sending them out to defend the Humvee. They were to try not to hurt anyone or let anyone get hurt, but do whatever it took to stop anything following them. He couldn't control them directly, not now, so they'd have to…do their best.

"We're gonna hit a fence, it might rock us around a bit, so hold on." He glanced at her, hoping this risk turned out to be worth it. Of course, the look on her face when she'd seen the sun bolstered him. Nobody deserved what she'd been through, nobody. With her in tow, he'd be able to convince Liam, too, even without Elena. They'd still find her, somehow, because he'd promised.

His dragons swarmed the drone and chewed it up. They hit the fence and plowed over it without issue. None of the tires blew out on the razor wire at the top, and he could only hope none of them took on a slow leak. They had a long way to go yet. He had to somehow get Asyllis across the country to meet up with Liam, Paul, and Kaitlin without anyone noticing and with no money. Damn, he wished Stephen could be here to carry her.

His dragons returned, allowing Asyllis to take her hand back. All things being equal, he preferred having both his own hands on the wheel. She did nothing wrong, except give him one more thing to worry about while escaping from a covert military project.

Actually, he didn't think for one second they'd *really* escaped.

Someplace like this probably had a satellite pointed at it all the time, or a giant radar installation staring at it. Heck, they might even have a tracking device in the Humvee. They needed to get lost in Vegas.

"So, I gotta ask you about what you're capable of and stuff. You seen me, how I turn into dragons and all. We gotta cover a lot of distance, can you do anything to make that go quick?"

Startled by his voice, Asyllis jumped, then curled her legs up and stopped looking out the window. "I'm not sure I understand the question. I have no special abilities. My mate and I, we were rangers, trackers and hunters, not magi. If I've ever been out of the ordinary, it was only in my skill with a bow. That you can do what you can do is fantastical to me."

Bobby frowned and tried not to let this distract him from driving. They hadn't reached a road yet, and he had to avoid the big bushes and things. "A bow? Like, you can control the arrows with your mind or something?"

"No, nothing of the sort. I am merely a good shot. Or, I *was* a good shot, anyway. The muscles have certainly withered from disuse by now. I could probably still hit a target—I still know how to do it—but not exceptionally well."

What did that mean? The Humvee bounced over a particularly rough bump, neatly distracting him from the quandary, and he spotted a road off to the left, which he turned to head for. They'd go much faster on it. "Okay, so, how's it that if you're normal, we're all not?"

"I have no idea. I knew nothing about what they were doing. Perhaps if we knew more, we could make educated guesses."

They'd done plenty of guessing so far, and seemed to have done a decent job getting close, if not right on. "Pretty sure all our daddies are different and human, else we wouldn't none of us look more human than you. Ain't a single one of us got pointy ears, we only got your eyes."

"Then it is reasonable to suspect the mixing of the two races is the cause of your strange abilities. Tell me, what of the others? You said there are thirty-five."

"Most of them are locked up in boxes right now, by a guy name of Privek. I can't figure why he's doing it, except maybe he wants control over us. The ones're out, aside from me and a couple others, they're working for him. But of the ones I know, there's a girl what can make fire, another can make ice. Hannah can make a force field, Jasmine can turn into a squirrel, Kaitlin sees the future, Violet can fly, all kinds of stuff like that. Some of them are harder to explain, but it's all stuff that don't make no sense, not really."

Asyllis nodded and went quiet for a few minutes, curled up in her seat.

Bobby had to pay attention to driving anyway. The way over to the road was bumpy as heckbiscuits and he had to keep a sharp watch to avoid putting them in a ditch or hitting something too big to give way. He let out a breath of relief when they reached the road and the drive smoothed out.

"I first arrived here in my sleep beside Tarilyr, my mate. You would use the word 'husband'. We slept in a hammock for the night, bound between two trees. Our son had just reached the age of adulthood, and we went off to spend time together, just the two of us, as we had not done for so long."

She sighed heavily. "I had a very strange dream. It happened so long ago, I barely remember it. Blue light, a feeling of being stretched. When we woke up, we were in a strange place, and there were men, human men, approaching. Everything happened so quickly. We tried to speak to them. We were frightened and confused, but their language was so thick and strange. More and more men came. They had guns. We didn't know what guns were until they demonstrated by shooting one.

"There was nothing to be done. Neither of us could resist them with such weapons, not with our two bows. They separated us, locked us in cages. Tarilyr went mad, he tried to escape and they cut him down. I saw it happen, I watched him die. I have been locked in a box ever since, though not long after that, they moved me to this place. I was drugged for the trip. I saw nothing. I learned English, they taught me so they could question me.

"They want to open a way between our two worlds. They've been trying to reproduce whatever brought us here ever since they realized what must have happened. I know this because of the questions they asked. There is no other possibility. After a while, they must have realized I'd told them everything I could, because they stopped asking questions and all I was left with were guards. They grow older and get replaced. My people, we live much longer than humans do. I couldn't say how much longer, but quite a bit."

Bobby listened and kept quiet until she left a long silence. "I'm sorry about your mate, that musta been a real hard thing to see. And being all locked up like that…pretty amazing you didn't just lay down and let yourself die." He saw her turn away to look out the window. "That's what they're doing at White Sands. They want to open up that path and make contact with your world. It happened once, they must figure it can happen again."

What would they do when they managed it and went through? He could just imagine a tactical team with some kind of translator crossing over and deciding the only safe thing to do would be blowing the other place up. Or worse, they'd find it great and send settlers through after that. Like humans hadn't done that before. He'd seen some movies that made it pretty clear what had been done to the Native Americans. Only this time, the people on the receiving end wouldn't actually be human beings, they'd be people like Asyllis and her mate.

Not on his watch. Those people? They were his people, too. He couldn't say if he really believed in God anymore, but he'd been raised Christian, and as far as he saw, that meant he ought to do whatever he could to keep it fair, at the very least. Now, more than ever, he knew they had to go public, and they had to do it as a group, not as one cowboy taking matters into his own hands and doing it his way. Granted, if he wasn't careful, he might not have a choice.

He glanced at Asyllis again, still watching out the window. The question of how to get her across the country without anyone seeing her still had no— Wait a minute. He wasn't alone, he wasn't the Head Cowboy. He had Liam's number and could find a phone. Maybe they could come here, or Kaitlin would have an idea, or Paul could do something. They could talk it out and figure something. Or Liam would tell him to stuff it because he couldn't find Elena. Still, at least then he'd know he had to stand on his own.

Part of him thought he should go back to the Monte Carlo and hit up Beverly again. She'd been nice, and he could lay it all out for her. If he meant to spill it all publicly anyway, what difference did it make if he told a person or two here or there along the way? He wouldn't be able to find a phone anywhere without letting people see Asyllis anyway.

Something else popped into his head, and the words spilled out before he could stop himself. "Hey, I wonder, do you know why they called your project 'Maze Beset'?"

Asyllis snorted. "Yes. One of the men, he was so pleased with himself for it, thought it was horribly clever. The two words are unrelated. 'Maze' is a wordplay. It sounds like 'maize', Spanish for corn, which has yellow silk, like my hair. Also, it is a maze to get through the bureaucracy and red tape and whatever else to find out about me. And, as you saw, I was kept in a maze of a prison. As for 'beset', it refers to how I am surrounded on all sides, and a bizarre notion that humanity is under threat of invasion or attack from my people. That threat is preposterous, of course. We have bows and swords, you have machine guns and nuclear bombs. Tarilyr and I were not advance scouts for an assault, either. They never believed me that my people pose no threat."

Unexpected noise distracted Bobby from thinking about any of that right now, and he looked all around before spotting the helicopter heading straight for them. "We got a little problem," he said as he floored the gas, knowing they had no chance of outrunning it. The Humvee flew down the road.

"Can't your *drathikén* handle it?" She turned to face forward, full of grim determination, and braced herself again.

"That there is full of soldiers. I ain't keen on killing soldiers, so no, there ain't a whole lot I can do about it. If'n I knew how to disable it without sending it crashing to the ground, I'd do that, but I sure don't." The Humvee slowed and bucked, making sputtering noises. Bobby looked all around in a panic and noticed a needle that might be a gas gauge. The needle sat all the way to the empty side. "I take it back," he said grimly. "We got a big problem."

"Is that the city ahead?" Asyllis pointed down the road. They'd just crested a rise high enough to see the taller buildings of Las Vegas in the distance. More importantly and usefully, a residential subdivision perched not too far away. If the guys in the helicopter had orders to capture instead of kill, and they could run fast enough, they might make it to the houses. Once there, they might be able to evade the soldiers.

That many of ifs and mights gave him little confidence. The alternative, though, force him to kill people, and Bobby wasn't ready to let his dragons do that again yet. Maybe he wouldn't be ready for that ever. Maybe that was a good thing. "Yeah, it is. We're gonna jump out and run like heckbiscuits for those houses nearby without stopping the vehicle. I'll help you, just jump for it."

Asyllis nodded her understanding and took off her seat belt. The helicopter came around in front of them, making this plan even better. He shifted the thing into neutral and took a deep breath. "Now." As the word left his mouth, gunfire sprayed across the windshield. He burst into the swarm and flew out with her, cushioning her fall as he'd done for Kaitlin in that car crash. The dragons found her light enough to carry a short distance, so he kept going, unable to pull her up higher than a few feet off the ground. Not that doing so would get the helicopter off their trail, but with luck, his speed would give them enough of a head start to get somewhere worth getting.

Some dragons noticed her breathing strangely, and a few caught sight of blood. Did she get hit by the gunfire or flying glass? Needing every last dragon to carry her, he couldn't check right now. Behind them, the helicopter let two soldiers out to scramble after the Humvee, then followed after the dragon swarm. That Bobby and Asyllis went into a residential area had to reduce their options. They couldn't just land a military helicopter on the street and send soldiers door to door. Right?

All the houses in the subdivision looked the same. In this particular part, they weren't trying to grow grass among the scrub, they just filled the yards in with rocks or covered the dirt with some kind of low growing creepers, a few shrubs or trees mixed in to make the yards actually worth looking at. Some had rock walls, most had no fencing of any kind.

When he reached the closest houses, Bobby had to stop and let the dragons rest. He set Asyllis on her feet as gently as he could and re-formed just in time to catch her as she collapsed. Now that he looked her over, he sucked in a breath and felt like someone kicked him in the gut. Three separate blood stains spread swiftly on her clothing. Bobby had no medical training at all, but he knew that digging the bullets out and burning the tissues could save her life. It worked for Dan, anyway.

"I can fix this," he told her firmly. If he didn't, he'd spend the rest of his life wondering about her, wishing he'd had time to get to know her. Three of his dragons popped back off and dove at the three injuries.

She hissed with sudden pain. "It's alright," she said, voice breathy and strained. Her hand weakly gripped his arm. "You gave me back the sky. Like you said: go down in the sun, not waste away in the dark. You're a good man, Bobby. I'm proud to call you my son."

He'd found her an hour ago and had barely learned anything about her, yet the sight of her drifting away brought pain to his heart and tears to his eyes. The dragons yanked on bullets, pulling them out. One found itself flooded with blood for its efforts and he knew that he'd killed her instead of saving her. "I'm sorry," he said softly. "I'm so sorry."

"Save the rest. Stop them. Don't let them destroy my home." Her words slurred, her grip weakened.

Nodding, he held her close, his world shrunken down to the woman in his arms. "I promise. I'll put things right."

She smiled at him, then her eyes slipped lazily to the sky overhead. "I wish," she began. Her last breath left her before she could manage anything else.

"Put your hands up," he heard behind his back, the voice exasperated and tense, like he'd already repeated this a few times.

"Fuck off," Bobby said as he pushed Asyllis's eyelids down. Rage boiled inside him. They'd killed her. She didn't deserve to die, she deserved to be free. Now that she was dead, they'd probably cut her up and pin her open like a frog in science class. They'd study every bit of her, trying to figure how she lived so long or something. He could see those damned scientists all relieved she could be treated like a thing now instead of a person. If that had even been what stopped them before.

"C'mon, buddy, let the lady go and show us your hands. Otherwise, we'll have to shoot you."

"She's dead." His voice came out flat and hard and cold.

"Damn, you killed her?"

Bobby turned his head, so angry he could barely think. "No. You did." They were soldiers, not much older than him. If he let this rage loose, he'd kill them. "Back off." He didn't want to kill them. The dragons did. They didn't care who these men were, they only cared about Asyllis being dead by their hands. Bobby cared, and he was in charge.

"Put your hands up." One of them kept a gun trained on him while the other took a tentative step toward him, attention flicking between Bobby and Asyllis.

"Turn around and walk away now, before I lose control and you both die." By the end of the demand, he found himself begging. "What you saw was real. Just walk away."

Both of them froze and stared at him. "Are you sure she's dead?"

"Yeah." Bobby closed his eyes and took a deep breath. "Was an accident, right? Guy busted her out and she got killed in a crossfire. He carted the body off, but you're sure she's dead." When he opened his eyes again, they had both taken a step forward and looked ready to try to take him down.

"Right. Sure. Look, just come with us." The one with the gun put it up to show he wouldn't shoot. "We can sort this all out back at the base. I'm sure you didn't mean any real harm, buddy."

Bobby didn't know what to do, just that he had to do

something. "I don't think you got the slightest idea what you're dealing with. I don't want to hurt any of you, but if you make me, I will." He heard the helicopter settle overhead, the steady thp-thp-thp of the rotor loud enough he had to shout. At least the wind from it helped him cool down.

"I don't want to hurt you, either, buddy. Just come along quietly and we can all avoid lots of trouble."

He put his hands up and thought about what he could do and still get out of here with her body. Like waiting in that geek's pocket, he had to watch for the best opportunity and take it, not bolt at the first chance. The helicopter moved off enough to land as the soldier gave him reassuring words about doing the right thing and he'd make sure to tell someone about it, and other pointless nonsense.

His opportunity came sooner than he expected. The helicopter door opened. Soldiers jostled in an attempt to surround him and load him up where he couldn't cause any trouble. Getting shot didn't scare him, leaving him free to act as he pleased. His left hand fell to dragons while he threw a punch at his captor with his right. Above their heads, two dragons sacrificed themselves in the engine, now making hideous screeches and crunches. More dragons burned and clawed whatever looked important.

Someone shot him while he shoved one soldier aside and knocked the other over. Dragons took the bullet and kept it from hitting anyone else. Thank goodness for that. The swarm blew out and carried Asyllis away again. Bullets flew around him. He ignored them.

What, exactly, should do now? By himself, he could fly for it and get to a phone. With a dead body, he needed a car. He broke into a random house and looked around. With luck, he'd have five minutes to find something that might help. Backup would come. Privek would find out.

Standing in the living room with Asyllis in his arms, he caught sight of a cordless phone sitting on a table. He first thought to call Liam. However, since Privek would toss a magnifying glass over everything here, the call would be traced, which could lead him to Liam. His attention went back to Asyllis, peaceful and still.

Setting her on the couch, he picked up the phone and called for an ambulance. The operator told him to stay on the line, but he hung up. He called information and got himself connected to a local TV station. "I seen a guy go into a house," he told the young woman who answered. "He had a lady in his arms, I think she was hurt, or maybe dead. Thing is, she looked kinda weird. I know this'll sound crazy, since we're so close to Area 51 and all, but I think she had pointy ears, like one of them elves in a video game. I'm just calling you in case it's something and they try to cover it up." He hung up on her before she could ask him any questions, then did the same thing with the local newspaper.

Tears sliding down his cheeks, he brushed his fingertips across her pale face. For some reason, he thought of the camera in his pocket and pulled it out. No one would believe a picture like this on the internet or news, not these days. He'd do it for Liam and Paul and Alice and Hannah and the rest, so they could see her face and know where they came from. Not only that, they'd help him keep his promise. Head Cowboy needed help. He took a few pictures, feeling ghoulish for doing so.

He heard sirens coming and thought about leaving a dragon behind to make sure she didn't get swept under a rug. Would that actually accomplish anything? He could burn the house down instead. No, the folks who owned the house didn't deserve that. His eyes strayed to a patch of sunshine on the carpet, and he picked her up, knowing what to do. If any press folks showed up, they might be able to get a picture.

As he laid her out on the driveway, a small white flower caught his eye and he picked it. “I done barely knew you, Asyllis. That ain’t fair. S’all I got to say about it.” He curled her fingers around the flower and sniffled. At the sound of screeching tires, he burst out into the swarm and flew up, unwilling to be further involved in this. Not now.

Since he had nowhere else in particular to go, he broke into a room at the Monte Carlo and used the phone. Liam told him they’d gone to the farm and let him hang up without talking much. Bobby stared at the phone for several minutes, still dazed by the roller coaster he’d ridden out here. He thought about taking a nap on the bed in the room with him. If he went to the farm, though, he’d be able to sleep in his own bed.

Seven or so hours later, the farm looked a tiny bit better than it had the last time Bobby saw it. None of the cars had been towed away, which surprised him. He recognized the spots where Jayce had been put down, where Stephen got shot, where Sebastian had been carried through and where his own dragon had been smashed. Since the lost dragon remained lost, he wondered if they’d taken it someplace.

Glinting metal caught his eye, surprising him again. The swarm set down there and devoured his missing dragon while he re-formed. For once, his belly didn’t rumble, having been filled an hour ago in Denver. He drooped, though, weary from going so long without sleep and from everything he’d done and seen in the past day.

Scuffing the dirt with a shoe, he thought about lying down right here and taking a nap in the mid- afternoon sunshine. Inside would be more comfortable. Comfortable felt wrong, like a betrayal of Asyllis. The familiar squeak of the front door opening interrupted his brooding.

"Hi, Bobby." Kaitlin gave him a sympathetic smile from the front stoop.

"Hey." It came out as more of a grunt than an actual word.

"Don't worry, we're safe here. For at least another twenty-four hours."

He grunted again, noting that, if he wanted to avoid talking about it, he could fly away and do something stupid or stand here like a dumbass. He had a peculiar talent for both. His feet moved. So did his hand. As he passed Kaitlin, he slapped the camera into her unexpectedly waiting palm. With that gesture, he'd passed on the responsibility. She would make sure it got taken care of somehow without him screwing it up.

Riker and Hegi worked in the common room, picking up debris and dumping it into a wheelbarrow. He grunted in greeting and kept going until he found some strange guy lying in his bed. Frowning, he stepped into the tiny space and looked the guy over.

"He was in the same place as Elena." Until she spoke, he hadn't noticed Kaitlin following him. "Adelphi."

So, they found Elena. He listened while she rattled the gist of what had happened there, staring at this new victim of Privek's plans. Or Kanik's. Maybe both. Another place to hit after they freed the others. "We gotta stop them."

"Who's this woman, Bobby?" She held up the camera, he turned to look.

"Our real momma." He found himself unwilling to wait for the others before telling the tale of what happened at Groom Lake. Words poured from him, like they could draw out the impossible ache inside. "They'll know it was me," he ended with. "Ain't no way they won't."

"I'll pass all that along for you, so you don't have to explain it again."

"Thanks. You know this is my room?"

Kaitlin made a face. "No, I didn't realize that. Sorry. I would've made them pick another one."

"S'alright." He bent to scoop the guy off the bed, and froze when he groaned. Part of him wanted to turn around and walk away, to flop down on Lily's bed and sleep and not worry about anything until tomorrow. The rest of him pointed out that he'd made promises, and ignoring them would be cowardly and rude.

Time to get a grip and deal. "Hey there." Setting the guy back down, he leaned in and kept his voice down in case the guy had a headache. "You're safe and all."

"What happened?" His voice started weak and slurred. He gained strength with each second that passed. "One minute I'm…" He blinked several times and reached up to rub his face. "Where am I?"

"Colorado." Kaitlin moved in closer and peered over Bobby's shoulder. "We found you tied up and knocked out."

"Huh?"

Bobby held up a hand to stop Kaitlin from saying anything else. "What's the last thing you remember?"

"I thought I was taking a job, sort of. I guess not."

"Right. Okay, I'm Bobby, this is Kaitlin. We're looking to know details and stuff."

"Um, Shane." He took a deep breath and looked away. "I, uh…was a little… It wasn't like I wanted to be, you know, it just happened."

Bobby had enough shame of his own to recognize it in someone else. From the roughness of Shane's hands, to how skinny he was, to the look in his eyes, the source seemed obvious. "Living on the street?" He waved off Shane's meek little nod. "I eat outta dumpsters on a regular basis. Ain't nothing to be worked up over with me. What kinda job was it supposed to be? Where'd you meet whoever done hired you? "

As he suspected, Shane raised his chin again. "I was in a shelter. It was morning, over breakfast. A guy in a suit with sunglasses came in and told everybody he was looking for volunteers for a sleep experiment. Anyone who went with him would have a safe place to sleep for a week, plus food and some cash at the end. Guy got more volunteers than he wanted. He picked out all of us that were kinda in the same age group. Got ten from there, I think. We all piled into a van. They drove us around some, but after that, it's all blank. I don't remember why I blacked out."

"It's 'cause they drugged you up," Bobby nodded. Bobby nodded. Grabbing homeless people meant no families or paper trails to worry about. What for, though? Looking for ways to replicate their abilities with adults, maybe? That was a creepy idea, one that made too much sense. "Okay, you feeling weird or anything? Got any funny itches or urges or anything?"

"Funny…how?" Shane's eyes went wide as Bobby popped a dragon off his thumb and let him get a good look at it. "No, nothing like that." Halfway through the gesture, he stopped and frowned. "Well, actually, there is one thing that's kind of weird. Not like *that* kind of weird but, well, um, I think I can see an extra color. I don't know what color it is, but I've never seen it before. It's like black, but not. Really hard to explain."

"Yeah, that's kinda weird." But, like he said, that came nowhere near to the level of what Bobby and the rest of them could do. Seeing an extra color sounded downright tame. It did probably match up with something regular people couldn't see. Unlike being a swarm of dragons, though, the power to see black- plus gave him no special defensive benefit. "Welcome to the club."

Shame gave him a small smile. "Thanks. I don't know what to

do now, but thanks."

"We'll figure something out soon as we can. There's a bunch of us with crazy stuff we can do, and we aim to stick together and help each other out. Even if all you got's a new color, you're one of us. Somebody'll bring something and help you eat, yeah? Rest until then, we'll get you up and about soon." He patted Shane on the arm as he stood up.

"Okay." He looked up at the ceiling. "Were other people there, where you found me?? "

"Yeah," Kaitlin said from the doorway, "and we're going back for them as soon as we can."

Bobby rummaged through his closet, pulling out clean clothes. "That's a fact. You don't gotta do nothing 'bout that, though. Just get back on your feet and relax for now."

"Thanks."

Leaving him behind, Bobby pushed past Kaitlin to head for the bathroom. Under the hot water of a shower, he tried not to think about Asyllis, how she died. It was his fault. The guys in the helicopter probably only knew that someone stole the Humvee and had maybe been told the thief might be nuts. Shooting at the vehicle probably seemed to be the best option they had to stop him, especially when it had to look like he meant to ram the helicopter with it.

Why exactly her death hit him so hard, he had no idea. He remembered when they came to say his Daddy was dead. The man had been part of his life for as long as he could remember, and when he was gone, Bobby mostly felt relief. They didn't have to worry about him anymore. Momma didn't have to answer the door with dread anymore. Their lives could go on without wondering if they should make plans with him for his next trip home or not. No more writing letters they didn't know if he'd ever get.

Asyllis, though, was just some woman he shared blood with. The dragons liked her immediately, and she affected him so deeply. He'd caused her death, he had to shoulder the blame for it. If he hadn't broken her out, she'd still be alive. In a box. Underground.

At least he gave her the sun.

A knock on the door startled him out of his thoughts. "Bobby, are you okay in there?" Liam's muffled voice actually sounded concerned.

How long had he been in here? He knew as well as anyone else that no amount of water could wash away his sins or make him stop seeing anything. Shutting off the shower, he grunted. "Yeah, I'll be out in a minute."

"We'll be in the kitchen. Things to discuss."

"Alright." His stomach rumbled at the mention of something related to food, and he scowled at the fogged up mirror. It never let the stain of death get in the way of hunger. Maybe Privek was actually right about him being a dangerous monster. He'd still do everything he could to get the others free.

He shrugged into a fresh pair of jeans and t-shirt and went barefoot to the kitchen. Riker and his men sat around the picnic tables with Kaitlin, Liam, and Paul, and Elena. Liam's girlfriend looked the same as he remembered her, aside from not wearing a suit. She hung on Liam's arm the way he wished Lily would do to him. All of them had bowls of thick soup and biscuits. Without tasting it, he knew none of it measure up to what Momma made. The thought made him frown.

Kaitlin patted the empty space beside her on the bench and waved him over. "C'mon, Bobby. Stuff some food in there before your blood sugar drops so low you fall asleep standing up."

"It's okay," Platt said with a cheery grin. "We can carry him."

One side of Bobby's mouth tugged up into an answering grin.

"I don't need nobody to carry me." Taking the seat, he looked from one person to the next, ending with Kaitlin. "Y'all got a plan already, or am I supposed to come up with it?"

"We're still on the objectives part." Riker set his spoon down and fiddled with a biscuit. "We talked it over, and we're in this thing, Bobby. What we saw, that's not the kind of thing you can unsee, and it's not what we pledged ourselves to defend. There's no doubt we're already on a list of enemies of the state, but sometimes you have to be the bad guys to be the good guys. Besides, you saved our bacon, and there's nothing we like better than bacon."

"Here, here." Hegi raised his glass of water in a toast. "Well said, Sarge."

Bobby managed a single little huff of amusement. "Objectives, then. One, we gotta get the others loose. Two, we gotta free everyone we can of Kanik's influence. Them pictures make it pretty clear he can do whatever he wants to."

"If you ask me," Riker said, "that Kanik guy should be a target. There's a saying about power and responsibility, and he's got one without taking the other."

Paul gulped. "We should at least try talking to him. He's one of us."

"Yeah, we'll try." Bobby dipped his biscuit into his soup and swished it around. "Look, there's something I need to say. We gotta go public. Ain't nothing else gonna work. So long as we stay quiet, they're gonna be able to keep doing this. It's gotta look to folks like we ain't a threat and can police ourselves, and what we want is to be citizens of our country and have all the same rights as everyone else. Now we know for sure we're products of military experimentation. We gotta focus on that angle, I think, on how this happened because there's folks running amok, doing without thinking and that sort of thing. Also, we been hounded and treated like animals, and that ain't okay."

"We can't just step up to a microphone and say 'I'm a superhero!'," Liam said with a frown. "I know you think this is the right way to go, but what about those of us who don't want to be public? I don't want to be mobbed by people, which I will be. Seriously, they could decide I'm some kind of second coming of Christ, it would be horrible. I just want to have a life, not kill myself healing the world."

Bobby nodded. "That's fair, and I understand. Kaitlin's gonna be in the same boat, and I'm pretty sure there'll be lots of folks who ain't so keen to know there's folks what can mess with their heads. That's why I ain't gonna ask anybody to come forward aside from myself. What I can do, it's good for people to not know about it, but somebody's gotta break the silence, and I'm okay with being that somebody. Nobody gets outed without their consent. I'm pretty sure that list of names'll get out at some point, one way or another, so my second plan is we set up the farmhouse here again, as a secure commune for all of us. Anybody what wants to live away from all that, come here and be safe."

At the surprised looks all around him, Bobby snorted. "I had some time to think about all this stuff here and there. Y'all don't think I just sit there brain-dead when I'm not talking, do ya?"

Liam cleared his throat delicately after a few awkward moments of silence. "We were kind of led to believe you aren't the brightest bulb in the box. But no matter. I see your point, and agree. All the money in the world won't stop someone from targeting us one way or another so long as we all stay hidden and secret. Silence is helping them more than us."

"Then there's the wormhole thing," Kaitlin said. "Maybe we should go after that first, shut down that research."

Bobby took a bite of soup-drenched biscuit and chewed while

he happily considered something besides his own failings. "I don't think we can stop it. We can slow it all down, we can make it public so folks know what's going on, but once science figures something out, it's figured out. Attacking there would just be to stop whatever they done got cooked up right now. I expect they won't have no serious problem building another one."

Liam nodded and frowned. "Publicity is the most likely foil for that. Carefully crafted publicity."

"Maybe we could film all of it," Platt suggested. "The breakout, I mean. Post it on the internet."

"People will think it's a joke," Liam said with a roll of his shoulders, "that it has special effects."

"That's fine." Riker looked off at the wall. "It doesn't matter if they believe it or not right away. What matters is we start showing it to the world. Platt, Carter, your jobs are to film the breakout. We need gear and supplies and a little more of a plan. You guys know the layout of the place with the freezer drawers full of people?"

Bobby stared at Liam without really seeing the healer. "I know it well enough. Actually, I can wake them all up myself. Where I'm gonna need help is the getting them out part. Everybody's gonna be groggy at the least, maybe not be able to do their thing. In some cases, that's maybe for the best. I'm sure Lizzie'd blow up the whole building if'n she could. It's worth saying here that we ain't harmless, we ain't all puppies and kittens, and everyone's gonna be pissed about the whole being taken prisoner thing."

"In which case, you setting them free is for the best," Riker agreed. "We'll still need a layout for an exit plan."

"Do we?" Kaitlin asked. "Don't we really just need to know who's going with who and has what job and where to meet up?"

"Aw, you can't make the Sarge go without a plan," Hegi grinned, "that's just mean."

"Paul?" A girl, maybe sixteen, stood in the doorway. She had pale skin and more piercings than Bobby considered attractive. Panting, she leaned against the door frame and clutched a sheet to her chest. "What's going on?"

Paul jumped up. "Sherrie, you're awake. Are you alright?" He rushed over and wrapped his arms around the girl.

"Where are we? Why are you here? What's going on?" She let him help her to the table to sit and leaned against him.

Paul pointed to everyone, offering their names for her. "You're safe here. I just need you to tell us what happened to you. Please. It's important."

Everyone stared at her. She looked down at the table. One hand snaked out and snatched two biscuits in a way that made Bobby take notice. Kaitlin said earlier that they had Paul's sister, and this must be her. He paid attention to the way she shifted her eyes around and wouldn't look at anybody.

"S'alright. She ran away from home, I'm guessing, and got picked up like Shane did. Some kinda promise of money or shelter or whatever, and once she was in the car or van, they shot her up with drugs that knocked her out."

"Yeah." She flashed guarded gratitude at him. "That's pretty much what happened."

In an effort to get her to trust him, he popped a dragon off his thumb and sent it to her. "Ain't nothing to fear here. Ain't nobody gonna take you again." Part of him knew he shouldn't promise that. This very place had been raided, and everything they'd just planned to do would make some folks eager to try it again. "Not 'less they kill me first."

The dragon landed next to her bowl and nudged the spoon towards her hand. She stared at it with awe and wonder. "I didn't actually wake up yet. This is a really weird dream."

Bobby shrugged. “You got any weird urges or itches or anything what feels or looks different than before?”

Sherrie gulped and looked around, finally actually seeing all the people in the large room, watching her. “I…um…I knew where Paul was before I saw or heard him.”

When she failed to follow that up with more explanation, Liam took a break from translating for Elena out of the side of his mouth to ask, “Can you be more specific? How did you know?”

She still hesitated. Bobby dipped his biscuit again and swished it around. “Look, my whole body can fall apart into hundreds of those little critters. I guarantee it ain’t weirder than that. Nobody here’s gonna judge you for whatever it is, so just tell us.”

“Seriously?” Her jaw dropped open.

While taking a bite of the biscuit, he held up his hand and let dragons off until he had nothing past the middle of his forearm. The four dozen or so dragons landed all around her and on her shoulders. They trilled at her in unison. Five picked up her spoon and stuck it into her hand. One peered into her glass of water from the rim, then leaned too far and fell in with a plop. It sank to the bottom and looked all around.

All around the table, he heard stifled chuckles and giggles and laughter.

“Ah, come on,” Bobby said with a roll of his eyes. “Get your little metal hide outta there. You ain’t no ice cube.”

“They don’t need to breathe,” Sherrie said with wonder, watching the dragon swim with all four little legs to the surface. It beat its wings, spraying water all around the cup, and managed to get into the air again.

Bobby could tell it felt sheepish and he called all the dragons back. He knew so much more about what they were capable of than he did when he first discovered them. “Yeah. That’s handy sometimes. What's important right now ain't what I can do, it's what you can do. I showed mine, let's have yours."

"Uh, I don't think I can demonstrate." Sherrie gulped and watched with fascination as his hand re-formed. "I can…see minds? Not like read them or anything, I just know they're there. Sort of. All your dragons have separate little minds, but when you're you, you're kind of a weird jumble."

"That's exactly what I see," Paul nodded his approval. "Don't tell our parents, but I'm a telepath. I see them as little sparks and other people as bright lights. Except Kaitlin, but never mind that. You?"

"Um, it's not that…defined? I don't know."

"Makes sense." Bobby nodded. "It's like you're seeing heat, maybe, or feeling it or something, I bet. A little more useful than black-plus, but still a lot less than the rest of us. Folks, they're trying to cut corners to make more, and either they don't got it all sorted or you pulled these two out before the dose was all complete. Either way, every single one of those people you saw in Adelphi is one of us now."

Riker, sitting on Kaitlin's other side, nodded in agreement. "That makes Adelphi a high priority target. Once we have more hands on deck, we'll be able to split up and tackle both Adelphi and White Sands at the same time. A basic plan is taking shape, we'll just need to work up the details. Kaitlin and I can handle most of that."

Was it his imagination, or did Riker look at Kaitlin like he imagined her naked? Not that Bobby cared, she wasn't his sis— Er, actually, she was. That didn't change how little he cared about who she did or didn't shack up with. It only struck him as interesting.

Liam frowned. "I don't understand why they don't just use military personnel. Isn't experimentation something you sign on for when you go in?"

Riker shrugged. “Not exactly. We can refuse, and there would be a paper trail, and we have families. Families ask questions and file lawsuits.”

Nodding, Bobby looked off at nothing in particular He wound up staring at Liam’s eyes. Family. He had his Momma already, and now he had a bunch of brothers and sisters, plus Riker and his men from the sounds of it. “What about you guys? You got families what ask questions and file lawsuits, too.”

“We all do, Bobby,” Kaitlin said with an arched eyebrow.

“Yeah, but—”

Riker laughed without letting Bobby finish. “My family thinks I’m still in Afghanistan. We were told not to say a damned word, none of us said a damned word. Fortunately, none of us has a wife to lie to.”

“Alright, glad to hear it.” Bobby grinned and sat down opposite the two of them. “Is that gonna be a problem when we get on with the part where we go public?”

“Yes, but we’ll live. Contacting them now would be detrimental to mission success.”

“Ayup, that’s how I feel about it.” He really did want to call Momma and talk to her about the things he’d done. Most especially, he wanted to hear her tell him it would be okay, and he wasn’t a bad person. Whether it was true or not, he’d like to hear her say it.

Chapter 9

After the meal, Bobby stood in the doorway of Lily's room, leaning against the frame. Everyone else batted around ideas for a detailed plan, or caught the last few rays of sunshine, or cleaned up. He'd told them through drooping eyes that he needed some sleep and no one gave him a hard time about it. Shane still lay in his bed, recovering from the drugs. Bobby had a thought to use Stephen's room, but couldn't stop himself from taking the detour to Lily's.

Sebastian had been grabbed right out of that little toddler bed, and his wailing screams for his mother still echoed in Bobby's head. They merged with the face of that little girl, making him want to hit himself with a baseball bat. Then he saw piles of shredded meat that had once been human. Asyllis, dead. The parade of images marched around him, over and over.

"I ain't a bad person," he told the room as he sat heavily on her bed. If he could make himself believe it, then it might be true. Stephen would agree and call him a dumbass with power he hadn't yet figured out how to control. That had to end now. People kept dying because of it.

"I'm in charge. Nobody dies 'less I say so. It's gotta be that way. More damage we do, more likely they lock us up in a box for good. All they really gotta do is stick us in a box with no vents while I'm dosed on that drug and eventually, we all starve to death. So listen up. We gotta have rules to protect us as much as them."

They didn't answer—they never did. But he felt something. The only other times he ever felt anything from them while in full human shape had been when their rage threatened to rip them right off his body. This time, he got acceptance from them. Understanding. Almost drowning with Stephen maybe showed them how it could really all go to heckbiscuits.

"Okay. Good. Best to try not to injure anyone too seriously, neither. What I say goes, and you follow my lead. I know how people think, so you gotta trust me to know what I'm doing."

They got that, too, even if saying those words out loud made him want to laugh at himself. Yeah, he knew what he was doing. Completely. Regardless, he could trust the dragons now.

Still barefoot, he rolled onto the bed and shut his eyes, breathing in Lily's scent. It felt like no time passed at all before a rapping knock on the door woke him. Somehow, he had no nightmares. Maybe Lily chased them away.

"Rise and shine, Sleeping Beauty!" Hegi's too cheerful voice echoed in the hallway as he walked away. "Thirty minutes 'til we leave."

Bobby groaned and rubbed the sleep out of his eyes. He got up and got dressed, choosing his desert camouflage pants and combat boots with a regular white t-shirt. He downed a breakfast on the go without tasting it, let alone looking at it long enough to figure out what it might be. In a few hours, they'd be freeing everyone else, and that thought rammed everything else aside. All along, this had been his goal. Finally, he got to do it. Granted, he'd thought he'd be liberating only eleven people.

One tense, quiet car ride later, Bobby dropped down into a

seat on Liam's family plane and stared out the window. Half an hour into the flight, Liam, more cool and collected than he'd been in Virginia, cleared his throat and asked politely for everyone's attention. It had to come from having Elena's safety assured. Bobby wanted that, too.

He swiveled his chair to see Kaitlin rubbing shoulders with Riker. Liam sat across the small table from the pair, next to Paul. They'd left Elena behind to watch over Shane and Paul's sister. Hegi, Platt, Hansen, and Carter sat in the rest of the chairs, all close enough to hear so long as no one whispered.

"We got a plan now?" Bobby asked.

Kaitlin nodded. "Yes, but first, I wanted to share something that I ran across while searching for stuff last night. Hannah must have seen it if she spent even two minutes looking, though she might have ignored it because of the date. It's a forum post about an article in the Juneau Empire, the paper there. Most of it's an environmentalist rant. There was a chemical spill in the city five years ago, caused by a train accident. It affected a mostly Inuit area the worst. A few people were killed and a bunch were hospitalized. This poster mentions Kanik Okpik as if he's some kind of martyr. He was injured and got acid burns on part of his body, but survived, at least up until this posting was made."

Something about that tugged at Bobby's memory. "You got them pictures I gave you?"

Nodding again, Kaitlin tapped and clicked on her laptop, then spun it around so everyone could get a good look at the pictures of Jayce. "Where did you get these, anyway?"

"I found the camera in Jayce's apartment." Bobby shrugged and peered at the much larger version of the image on the screen.

"What were you doing in Jayce's apartment?"

"I was in Vegas anyway," Bobby shrugged, "figured I'd have a look. Cops went through it something fierce. Kinda like they done did at the farm, only nobody was there to resist." He pointed at the screen. "Look at his hand."

Riker flipped between the before and after pictures for everyone. "That's freakish. I saw these before, but it's still just plain… freakish."

"It's the result of mind control," Kaitlin corrected. "But yeah, the hand. That could be acid burns."

Bobby noticed Riker putting his arm on the back of Kaitlin's chair, and his body shifting to lay claim to her. He thought Kaitlin noticed. Yep, these two definitely had something going on. "You know, I kinda wonder if there's something about the human-alien cross we are that makes us all more…frisky than usual folks."

Liam coughed, hiding a half a grin behind his hand. Paul blushed. Riker looked up at him with an arched eyebrow and said nothing. Kaitlin grinned. "I wouldn't be surprised, but we are all in the same age group, you know. Confined area. Shared doom and freakishness. So, you decide to get all up on Lily and—"

"Hey now," Bobby pointed at the screen with a chuckle. This foreign feeling, of being amused and wanting to laugh, made him hope they could all keep things light for now. They'd all have plenty of time for brooding later. "Plan time."

"Yeah, yeah." Kaitlin took control of the laptop back. Between her and Riker, they had good ideas, complete with maps. "The important part is we're up against someone who can do that kind of mind altering to probably anyone."

Paul cleared his throat uncomfortably. "Technically, I can do things like that, too. I used it to get us out of the facility the other day. I can probably defend against it, I've just never tried."

Hegi leaned in and fixed Paul with a suspicious glare. "How do we know you didn't put a mind whammy on Sarge to get us all to go along with this?"

Paul shrank back from him. "I, uh," he gulped, "just because I *can* doesn't mean I *would.* I haven't really let loose and seen what my limits are because I'm afraid to. I don't want to be a monster with a horde of zombie drones to do my bidding. That's just…wrong."

If only Bobby had ever felt that way for more than a few minutes, a lot of people might still be alive right now. He crossed his arms and tried not to scowl too much at Mr. Goody Two Shoes. "This whole shebang may be up you and Stephen and Andrew and me, then. All of us can resist Kanik. We gotta change the plan on account of that?"

Riker thought about it and glanced at Liam, who shrugged. "Yes, I think we do."

"Let's get on that, then. We got, what, three more hours? There any food on this here plane?" Bobby spent the rest of the flight eating and trying to memorize what he needed to do. They had a plan, a backup plan and a retreat location. Here was hoping Stephen got his stuff back as quick as possible, because out of all of them, the vampire would probably be the biggest help.

They touched down in DC at 12:11pm, and found Riker and Platt's two cars waiting for them at the airport with sizable parking fees. Liam covered them.

"You know, in all this," Bobby said, "I don't figure why that pigtailed girl was so important."

Kaitlin shrugged. "Maybe it was just so you could feel justified killing that agent."

"I s'pose."

"Is that really the only detail that's bothering you?"

He rolled his eyes. "A'course not. Everything else seems bigger, though, like it matters. That one little girl, she weren't much. Just a kid."

"Are you talking about the little girl at Hill Air Force Base?" Liam, also in the back seat, leaned forward to fix him with a stern glare. "The one you tried to abduct?"

Bobby opened his mouth to agree with the first question. Before he could, the second one made him glare at Liam. "After what you seen, you still buy that line?"

Liam frowned. "Yes, and I guess I shouldn't. Her name is Elizabeth, she's the granddaughter of the Chairman of the Joint Chiefs, General Hanstadt. Her father is a Major in the Air Force. Elizabeth was there that day because her mother was recovering from surgery."

"Privek tell you that?"

Still frowning, Liam nodded. "Yes, actually. He was very forthcoming with certain kinds of details."

Riker and Hegi glanced at each other. Since Hegi happened to be driving, Riker turned around to face Bobby. "That little girl saw you turn into dragons?"

"Yeah." Bobby scratched his chin idly, watching the scene replay in his head. "That agent thought she was my kid, or Stephen or Dan's. He shot at her, not me. I took that bullet for her and killed him." His now jaded self marveled at how shiny and naïve he'd been only a few weeks ago.

"That might be the one thing that winds up keeping all our asses out of a sling here." Riker glanced at Hegi again, then back out the rear window at the car with the others. "We should take the party to his doorstep once we've gotten all your people out."

"What about the people at Adelphi?"

"He's the Chairman of the Joint Chiefs," Riker shrugged. "If he can't get that sorted out, no one can."

"I agree." Liam pulled out his phone and futzed with it. "There's no way we can just waltz back into that facility now. They'll be on alert and have pictures of us handy. I'm sure there was security footage of every one of us that went in, and it's been examined by now. Privek's suspicions about Paul and me have been confirmed, and he knows Riker and his men are on the other side, as well as knowing Kaitlin is with us. By now, he's checked and knows you're out, too, and that you freed Asyllis."

Bobby looked out the window and tried to think of what Privek and Kanik might do, if they'd change things a lot based on what had happened over the past few days. The problem was, he didn't understand them, not really. What did they want? He had no real clue. Probably, if no one explained it all to him, he'd never understand. "I think the question we gotta find the answer to is why he took everybody from the farm. The real reason, I mean. Once we know that, seems to me we'll kinda have a handle on the why for everything else."

"I'm going to see what I can do to get us a meeting with the good General." Liam tapped his phone and held it up to his ear.

Bobby gaped at him. "Just like that?" Apparently, the company he currently kept was more rarefied than he knew.

Liam snorted. "We'll see."

Bobby went back to staring out the window, watching the scenery go by. If not for the need to be able to coordinate, he'd be out there flying instead of in here squished between Kaitlin and the door. Actually, he'd be there by now. In the background, he heard Liam on phone.

"Hi, uncle Glen, it's Liam. I was wondering if you could do me a favor." He chuckled at whatever Uncle Glen said. "No, nothing like that. I have a *friend* in the Army who's gotten into a little bit of trouble, and I was wondering if there's any way you could set us up with a meeting of some sort with General Hanstadt to discuss it as soon as possible. … Yes, I understand that, but this is a fairly unusual situation. … Tell him it's about Elizabeth's Hill dragons." From Liam's face, Bobby got exactly nothing. The guy must clean up if he ever played poker. "Yes, those words exactly, … No, I can't explain right now. … Sure, lunch next week would be great. I'll see you then."

"Next week?"

Liam kept his phone in hand, scrolling through his contacts again. "I'll meet my uncle for lunch next week. He'll text me back if he can get us in to see Hanstadt."

Reassured about the time frame, Bobby nodded. "Is that the price you gotta pay for a favor like that?"

"Depends. My Uncle is a Senator on the Armed Services Committee. If he has to call in a favor, then I'll have to make it up to him somehow. More than likely, though, when Hanstadt hears the message, that'll be enough."

The idea of meeting the top dog for all the military made Bobby squirm. Maybe if his Daddy hadn't been a Marine, it wouldn't be a big deal. He rubbed his face, wishing it could be a secretary or something instead. Liam's phone chirped a few minutes later. Bobby turned at the sound and watched the other guy read the message, then nod with satisfaction.

"Hanstadt will meet with us tonight at eight. Do we want to change the plan?"

For whatever reason, everyone looked at Bobby for an answer. Even Hegi flicked his eyes up to the rearview mirror to check on his reaction. Head Cowboy liked that. Bobby wasn't so sure. The boots seemed to fit, though, so he pulled them on and took a deep breath. "Nope. Us being quiet's got to not even seem like a thing he's got the ability to ask for. I ain't going quiet-like nowhere never again if'n I don't want to. Plus, if'n we're gonna face down Kanik, I want Stephen at my back."

Liam pursed his lips, like even though he'd expected that

answer, he'd hoped for a different one. "What if Privek or Kanik are there?"

"I got a few things I'd like to say to Privek," Bobby growled. "Most of it's about him eating dragons."

"Bobby." Riker's tone reminded him of his Daddy. He looked up to find the Sergeant staring at him intensely. "Don't walk in there looking to kill him. The job is to save lives, not take them."

Bobby turned away and tried to stop thinking so hard about kids with their chests blown out. He wanted, so badly, for all of that to be Privek's fault. Privek set the whole thing in motion by grabbing him in the first place, by framing him for Mr. Patterson's murder, by sticking them all into those cells and the rest of it.

Actually, what he wanted more than anything right now was to go home and have Momma tell him all this had been nothing more than a crazy nightmare. Then he could wake up tomorrow and go back to work with no dragons or vampires or precogs.

Except he couldn't, and right now, he needed to get his head on straight. When they reached the building, the nine of them would break in and free as many of the others as they could. God, he missed Lily. Having her smack him upside the head, or glare at him, or throw his gifts back in his face was so much better than not having her around at all. He'd give a lot right now even to have her look at him the awful way she did when he showed up in uniform.

He rubbed his face with both hands, trying to make the images go away. It didn't help. Pulling his hands away, they broke apart into dozens of dragons, all of which sat on his legs and looked up at him. They didn't understand right and wrong, not like he did. Each of them was too tiny to get the whole picture, that's why. They were fragments of him, little pieces of his soul.

No, he didn't really believe in the idea of a soul, not anymore. His stains weren't there to be judged by anyone or anything else.

They were there for him to judge himself. Could he find a way to bleach them out? Maybe not, but he'd for damned sure try. For however long he had left in this world, he'd do whatever it took to atone for those people. Like Riker said, he had to walk with the goal of helping, not hurting. For Sebastian, for the world to be a place where a little boy could grow up not worrying about some asshole made of dragons swooping down out of nowhere and killing him and everybody he ever knew for no reas

It was his fault and it would always be his fault. No one else deserved the blame for what happened. Privek bore some responsibility, too, just not for any of the things Bobby did. Same for Kanik. Without them, he never would have been in those situations. He still might have done horrible things on his own.

"We gotta step light, hear?" He said it quietly, talking to the dragons and knowing the whole car could hear him anyway. He'd already said these things. This time, he did it for himself more than them. "Too many died already, let's not make more bodies if'n we can help it." The dragons nodded and re-formed back into his hands.

"It'll turn out okay," Kaitlin said with firm conviction.

He glanced at her. "You saying that 'cause it's true or 'cause you think I gotta hear it?"

Her mouth curled into a smirk. "I'm going to live through this."

"I think that means 'yes,'" Riker said with a half-grin.

Bobby snorted. "Reckon so." To keep his sanity, he focused on his best memories of Lily while the scenery went by. There would be new ones at some point. Hopefully.

Chapter 10

The building showed no sign of heightened alert or extra security. Bobby broke into the swarm as soon as Hegi parked the car, eager to get inside and do his part. His dragons flew around, looking for a vent. As they poured into the first one he found, one noticed something strange: a squirrel sitting on a branch of the nearest tree, watching the swarm with more interest than a critter ought to have. He dove into one dragon and sent it that way, trusting the rest to find the drawers and open them up.

One paw waved at him excitedly, confirming he'd found Jasmine. She put out her paws and the dragon, still quite small compared to her squirrel shape, landed in them. He had no real way to explain the plan, and she presented an unexpected wrinkle. Did that mean Will was loose? Did they miss noticing Will at Adelphi? Kaitlin might not have recognized him, especially with so many bodies there.

He needed to get her to the others, because he needed them to be able to talk to her. Not just for Will. She could screw up the whole operation by trying to help. The dragon gestured to try to get her to stay put, but she ran down the branch to the trunk of the tree. Once there, she changed into Jasmine and held out her hand.

"Hi, Bobby," she whispered, not as cheerfully as he remembered her being. "They have Will. They said they were rescuing him, but they tried to shoot me and now he's inside. I followed them here, but I don't know what to do. Are you a dangerous terrorist? They said you were a dangerous terrorist, but they lied to me about Will. Did they lie to me about everything else, too?"

Bobby nodded, grateful for finding her so focused and able to get to the heart of things. He wished he could give her all the details.

"Are you getting everyone else out?" Nod. "Is there a plan?" Nod. "Can I help?" Shrug. "Okay. I'll wait here, then. If I see a way to help, then I will."

He never expected something that useful and coherent to come out of her mouth. She'd always struck him as flighty. An intelligent, capable woman lurked inside, and he'd never bothered to look. Will probably knew already.

The dragon patted her hand as it nodded, then pointed off in the direction where she could find the others. That done, he took off to go keep the people that ought to be waking up soon from freaking out without him actually there. Jasmine turned back into a squirrel behind him and ran down the tree trunk.

Jumping out of the one dragon, he re-formed most of his body in the freezer drawer room, where he found the doors already open. As he pulled the slabs out, he found the collection of people stashed her interesting: Stephen, Jayce, Owen, Anita, Dan, Lizzie, Matthew, and Andrew. Considering he'd been in this bunch, Privek might have chosen all the ones he considered the most dangerous to put here. Or, he thought with a smirk, the most difficult.

Stephen groaned first. Bobby grinned and thumped his arm. "Who's the dumbass now?" he chuckled at the vampire.

"Jesus, Bobby," Stephen breathed as he cracked an eye open.

"I will never, ever doubt you again." His voice was a hoarse rumble.

"Where are we?" Jayce rolled and fell off his top rack drawer, crashing into Lizzie, Anita, and Matthew. The four of them landed in a heap on the floor. The girls and Dan wore nothing. The rest had some sort of pajamas on, except for Stephen, who still had everything he'd been taken with.

"In the guts of a Federal building," Bobby told them, trying not to laugh, "working on escaping. Less crashing and noise would be a good idea, since you're all drugged, and can't do nothing but stumble around like idiots."

"You want to give pointers, then?" Anita flopped and glared at Stephen when he dropped a sheet on top of her.

"Sure," Bobby shrugged, still smiling. "Relax and let it work its way outta your system. I got a plan, and we got others on the outside. Kaitlin's free and I got two guys what were on the other side to help. Plus Jasmine is out there. Plan allows for none of you being able to use your stuff, so just take a minute to be able to walk on your own."

Dan sat up slowly, careful to avoid hitting his head on the bunk above him. "I don't suppose you thought to bring clothes for us?"

"Thought of it, sure. Couldn't manage it." Bobby gave Stephen a hand getting down. The vampire felt unusually heavy. "There's some waiting outside, in the car."

"Ung. I'm *starving*," Stephen rasped out. "Any volunteers before I go on a rampage?"

"They done knew you drink blood and they didn't give you none in the drip? That's kinda messed up." Bobby shook his head and waved him off. "Y'all been under for near on a week now. I done got ya out soon as I could. I got no idea where the rest are, there's only just this one bank of drawers, but everyone done got took, so they're someplace. Hopefully here. We gotta find 'em and get out, at any rate.

"There's still a few of us on the other team what might be around to try and stop us from leaving, and the guards here got them dart guns what they used to take us down at the farm in the first place. Out of the eleven they got, I got three, and I think the one named Kanik is actually Privek's master, or maybe his slave. So, we got seven folks to convince they're being used and one what probably ain't gonna be convinceable."

While he explained, Stephen scanned the room, his eyes flitting from one person to the next. He took a step towards Lizzie, but Bobby stepped in the way. "You need fresh blood, ya idjit. Without this stupid drug in their system."

Anita, now wrapped up in the sheet, held her arm out. "Here. You need enough to be sane, right? Take that much."

Looking her over with suspicion, Stephen asked, "Are you volunteering to take one for the team? "

She pursed her lips and looked away. It had to be hard to find something to rest her eyes on that didn't include Dan and Lizzie checking each other over more carefully might be considered tasteful, a shirtless Owen on his hands and knees and breathing deeply, an equally shirtless Jayce sitting and rubbing his face, or Andrew sitting in a tight white shirt and briefs and staring up at the fluorescent lights. The scene reminded Bobby one of those weird underwear or cologne ads.

The long pause meant everyone watched her, even Lizzie and Dan. Bobby pitied for her, realizing that must have been a weird thing for her to offer.

Her hands all over Dan, Lizzie smiled. "It's okay, Anita, we can still all think of you as a raging bitch if you want."

Jayce snorted out a laugh. Matthew and Stephen both chuckled. Dan kissed Lizzie's neck with a dirty little smile and pulled a sheet down for her. Andrew and Owen both grinned, and so did Bobby.

"Fuck all of you," Anita snapped, She left her arm out, though, still offered to Stephen. The vampire took it and bit her. She gasped and collapsed into him while he drank. Still weak himself, he had to sit down to hold them both up.

"Do we know what Kanik can do?" Jayce stood up and stretched. Bobby could relate to the impulse. More importantly, it took attention off Stephen and Anita.

"He can mess around with your head. In fact, I got pictures proving he done it to you before, in particular. No idea why you and not me, but if you don't remember it, maybe he did do it to me and Alice and Ai, and we don't remember it neither. Then again, Paul—he's one of the two of them I got convinced—couldn't do nothing with my head, and he's a telepath, so maybe he didn't hit me with a head whammy."

Jayce nodded and held up a hand curled into a fist while his other hand braced on the steel of drawer. Nothing happened. "Nope, I can't do my thing yet. How long did it take you to get this crap out of your system?"

"I dunno," Bobby shrugged. "Ten minutes, maybe."

"It'll probably take us all twice as long, then." Stephen set Anita down on the floor and straightened. "I feel so damned heavy. I forgot what it's like to not be able to fly." He poked himself in the gut for no apparent reason, then swore. "I can probably be killed like this. All of us can."

Bobby shrugged. "So long as we stay in here, ain't nothing to worry about, not really. Least, I don't think so. I done planned on it taking a while to get out like this, expecting to have to explain everything and folks needing help. This room ain't got cameras so far as I could tell, and it don't get checked by the guards. There's a guard post right outside it."

The door behind him, however, opened, and a guard stood there. Liam said— But then, Liam also said he thought maybe Privek knew to expect something. They must have changed the routine because of it. Fortunately, not having their powers failed to make these people useless. Bobby broke into the swarm to prevent the guy from leaving, Jayce stepped up and grabbed him, Stephen decked him, Owen yanked the radio and dart gun off his belt. Once they had him under control, Bobby re-formed to shut the door again. The poor guy hadn't stood a chance.

"So much for your intel, Bobby," Jayce grunted. He shoved the guard up against the wall.

"Great." Bobby grabbed the guard's other gun, the real one. "You know who we are?" The question was directed at the guard, who held his hands up in surrender.

The guard held his hands up in surrender. "N-not really, no. I was just told to check the room."

"He's lying," Stephen snarled. "Break his damned neck."

"Wait, no! I'm just a guard, I'm not worth it." The guard's voice went high pitched and panicked, his eyes wide and darting from man to man. "They said the people in the drawers were dangerous. I'm supposed to check to make sure all the dosing packs are the same and the drawers are locked. That's really it, I swear!"

Bobby nudged Stephen to get him to back off, hoping the guard would see it as him being in control. He wanted the guy to believe he'd be fine so long as he played straight with them so no one had to think too much about how far they wanted to go to get information. "How long before you get missed?"

"Um, a few minutes. There's another guard outside. I check in with him on the way out and go on the rest of my rounds."

Owen passed the radio to Dan, keeping the dart gun for

himself. "What's on the rest of your rounds? "

The guard blinked and bit his lip. Jayce tightened his grip on the guy's shirt. He gulped. "Um, there's a pair of separate rooms. Just down the hall. One has a woman and a kid, the other has just a woman."

Bobby's jaw clenched, because he knew exactly who the woman and kid had to be, and could have found them when Liam broke him out. He wanted to kick himself for not doing it, but then, what would that have accomplished? It would have pissed him off even more. At the time, it probably would have made things worse. "Which way? Be specific. And what guards are between here and there?"

"Down the hall to the left, first door on the right. One guard outside this room, one more outside theirs. No others on the way. Two down by the elevators."

Glancing around, Bobby could tell no one else had any brilliant ideas. The guard needed to be handled, and every option—letting him go, taking him hostage, killing him, sticking him in a drawer—seemed stupid and counterproductive. "Jayce, let him go, he's got the point. Unload this and give it back to him. Owen, unload that dart gun, too, and give that back. Dan, give the man his radio back. He's gonna walk right outta here like he's s'posed to, and he's gonna finish his rounds, then he's gonna take a break outside."

"Head Cowboy," Lizzie said, like she found it both annoying and delightful.

"This ain't no time for that. None of you got your stuff back yet. I do. He ain't going alone." Bobby popped a dragon off his thumb and held it up for the guard to get a good look at it. "You see this little guy? He's kinda cute, looks real harmless." It danced and flapped its wings, pretending to be a kiddie toy. Then it stopped and fixed the guard with a hard stare, one that matched Bobby's own. "He ain't even close to being harmless. You even think about tipping the other guards off, he's gonna blast his way into your mouth as hard as he gotta." The dragon let off a puff of fire and flashed its fangs. "Then he's gonna crawl down your throat until he reaches about where your heart is, and he's gonna rip his way outta your chest. We got an understanding?"

Standing there, the guard stared at Bobby, his mouth hanging open. "Jesus Christ."

"He ain't gonna help you," Bobby growled. "You do what I done told you to, and you get to walk away. We ain't got no real beef with you, it's with your bosses. Just on account I ain't sure I can trust you, I'm sending a few others with you, and they'll be happy to just burn and claw you wherever they can reach." He let off the rest of his hand, and they dove into his clothes. Bobby made sure at least one went into a pants pocket to threaten the guy's manhood, figuring that would be plenty motivating.

"O-okay, yeah, sure. I got it." The guard squirmed uncomfortably. "Finish my rounds and take a break outside."

Bobby shooed him off. "Get going."

The door closed behind him and Bobby turned around to see everyone but Stephen staring at him in shock. Actually, Lizzie seemed aroused more than disturbed.

"Stop it," the vampire said with a roll of his eyes. "Just because he's learned how to kill people efficiently doesn't mean he's suddenly a psychopath."

Giving them all his back again, Bobby rested his hand on the doorknob. Of course they thought he'd jumped off the sanity cliff. Right about now, some of them had to be wondering what exactly he did while they were out, maybe even back in Afghanistan. Jayce and Matthew could probably find all the right conclusions. "C'mon, we ain't got time for this. We're gonna knock the guards out without killing them, and get as many outta here as we can find."

"Are we going to blow the building up?" Lizzie asked hopefully. When he looked back, she licked her lips.

"Not unless we gotta. We're in the city here, DeeCee to be precise. Blowing it up'll get folks hurt. This ain't a base with a fence round it, nor a house in the middle of nowhere. It'd be best if we don't actually hurt nobody."

"Aww." She pouted as she held her sheet close. "When you threatened the guard, I thought you were—"

He cut her off, not interested in hearing it. "I ain't. You thought wrong. I want us to be safe and free. They ain't never gonna leave us alone if we go around killing and destroying and all that."

"They won't leave us alone regardless." Jayce put a hand on his shoulder and gripped it firmly. "The idea they will is a fantasy."

Bobby stopped and rubbed his forehead. "Look, yeah, I know. I got a plan. Most important thing right this minute is to get outta here. After that, we get into the rest. Ain't keeping ya in the dark, just trying to keep from explaining over and over so much."

His attention went to his dragons with the patrolling guard, because they saw Lily. "I'll be right back," he told Jayce, then he threw himself into the dragon doing its best to hide behind the guard's ear. Lily sat with Sebastian in a living room, reading a picture book with him. They looked normal and happy, and had no signs of any sort of mistreatment. He didn't know what to make of that. Lily noticed the guard and smiled, then ignored him. Sebastian completely ignored him. He jumped his dragon off the guard's ear as the man left, sending it to land on the book.

"Look, Mama, Bobby!" Sebastian scooped the dragon up and presented it proudly to Lily.

"Yes, that's one of his dragons. We should call Mr. Privek to let him know." Lily scooted Sebastian off her lap and, to Bobby's horror, went for what must be some kind of intercom.

Bobby wriggled out of Sebastian's grip. He darted to Lily, trying to get between her and the button on the wall. "Mama, Bobby wants you. "

"Yes, well, Bobby is—" She sighed and put her hand on the button. "I know, Sebastian. Mr. Privek said he might act strangely if he came here." Despite Bobby landing on her hand, she pushed the button. "Please inform Mr. Privek that Bobby is here. One of his dragons just showed up."

A male voice responded, "Yes, Ma'am. Thank you, Ma'am."

Why did she do that? Bobby had no idea why Lily would do that. She was mad at him, yes, and he knew it. It boggled his mind that she could be *that* angry just because he did a few dumbass things. His stupidity didn't rate siccing Privek on him.

"We got a problem." He told the dragon to get out of there and threw himself back into his body. "Lily just done told Privek I'm here. Any of you getting your stuff back yet?" He watched Jayce put a hand on the bank of drawers. A silver sheen slowly crept up his hand.

"Mine is coming back, but it's sluggish. Doesn't feel solid, either." He swatted Lizzie's hand away as she reached over, probably to squeeze his butt. "Take my word for it," he told her with a smirk. "It's just a thin coating on the outside.

She gave a husky chuckle and turned her palm up. It threw some tiny, harmless sparks. Her amusement died and she pouted."It's so pathetic."

"It's okay, baby. It'll come back, we just need more time." Dan put his arm around her waist and kissed her neck.

"We don't got no more time." The rest of the dragons with the guard let him know Lisa was the woman in the other room, currently taking a nap. He had no idea why they singled her out. Nor did he understand why both women stayed with the door unlocked. Had

Lily poured out her anger to Lisa? How would he ever get either of them to forgive him?

"I can still punch people," Jayce pointed out. "I just can't deflect bullets or break walls."

"Same here." Stephen stood on his toes, still unable to leave the floor.

"Don't look at me," Andrew grunted as he got to his feet. "I can scrap a little, but not nearly well enough to deal with trained guards. And if I help anyone walk, we'll never know when their powers come back. Why am I even in here with you guys?"

Bobby had no answer. Wait. Yes, he did. "Kanik. He does some kinda mind control. You turn powers off. Stephen's immune, too." Now that he got rolling, he understood why every last one of them had been stashed here. "Jayce, you were really hard for them to put down. Dan, you were on camera making people shoot themselves. Lizzie done blew up Hill good, and Matthew got seen there as a werewolf. Anita, they knew you wrecked up that house. Owen, you woke everyone up at the farm. All of us're the ones they see as threats. Nobody else caused 'em no trouble, just us. We're the ones they used to motivate the others.

"Lily's gotta be under his thumb, that explains why she just called Privek on me. We gotta expect the rest are, too. That means we're gonna be up against our own. Worst of 'em is gonna be…I dunno. Maybe Alice, Andrea. Sam, depending on what they got set up here. Hannah's smart, Greg maybe built them something. 'Course, we got no idea about the ones we never met. My gut says they got some of 'em here, expecting this jailbreak. Lizzie, you're gonna have to deal with Alice's ice. Don't blow nothing up you don't gotta, since there's ordinary office folk here.

"Jayce, Stephen, you gotta protect Andrew. He's the one what's gonna get everybody outta Kanik's grips." He hoped so, anyway.

"We're going for Lily and Lisa first, on account we know where they are. Owen, I don't know what to suggest for you, just do whatever seems right." His eyes went from face to face as he spoke, ideas coming to him in the moment. "Anita, Dan, keep folks from shooting any of us soon as you can."

Matthew, who Bobby found himself staring at, used the rolled-out slabs to haul himself to his feet. "I know, I'm just a wrecking ball. I'll do my best to keep a lid on it. What're you going to do? "

Glad he didn't have to be the one to say it out loud, Bobby nodded. "Folks on the outside're gonna set up a diversion soon as they get the word from me. I'mma leave a couple dragons behind with y'all. When they squawk, get moving. I'll be spread over the building, getting you some warnings when I can." He dearly wished they had Sam. "If'n you hear a voice in your heads, it's just Paul and don't freak or nothing."

With that, he blew out into dragons and left through the ventilation system. Four stayed behind—one for Stephen, one for Jayce, one for Matthew, and one in case someone else had to split off. Most of the dragons broke off to search the building from top to bottom while a handful went out to where Riker and the others waited. Along the way, he found Jasmine again and beckoned to her, getting her to follow him. She'd be able to tell them at least a few things.

"Liam!" Jasmine stood into her human shape and threw herself into a hug that took Liam by surprise. He'd been squatting behind a shrub and she knocked him onto his butt. "Are you helping Bobby now?"

"Yes." He hugged her back as he got his feet under himself again. "Is Will inside? "

Bobby wanted to give her a real hug when he saw the fierce,

unhappy determination on her face. More, he wanted to give her Will back. "That's where they took him after the helicopter ride. I haven't seen him come out yet. I saw them put a gun to his head. Do you think he's okay?"

Liam patted her shoulder. "I think he's alive." In one of the dragons, Bobby chirped and danced on Liam's shoulder. Another dragon sat on Riker's shoulder, and another on Paul's. He figured Kaitlin would be fine without. "Paul, can you reach the dragons individually?"

"Bobby, or dragon, or whatever, can you hear me?"

"Yeah, I hear ya." Relieved to hear Paul's voice in his head, Bobby passed along the important points quickly, and heard Paul repeat it all out loud for the rest.

Riker stared at the building hard enough to peel paint. "Are Privek or Kanik here? Can you tell, Paul?"

"There are too many people here for me to tell if anyone in particular is around, so I can't say who's here and who's not." Paul sighed heavily. "I want to help more than that, but I just can't."

"Do what you can," Riker said.

In unison, his four men finished for him. "Don't waste time worrying about what you can't." They all grinned.

"It's a Sarge-ism," Carter said with a chuckle. "How long should we wait?"

Distracted by goings-on back in the freezer room, Bobby paused and thought about it. Jayce smacked one of the cabinets again, checking his power and finding it still sluggish. Stephen rolled his head, neck cracking, and lifted half an inch off the floor. Seeing that, Lizzie cupped her hands and a little ball of fire boiled in the center. *"I don't know. It's gonna be a—"* The door slammed open.

The guy with the icy blue eyes standing in the frame had short brown hair and skin tanned from time spent outdoors. He wore a pair of jeans and a plain t-shirt."None of you are going anywhere." His body melted into water and expanded to fill the doorway.

Inside the room, a strange metallic whump noise came from the back wall. When his dragon turned to find the source of the sound, Bobby caught sight of a person-sized blue-edged disc on the wall, outlining a view to someplace else. That other place had a dozen men in body armor with dart guns pointed into the room. Behind them, Alice stood in front of a wall of ice, probably intended to cut off anyone who tried to escape that way.

They'd set a damned good trap. Bobby let out an expletive for Paul's benefit, then threw himself into the dragon Stephen's shoulder and trilling in alarm. He sent an urgent call for the dragons to converge in the room again. A barrage of darts streaked into the room. Everyone dove for the sides to avoid them, or tried to. Anita, too slow, took two darts and groaned. One hit Dan in the shoulder, another tagged Matthew in the leg.

Jayce ducked out from behind the open door and punched the nearly transparent barrier blocking their escape, only to recoil in pain from the impact. The swarm poured into the room and settled over the blue disc opening to catch any more darts they might shoot.

Venomous rage settled over Lizzie's usually smirking face. She glared through the swarm, ready to run in and murder their attackers with her bare hands.

Owen opened his mouth and shouted, "Let us go!" He only managed to be a tiny bit louder than a normal voice.

Everyone seemed so stymied by this. Add a little stress to a situation and everyone panicked. Stephen, at least, had his back plastered to the wall beside the blue disc, and seemed to be trying to think.

For some reason, none of these people could come up with

the answer that seemed so obvious to Bobby. He needed to be able to…to give orders. Damn, Head Cowboy had climbed up on his high horse. A handful of dragons flew to Andrew, trilling at him where he cowered in the corner, urging him to his feet. They pointed frantically at the water-guy in the doorway.

Andrew took forever to get the idea, then he lunged out and slapped his hand on it. Him. Whatever. Bobby had his own problems. Alice shot shards of ice at the swarm, ripping through the tiny bodies. Most of it, they dodged. She managed to hit twelve head-on, and encased twice that many in ice.

Stuck there to defend against the darts, Bobby had to let the dragons take it. While the guy in the doorway slowly oozed back to his body, Alice kept shooting the dragons with globs of ice. Lizzie stood in the middle of the room now, staring so hard through the swarm he thought laser beams might shoot out of her eyes to hit Alice in the chest any second. She took deep breaths, her hands held out with tiny flames dancing in her palms. Slowly, they crept up her arms, but she needed more time to be able to fully counter Alice.

Stephen lunged at the water-guy and bit him in the arm. Water-guy moaned and dropped to the floor, revealing the girl standing behind him with a dart gun in her shaking hands. Bobby recognized her as the one who shot him at the farm, and she seemed as terrified now as she'd been then.

She squeezed the trigger while Jayce hopped over Stephen gulping down water-guy's blood. The gun clicked—she'd forgotten to switch the safety off. In one smooth motion, Jayce took the gun away from her, flipped it around, thumbed the safety, and shot her before she managed to do more than stumble back.

he blue disc and the view of the other room disappeared. As Lizzie screamed out a rage-filled cry of challenge, Bobby re-formed in agony, one arm missing because of all the ice encrusted dragons littering the floor. “Little help, Lizzie,” he grunted. So many of his dragons had been smashed that he felt like a walking bruise.

“Baby,” Dan said, still on the floor, “Calm down and help Bobby. C’mon, heat up the ice. You’ll get your chance later when you’ve got more fire to burn.”

“Nobody shoots you but me!” Flames flashed out, engulfing Lizzie’s body and making everyone flinch away from her.

Bobby held an arm up to shield himself from the fire. “Lizzie, get a—” He bit back a few choice swearwords, instead making a wordless noise of exasperation. “—grip. We still gotta get outta here.” Since she kept doing what looked to him like throwing a temper tantrum, he scooped up and chucked his frozen dragons at her. The ice sizzled and popped, and it seemed to soothe her.

Stephen sighed in contentment and sat up. “That’s more like it. No drugs in that blood. I think it’s chasing the rest of it away for me.”

“We should take these two with us. How long will he—” Jayce used his chin to indicate Water-guy. “—be out?”

“A while.” Stephen floated to his feet and picked Water-guy up easily. “Oh, yeah.” Rolling his neck around made it crack loudly. “I’m good to go.”

“Jayce, how you doing?” Bobby lobbed a large chunk of ice at Lizzie, and melting it both released five dragons and got Lizzie back under control.

“Not solid yet, but getting there.” He picked the girl up and hefted her over his shoulder. “I should be able to repel the darts, but maybe not bullets yet.”

“Good enough for now,” Bobby nodded. “You, me, and Andrew are going to get Lily and Lisa. The rest of you go clear a path to the elevators and get a car for us. Do what you gotta, but remember not to hurt no one too much.”

"We're the good guys, Baby," Dan said as he got gingerly to his feet and grinned. "At least for now."

Jayce handed the girl off to Matthew. The werewolf had a fresh dose of the drug, making him unsteady. He shouldered the girl well enough anyway. Bobby and Andrew followed Jayce down the hallway. A small group of guards clustered around the door they needed to go through and Jayce kept walking, letting their darts bounce off his metal flesh. Bobby burst back into the swarm and surrounded the poor guards, biting their hands and ripping guns away.

The pair of them knocked all the guards down in half a minute. "Good work," Bobby said as he re-formed, proud of his dragons for avoiding killing anyone. They listened to him. That mattered. He pushed the door open, beckoning Andrew to follow, and took the first door in the new hallway to get to Lily.

Chapter 11

Paul swore. "Go, go, go! They're under attack, I think."

Riker nodded and led his men through the parking lot at a jog. Liam didn't like this part of the plan very much, mostly because it involved a high probability he would have to heal people. A shame that just asking Privek nicely to let everyone go would never work. He stuffed Jasmine the squirrel into his pocket and led Paul and Kaitlin up to the front doors, only to find them locked.

Liam frowned as he rattled the door again, refusing to accept their condition. "Why are the doors locked? These doors are never locked. Not even in the middle of the night."

"There must be an alarm going." Kaitlin made a face. "I didn't see that coming."

The wind kicked up, tossing small debris into the air. All three of them looked up to see two women dropping down out of the sky. Chelsea's feathery wings caused most of the breeze, and Dianna's ability to control the wind made it worse. They landed together, one on each side of the trio.

"What's going on, Liam?" Dianna put a hand on one hip and regarded her fingernails casually. The attractive black woman had taken to wearing spandex bodysuits now. Liam supposed that being able to fly would make skirts particularly unattractive, and loose clothing would get in the way. It made her look like she dropped off a comic book page. This particular outfit was dark red with a yellow sash across her waist and subtle black stripes up and down her body that brought a tornado to mind.

Chelsea, a pretty blonde with sparkling green eyes, turned her head in sharp, abrupt movements that reminded Liam of a bird studying a worm. "Where've you been for the past few days?"

Privek had arranged a welcoming committee, apparently. Liam shrugged, knowing he could fool these two at least well enough to keep them from doing anything regrettable. "Just enjoying the fact I'm not in Afghanistan."

"Uh huh. Who's this?" Dianna stared at Kaitlin.

"Kaitlin Tremont, here to meet Privek and hopefully join the home team."

Kaitlin gave them a good impression of a chipper person smiling and waving. "That's me, just looking to be on the winning side and all."

Dianna and Chelsea shared a look. Chelsea wrapped her arms around Kaitlin and snapped her wings out. "Let me help you with that."

Dianna put her hands out and the winds kicked up again. "The building is on lockdown until Mitchell is taken down, so we'll get you all in to see him."

Behind him, Paul made a little *eep* noise. Liam stifled a sigh. "That's really not necessary, ladies. We don't mind climbing stairs."

Kaitlin screamed out, "Riker!"

Idly, as his feet lifted off the ground, Liam reflected that when the precog screamed, it was really more of a frantic yell without the shrieking high pitch some women are capable of. Nothing he could do would stop Dianna, or anyone else, so he tried to keep his feet under him and not provoke her to drop him. Gunfire took him by surprise, though it shouldn't have. Riker was a soldier and he had a gun. Obviously, when a girl he liked made noises like Kaitlin did, there would be shooting.

Liam curled up to avoid getting shot and saw nothing. He went downwards abruptly and slapped to the ground, letting out a grunt as something crunched under him and a sharp pain stabbed into his leg. Something small and furry tapped his face. In agony, he opened his eyes to find himself lying on the concrete with a squirrel trying desperately to wake him. Beyond Jasmine, he saw Paul lying on the ground, unconscious. The gunfire had stopped, so he looked around and caught sight of Chelsea crumpled on the ground, bleeding and gasping for breath. Next to her, Kaitlin got unsteadily to her hands and knees, shaking her head.

He saw Dianna at least thirty feet up in the air. Someone else up there flailed one arm while the other clutched at his neck. Taking in the assault rifle dangling from its strap and military fatigues, he guessed it to be the man who'd been shooting: Riker.

More gunfire made Liam flinch down again, giving him a fresh rush of adrenaline. When nothing hit him, he rolled to see Riker's men shooting up at Dianna. Propping himself up on one elbow, he saw that his leg stuck out at a funny angle. Seeing it made it hurt, and he groaned, wishing he could heal himself.

Jasmine became human again beside him and pulled on his arm. "You have to help Paul!" She dragged him to the telepath and slapped his hand on the closest part, his knee.

The telepath could have prevented all of this if he'd only been prepared to handle this kind of stress. Now, he lay on concrete, bleeding to death on the inside with a dozen or more cracked bones, including his skull. Liam braced for the pain and still let out a tortured cry when his bones ruptured and repaired themselves.

Someone screamed, masculine and shocked, and then it stopped abruptly. Shouting followed while Paul groaned and Liam lay there in agony from his leg that stubbornly refused to heal. How high up did they get before Dianna threw them back down? It must have been at least twenty feet.

"Bring him here, quick," Paul called out.

Liam took deep breaths to keep from hyperventilating, knowing what to expect next. Even prepared for it, the intense torture of Riker's injuries overwhelmed him. Dianna had definitely tried very hard to kill him.

"What about Dianna?"

"The wind chick? She's toast," said Carter, or maybe Platt. They sounded too similar to tell through the pain. "Body's over there. This winged girl won't last much longer, either."

"Chelsea," Paul said, voice full of anguish.

Jasmine sniffled. "She seemed so nice."

Liam shut out the rest of the chatter to focus on not letting himself go mad. Sure, he'd healed men in bad shape before. No amount of experience would ever make it pleasant, fun, or easy the next time. "I'll heal Chelsea," he grunted as Riker's injuries faded from his own body.

Someone dropped her hand into his. He found three bullet wounds, one serious enough to kill her. Liam gritted his teeth and healed all of it. With the others, the injuries had been all internal. Hers made holes in him and put blood stains on his shirt. She coughed and sucked in air while Liam gasped and wheezed. He heard the soldiers threatening her, Paul and Jasmine trying to ward them off, and Kaitlin fussing over Riker. No one, it seemed, felt he needed any attention.

The pain of everyone else's wounds faded, leaving only his own leg tormenting him. He needed someone to give it to. No one here qualified, until he listened to the tone of Chelsea's voice as she protested her treatment. It grated on his nerves, and he knew there would be no talking sense to her. Having a broken bone would keep her out of trouble. He opened his eyes and grabbed her arm. Her squeal of surprise bothered him as he pushed the bone break onto her. It scared him that he could do this.

"Liam, what are you doing?" Paul gasped.

He let out a sigh of relief. "Experimenting." To see what would happen and assuage his guilt, he tried to heal her. Nothing happened. "Sorry, Chelsea. You shouldn't have tried to take Kaitlin." Thankfully, she wasn't up to retorting right now. "Tie her up to be on the safe side, and let's get inside. They're bound to need help by now."

Getting to his feet, he averted his eyes from Chelsea, now curled up in a ball and crying over her own broken leg. That left him noticing the heavy stares of his team. He wondered if Bobby felt the same way when people gave him these looks. He'd done something horrible and he knew it, and everyone else knew it, and he knew they knew and judged him for it. Maybe, the next time he saw Bobby, he could cut the guy a break.

Riker sprang into action, pulling a rope out of who knows where and tying Chelsea up. Hegi hurried to the door and pointed his gun at it. A few short, sharp reports announced his method of lock picking. Carter grabbed what remained of the handle and yanked it open. The five soldiers assaulted the entrance, taking gunfire and returning it.

"*You shouldn't have done that,*" Paul's mind voice accused him.

"*I thought I could take it back and heal it, but I guess I can't.*" He winced at how defensive and petulant that must have sounded. "*Can you contact Bobby? We need to know what's going on.*"

Chapter 12

Bobby opened the next door to find Lily and Sebastian as he'd last seen them, sitting with the book again. Sebastian lit up with a broad smile at the sight of Bobby and Jayce. Lily's face twisted with fear and she grabbed the boy up. Sebastian chirped with surprise and waved cheerfully.

"Bobby!" Sebastian tried and failed to wriggle free of his mother's grasp. "Mama, it's Bobby. Want a hug."

"Lily, what're you doing?" The expression on her face hurt. She hated him, enough to see Privek as better. "I ain't gonna hurt you or nothing. We gotta get outta here. No time for this kinda thing."

"We're not going anywhere with *you*." She said 'you' like he was the lowest of the low, something she scraped off her shoe. It hit him in the gut, worse than her slapping him and still being mad, worse than trying to accept there couldn't be anything between them, worse than just being avoided by her.

"Lily," he said helplessly, "please. Privek's gonna do things to Sebastian, you know that."

"Mama, let go." Sebastian squirmed in her arms, struggling against her desperate grip. He broke free and ran to Bobby, who bent down and picked him up. He settled the boy on his hip and small arms wrapped around his neck while he snuggled close.

Lily jumped up and screamed at Bobby. “Don’t you dare take him away from me!” A white brick formed in her hand, and she threw it at him.

“What in—” Bobby curled away from it to protect himself and Sebastian from the brick. It hit him in the back, and it hurt. “Lily, what’re you *doing*?”

She raised her hand and another brick formed. “You can’t take him, he’s not your son!”

He ducked away as she swung for his head. Thank goodness she’d never learned to fight. Setting Sebastian down, he turned to face her. She slammed the brick into his head hard enough to blow it into dragons. They snapped back into place and he grabbed her wrist to make her stop. Shoving his body at her, he pinned her against the wall, brick-holding hand over her head and the other bouncing around and smacking him ineffectually.

“What’s going on, why in heckbiscuits are you hitting me with…bricks…” She had her power and wasn’t sedated. Why did she have her power without being sedated? That made no sense. Privek wouldn’t leave her like that unless he trusted her. He stared stupidly at her face as she screamed and raged. Things clicked into place. Kanik. He messed with heads. He must have made her think they’d protect her from that evil Bobby who wanted to take her boy away.

How was he supposed to break that? Could it be broken? Was she stuck like this forever? No, there had to be a way. “I’m sorry for this, Lily.” He forcefully covered her mouth. “You gotta pipe down, just hear me out.”

She bit him and his hand dispersed into dragons. “Get off me, you perverted freak,” she snarled. “If you take Sebastian, I’ll kill you.”

In a storybook, kissing her would work. Bobby had a feeling she’d bite him again if he tried that, which wouldn’t solve anything.

"Lily, knock it off. I ain't taking your boy. I just come to see you, right? I know he ain't my son." She'd called him a 'perverted freak', so maybe it would help if he explained and apologized. "I also know you're pissed at me on account I done some stupid crap. I didn't mean to spy on you, I just didn't think first. And I shoulda left you a note. I never seem to do nothing right, not for you, and I'm sorry."

While he kept talking, Bobby noticed Jayce slip in and, with a finger to his lips, snatch Sebastian up and out of the room. "I ain't never tried to take Sebastian before, why d'you think I would now?" He did everything he could think of to get Jayce to understand he wanted Andrew to come in and stop Lily from making any more bricks.

She must have caught Andrew running towards her out of the corner of her eye, because she turned with another shriek and a white glob formed in her hand. Andrew barreled into them both, knocking all three of them to floor in a tangle. Bobby opened his eyes to find himself face to face with Lily.

"What…happened?" She blinked and squinted, then her eyes went wide in horror. "Oh my gosh. I walked right in here, I let them lock us up. And I called Privek on you. Why did I do that?" Squeezing her eyes shut, she pressed her face into Bobby's neck.

Bobby slumped in relief and held her close. "Andrew, go get Lisa. Next room."

The Creole nodded and scrambled to his feet. They knew now that he could cut off whatever control Kanik had over a person without having to get at Kanik himself. That didn't really make sense, but Bobby's own dragons didn't really make sense, so he had no room to cast that kind of stone.

"It's okay, Lily. Your head got messed with. Ain't your fault, ain't nothing to feel guilty for." He reveled in the fact that she didn't pull away or punch him, or hit him with a brick again.

When she did finally pull back from him, he brushed tears from her cheek and tried to guess how this would work out. He never could quite figure out women, not really, especially this particular one. For all he knew, she'd wriggle away and focus on her son. To his surprise, she broke into a smile and kissed him.

Jayce cleared his throat. "Much as it pains me to stop you, we do still need to escape with as many of our people as we can."

"Yeah." Bobby lay there on the floor with her, marveling at how something so simple could wipe away everything else. All the doubt and guilt still huddled inside his head, of course. Somehow, the feel of her soft, warm body against his made it matter a lot less. He had a job to do and he'd get it done.

"We'll talk later," Lily said. She wriggled away from him.

The way she moved put all kinds of ideas into Bobby's head, enough so he had to adjust his jeans as he hauled himself to his feet. "Right. Yeah. Okay. Right."

Jayce grinned. "Do you need a minute?"

"Shut up," Bobby grumbled. "There's still a lot to do here, and we got places to go and all. Dragons outside're telling me they had some trouble, and one of ours is dead. They're coming in."

That wiped the smirk off Jayce's face. He turned without another word, leading them all back to the elevators. Everyone else waited while recovering from the drugs, some more patiently than others. Bobby saw no guards and figured they'd been stuffed, unconscious, behind doors.

Lizzie showed off a ball of fire in her hand, lighting up her pleased grin. Stephen punched the button for the elevator. "Everyone is doing alright now, except Dan and Anita." Those two both drooped, in need of a nap or a shot of caffeine. Behind him, the elevator dinged and the doors slid open.

Kaitlin stood there, in front of Jasmine, Liam and Paul.

"Howdy, campers. We're holding the lobby. I see we have a bunch, but not everyone. These two are on our team, no molesting them."

"You have Maisie and Brian," Liam said, "Chelsea is out of commission and Dianna is dead. That leaves Kevin, Camellia, and Ray, plus the rest of your people. Kevin can turn invisible, Camellia does a chameleon thing, and Ray can make a protective shield. He's also good at punching."

Bobby nodded and thought about the situation. "Everyone get to the lobby and get out. Stephen, Andrew, Jayce, and me are gonna go through this building and get whoever else we can find." He ignored Lizzie's pout in favor of glancing back at Lily with Sebastian on her hip. "Don't bother being quiet. See what you can do to get us all outta here."

Lily smiled and kissed Bobby on the cheek on her way to the elevator. It warmed him to his toes to know she still wanted to be on his team Somewhere inside, he'd been half worried she'd slap him once she had a minute to think about it. She'd put a dumb grin on his face, and he didn't care that everyone could see it.

Stephen grabbed the door to the stairwell and hauled it open. Bobby gave Andrew an encouraging pat on the arm and led the way up. The room they'd seen through the portal had to be here someplace, and the upper basement seemed the most likely, making it their first stop.

"I'm gonna—" Bobby stopped on the landing for the next floor when he saw Lizzie step up next to Andrew. She had a hand on her hip and her expression dared him to challenge her. "What're you doing?"

She rolled her eyes. "I'm coming with you, duh. What are you going to do when you find Alice? Run really fast so she doesn't ice you up?"

"What're *you* gonna do when Kanik tries to take over your

mind? Burn him up first? "

"That's an idea." She grinned and held up her hand, now engulfed in flames. "Jayce can't defend against it, either."

Jayce shrugged. "If he gets me, he can't blow up the building."

Pushing the door open, he burst into the swarm as an unexpected volley of darts flew at him. Ice filled the space along with his dragons, catching and encasing more than half of them. Fire roared into life behind him, then Jayce's metal fist slammed through the rapidly melting sheet of ice, followed by his body.

"I really don't want to hurt anyone," Jayce said as he barreled into the group of men in tactical gear. In the time it took the dragons to get through the space now hosting a duel between fire and ice, Jayce knocked two of the shooters down and out. The swarm streaked in and shoved guns around, forcing several to clatter to the floor. Stephen stayed back for the moment, ready to knock Lizzie aside if he needed to. Andrew kept his back to the wall and out of sight.

Jayce clocked a third man with his steel fist, then a fourth with his elbow. "Why can't we just all be civilized?"

Bobby spotted Alice and went for her. She stood behind the men, peering around a corner to throw ice. They needed to get Alice and Andrew together. Hoping to circle around behind her, the swarm streaked up the hall, away from the fray. By the time he found her from the other side, Alice screamed with wordless frustration. He slipped up behind her and re-formed in the act of grabbing her arms and pinning them behind her back.

"Come on, Alice, why're you fighting us? Andrew's cooking ain't that bad, is it?"

"Dammit, Bobby!" She squirmed and struggled, kicking out and flinging her head back. His head blew into dragons that re-formed again immediately. "Let me go!"

"Lizzie, cover Andrew over to here!" One slow, difficult step at a time, he hauled Alice in that direction. Her body chilled in his arms, and his breath came out in little white puffs. If she kept that up, he'd wind up in the swarm again.

A curtain of fire sprang up, forming a curve around Jayce and the last few men still resisting him. Andrew sprinted around it and crashed into Bobby and Alice, not bothering to try to stop on the now slippery, icy floor. Without Alice affecting it, and with Lizzie's fire roaring, the temperature shot back up.

"What the..." Alice shook her head to clear it and Bobby let go of her.

"Welcome back," Bobby said as he relaxed onto the floor. "We're gonna need your help getting folks outta here. You up for that?"

Panting, Andrew wriggled out of the small heap of bodies and sat up on his knees. "I hope the rest are easier."

Alice sat up and stared stupidly at Lizzie, now by their side and offering her a hand up. "All I wanted to do was freeze everyone except those guys."

"Yeah, we know." Lizzie grabbed Alice's hand and yanked her to her feet. The fire dropped and disappeared, revealing Jayce standing in the midst of ten bodies in black tactical gear. Her eyes flicked from body to body and she licked her lips. "Isn't he great to watch? All those bulging silver muscles. It's all over, you know. *Everything* is metal. Can you just imagine?"

Jayce ignored her and, with Stephen's help, pulled weapons off the unconscious men. "I hate these darts," Stephen said with a scowl. He dropped a handful of them on the floor and stomped hard, smashing them. "Like we're rabid dogs that need to be controlled."

"Using them against our own may make things easier," Jayce said with a nod, "but I'm feeling like we shouldn't actually do it. I know I shot that one girl downstairs with her own dart gun. I just don't like it." He unloaded the one in his hands with a smooth motion, popping the loaded dart out and letting it fall to the floor. "Lizzie, can you burn them all up without hurting these guys? "

Instead of answering, small pops announced her doing it.

"Good deal." Bobby got to his feet. "Alice, there anyone else on this floor?"

"No, it was cleared out two days ago. Ever since they realized you were loose, they've been prepping the building for when you come back. Security was tightened and all nonessential employees were told to stay home. Some of us are here, some went to another facility. Sam's got the building wired, I'm not sure what all for. They're using Greg for something, too."

Aside — Privek

Everything was not precisely going according to plan, but it came close enough. Privek glanced over at Kanik, hoping the lunatic would stick to it. Right now, the kid paced back and forth frantically across the thick shag carpet, ignoring the monitors and muttering to himself. He did that a lot and Privek had learned to ignore it a while ago.

Those monitors, with the camera feeds provided by Sam, showed a large group of them converging on the lobby, along with those five soldiers helping them. He should have known better than to post those men anywhere near someplace Mitchell might show up if he ever got loose, but their involvement wasn't any more of a disaster than anything else.

His eyes zeroed in on the actual problem: Moore and Pearson. He didn't expect either of them to want to wake Mitchell up, and definitely didn't expect Moore to find Elena. The telepath shouldn't have been persuaded away from their goals, either. He should have seen through Mitchell just like Kanik's implanted suggestions told him to. Kanik's ability, apparently, wasn't as foolproof as he thought. At least it had kept Pearson from successfully reading his own mind.

Actually, in some ways, the worst part had to be Kanik losing his control over Jayce early. After making the effort to set those first four up to flee those ridiculous experiments, and planting those lists so they'd do half the work for him, he'd lost his ace in the hole. At least everything had gone well prior to losing him. If the suggestions had only lasted a little longer, he wouldn't have had to send Camellia to find them. Things would be much better if he had Jayce now, too.

Privek pulled his phone out and sent Sam a short text, trusting the improvements she and that Greg kid made to the structure to be enough to handle the escapees. In a minute, several would be dead, and the rest would blindly flail around, blundering into the rest of his trap. Good thing Mitchell decided to take all the ones who could actually survive this sort of thing on his side trip.

He imagined himself slapping glossy photographs down in a line on the President's desk, each showing Mitchell's handiwork, or that of one of his band of freaks. The fireballs wouldn't be terribly compelling, but the corpses with their chests ripped out would make a statement. Agent Kaffer's body, too; all those tiny bites and scorchmarks hinted at a slow, painful death of a thousand cuts.

The President and all his advisors—the Vice President, the Chief of Staff, the Chairman of the Joint Chiefs, the National Security Advisor, and more—gaped at the pictures, sucking in breaths and riveted by the grotesque images.

"These things represent a clear and present danger to the security of the Unites States, Mister President."

The President kept his hands to himself, as if refusing to touch the photos would make them less real. He was a weak man, a politician. A few long, stunned seconds passed before he reached for the one showing Mitchell and a few of the others. Picking it up, he stared at the faces, imagining his own teenage children in their place. "They're just kids," he protested.

Privek slammed a hand on the desk, making all of them jump. "Don't let them deceive you, Mr. President. They may look like ordinary humans, but I assure you, they are not. They're dangerous halfbreeds, too alien to handle the power they've developed without letting it consume and corrupt them. We need to hunt them down before they kill like this again. I have the tools to do the job, I just need resources to deploy them."

The President nodded and sighed in resignation. "Give him whatever he needs to deal with this. I'd give you a Cabinet position, Mr. Privek, but then you'd be subject to Congressional approval. This should be kept quiet, and your vigilance and patriotism will be rewarded. Handsomely."

Kanik's voice broke into his fantasy, dispelling it for now. "I don't understand what we're doing anymore." He seemed to have regained some measure of lucidity. When he'd first found the kid, he'd been paranoid and ranting and obsessed with revenge against the executives of that rail freight company. He saw the potential immediately. Kanik was his golden ticket. So sad he'd probably need to kill the kid to seal this deal. Someone would have to take the blame for everything. Privek would miss having such a useful tool at his disposal, though.

"We're getting back at the men who hurt you."

Bringing up his old hurts never failed to distract Kanik. He went off on a spittle-flecked, incoherent rant about injustice and the marginalization of the Inuit people, and all the rest. Funny how out of all these freaks, the one who could plant suggestions in others' minds turned out to be the easiest to manipulate.

"The test subjects," Privek said loudly enough to interrupt, "will be waking up soon. You should go and make sure all of them are under your control. We'll need them to keep you safe."

Kanik paused in his pacing and nodded fervently. "Yes, yes, the railroad men are coming. They won't get me. No one will get me. We'll stop them and their pawns." He hurried out of the room, rubbing the old burn scars on his hand.

Privek smirked and turned his attention to the monitors just in time to watch the real show begin. With proper motivation, Sam and Greg did good work. Maybe he'd keep them around. Just because they were freaks didn't mean they couldn't be controlled for the long term. It depended on how this whole thing went down.

Chapter 13

Packed with people, the elevator dinged and the doors slid open. Liam stood away from the back wall, ready to pile out with everyone else, when he noticed Paul roll his shoulders uncomfortably. His eyes darted to Kaitlin. Her eyes closed and her lips parted.

Paul shrugged it off and stepped out of the elevator with the others. Owen carried Maisie in his arms and Matthew had Brian slung over his shoulder. Lisa helped Anita. Lily let Dan lean on her while Sebastian walked beside her, holding her hand. Jasmine sat in Liam's pocket again, trying not to take up space.

"Wait," Kaitlin said.

Fearing the worst, Liam reached out and missed Anita's arm.

"Come back." Kaitlin grabbed Lily's shirt.

Outside the doors, Liam heard a mechanical whirring. It sounded very different from Bobby's swarm. His foot moved back and he had a sinking feeling he knew what Kaitlin had seen.

The lobby erupted with gunfire.

"Get down!" The voice came from the lobby, and Liam thought it might be Riker. "We need cover!"

Liam grabbed Dan and hauled him back in, healing the fresh

injury to his leg without thinking. How many bullet wounds would he heal today? At once, he hoped it would be a lot and only a few—the lobby had few places to hide and that sounded like a lot of weapons firing. Apparently, Privek had expected something like this.

The deafening roar of guns trampled over voices shouting in the lobby. Jasmine crawled out of Liam's pocket and raced out of the elevator as the doors slid shut, cutting off the clamor.

"What are we supposed to do?" Liam looked to Kaitlin, begging her to have an answer.

Her eyes darted around wildly. "I don't know. It's like with the assault on the farm. I only know what to do for me, not anyone else, and only at the last minute."

"What about Riker and his men?"

Kaitlin went pale. "I…I don't know," she whispered. "They were in the lobby last we knew."

Sebastian reached a little hand up to the buttons. "Mama, don't run away." He pushed the number one and watched the doors open again. The fire sprinklers hissed, soaking everything and putting a metallic tang in the air. They heard a gun sputter and stop. Lily grabbed her son, pulling him away from the doors and shielding him with her own body.

"I got it," Anita's voice, strained with pain, called out. "One left."

The last gun clicked, still shooting without bullets. "Clear," Jasmine's voice shouted from near the ceiling. "Is everybody okay?" A lot of silence answered her.

Liam pulled himself to his feet and poked his head cautiously out of the elevator. "Hold the doors open." Dan stuck a hand in the way and peered out, too. A haze of dust and smoke hung in the air, the walls riddled with bullet holes. Chunks of concrete or plaster, or whatever the walls and floor were made of, littered the floor.

Everything was drenched. Brackish water formed small puddles bounded by debris.

Flinching away from the rain, Liam held up a hand to shield his eyes so he could see. He caught sight of Anita, huddled on herself and shivering behind a pillar, her power holding up a broken piece of bullet-ridden plexiglass from the security station as a shield.

Jasmine clung to something on the ceiling, dangling next to the empty machine gun still chattering away. She must have disconnected the ammunition somehow. As he watched, she shrank down to her squirrel shape again and raced across the wall to get down.

The front wall remained intact with only the glass door damaged. He saw Riker standing there, doing the same thing as him: checking the situation for safety and survivors. A wide smear of blood on the floor suggested all his men didn't get out in one piece. So long as they all lived, he could take care of them.

Thanks to the sprinklers, the air cleared quickly, and Liam made out a limp hand in the debris. "Can someone shut off the water?" He hopped and hurried over to that hand, hoping he'd find it attached to an arm.

"I can only affect people," Dan grunted from close behind him. "Anita, did you get hurt?"

From what he'd seen of the Hill footage, he never would have guessed Dan would show concern for anyone else. Yet here he was, offering Anita a hand up and looking her over. The Hispanic girl took his help, letting out a squeak as she tried to put weight on her foot. Distracted from his other goal, Liam leaned over and took her other hand. Another bullet wound added insult to all the injury his pants had suffered already. The pain made him grit his teeth as it flashed in his leg and rapidly slipped away.

Riker, Hegi, and Platt reached the other people first and

shifted the debris off them. "Liam," Riker called out, his tone sharp enough to cut through shock, "what can you do about dead?"

"Nothing." Liam took a deep breath and forced himself to go find out who Riker had found, knowing he only asked because he found a body. What he wouldn't give for an umbrella right now.

"Day-umn." Dan's comment covered the situation. Paul was dead, his body riddled with bloody holes. Alongside him, four more: Lisa, Maisie, Brian, Owen. It looked like they'd been used a thousand times as targets in a shooting gallery. The guns broadsided them, because Brian should have been able to shield them, and Maisie should have been able to get them out of there.

"Wait, where's Matt?" Dan looked around, then he pointed at a hole in the wall, big enough for a person to get through. "Never mind. We don't want to find him right now. He's got no control as a wolf."

"Liam, quick," Platt said, holding two fingers to Maisie's neck, "this one is alive." Riker gave up on Owen and crab hopped to grab Maisie's hand to shove it at Liam. Debris drunkenly flopped off of her, probably Anita's doing.

In a daze, Liam took it, then he collapsed to the floor, overwhelmed by all the damage done to her body. Bullet wounds and cracked ribs and internal bleeding all warred for his attention, and he let out a gurgling scream as it washed over him. Something else kept her unconscious, but she'd be fine.

"What do we do now, Sarge? Guns popping out of the ceiling wasn't anything we expected." Platt picked Maisie up.

Riker pushed Paul's glassy, staring eyes shut and scowled. "Outside. Liam, take care of Hansen. He'll live, but we could use him at one hundred percent."

"Lisa's pregnant." Kaitlin shook, hugging herself. "I didn't see this coming. Why didn't I see this coming?"

"You're not per—" Riker cut himself off, and he, Platt, and Hegi all cocked their heads to the side and listened to something. "Change of plan."

Carter helped Hansen, cradling his arm and limping, hurry in through the door and looked to Riker. "There's four of them."

"Elevator, now!" Riker barked.

Everyone else hurried that way. Liam stood there, staring stupidly at Paul's corpse. He risked everything because Liam asked him to. Consumed by his need to find Elena, he begged and cajoled until Paul relented and helped him wake up Bobby. His death was Liam's fault. Elena was safe and Paul was dead.

Someone shouted his name, maybe more than once. It made him look up. Three women he'd only previously seen pictures of filed in through the door, accompanied by Raymond. He thought the thin, waifish Asian wearing blue leggings with white polka dots and a matching blue top might be Ai. The second, a blonde with curves in black pants and a red blouse and boots could either be Hannah or Violet.

As for the third, they only had two black women among them that he knew of, and Dianna's body still lay outside. That made this one, with her hair swept up in an elegant bun that clashed with her plain shirt and jeans, Tiana. Ray looked like he usually did: a burly black man in military camouflage pants and a dingy white tank top, holding a large silvery shield.

It took him a long second to register the strange, futuristic guns they each carried. By then, the foursome had those weapons raised. Each showed him cold indifference, a willingness to cut him down where he stood and be unmoved by it.

Something took control of his body and made him run, ducking down and hopping around to be harder to target.

The guns threw pulses of sickly greenish light across the

lobby to slam into the already broken surfaces. He heard sizzling where they hit, the light either cooking or eating the surfaces it struck. Liam's mouth went dry as he considered what that would do to flesh. Where did they get guns like that? His body ducked into the elevator and the doors slid shut behind him.

"Jesus fucking Christ with a biscuit," Dan spat. "Run next time, ya idjit."

Riker grabbed Liam's arm and smacked it onto Hegi's, causing his healing gift to activate and take the soldier's pain as the elevator trundled upwards. "They might have been there to herd us, I'm not sure. Rundown of superpowers here?"

Sebastian, the cute little boy holding Lily's hand, pointed at each person and recited all their abilities as if he had the list memorized somehow. "Healing, precog, telekinesis, body control, weapon creation, portal-based teleportation, squirrel shapeshifter. Uncle Matty is a werewolf."

Everyone stared at him except Jasmine, who sat in Kaitlin's hand as a squirrel. Liam didn't blame her for not wanting to be in his pocket anymore.

"Right." Riker recovered from the surprise well before Liam did. "Thanks. What kind of weapons?"

Lily she sighed as she pulled her son into a bewildered hug. "So far, I haven't tried a lot. I can make functioning bullets of any kind you show me, bricks, blades, hand tools, and inflexible sheets. None of it lasts more than an hour."

Riker nodded and pulled the clip out of his rifle. Popping one bullet off, he handed it to her. "We may need more of these before we get out of here. Anybody get an empty spare clip, give it to her so she can fill it up. What's wrong with the teleporting girl here?" He slammed the clip home and checked his pistol. His men followed suit, checking their weapons, too.

Dan shrugged. "Jayce shot her with that drug stuff. She was on the wrong team. She'll be out for hours."

"She's not a threat to them, then, so she's low priority if we need to bug out. What button did you push?"

Platt shrugged. "I didn't."

Sebastian beamed up at him. "I pushed the six!"

Chapter 14

"The elevator just went past. I heard it."

Bobby nodded. He shouldn't have called back *all* his dragons. The situation go out of control so much and so fast that he thought he needed all hands…er, claws on deck. Now he had no idea what else might be going on with Riker and Kaitlin and the rest. That needed to change. "I'm gonna scout ahead and go see who's in the elevator and what's up. Stick together and don't do nothing stupid."

"That's your job." Stephen finally sounded like himself again.

"Yeah." He blew into the swarm and left a few behind. Most of the dragons poured down the hallways of the second floor, searching through the place. A handful went to find a way to wriggle into the elevator. Another handful went down to check the lobby. Since they hadn't gone past the second floor yet, the dragons heading for the lobby reached their destination first.

They streaked out into a war zone.

Bobby threw himself into one of those dragons, stunned by what he found. Tiana, Ai, Violet, and a man he didn't know picked their way through, holding weird looking guns. Violet stooped to check the bodies.

"These are dead. Leave them."

Tiana peered into the giant hole in the wall. “Should we check this way?”

“Nah,” the black man said with a shake of his head, “our job was just to get them to take the elevator. Mission accomplished.”

“I’m going up the stairs to make sure they get a proper greeting.” Ai blurred as she ran to the stairs.

“Andrew!” Bobby had enough dragons near the Creole to at least form a kind of mouth. It was weird and freakish. He chose not to think about it in favor of grabbing a chance to get Ai. “Stairs! ”

Fortunately, Andrew hadn’t gone anywhere yet and decided not to be disturbed by what he saw of Bobby. He tossed the door open and flung himself through it, just in time to collide with Ai as she sped up the stairs at a hundred miles an hour. They tumbled together in a squawking heap, her gun clattering to the floor and shooting off a pulse that singed Andrew’s arm. He groaned. He also slapped a hand on Ai’s arm and squeezed so she couldn’t get away.

“Oh, my head.” Ai groaned. “What did I just hit?”

“Me. And the floor. What’re you in such a hurry for, anyway?” Andrew let her go and they each leaned against the other and the wall to get to their feet.

“I was…” She frowned and shook her head. “Why did I even care about that?” Her eyes went wide and her mouth fell open. “Oh, Andrew, Lisa is dead! And Owen. Down in the lobby, with some of the others I don’t know. I tried to shoot one of us, too! Oh my gosh, why did I do that? ”

“Easy, easy.” Andrew hugged her. “They’re using some kind of mind control. I’m the antidote.”

Bobby wanted to hear everything she had to say, just not right now. He sent his dragons back to their search and threw himself into one racing to the top floor. They streaked out into a hallway near the elevators, where he saw Andrea pacing impatiently. The dragons crawled across the ceiling, trying to go unnoticed. Though she couldn't disintegrate people, that wouldn't stop her from disintegrating the elevator.

He watched in horror as panels in the ceiling slid down to reveal guns. The elevator dinged to announce its arrival before he could come up with a plan. Bobby dove inside it the moment the doors opened with the rest of this small group. Five dragons pushed on the second floor button frantically as bullets flew through the air. Fortunately, everyone had already ducked down, probably Kaitlin's doing.

The doors slid shut, cutting off the gunfire. The first two hits made small dimples in the metal doors. The next two thumped in farther, somehow meeting less resistance. Bobby could see how this was going to go and threw himself back downstairs, calling his dragons together and re-forming most of himself near Jayce. "Elevator! It's about to fall."

Jayce opened his mouth, then shut it and sprinted for the elevator, with Bobby right behind and calling out for Stephen. The three men cranked the doors open and looked up.

"I'll slow it down." Stephen jumped into the shaft and flew up while Bobby helped Jayce brace himself so he could stop the falling car and hold it.

How were they going to get Andrea to Andrew? It sure wasn't going to happen with them all standing around waiting for disasters. "Keep everyone together," he told Andrew, pointing at him to make sure he knew that was his job. Before he could respond, Bobby burst back into the swarm and streamed up to the top floor.

The swarm poured out through the same vent as before and streaked towards Andrea, now standing at the gaping hole where the elevator doors should be, peering down the shaft. He would never get a better chance. The swarm shoved her, hard, and watched her fall.

Someone down there would catch her. They had to. She screamed up enough of a storm, they wouldn't be able to ignore her.

In that moment, watching her swallowed up by the darkness, hearing her terror, he knew what they had to do. The swarm dove after her and noticed she stopped screaming with a sound of confusion. Anita caught her. Dragons flew around her and out through the gap as Riker and his men climbed down and helped everyone else.

"Andrew, take care of Andrea soon as you can." Bobby re-formed again, feeling like he kept going in circles. He'd had about enough of that. "Lizzie, you remember how I said not to blow up the building?"

"Yes." Lizzie pouted at him with a sullen nod.

"Forget it. Set the whole damned thing on fire." He watched her face light up with glee.

"Bobby," Andrew said as he hurried to the elevator, "we're kind of *in* the building right now."

"Yeah. Not for long. Blow out a window, and we're getting outta here." Pointing down a hallway, he stayed put while she ran off. "Time to get outta here. Jayce, Stephen, and Anita're gonna ferry whoever they gotta. You see anybody what needs to be helped out, you help 'em out, but get 'em straight to Andrew. We ain't playing this maze of death crap, and we're getting our people back."

He picked Sebastian up, who hugged him around his neck. "You wanna take a ride with the dragons? "

"Is Mama coming?"

"I'll be right behind you," Lily said, smiling at them both.

Lizzie shouted, "Fire in the hole!" She sounded positively rapturous. An explosion rocked the building.

"That's my girl," Dan smirked, the last one out of the elevator. The second he got clear, Stephen and Jayce let the car go. Everyone hurried to find Lizzie. She hadn't gone far, and the size of the gaping hole in the side of the building surprised Bobby. The pile of rubble strewn across the ground below it attested to how much force she put into the fireball that caused it. He could see chunks of masonry at least fifty feet away.

As soon as she saw Dan round the corner, Lizzie ran and jumped into his arms, planting a kiss on his lips as he spun her around. Bobby ignored them in favor of peering out through the hole. He saw a small horde of animals converging right where they'd land if they jumped out from here. Tiana must be nearby, which meant— Something green and painful tagged him in the shoulder. Sebastian, protected by the wall, was fine.

Whatever that gun shot, it made his entire shoulder burn. Dragons all around the injury popped off, some of them dissolving. "Stay back! Andrea, can you get that thing? It's Violet, so look up."

Andrea, still near Andrew, was about to move closer when Violet swooped right up and started spraying the area with that weird green stuff. Bobby's arm came back together and he threw a punch at her face. It probably hurt him more than her, but it distracted her long enough for Andrea to make her gun disintegrate into a fine layer of dust. Violet squealed and flew away.

"I'll get her," Stephen growled, a burning streak on his face healing over. He ran for the opening and jumped into the air behind her, chasing after her. Stephen and Jayce seemed to have taken the brunt of the burst she fired in, and Liam healed Jayce.

Bobby peered out again and spotted Tiana. "I ain't keen to get chomped to death by rats and cats. Anybody got any ideas?"

A squirrel zoomed up and changed into Jasmine lying on the floor, peering out. "I can help!" She screwed her eyes shut and pressed her lips together.

Liam blinked and stared at her. "Do we want to know what

she's doing?"

"Probably not," Jayce said with a smirk.

Kaitlin cleared her throat. "Bobby, if we set the building on fire, there are some people who'll die in here."

Of course there were. Nothing about this could be easy. No, that just wouldn't be right. Bobby sighed and set Sebastian down. "You know where they are and what's guarding them?"

"Fourth floor, four of our people, no guards. Just locked doors."

"Alright. I got that. Stay with your Momma," he told Sebastian.

The boy nodded gravely. "Come back."

He ruffled the kid's hair affectionately and gave Lily a sheepish grin. "That's the one thing I seem to be pretty good at." The sight of her grinning at him warmed him to his toes as he blew into the swarm again and streamed up to get to the fourth floor. Somehow, he knew it wouldn't be as simple as Kaitlin said, so he took the time to fly through the fourth floor, looking all around for anything that might be amiss.

There were no hidden guns or trapdoors, no people, nothing. He did find some cameras scattered around, and smashed all of them. That done, he set to the task of breaking the four doors open to find Greg's boyfriend Albert, Lisa's husband Clive, Jasmine's fiancee Will, and, strangely, Christopher the empath. Chris had been either drugged or controlled, he figured.

Once the doors were all open, Bobby re-formed in the middle of them. "Time to go, guys. They're trying to—" Chris and Albert flung their arms around him and hugged him tightly. Clive and Will gave him strained, anxious smiles.

"I don't care how uncomfortable this makes you, Bobby," Christopher said with a teary warble in his voice. "I'm really happy to see you."

"Um, yeah, look," Bobby squirmed, "I'm glad you're free and stuff, but we gotta get outta here."

"Where's Greg?" Albert let go first. "Is he okay?"

"I don't know. Stairs are this way." He avoided looking at Clive while herding them. "Jasmine's okay, she's helping us. Ain't seen Greg yet."

"What about Lisa?"

Bobby scratched his cheek and wished he had better news. More, he wished he knew Clive better so he could break it to him in the easiest way possible. So many people lived at the farm and he'd spent so little time there that he hadn't really met everyone yet. He opened his mouth to say something, not sure what it would turn out to be.

"You're not getting out." Although well timed, Bobby curled his lip at this distraction. Sam and Greg stood side-by-side, blocking the hallway. Sam had her arms crossed over her chest, showing a completely uncharacteristic amount of confidence. Though she had no weapons Bobby could see, he figured she meant to use his dragons. Greg, on the other hand, had adopted a genuine mad scientist look with red tinted goggles, a lab coat, work gloves, and a really big futuristic gun held in both hands.

Bobby put up his hands in surrender. "These guys was just bait for the rest of us. I know it and so do you. Let them go."

"Greg? What are you doing?" Albert pushed past Bobby to stand in front of him. "Did you make…a gun?"

Greg's face contorted in confusion. "Two different kinds," he said.

"But…you refused when those guys from the Pentagon came. Remember? Last year, two men came and tried to recruit you, to work on the next generation of weapons. You said no, that you'd never make a weapon. That was a perversion of science, that's what you told them."

"This is all very nice," Sam said, "but you're still not going anywhere. Get into that room, all of you in the one." She shooed all of them with both lanky arms. No one moved.

"Greg, this isn't you, it's not who you are! Why are you doing this?" Albert stood there defiantly, his hands held out in invitation.

Sam's eyes narrowed and Bobby had some suspicions about what she might try. He took a swift step around Albert and punched her in the face, hating himself for hitting a girl. Again. She stumbled back to hit the wall and Bobby followed her, vaguely registering that Albert grabbed at the gun, and Clive and Will helped him overwhelm the super-geek. Chris stepped aside with his hands held up, useless and panicky. Sam pulled something out of her pocket, and Bobby didn't realize he needed to dodge it until she jammed it into his gut and jolted him with electricity.

He broke apart into the swarm, losing a few more dragons to everything Privek set up in this stupid building. That must have been what Sam wanted, because he immediately found himself fighting for control of his dragons. He wanted them to get Sam to drop the taser and keep her busy so she couldn't interfere with the others. They all wanted to fly off into that room and stay there. Neither happened. Instead, they buzzed around in the air, doing nothing but taking up space.

"Don't hit him," Albert wailed as Clive slugged Greg across the chin. Greg fell to the floor, stunned by the blow, and Albert followed him down, protecting his head.

Clive grunted and shook his hand out. "Do something, Chris!"

"Like what?" Chris wrung his hands together and kept his eyes screwed shut against all the violence.

Bobby wanted to grab him and slap him. Sam wouldn't let him re-form. At least they refused to do what she told them to. That was something.

"You do emotions, don't you?" Will grabbed Chris's chin and turned his face to look at Sam through the swarm. "Open your eyes and make her…I don't know! Scared or something. Distract her. She's obviously doing something to Bobby."

Chris breathed fast and shallow, opening one eye tentatively and wincing away from the whole episode. "I've never done that before!"

Clive picked up Greg's gun. "Try, dammit! She wants to kill us all."

Will squeezed Chris's shoulder. "Come on, Chris, you can do this. We need you to do this."

Gulping audibly, Chris nodded and stared at Sam so hard Bobby thought his head might explode. She shrieked and scuttled away. Bobby got control of his swarm back and they re-formed fast enough for him to chase her down and grab her. At least he didn't have to hit her anymore. "Good job and keep it up Chris. We gotta get 'em both down to Andrew, he'll fix it so they're themselves again. Don't leave that weapon here."

Clive stopped fiddling with the gun, keeping a firm grip on it. "She's dead, isn't she? That's why you won't answer."

Unable to look at him and say it, Bobby hauled Sam towards a window on the side of the building where the others should be. "I'm sorry, man. It happened in the lobby." Considering what the dragons saw down there, he figured Sam and Greg might be responsible. He had no intention of saying so. Not when it wasn't really their fault. "Privek and Kanik done it." How he wished he could blame those two for everything.

Clive pressed his lips thin and nodded, then pushed Chris to get him moving. Will helped Albert pick up the still stunned Greg and carry him. At the window Bobby found, he grabbed a lamp and smashed it into the glass, shattering both. He stuck his head out to see a massive pile of squirrels converged at the base of the building with almost everyone else in the center of it. Jayce stood under Andrew, ready to catch him if he fell while climbing a rope to get down to the ground.

"I got six more up here," he shouted down.

Stephen shot upwards and gave Bobby a smirk. "It's possible you may never realize how much I appreciate you picking the shady side of the building for our escape path."

Bobby chuckled as he wrangled Sam through the window and into Stephen's hands. "Hey, man, Head Cowboy takes care of the herd. Make sure to get Andrew on Sam and Greg. They done tried to kill us. Have him hit everyone else, too, just to be on the safe side."

"Aye, Cap'n. I can carry two at once." They pushed Greg through and Stephen carried both down, then returned for the rest. Bobby's swarm flew down with him the last time, and he got to see Jasmine jump up and send squirrels flying as she ran for Will and flung herself at him. Thanks to Liam, Greg and Albert got to be reunited, and Sam collapsed into a heap of sobbing as soon as Andrew touched her. Matthew lay in the grass, off to the side with no squirrels near him.

All of that mattered, just not right now. Bobby had a feeling he'd come to hate the word "prioritize". It made him feel like a dick to interrupt everyone while they reunited and took stock and watched Lizzie gleefully blow up the building. He had to do it anyway.

Lily, he noticed, glanced at him, gave him a tight-lipped smile, then put her arm around Clive's shoulders. He hoped she'd done that because she could tell he had something to say and needed to get it out sooner rather than later. Striding to the center of the group, he cleared his throat and found almost everyone staring at him as a result.

"Folks, we can all hear the sirens a'coming. Some of us're still missing, and we still gotta get to Adelphi and free all them people, but there's another thing we gotta do first. Today, we gotta let folks know we're here and we ain't gonna let ourselves be locked up, nor experimented on, nor treated like we ain't worth the same as humans. If'n you don't want to be public, get scarce. I got lots to say, and it's gonna be heard, and that's that, but ain't nobody else gotta be seen or known about if'n you ain't comfortable with it. No shame either way."

Stephen stepped forward first. "I'm in, for all of it." He flashed his fangs in a grin. "I can hardly wait to have teenage girls climbing all over each other to let me suck their blood."

Jayce nodded and so did a few others. As expected, Liam wasn't interested, and he didn't hold it against the healer. When they were sorted out, Riker and his men stayed, along with Jayce, Stephen, Lizzie, Dan, Ray, and Matthew. None of the rest wanted to be seen right now. Several said they needed time to think about it rather than outright refusing.

Lily waved to him as she carted Sebastian off, pointing to the boy as the reason she wouldn't stay, and Bobby nodded. He understood. He also sent a dragon with them so they'd be able to find each other later. By the time the fire department showed up, all of them managed to get at least a few blocks away and the building had become an inferno.

Ignored by the firefighters, the twelve of them stood there, watching it from the curb. "Riker, you guys sure you want to have your faces flashed on TV?"

Riker shrugged. "If we're going to be court-martialed and charged with treason anyway, we might as well try to control the media coverage a little."

"My mom is going to kill me for this," Hegi said with a sigh.

Bobby snorted. "You always got a place with us, even if I gotta smack heads together to make sure of it." He turned, because the first news van screeched to a halt mere yards away from them. "Man, they musta been in the neighborhood already."

Stephen sneered. "Vultures."

"Says the vampire," Jayce chuckled.

"Excuse me!" An attractive woman in a skirt suit jumped out of the van and looked right at them. "Did you see what happened? Would you be willing to talk about it on camera, live?"

Bobby smiled warmly. "Sure thing, ma'am. I done saw the whole thing, and I'd be right happy to tell the whole world all about it."

The reporter's eyes lit up with a jackpot smile and she beckoned frantically for her cameraman to get set up.

Chapter 15

Liam clicked the radio on in his car. Since he had his keys and the car still sat in the parking lot, he figured he might as well get it while he could. The Roadster had only one passenger seat, and he brought Clive with the rather large gun he refused to let go of. A few others took their own cars, too, he noticed, and everyone who wanted to got away from the site without a problem. Chelsea, as it turned out, regenerated slowly. Once Liam explained that to her, she flew away.

He glanced at Clive, wondering if he'd been stupid to take the only other person suffering an acute loss. They had something in common right now, so he figured they ought to stick together. Granted, Elena hadn't been the one he lost there, so he had no idea how to relate to Clive on that level. Paul, though, had been his friend, a *real* friend. All his life, people had valued him for his parents' money, or his ability to get them out of trouble or do them favors, or his looks. Paul had asked for nothing and gave everything.

"...According to eyewitnesses," the radio voice told them, "part of the building exploded out a minute or two before the entire structure was engulfed in flames. People were seen jumping out from the second floor, and the area is now swarmed with first responders.

Several unconfirmed reports— Hold on, I'm just being handed additional information about this, which is kind of a surprise. Usually with something like this, it's just a standard…sort…oh my God." The radio personality left two seconds of dead air, then a commercial started.

Clive reached over and snapped the radio off. "Bobby's really spilling it all."

"He said he would. If there's one thing I've learned about Bobby over the past few days, it's that he keeps his word." Liam let the car go quiet again. The electric engine didn't even make any noise, leaving them floating down the road in a tense, heavy bubble. After a long pause, he asked, "Can I take you anywhere in particular?"

Clive stared down at the weapon on his lap, one hand idly patting it. "Adelphi."

Liam regretted asking the question. "I was thinking more of a bar or something."

"Why? Do you think getting drunk will bring her back?"

"No. It's just what I could use after all of that. I've never healed so many people at once and been so utterly useless at the same time. I couldn't save your wife, and for that, I'm sorry."

Clive turned to stare out the window. "I want Privek to…to hurt."

"I can relate to that." It was a bad idea, but he got onto the highway that would take them on as much of a roundabout route to Adelphi as he thought he could manage without Clive getting suspicious. Privek probably had that place set up with even more defenses. They'd need backup. Of course, Bobby planned to assault it. They just needed to wait until he got there. A handful of them would probably be able to trash the place in minutes. He remembered the footage from Hill. That's what happened when a small group of them worked together. This would be a bigger group.

The scenery flashed by. Liam expected Clive to break down and cry at some point. He didn't. The man struck him as the mild-mannered type, with a boring job he did to pay the bills rather than out of love for it. The way he kept patting the weird gun seemed out of place and disturbing.

Liam's phone rang as he rolled to a stop for a traffic light at the end of the off-ramp in Adelphi. Glancing at it, he didn't recognize the number. Once, he would have assumed it unimportant and ignored it. Now, he sighed and answered it, expecting it to shatter his expectations or world yet again. "Hello? "

"Hi, you don't know me. My name is Mike." He spoke in a hushed voice. "I work at White Sands Missile Range, on the Maze Beset Space-Time Anomaly project. I know Sam, and Bobby Mitchell gave me your phone number. He asked me to call you if I wanted to help all of you. This has been my first real chance to do that, and I don't have long. They just successfully sent a penny through the wormhole and it didn't collapse. When they shut it down and opened it back up, they got the penny back, along with some other stuff. A little scoop of dirt and plants, maybe some small animals or insects."

Liam's heart sped into overdrive. They'd done it. They'd created a wormhole to another world. An insistent horn from the car behind him startled him back into awareness of his surroundings. He flipped off the guy behind him and got the car moving. "Um, okay. Thanks for letting me know. Do you think they're going to keep trying today, or be sidetracked by studying the dirt?"

"Best guess, they're going to poke at it for a few hours, then go back to tweaking the machine and try it again as soon as possible."

"Good to know. I don't suppose there's anything you can do to maybe slow them down a little? Like, a day or two, I mean. Not grand sabotage or anything."

"Oh. I don't know. I'm already taking a pretty big risk by calling you. Can you tell me something? How's Sam? Bobby said she was in some kind of jail."

"She's okay." Liam hated lying to strangers. He assuaged his guilt with the knowledge that he'd only lied in one sense—physically, she was okay. Kanik's gift was all the more horrific for letting his victims remember everything they'd done under his influence. She'd done quite a bit. "We got her out. She's free. You might want to give her a little time to recover from what happened."

"Sure, yeah. That's cool. I'll just email her and let her know I'm here if she wants to talk or anything. Thanks. Oh, crap, I gotta go. I'll do whatever I can here." Mike hung up.

They reached the facility. Liam stopped the car on the street about ten yards from the driveway, acutely aware he had no real way in on his own. "We can wait here for the others. With them—" He stopped because Clive tossed the door open and got out. Liam hit the button to shut the car off and stepped out, too.

Clive pointed the gun at the guard shack and fired. Liam expected a laser beam or some sort of projectile. Instead, the ground trembled and some force churned up and tossed a wide cone of asphalt, dirt, concrete, grass sod, and everything else in front of Clive. The gun pitched upwards in his hands from the recoil. Some kind of shockwave flung the debris at the guard post, crashing into it and ripping it apart.

Liam cringed away instinctively. He also screwed his eyes shut, not wanting to see what happened to the soldier inside. That guy had been doing his job a few days ago, and Liam had blustered their way past him. Now, he probably had been battered to death by one man's grief.

Looking down at the gun, Clive fiddled with the levers and fired it again. This time, he held it steady. He'd made the cone more precise: narrow, focused, and longer.

"Clive! Stop, you're going to kill people." Liam hurried around his car to find the gun pointed at him. "What are you doing? I'm on your side."

Now, when he'd found the perfect tool to vent his rage, tears streamed down his face. "Leave me alone. You sit in your fancy car and wait for the others. I'm going to take care of this, once and for all."

Liam raised his hands in surrender and tried to imagine how the other man felt, tried to stand in his shoes. "This isn't the way, Clive. If you go in there by yourself, you're going to get killed." The moment he said the words, he realized that was the plan. "At least try not to hurt anyone else, Clive. They're just doing their job. Most of them don't even know what's going on here. It's a research facility, not an evil mastermind lair." How long would it be before the others showed up? He had no idea how long he could keep Clive from rampaging by talking to him.

"Ignorance is no excuse!" Clive shot the gun at the ground between himself and Liam, then turned and ran for the gate.

Wiping his face made things worse, smearing the dirt into his mouth and eyes. He rolled to his hands and knees, coughing and spitting and blinking. Something plastic scraping on the asphalt reminded him that he'd managed to keep his phone in his hand. There had to be someone he could call that would actually be helpful somehow. Paul was dead. Dianna and Brian were dead. Ray had a phone. Andrew had freed him and those three women, so he'd be safe. He'd stayed with Bobby, so he'd also be useful.

"Answer, Ray, pick up. Pick up, c'mon, pick up." When he really needed them, where were they? Ray picked up on the third ring. "Ray, listen to me. I need help at the Adelphi facility. Whoever can get here fast. No time to explain, just grab whoever can fly and get them here, now." He hung up without giving the other man a chance to ask questions and hurried over to the guard post.

Picking himself up off the ground, he surveyed the area and caught sight of dust clouds leading deeper into the base. Clive had a plan, apparently, and it included causing a lot of damage. Liam had no way to stop him. Movement at the guard post caught his eye, and he forced his feet to carry him in that direction.

Someone bigger, faster, or stronger would have to stop this. Meanwhile, he'd slog along in Clive's wake and heal anyone he left alive.

His superpower sucked.

Chapter 16

“You can stand there and try to deny it, but we ain’t special effects, and we ain’t going away.” After only ten minutes of media circus attention, Bobby wanted to smash a camera or shove a microphone someplace unpleasant. A sea of both devices had been shoved at him, their humans jostling and shouting at him to be recognized and have their special question answered. Past them, a fleet of vans with TV station logos blocked them all in.

They’d put on a show already, and kept it up. His left arm being dragons meant every single cameraman had a chance to get a close-up of one. Lizzie let fire dance across her hand and arm and body over and over again. Jayce changed from steel to cloth to concrete and back again and again. Ray held up his shield and changed its size, color, and shape. Stephen lounged in the air, not touching the ground.

With all of that, every reporter asked the same stupid questions.

Someone’s phone buzzed behind him, and he turned to see Ray holding his out, looking to Bobby in question. Bobby nodded. For all he knew, it could be important.

“Are you the leader of all of these ‘superheroes’?”

Someone had already asked that question. He answered it again anyway. "I'm the group spokesdragon." The loose dragons trilled in glee. While an amused chuckle ran through the small crowd, Ray touched his shoulder.

"Everyone who can fly needs to get to—" Ray looked up at the cameras and microphones. "The other A site. One's there already, and there's a problem."

Not sure what to make of that, Bobby nodded and turned back to the cameras. "Sorry, folks, we got more work to do. Like I said, some of us are still prisoners, and we gotta do what we gotta do to be free. We'll be available for questions again soon." Turning away from the reporters, he smirked and waggled his eyebrows at Lizzie and Dan. "Keep 'em off our back for a minute. Don't hurt nobody." The rest, he waved to follow him.

Lizzie squealed with delight and Dan wrapped an arm around her waist. The pair of them would be enough to tie up those reporters for a few minutes. "It's Adelphi, everybody get there fast as you can. Stephen, take Jayce and get there already. Riker, you guys drive the rest. Ray, if'n you got phone numbers, use 'em. I'll round folks up and be there soon as I can."

Head Cowboy watched in satisfaction as everyone leaped into action without arguing. They'd decided to accept that he had a level head and wouldn't knowingly lead them into disaster. Even better, no one questioned his suggestions—he delicately avoided admitting the word "orders" fit better—for how to get things done.

He let his dragons peel off for pure showmanship and scattered the swarm. It was a real shame he couldn't spare the time to ride over with Lily. They had things to talk about.

Chapter 17

Liam coughed on the dust and dirt covering the base in a thick haze as he knelt by a downed soldier and checked his pulse. This one had a concussion that Liam took from him. The one next to him had no life- threatening injuries and already had gotten to his hands and knees. They'd both be fine. He left them both without a word as soon as the splitting headache faded.

Clive still ran rampant, smashing and chewing up walls and vehicles with that weird gun. At odd moments, Liam caught his voice screaming Privek's name in rage-filled challenge. Then he'd destroy something else, filling the air with more dust, more dirt, and more noise. Eventually, he'd have to stop on his own, too torn up and frustrated to do anything but collapse and weep for his wife. They could all hope so, anyway.

"Liam, what's going on?"

Looking up to find the source, Liam had to blink several times to understand what he saw. Cant—Stephen, the vampire—dropped down out of the sky, carrying another of them and with some kind of strange, thick cloth thing covering his head and hands. They landed in the shade of a partially destroyed wall. Stephen set the man aside and pulled the cloth off. It shimmered with silver and stood as a person.

He racked his brain for their names and came up blank. Too many names and faces too fast and in the midst of chaos and crisis left him unable to place the two other men. Paul would've remembered them.

"It's Clive. He's…upset. He has that gun-thing." Waving his hand around, he hoped they didn't need any additional explanation. "So far, he hasn't killed anyone."

The silver one nodded grimly and ran off. Stephen grabbed the other guy before he could follow and took him by the shoulders. "I know you can control yourself while you're in wolf mode, Matthew. I know you can. Believe it. If I can keep my blood lust under control, you can tell your wolf to fuck himself. We don't want to actually hurt anyone, remember that. Hold onto that."

Matthew nodded, took a deep breath, and curled his hands into fists. "I'm in charge. I run this body, not the wolf. I make the decisions."

Uncomfortable with overhearing the conversation, Liam turned away to give them the illusion of privacy. Matthew reminded him of Bobby asserting dominance over his dragons. How many of them had that kind of control problem? More than would admit it, probably.

That one word, *brother*, made him feel a twang of something. As much as Paul's death left a gaping hole in him, he'd only known the telepath for a couple of weeks. Time, he knew, would have given them inside jokes and shared struggles. They'd complemented each other well enough that he felt confident they would've become great friends.

His parents loved him and would do nearly anything for him, and the same for his sister. Elena held his heart so completely, he had no need to wriggle away form her. None of them offered the same thing that Stephen just promised to Matthew. They couldn't understand it. He couldn't explain it with words and hope for them to help in the ways he needed. Elena would try, but even she'd fall short.

This sense of family they shared, he realized, explained why Bobby fought for them all, why he was so hell-bent on sacrificing himself to save them all, why he willingly stuck his neck out and risked everything, even for the ones he hadn't met yet. If he chose to be honest with himself, recognizing that in Bobby had led Liam to give him the benefit of the doubt in the first place. He remembered calling Bobby a dangerous man an eon ago, and although he hadn't fully grasped it at the time, this was exactly what he meant.

Bending down to check on a man with blood staining his uniform, he caught movement out of the corner of his eye and ducked. The silver man sailed through the air and slammed into a wall hard enough to knock a hole through it. Clive must have shot him. That gun had a hell of a punch. He straightened to go check on the silver man when the guy stood up out of the debris and ran back to the fight, unaffected by the impact. Being silver apparently had advantages.

"What happened?" The man with a short length of steel rebar through his thigh groaned and tried to prop himself up on his elbows.

Liam held out a hand to get him to stop moving, because a length of steel rebar had impaled his leg. If he could keep him from seeing it, the guy would never know. "Lie down, you took a knock to the head." He grabbed the rebar and yanked it out, doing his best to ignore the soldier's sharp, grunting scream, then put his hand on the leg and healed it. A brand new bloodstain spread on his pants while he clenched his jaws shut to endure the pain.

While he found himself looking off in a random direction, he noticed people stumbling out of one of the partially demolished buildings. They stumbled and flinched away from the sunshine, moving in a shambling, uncoordinated blob. When he noticed that every last one of them held a sheet up to cover their bodies, his eyes flicked to the building. With a jolt, he recognized it. They'd found Elena in that one.

These people had been the ones on the gurneys.

These people each had a superpower.

These people had to be under Kanik's influence.

His phone chirped with a text. Tearing his eyes away from the sight, he checked the message. It made him want to laugh. Standing this close to a growing mob of potentially hostile people, he didn't dare.

Chapter 18

Thick haze drew the swarm from miles away. One regular guy with a funky gun sure did manage to wreck up a ruckus. A plume of dirt or smoke shot up into the sky, with several large things flying up, then falling down again. Jayce, Stephen, and Matthew clearly hadn't been able to stop Clive yet, and they'd had a ten minute head start on him. Violet and Chelsea should arrive with their passengers shortly, too.

Reaching the base, he dropped the swarm down lower to survey the situation. Soldiers moved around, clumping together and checking weapons. That complicated things. He'd been hoping to blow into the base with a distraction timed to provide cover for the evacuation. Of course, he'd been hoping to do this later, after they had a chance to breathe and sketch out a plan. Food would've been nice, too.

Moving on, he came across a huge number of people walking around, none of them in uniform. Jayce flew into sight and hit a lamp post, breaking it in half. In the distance, Bobby made out Clive, back to a wall. His face twisted into rage-filled agony, he blasted the gun in every direction, showing off how little time it took to reset between blasts.

Bobby landed where Stephen lurked in the shadows and re-formed. "What's going on, exactly? "

"Exactly? I can't get involved. I'll burn up. Matthew and Jayce are trying to talk sense to him, but he keeps shooting them for distance with that gun. They can't get close. Ai could probably take it from him, Dan could get him to put it down. I'm sure we'll have plenty of options when the others get here. He wants to kill Privek, so far as I can tell."

"He can get in line," Bobby growled.

"No kidding. I'd like to throw him off a building, personally. Then maybe catch him and do it again a couple of times before I 'accidentally' forget to catch him once." Stephen sighed wistfully, and Bobby cleared his throat to get him back from revenge fantasyland. "Liam is off in the aftermath someplace, healing the people Clive hurt already. At this point, Clive's not really harming anyone, so there's no point in making a grand effort to stop him. Contained is good enough until we can get him without much risk."

Nodding his agreement, Bobby watched Jayce and Matthew run in at Clive together and each get tossed for distance before they got close enough to do anything. He opened his mouth to say something when gunfire erupted in the distance. "Heckbiscuits, they found someone to shoot." It could be Liam, so he blew back into the swarm and flew for the sounds.

He found chaos. That bunch of people he saw before, had actually been wearing nothing but sheets. Some of them were buck naked. They swarmed the armed soldiers, and bodies already littered the broken ground. None of this made any sense until he noticed one of the unarmed people had mottled green-brown scales instead of skin. Another one glowed all over with red light. A third made sparks shoot from her fingers in a muted, more colorful copy of Lizzie's ability.

No need to break out the formerly homeless test subjects, because they'd escaped on their own. Their powers were all over the map, and minor, like Sherrie's and Shane's. He needed to stop this fight. He had no idea how. His dragons couldn't stop this many people without killing them all. Time, he needed more time. With more time, more of his side would show up and could take control of this.

Landing and re-forming, he gave his best shot at some kind of command voice. "Fall back! There's too many of them." He thought it sounded fake and weak. The soldiers bugged out anyway. Either Head Cowboy did a better job than he guessed, or these guys were only too happy to be ordered out of this mess. He caught sight of Liam being stupid by running into the throng to reach the ones bleeding on the ground. Hands and feet and claws got in his way, punching and grabbing and kicking and shoving and stomping.

"Quit it," Bobby snarled, "he's trying to help." The ones nearest him turned to give him the same treatment. It gave him a good view of their faces. Every one of them had the same slack-jawed expression of empty-eyed, mindless determination. They reminded him of zombies, and he didn't have one single clue what to do about it. As the swarm, they couldn't hurt him. Liam, on the other hand, had curled up into a ball while they beat the crap out of him.

A dragon streaked off to get Stephen while the rest of the swarm did what it could to surround Liam and keep them off him without hurting them. They had to be under Kanik's influence, which meant they had no control over their actions. After all, Sherrie and Shane hadn't acted like this when they woke up. The mutation hadn't caused this.

Leaving a smoke trail behind himself, Stephen zoomed in, grabbed Liam without a word and fled for the safety of shade. Bobby shifted his attention to trying to corral the zombies, but he'd come too late to the party for that. He watched helplessly as they ran in all directions, some shrieking, some yelling, all seemingly out for blood.

Violet and Chelsea arrived, carrying Lizzie and Dan, and landed on top of a nearby building. Why couldn't one of them have brought Andrew? Because they wouldn't be able to fly if they were carrying him, that's why. Even if Andrew was here, how would that help? It would take a while for him to reach all of these people. There were over a hundred of them, maybe as many as two hundred.

He went up to where the four of them stood and re-formed, offering a quick explanation of what he thought was going on. "Best I can think is we need to find Kanik and make him stop."

"That's great, Bobby," Violet said, her Alabama twang making him miss home right now, "but how do we find him?"

Bobby scratched his head and turned to watch zombies streak past, literally and figuratively. Quite a few hadn't bothered keeping a grip on their sheets. "I'm gonna go hunting. See if'n you can help Stephen find a coat or something, and go hang by the entrance to direct traffic when the others get here and try to keep this contained in the base." The swarm spread out, looking for any sign of the source of all this madness.

He saw Matthew, in his werewolf form, watching Jayce's back without rampaging or attacking for once. Good for him for getting a grip on the wolf. Clive's gun lay on the ground. The poor guy had fallen to his knees, sobbing, holding onto Jayce like a drowning man about to slip under.

Since he couldn't see Stephen and Liam, he hoped they'd found a hole to hide from the sun and random zombies. Violet had gone off to the front gate with Lizzie. Two cars screeched to a halt, and the newcomers worked on setting up a blockade.

Privek. He found Privek. The man walked through a door as dragons buzzed past it, and the person behind him could only be

Kanik. Along with them, Hannah, Tony, Javier, and John left the building, following like lost puppies. He'd chosen a weird group to keep for himself. Hannah, he could understand. She could make a force field and had more organizational skills than Bobby could shake a barrel of biscuits at. The rest, though, he didn't get. Tony could turn himself into objects, Javier could climb walls, and John controlled plants. Against Matthew and Jayce, those guys had no chance.

Bobby called the swarm in while Privek swaggered through the zombies threatening Matthew, his entourage in tow. Landing next to Matthew, the dragons flew together until Bobby stood there, hands in his jean pockets, unafraid of whatever might happen next. Privek pulled out a gun, pointed it at Matthew, and fired. The werewolf could heal his injuries, so Bobby didn't even flinch as three shots went straight into Matthew's chest. He took a step back from the impacts and growled.

Bobby lifted an eyebrow. "That the best you got?"

Beside him, the werewolf threw his head back and roared. Whatever control Matthew had, it must have been tenuous, and getting shot broke it. Bobby saw Privek's mouth quirk up in a smug smirk. He saw Kanik, the left half of his face covered with queer burn scars, dart forward with a mild limp and grab Matthew's furry arm. Bobby blew out into the swarm and went for Kanik. Take him out, and everybody would be free of his influence. In theory.

The second his dragons touched Kanik, he lost control of them. Kanik laughed maniacally. Bobby had no idea what to do. He was still himself, still had his mind, but the dragons refused to do what he wanted. They launched off of Kanik and went for Jayce, and there was nothing Bobby could do about it. He saw out of their eyes and felt the press of them without having the ability to control or direct them. This, here, now, became his new worst thing imaginable:

his tiny little machines of death under the control of a madman.

Jayce's eyes widened and he grabbed up Clive and the gun, then took off running. At least he had enough sense to see what happened. He didn't, though, have enough speed to get ahead of the swarm. Dragons caught up with him in seconds and poured into his mouth, and into Clive's. Bobby's mind screamed out to stop them. They kept going, ripping Clive apart and clanging around inside Jayce's steel innards.

"You can't stop us, Bobby." Privek grinned, stepping up to pat Matthew on the arm. "No one can. Kanik, send the dragons to kill the rest of them. Leave the healer, he's useful. We'll control him this time, though, to avoid any more *incidents*."

A blast of air and dirt and concrete tossed them all back and off their feet. Dragons got tossed for distance, and Bobby's consciousness moved that way, staying in the center of the swarm. Jayce had the fancy future gun in his hands and fired it again. This time, a blue force field sprang into existence, sending all the debris flying around the group of six. Privek got to his feet and dusted himself off in the safety of Hannah's power. The rest of them followed suit.

Yeah, sure, easy fight. With just himself to worry about, Jayce took off running again. He'd have figure something out, because Bobby couldn't imagine how anything would stop Privek now. Jayce and Stephen were probably the only ones he couldn't kill right now. As soon as the dragons formed back up, they were going to leave a sea of corpses in their wake.

Again.

Chapter 19

"Stephen!" Liam turned to find the source of the urgent shout, only to see that shiny metal man charging straight for him and the vampire standing next to him. Stephen had found enough cloth to cover up, and they'd just stepped back out of the building they'd been sheltering in to survey the scene.

He'd never seen so much chaos. People ran around all over the place, bouncing off the walls in some demented game of human pinball. Liam clung to the wall, hoping no one noticed and attacked him.

"Bobby's under mind control," Shiny Metal Man called out as he kept running, carrying that big gun Clive brought. "Kanik has to touch you to take control. We need Andrew, can you find him and get him over there?" He stopped next to them and fired the weapon as he panted, tossing people around like ragdolls and kicking up dirt and small things that glinted in the sunlight. "You're faster than me."

"Understood, Jayce." Stephen nodded and flew away from them, towards the front entrance.

"Maybe I should just hide until this is all over," Liam suggested with a gulp.

"Time to grow a pair." Jayce grabbed the front of his shirt and dragged him deeper into the base.

Liam stumbled along behind him, unable to resist such a massive force of steel, and glared at his back. “What do you expect me to do? Heal them into submission?”

Jayce fired the gun again, and Liam noticed more glittery things being forced back. “Privek wants you, he thinks you’ll be useful. That means the dragons aren’t going to hurt either of us. You need to be up in this.”

With more than one reason now to be apprehensive, Liam’s eyes went wide and he gulped again. “Are those…Bobby’s dragons you’re targeting with the gun?”

“Yes. I’m slowing some of them down.” He kept going, pushing the small clump of dragons back with repeated shots in their direction as they went.

Liam spotted Privek and his entourage as Jayce fired directly at them, knocking the whole group over. Before they had a chance to really recover, he yanked Liam behind a wall, thumping him into it face first hard enough to make him grunt, and they took cover.

His nose felt like it was running, so Liam swiped a hand under it only to have it come away with a small smear of blood. “I don’t heal my own injuries.”

“Huh. That must suck.” Jayce’s skin tone shimmered and changed to be the same as the wall, complete with texture. He leaned out only enough to see.

“Yes, thank you, it does.”

Jayce leaned back and stared at the gun, his masonry brow furrowed. “I have an idea.” The grin Jayce gave him as his expression cleared made Liam want to get up and walk in some other direction. “Go out there and distract them. Don’t let Kanik touch you. I’ll circle around and come in from behind.”

“I don’t really like your ideas.” Liam crossed his arms over his chest, perfectly aware of how petulant it made him look. He didn't care.

"You have a better one?"

If only he had a way to smack that look off Jayce's face. From the raised eyebrow to the mild amusement to the challenge, Liam hated Jayce a lot right now. He grunted. "Fine. Just hurry. I doubt I can keep him distracted for long before I become Kanik's new pet." He pointedly did not think about the very real possibility of that actually happening, or what it might be like.

Jayce nodded and jutted his chin out for Liam to get moving, then crept away. Liam rubbed his face and stood up with his hands out in surrender. Within seconds, a small flock of dragons swarmed him, landing on his head, shoulders, and arms. It was like…having a bunch of large spiders crawling over him. He shivered at the comparison and brushed a few off.

The dragons chirped angrily at him. A few blew out little puffs of fire. "Okay, okay, I get it," he said, not having to feign a mild panic. "Don't hurt me, I'm ready to talk." He had to force his legs to take him in the direction the dragons obviously wanted him to go, and he noticed himself hyperventilating. Were those awful stuttering, chattering noises really coming from his own mouth? He gibbered in terror, and it was no act. He needed to focus, to think about Elena, safely tucked two thousand miles away from here.

Privek looked sharp in his dark suit. For once, instead of cool detachment, his mouth and jaw below his sunglasses had tightened into impatient annoyance. He held a pistol pointed at the ground. "Liam, how nice of you to stop by." He turned to Kanik. "Send the dragons to find Westbrook."

So much for being a distraction. "I'm sorry I lied to you." Nothing like an apology to break the ice.

Privek's face smoothed over to a cool neutral. "Are you a

distraction, then? Kanik, take him. Everyone else, stay alert."

Liam had two choices: stand or run. A true coward at heart, he turned and fled. He managed to get only a few steps away before a blue field formed right in front of him. Unable to avoid it, he slammed into it and bounced back. Hitting the ground hard with his hip, he groaned and wondered if he'd be able to pass that bruise on to someone else.

Kanik approached, staring intently at Liam and holding his hand out to grab him. In the distance, Liam saw Jayce bounce off a blue barrier.

"Are you a conductor?" Kanik's half-melted face filled Liam's vision.

The burns made Liam pity him, but the mad gleam in his eyes made Liam scramble away. Never mind scrapes and bruises, he needed to not be close to Kanik. Ever. "No. I'm a healer."

Kanik walked beside him, refusing to let him escape. "Can you heal my burns?" His eyes glittered with an alien sort of curiosity, as if he'd never encountered anything quite like Liam before and yearned to dissect him.

"Uh." After what he saw himself do for those soldiers a few weeks ago, he wasn't really sure. "I, um, maybe? We'd probably have to cut off the affected areas."

Kanik's eyes slid shut and his whole body shivered with some kind of ecstasy for a few seconds. "You could make me whole again."

"I think so, yes." Liam hit debris big enough to stop his backwards scuttling. He flinched back as Kanik lunged for him and stopped with his two hands poised an inch away from Liam's face, ready to press them onto his flesh.

"Hurry up," Privek groused.

Kanik's eyes darted all around, then settled on Liam again. "Would you heal me willingly?"

“Of course.” Unable to keep himself from doing it, Liam stared at the too-close fingers and braced for the part where he lost control over his mind. “You’re one of us.”

His eyes narrowed. Actually, the one eye, affected by the scarring, puckered more than anything else. “Am I?”

Keep him talking.

Liam knew how to keep people talking. He’d once thrown so many words at his mother that she gave in and let him have the keys to the antique Jaguar for a date at the tender age of sixteen. He’d convinced a girl she’d been the one to dump him so they could stay friends and he could still crash her parties. He’d…talked Paul into helping him wake Bobby.

Thinking of Paul and Bobby gave him the angle he needed. One more thing to be grateful to them both for.

“We’re brothers. You and me. We had the same mother. Privek is the outsider, the one we can’t trust. He’s using you, Kanik. He’s using all of us.”

Chapter 20

Bobby watched through the eyes of the dragons as they slipped through the zombie swarm, checking each one to make sure they continued to follow orders. The swarm reached the other side of the throng and his dragons saw everyone, his brothers and sisters. All of them came and they stood together, doing what they could to keep the zombies from escaping and wreaking havoc outside the fence.

His dragons arrayed themselves in a long line and surveyed the assembled superpowered people. He counted and came up short. There should be twenty-two now, plus one if that portal-teleporting girl woke up. He counted eighteen. Four of them had to be up to something. He hoped it turned out to be the right four.

Scanning the crowd, he ticked them off in his head. Stephen's absence stood out. He thought Andrew might also not be there. With luck, everyone understood his importance and worked to get him in a position to stop Kanik. Either that, or someone would have to kill the guy, and that someone wouldn't be Bobby.

The dragons surged forward as a long cloud of silvery motes winking in the sunshine. Violet figured it out first. She grabbed Andrea, standing next to her, and flew away. Others turned to look. Chelsea flew off on her own. Heavy pieces of debris jumped up to form a barrier. Ice shot up from the ground. He saw the blurred form of Ai racing around another small group.

Kanik's dragons rushed the defenses. They clawed and burned and scraped at what got in their way. One group stopped in its tracks, probably because of Sam. With horror, he saw one squirm and struggle through a small gap and dive at Lily.

Bricks formed in both her hands, and she smashed them together, crushing the dragon just inches from her face. Two more followed it through and she only caught one before the other burned through her cheek and dove into her mouth, choking her.

If Bobby could've screamed, he would have. He pushed as hard as he could to jump into the dragon in the lead to try to stop it. As it wriggled down her throat, he found himself pulled into the dragon. Suddenly, he had a burning need to kill everyone with the icy blue eyes. All of them had to die. He'd been made for this job. He did it without hesitation.

Chapter 21

Staring intently at Liam, Kanik stopped with his hands still hovering an inch from his face."

"He promised to help me, too. But it was a lie." Liam took a deep breath, sure this had to be at least as bad as having a gun pointed at his head. His hear pounded so hard in his chest that he could barely think. "Kanik, he's using you. Look into my eyes and you'll know I'm not lying."

Kanik's eyes bounced back and forth between Liam's. "I just want myself back." He lowered his hands.

"That's what we all want, too. Can you stop everyone from fighting and all that? We don't want to hurt anyone, none of us do."

Kanik's face fell, and he rocked back onto his heels. Both of them jumped, startled by gunshots. Someone fell onto Kanik, and shoving him into Liam. He gasped, suddenly struck with an overwhelming sensation of drowning. Only a second later, it abruptly cut off.

"You can't kill me with a gun, asshole." The vampire's voice held so much angry darkness that it sounded like he might rip Privek apart with his bare hands.

Kanik's eyes went wide with shock at the same moment when

Liam realized Andrew had been the one who crashed into them. He held Kanik's arm with one hand and his own leg with the other. Blood seeped out of the leg to stain his jeans. Privek must have shot Andrew, which Liam had no way to heal.

"Don't kill him," Liam shouted. "Not yet." The fighting had stopped, and everyone in Privek's entourage stood there, disoriented and confused.

he vampire took another shot to the chest before he batted the gun away and grabbed Privek by the front of his suit, lifting him off the ground. They went twenty feet up and Stephen chose not to bite him or break him in half. At least he responded to orders.

Utterly flabbergasted by this turn of events, Privek flailed in the air. "How? You can't overcome—? This is impossible! You're all mine! Kanik! We can still rule this country, side by side, as the power behind the President!"

Kanik lifted his head. "Who cares about that?"

Chapter 22

The dragon burned and bit and scraped. Lily's gurgles and whimpers echoed all around Bobby, the world shaking as she writhed around in reaction. He burst through Lily's chest in a blast of fire, spraying blood and gore everywhere and already looking for his next target. It focused on Anita as she turned to watch Lily fall into Tiana's arms. In that moment when her body went limp and her eyes glazed over, he suddenly got control over his dragons again. They stopped attacking and backed off, all of them confused.

He pulled the swarm together and re-formed on the other side of the barrier between him and her body, unable to do anything but pound on it with one fist. Sam still had control over enough dragons to deny him his other hand and arm up to the elbow. "Let me through, please, Anita! I ain't controlled no more, I swear, let me see her!" Tears stung his eyes. She could still be alive, he had to hold onto that. "I gotta take her to Liam! Help me save her!"

The debris parted and he saw nothing but Lily, lying there, bloody and still. He grabbed her up and ran for it. The swarm broke out and carried her faster than his legs could, and he felt Sam release the rest. She wasn't dead, not yet. He couldn't do anything about Clive, he couldn't do anything about that little girl or her people, but he could save Lily. He *would* save Lily. Somehow.

All around him, the zombies looked around, confused. Every last one of them must have been under Kanik's influence, and now they were free and had no idea what happened. But it didn't matter, because he needed to save Lily.

He found the smaller group, Stephen holding Privek up in the air. Kanik looked less like a threat than a confused person. The swarm set Lily down beside Liam and Bobby re-formed on one knee between them both. Picking up Lily's hand, he shoved it into Liam's. "Heal her, you gotta."

Liam looked up at him. As he sadly shook his head no, Bobby heard a thump, a clatter, and a shout. Bobby looked past Liam and saw Stephen on the ground, yanking a dart out of his arm. Privek scrambled to his gun, picked it up, and fired all around, hitting Javier in the arm, Liam in the leg, and Kanik in the back. Bobby jumped up and ran straight at him, taking a bullet in the gut and not caring as he leaped and tackled Privek.

"You did this, all of this," he said, tears rolling down his cheeks. He grabbed two handfuls of Privek's suit and dragged the man to Liam. "Look at what you done, you—" He shoved Privek's face down at the ragged, bloody hole in Lily's chest. "There ain't no words strong enough."

Chapter 23

Liam knew Bobby didn't mean to shove Privek at him. It was incidental. What happened was something he had no control over. The woman Bobby shoved at him—one of their kind—was dead, but so freshly dead, he wasn't sure if she was beyond his ability. All he really knew for sure was that he had no intention of sacrificing himself for someone else, not like that. But Privek wasn't him. More importantly, he hated Privek.

His power swept him up, daring him to try to resist. What would happen clicked in his head, and he let it. A connection formed as he reached out and grabbed Privek. Liam took Lily's death on himself, then passed it—along with his own bullet wound—to Privek.

The agent gasped and gurgled and goggled. The woman's chest healed over. He collapsed and she drew a breath.

For a moment, Liam stared blankly at what he'd done. It filled him with awe and wonder and horror all at once. As he lay back again and stared at the sky, he thought perhaps Privek had gotten off too easy. That bastard deserved something much worse for all he'd done. With that happy thought, he blacked out.

Chapter 24

Camellia stayed still, perfectly camouflaged as she leaned against the wall, watching everything happen. Kevin's body heat gave him away, standing beside her. "I'm glad we had orders to stay out of this." Mitchell dove to his knees and shoved the now dead body off the now live one, taking her up in his arms and kissing her.

"Me too." He sounded noncommittal. She imagined he leaned there casually, arms crossed and aloof. He spent so much time invisible, she had no idea what sort of mannerisms he really had, and made them up in her head.

"I'm thinking maybe I don't want to be part of the group."

"No? I'm thinking it's pretty incredible how they'll do just about anything for each other. Wouldn't mind having an in to that."

Camellia shrugged, distorting her camouflage enough that anyone looking could see her. "A lot of people die around them. Lots of chaos, destruction. Privek was only the first person who wanted to control us. He won't be the last." She watched the shiny guy and the vampire checking on everyone over there.

"Maybe so, but even I know that being invisible only keeps people from seeing me. I'm pretty sure I can be detected. I also have a feeling that if I go off on a crime spree, these guys will be the ones hunting me down. For their own safety, if nothing else."

"I guess you have a point." Camellia shrugged again. "I suppose it won't hurt to give them a try, at least."

"No, I don't think it will."

Chapter 25

Bobby got out of the car with Riker, Stephen, and Jayce. Nearly everyone else either needed to rest or had volunteered to deal with all those people. Getting nearly a hundred and fifty formerly homeless folks with minor superpowers across the country without attracting too much attention to the destination presented a complicated problem. Hannah said she'd take care of it, which Bobby appreciated. He didn't have the first clue how to even start on it.

Lily was fine (thank goodness she left Sebastian in the car, so he didn't see much of anything), so was Liam. He healed up everyone who'd survived, the drugs wore off for Stephen and everyone else, and they had to figure out what to do with Kanik. The guy needed help, and they'd find a way to get it for him. They'd take care of their own, and that was that. Liam said his parents would help financially, and a few of the others had some money, too. The farm would be in good shape soon enough, and they might just start their own little town.

The only other loose end besides the one they'd come here to take care of was the wormhole stuff. Bobby felt pretty confident a bright light of publicity combined with some sabotage would slow that down enough to trigger all kinds of bureaucracy. Folks would learn more about Asyllis than the few blurry shots a reporter managed to grab, too. He had a lot to say still, and nobody could shut him up about any of it.

General Hanstadt had a really nice house with a really nice front yard. Everything was precise and as close to perfect as nature would allow. It felt artificial and sterile, but that didn't matter. Bobby led them all up the front walk. The door opened before he had a chance to ring the bell, which didn't really surprise him. After everything that happened today, they had to be expecting a ten pony circus to ride up to the door and blow it up, or something equally dramatic and destructive.

"Mr. Mitchell." The General answered the door himself, in uniform. "Please, come in."

Bobby gave him the most polite smile he knew how and stepped inside the house. "Everybody calls me Bobby. This here's—"

"I know who your friends are." His interruption sounded less than friendly without turning the corner to ugly. He gestured for them all to use a particular doorway from the well appointed entry. Inside it, they found unexpected visitors already sitting on the couches and chairs.

The two men in dark suits standing in the corners reminded Bobby too much of ones he'd faced before to be comfortable, but he didn't suppose members of the Secret Service would leave just because he asked nice. Not when the President of the United States was in the room. Though he didn't recognize anyone else in the room, he figured they must be important.

"Is it alright if I call you Bobby, too?" The President gave him a perfunctory smile as he stood up and extended his hand to shake with all four of them.

"Yessir, that's fine. You are part of 'everybody' and all." For some reason, he expected the President to be something more that the ordinary man standing before him. He ought to be big, or shiny, or somehow larger than life. The guy was just a man in a suit, really. Taller than him, sure, and probably twice as smart, but not a superhero. Realizing that made it easy to talk to him. "We weren't rightly expecting you, sir, or we mighta dressed up a touch." At least they took the time to clean up all the blood, and Liam sprang for new jeans and shirts. Except for Riker, who insisted upon wearing his Army fatigues.

"Don't worry about it. You've had a rough day." The President sat back down and gestured for them to follow suit.

Bobby heard Jayce and Stephen both make little noises and mutter to each other as they stepped around the furniture and sat. A glance back showed him Riker found whatever they said funny, too, but he kept it mostly stifled back. The soldier didn't sit with the three of them—he stood at parade rest behind the couch they took. "That's one way of putting it, I reckon."

"We were expecting William Moore to be with you. Is he alright?"

"Yessir, he's just exhausted. Bunch of us went through a wringer, and the only reason you got this many is on account we figured if no one came, y'all'd get a touch ornery. Sergeant Riker here insisted on coming, too."

"Buffalo soldier Sergeant Cory Riker, Sir." Riker saluted. "I want to know how my men and I will be treated after all this."

General Hanstadt stopped a few steps away from him. "You're not going to be arrested, if that's what you mean, Sergeant."

"We'll get to that," the President said with a nod. "First, I want to talk about where we go from here."

Bobby felt everyone turn and stare at him. His eyes dropped to his lap, where one of his hands rested on his leg, and it fell apart into dragons. The bunch of them turned to watch the President, then all sat obediently in silence. They drew the attention of all those who'd never seen them in person before. It was a kind of power, one Bobby had yet to decide how to feel about.

"You'd be stupid not to be thinking about how you could use us, for the country, for yourself personally, for whatever else, but I'm telling you right here, right now, flat out: ain't gonna happen. You can't control us. Even if you could, we won't let you." As he spoke, he raised his eyes until he met the President's gaze, as serious as he ever got. "If'n you try, we're gonna rain fire and brimstone down on whoever and whatever we gotta to make it stop. We ain't toys. We're people."

"That sounds like a threat," General Hanstadt growled. He seemed coiled and ready to leap over the couch to protect his Commander In Chief. Bobby noticed the Secret Service agents tensing. Stephen stayed calm, draped on the couch like a coat, and Jayce looked thoughtful as he flipped a small piece of steel over in his fingers.

Bobby nodded. "Point is, you deal square with us and we'll deal square with you. You mess with us, and you won't know what hit you."

Now giving Bobby a calculating stare, the President sat back in his seat, a picture of rigid, forced relaxation. "I came here in the hopes we could work something out for mutual benefit, Bobby."

Letting out a light snort, Bobby shook his head. "I ain't stupid. We been abducted, stabbed, shot, poked, prodded, lied to, even killed, all by people what wanted us to 'work something out for mutual benefit'. I got no faith the US government has our best interests at heart, and ain't listening to whatever you got to say all doe-eyed." He stood up, his dragons re-forming his hand again. Stephen floated to his feat and Jayce also stood, shimmering into steel. "Sergeant Riker and his men are under our protection, so're their families and ours. We ain't rightly sure if we all still want to be American citizens anymore, we'll get back to you on that."

The President frowned. "You can't just take American land and declare yourselves sovereign. You do that, and it'll be interpreted as an attempt at secession."

This wasn't exactly how Bobby envisioned this meeting. He had a point to make and he made it, and now it was turning into some kind of pissing contest. "I ain't your enemy, Mr. President. None of us is. Just remember this when you deal with us: we got among us folks what can make fire, disintegrate anything, break a body in half, and fly. You give us a little time, say a month, to bury our dead and set ourselves up, then you send someone out to talk polite-like and we'll listen." He tipped an imaginary hat, like Jayce often did. "It was nice meeting you, Mr. President."

"That went well." Stephen smirked as the front door closed behind them.

Jayce cracked a grin and chuckled. "You might have told us you were planning on threatening the President of the United States with war."

"Wasn't rightly planning on it."

Stephen clapped him on the shoulder. "That's what I like the best about you, Bobby. Full speed ahead and damn the consequences torpedoes."

Riker snorted. "They're going to try something, just to see if they can get away with it."

"We'll be ready for it."

Sam had ideas about electronic surveillance, and Tiana said something about animal sentries. Even John had thoughts about using the plant life for security.

Bobby opened the front passenger door of the car and climbed in. Jayce got into the driver's seat and the other two climbed into the back. "Ain't nobody gonna sneak up on us never again."

"Yessir, Head Cowboy." Riker saluted Bobby.

Jayce grinned. "I like 'Spokesdragon' better."

"You would," Stephen said, shaking his head. "Injun."

"Fifty percent," Jayce nodded. "So, technically, I'm a Space Injun."

Riker grinned. "That makes Bobby a Space Cowboy."

"Some might call him the Gangster of Love. Or even Maurice."

"Oh, whatever, just stop someplace so I can get a burger or something." Bobby laughed with them all, happy he could finally settle down and relax for a while. Then they passed a billboard with a woman dressed like a housewife on it, advertising a maid service. The woman looked a lot like his Momma, which made him think of her, and his smile faded.

He thought about it for a few minutes, scratching his chin. He hadn't gone to see her since that one day. Time had been tight. Danger had chased him. He'd worried about getting her mixed up in all of his problems. Now, he all that lay behind him. They stopped at a fast food place and got something to eat, and he still thought about it.

"Guys, I gotta bail."

Jayce took his eyes off the road to glance at him. "Car too slow for you?"

Bobby grinned and shook his head. "Naw, there's something I gotta do."

"I'll go with you," Stephen offered.

Bobby waved the vampire off. "I'm just going home. Ain't no big deal. I'll see y'all back at the farm in a few days. You ask me, I think it's a good idea for folks to take a buddy when we go home to visit, but I think I'll be okay."

"Head Cowboy only makes the rules," Jayce smirked, "he doesn't follow them."

Rolling his eyes, Bobby pushed the button to roll the window down. "Yeah, whatever. I got someplace to be." He let the dragons peel off and dart out the window. He heard Stephen say something about him cheating, then he streaked up and away from the car.

Chapter 26

When he reached his Momma's house, Bobby saw a van from the local news station parked outside, even though it was the middle of the night. National news would probably be here in the morning. That aspect of going public hadn't actually occurred to him until this moment. Since no one else brought it up, figured no one else thought about it, either.

To avoid attracting attention, he dropped down and re-formed on the back step. The door was locked, of course. He broke in and relocked the door behind himself. He grabbed a banana off the counter in the dark and ate it, then he dropped down on the couch and rubbed his face. How was he supposed to tell her about everything that happened? What would she say about it all? She accepted him for what he was, but that was before…

He saw that girl again. He saw Lily with her chest ripped open. He saw shredded piles of meat. He'd done that, all of it. A hand on his shoulder interrupted his thoughts and made him look up. Momma stood there in her nightdress and slippers, a weary smile visible in dim light coming through the window.

"You look like your Daddy, boy." She sat next to him, putting her arm around his shoulders. "He used to come out here and sit like that sometimes."

Bobby leaned into her, grateful he could still have this, at least for the moment. "There's reporters parked outside."

"They been there since about a half hour after you went on TV. I saw that, by the way. It's all over the place. Some folks are saying it's fake, but I know better."

"I'm sorry I brought that to your doorstep."

Momma tsked at him. "I can take care of myself. Though I will say this house is whole lot quieter with you gone. Empty-like."

What he wouldn't give to be able to waltz right back into his life. Bobby sighed. "Did Daddy ever tell you about the stuff he did as a Marine?"

She squeezed his shoulders. "That's how he stopped having nightmares. He talked about it. He never wanted you to hear any of it, so he'd tell me when he woke up and couldn't sleep, in the middle of the night. Like now."

If that wasn't an invitation, he didn't know what was. Bobby started talking, telling her the whole story, from start to end. Once he started, it came out in a flood of words, and he didn't leave anything out, not a single thing. Through it all, she sat there and listened to him and didn't let go. It was what he needed, more than anything else.

When he stopped, the silence was deep and wide. Momma pulled him into a hug and rocked him like she used to when he was little, until he fell asleep. He woke up later to the smell of bacon and eggs, a pillow under his head, and a glass of orange juice on the coffee table. Sitting up and rubbing his eyes, he took a long drink of juice. As he stood to take it to the sink, someone knocked on the door.

"Ignore it," Momma called from the kitchen.

He grinned and ambled to her. "You figure they'll get bored

and go away?"

She set everything aside and wrapped him in a hug. "I figure my boy's belly is more important than anything they want to know."

Until that moment, he hadn't realized how much he still worried about her acceptance. He hugged her back, reveling in the embrace. "I love you, Momma."

"I love you too, Robert. You're my boy, and that won't never change."

LISTING OF SUPERHEROES

Robert Mitchell (Bobby)
Age: 19
Occupation: Appliance delivery person
Hometown: A semi-rural suburb of Atlanta, Georgia
Superpower: His entire body is made of tiny robot dragons, which he can separate and re-form at will. The dragons have individual minds that operate on a simplistic level, and are each part of the hive mind that is Bobby. They can all breathe fire and fly.

Jayce Westbrook—Native American/Yavapai
Age: 22
Occupation: Hotel security guard
Hometown: Las Vegas, NV
Superpower: The ability to change the composition of his body to any material he touches with his hands. He tends to choose steel or similar metals, which give him additional strength along with defenses against most kinds of weapons.

Ai Dazai—Japanese
Age: 22
Occupation: Not stated
Hometown: San Diego, CA
Superpower: Speed, 100mph.

Alice Fielding—Chinese
Age: 21
Occupation: Pre-med student at Stanford
Hometown: San Francisco, CA
Superpower: Creates ice. Her body is immune to the harmful affects of cold.

Jasmine Milani—Iranian
Age: 22
Occupation: Waitress
Hometown: Washington, DC
Superpower: Shapeshifter—squirrel form only. She can also run at unusually high speeds and exercise a mild form of mind control over other squirrels.

Hannah Parson
Age: 23
Occupation: Secretary in a real estate office
Hometown: Philadelphia, PA
Superpower: Makes a force field of blue energy that deflects everything she's ever encountered, and can catch or carry people and objects.

Elizabeth Caulfield (Lizzie)
Age: 19
Occupation: None
Hometown: A small town near Little Rock, AR.
Superpower: Creates fire. She's immune to fire and suffers no ill effects from exposure to heat.

Daniel Jarvis (Dan)
Age: 19
Occupation: Not stated
Hometown: A small town near Little Rock, AR.
Superpower: Body control (others). He can control the physical actions of others as if they were puppets for his mind.

Andrew Roulet
Age: 23
Occupation: Sous-chef in a fancy restaurant
Hometown: Baton Rouge, LA
Superpower: Nullifier. Whoever he's touching is completely incapable of using their own power until he lets go. He also can remove the effects of a mental power from a victim/target.

Stephen Cant
Age: 20
Occupation: College student
Hometown: Dallas, TX
Superpower: Classical vampire. He can fly, has unusual strength, regenerates, and his saliva can overload the senses with pleasure. Unfortunately, he also can only ingest blood and burns in sunlight.

Christopher Gonzales (Chris)—Tejano
Age: 23
Occupation: hairdresser
Hometown: Austin, TX
Superpower: Empathy. He can sense and alter the emotions of others.

Tiana Brown—African-American
Age: 23
Occupation: Zookeeper at the LA Zoo
Hometown: Los Angeles, CA
Superpower: Animal telepathy.

Matthew Garrison
Age: 22
Occupation: Marine veteran
Hometown: Los Angeles, CA
Superpower: Werewolf with regeneration. The alternate shape is tied to his PTSD. When in werewolf shape, he's unable to control himself and rampages until stopped.

Lily Thatcher
Age: 20
Occupation: Mom to Sebastian (age 2), employee at her parents' garden center
Hometown: San Jose, CA
Superpower: Creates objects out of a hard white material. She has the most success making weapons and tools, and can create fully functional bullets.

Anita Martinez—Hispanic
Age: 21
Occupation: Casino pit boss
Hometown: Reno, NV
Superpower: Telekinesis.

Kaitlin Tremont
Age: 20
Occupation: Online day trader
Hometown: Shelby, MT
Superpower: Precognition. She sees the future, both on demand and whenever her own safety is in jeopardy.

Andrea Foster
Age: 21
Occupation: Not stated
Hometown: Indianapolis, IN
Superpower: Disintegration. She can destroy any inanimate object, rendering it to fine dust, but cannot affect living things.

Greg Mezilis
Age: 20
Occupation: Graduate student
Hometown: Madison, WI
Superpower: Gadgeteer. He is a supergenius in the subject of applied science and engineering.

Violet Grace
Age: 21
Occupation: Graduate student (Law school)
Hometown: Mobile, AL
Superpower: Flight, 100mph.

Owen Johnson
Age: 22
Occupation: Garbage collector
Hometown: Denver, CO
Superpower: Sound control. He can manipulate the sound of his own voice in any way imaginable.

John Tseng—Chinese
Age: 21
Occupation: Florist
Hometown: Raleigh, NC
Superpower: Plant control. He can manipulate plants to change their characteristics, supply them with nutrients, and communicate with them.

Javier Ortiz—Hispanic
Age: 19
Occupation: Auto mechanic
Hometown: Los Angeles, CA
Superpower: Wall crawling. He can walk across any surface at any angle, including water.

Maisie Polape—Native Hawaiian
Age: 20
Occupation: Hula dancer
Hometown: Honolulu, HI
Superpower: Portal throwing. She can create a wormhole between any two points, so long as she has a surface to put the portals on. The two portals she can create are person-sized and allow anyone to pass through.

Paul Pearson
Age: 20
Occupation: College student
Hometown: Seattle, WA
Superpower: Telepathy

William Moore (Liam)
Age: 23
Occupation: MBA student at Harvard
Hometown: Chicago, IL
Superpower: Empathic Healer. He takes the injuries of others onto his own body, then regenerates them himself. Injuries he sustains personally do not regenerate, but can be given to someone else.

Samantha Green (Sam)
Age: 20
Occupation: Webmaster, college student
Hometown: New York City, NY
Superpower: Accesses and controls any type of device that runs an operating system, including peripheral devices, like cameras and microphones.

Antonio Benti—Cubano
Age: 21
Occupation: Not stated
Hometown: Miami, FL
Superpower: Shapeshifter—inanimate objects of a size similar to his own body only.

Lisa Brewer
Age: 23
Occupation: Kindergarten teacher
Hometown: St. Paul, MN
Superpower: Accesses a pocket of extradimensional space with unknown dimensions. She is able to climb into the space herself, and can theoretically stuff something as big as a car inside it.

Camellia Androvitch
Age: 21
Occupation: Customer service call center drone
Hometown: Phoenix, AZ
Superpower: Chameleon. Her body can shift what it looks like to match her surroundings. When she stands still, she's effectively invisible.

Dianna Jackson—African-American
Age: 18
Occupation: None, recent high school graduate with no plans
Hometown: Chicago, IL
Superpower: Controls the movement of air and can propel herself, others, and objects through the air.

Chelsea O'Malley
Age: 18
Occupation: Mental patient (institutionalized)
Hometown: Boston, MA
Superpower: Has two feathery, angel-like wings that allow her to fly.

Kevin Astrid
Age: 21
Occupation: Apartment complex security guard
Hometown: Dallas, TX
Superpower: Invisibility

Brian Arralt
Age: 20
Occupation: College student—marine biology
Hometown: Portland, OR
Superpower: His body can melt into clear water bounded by a transparent membrane as tough as steel.

Raymond Beller (Ray)—African-American
Age: 23
Occupation: Construction worker
Hometown: New Orleans, LA
Superpower: Creates a physical shield that he cannot be separated from against his will. It can range in size from covering only his fist to a ten foot square, and he can lift it easily no matter the size he chooses. The material is impervious to harm.

Kanik Okpik—Inuit
Age: 22
Occupation: None
Hometown: Juneau, AK
Superpower: [redacted]

About the Author

Lee French lives in Olympia, WA with two kids, two bicycles, and too much stuff. She is an avid gamer and active member of the Myth-Weavers online RPG community, where she is known for her fondness for Angry Ninja Squirrels of Doom. In addition to spending too much time there, she also has a nice flower garden with one dragon and absolutely no lawn gnomes, and tries in vain every year to grow vegetables that don't get devoured by neighborhood wildlife.

She is an active member of the Northwest Independent Writers Association, the Pacific Northwest Writers Association, the Science Fiction and Fantasy Writers of America, and the Olympia Area Writers Coop, as well as being one of two Municipal Liaisons for the NaNoWriMo Olympia region.

Thank you for reading! If you enjoyed this book, please consider posting a review wherever you buy your books.

www.authorleefrench.com www.clockworkdragon.net

Books by the Author

Spirit Knights

YA urban paranormal adventure

Girls Can't Be Knights

Backyard Dragons

Ethereal Entanglements

Ghost Is the New Normal

Boys Can't Be Witches

The Maze Beset Trilogy

Superheroes in denim

Dragons In Pieces

Dragons In Chains

Dragons In Flight

In the Ilauris setting

Standalone fantasy tales

Damsel In Distress

Shadow & Spice (short story)

Al-Kabar

www.authorleefrench.com www.clockworkdragon.net

The Greatest Sin

Epic fantasy co-authored with Erik Kort

The Fallen

Harbinger

Moon Shades

Illusive Echoes

A Curse of Memories

Darkside Seattle

cyberpunk as L.E. French

Street Doc

Fixer

Mechanic

Anthology Appearances

Into the Woods: a fantasy anthology

Merely This and Nothing More: Poe Goes Punk

Unnatural Dragons: a science fiction anthology

Missing Pieces VIII: short stories from GenCon's Author's Avenue

Artifact

What We've Unlearned: English Class Goes Punk

Bridges (editor)

Enter the Aftermath

Undercurrents

Hideous Progeny: Horror Goes Punk

www.authorleefrench.com www.clockworkdragon.net

www.ingramcontent.com/pod-product-compliance
Lightning Source LLC
Chambersburg PA
CBHW030345310726
48979CB00001B/194

9781944334055